Praise for Starhawk's
The Fifth Sacred Thing

"SLATED TO BE ONE OF THE GREAT VISIONARY UTOPIAN NOVELS OF THE CENTURY."
—Marion Zimmer Bradley, author of *Mists of Avalon*

"A RIPPING GOOD READ."
—*Los Angeles Times Book Review*

"A STUNNING PHILOSOPHICAL FANTASY ABOUT LIFE IN THE NOT-SO-DISTANT FUTURE."
—*Interview* magazine

"PROVOCATIVE AND MAGICAL, POLITICAL AND SPIRITUAL . . . AN EXTRAORDINARY BOOK THAT STANDS IN THE GREAT TRADITION OF POLITICAL AND PHILOSOPHICAL NOVELS."
—Margot Adler, author of *Drawing Down the Moon*

"EXCITING, MAGICAL, AND RICH WITH EXTREMELY IMPORTANT TREASURE MAPS FOR THOSE WHO REALLY CARE ABOUT LIFE AND THE SURVIVAL OF OUR PLANET."
—Merlin Stone, author of *When God Was a Woman* and *Ancient Mirrors of Womanhood*

"EQUAL PARTS URGENT TESTAMENT AND FERVENTLY HOPEFUL VISION . . . A VALUABLE CONTRIBUTION TO ECOTOPIAN LITERATURE."
—*San Francisco Chronicle*

"AN ANTHEM OF HOPE. GENERATIONS TO COME WILL BLESS THE NAME OF STARHAWK."
—Daniel Quinn, award-winning author of *Ishmael* and *The Story of B*

Bantam Books
by Starhawk

ॐ

WALKING TO MERCURY

THE FIFTH SACRED THING

Walking to Mercury

STARHAWK

BANTAM BOOKS

NEW YORK
TORONTO
LONDON
SYDNEY
AUCKLAND

WALKING TO MERCURY
A Bantam Book

PUBLISHING HISTORY
Bantam hardcover edition published March 1997
Bantam trade paperback edition / July 1998

Grateful acknowledgment is made to Curzon
Press Limited for permission to reprint excerpts
from the book *The Wisdom of Buddhism,* edited
by Christmas Humphries.

Other excerpts taken from *The Tibetan Book of
the Dead,* translated by Francesca Fremantle and
Chogyam Trungpa. Shambhala Publications, Inc.,
1992.

Book design by Ellen Cipriano.

Bantam Books are published by Bantam Books, a
division of Bantam Doubleday Dell Publishing
Group, Inc. Its trademark, consisting of the words
''Bantam Books'' and the portrayal of a rooster, is
Registered in U.S. Patent and Trademark Office
and in other countries. Marca Registrada. Bantam
Books, 1540 Broadway, New York, New York
10036.

PRINTED IN THE UNITED STATES OF AMERICA

BVG   10 9 8 7 6 5 4 3 2 1

Acknowledgments

Many people have contributed to the writing of this book. Isis Coble has read every draft of the manuscript, and her comments and insights were invaluable. Marie Cantlon worked with me on the development and editing of this book, as she has on all my other published works. As always, I am deeply grateful for her guidance and appreciative of her eye for structure and language. I thank Linda Gross, my original editor at Bantam, for her warm support and encouragement, and Beth de Guzman for her help in guiding the story to its final shape.

The Red Rock Writers suffered with me through all the early drafts of the story, and I value the constructive criticism given to me by Craig McLaughlin, Cristina Salat, Cynthia Lamb, George Franklin, Mary Klein, Sheila Harrington, and T. Thorn Coyle. Tom Hayden offered encouragement and valuable advice. I also thank Chris Kolb for his reading of the manuscript and his insights about Nepal.

Some scenes in this book were originally drafted as long as twenty years ago. Bill Menger, my writing teacher long ago at UCLA, gave me crucial encouragement at an early age. My ex-husband, Eddie, provided tangible help and encouragement.

In 1992 I actually did make a trek through Nepal similar to the one described here. I am grateful to our guide, Karma Lama, for his care and for introducing me to the rich culture of the Sherpas. The characters in this book were not based on the members of my trekking group, who were an amazingly interesting, flexible, and congenial group of people. I especially appreciate Ceres, who put up with my coughing in the tent at night, did most of the trek with a sprained ankle, and has been my good friend since the time we nearly drowned together—but that's another story!

I also honor the work done by the various groups who over the years have organized opposition to nuclear testing at the Nevada Test Site. I want to acknowledge the ongoing activism of the Western Shoshone Nation, whose sacred land has been appropriated as the bomb site. In particular, I thank the elders who have graciously shared ceremony as well as political alliance.

Although I have many times blockaded at the Test Site, nothing in this account, except for the name "Circle A," is based on any of my actual affinity groups, nor are the characters here taken from any living person. However, I do thank all my blockade buddies through the years for their work, their humor, and their support in moments of crisis.

Unlike Maya, I do not feel isolated in my own life and work. The Wind Hags have sustained an ongoing women's circle that I've been proud to be a part of for more than fifteen years. I am also grateful to work together with the Reclaiming Collective and our extended network of teachers in the U.S., Canada, and Europe.

Jodi Sager has for many years been the keeper of my teaching, speaking, and travel schedule, providing me with time to write. Kim Jack has recently turned her amazing organizational talents on my office, allowing me to find my files, my desk, and to answer some of my mail.

I have taken the novelist's license to rewrite history in the matter of the burning of the Tengpoche monastery. The *gompa* did burn, but in January 1989, not at the time the incident takes place here. Aside from that, the descriptions of places and customs are as accurate as I can make them, but I do not make any claims to being an expert on Buddhism, Nepal, or Sherpa culture, and I apologize for any misrepresentations that may have crept in.

This is a work of fiction, not biography or autobiography. None of the characters are meant to "be" anyone in real life—even me. A novel is like an extended dream, and all the characters in it arise from the consciousness of the dreamer, mixing scenes and memories from life with pure imagination until the boundaries of real and unreal blur and the characters take on a life of their own.

In some scenes I have used the names of real institutions for verisimilitude. The events in this book are not meant to reflect on those institutions. Johanna's birth scene, in particular, is pure fiction and while it reflects common obstetric practices of the sixties, I have no reason to believe they would have been practiced at UCLA, where I and members of my family have always received excellent care.

I thank my husband, David, for his constant love and support. And finally, thank you to Bob and Brian, who picked the manuscript off the road when it fell off the back of the truck on the Pacific Coast Highway, and didn't lose a page!

This book is dedicated to the memory of my mother, Dr. Bertha Clair Goldfarb Simos.

1

The Mountain

The mountain demanded that she let all the barriers, the layers of protection, even the names of things, dissolve. She was trying to let cold dissolve as she stepped out of her frayed blue jeans, slipped off her shirt, and stood naked under the pink dawn sky. Snow-licked peaks held the lake suspended above the canyon in cupped rock hands, letting a trickle of stream cascade down to the riverbed a thousand feet below. She stood on a narrow strip of lake sand, an edge. She was pursuing the place inside her that was beyond the edge, any edge, every edge. She was very young, but she had been alone for a long time.

The water was a still and perfect mirror, doubling every knob and crevice of the granite rocks that lined its shore. Tall pines grew downward into a well of blue sky. The woman in the water was a collection of forms and shapes and colors, no more, no less, than the rocks or the trees. A smudge of dark hair, two dark holes for eyes, a pale, lean body that had shed its cushioning as she had shed every superfluous comfort. Image without substance. If she entered the mirror, she would disappear.

She stepped into the water. The mirror rippled, shattered. The water's edge moved slowly up her ankles, her calves, a burning line. She was a woman sawed in half by cold, as she waded deeper, letting the edge pass her knees, her vulva, her rounded hips and belly and navel, the hollows of her spine, each separate rib, breasts. She stood for a moment, the edge at her nipples, letting her arms and hands rest lightly on the water, feeling her legs and feet first burn, then numb. She gave them to the cold and the water, and the water received them. Taking a sudden, deep breath, she plunged. The water took all of her, the cold so fierce that everything else ceased to exist. Under the water lived the silence, and she let herself dissolve.

It was her daily ritual. Purification, like the mikvah of her grandmothers.

She had given herself to the silence, and in the silence she heard the Eternals that were in things and through things, presences to merge with, that spoke not in words, but in a subtle shifting inside her.

And though she was struggling to abandon words, they came to her out of the silence: words of power, names that evoked the shifting pulses of what beat through her, of what she knew without words, names that could let her call the Eternals. She named her presences, as people had always named their gods, drawing arbitrary lines around her constellations of power, fixing them into crystallized forms that she could beckon at will.

What pulled her on, up to the high, lost meadows far above the trails and the granite ledges of the high peaks, she called the Seer. What asked her to merge, dissolve, and enter the mountain's heart she called the Singer.

What beckoned at that heart, gaping over the edge of going too far, she called the Reaper.

When time ceased to exist, they measured the rhythm of her heartbeat and told her when to come out. She shook her head clear of the water, felt the day's first rays of sun on her arms and breasts, stepped out on the shore and stamped her feet until blood pulsed again.

It was enough, for now, this mountain-cradled bowl of granite with a fringe of trees and a lake like a clear blue eye. It was all she needed.

But it would not always be enough. She had discarded the word for cold, but the winds that whipped down from the pass grew more frigid daily. She had fled time, but it pursued her in the rains of autumn.

She had evoked power, and already she began to hear its whispered demands.

"Be my eyes."

"Be my voice."

"Be my hands."

To have a vision was to become its servant. Young as she was, she had learned that already.

Naked, she shivered in the cold wind. Soon, she knew, she would feel her loneliness again. One day the Eternals would whisper, sigh, and she would know that the time had come to leave the mountain, and go home. She would carry power with her, and the Eternals would follow her down. They were old powers, embedded in mountains, and she had wakened them from sleep. They would pursue her until she learned how to make a place in the world for them.

Soon. Soon. The word itself evoked the relentless forced march of time, called back the other world where she was a twenty-one-year-old girl in flight from a broken heart and nothing was eternal, certainly not love.

She shivered again. For just one moment, she was afraid.
She had left fear behind her.
It awaited her return.

—Maya Greenwood,
From the Mountain

2

Letter

Committee to Ban Nuclear Testing
Nevada Test Site Peace Camp
February 15, 1988

Dear Maya:

    You probably wonder why I'm writing to you after all these years. Maybe I shouldn't be. Since you never answered my last letter, I took that to mean you didn't want to hear from me. I can certainly understand that, and that's why I never wrote again. I respect your privacy.

    But when I heard the organizing committee had called to invite you to the action, I knew that I had to let you know that I'm here. It was only fair to you, and although I was tempted to let you come, and surprise you, that wouldn't be honest. Right now what keeps my life liveable is simply trying to stay as honest as I can.

    They don't know, of course, about our history together. Nobody does, as far as I know, except you and me and a few people who are dead. I certainly understand if you want to keep it that way.

    Most people here don't even know who I am, although I haven't changed my name or tried to disguise the past. History moves fast in the age of MTV, and the heroes and the antiheroes of the sixties are just old, faded ghosts. Hell, the younger ones only know Bob Dylan as somebody their parents used to listen to.

    I'm here working with a group called Grains of Truth. We serve food for the homeless and for a lot of political actions. So I spend my days chopping vegetables and washing pots and pans. You'd laugh to see me. As I recall, when we lived together any dishwashing that got done, got done by you. Well, times have changed. I've changed, anyway, as you can imagine.

    We do good work. It's simple, basic work, and I'm proud to do it well. I'm happy, feeding people.

    I've come through a lot to be able to say that. Some of it you know and some of it I hope you can't even imagine. What has it been—seventeen years since we were last together? They've been filled with good days and bad days, a lot more bad than good. When I wrote you a few years ago I thought I was on my way up, but it hasn't been a smooth rise. More like a roller coaster. Now I feel I'm on an even keel, but I never assume that'll last. I owe debts that can never be repaid.

Still, right now, here in this desert, I'm happy. There's a secret they don't tell you about the Nevada desert—how beautiful it is. Wide, wide skies and bare round hills colored red and gold and purple. That's classified information. If they let it out, people might start thinking about this place as more than a wasteland we can blow to hell and a dump for our nuclear garbage.

You see, I'm trying to entice you into coming here. As soon as I heard the committee was contacting you, I started to think about how much I'd like to see you again. Maybe this is just my fantasy, but I feel like we'd have a lot to talk about. There's a history only you and I are still alive to share.

Of course, I have an unfair advantage, because I've been reading your books all along and so I feel I know you. Maybe that's a common illusion people have with authors—that you've been carrying on a conversation for years. I have to stop and remind myself that the dialogue's been one-sided, that you don't know me at all, at least not who I am now. Only what I was. You have no reason to care what I want or don't want. Why should you?

Still I can't help believing that we could be friends. I'd like that so much. Is seventeen years long enough for old wounds to heal?

To be honest, though, I have to admit that while I've learned to do good work I still don't do relationships very well. For most of those years, I didn't have a hell of a lot of opportunity to practice. The time we spent together is a lot more present for me, a lot closer than it probably is for you. Because you were the woman I loved before I got sent up and you were the woman I thought about for so long.

So this is a small warning—that your memory carries more weight for me than mine can possibly carry for you. I'm aware of that. I promise not to let it get in our way. And if you want to come here and not have anything to do with me, I'll understand. You can have all the space you need. I won't even say hello unless you greet me first.

But maybe I'm not wrong in thinking there's still something we need to complete together. If there's anything you still need or want from me, anything I can do for you or be to you, I'm here. I'm ready.

Not meaning to haunt you,
Rio

3

Phakding to Namche

Bright skies and crisp air greet us our first morning
on the trail, where primroses and rhododendrons
wave you on your way past fields and farmhouses to
the entrance of Sagarmatha National Park. You'll
stop for an early lunch. Eat hearty, because
afterward it's a four-hour climb to the village of
Namche Bazaar. You'll sleep well tonight!

—*Mountain Co-op Adventures*
brochure

The bridge swayed as Maya stepped out on it. For a moment she felt a
sharp sense of vertigo, as if the poles of the earth might shift and a new
dimension open up at the far side of the gorge. Maybe there, she thought,
where the bridge ends, I'll walk out of this world and find—what? The
elusive fairy call that I've been following all my life, that lately seems to
have stopped calling? Maybe I'll step into the Otherworld, and never go
home again.

Again the primitive suspension bridge shuddered in the wind, and
instinctively Maya grabbed one of the rusty cables that supported the
narrow, wooden span. Get a grip, she told herself. More likely to step
through a hole in the bridge and encounter new dimensions of mortality.
Here and there a board was indeed missing underfoot. Through the gaps,
Maya could see the milk-white foaming waters of the Dudh Kosi River,
rushing down from the high, high mountains that waited, somewhere
above.

Surely this is safe, she told herself. After all, she was following
behind a train of heavily laden porters: small, lean men carrying high
loads in the baskets they supported by tumplines across their foreheads.

They were joined by equally burdened young girls in gold nose rings and saris or the wool jumpers and striped aprons of Tibet, and young boys in flip-flops and T-shirts proclaiming I ♥ New York, all carrying loads that towered above them: drums of oil and stacks of cooking pots and piles of duffel bags and crates marked Japanese Everest Expedition. And the porters were following a train of yaks, laboring under bulging packs and high loads of wood.

The bridge had withstood all that weight; surely the cables would hold for one more woman, on the hefty side of slender, granted, but not nearly as heavy as a loaded yak. She carried only a small day pack, whose contents held a weight that was emotional rather than measurable in poundage. An old journal, a collection of letters, a gift for her sister, Debby, who might or might not be waiting to see her. And a plastic bag filled with her mother's ashes.

Don't think about it, just do it, she told herself, walking on. What was wrong with her, anyway? She had never been concerned with safety. She had never been afraid of heights.

When she reached the opposite side, she breathed a deep sigh as she planted her feet on solid ground. Turning, she waited for the rest of her group. Jan and Lonnie had gone on ahead with Tenzing Sherpa, their head guide, but the others would be following behind her. On the level stretches, she could take the lead, but on the uphill climbs, she fell behind, coughing and stopping for breath. The cough had begun on the airplane, gotten worse in the dust of Kathmandu, and didn't seem inclined to go away.

Forests of blue pine climbed the steep slopes of the gorge. Every patch of remotely level ground was terraced and farmed, supporting small villages of stone houses. The river was a white thread at the bottom of the gorge, the bridge a metal spider's thread. She took out her camera. I look like a tourist, might as well act like one. Take a picture. Maybe a series. Scary Bridges of Nepal. It would make a nice coffee-table book.

The picture would have been better with the train of yaks crossing, but she was not the sort of photographer who managed to find herself in the right place for the ultimate shot. No, she could focus and get the needle of the light meter in between the notches—that was about her speed. But here came someone walking on the bridge, a human figure to add scale. Maya snapped, and then lowered the camera to watch as a young woman stepped confidently out onto the first of the wooden slats. Maya recognized her; she had seen her yesterday in Lukla, in the café where they'd waited as their pack train was loaded. The woman was young, barely more than a girl, really, and Maya had caught just a scrap of her conversation with an older couple.

". . . and at night my legs ached so badly, I couldn't sleep well," she'd said. "We hadn't found much food at the teahouse, only some dhal, and I'm still growing, you know, so if I walk too far without eating, I feel it."

Still growing. Maya had stopped growing, vertically at any rate, at thirteen.

"Everyone told me not to try the pass over Cho La, but I went anyway . . ."

Once I was like her, Maya had thought, daring the passes that everyone warns you against. What am I doing here now, preparing for this prepackaged adventure?

But I've done that—the life-on-the-line challenge. And that's not what I wanted. I wanted time to walk and rest and think things through. Still, I'd like to know more about that girl. Woman. Oh hell, girl—she can't be more than eighteen. I could be her mother. She's just about the age Johanna and I were that summer on the coast with Rio, when we were still sweet and wild as beach plums, unmarred, our skins unbroken.

I'll speak to her, Maya had thought, but when she turned around, the girl was gone.

Now here she came, a young woman in a green wool sweater with a small rip in the left shoulder, and a long Tibetan-style wool skirt over her heavy hiking boots. Her dark hair was pulled back with a brown scarf, her cheeks ruddy and windburned over a deep tan, her gray eyes big in her thin face. A full pack was strapped to her back, and her right hand gripped one of the T-shaped sticks the porters used as walking sticks and as supports for their load when resting. She walked with an easy balance over the swaying span, as if she were used to instability.

Good, Maya thought, now I'll speak to her. She nodded and smiled as the girl reached her side of the gorge.

"Hello."

"*Namaste*," the girl said, dipping her head in greeting and moving past Maya on the path. Maya spoke up quickly.

"I took your picture. I hope you don't mind."

The girl shrugged. "It's okay."

I feel shy with her, Maya thought. Like the time I met Alice Walker at the homeless benefit and couldn't bring myself to say anything. Or with someone I've fantasized about, as a lover. What do I say to her? She's walking away.

"Where are you going?" Maya asked quickly. It was the standard Nepalese greeting, one of the phrases she'd learned from the language tape she'd studied on the plane. But of course she said it in English. The girl was American, by her voice, from somewhere west of the Mississippi.

"To Namche, today," the girl said.

"And after that?"

She shrugged, an eloquent gesture.

Oh yes, Maya thought, that's what I need, to not know where I'm going, to wander in the wilderness without a route and a schedule and a set destination.

"Are you traveling alone?"

"Yes."

Once I was like you, Maya wanted to say. Young and alone and free. Look at me, I want you to know me, know how alike we are, how I belong with you.

Instead she said, "Aren't you afraid?"

Instantly she could have kicked herself. The girl just smiled. "I like traveling alone," she said, and walked on.

How could I ask her that? Me, Maya Greenwood, author of *From the Mountain*? Me, who's been asked over and over and over again, "Aren't you afraid?" What was I thinking of? What's wrong with me?

Afraid! I'm the one who was afraid—afraid to try to find my sister without a guide or to be too dependent on her uncertain welcome. Afraid to struggle up these mountains with a thirty-pound pack on my back. And just well off enough to be able to afford to let someone else carry it for me.

And what's wrong with that? I'm not eighteen anymore, I'm not twenty-one like I was that summer on *my* mountain. I'm pushing forty. I've some sense, and I've earned my comforts.

Ang was now crossing the bridge, leading the train of yaks, their sides bulging with duffel bags. No, not yaks, she must remember to stop thinking of them as that. They were *zopkios,* a cow-yak cross, indistinguishable as far as Maya could make out from the real thing, but happier at lower altitudes. So said the guidebook, her Himalayan bible.

Ang was their sirdar, in charge of all the porters and the practical details of the trip. Their four stolid animals followed him, and behind them came Ila, the driver, a heavy-browed, square-faced man of forty with hair as shaggy as that of the beasts he cared for.

"Now much uphill," Ang said to Maya, with a nod and a grin. He was also in his forties, spare and wiry with a broad, smooth face, close-cropped hair, and a calm smile.

She smiled back at him. "Then I'd better get started." She turned and began to climb up the path.

Winding its way up the sides of the gorge, the path was a series of steep climbs broken by steeper climbs, interrupted by stairs carved into the hillside and occasionally relieved by switchbacks. Maya began by trying to keep a good pace, one that would let her stay ahead of the group. After the first few hundred feet, her lungs began protesting. When she moved, she felt as if she couldn't catch her breath. Periodically she had to stop while a spasm of coughing shook her body. Ang passed her, and she clambered up to a small outcropping of rock to let the *zopkio* train go by.

"Never stand on the outside of the trail while being passed by yaks," the guidebook had said. "People have been knocked off the trail and died."

What a humiliating way to go, she thought. Whacked by a yak. It formed a refrain in her mind: Whacked by a yak,/She didn't come back. . . . A mantra, she thought as she struggled up what seemed to be an endless series of switchbacks. What kind of spiritual awakening will *that* bring me?

Carolyn and Peter passed her, deep in conversation. They were the married couple on the trip, two psychologists from LA. They seemed nice enough, Maya admitted to herself, in spite of resembling so closely everything Maya's mother had wanted her to be. Professional, married, and slim. But that was no reason to dislike them, Maya told herself firmly as they cruised by her, talking easily to each other, not even out of breath, while she had to stop again and cough. Carolyn was affable and smiling, and Peter exhibited a good-natured sense of humor, plagued as he was by Sherpas eager to try out their Japanese on him, so that they could be ready for the next tourist boom. Patiently, he'd explain to them that he was third-generation American, and the only Japanese he knew was confined to menus, but they still greeted him with *"konnichiwa."* "Sushi," he'd reply gravely, or, "Sashimi."

He and Carolyn were so much a couple, so wrapped in each other's energy fields. They made Maya feel alone.

It would be nice to have a lover who would climb mountains with her. Johanna never would. She had been avoiding exercise ever since the two of them ducked out of running laps on the Harding High ball field, hiding in the hedge while the other girls ran around and around. No, Johanna was no jock. Just as well. Women who climbed mountains tended to do other things, like play softball and work out with free weights. Maya couldn't see herself in that picture. And men? She was not averse to men, especially if they had arms that resembled Peter's, golden brown and smooth skinned, with muscles that were well defined but didn't bulge in an unseemly way.

But of course, men like that wanted women like Carolyn, who was fit and petite and made Maya think of all the old fairy tales where someone wishes for a daughter with hair black as a raven's wing and cheeks as pale as the snow. Beautiful. Maya considered her own charms. She was attractive enough, she supposed. There was certainly nothing wrong with her. On a good day, when her dark curly hair was newly cut so it framed her face, and she'd had enough sleep so that there were no puffy bags under her eyes, and enough sun to put some color in her cheeks, she was quite good-looking if you liked mature, full-bodied women. But she was definitely not in Carolyn's class.

And any lover who climbed mountains would see her on days like today, wheezing and sweating, with her hair all matted down from the yak-wool stocking cap she'd worn in the morning chill. Hat hair, one of the untold hazards of the Himalayas.

Enough. I should be thrilling to the spiritual resonances of the mountains, not rating my looks against Carolyn's. Good feminists weren't supposed to do that, anyway. But of course we do. We just don't admit that we do.

She stopped at the top of the switchback to take a long drink of water. The trail climbed on above through a jumble of boulders. Goddess, the damn thing went up and up forever! It probably didn't stop at Namche but continued on to the moon at least, if not the far reaches of the galaxy. She wiped the sweat off her face with the front of her T-shirt, just as Howard climbed up past her.

"You okay?" he asked.

"Just slow. Go on ahead, I'll be fine." She didn't want to walk with Howard, not today, not while she was wishing to be alone in a remote, unpeopled wilderness while her body was protesting that three hours a week of aerobics class had not been enough preparation for a four-hour climb at eleven thousand feet with a cough. Howard was nice enough. It was just that he represented something she'd always tried so hard not to be. The first night, when they'd all had dinner together at the hotel in Kathmandu, he admitted that he'd come on the trip because he was thirty-five years old and had never had an adventure. That made Maya infinitely sad, and worried. Worried about herself. How had she ended up on a packaged tour with someone who'd never had an adventure?

This tour might prove to be too much for her, however. Forty-five minutes into a four-hour climb, and already she wanted to stop. But she'd better get a move on. Not that she could get lost—Tashi was still somewhere back on the trail, sweeping the rear. She was well cared for. But the sooner she went up, the sooner she'd *be* up, and could stop. Tomorrow was a rest day. And if Debby had gotten her letter, maybe she'd meet Maya in Namche. She might already be waiting there.

Grunting, Maya tucked her water bottle back in its waist-belt carrier and forced her right foot to take one step onward. Then her left. The sides of the mountain were dotted with primroses and spreading rhododendron bushes, as the Mountain Co-op Adventures brochure had promised, although the rhododendrons were not yet in bloom. She tried to focus on the infinite small beauties around her, to let her mind roam beyond the confines of the body. A good place to practice Buddhist detachment—these mountains. To think about getting off the wheel of birth and death, the endless up and down, up and down, climb and descend only to climb again—that was life on these trails. That was life, for that matter. Granted, in the books she wrote about the Goddess, she'd always preached that life itself was the goal, that the wheel itself was liberation. Hah. A philosophy for the flatlands, not for these heights.

The impact of altitude on theology—there would be a nice graduate thesis for someone.

She stopped for a moment, wiping her face. Her arms were damp, and she could feel the sweat pooling under her breasts, dripping down her legs under her black skirt which she wore because the guidebook said Sherpas disapproved of women who wore pants. In fact, this stretch of Nepal was so well trekked, its Sherpa population so cosmopolitan, that she could have worn a clown suit without causing much comment. And not be starting to suffer from the rawness between her legs that plagued fat girls, or more properly said, Women of Size.

Not that she was all *that* fat, just Rubenesque enough so that her thighs rubbed together as she walked.

"A skirt!" she had complained to Johanna as she was packing. "Stephen Berznewski wants me to hike in a skirt! What does he know? I bet he never suffers from the Terrible Thigh-Chafing Problem."

"Who's Stephen Berzwhatski?" Johanna had asked.

"Author of *Trekking in Nepal—the* definitive guidebook. Everyone says so. I bet he has thighs like chopsticks. I bet they not only don't touch, they've never even met. When he wants to cross his legs, he has to introduce them to each other. Left Thigh, I'd like you to meet Right Thigh. Right Thigh, meet Left Thigh."

"You *are* going to take a pair of blue jeans, aren't you?" Johanna asked, sorting Maya's socks and rolling the pairs up together.

"Blue jeans! Blue jeans are death traps."

"How is that?"

"You get wet, and they conduct heat away from your body. Then you die of hypothermia."

"Don't tell me. Stephen Whoski says so, in the guidebook."

"You got it. I guess I'll either have to offend the Nepalis or waddle up the mountain, bowlegged as a bull rider after one too many rodeos. Why is it that nobody ever addresses the Terrible Thigh-Chafing Problem?"

"Medical science has an answer for you," Johanna assured her.

"Liposuction?"

"Talcum powder. I've got a tiny can of rose-scented talcum powder you can carry in your day pack. Just apply a little, discreetly, when you go to the bathroom."

"Bathroom! I don't think they have bathrooms in Nepal."

"You really know how to take a pleasure trip, is all I can say."

The bed was piled high with a mountain of supplies that Maya was

convinced could never fit into one duffel bag. "Stephen Berznewski rec-
ommends a pair of light wool slacks, which I purchased at the Mountain
Co-op along with the thermal underwear and the fifty-dollar pile sweat
pants. Now where did I put my second pair of hiking boots?"

"Over here." Johanna handed them to her.

"What would I do without you?" Maya said. "I wish you were
going with me."

"You take a nice cruise on the Caribbean, I'll go with you. Drinking rum punch on a tropical beach—that's what I call a vacation."

"I'm not just going on vacation," Maya said sharply. The sharpness
covered something they both knew: that she didn't really wish Johanna
was going on the trip. "It's a pilgrimage."

I am taking my mother's ashes to the holy mountain, she thought,
but she didn't say so out loud. "Anyway, I need to see my sister. Betty's
dead. Debby will need me to comfort her."

Johanna gave Maya her Look, chin tilted down, eyebrows up, full
lips slightly pursed, the heavy, twisted coils of her hair swaying gently to
and fro as she shook her head. "Uh-huh. She may or may not need you,
but are you sure you need her right now? You know how critical she can
be."

Maya turned away and began folding T-shirts.

"She's just never forgiven me for running away and leaving her
stuck at home with Betty. But we're sisters. It doesn't matter whether or
not we get along well. We still need each other."

Johanna picked up a T-shirt.

"She should come here," Johanna said. "She should have come
home when your mother died. Even if she is the only doctor in all the
wilds of what-do-you-call-it?"

"Khumbu. The region is called Khumbu. And she's got a partner
who works with her."

"So she should have come."

"I agree. Of course, she didn't realize how soon Betty was going to
die. We thought she had more time. But the point is, she didn't come. So
I have to go to her."

"Your reasoning escapes me." Johanna stacked the shirts on the
bed beside the suitcase. "But whatever. Are you even sure she knows
you're coming?"

"Nothing's ever sure when you're trying to communicate to the
wilds of Nepal." That's true enough, Maya thought, and of course it's
equally true that I could have telegraphed instead of asking the trekking
company to get my letter to her. But I didn't want to tell her in a telegram. So cold, so abrupt. "Coming to Khumbu March 15. Stop. Mom
dead. Stop." But damn if I'm going to justify myself to Johanna.

Maya looked down, counting her pairs of socks. She had three pair of hiking socks, three pair of liner socks, two pair of wool socks. Johanna had seated herself on the edge of the bed and was opening her mouth to say something Maya suspected she didn't want to hear.

"Do you think I need another pair of socks?" she asked quickly, hoping to distract her.

Johanna ignored the question. "And you're still intending to drag your poor mother's ashes off to the back of beyond? She could have been buried in a nice, quiet grave in LA, you know, the one place on earth your mother was ever comfortable in. A grave you could visit once a year, and put flowers on. Not a godforsaken mountain in the wilds of Tibet, where you may never go again."

"Not Tibet, Nepal," Maya snapped. "You know it's Nepal, I've told you fifty times. You keep calling it Tibet just to irritate me. Admit it." She turned and faced Johanna. That was the way—put her on the defensive.

"I don't have to *try* to irritate you. You are as itchy as a performing dog in a flea circus."

We could fight, Maya realized. But I don't want to. Bad enough that I'm leaving.

She forced a smile. "I am, aren't I? I can't help it. But anyway, it's not a godforsaken mountain, it's a holy mountain. The ultimate mountain. Sagarmatha. Chomolungma. Goddess Mother of the Universe. Funny, I always thought of Tibetan Buddhism as a male-dominated system, but I bet there's a lot of underlying Goddess imagery, if you look for it. Anyway, I'm named after the Buddha's mother."

"Now who's talking about Tibet?"

"According to Stephen Berznewski, Tibetan Buddhist culture is best preserved in Nepal, since the Chinese invasion."

"And where, in the gospel according to Stephen Berzwhoski, does it say a person like you is supposed to work off her grief by climbing Mount Everest?" Johanna leaned back against the wall. "Couldn't you just tear your garments, or go see a therapist like normal people? Girlfriend, I've heard you moan just climbing up these stairs with a bag of groceries!"

Maya laughed. "I'm not going to climb up Mount Everest. I just want to get close enough to see it. That's my goal. And what better place to leave my mother's ashes? She never got to see the Himalayas in life, why not in death?"

"She never *wanted* to see the Himalayas, as far as I knew. She had a nice trip to Israel a couple of years back, and Hawaii—she enjoyed that."

"But Debby's in the Himalayas." Maya placed her socks in a small stuff sack and jammed it down into her duffel bag. "Together we'll find some beautiful place to leave Betty."

"Someplace you'll never see again. A grave that you'll never sweep or tend or place a few roses on."

"Jewish people don't *do* flowers on graves, or lavish wreaths on the coffin, or set up banks of bouquets at the funeral. I'm sure it's a constant heartache to the entire Floral-Tribute Industry."

"Since when do you only do what Jewish people do?" Johanna stood, picking up one of Maya's boots and wrapping it in a plastic bag.

"There's something about death," Maya replied, taking the boot from Johanna and staring at the duffel bag, wondering how to fit it in. "Brings you back to your roots."

"Maybe so, but the rest of you was a flaming Pagan, last time I looked." Johanna handed her the second wrapped boot. "Somebody who sets up altars for your ancestors every Halloween and calls them into your circle. If your mother's not your ancestor, who is? You ought to lay her to rest in a place you can reach."

Maya sighed wearily and dramatically. She stood for a moment, contemplating her wool slacks. Should she pack them flat or roll them up? Would they wrinkle more one way than another? Did it matter?

Johanna leaned over, took the slacks out of Maya's hands, and rolled them into a tight cylinder.

"There. That's the way to pack them. They'll take up less space, and they won't wrinkle so much." She stopped for a moment, looking at the expression on Maya's face. "All right, call me bossy if you want. But you're just standing there, looking like a dying cow."

Maya took the slacks and stuffed them into her duffel bag. "Johanna, why do you think Betty wanted to be cremated? *That's* not traditional, you know."

Johanna, surrounded by piles of Maya's T-shirts, began rolling them up.

"She just didn't like the idea of burying people. Thought it was a waste of space. She was never one to waste anything."

"Look, I've thought about this a lot," Maya said, her head down as she arranged her clothes inside the duffel. "I think Betty was telling me that she wanted me to take her with me, to carry some piece of her to Debby. She knew we'd never make a pilgrimage to Mount Sinai Park in the San Fernando Valley. I think, at the end, she was saying that she wanted to adapt to us, to our lives. She wanted us to be able to take a bit of her wherever we went."

Johanna shook her head. The metal rings that bound the ends of her heavy coils of hair danced on her shoulders, and her dark skin gleamed. Johanna had beautiful skin, as smooth and glossy at thirty-eight as it had been at seventeen, and for a moment Maya was distracted from their argument. "She would have wanted to be laid to rest among her own people, is what I say."

"You've said it five times, now just shut up about it, okay?" Maya snapped. "She's my mother, they're my ashes, it's my trip." She grabbed the shirts Johanna had carefully rolled and shook them out, stuffing them roughly into the bag.

Johanna took them out gently and rolled them again. "Look, love, you may be mad at me, but that's no reason to wrinkle your clothes."

Oh, go away, let me pack by myself, leave me alone, Maya thought, but she held her tongue. It's not Johanna, it's my problem. I shouldn't take it out on her. Goddess, Goddess, Goddess, I need to get away!

Johanna put her arm around Maya's shoulder. "You are edgy," she said. "I'll stop riding you. I know you need to get away. I just wish you didn't always have to do everything in a way that's so hard on yourself."

Oh, don't be sympathetic, Maya thought. You'll make me cry, and I won't want to go.

"It'd be easier to climb Mount Everest than to stay here, the way I've been this last month," Maya said quietly. "I can't write, I can't work, I can't even think."

But of course Johanna didn't know what it was like. Maya would have to tell her, to say, "Jo, there's something I've been following for twenty years. Sometimes it's as clear as the whole Hallelujah Chorus thundering in my ear, sometimes as subtle as the hint of a hint of a faraway drum, but constant, always there. That's what I write from, that's how I make my magic, that's the presence I'm pledged to make an opening in the world for. But now it's gone. It died when my mother died, and now when I sit down to put words on the page, or I stand up in front of a roomful of expectant eyes, nothing comes."

And it wasn't that Johanna wouldn't understand. She knew; she knew the rhythm and the backbeat and some harmonies of her own. But to talk about it was to name it, and to name it would be to admit that the melody wasn't soaring for them any longer. And once they admitted that, what would hold them together? She couldn't risk that loss, not right now, so soon after losing her mother. And yet some part of her longed for it, yearned to be cut loose, to fly free.

Space. She needed space to sort herself out.

"Your mother just died, love," Johanna said. "Why be so hard on yourself? So you don't finish your book this spring, there'll be time."

"There won't be time," Maya said, shoving the duffel bag over and sitting down abruptly on the bed. "There's never enough time. These three months were all I had off this year to write, before I'm all booked up with lectures and teaching and workshops. And you know how that goes. I can't write on airplanes. I cannot."

"So you won't," Johanna soothed her. "It's not that I object to you going off, I just think you're putting another pressure on yourself, when you could stay here and take it easy and get yourself some rest. Enjoy staying home, slowing down.''

"But I can't. I can't rest here, Johanna. People call me on the telephone.''

"So don't answer.''

"But it's not just that.'' Maya looked away, staring at a crayon drawing Johanna's daughter, Rachel, had made years before. The picture showed two large figures, one painted brown, one painted pink, and a small brown figure between them with a big smile on her round face. When had Rachel done it? About a year after Maya moved in. The brown figures had a smooth, round bubble of darker brown hair surrounding their heads; the pink figure had snaky dark curls. Maya had framed it because of the smiles, but now they seemed merely curved lines, grimaces. "Everything's gone dead, here. I can't get it together to clean up my room or do my laundry. I thought about scattering Betty's ashes in the garden, but the weeds are too damn depressing, and I haven't turned the compost.'' Maya looked around at the rest of the debris of her belongings, which suddenly seemed too chaotic to organize. "It's all too much. It all wants something from me. And nothing's . . . speaking. Nothing's singing inside. I've lost my power.'' There, she had said it. Now maybe they could talk.

But Johanna just smiled, sitting down beside Maya and patting her shoulder as if she were comforting a child. "Oh, I doubt that you've lost it. Maybe just misplaced it for a bit.''

No, they couldn't talk. Some things could not be said; they evaporated as soon as you tried to pin them down in words.

"I've got to get away,'' Maya said again. "Everything depresses me.''

"How about me? Do I depress you?''

Maya was silent.

"I do, don't I? That's what this is really about.''

"You don't depress me. But—'' she stopped.

"But. That's what it is, isn't it? But.''

Maya sighed. "I don't want to fight.''

"I know. You just need your space. I've heard it before. And hey, that's cool, girlfriend. You know whatever you need is okay by me.''

"I know.''

"I love you,'' Johanna said, pushing the piled clothes and the duffel aside and reaching for Maya. "Just don't forget that.''

Maya took her hand. "I never forget that. I never doubt that you love me, or that I love you. But you don't fantasize about me. I don't drive you wild in the middle of the night. When I'm away from you, you aren't lusting after my hot thighs. You're lusting after Raymond, or Verne, or Lillian.''

"I can't help what I am." Johanna squeezed Maya's hand. "I'm not a one-woman dog. Neither are you, for that matter. You gettin' jealous, all of a sudden?"

"Not jealous, exactly. I just want to feel alive again."

"Maya, honey, we've been together for a dozen years. You can't expect fireworks. At our age, love presents itself differently. You've got to learn to recognize it in other feelings besides nonstop lust."

"What feelings?" Maya said. "Name three."

"Comfort. Familiarity. Irritation."

Maya smiled. "If irritation is the measure of our love, it runs deep."

"What we've got *is* deep! We've built a life together. We have a history. Don't discount that. We've stood by each other and defended each other and hung together through the hard times. We've fought for our love!"

"We have done that," Maya admitted. "My poor mother! Your poor mother, too!"

"Hey, my mother is a blessed woman. So was yours, if she could only have let herself see it."

"I feel so strange, now that she's gone." Maya let herself lean back against Johanna's shoulder. "As if I've been pushing against a closed door all of my life, and suddenly it's disintegrated, and I'm left sprawling in the dust. I need some space to pick myself up and figure out who I am."

"Space, always space," Johanna crooned, stroking Maya's hair. "For you it's not the final frontier, it's the first line of defense."

Maya pulled away. "I can't help what *I* am, either."

"What's that?"

"Let's just say I'm not fully domesticated."

"Kind of wild, huh?" Johanna winked at her. "That's what I like about you. Run wild, run free. Just remember, you can run from your troubles, but you can't run away from yourself."

"Oh, great, Johanna." Maya stood up abruptly, pulling away from her. "Shall we see just how many of those clichés we can come up with? How about, 'Wherever you go, you take your problems with you'? How about, 'Anywhere you go, there you are'?"

"Those are proverbs, not clichés."

"I don't care what they are, I don't find them to be true. Frankly, the geographic cure has always worked for me."

"So far."

"Far enough."

Johanna stood and kissed Maya gently on the forehead.

"Okay, love, I'll stop harassing you. Go to Nepal—that's good. You'll have the time of your life. I just hope you're not setting yourself up for some misery with your sister."

"Maybe I am, but if so, I'll survive." Maya let herself be pulled into Johanna's arms, and rested her cheek against Johanna's. "I don't know why, I can't think of what else to do. I need to complete Betty's death, to bring the three of us together, one last time."

"A precious family scene, I can see it now—you, Debby, and the Urn."

Maya gave a small smile. "Hey, play what you're dealt, right?"

"I just hate to think of you being unhappy, so far away from me."

"You'd rather have me unhappy right here, in your face?"

"Sure. Where I can watch."

"I'll be all right," Maya said. "Whatever happens with Debby, it'll be a good trip. Mountains are there. You know I always feel better in the mountains, and those are the highest mountains in the world."

Maya dug Johanna's talcum powder out of the small pocket in her day pack, and ducked into the bushes to apply it discreetly. She resumed climbing. I guess Johanna was right, Maya thought. I wouldn't exactly call this a pleasure trip, so far. But just then she rounded an outcropping and looked back where the gorge stretched, deep and blue, the river a white cleft far below her. On the opposite cliff, the afternoon light caught the pale, pale green of terraced fields so that they glowed like wet transparent leaves. The beauty of the warm light in that vast space made her forget the effort of the climb. For a moment, she was young and weightless and free.

I *am* on a pilgrimage, she thought. And I have come to the right place. To be here, to see this, is worth the sweat. Whatever Johanna thinks, I do need space. Literal, physical space. And silence. I used to know how to be silent, when I was young, like the girl on the bridge. I learned that in the mountains. But now I'm thirty-seven, an indeterminate sort of age. Not old enough for wisdom, just old enough to carry around a clamorous history. It's so loud in the back of my mind, no wonder nothing else can speak through me.

She turned to climb again. Maybe that's what death does, opens a door into the spirit world so all your old ghosts come rushing back. Even Rio, writing to her after so many years. He wasn't dead, but she'd thought of him that way. His letter was in her pack, along with old ones from long ago, haunting her with the ghost voices of unwritten replies, clamoring at her to make a decision, accept or decline his invitation. Well, she could contemplate the problem as she climbed. That was the way to get up the hill—think about something else. Not Be Here Now, but Be There Then. Not mindfulness, but mindlessness. Distraction.

But her mind refused to focus. As her body plodded up the hill, her thoughts slipped, leaped, danced ahead, and soared above and beyond, staying away from all serious questions. Hours passed as she slowly climbed.

At last she rounded a shoulder of the mountain, where the path leveled out. There below her were whitewashed stone houses with painted window frames and doors curved in a perfect arc around the terraced fields that covered the hanging valley of Namche Bazaar. To the west, a gorge separated the town from a massive granite mountain with patches of snow clinging to its sides. To the north, east, and south, gentle mountains cradled the town, while behind them rose stark, high peaks. Maya caught her breath in delight. The town seemed magical, something out of an old dream or an earlier time. She felt that she'd stumbled into the midst of a fairy tale, where the heroes, wandering through the wastes, find shelter beckoning.

She had done it. She had survived the hill. Suddenly she felt a surge of pride, a wild desire to whoop and dance and let out a victory yell. The summit of Sagarmatha herself could hold no greater sense of achievement. The misery of the climb fell away, and she basked in the beauty before her.

Now she deserved every comfort provided by Mountain Co-op; her warm sleeping bag, a cup of tea, time to rest while someone else made dinner. She deserved to have every desire gratified, every wish fulfilled. Surely she would be rewarded for her magnificent climb. Her sister would be here, waiting in this magical place, and they would heal together and comfort one another.

"Namche Bazaar," said a voice behind her. Tashi, their twenty-one-year-old Sherpa guide, had appeared suddenly, like a wood sprite. "Nice town, yes?"

"Yes!" Maya said. "It's beautiful!"

"You like?" He brushed a shock of hair out of his eyes and flashed his wide, ironic grin. "Western people like very much."

"I do. It was worth the climb."

"I do not like," Tashi said, pulling a pair of dark sunglasses out of the pocket of his blue-and-purple ski jacket. "I do not like mountains."

Maya laughed. "Tashi, how can you say that?"

"It is true. I like the large, flat valley, with the deep river, to swim."

"You're jaded."

Tashi shrugged and, over her protests, lifted her day pack off her shoulders and slung it by one strap over the pack he already carried on his back.

"No, Tashi, I'll carry that, really—I want to!" It was her life he was carrying away, her past, her letters, her mother's ashes. She needed to carry them herself. That was part of the pilgrimage, the penance, the magic.

But he was ahead of her now, smiling, her life disappearing with him around the curve of the trail.

"Now you are tired," he called back. "I will carry to Ang's house. Come with me."

She followed, entering the magic town with a sense of failure.

4

Namche Bazaar

At an altitude of 11,300 feet, Namche Bazaar is the
largest Sherpa village. Spectacular views of snowy
peaks include Khunde (21,741 ft.), Thamserku
(21,679 ft.) and Kantega (22,240 ft.). You will most
likely stay in a traditional Sherpa home, guests of
one of Mountain Co-op's many friends here.

—*MOUNTAIN CO-OP ADVENTURES*
BROCHURE

Maya sat on the bench that lined the south side of the main room of Ang's
house, her back against the wall, her feet tucked into her sleeping bag.
Her pack had been restored to her by a smiling Tashi as soon as they
reached Ang's house on the far side of Namche. Her journal lay beside
her, but she was too distracted to write. Debby was not there. Ang had
gone out to see if he could track down any message from her, and Maya
had wanted to go with him but her feet and lungs protested.

"You wait, rest," Ang had said, smiling kindly at her. "Much uphill,
today. Better to rest."

Maya had not argued with him. Now she sipped tea, watching Jan
and Lonnie, who sat back-to-back farther down the long bench. Jan was
drawing the view from the small window, which looked out over the
terraced fields and the sheer ice faces of the mountains across the small
plateau where Namche perched. Maya also had a window to look
through, but her view was partially obscured by potted plants and a
calendar decorated with tankas.

The light was dim, filtered by vines as it passed through the windows, but not so dark as the interiors of the houses she remembered in
Mexico and Central America, those windowless rectangles of adobe or

concrete blocks where big-eyed children seemed to peer endlessly from doorways.

Of the three goods—material wealth, spiritual wealth, and natural beauty—the room was set up to keep the evidence of material wealth before the eyes of guests. All the benches faced away from the views of the mountains, as if they were far less interesting than the display of large copper pots, aluminum pans, trunks, folded blankets, cans, plastic storage containers, folded sleeping mats, and drums that crammed the wooden shelves on the opposite wall. Maybe here natural beauty was so ubiquitous as to be unimportant.

The symbols of spiritual wealth, Maya noted, were all human in form. On the west wall, a wooden cabinet stood before a series of color pictures: the tantric deities coupling in ecstatic union, the Dalai Lama, Buddhas, and Rinpoches. Silver cups marched in a line across the top of the cabinet. From the ceiling hung a gold foil canopy bordered by a cloth patchwork fringe and strung with cut-paper garlands.

Odd, she'd always thought of Buddhism as the most abstract and rarified of religions, without a deity or a Supreme Being. But here, ultimate mind was everywhere manifested by things: statues and images and paintings in bright colors that stood out shockingly in a spare world where nature provided a palate of greens and grays, blacks and whites. The Bible says we are made in God's image, she reflected; *au contraire,* we seem to need to make our gods in the image of ourselves. Even our goddesses, Maya admitted. Maybe that was my mistake. Maybe I should never have let the powers take on names for me, never given them form, called them Goddess. To name them is to limit them, and to limit them in any way is to be restricted by those same boundaries.

But that's what we do, because we can't wrap our minds around the reality of that mountain out there, the sheer mass of granite lifting itself to split the sky. We have to make the mountain mean something, to bring it down to human terms, climb it or log it or photograph it, because we don't know how to simply stand in awe of what is.

Or maybe the Sherpas do know. Maybe when wonder is an everyday phenomenon, it becomes embedded in the ordinary. You no longer need to make a fuss, point out every extraordinary feature, erect neon signs in the psyche shouting, "Look! Look here!" An ordinary wonder is like an old, comfortable relationship, someone you've been with so long, known so intimately, that actually making love seems redundant.

Like me and Johanna. Maybe we've become so familiar with our mountain that we no longer look at it. We just climb its back and shelter under its trees.

Pembila, Ang's sweet-faced wife, came out of the kitchen and replaced the metal teapot with a fresh thermos. Maya refilled her cup, cradling it in her hands, grateful for the warmth, wishing her sister were there with her.

What could have happened to Debby? Only about a thousand things. She could be stuck with a medical emergency or sick herself or away. What if she hadn't gotten Maya's message? What if she didn't come at all?

Down the bench, Jan was biting her lip in concentration, brushing back her long, pale hair, glancing out the window and then back at the sketchbook on her lap, making lines and rubbing them out again. Lonnie's dark curls framed Jan's sleek head like a halo, and Maya could feel what passed between them, the awareness in every nerve and cell of the touch of the other, the heat passing from back to back. Yes, surely they were the mountain, they were Sagarmatha, Chomolungma, Ama Dablam, the Mother's Charm Box, to each other. How long had it been since she and Johanna had generated that pure intensity?

Years, maybe. No, that wasn't fair. They had interludes of passion, but they came and went. Maybe that's all we can expect, Maya thought. Maybe passion can never be constant.

Lonnie shifted her position and Jan let out a soft cry of protest.

"Don't move! Don't move yet! I'm almost done."

"My ass is turning into ice," Lonnie said.

"Don't jiggle."

"I miss my sofa. I miss my central heating. I miss my bathtub!"

"Don't whine."

Lonnie's hand reached behind her and subtly, almost invisibly, traced the seam of Jan's jeans as it curved over her hips and down the outside of her thigh. Maya wondered if she should leave them alone. But this big, open room, where anyone could walk in at any moment, was no place for privacy.

"You better be producing a great work of art, is all I can say. Did Van Gogh's wife ever do this for him?"

"Van Gogh didn't have a wife."

Now Jan reached down and gave Lonnie's hand a quick, hard squeeze. Maybe Maya should leave the room for her own sake, not theirs. She could feel them wanting to embrace, so strongly that it made her teeth ache. But there was no place else to go. Ang's kitchen was too smoky for her cough, and even if she hadn't been so tired, she didn't want to leave until Ang came back. Maybe he would have a message from Debby. Maybe Debby herself would still come tonight.

"Gauguin, then."

"Gauguin had a wife and four children he left to starve in France while he went off to Tahiti to paint and infect half the island with gonorrhea," Jan was saying.

"Send her to me," Lonnie said. "I'll sue the bastard for support. Lawyers' fees and court costs, too."

"Quiet, I'm concentrating," Jan said.

Maya opened her journal, then shut it again. She didn't feel like making the effort to push her pen around the page.

What if Debby resented Maya coming to Nepal, intruding on her private world? Obviously, she liked having ten thousand miles between herself and her family. And she'd always questioned Maya's motives, expected the worst from her.

Maya smiled suddenly, remembering one afternoon when she was about twelve years old and Debby seven. Maya, who was still called Karla then, had started menstruating a month or two before. She was having terrible cramps that day and a heavy flow, so she'd decided to take a hot bath. Her friend Joyce Levine had told her that the bleeding stops in water. Nobody, however, had informed her uterus of that fact. As soon as Maya had lowered herself into the bath, the water turned bright pink. The heat loosened her cervix and she felt as if she were gushing blood, drowning in it.

"Mom!" she'd screamed. "Mom, come here!"

Betty was on the far side of the house, and Debby had come instead, peeking in through the doorway.

"Go away!" Maya had yelled. "I want Mom!"

Debby, who had recently seen some old movie in which a Roman senator opened his veins in the bath, saw her sister immersed in a tub of bloody water and began to cry. "Mom! Karla's dying!"

"I'm not dying," Maya had yelled, but Debby's wails had drowned out her voice. The door slammed, and Maya could hear screams and running footsteps.

"She's bleeding to death! She's killed herself in the bathtub!"

"Karla!" Betty had screamed, bursting into the bathroom. "Karla! What's wrong? Oh my God, why did you do it? Why did you do it?"

"I'll call the operator and get an ambulance," Debby called from the hall.

"NO!" Maya screamed, certain she would indeed die shortly, of embarrassment. "Mom, stop her! Stop her! Mom! I'm not dying!"

"Let me see your wrists. I'll get a towel. I'll get a bandage. Don't move." Betty hovered over the tub, frantic.

"Just get me a Kotex!"

"That won't do any good, we need to put pressure on the veins. Just stay calm."

"It's not my veins, I just need a Kotex!"

Betty blinked.

"A what?"

"A Kotex."

"That's all? You nearly give me a heart attack, over a Kotex?"

"I didn't do anything, it was Debby!"

"It was not!"

"It was so!"

"Shut up, both of you!"

"Make her get out of here and leave me alone!" Maya had pleaded.

"You shut up! You can't be dying if you can yell like that."

There was a moment of quiet. Debby calmed down.

"If Karla does die, Mom, can I have her room?" she asked.

"I am not dying!" Karla snapped. "And I would appreciate a little privacy. All I want is a Kotex so I can get out of this tub without bleeding on the floor."

"Gross," Debby said.

"I didn't ask for your opinion. What do I do now, Mom? Joyce told me it would stop in the water, but it didn't!"

"Pull out the plug," Betty said, sitting down on the toilet. "Just let the water drain." Then she began to laugh, and Karla, catching sight of her, started to laugh, too. Soon they were both laughing so hard they were crying. Debby merely looked disgusted as they tried to explain.

"Every month?" Debby had said, appalled. "That's going to happen every month?"

"You know about it." Betty had slipped an arm around Debby's shoulder. "I've explained it to you before."

"Yeah, but you didn't tell me how gross it was."

Remembering, Maya laughed to herself. She would have to remind Debby of the scene; it was one of the good times with Betty, one of the moments when they felt bonded, three hysterical women together.

Jan let out a long breath, held her picture out, and pronounced it done.

"Let me see, let me see." Lonnie bounced up from the bench and knocked into the long, low table that fronted it. "I've got to see if it was worth the sacrifice of my rear end."

"It's okay," Jan said. "It's getting there."

"It's beautiful!" Lonnie exclaimed. "Maya, come and look."

Maya uncurled her legs and removed them from the warmth of her bag. She went over to where the other women sat, and looked at the sketch in the fading light that came in from the window. Jan had drawn the *stuppa,* the small Buddhist shrine, a hemisphere of whitewashed stone crowned by a white cube decorated with painted eyes and a strange question-mark-like symbol where a nose might have been expected. In the drawing, the whiteness of the *stuppa* stood out against the textures of the ground and the rough rocks and forms of women bent over to hoe the fields. Light played over the surface, caught in the edge of a stone here, the profile of a face there, and the *stuppa* seemed to be both its source and its main reflector.

"It's lovely," Maya said. "You've caught the magic."

"I wanted to put in the mountains behind," Jan said. "I wanted that contrast of intimacy, in the fields and the village and the structures, and sheer, immense space. But the paper isn't big enough. Or I'm not good enough."

"Don't say that," Lonnie protested. "You are good. Damn good!"

"Not as good as I want to be," Jan said.

"No artist ever is," Maya said. She looked out the window again. Ang's house was built on a terrace. In the fields below, the women were packing up their hoes and hoisting their babies onto their backs as the light began to fail. They reminded her of other women she had seen, long ago, carrying their babies wrapped in shawls, gathering firewood or maguey, following their menfolk to the fields of corn. She had spent a lot of her life looking at other people's fields, other people's bending and stooping and sweating to feed themselves, while she watched and dreamed and wrote. Without doubt she was among the privileged of the earth. What had she done, what could she do, to deserve it?

She sighed. Maybe Debby thought she was frivolous, coming on a pleasure trip to the place where her sister worked hard and made sacrifices to give these people care. Maybe she wouldn't want to reminisce about Betty, to talk with Maya the way Maya needed to talk with her.

Across the fields, where the dirt streets curved around to the other bar of the horseshoe, Maya caught a glimpse of green. The girl in the sweater walked purposefully down the street, looking at home, looking as if she belonged. She was revealed, just for a moment, in a gap between two buildings.

What was she doing? Maya wondered. Where was she going? The mountains rose behind her, promising an unattainable purity, clarity. If only Maya had the strength to run out of this building, up to their beckoning white slopes. Still she could feel the call, the desire, the need to climb beyond the trekking paths, above base camp, into the ultimate altitudes, the unvisited heights.

The door opened and Ang came in, smiling. That could mean good news, or that could mean nothing: Ang smiled whenever he looked at Maya, his kind eyes crinkling into narrow creases in his leathery face.

"Did you find out?" Maya asked, trying not to sound too anxious. "Is she coming?"

"I have found a letter for you," Ang said, handing it to her.

"Thank you. Thank you so much."

"No problem."

Maya sat down again on the bench, and read:

Dear Karla—excuse me, I mean Maya. I never can get used to calling
you that. I got your message, and I had really hoped to get down to
Namche to meet you, but my relief partner, Jim, isn't back yet from
an emergency he was covering a day's walk from here. Actually,
everything's a day's walk from here, if not farther. I hope he'll be
back tomorrow, and I can join you, but if not, I'm sure I'll catch you
at Tengpoche.

The trekking company said they had a letter from you, but it
seems to have gone astray, and the message they gave me didn't say
anything about Mom, just that you were coming. I'm assuming that
means bad news, or you wouldn't have left her to come here. What
can I say? I wish you'd telegrammed—you know how unreliable the
mail is here. But we'll talk when we see each other.

Love,
Debby

Maya set the letter down. Maybe it's just as well, she thought,
trying to control her disappointment. I'm so tired, now, and she's decided to be mad at me. I don't have the energy for arguments and expla-
nations. Tomorrow I'll be rested and fresh. Still, she could have said
something to indicate a little warmth, a little excitement that I'm here.
Instead she makes me feel like I'm just another scheduling problem.
Maybe I was wrong to come.

She felt a cold pang in her gut. There's nobody to pull us together,
now, she thought. If we don't make the effort, we could spin off into
space and never connect again.

Suddenly Maya felt terribly alone. She ached to feel Johanna's hand
smoothing her forehead, to hear her low voice crooning comfort. Or
Rio—she would even have welcomed him. She longed for someone who
had shared something real with her; a love, a past, a tragedy.

The room was cold, and she tucked her feet up under her sleeping
bag. Yes, even if she wanted nothing to do with Rio now, he was embedded in her life like shards in soil strata, part of her archaeological record,
her Formative period. Maybe she should go to Nevada. She would have to
decide on this trip. Maybe she'd made a mistake, trying to leave him in
the safe, entombed past.

She sighed softly. If she could only dig deep enough, explore far
enough, long enough, high enough, if she could track the Milk River to
its source, maybe then she would at last understand how everything
began and how it all got so tangled up together, her and Betty and Debby,
Johanna and Rio, too. Maybe then she could pick up the trail she had lost.

Now, before the last of the daylight was gone, before the kitchen boys brought up pots of tea and bowls of steaming soup and a dinner of lots of different things, all fried—now she would read Rio's old letters. She would decide what to do about Nevada, about her life. Reaching into her pack, she pulled out a bundle and settled it on her lap, leaning back against the window to catch the last of the light. She looked down. But it was not the packet of Rio's letters she held in her hand. Instead, she recognized Johanna's handwriting, her almond-colored writing paper. She pulled the top sheet off the bundle.

"Love," she read, "you say you want to get away and think, to sort out our relationship and our history. I can't go with you and I can't help you. I can't even say clearly what I hope for when you return. All I can offer is a touch of perspective, a few pages torn from my journals here and there. Enjoy. Johanna."

Enjoy. She wasn't sure that was the right word. Instead, as she opened the papers and spread the first section out before her, she had the sensation of starting on another climb, a laborious journey through a landscape of memory. People always talk about delving down into the past, she thought. How much better to ascend, to haul yourself up above it, where you can get an overview.

She skimmed through the pages Johanna had given her, noting the dates. Yes, if she put them together with Rio's old letters, she would have a series of overlooks along the memory trail.

I guess I'm not the sort of person who can just take a vacation, she admitted. I've brought along my own mountain to ascend in tandem with the terrain. A double pilgrimage.

Pulling her bag up closer around her body, she began to read.

5

Johanna Weaver's
Diary

May 20, 1967

Dear Sheba:

    Well, we're in trouble now! Marian is screaming and we're both grounded for the rest of the weekend and next weekend, too. And it's so unfair!

    Yesterday was the big demonstration against the war, over at Century City, not too far from here. Karla and I really wanted to go, and we both weren't supposed to, for different reasons. Mama—I mean Marian, I'm trying to remember to call her that in this diary even though she'd whop me upside the head if I called her that to her face. Or at least *Mom*—*Mama* is so old-fashioned. *Marian* wouldn't let me go because of Uncle Marcus, who is over there fighting. Mom prays for him every day, and I can see her wince whenever the doorbell rings unexpectedly, in case it's a telegram. That's how she found out about Daddy, when he got killed in Korea when I was just a baby. And in spite of what Sue Mansfield's nasty father says, I know they were married because I've seen her ring and the look she gets on her face when she talks about him, not to mention the fact that we get money from the VA. Still that was a long time ago and I wish she'd get married again. Otherwise who's going to take care of her when I grow up and go away?

    The men in our family run to warriors, Mama says, but I say that maybe they don't always fight for the right things. I love Uncle Marcus, and because of that it took me a long time to come around to be against the war, but I can't close my eyes forever to what's going on there. So Mom and I had a big fight. I told her I was entitled to my opinion, and she said as long as I was living in her house I would respect her views, and how would Uncle Marcus feel, risking his life in Vietnam, knowing I was out in the street working against him? But I said, first of all, he wouldn't know I was out demonstrating unless she told him, and secondly, I wouldn't be working against him, I'd be working for him, trying to get him brought back home before he gets killed. Or before he does something awful. I know they're killing women and children and babies over there. I've seen the pictures and heard the stories. But I can't believe my uncle is doing it. He loves kids. When I was little he always used to take me and my friends out and play softball, and he would bring me the best presents. Like I remember when Troll Dolls were the in thing and Mom wouldn't get me one, but he did.

Anyway, it didn't matter how much we yelled or how logical and fair my arguments were, Marian still wouldn't let me go. Betty wouldn't let Karla go for another reason. She said she was afraid Karla would get her name on a list, that they had lived through enough of that with her father during the McCarthy time. Karla was really furious. She called Betty a hypocrite, and I had to agree with her, although I didn't say so to Betty. That would only have made things worse.

Betty is against the war herself, she just doesn't want to do anything about it. I guess that's her right, but she shouldn't try to stop Karla. It's her life. Just because you're only seventeen—or sixteen in the case of Karla, her birthday's next month—just because you're young doesn't mean you can't have an opinion about things and a right to speak your mind. Really, we should have more of a right to speak out because we've got to live in this world a lot longer than the grown-ups. We'll be around long after they're dead.

So we were mad. Ordinarily, I don't like to deceive Mom, but in this case I felt it was my moral duty. So Karla and I told Marian and Betty that we were going over to Joyce Levine's to study. And Joyce said her older sister would cover for us, and say we had gone out for a burger if anybody called. Joyce herself was supposed to meet us at the demonstration, and Karla and I took the bus down to Century City.

There were thousands and thousands of people there, the biggest crowd I'd ever been in. We never did find Joyce. The whole street was blocked off in front of the Century Plaza Hotel, and we had to walk a long way down to get to the back of the march and join in. There was just about every kind of person there, old and young, although not too many other black people besides me. Some people looked like hippies, with long, stringy hair, some of them were in blue jeans and work shirts, but a lot of people looked like they had dressed up to try to appear respectable. That's what Karla and I did. We'd talked it over, and she wore her plaid skirt and a white blouse and I wore my summer dress with the pink flowers and my half heels, the white sandals. That was a mistake. I'll never wear high heels to a demonstration again, if I ever get out of this house and get to go to one again.

We marched up the road until all the people came together in front of the hotel, where supposedly President Johnson is staying. Some of the

time we were singing "Ain't gonna study war no more" and some of the
time we were chanting "Hey, hey, LBJ, how many kids did you kill
today?" Then they had the rally, and different people got up to speak.
Most of them just did the usual thing, yelling about how bad the war is
and trying to work up the crowd. But then this Vietnamese woman got
up on the stage. She was so tiny you could hardly see her above the
crowd, and she had spent five months in the tiger cages, these pits that
are so small you can't lie down or stand up or move very much. They just
throw you down a little food to eat and hardly any water in the broiling
heat, and you have to go to the bathroom right there where you are. And,
Sheba, they had tortured her, because they thought she had been helping
the Vietcong. They'd whipped her on the soles of her feet and burned
her breasts with cigarettes.

I felt sick. The war suddenly got very real to me. The problem is,
you know, when something is going on halfway around the world, it's
hard to feel it. You see the story on TV, and it's just another story. And
meanwhile, real life, your own ordinary life, is kind of pleasant. I live in a
nice house, and Karla's next door is even nicer and bigger. Not rich or
fancy, but clean and comfortable and we each have our own bedrooms.
We go to a good school. Some of the classes are boring but it's better than
a lot of schools. Everybody expects that we'll go to college and marry
doctors or teachers or lawyers and have plenty of money. That's what life
is supposed to be like—comfortable. Supposedly everybody can have a
life like that if they want it and work for it, in this country at least.

But that's a lie. All this comfort is a lie. It stops at the gates of the
ghetto and the Mexican border. It's bought at the price of somebody
else's pain. Some child goes hungry for every mouthful I eat.

They shouldn't have lied to us, Sheba. They shouldn't have fed us
all that crap about liberty and justice and the land of opportunity. Because the thing is, we believed it, and now when we find out they're
torturing people and murdering children and letting little babies go hungry, we can't believe in anything they say anymore. And we're mad! I'm
mad. I'm angry every day. I don't want to feel like this—I don't want to
feel like everything good I have is taken away from somebody. I don't
want to be the Exceptional Negro, the one who proves that the system
can work because after all, it lets me go to a good school and get good
grades.

Mad, mad, mad, angry mad and crazy mad. Sometimes I think I *will*
go crazy, living my ordinary comfortable life with nothing to complain
about, and all the while I'm hearing the scream below the surface.

Anyway, I'm glad I heard the tiger cage woman speak, even though
she made me cry. Because she's real. Just then a whole busload of cops
came up and made a line across the roadway. They were dressed in heavy
leather jackets and gloves and carried big plastic shields and clubs, and

they looked scary. For a moment there I wished I'd listened to Mom, but when I thought about what that Vietnamese woman had gone through, how she'd suffered, I felt ashamed to be such a coward.

The sheriff got up on the back of a truck with a bullhorn and ordered everybody to disperse. Now the thing is, Karla and I couldn't have dispersed if we'd wanted to because we were smack in the middle of about ten thousand people, and we couldn't move very far. Some of the demonstrators were arguing with the cops and a few of them sat down and linked arms, and then the line of cops began to move into the crowd, bashing people with their clubs. Some people started screaming and other people were just yelling and swearing and half the crowd started easing back but the other half was trying to push forward, and I thought we were going to be trampled in between. The stupid cops kept beating people for not leaving, but the people they were beating couldn't go anywhere because the people behind them weren't moving away. It was like a nightmare. With those stupid shoes, I couldn't even walk too well, let alone try to run. Karla grabbed my hand, so we wouldn't get separated, and towed me along through the crush. There were a few moments when I thought I was going to fall and get the breath crushed out of me, but she led us out to the side, to an open spot where we could make our way down a small hill to the next street below. She held my hand and kept me steady, but once I did slip and twisted my ankle. Luckily it wasn't bad. I swear I'm going to give those shoes to the Salvation Army.

We made it down to the other street, where a few cars were driving by. I could still hear the shouts and the chants and the bullhorns, but we figured we had done enough. Karla stuck out her thumb and caught us a ride with some UCLA students going back up to campus. Ordinarily I don't hitchhike. Mom says it isn't safe and I don't want to prove her right, but this was a special occasion.

Joyce's house isn't far from campus, and we arrived at her door just in time to get a telephone call from Betty, checking up on us. I only heard Karla's end of it.

"No, we've just been hanging around here all afternoon. Nothing special."

Pause.

"Yeah, we were out in the yard for a bit. I guess we didn't hear the phone."

Pause.

"We were thinking of getting a pizza and taking another crack at Spanish. Okay? See you later, Mom."

So, we thought we were cool, until we watched the six-o'clock news. They had great shots of the demonstration, the cops beating on people, everything. Including a gorgeous, full-face shot of me and Karla,

holding hands, picking our way down the hill, a perfect picture of interracial harmony.

"Shit," Karla said. "Oh, shit. What do we do now?"

"Pray," I said. "Please, Jesus, don't let Betty or Mama watch the
news tonight."

But Jesus was not on our side.

Sure enough, ten minutes later we got a call from my mother
telling us to get home at once. Her voice was icy cold. Joyce's house is
about a mile away and we could have walked, but her brother offered to
drive us. I wasn't sure if that was good or bad—I would have liked to
postpone the scene, but we had to face it eventually. Better to get it over
with.

My mother and Karla's mom were both waiting at her house. They
looked really mad when we walked in.

"You lied to us," Marian said right away. "We trusted you and you
lied to us."

Karla tried to explain, quite reasonably I thought, that we'd had to
lie because if we'd told them the truth they wouldn't have let us go. But
they weren't buying that.

"The government is lying to us," I said to Marian. I told her about
the tiger cages, but her face just closed up as if she'd shut her eyes and
ears and nothing could penetrate.

"Your uncle would not participate in anything like that," Marian
said. "That's communist propaganda."

But I could hear something in her voice, Sheba, just a little quiver
of uncertainty, and I realized that deep inside she did hear what I was
saying. Maybe she even believed it. Still she had to try not to, because she
loves her brother. She was holding on to the lie so as not to lose the love,
and it scared me to realize that love can make people do that.

Betty was looking at her kind of sadly and I felt bad for Betty, too.
Because she did believe us, she's hip enough to know that the torture is
real. And she knows that we *should* stand up against it, but she's afraid.
That's what it comes down to. So she seemed kind of pitiful to me. I
don't want to end up like her, being afraid to do what I believe. And I
don't want to end up like Marian, closing my eyes to what's real in order
to love.

"The war is not the issue here," Betty said. "The issue is that you
lied and disobeyed us."

"The war is the issue," Karla said. "You had no right to tell us not
to go to the demonstration."

"We are your mothers. We are responsible for you," Betty said.
"When you grow up and leave home, you can do whatever you like. But
until then, you'll do what I say."

"I won't," Karla said. "You're wrong. You have no right to stop me from standing up for what I believe in. It's like in Nazi Germany—I'm not following orders if they're wrong."

"Don't give me Nazi Germany," Betty said. "You know nothing about it."

"I do know! I've heard about it my whole goddamned life! You won't buy a Volkswagen or a German camera because of what they did in the war . . . well fine. I'm not going to be a good German. When my kids ask me what I did during the war, I want to say I did everything I could to stop it!"

Betty shook her head. I could see that what Karla had said struck home, but Betty tried to fight it off. "I admire your spirit," she admitted. "But it's my job to protect you. Look at what happened—your picture on the news like that. How do you know it won't go into a file for them to use against you when you want to get a job? You know what happened to your father."

"He's doing all right," Karla said. "Why don't you call him, see what he says? He'll tell you I'm absolutely right."

Up until then, she'd been doing great. She might even have convinced Betty to come around. But dragging in her father—that was dirty fighting. Her dad was a communist back in the thirties, and he's still this famous radical lawyer, but he ran off with a younger woman he met at a hearing of the House Un-American Activities Committee and left Betty to raise the kids alone.

"Don't drag your father into this! What Joe Greenbaum thinks cuts no ice with me. He was no help in raising you, and he's not going to start telling me how to do it now."

"At least he acts on his ideals," Karla said. Oooh, child, I thought, that was mean. And not wise.

"His ideals!" Now Betty was really mad, and her voice kept rising until she was yelling, which she does a lot. "His goddamned pristine ideals—sure he acts on them. As long as somebody else pays the price, buys the groceries, cleans the snot from your noses. He can't be bothered with any of that. Oh no, he's got to go off and save the world. What does he care if his own kids starve, if I have to work my fingers to the bone? Well, I'll tell you something, Miss Idealism. You go ahead, go to every goddamned demonstration you want, have every ideal you think is so precious that it justifies hurting the people who depend on you. You're just like him! A liar and a cheat!"

Karla opened her mouth to say something else, but I figured I better jump in before she dug us in any deeper.

"I'm sorry I lied," I said to Marian, "but I'm glad I went to the demonstration. I won't lie to you again, but if I want to go to another protest, I will. I'm seventeen years old, and I have a right to think what I think, and you can't stop me."

Marian looked grim. "I put the food on your table," she said. Which is true, but that still doesn't entitle her to keep me from doing what I think is right. She stood up. "We're going home, now. You're grounded for the rest of the weekend, and next weekend too."

I shrugged my shoulders and followed her home. But she was on night shift at the hospital, and after she left, Karla called me on the telephone.

"I can't believe them," she said. "They're such hypocrites."

"Your mother is a hypocrite," I said. I was talking on the telephone in Marian's room, lying on her bed. Up on the wall were pictures of me as a baby and Grandma and Grandpa and Martin Luther King and my dad in his uniform and Uncle Marcus in his. "Mine is just a poor dupe of the system."

"My dad, too," Karla said. "He called, from New York. He saw us on the news—the picture went national. He was all proud and like, 'Nice going, Karla, I see you take after your old man,' but when I told him how mad Mom got, all he could say was, 'Well, Karla, I think she's wrong but she's raising you. You've got to respect her.' Bullshit! What's wrong with everybody, Jo? Do you think there's some secret laboratory where they take you when you reach a certain age and inject you with bullshit serum, so you can't recognize the real thing when you hear it?"

"It just hurts that my mother won't listen to me," I told her. "She won't admit that I can have an opinion that's worth something."

"We can't let them get away with it," Karla said. "We can't let them turn us into bullshitters, too. You were right, at the end there. We were wrong to lie—that just buys into the whole game. You were so strong, Jo—God, you were beautiful! When you said, 'I won't lie but you can't stop me doing what's right.' "

"The problem is," I said, staring up at the pictures, "they both do have ideals. They raised us to think. All our heroes were the people who stood up for what they believed in. Martin Luther King is like God in our house. But when we do, they get afraid."

"We can't let ourselves get afraid," Karla said. "We've got to keep our eyes open for the lies and use every tool we have to cut through them."

"Like what?" I asked, because a certain note in her voice made me think she had something specific in mind.

She spoke real softly, almost in a whisper. "Maybe it's time to do the acid."

Megan Ricci had given me two hits of acid for my birthday. She knew Karla and I'd been wanting to take some together. I'd only ever done that half a hit with Charles from the Baptist Youth Group—wouldn't Marian die if she knew? Poor Mom, she was so happy I was going out with a nice young man from the church—she never knew what happened while she was on night shift. And I never knew how much was the acid and how much was what we did to each other under its influence. Too bad his dad got transferred to Germany. Karla dropped once with Tony Klein when they went to the Jefferson Airplane concert. She said the stuff they had wasn't very strong. She didn't hallucinate, but she felt like she could see right through the surface of things, like X-ray vision, down to the reality below.

I had the acid in the bottom of my underwear drawer, two hits of Purple Owsley—supposed to be the best there is. We were saving them for the right time.

"We're grounded," I reminded her. "We'll have to wait another week or two."

"We can do it at school," Karla said. "Monday."

"Won't that be dangerous?" I asked her.

"Nah, we can maintain. Like I said, you can still do everything you usually do, it's just that you understand what it means at a deeper level."

"But I thought we wanted to go to the beach, or someplace nice."

"We can do that too, sometime. But what better place to see through the lies than in the heart of the lie machine itself?"

I couldn't argue with her.

So, Sheba, that's what we're going to do, Monday morning. I hope it turns out okay. And I really hope nobody ever reads this—especially not Marian!

Wow, I've written a lot! I guess that's the one advantage of being grounded—it gives you plenty of time to write in your journal.

Johanna

6

Dawn at Namche

Thou canst not travel on the path before thou hast
become that path itself.

—THE VOICE OF THE SILENCE
THE WISDOM OF BUDDHISM

The sun was just a hint, a glimmer of light behind the high peaks that
cradled Namche as Maya squatted on the ledge outside Ang's house to
pee. No one else was awake yet, and that was fortunate. Had someone
else been around, she would have had to negotiate the treacherous stone
steps up to the outhouse. Now she had the world to herself, the high
peaks ice blue against an indigo sky just beginning to lighten from black.

Almost dawn, she thought. A new day, a new beginning. I should
get up more often with the dawn. Maybe then I'd have more insight into
origins, into the roots of things.

But really, where does anything begin? Jo, you think it began with
that demonstration, with a lie we told in service of a bigger truth. Or did
it begin earlier—on the day your mother came looking for a place to rent,
towing a daughter with two long pigtails hanging down her back, and we
looked at each other and began to giggle while our mothers talked? Or
earlier still, maybe the day my father walked out the door and never came
back, or the night a bullet found your father's heart in Korea, or the day
they met, Joe and Betty, Herman and Marian? Or we could trace the
beginning even further back, until we find those first protozoa or
amoebas or whatever who liked the look of each other and invented the
exchange of DNA.

Then again, maybe all of that was merely a prelude to what we did
the next day. Certainly, when we were in the middle of it, we would have
sworn that six billion years of evolution were culminating in that one

event. The arrogance of youth allied to the grandiosity of LSD—a dangerous combination.

I don't think I'll go back to bed, Jo. I'm just going to huddle here on this ledge with my fists in the pockets of my down jacket, watch the sun climb mountains, and remember.

7

May 1967

"There was this man," Steve Baer was saying, "who kept having the same dream, over and over again, about this plane that was going to crash."

Karla lay collapsed on the lawn behind the music bungalows at Harding High, Johanna beside her. Their friends surrounded them, smoking and gossiping before the bell rang for class. The day had barely started, but Karla had already been high too long. Insects crawled between her lids and the surfaces of her eyes. When she opened them, the faces of her dearest friends leered at her and began to melt away.

Outside the school yard, cars cruised by like sharks—black, red, pink—like the '57 Chevy her mother still drove. Could it be Betty, checking up on her? No, Karla was getting paranoid. Betty had bought the car new, ten years before, when Karla's father went away. She remembered the thrill of that ride, piled in the front seat next to her baby sister, Debby, breathing in that vinyl, new-car smell. It had seemed to make up for something. Her mother had been weeping silently while she, Karla, read all the signs on the freeway. She was only seven years old, but she had always been good with words. Except the hard ones. She remembered having trouble with *exit*.

Karla turned over onto her stomach. The grass smelled good, earthy and sweet. Above her, ominous conversation buzzed on.

"Night after night, he dreamed the crash. So finally he called the Van Nuys airport and found out they had a plane with the same identification number. Do you know what the odds against that are?" Steve asked and Karla was sinking. She couldn't understand why he was tormenting them all with this story that went on and on, about how the man had begged the plane's owner not to take it up, and the owner had said it was being repaired and was grounded, but that night the man dreamed it crashed through the wall of his house.

She knew the story meant something, but she didn't know what. It was a message she couldn't read.

Someone tapped her on the back. She sat up and Megan Ricci handed her a joint. Karla stared at it, pondering the name, wondering why they called it a joint. Who or what did it join?

"Stay out of your head," Johanna told her, taking the joint away from her and inhaling.

". . . and so the man and his wife moved to a motel," Steve said, "and that night the plane crashed into the motel room, the room where they had gone to escape it. Just exactly like in the dream."

Suddenly Karla wished, more than anything, that this were a normal day, that the leaves of the oleander would stop speaking to her and that she could be the good girl she was supposed to be, with her homework done, and cocoa waiting for her at home when school was over. We've blown it, she thought. The acid is too much for us, too strong. It wasn't like this when I tripped before.

"We're all going to die," Johanna said.

Karla turned and looked at her. Johanna's eyes were round and too big, two dark staring lamps, and her hair looked funny. Every month or two her mother took her to have it straightened at the beauty parlor on Florence Avenue. She wore her hair in a smooth cap that hugged her head, but today the edges were separated into stiff spikes. Karla straightened her own hair by setting it on big orange juice cans or, when she got desperate, ironing it, but it never would hang in long, smooth sheets like the girls in the magazines. Right now it curled in dark snakes around her neck and hung from her temples like the forelocks of her ancestors.

We're coming apart, she thought. The acid is doing it to us. We're fakes, trying to cover our heads and turn ourselves into what we're not. We thought the acid would show us the lies, but we're the liars.

"I've heard this from a lot of people and I know it's true," Joyce Levine was saying behind them, "that they just can't communicate . . ."

"Maintain," Karla whispered. That was their only hope. Maintain the illusion, maintain the game, make the proper responses that were important for a reason she could no longer remember.

". . . with anyone who doesn't use drugs."

Johanna's voice jerked Karla back.

"Why?" she asked. "It's a lie."

Karla knew there must be an answer but she couldn't remember what it was. And there was something important she was supposed to do but she couldn't remember that either. Her throat was dry and a clutch of eggs seemed to be hatching in her belly. She could feel the birds peck and scratch. It was fear, she realized. She was afraid of what would happen if she couldn't maintain. Fear kept the game together.

She began to follow that one around.

"And do you really think," Joyce was saying, "that if you turn on, and your friends don't . . ."

"You can't laugh off a thing like that, you know," Steve went on, his eyes earnest behind his thick brown-framed glasses. "You can't pretend it didn't happen, that those things don't. Of course everyone knows someone they respect, his mind and his emotions, who's had something like that happen to him."

". . . that you won't drift apart?" Joyce said. "That it doesn't create a gulf?"

Joyce loomed above them, her brown cloud of frizzy hair flaming in the sun. She worked her mouth nervously, biting her lips and chewing the insides of her cheeks. She had a broad mouth, a generous mouth, a clown's mouth, and Karla knew how Joyce hated it, how many hours they had spent together, two years back, practicing with Joyce's older sister's makeup, striving to hide their flaws. Suddenly that made her infinitely sad.

"You're beautiful," she said to Joyce. "You're really fucking beautiful."

"Oh my God! Karla!" Joyce said, turning to look at her for the first time. "How did you get so stoned?"

Johanna sat up, looked at them both, and beamed beatifically. The early sun flared in a halo behind her head. "Jus' lucky I guess," she said. Then she began to laugh, and Karla joined her. Tears in their eyes, they rolled on the ground.

". . . and if you call that coincidence," Steve Baer went on, although nobody was listening to him any longer, "then you're saying that anything can happen."

"This is incredibly self-destructive," Joyce said. "I don't understand."

She had never dropped acid, she couldn't possibly understand. Joyce was yammering like a monkey. Karla looked at her with pity, and for a moment, she knew Joyce hated them. A wave of ice rolled toward her, broke over her head, pushed her down. It was true that there were times when she just could not communicate.

This was one of them.

The monkey was a mirror, Karla thought. A mirror of fear. Fear/mirror. Mere fear.

"Stay out of your head," Johanna said.

"You should go home," Joyce said. "You should both go home while you still can."

But they couldn't go home. On Mondays Betty saw her private clients in the living room, and Marian would be getting home from the night shift, reading the paper before she slept.

"We're safer here," Johanna said. "We're like the purloined letter."

"What?" Joyce asked.

"They won't look for us here because this is where they expect us to be."

Tony Klein, who edited *The Other Side,* their underground school newspaper, and was almost but not quite Karla's boyfriend, plopped down next to Johanna. He shook his head, and with his finger traced the letters *L-S-D* on her forehead.

"Neon," he said sadly. "It's written in neon. You can see it flashing half a block away."

Johanna's hand went slowly up to her forehead.

"For God's sake, Tony!" Joyce exploded. "Don't mindfuck. This is serious."

Karla could feel her own forehead throbbing, like the fluttering pulse inside when she touched herself, and yes, she wanted to mindfuck, to melt, shuddering mind into mind, flesh to flesh, and dissolve.

"You're beautiful," Johanna said to Karla and Joyce. "You dance with the angels. You shine like the stars."

Everything shifted. Reality was a toy made of plastic with a little picture on it that moved when you changed your angle of view. Joyce loved them. She cared, and her caring stretched tendrils across the cold reaches where things hurled unexpectedly out of the dark. Karla wanted to laugh and cry and reach for her.

The bell rang.

The numbers danced all around, 8s rolling and flopping on their sides, fat teddy bears, 9 a delicate dancer balanced on one toe. Karla was trying to solve this quadratic equation:

If infinite mind (A) is projected into infinite emptiness (n) and eternally (X^n) trying to return . . .

She was riding on an infinite plane that was somehow doomed to crash. Lines, sharp and cold as shards of ice, extended forever, through a void that was pointless because a point had no substance.

How long would the journey take?

"Karla?" Mrs. Ito, the math teacher, was asking a question.

The name fetched her back from the edge. Ito was waiting. Karla was scared. She had no idea what was going on back in Reality, USA.

"Well?"

A well is a hole in the ground. A well is a long way to fall. Just before she hit bottom, her mind, O well-trained dog, fetched a bone of a phrase.

"I'm sorry," she said. She was sorry for them all. They were all sliding down a hillside in an avalanche no one could stop, grasping at the underbrush that broke off in their hands. They were all going to die. She said it aloud.

"We're all going to die."

"Excuse me?" Mrs. Ito was not prepared to hear it. Megan Ricci who sat behind Karla kicked her chair sharply.

"My mind was wandering," Karla said. It was more true than Ito could guess.

The class exploded with laughter. Mrs. Ito looked perplexed.

"What is happening to this class?" she asked.

The bell rang, and so she never knew.

Habit remains where thought fails. Muscles contract, vessels pump, one foot follows another. Marvel at the intricacies that don't have to be thought about.

"You're skating a little close to the edge," Megan said in passing. "Take off. Go to my place. You know where the key is."

Megan was eighteen. She had moved out of her parents' house and lived with her boyfriend above the carousel at the Santa Monica pier. Karla wished she were there, listening to the tinkling music under her feet. She wished she could find Johanna; she had something to tell her.

Her feet seemed to know where they were going; they carried her. Habit remains when thought fails.

The thing is, she wanted to say, that I have seen beyond the lies and nothing's there. Can we please stop now? Go home and curl up on the sofa and drink hot tea? Do something, anything, to distract ourselves from this hollow place. But now she had seen it she could never go back. She could never again believe in all the things people pretend mean something.

Johanna was out of reach. She was sitting across the room, a world away. Frank Harvey, their English teacher, was writing on the board, and Karla couldn't reach her to ask how she was supposed to live, now that she knew.

Across from Karla, Marina Colby was distracting herself from the emptiness by rubbing lip gloss on her beautiful mouth, and John Weir barricaded the terror with a book, and behind her there was chatter to keep it away.

"You can carry back here and never know. I knew a girl once who was in her seventh month before she found out."

"She should have admitted to herself what she knew she was going to do and taken precautions."

"Stay out of your head," Johanna mouthed at Karla silently.

But when Karla fell out of her head, oh God, she was crawling through the dark. It was all she could do to keep from sinking to her knees.

They had not taken enough precautions. Perhaps precautions were impossible. The fact is, there was nowhere they could go to escape. Karla wanted to come down, she wanted to want to eat and sleep again, to want a scholarship to Columbia, to want her mother. But everything rang hollow when you touched it. There were no nets, no anchors, only ropes of cotton candy flung across the abyss. What was real lay in the waters below. What was real had jaws.

Frank Harvey was writing on the board. He had silver hair and a pointed beard and he looked like a dog, a fox terrier, grabbing strings of words and shaking them, barking at the wheels of meaning.

On the board, he had written a passage from the Upanishads: "Who sees all beings in his own self / and his own self in all beings / loses all fear."

Karla was drowning and he had thrown her a lifeline of words, and yet when she grasped for it she fell short. All around her, yes, she saw her own being. Frank Harvey was her defending herself with words and Danny Fields was her posturing and trying to dodge it and Sarah Borko was her trying to stay ahead of it by running everybody else down and everyone else was a mocking funhouse-mirror distortion of the ugliness. But what was wrong wasn't them but her. She should be finding the kingdom and glory, but instead she was finding nothing. No one home.

"Who has something to say about that?" Harvey asked, gazing down the rows as if taking aim.

The class was universally silent.

"Karla?" he asked. She was his favorite student, the one he could count on when everyone else went blank. He sent her papers back to her scribbled with compliments and exclamation points. He had the secretaries retype them and mimeograph them to show to his future classes. He believed that she could write.

Karla stood up and said the only thing she could say. "We're all going to die."

Harvey's eyes widened and he smiled, rubbing his hands together. "Exactly! We're all going to die—so how can we fear each other, fear another doomed and mortal creature like ourselves?"

He turned back to the board and went on. "A title will tell you everything, if you really look at it. Upanishads—what it means, literally, in Sanskrit, is 'sitting under.' Sitting at the feet of the masters, right? So what we have here are the teachings you'd get if you were sitting at the feet of the guru, the enlightened one. Makes sense?" He paused significantly, while the class dutifully nodded. "But let's look a little deeper, if you think that's possible. I wouldn't want to tax anybody beyond his strength. Hello out there! Is anyone awake? Any ideas? Any sudden flashes of illumination?''

They played the game together, Harvey and Karla, thrusting and parrying in a formalized mental combat. Mindfuck. Tense and relax. But she no longer wanted to do that dance. She wanted the grass and the sun and what called to her from the jacarandas and the curving arch of Marina Colby's breast under her Lanz jumper, or the muscle in Jeff Brown's upper thigh under his faded Levi jeans.

"It's like understanding," Karla said. "Undersitting."

"Hey, that's good. That's very good!" Harvey said in a tone Humphrey Bogart might have used to Lauren Bacall. "And doesn't that just hit it right on the head in terms of the essential difference between Eastern and Western thought? Because when you're sitting, you're passive, receptive. You're just being. But when you're standing, you're ready for action, ready to do something. And that's the Western concept of understanding—being able to do something, manipulate something, fix it, control it, use it. But the ideas we're talking about here aren't the ones you *do* something with—they're the ideas that act on your state of being."

His ideas were acting on Karla's state of being, and she found herself getting angry. He was just like her father, another priest of the head, seducing her with words, ideas, the magician, the trickster, the tambourine man, the ultimate illusionist saying, "Look here!" when it was happening over there. But over there, nothing was happening, and that was what he didn't want to face.

"Who has something to say about that?" Harvey inquired.

No one answered.

"Johanna? Perhaps you could expound a bit for us."

Johanna stood up. She looked like someone trapped in the wrong place, surrounded by the wrong people, where it was all about to crash through the wall.

"I think you're full of bullshit."

Harvey's eyes widened. "Oh? Back up your statement."

Johanna shrugged. "You say it, but you don't mean it. Because if you mean it, you got to live it. And you don't. If you did, you wouldn't be doing what you're doing. You wouldn't be here."

"And where, pray tell, do you think I would be? Alone in some mountain fastness, contemplating?"

"This is all from the head," Johanna said. "But where is the heart? Nothing here has to do with the heart."

"Aha!" Harvey said. He was enjoying himself, and Johanna looked angry.

"So now we come to it," he went on. "Where is the abode of the heart? How's that for a homework question, class?"

There were a few titters, but only a few.

"Where would the enlightened man be—not, mind you, that I'm making any such claims. You can't pin that one on me! But wouldn't the man of the heart choose to be right down here in the muck, among the slaves?"

The word conjured spirits. Karla could feel them, lashed to huge blocks of stone, groaning under the whips of the overseers in the bone-dry deserts of her brain. She looked across the room and knew Johanna could see them, crammed into stinking holds, shackled together, sailing up and down the tides of her blood looking for freedom.

"I can tell you don't like that concept," Harvey said, "but it's true. And I'll tell you why. You are slaves because you don't think. I'm not saying you can't think, but by and large you don't. You think like your parents or the people you see on TV, but that's just reflex action. It's not freedom. Freedom is reason, independent judgment. And that, friends, is how I perceive my job in this place, as prodding you toward freedom."

"Then live it," Johanna said. "Take us out there. Take us out from behind these walls."

"Ah, but no one can take you there. Maybe I can point the way. But only you can take yourself there. The door is open."

Johanna stood, a dark, glowering presence. And then suddenly she grinned, and then laughed. The door *was* open. "Right on," she said. "Catch you later." And she was gone, out to the sun and the grass.

Karla sat, clamped to the chair. She knew (in her own self) that the door was open, and she was afraid to walk through.

Harvey sat down on the top of his broad desk. He stared out of the window for a long moment, thinking. Everybody watched him.

"I worry about you people," he said. "What's it going to come to, all this intensity?"

The bell rang.

Jacaranda leaves traced embroidery patterns on the sky. Karla felt better outside, letting habit carry her along the walkway toward the auditorium. A special assembly was called for third period. The air gave her back a breeze of hope that she might yet make it through this one.

Habit carried her past the steps where the Mexicans ate. She walked past, averting her eyes as she always did, trying to blend into the swirling patterns of the air and become invisible so they wouldn't shout at her or laugh at her or call out things in Spanish that she didn't under-stand.

"Hey, Karla!" a girl's voice called out. Karla wanted to run away but she couldn't because they might have thought she was prejudiced. She turned around.

"Haven't seen you in a while, Karla. You not taking typing this semester?"

Dolores Rodriguez, who'd sat next to Karla last fall as they struggled through finger exercises and letter forms, smiled at her. She was a sweet, pretty girl, plump as a small bird with bright brown eyes and glossy black hair pulled up from her forehead and falling in soft waves down her back. She was wearing a red sweater, and as Karla watched she turned into a bird, with bright chirpy eyes and a red-feathered breast.

"No," Karla said, and stopped. She knew she should speak, but Dolores shifted her book bag and fluttered and peeped. Karla was quite distracted. She couldn't get her mouth to work. Two of Dolores's male friends were sitting next to her on the picnic table bench. They were wearing jeans and boots and black leather jackets, and their hair was slicked back in high waves. They watched Karla, their eyes half-closed, expressionless. Lizards, Karla thought, basking in the sun, their jeweled scales flashing patterns that shifted and tumbled through the air, turning the whole world into a kaleidoscope of menace. Lizards eat birds. She wanted to warn Dolores, but still the air wouldn't push past her vocal cords.

Everything was melting, and Karla was starting to melt, too, to ooze away into some fluid substance that would freeze and turn to stone. Maintain, she told herself desperately. You've got to maintain. By sheer will she made her flesh cling to her bones, blinked her eyes, forced herself to an island of lucidity where the world became solid again, where on the other side of the bench a girl with high, ratted hair was passionately kissing her boyfriend. Behind them, Raul Jimenez lobbed a rock at a seagull. Karla knew who he was because Tony had wanted to do a story on him for *The Other Side* when he got kicked off the football team for telling Coach Davidson to fuck off. But Raul told Tony to fuck off, too.

The rock flew out of his hands toward the bird, making a trail through the sky as it flew. He missed. The bird flew off, making a trail in another direction. A hundred rocks chased a thousand birds; one of them was bound to connect.

"Don't," Karla said involuntarily. "Don't hurt the birds."

All of them turned to stare at her. She could feel their hostility, like a cold wind. Dolores was still smiling. Karla wanted to smile at her, but she couldn't. She was afraid. They could surround her, stone her to death. She was an intruder, an outsider, different.

And she, who had felt the sky sing in her blood and the leaves etch patterns in her brain, she (who sees all beings), could not look (in her own self) into the face of Dolores Rodriguez, who smiled at her (and her own self) and waited for her (in all beings) to respond.

She was different; Karla was afraid of her.

"Don't hurt the *birds,* Raul," one of the guys mimicked, and then they were calling out to each other in Spanish, things that made Dolores look embarrassed and flushed. Or maybe she was only looking hurt, hurt that Karla wouldn't speak to her, acknowledge her. Now she was turning into a puppy, a big-eyed spaniel with floppy ears, and the rest of them were hounds, closing in. Karla wanted to run but she was frozen to the spot; she wanted to smile at Dolores but all she could do was grimace in shame. The patterns of color in the air looked like a net, like a trap.

Johanna walked up.

"Hey, Raul, how ya doin', man? Dolores, baby, old Jacobsen still got you pounding those keys? What's your speed up to these days—a hundred and forty-two?"

In Johanna's wake, everything changed. The air brightened, the strands of the net splintered into shards of winged color that wheeled and turned and flew off.

Dolores turned away from Karla and trained her smile on Johanna in relief. "More like sixty," she said. "And you?"

How could she do it, Karla wondered, how can she stand here and banter with them, stoned as we are? But they were no longer watching her; she could breathe again. Yet she felt a different unease. Johanna was so at home with them. Karla was excluded. She wanted Johanna back. She wanted Johanna to be the same as she was, her mirror, her twin, no different in any way that mattered. She couldn't bear to let her not be the same being (in her own self) as Karla (in all beings).

But yet Johanna *was* different. She *was* black. But that wasn't important, Karla thought. All her life she'd been taught and trained to believe that it wasn't important, that to even notice it was prejudiced, but now the acid was like a drill probing into the heart of every thought she'd had, and maybe she was wrong. Maybe, just maybe, there were parts of Johanna, oceans and continents, trails and pathways, rivers and deep caverns, that Karla had never seen. That she had made herself *unsee,* and in so doing had annihilated her own best friend.

She felt sick, sick of herself.

"Come on," she said, grabbing Johanna's hand. "We'll be late, late to the assembly." Johanna gave Karla a slightly puzzled look, shook her head at the others and shrugged. But she turned and walked away with Karla. The rest of them followed. Together they crossed the lawn and climbed the steps to the auditorium. Karla fought down waves of panic and disgust. She was a white face in a dark sea, alone, vulnerable, trying to stem something, hold back some alien force. But she was disgusted with herself for being afraid, for not being able to be easy and natural and real, like Johanna. What would she do to protect herself? Turn the hoses on the Mexicans? Set dogs at Johanna's throat?

With relief, she ducked into the auditorium. Dolores and her friends took seats down below, but Karla climbed up high, to the highest balcony, and Johanna followed.

"What's the matter with you?" Johanna asked as they sank into their seats. Someone up at the podium was speaking in an incomprehensible tongue, mouthing senseless phrases, senseless at least when viewed against the truth that we (in all beings) were all (in our own selves) going to die.

Karla didn't reply. If she opened her mouth, all the ugly places would show, and Johanna would know her and hate her and, worse, be hurt by her. Karla would never speak again. Fuck college. Fuck Columbia.

Johanna radiated sunlight and smelled of new-cut grass. "Talk to me," she said. "Tell me what's wrong."

Karla swallowed hard, fighting not to sink and melt, to hold on to the island where the acid merely sharpened the edges of everything. "I was afraid," she admitted. Yes, that was the word for it, the buzzing, stomach-churning throat-closing thing that had happened to her. "I was all alone with them, until you showed up. I didn't know what they'd do."

"Alone? What do you mean, alone? Dolores was there, and she's your friend, isn't she?"

Karla was silent. The voices at the podium droned like not very good music. Elevator music.

"Or do you mean," Johanna said, drawing each word out slowly, "that you were the only white girl in a crowd of greasers? Is that your problem?"

"It's not that they're Mexican," Karla protested. "It's just that they're not like us."

"What do you mean by that?" Johanna asked.

What did she mean? That they took Business English instead of World Lit? That they didn't read Herman Hesse or Tolkien, and ratted their hair instead of ironing it? Karla could form the thoughts, but each one carried its own mocking, judging echo, and she couldn't get them out of her mouth.

"And who do you mean by us?" Johanna asked, when Karla didn't answer. "Are we alike?"

"In all the ways that count," Karla said. "Inside us, we're alike."

"Is that so? What makes you so sure?" She didn't wait for an answer. "What do you think it's like for me? I've got one of the few black asses *in* this school. I'm always surrounded."

"But that's different," Karla protested. "I mean, you don't have any reason to be afraid of us."

Johanna looked at her as if she had just said something so incomprehensibly stupid that she couldn't believe the words had come out of Karla's mouth. Stupid, said the mocking voice in Karla's own mind, and the word echoed out through the air, leaving trails like flying stones. Stupid, stupid, stupid.

I'm not part of that, Karla wanted to say. Look at my father, down there with the Freedom Riders. Look at my mother, willing to rent to you and your mother, the only Negroes in our neighborhood.

But no, no, no, that was wrong. Karla was wrong. She was part of it. She had done her wrong. She was a liar and a killer and a fraud.

"I'm sorry," Karla said miserably. "I'm sorry, sorry, sorry."

"Sorry my ass is black?"

"No. That's not what I mean! I'm the problem." When she said it she could see THE PROBLEM emblazoned inside her in giant capitals, in flaming neon. That's what she was and who she was, THE PROBLEM.

"You think maybe you ought to be black, too? Keep me company, maybe? Being stoned out of your mind and crazy isn't enough of a handicap for you?"

Karla turned to look at her. I need you, she wanted to say. I need you to be like me, inside where it counts, to let me see myself in your being. Because if we're separate there, then I'm all alone, and something is sucking me down and down and down. A new wave of the acid washed over her, and she was going to drown or rise, depending on what she read in Johanna's face.

Eye met eye.

"It's okay, child. Really," Johanna said, and suddenly she began to laugh.

Karla wanted to cry, but the acid pushed her over a different edge. Suddenly it seemed so funny, that they were worrying about their skin when their bones were dissolving and the threads of reality were unraveling all around them. The two of them caught laughs from each other, passing them back and forth like crab lice.

"Shut up," someone hissed from the end of the row. They tried to stifle themselves but the effort only made everything funnier.

Then the energy changed. Peter Pierce, the student body president, was speaking. His voice rang with determination and defiance.

"We of student government have tried to work with this administration, but they have obstructed every attempt we have made to institute reasonable changes. We believe that we cannot be educated for democracy in a fascist system."

"Did he really say 'fascist'?" someone whispered behind them.

"That can't be his approved speech."

"Goddamn! He's turned radical."

"We are not children!" he went on. "We are young adults, some of us old enough to be expected to die in our country's wars. We have a right to dress how we please! Something is wrong with a system in which teachers are more interested in the length of their students' hair than in their minds!''

"Right on, Peter!" someone yelled. People were cheering and shouting.

Karla could understand him. He was making sense, and his sense drew her out of herself. She could understand him, because he spoke the truth. It was a brilliant insight: She pulled out her notebook and wrote it down. Truth makes sense. But that wasn't exactly what she meant, she could see that when the words were written out.

Truth is what you can understand on a heavy hit of acid.

She put that down in her notebook. It might be important. Maybe she would write about it for *The Other Side.* Someday one of their readers might find themselves wandering in this same wilderness. They should leave signposts for each other.

Truth stops things.

The students (who were all going to die) were roaring. Peter Pierce was calling for action, for a rally at lunch.

He was shining and unafraid.

They escaped to the lawn, to wait out their short break before physical education. They lay on their backs in the grass. Megan Ricci gave them a box of strawberries.

"Enjoy," she said.

Johanna flicked her tongue over red flesh. To Karla's eyes, the fruit seemed magnified. Each seed had a tiny, hairy tail, like a sperm stuck to the ripe, sweet ovum. Johanna put it to her mouth, ran her lips over its round, swelling shape. A stab went through Karla, not quite pain, not quite pleasure.

"Did you catch that? Did you see that?" Tony Klein rushed over, excited. "Marcher called Pierce to the office right afterwards. You watch—this whole place is going to explode."

Joyce Levine joined them. "What's happening?"

"We'll know at lunch," Tony said. "If Marcher suspends Pierce, it'll be the worst mistake he ever made." He turned his attention to Karla and Johanna. "How's the outer space exploration team?"

"We're all going to die," Karla said.

"Granted. But not, I hope, before lunchtime."

Joyce still looked worried. "I just wish you'd go home, before something happens."

Johanna looked up. She began to sing.

I ain't got no home in this world anymore,
Ain't got no home in this world anymore,

Farewell sorrow, praise God the open door,
I ain't got no home in this world anymore.

Karla knew the song from the Incredible String Band album. It was
a hymn, Johanna told her, that they sometimes sang in church. But Karla
could only hear it in reedy, Celtic voices. Yes, she was in the wrong
world, born on the wrong planet. But where was the door?

The bell rang. Joyce and Tony walked off.

Johanna lay on the grass, with the sunlight like hands on her body
and half the strawberry still held in her lips. Her eyes were closed. She
looked peaceful, like someone born at the center of things, like someone
at home.

"Come on," Karla said. "We've got to go." As the space around
them emptied, she began to feel a terrible uneasiness. They were supposed to be somewhere else, doing something else. It was dangerous to
be where they were.

"I'm staying here," Johanna said, "in the sun."

"You can't."

"Why?"

"It's just the way it is. You've got to play the game." The game was
all there was, Karla realized now. Without it there were no shields against
the void.

"No more," Johanna said.

Karla shook her. "You've got to! It's not over yet."

When she touched Johanna, she felt as if her hand passed through
the layers of blouse and sweater and cleaved to the flesh of her shoulder.

"Trust me," Karla said. Somebody had to maintain, to stay in control. Why did it have to be her?

Johanna did trust her. Karla knew that. Johanna had trusted her
with her childhood oracles and visions, with her sexual fantasies about
John Lennon and Little Stevie Wonder, with the secret stains of her first
menstruations, with her belief in spirits and with the hiding place of her
birth control pills so that Karla could remove them if she, Johanna, were
suddenly to die. She would trust her now.

She did. She followed Karla across the grass where the light
danced in the trees.

Karla had given herself to the mocking inner voice that taunted
and demanded. "Obey," it said. "Get in line." She knew that she had
forgotten something, something important, or missed it somewhere, but
the voice kept on, filling all the space in her mind, saying, "You'll get in
trouble," and she couldn't remember what she was trying to forget.

When they reached the heavy double doors that led to the girls'
locker room, Johanna balked.

"I don't want to go in there."

"You have to," Karla said sharply, almost sadistically. She was angry at Johanna for needing to be dragged around like a child and yet pleased, in some part of herself, that Johanna would do whatever she said. Karla had proved once again that she was the strong one.

Johanna gave her a long, sharp look, as if she could see something gripping Karla's shoulders, something grim, devilish. But she followed her down.

The locker room was gray and dead and Karla felt at home there. She understood why they built such places; what they were buttressing, what they were shutting out. Johanna had a grim look, like a warrior sizing up the terrain of battle. Karla felt scared. She wanted to be the warrior, the protector. She didn't (and yet so badly did) want to be protected. Around them girls were shrieking and calling and banging metal doors. The high voices echoed on the concrete walls. Karla was in prison, where she belonged, where nothing could get at her.

Habit led them to the narrow wooden bench beside their lockers. The other girls were pulling off their bright dresses and pulling on black shorts and white blouses. Johanna sat down and pulled off her sweater. One by one, deliberately, she opened the buttons of her blue cotton shirt, to reveal her naked breasts.

Karla reached for the dial of her locker and then habit failed. The acid hit her like a tidal wave and she went under. She couldn't move. They were coming for her; the chariots were on the horizon and she felt the thunder in her head, but no Red Sea would open for her, because she had no faith. The devil had undone his own. She had sold out for the safety of these cool gray walls and even as she looked they were melting. Something was about to crash through them, to find her even where she had gone to hide. She had given in to fear, and fear had betrayed her and Johanna, too, leading them into this pit. Karla was a coward, and they were both lost.

Having begun to take off her clothes, Johanna continued. She stepped out of her denim skirt and slid her underwear off. Open, she faced Karla, offering something, holding out her hand to touch.

Karla was still scrabbling, wanting to cover Johanna up, as if that would make everything all right, as if that would allow her to remain hidden. If she could only open her locker (but she couldn't remember the combination), only get out of her clothes and into her gym clothes (but it was impossible), only get out to the lines of girls in the field (but it was too far), then she would be safe. But she would never be safe again. She had seen too deeply; she knew what underlay the game.

The bell rang, and the shrieking girls rushed out like a flight of birds. They were alone while the clock ticked eternally on.

Johanna reached for her.

"Time!" Karla said desperately. "We—they'll . . ."

"Forget all that," Johanna whispered. "It doesn't matter now. What matters is the heart."

A crack opened in the wall, and suddenly Karla hated her for opening it. She wished she were somewhere else, anywhere else. With her squad doing exercises. Answering essay questions, telling lies.

"Touch me," Johanna said.

And although she had thought that the acid was as strong as it could be, a new wave hit, and Karla no longer knew where she was, except that it was closing in on her, or who she was, except that she hurt. There was nowhere to go; it was coming from every direction and there would never, as Johanna reached out her hand, be anywhere else to go, as she waited, except to face that demand. The demand, as Johanna the sky the leaves the sunlight the faces of Mexicans and Harvey and Joyce and her mother her father her demon self all made it: "Touch me! Touch."

And something in her didn't want to touch, didn't want to be touched, wanted to remain separate, inviolate, safe.

Johanna's breasts glowed in the gray place like luminous, dark beacons. When she allowed herself to look at them, Karla felt a longing like a hot thread up her spine, for something she could never put a name to or touch or reach. Because she was afraid to reach for it, afraid, afraid. Her fear erected walls, brewed cocoa, saved her father's letters, won scholarships to Columbia. Her fear would never allow her to look another human being honestly in the face.

Johanna's face was still, patient, sculpted in strong planes. Johanna's eyes were dark, like her own eyes, and they were open, and Karla could fall into them, if she let herself, into the place where all the separations disappeared. Johanna's eyes could save her life.

Slowly, slowly, Karla reached for her. She placed her hand on Johanna's heart. And she (who sees all beings) touched her (in her own self) and she (and her own self) was touched (in all beings).

Praise God the open door.

Softness wrapped them, hands like sunlight on velvet skin, fingers delicate as bird wings and moist tongues touching, seeking, finding the secret places where everything flowed together, and the wings beat, beat, and the birds took flight.

The fear was gone in the touch of the heart.

8

Johanna Weaver's
Diary

May 23, 1967

Dear Sheba:

It's four o'clock in the morning, and I can't sleep. I'm writing under the bedclothes with the flashlight, so my mother doesn't come in. I'm still high, but it's gone all wrong. My teeth are buzzing in the back of my throat and I feel all shaky, like I might throw up. Oh, Sheba, I feel bad, bad, bad—and worse when I remember how Mama looked at me. If only I could wake up in the morning and start today all over again. I would stay home in bed. I swear.

Oh, God, what have we done?

I'm getting ahead of myself. Let me try to write this down in some coherent fashion. Okay, begin.

We did the acid. That much should be clear already. And to start with, it was good. As long as we were all hanging out behind the music bungalows. At least whenever I was in the sun, I felt okay. It was a weak kind of sun, because the sky was lead-gray smoggy, but I could still feel the rays. I was thinking about how Uncle Marcus always used to tell me about the Egyptians, how they worshiped the sun, and they were black, Africans. He'd call me his sun queen, his princess.

On the acid I felt Egyptian. I felt like a priestess, like a queen. As long as I stayed in the sunlight, I felt sure everything would be all right.

Still, there were some bad moments. Everybody around me had a tendency to turn into ghosts right before my eyes. There was their color, to begin with, and the way their faces kept dissolving and their bodies melting away. Underneath I could see the bone. White bone, the same for everyone. We were all going to die. Color on the outside made no difference to the bone below, or to the whirly skirly air above where the angels were dancing in the sun, leaving trails behind them.

Even on acid, of course, we had to go to class. Karla had said that was good, that we'd be seeing through the lies. But it was hard, sitting there listening to Beckerman drone on in History and Harvey do his trip in World Lit. Because what I was seeing wasn't lies so much as a game I didn't really believe in anymore. But hey, you know, I could handle it. Until the trouble with Karla started.

I was walking across the field, toward the benches on the way to the auditorium. I'm trying to remember when, or why, but it's all a little vague. Oh yeah—there was an assembly called for third period. Anyway, a lot of the Mexican kids hang out there, Dolores and Raul and Ramon and some of the others I don't know. I walked up and said "Hi, how ya doin'," kind of grooving on being able to maintain, you know, to talk that talk while the angels were dancing all around me, and the jacaranda leaves turning into lace. But Karla was there, just standing there staring at Dolores like a bug trapped by a light, not saying a word and looking pretty weird. Shit, I thought, she's going to get us busted, but then I realized she was scared. It took a while for it to sink in, but finally I got that she was scared of Dolores and the Mexicans.

I couldn't believe it! Jesus Christ (if you'll excuse the blasphemy)—how can you be scared of Dolores Rodriguez? It's like being scared of a muffin. A sweet roll. A glazed sugar doughnut. What the hell was going on in Karla's mind? And I didn't want to believe what I thought it was, but as we turned and walked on toward the auditorium—because I really didn't want to get busted and I knew we had to maintain—I began to have my suspicions.

And then it was like she was looking at me as if she'd just for the first time noticed that I was different, too. Now I always would have said Karla's not prejudiced. She always sticks up for civil rights and her daddy's all involved in it. A couple of years ago we spent days begging Betty and Mama to let us go to Mississippi but of course they said we were too young. I remember Karla wailed that it would all be over by the time we grew up, and we would have missed it. Mom laughed. "Child, I wish that were true," she said. "But this battle won't be over in a summer or a year or a lifetime. It was going on long before you came into this world, and it'll still be going on when you're ready to leave it again."

If Frank Harvey were grading this, he'd say I'm digressing. Anyway, I started to wonder, for the first time, what was really going on inside Karla's head about it. Race, I mean, and there I've said it. That's a bad thing to wonder on a heavy hit of acid. We never talk about race except sometimes we make remarks about hair or something like that. But most of the time we just act like there isn't any difference, or none that matters, and that's how I always thought it should be. But when Karla said it—what she said was, that we were alike in the way that counts, on the inside—I got mad.

The thing is, the difference is there, whether we talk about it or not. I'm black, she's white—the two of us are not the same. The world won't let us be. And I suddenly started to feel bad. I started to wonder if the reason we don't talk about race is not because it doesn't matter, but because it does. Like, maybe it isn't me, Johanna Weaver, in all my nappy-headed glory that is Karla's friend, maybe it's like they say, inside every fat person is a thin person trying to get out. Like to her, inside black me is a white me that she thinks is the real me, that's her *real* friend, and the blackness is just something to politely ignore, hoping it'll go away. I'm not expressing this well, but I started to feel sad and mad and to spiral down and down, and it wasn't even Karla any longer or anything I could name, but everything and everyone in the whole shithead world.

I asked Karla if she'd ever thought about what it was like for me, always being the different one, and then she really made me mad. She said *I* didn't have anything to be afraid of. Then I was so mad I couldn't even speak, even though I could tell that right away she felt bad and she started apologizing like crazy. But at the same time I had to ask myself what I was so mad at. Wasn't that what Mama and I argue about all the time?—her always telling me to watch out for white people, not to trust them, and me trying to tell her she's old-fashioned and paranoid. Karla's mother is the same way about men—"Make sure someone walks you to the car, and look in the backseat before you get in in case someone's hiding there." We laugh about them all the time.

"I know Karla is your good friend, but why don't you make friends with some nice black girls, who you could really count on," my mother always says. "But Mama," I say, "why did you move us into a white neighborhood if you didn't want me to be friends with white girls?" "I didn't say that, I just said that I wish you had some friends of your own kind." "Karla is my own kind!" I've said it a hundred times. And now when she said the same exact thing to me, I wanted to kill her.

Then I started to feel afraid. Because without her, I was all alone, really alone. We'd gone together into this place where nobody else could follow us, and now we'd found what divided us. It seemed like a test, like our lives depended on what we did right then at that moment. Either we would have to live in the world where that difference mattered, or we had to wipe it away. Go beyond it, touch through it. And if we could, if just once it could be done, all that old world would shatter.

That's the real problem with acid, the worst hallucination. Not anything you see, but the hallucination that whatever it is you do matters so damn much.

I guess that's the real reason I did what I did in the locker room. I still don't exactly understand it. All I know is we were undressing for gym after the assembly was over. The acid really kicked in and Karla and I sat on the bench by our lockers. We couldn't move, all we could do was stare at each other. I knew I had to reach for her. I had to touch her, to let her touch me, to get so close that the differences could dissolve. I felt this incredible power rushing through me, like I really could change the world, and a phrase came to me—like a voice, saying—"You are here to fight for the heart."

A warrior for the heart. Heart warrior.

Suddenly I knew it was important, it was the most important thing in the world, for us to touch. Really touch. Touch deep, below the skin, below the bullshit and the separations. If we could touch, we could save the world.

So I reached for her. And after a long time, she reached back for me. And oh, Sheba, it was sweet. So sweet.

I can't write about it. Letters on a page can't do it justice. It was like slipping into another world, a world so perfect and right and magical that once you've breathed its air you can never be the same again. Even though nobody ever told you, even hinted to you, that that world existed.

But I guess you can't stay in that world very long. While you're there, it feels like eternity, but outside time goes on.

So eventually we heard a voice, and looked up. Miss Wright, the physical education teacher, was standing above us. She's a kind of square woman, in her body, I mean, with her hair cut short and her ankles thick and her calves bulging with muscles, and as I looked at her all that squareness started to melt away.

She asked what was going on, and we started to laugh. God, did we think that was funny! What was going on was so far beyond anything she could imagine, and we really thought that everything was going to change in that moment, that not just us but nobody else would ever be the same again. So it was like being on the *Titanic*, with someone asking, "Is there a slight problem with the ship?" Or like a kid wanting you to explain the game when it was over, over. Olly olly oxen free.

"Are you on drugs? What drugs are you on?" she asked, and we just laughed again. We couldn't stop ourselves. Every time we looked at each other, we laughed more and more. Miss Wright came back with Miss Darley, Miss Barbie-Doll Face, we call her, with her bright red lipstick and her blue eye shadow and she looked like a doll to me, or a clown. I almost pissed my pants—except I still didn't have any on. She looked so funny to me. I thought she must look that way on purpose, as a joke.

They told us we'd feel better if we got dressed, and we thought that was really hysterical because nobody could or ever had felt any better than we did at that moment. The girls came in from the field and started to turn into different animals, and Wright and Darley were scurrying so hard to keep us away from them, as if we could contaminate them. And we laughed because we knew they were trying to protect something that was already gone, dead, over and done with.

Wright and Darley managed to get us dressed, and then they clamped their hands around our wrists and dragged us out toward the principal's office in the administration building across the lawn. Even through the smog, the sunlight felt so good, licking my face like a cat, and I laughed because they had brought me back to where I most wanted to be.

All in all, as you might gather, we thought the whole thing was pretty damn funny. At first.

A crowd of students was gathered in front of the doors to the administration building. On the ledge to the right of the concrete steps, Peter Pierce was speaking. The sun lit up his blond hair, it almost seemed to crown him, and I felt like the game was really going to break apart. Everybody was going to burst free, even the girls with the plaster hairdos and the sweetheart sweaters and the guys with slide rules sticking out of the pockets of their polyester pants. They were going to change; they were going to roll in the grass and paw each other like animals on the administration building lawn.

What mattered was to stay in the sun. I knew that. In the sunlight, I couldn't be beat. I'd gone down below to fight a battle and I had won, and now the battle for the heart was being fought all around me, and I was part of it. Wright and Darley tried to drag us through the center of the mass of students. I sat down on the grass and jerked my arm free from her grip.

"Get up! Get up! I'm ordering you to get up," Darley yelled. But the acid had taught me a lot about dissolving. I lay down on the grass and let my body become part of the earth, so heavy that Darley couldn't move me. Darley yelled, Wright yelled some more, but then Karla was on the ground beside me, and Tony Klein was up on the ledge shouting, "Protect them! Don't let them be taken away!"

Joyce Levine wrapped her arms around my waist, crying and yelling, "Leave them alone! Leave them alone! Can't you see you're hurting them?" Tony leaped to the ground and held Karla's ankle and began chanting, "Hell no, don't let go!" and the crowd took up the chant. I felt hands all over me, holding me as if the whole crowd was claiming me for its own. Wright and Darley moved away. I caught Karla's eye, and we started to laugh again. I was a warrior, and I had won my first victory, and everything was going to change. Everything.

We held on to each other, laughing and shaking, with the sun pouring diamonds all over our heads and the angels beating their wings in heaven, while the crowd grew and the speeches grew louder. We laughed while different kids got up shouting demands and everyone yelled back. We were still laughing when the cops formed a line down the field, marched in, and started swinging nightsticks.

The nightsticks pried Joyce loose and made Tony drop his arm.

The police snapped handcuffs around our wrists, Karla's and mine, and shoved us until we got up. And I was still laughing. I still thought they were so, so funny, trying to hold back what we'd let loose. Until a big white heavy fist smashed me across the mouth.

I was too high to feel pain. But suddenly the whole universe shivered and came apart. Like looking in a mirror when someone throws a stone at it. Someone was screaming and the cops were hitting me, jabbing their clubs into my belly, jerking me up when I started to fall.

They kept on beating me. Every place they touched me was singing in a high, shrieking voice. I understood that they needed to reach for me as I had needed to reach for Karla, needed to touch me in the real core just because I was different from them, just to reassure themselves that they were not truly alone. But they didn't know how to do it, didn't know how to touch across the barriers of the heart.

Karla was staring at me, her eyes like big round wounds, not laughing anymore. I wanted to say something to make her feel okay but I didn't feel that okay myself. I was afraid.

Then they stuck me in a patrol car, with my hands cuffed behind me so that I had to keep leaning forward to try to keep my weight off them. Blood was dripping from the corner of my mouth. I could taste it. Karla was gone, off in some separate car. Around me I heard the buzz and crackle of police radios, and cold voices, and they flew around like dragged-out fallen angels.

I was trying to understand what was real. What we had on the locker room floor, that sweetness, had seemed so strong that it could stand up to anything. But the blood and the fists and the nastiness in the voices around me, that was *really* real. That was the world my mother warned me about, and I didn't want her to be right. I wanted to believe in the magic and the sweetness. But I had to fight hard even to remember it, to hold on to a glimpse. All I could hold on to was the phrase *heart warrior*.

I was a warrior of the heart. I would have to learn to bear pain.

They took me down to the police station and brought Karla in and sat her next to me on the bench. We huddled together, still cuffed. The walls of the station were gray-and-green concrete blocks. The cops kept asking us questions and more questions. Names. Addresses. Parents' work phones.

Karla was looking at me, at the blood on my lip, at the bruises starting to color around my eye. But for a long time I couldn't look back at her. The cops hadn't touched her. I wondered about that. I mean, there was an obvious explanation as to why they beat *me* up and not her, but I was still whacked out of my skull on acid so I had to wonder deeper, to wonder down. Why? Why is there this difference, what does it mean to them that I am black and she is white? Why should that loosen their fists in my direction? I had been harmless enough, simply laughing, not at them so much, but at everything. But that wasn't what they saw. They saw a black girl laughing at them. No, let's be honest, they saw themselves being laughed at by a nigger. And that had to be stopped.

"Johanna," Karla whispered to me, "we can't let them make us think we were wrong. That's how they win. It was real. Don't lose it."

I wanted more than anything to be able to say, simply, yes. Yes, it was real, that sweet, sweet moment, yes it was more real than those fists and my throbbing face. My mother is wrong, your mother is wrong, the world is a beautiful place, not full of danger and ugliness and hate.

But I couldn't say it.

"It was real," I said, "but it's not all that's real." That was all I could manage.

"We'll fight all that together," Karla said.

And again I wanted more than anything to believe her, to trust her, to trust that she would always be a strong shield at my back. But I had seen her scared shitless of Dolores Rodriguez. What kind of ally was that?

"Mm," I replied, just the same kind of murmur that my mother would make, and my mother's mother too, and suddenly I felt as if they were there inside my skin, a long line of ancestors, going back to slavery days and beyond, women with nothing to leave their daughters but one sound and a quizzical look. I was them; I carried them on—for all I knew, "mmmn" was a word back in Africa, or the name of a queen, or a battle cry. And suddenly I felt ashamed. I had tried to escape them, those women in their aprons with their big black hands. Maybe I was the one who had tried to unsee myself, un-be myself, not Karla who sat looking sick and fierce and mad, saying, "I want to stand with you."

I knew she meant it. I knew she felt just terrible that I was bruised and bloody while she sat there unmarked. If she could have split her own lip, she would have. And yet, *I* was the one with the bloody lip, the one sitting inside the body that hurt and throbbed and ached as the acid started to wear off just a bit. Maybe they had done me a favor, those cops with their fists, making the difference visible, marking it out for us both to see, so that we couldn't ignore it, couldn't pretend.

"They didn't beat you up," I said, and I could see that hurt Karla, maybe as much as the cops hurt me.

"Shut up over there," the desk sergeant yelled. "No talking, or we'll stick you in separate holding cells."

Then I felt bad. I met her eye. We were forbidden to talk, so we just looked at each other, and it was okay again. Except deep, deep down, where something had changed that couldn't be unchanged.

It's really, really late, now—it must be four in the morning. I can't believe how much I've written—pages and pages. I hope nobody ever, ever sees this until after I'm dead. But I'm still not sleepy and if I just lie here and think, I'll go insane, so I might as well try to finish and tell how it ended.

As soon as my mother walked through the door of the station, I knew it was going to be a bad time, one of the times you just have to live through somehow. I tried to tell myself we had nothing to be ashamed of, to feel as righteous as I did after we got busted for going to the demo. But when Mama looked at us and kind of drew into herself, I couldn't look her back in the eye. She's a big woman, but she looked small next to the cops, and sort of innocent, still dressed in her white nurse's uniform under a white sweater, her hair so carefully arranged. She looked me over and turned to the sergeant behind the desk.

"I am Mrs. Marian Weaver," she said, "and I want to know what you have done to my child."

"I think the question is what she has done," the sergeant said.

"I will deal with her for what she's done. But I want to know why she is sitting there in your police station with a bloody lip and a black eye."

"Resisting arrest." The officer shrugged.

"This is not the end of the matter."

That's my mama. She might wallop the daylights out of me herself when she got me home—or threaten to, because she never really hits me. But she'd defend me to the world. I felt bad. My body hurt all over, and I hurt watching my mother try to protect me. It came to me that she's a warrior too, fighting the everyday battles of just staying alive. And I'd deserted her, let her down.

The time seemed to stretch on forever while she talked to the cops. Finally they uncuffed us and released us to her custody, with a court date set for next week. Karla and I were quiet in the car. We didn't say a word while Marian parked and we went into our house. Marian set her purse down on the Formica table in the dining corner of the living room, folded her arms, and fixed me with her eye.

"All right, Joanne." She never will call me Johanna even though I've asked her to a million times. You wouldn't think it would be such a big deal. I mean, whose name is it? "Now I want you to look at me and I want you to tell me the truth. What have you been messing around with?"

I couldn't answer her. It wasn't like the other time, when I could fight back and argue and justify what we did. I had no words that could possibly make my mother understand.

"What drug are you on?"

"Acid," I said. At least I knew the answer to that one.

"I want to know. Do you need a doctor, do you need a psychiatrist, or do you need a strap across the backside?"

Karla began to edge toward the door. My mother turned on her.

"You sit down, young lady! You're not leaving my sight until your mother gets here. I've talked to her, and we've agreed about that."

Karla sat down. When my mama gets that tone in her voice, you don't cross her.

"Open your mouth, girl."

"I'm sorry," I said. It wasn't what I wanted to say. I wanted to say, Mama, I understand you, all the battles you fought on my behalf, all the long nights studying after a hard day at work when I was small so you could get your nurse's cap, all the miles of corridors your feet have walked and the hours on the night shift, all so you could give me something. But what you've given me isn't what I want. That's not your fault. You gave the only thing you know to give, everything that to you stands for not having to bow and scrape and bend, but I wanted to soar. I wanted to see behind it all and turn it inside out in great blossoming waves of love.

"I'm sorry," I said again.

"Sorry! I believe you're sorry! How sorry will you be when they kick you out of school? How sorry will you be when you don't graduate? How sorry will you be when you don't go to the university, when you're stuck in some low-pay job the rest of your life, cleaning up after the ones who did graduate? How sorry will you be when you have a police record that follows you the rest of your life? Don't tell me sorry now!"

Her words left trails behind them, trails of blood. I can never be sorry enough, now, never make it up to her, never come back. A gong was ringing in my head, wrong, gone, gone, wrong, and my head hurt like anything, and I wanted to throw up. Karla, whose daddy is a lawyer, after all, even though he's in New York and never comes to see them and they don't get much good out of him, but still she thinks in that way, she told Mom that the court seals your records when you turn eighteen.

"I don't want to hear from you," Mama said to her. "You have forfeited your right to talk to me. Maybe you can afford to mess around with craziness, with your daddy a lawyer and your mama a Ph.D. psychologist. But you have no business dragging my girl into it."

"She didn't drag me!" I said, with the gong still ringing between my ears. "Whatever we did, we did together."

"Well, it is the last thing you ever will do together. If you don't have any more sense than that together, you had better stay apart."

Then we were quiet for a long time, until finally we heard the doorbell and Karla's mother rushed in. She always looks nervous, Betty does, rushing here and there and chewing the inside of her cheek when she thinks nobody's watching. Today she looked gray and wrecked, like somebody had taken her skin out and stretched and bleached it, and her hands were twisting in the air.

"Are you all right?" she asked Karla. Karla nodded. "You're not all right. You're on some drug. What's wrong with you? What are you on?"

"Acid," Karla said. It was her turn now, and I sat back to watch her go through it. "We're pretty well down by now." But that was only partly true, because even as I watched, Betty's face began to change, her chin getting long and sharp, her eyes glittering in a mean way, her thin lips stretching into a crocodile grin. It struck me how easy it is to turn into a reptile, if you're not real, real careful. It can happen in a moment—it could happen to me.

"You don't look down. You don't look normal."

"I'm fine, Mom. Okay?"

"Fine! You get in trouble at school, you get arrested by the police, I get called at work with some story I can't even believe, you sit there looking like some drugged-out delinquent, and you try to tell me you're fine?" Snap, bite, snap, went the jeweled crocodile jaws. Beware the Jabberwock, my friend, the jaws that bite, the claws that snatch. "*Fine?* Is that what you think about your behavior, that it's just *fine*?" And the madder she got, the more the jewels in the air spun around her. Oh, I guess we weren't really down at all.

"*Fine!*" Betty yelled. "I'm calling your father in New York."

"Fine!" Karla stood up abruptly and screamed back at her. "Fine! Fine! Fine! Call my father! Call him and tell him how the cops beat Johanna up. Why aren't you mad about that?"

Betty looked at me, I could feel her eyes travel all over my bloody lip, and she stopped for a moment, taking it in. Then she got herself back on track and started in on Karla again. "Don't change the subject! We're talking about your behavior!"

"Then talk about the fucking world we have to behave in! We haven't hurt anybody. We haven't beat anybody up. We haven't napalmed any babies!"

"Don't give me politics about this! Politics is not an excuse for self-destructiveness! Just because your father never learned that, doesn't mean you have to act out too."

"This has nothing to do with my father!"

I admired Karla for standing up to her mother, but I couldn't join her. It was another difference between us. I was feeling bad, now, bad that I'd hurt my mother, while Karla was feeling bad that Betty was hurting her.

Betty took Karla home, and we were forbidden to speak to each other.

I went to bed and tried to sleep, but I couldn't. I lay here for a long time, feeling like I was in a battle for my own heart. Because I felt worse and worse and worse, and the more I went into that feeling, the lower I sank down. How could we be so stupid? We had never been in real trouble before, but now we'd never get out. My mother was right. I had failed her, betrayed her and that long line of women behind her who had suffered and survived so that I could stand in the sun. My head hurt and my back hurt and my stomach was bruised and sore. I curled up on my bed, hugging the pain as if it were a lesson I needed to study and memorize.

By midnight I was sobbing into my pillow, trying to muffle the sound of my voice. The door to my room opened, and my mother came in. She sat on the edge of my bed and laid her hand on my back, the way she used to when I was a little girl and had a fever and couldn't sleep. I wanted to sob out loud but my breath was stuck in my lungs and I couldn't release it. I didn't deserve to release it, to feel my mother's comforting touch.

"I didn't want you to ever be hurt that way," she murmured, her voice low as if she were confessing some shameful thing she had done. "I can bear suffering, but I can't bear for you to suffer."

The sob came out, and I turned to Mama and let her rock me and hold me like a child. "I wanted things to be easy for you," she said. "I never wanted you to feel a fist in your face."

"But it's real, Mama," I whispered. "You can't protect me from what's real. And maybe easy isn't what I want."

"Whatever it is you want, child, you can't shake it off the tree before it's ripe. It takes time, Joanne. And work, and patience. You got to tend the ground, and bring water to the roots."

I was crying now, full out, loud and plain. I wondered if Karla could hear me through the open window.

"Hush, child," Mama said. "It's not as bad as all that. You'll see. We'll get by. We'll survive. We always have."

When she left, I lay there for a long time, looking at the camellia bush outside my window. In the moonlight, I could see the flowers, buds, and open blossoms and the ones with their petals already shriveled and ready to fall. They're the first to bloom in spring, and the first to rot. And what I'm trying to understand is how the same world can hold them both—all that beauty, all that decay. That pink star moment when Karla and I touched—already it was turning brown at the edges. We couldn't hold it. The petals were dropping off in our hands. We had failed, failed, failed, and now we were separated, and the blossom would never open again.

I thought I heard a voice, like that of an old, old woman. I could imagine her face, dark and kind and wrinkled.

"Hush, child," she said. "What's important is your attempt to touch truth, not your failure to hold it. Nobody can hold it."

Then I realized that somebody forgave me. One of that long line of women behind me: an old witch-woman who brewed potions to slip into the food of the slaveowners or an ancient priestess by a green jungle river, or a queen who worshiped the sun. Somebody knew how it was, someone had been here before. And maybe, just maybe, I would find it again—the star, the flower, even someday the fruit. It would be my warrior's quest, my holy grail. Because we would always know it was possible, Karla and I. We'll remember that once we'd had a glimpse of it, and that moment will haunt us and get in the way of everything else that doesn't live up to its promise. We'll have to keep reaching, searching, finding and losing, and finding again, over and over, over and over. Because we won't be able to settle for less.

Whatever it costs. However long it takes.

Johanna

9

Rest Day at Namche

I will adopt only the attitude of the enlightened
state of mind, friendliness and compassion, and
attain perfect enlightenment for the sake of all
sentient beings.

—THE GREAT LIBERATION THROUGH
HEARING THE BARDO
THE TIBETAN BOOK OF THE DEAD

Maya was sitting in the dusty waiting room of the small wooden structure
that served as Namche's only bank. She faced a long counter where the
one clerk seemed engaged in an endless transaction with an older Sherpa
man. Outside, the morning sun was making an arc over the high peaks,
illuminating ridges and canyons and banishing shadows, while she sat
trapped in a dim alcove.

My timing is all wrong, she thought. Debby still hasn't come. The
rhododendrons won't bloom for weeks yet. They're akin to camellias;
how can I expect a new blossoming when all the buds are shut tight?

She sneezed. Around her dust swirled, and she coughed softly. The
dusty room was not helping her lungs, and the clerk seemed no closer to
finishing his transaction.

Why did I offer to do this little chore? she berated herself. There
must have been a better way to try to be a helpful member of the group.

The night before, Carolyn and Peter had precipitated a minor crisis
when they returned from their walk and enthusiastically described the
shops of Namche, where yak wool sweaters, knitted hats, rugs, blankets,
handbound books, hammered silver bracelets, necklaces, earrings, and
nose rings that would turn skin green in a few days, yak bone carvings,
bejeweled daggers, and chalices made of human skulls awaited buyers.

"Tenzing, Tenzing, why didn't you tell us there were places to shop!" Lonnie lamented. "I didn't bring any extra money!"

Tenzing smiled. His dark eyes crinkled up into two narrow slits, surrounded by the radiating tracks of a thousand other smiles that had spread across his broad good-humored face. He had a glossy mandarin mustache that framed his full mouth, and a thick thatch of black hair that fell over his forehead.

"You come all the way to the Himalayas, in order to go shopping?" he teased. He spoke English fluently, but with a sweet accent that transformed "she" to "see" and "shopping" to "sopping."

"We are Americans," Lonnie informed him. "Shopping is what we do."

"You are what you purchase," Maya added. Peter grimaced, and Carolyn pursed her lips. All right. It wasn't that funny. So what? She was just trying to be pleasant, to joke and laugh with the others instead of staring blankly at the pages of Jo's journal, lost in her own memories.

"Don't you think people have enough stereotypes about rich Americans without deliberately fostering them?" Peter said.

"I don't have to foster anti-Americanism," Maya snapped. "My government takes care of that for me." Everyone was tense suddenly, frozen in a succession of snapshot poses about the room, for just an instant, a beat. We could have a conflict here, Maya thought. How did I do that? Is it my breath? My personal charm? Why does this keep happening to me in groups? I'm okay as long as I'm leading them, but let me try just to be in one . . .

She remembered the last horrible meeting of the ritual circle she'd hoped to start a few years back. Johanna had dropped out after the first meeting, saying she was tired of being the only black girl in a sea of white. The group had met for a few months, and then begun to fight.

"You dominate the group," Phyllis had accused Maya. "Either you're off on some trip, or you have to be the center of attention." Carrie had agreed; Barbara and Jeannie had just sat silently, looking uncomfortable. I need help, Maya wanted to say. I've just spent a weekend channeling forty women's pain. I'm tired. But everyone else was suddenly cheerful and happy, saying how good it was that they'd talked honestly at last. Maya had never gone back.

Was Phyllis right? she asked herself. Am I snapping at Peter like a wolf bitch challenging the dominant male for control of the pack?

Carolyn turned to Maya and smiled peaceably. "Don't mind Peter. He has a bee in his bonnet about the way Americans are viewed abroad."

She is trying to repair the fabric of the group, Maya thought. I should help her.

"I have about a hundred bucks in cash. . . . I could lend you some, Lonnie," she offered. "And I've got my traveler's checks."

"I suppose we do some good by shopping," Carolyn mused. "Bring money into the local economy."

"Yes and no," Peter said. "You could make the case that we distract the local economy from producing for local people's needs. Not that that will stop you ladies from buying all the cheap jewelry you can get your hands on."

"The bank will cash traveler's checks," Tenzing spoke up. "If they have enough money on hand. It is all carried up and down the mountain by yak trains, you know."

"Eat your heart out, Wells Fargo," Lonnie said.

Maya had little desire to shop, herself. Oh, she would certainly bring back something for Johanna and Rachel, but there would be time for that in Kathmandu. Americans in the Third World were subject to a kind of frenzy. She had seen it in the crafts markets of Mexico and the mountain villages of Guatemala, a glaze in the eyes, a feverish, labored breath in the presence of the bright, the colorful, the hand-tooled and handwoven goods, each counting for hours and hours of somebody's labor, and all cheap, cheap, cheap. Maya had been immune to the buying fever at the time. She'd had no money to spare and no home to send things back to.

And now she much preferred to experience Nepal first and shop later. But she would try to be helpful, to make peace. So she volunteered to cash her traveler's checks and lend some rupiahs to Lonnie, Jan, and Carolyn. In return, Jan had volunteered to take Maya's dirty underwear and T-shirts to wash in the river.

I should have angled for the laundry job, she thought, out in the fresh air, beating the clothes clean on stones beside the little stream that ran down beside the *stuppa*. Oh, well. At least she had a little time alone, to think about Johanna's journal.

The sections she'd read had opened up her memories and left her feeling raw, melancholy, half-caught in the acid vision that strips the false from the true, the mask from the face below. Or seems to. That was her problem, now. She had never lost the vision, but she had mislaid her belief in the vision's importance. Not just the adolescent belief that one vision could change everything, but the hope that it changed anything.

She closed her eyes for a moment, content to nurse her melancholy, enjoying the silence.

"They're not very efficient, here."

The voice jerked Maya out of her reverie. She turned to face Howard, from their trekking group, who had sat down beside her on the bench.

Howard smiled, and instantly she felt annoyed. He wasn't so bad, Maya tried to convince herself, listing his good points. He was tall and even-featured and his wavy blond hair showed only the slightest suggestion of thinning at the temples. His features were pleasant, and he was obviously smart enough to hold down a good job. Stable. Responsible. Overall he was a tall, strong, healthy man any mother would be proud to call her son. But he wore his body so uncomfortably, as if it were something he had borrowed and was afraid to dent.

"How long have you been waiting?" he asked, glancing at his watch.

"Not too long. Time works differently here," Maya said. Her impatience vanished in the face of his. Suddenly she was serene, accepting, a veteran of many slow transactions in the Third World. "They'll get to me when they're ready."

She sat up and adjusted her skirt. Underneath she wore her cotton sweatpants, not the greatest fashion statement, perhaps, but it alleviated the Terrible Thigh-Chafing Problem. And provided a bit more padding on the hard bench.

"We could be outside, enjoying the sunshine." Howard sighed.

Just what she'd been thinking herself, so why did she feel so irritated when he said it?

"Feel free to go," Maya said sweetly. "I'm really quite happy to wait by myself."

"Oh no," Howard said hastily. "I want to cash a few checks of my own. Besides, I'm quite interested to see how the bank operates under these conditions. You know I write software with banking applications."

"No, I didn't know."

"Yes, right now I'm working on a system for Citibank, for their mortgage division."

"How interesting," Maya said politely, wishing he would just go away and let her write in her journal.

"What the system does, is it helps the analysts sort through all the information on the loan applications it receives, to find out what is actually relevant statistically. What do you think is the biggest problem business faces today?"

"I don't know." Oh, Howard, please just shut up and let me think.

"Take a guess."

Maya sighed. "Reaching the end of our natural resources?"

"No."

"A crippling national debt?"

"That's a problem, but not the worst."

"How about eight years of totally irresponsible fiscal policy on the part of the Republicans?"

Howard shook his head. "Information," he said authoritatively. "Information overload is the biggest problem facing business today."

"You don't say." Howard's round blue eyes were fixed on Maya. When he talked, he blinked nervously. He's trying to be kind, Maya thought. He's trying to engage me and entertain me and save me from what he sees as a boring situation.

"You see, there's so much that we know, so much information floating around, but unless it's organized, you can't make use of it."

"I often have that problem," Maya said, willing herself to engage with him. "A lot of times when I'm writing, I'll need a reference in a certain book, and I know I have the book, but damn if I know where to find it."

"How do you organize your library?" Howard asked. "Alphabetically, or by subject?"

Maya laughed. "I use the RPJ system—for books, papers, accounts, everything."

"RPJ . . . What does that stand for?"

"Random piles of junk."

Howard laughed, a dry "heh heh" that acknowledged she was making a joke. "How does that work for you?"

"I only lose my tax files once every two or three years," Maya said. "I found my passport the day before I left for this trip, and I only misplaced the galleys of my last book for three or four days. I would say it works okay."

This last remark appeared to stun Howard into silence. Maya whipped out her journal. Maybe he would get the hint and stop talking to her. She began to write.

"It's funny what comes back to me, reading Johanna's journal, seeing my own life viewed from another angle . . ."

"I admire the way you keep your diary, so disciplined, always writing away," Howard said.

"I'm a writer." Maya closed her journal with a snap. If irritation were truly a measure of love, she reflected, she and Howard were far down the rocky road of romance. Still she didn't think that was quite what Johanna had meant.

"I've thought of writing a book," Howard said. "It'd be different than yours, of course. More of a technical journal. Is it hard?"

Maya bit her lip. Nothing but nothing annoyed her more than people who said they were going to write a book. She forced a smile.

"Have you ever written a term paper, Howard?"

"Of course. In just about every class I had, in college."

"Writing a book is just like writing twenty or thirty term papers. So you see, you've already done it, more or less."

"I never thought of that," Howard admitted.

At that moment, the clerk at last appeared behind the long wooden counter. Maya stood up, presented her traveler's checks, and waited hopefully for her money.

The clerk took her checks, looked at one thoughtfully, turning it over as if he had never seen anything like it before. He called a second clerk out of a back room for consultation. After a moment, they produced a long form for her to fill out and sign, and directed her upstairs to wait in a dusty room full of ancient leatherbound ledgers, for the attentions of a third clerk.

"This is fantastic," Howard, trailing behind her, murmured. "It's like something out of Charles Dickens."

"The Circumlocution Office," Maya said. Her impatience with Howard was beginning to spill over into a distaste for the entire banking system of Nepal. "Still, it's amazing that they have a bank here at all, where everything has to be trekked in and out on human backs or *zopkios,* like Tenzing said. Do you suppose they have armored yak trains?"

"I wouldn't think so."

"Makes you appreciate Karl Marx," Maya said.

"Marx?" Howard said, surprised. "Why does it make you appreciate Karl Marx?"

"The labor theory of value." She had started on this tack just to be saying something, but as she went on she began to convince herself. "You know. Makes a lot more sense up here, where sheer physical effort has to go into every simple act. Every stone in every building was carried in on someone's back. It's no accident that every successful Marxist revolution took place in what today we'd call an underdeveloped country. Even if it does totally contradict Marx's own belief that socialism would evolve as a natural development of capitalism."

Goddess, what was she talking about? If only Rio could hear her now, or Daniel, who'd called her anti-intellectual because she'd refused to slog her way through *Das Kapital.* He should have explained to her how useful the theory could be in unnerving the Howards of the world.

But why was she being so indirect? Why didn't she just make like Greta Garbo? "Howard, I vant to be alone."

From the interior of the building appeared a man with the even, dark features of the lowland Nepalis, sporting an official-looking cap. He took the sheaf of papers that by now she had filled out and signed, looked them over carefully, and handed them back to her, pointing out several places she had missed where her signature was required. He then nodded, took her checks, her passport, and the papers, and disappeared into a back room.

"This could all be computerized, very simply," Howard said, as he repeated each procedure right behind her. "Think of the time it would save. They could run this whole office with one man."

"Howard, they only have electricity here four hours a day, and it doesn't start until after six. And at that, it's enough to run one lightbulb per family."

"They could do it with solar, or beef up their hydroelectric capabilities."

"But they'd need someone to install the program, and service them, and program the computer, and delouse it, or whatever you call it whenever it goes down. I don't think so."

"Debug," Howard said. "Not delouse, just debug."

"Anyway, this way they employ half a dozen people, give meaning to their lives, standing around compiling dossiers on hapless tourists who want to cash a check. What do you think they're doing, back there? Radioing back to Kathmandu, to find out if we're wanted by the CIA?"

"Are you?" Howard joked nervously, as if he suspected she might be.

"Not lately," Maya reassured him. She had a sudden, adolescent desire to say or do something outrageous, something that would stun and shock him and prove irrevocably that she was different from him, that she was the sort of person who dares the passes everybody warns you against.

Grow up, she told herself firmly. Don't use the man in order to bolster your own self-image. Either be kind to him or ask him nicely to go away. Anyway, people weren't so shockable these days. Slightly unsavory pasts were quite commonplace, along with green hair and half-shaved heads. Rebel youth was forced to go to the trouble and expense of piercing its navel, its nipples, or its clitoris. She shuddered. No, thank you.

At length the man in the cap reappeared, retreated to the far corner of the room, opened a ledger, and began to copy out longhand much of the information Maya had provided. Howard watched in horrified fascination.

"Think of it as an adventure," Maya told him. "Something to tell the boys back home."

"I should write an article about it," Howard said. "For the LK *Newsletter*. I wonder if I could justify writing off any of the trip on my taxes."

"LK?"

"Lambert-Klein. Where I work."

"Look, I can't believe it. Here he comes, with actual rupiahs in his hand."

Maya received her rupiahs with appropriate gratitude, and then felt obligated to wait until Howard received his. They exited down the stairs and out the door into the cold, blue day.

"You're awfully patient," Howard said. "That nearly drove me crazy."

"I learned patience when I lived in Mexico, back in my twenties," Maya said.

"Oh. What were you doing there?"

She winked at him, and yielded to temptation. "Running from the law."

Debby had still not appeared when they got back to Ang's house. She had sent no further word. But Khunde, where her clinic was located, was a half-day's walk away. Unless she'd left at dawn, she couldn't possibly have reached Namche yet. Maya could still hope she'd come later in the afternoon.

The group distributed itself between the long bench and the small stools, clustering around the tiny tea tables of Ang's main room. Pembila, Ang's wife, pressed them to try some of her homemade cheese, a dry, chalklike substance with a strong, goaty taste made from the milk of the dzo, or female yak. She laughed at the faces they made, and teased them, offering to cook up other Sherpa delicacies. Jan sketched her, and Maya hoped she could catch some of the woman's beauty, her pride in her house, her skills. Pembila wasn't promoting any image, Maya thought, she was just who she was. Or at least, she admitted, that's how I see her. How the hell do I know? Maybe inside she's sneering at us. "Those wimpy trekkers, can't make cheese, can barely drag themselves uphill— I'm much cooler than they are, and I hope they notice it!"

The kitchen boys began serving steaming cups of *chiyaa,* hot tea with milk, and fried potatoes topped with fried eggs. It was altogether more frying than Maya was used to but she wasn't complaining. The fat would counter the cold. She moved her small stool to face the windows. Across from her on the bench, Tenzing sat between Carolyn and Lonnie. Jan was next to Lonnie, and Maya noticed their ankles pressed together.

Rather sweet, she thought. She admired their imagination; conducting romance in exotic places even though they lived a couple of thousand miles apart, Lonnie in Portland, Jan in Santa Fe. Lonnie had informed Maya on their first night in Kathmandu that she and Jan had met one year before on an Olivia Records tour to Greece. She had imparted this information with just the suggestion of a query in her voice, and a swift glance at Maya's face, to see what she might read there. Maya recognized the dance. By rights she should have made the next move, some light remark to let Lonnie know that *she* knew the Olivia cruises were a lesbian singles scene, should have let drop some casual reference to Johanna. She would then be labeled and accepted, and the three of them could form their own secret club, pals and buddies for the rest of the trip.

But Maya had kept silent. Not because she was ashamed of being with Johanna, but because nothing about her relationship with Johanna seemed to fit any mold. They'd had passion, certainly, moments of it that hit them like all of Sagarmatha dropping on top of them, milk rivers spewing, birds flapping, goats scampering, walls of ice crumbling into the avalanche. But they'd also had early frosts and long glacial freezes.

No, they'd never been able to define what they were together, to commit to some identity group. Whenever one of them had tried, the other resisted. Maya had occasionally longed for the comfort of belonging somewhere, but then Johanna would balk. She remembered the fight they'd had the time she tried to persuade Johanna to join a support group for interracial lesbian couples.

"Are we lesbians?" Johanna had asked. "Are we even a couple?"

"We live together," Maya had said. "We love each other. We have sex when the mood strikes. Do we need some kind of certificate?"

"We're friends before we're lovers," Johanna stated.

"Is that against the lesbian code?" Maya asked.

"No, but the fact that we each occasionally go out with men is. I know those women. They'll chew you up and spit you out alive for consorting with the enemy."

"The word still scares you," Maya said. They were lying in bed together, and Maya rolled over and murmured in Johanna's ear. "Lesbian, lesbian, lesbian."

Johanna pushed her away and sat bolt upright, angry. "No, the word doesn't scare me. But I am in a different situation than you. It's easy enough for you to call yourself a lesbian, make the great political gesture. Or a hippy, or a revolutionary, or any damn thing you please. But I am a black woman before I'm anything else, and the first word in that is *black*."

"Can't you be a black woman and a lesbian, even if you are kind of a closet bisexual? I won't tell. Think of Audre Lorde."

"I'm not sure it's the right thing for me to do, to claim some other identity that's going to separate me from most of my people."

"You're waffling," Maya said.

"I am not waffling, I'm thinking it out." Johanna turned to Maya. "And I have to think it out for myself, okay? Not for you, not for Audre Lorde, not for some Committee of Feminist Theory, but for me!"

"If being who you are separates you from people, isn't that *their* problem?" Maya had said softly. "Don't you need to educate them?"

"How can I educate them if I'm separated from them?" Johanna sighed. "Maya, my people need me! My work for this lifetime is to fight for the children. I've got to put that first. You're in a different situation, like I said before."

"How different? Ain't I a woman, to quote one of *your* people. And a Jewish woman, at that? Oh, I know that's not the same as being black, but it's also a dual identity. Or are you implying that *my* people don't need me?'' Do they? Maya wondered suddenly. Certainly, Jews in America seemed to be getting along just fine without her active aid. Yet she discovered a certain pain in thinking that they might not need her at all. Who did, then?

"That's not what I'm implying," Johanna said patiently. "You have a different role to play in this life. You get to shock people and challenge them and push their edges. I know that's not easy, either . . . but it gives you a latitude of freedom I don't have." She lay back down and slid her arm under Maya's shoulders. "Anyway, how did we get talking about all this? I don't need a support group to be with you, love. I just need you to be with me, when the mood strikes us both."

Maya pushed away the last of her fried potatoes. Any more, and she'd be too heavy for the poor Sherpas if she collapsed on the trail and they had to carry her out. It was important to think of others, after all.

Maybe Johanna was right, Maya thought. I've always believed my role in this life is to be the one who dares the high and dangerous passes. If so, what am I doing on this tour?

The question reminded her of the girl in the green sweater. She turned to Tenzing.

"Do many young people come trekking in these mountains?" she asked.

"Oh yes," Tenzing said. "I have myself, from time to time, guided groups of them. They come on school trips, or with the program that I used to work for."

"What is that?" Carolyn asked. She was still eating her potatoes, cutting them up slowly into small bites and chewing daintily while the others were already drinking their tea and eating their canned fruit. In spite of her petite size, she ate as much as any of them, Maya noted. So much for the calorie theory. Heredity must be the decisive factor. She reached for a cookie, which the Nepalis called biscuits, English style.

"It is a program for youth, between high school and college. They come to live in the Third World for a month and do projects to help the community. I used to be an adviser, but now I quit."

"Why?" Peter asked. He was perched on another low stool, on Maya's right. "Didn't you like it?"

Tenzing shook his head. "It was terrible!" he said. "Those youth! Like trying to corral a herd of unruly yaks. They did not want to work, they did not want to study. They like to smoke hashish and drink beer and party in their rooms all night, and then sleep half the day. 'Why do you come here?' I ask them. 'Your parents have spent thousands of dollars for you to come here—when you could get high and party and sleep at home in America.' Do you understand?'' He turned to Peter, but Carolyn answered.

"Drugs relieve pain," she said in a tone that annoyed Maya only because she sounded so utterly sure of the answer. Were Carolyn not married, professional, and slim, Maya admitted, were she, say, a three-hundred-pound ex-con speaking in an AA meeting, she could say the exact same thing and not annoy Maya at all. Context is everything.

"There's a lot of young people in pain in America, and they aren't all in the ghettos," Carolyn went on earnestly.

"That's for damn sure," Peter said. On the other hand, for Maya *his* good looks ameliorated his somewhat pompous, paternal tone. What does that mean? she wondered. Is it just the general social conditioning that favors men? Does it mean that I see myself in competition with Carolyn and see Peter as a sort of prize? Is it an inner longing for a strong father figure?

Oh, Betty, if only I could call you and chew this one over with you. It's just the sort of thing—the only sort of thing—we could really connect on. How you loved to do it, too—take one small reaction, one sentence, one misplaced word, and turn it inside out and upside down until you could shake some meaning out of it. I bet you were a damn good therapist, even if you were batty as an old barn in your personal life.

"Drugs provide pleasure, too," Lonnie said, shifting her body just a millimeter closer to Jan's.

"I wouldn't agree it's all pain relief," Maya commented. "I'd say people who use drugs are looking for something our culture doesn't offer. For magic."

"I just read an article about that," Carolyn said. "By a Jungian. He was questioning why there's such an upsurge of interest in astrology, crystals, goddesses, all the New Age stuff. So he interviewed two hundred people who subscribed to *Astrology Today*." She speared another piece of potato and gestured with it on her fork. "He claims the archetype of the mage is resurfacing in modern culture as an answer to our disappointment with technology in an age of nuclear weapons."

Peter smiled benignly at them all. "Carolyn goes for all that Jungian hocus-pocus. I'm more of a family-systems man, myself."

"I bet you're a Capricorn," Jan said brightly. "Or a Taurus, maybe. When's your birthday?"

"September twelfth."

"A Virgo, then. I knew it had to be an earth sign."

"And if I'd said Aquarius, would you have said you knew it had to be that?" Peter challenged her.

Jan shook her head. Her long pale hair framed her thin pale face and her narrow mouth drooped, then stiffened. "You have an earthbound quality. You could never be an Aquarius." Her voice was tight, offended.

Lonnie rushed to Jan's aid. "*I'm* an Aquarius. With Scorpio rising."

"It's a good combination for a lawyer," Jan assured them all.

Tenzing turned back to Maya. "So you believe young people want magic," he said. "Why?"

"Because they're looking for simple answers," Peter interjected. "Like everybody else, these days. Nobody wants to think anymore."

Maya attempted to give Peter what Miss Manners would call a Cold Stare. Good looks only excuse so much, she thought. He was edging close to the line.

"Nobody asked your opinion," Lonnie snapped.

"Excuse me," Peter said, drawing the words out sarcastically. "I was responding to what I thought was a general question."

"You were claiming turf," Lonnie said calmly. "Like men always do. Tenzing was speaking to Maya, weren't you, Tenzing?"

"It's not important," Tenzing said, his smile becoming slightly anxious. "Nothing to get upset about. But Maya, what do you think?"

Maya took a long, deep breath. "Dion Fortune defined magic as 'the art of changing consciousness at will.' There's nothing simple about that."

"Drugs change consciousness," Peter said. "Are you calling them magic?"

"I'm saying that ordinary consciousness is constricting. We all need relief, from time to time. We all need to enter the realm where everything comes alive. If our culture doesn't teach us to do it without drugs, then we'll use whatever comes to hand."

"So you're advocating drug use?" Carolyn asked.

Maya shook her head. "No. I'm advocating what I do."

"Which is what?" Lonnie spoke up.

"I teach magic."

The group was silent.

Finally Peter spoke. "I hope I didn't offend you."

"Ignorance doesn't offend me," Maya assured him sweetly.

"Greenwood, Greenwood . . . Are you Maya Greenwood, the writer?" Lonnie asked.

Maya nodded.

Jan's pale blue eyes shone. "Oh, I wondered if you were when I saw your name on the group list. I'm so thrilled!"

Dear Goddess, this was exactly what Maya had come on the trip to get away from. She was tired of admiration. It was a burden, a demand. She should have made up a different career for herself. I'm a diplomat, a private detective, an international spy. Yes, that's what she and Johanna had really wanted to be, all those long years ago, sprawled on the floor watching *The Man from UNCLE* on Marian's black-and-white TV and having sexual fantasies about Illya Kuryakin. The good Russian.

"I've heard of you," Carolyn said, pushing away her plate at last. "You wrote that book on Venezuela. Are you doing Nepal, now?"

"You've got me confused with someone else," Maya said. "I've never been to Venezuela. And I don't know if I'll write about Nepal or not. I didn't come here to write. I came for personal reasons."

She considered eating another cookie. If weight was determined by heredity, why not?

"How do you teach magic?" Tenzing asked. "To us, that seems very strange. Our *Iho-wha*—would you say, magicians?—are very secret. They do not give lectures."

"I'd love to meet one," Jan said. "That would really be something!"

Tenzing shook his head. "They are dangerous. You do not approach them lightly. We will meet the Rinpoche at Tengpoche. That will be a good experience for you."

"So you're on the New Age circuit," Howard said. "That kind of interests me."

"Do you do healings?" Tenzing asked.

"In a sense," Maya said. "Hands-on healing is not my primary talent. What I try to heal is our shattered cultural imagination."

Tenzing considered. "How do you do that?"

"Mostly through ritual. I teach people how to create their own rituals, and I teach the skills at sensing and moving energy that makes a ritual more than form."

"Now that sounds very strange," Tenzing admitted. "How can you create a ritual? Our rituals are very old things, handed down for many years."

"But somebody created them, sometime," Maya said. "Maybe thousands of years ago, maybe ten years ago, maybe yesterday. We can listen and invent as well as people did long ago. In our tradition, we say that the Goddess is always speaking to us."

Except in my case she seems to have clammed up recently. But no need to go into that.

"Which Goddess is that?" Tenzing asked.

"The old Goddesses of Europe," Maya said, "who are particular incarnations of the old Goddesses everywhere."

"I didn't know Europe had Goddesses," Howard admitted. "Except for the Greeks, of course. I guess the Romans did, too."

"You're not alone," Maya said. "The church did a good job of convincing people that any remnants of Goddess worship were Witchcraft, pure and simple. But the Goddess underlies all of European civilization, if you can call it that."

"That's a lovely theory," Peter said, bending down to the table to replenish his cup of tea. "But there's no archaeological evidence to support it."

"Bullshit!" Maya said. "There's volumes of evidence. Read Gimbutas. Read Mellaart."

"I just read an article in *The Journal of Anthropology* that contradicts you," Carolyn said. "According to the authors, no true matriarchy ever existed."

"Nobody ever said it did! We're not talking about some mirror image reversal of what we've got, with women on top instead of men— we just maintain that society was more egalitarian. Power wasn't yet structured according to gender. I know that's hard for academics to imagine—or maybe they just resist looking at evidence that might force them to take a fresh look at how power is divided in *this* society." Maya's voice rose. Calm down, she told herself. You're scarcely being a living example of the calm serenity the Goddess brings. On the other hand, who ever said that the great powers of life and death and transformation—Demeter, Hecate, Pele, Kali, or Aphrodite for that matter—had much to do with serenity? Rage, passion, sorrow, ecstasy, or heartbreak were more in their line.

Tenzing's smile was strained. Maya took a deep breath, wishing she'd never come on the trip, or had come alone. "I'm on vacation," she said. "I argue about the Goddess for a living. On this trip, I wanted to get away from it for a while."

Carolyn flashed a smile. "Peter and I enjoy a good argument. But I can hear you saying that you don't."

"Sometimes I do," Maya said, half expecting the discussion to degenerate into a Monty Python dialogue. No, you don't. Yes, I do. That's not an argument; that's contradiction.

"Anyway, let's not argue now." Carolyn smiled again. "I'm interested in finding out more about your work."

"So what exactly would you do?" Peter asked. "Suppose I came to you and said, teach me how to create ritual, what would you tell me?"

"I'd tell you that a ritual isn't so much what you do, it's about reading the energy and responding to it and creating a container for it."

"How?" Lonnie asked.

"Dancing, chanting, drumming—any of the old techniques for changing consciousness," Maya said. "A true ritual is always an enacted story of transformation. Maybe you're Witches dancing around the Maypole to celebrate the rising fertile energies of the spring, or maybe you're Jews sitting around a table eating unleavened bread to celebrate the liberation of your ancestors from Egypt, or monks dancing under the full moon in masks to celebrate Buddha's triumph over Ignorance. It doesn't matter what culture you're in or what religion you're practicing. If the ritual works, if the acts have power, something changes in you. Some creative energy is unleashed, or something is liberated, or some ignorance of your own is enlightened. I wish I could describe it better for you, but as often as I've tried, words can't really tell you what happens. You have to experience it.''

"Let's!" Jan said eagerly.

"Why not? Do some magic for us," Peter said.

"I don't do tricks," Maya said sharply. "I don't pull rabbits out of hats. And I don't do magic *for* anyone. When magic happens, it's because the time is right and everyone is creating it together.''

"When do you think the time might be right?" Jan asked.

"We'll see.''

By the time lunch ended, Debby had still not arrived. The group left to visit the Sherpa museum, and Pembila promised that if Debby showed up, she'd tell her where they'd gone.

The main street of Namche Bazaar curved around the horseshoe ledge that supported the town. Just wide enough for a loaded yak to pass, the narrow street boasted a small dusty post office and the bank. At the bend, it stepped down a level, and below were shops and the stalls of street vendors, offering small necessities—batteries, oil, soft drinks, as well as camping equipment, jewelry, crafts, and other tourist treasures. The upper branch of the road headed uphill, out of town toward the museum and the trail to Tengpoche Monastery.

As Maya puffed her way up the steep hill, she couldn't help but wish that they'd located the museum somewhere lower. But the Sherpas thought nothing of a climb like this, and in theory, neither should the visiting trekker for whom the museum was built. A confraternity of the physically fit. I'm on this trip under false pretenses, Maya thought. I'm not a Naturally Fit person, and it shows. The blood of generations of pale scholars flows in my veins. On the other hand, the same blood flows in Debby's veins, and she undoubtedly could cruise up this hill with fuel to burn and had never needed to watch her weight like Betty and Maya did. Maybe Debby was a changeling, swapped in her cradle for the chubby infant who was meant to be Maya's true sister.

Below, Namche hugged its U-shaped plateau, and behind, range after range of mountains dwarfed and cradled the hanging valley. The view reminded her of other villages she had known, other towns that seemed removed in time, off the road. But this one had a special beauty and integrity, in its stone walls and tile roofs, its harmony of shape and form. Here were none of the tin roofs and cement-block walls that marred the little hill towns of Guatemala, none of the mammoth outsize churches that dwarfed the villages of Mexico. The white *stuppa* that stood in the lower fields was small, comfortable, embedded in the town rather than dominating it. The prayer wheels in their little stone houses that lined the stream blended in with the dark untilled earth of early spring.

For a while, Maya wandered through the rooms of the small museum, looking at the collection of traditional Sherpa garb and tools and cookwear. But the exhibits made her sad. Already so much had been eroded. Instead of felt boots, modern Sherpas were likely to wear beat-up Nikes. The women topped their traditional jumpers and striped aprons with hand-me-down sweaters and down vests, and young boys sported T-shirts from the Hard Rock Café. They cooked with aluminum pans instead of their round, copper pots. Yet what did she want, for them to remain preserved in preindustrial purity, like figures in an outdoor museum, to feed the romantic fantasies of tourists like herself who longed for a world that had not yet been ruined? What a pleasure it was to walk through a land with no roads, only trails, to stroll through a town where no cars emitted fumes and no radios blared—yet she could see the unremitting physical effort it took to live this way. However much she might admire the unspoiled landscape, she had no doubt that the Sherpas, offered cars and washing machines and television, would seize the day and never look back any more than she would trade in her word processor for a quill pen.

It was all too much for her. She slipped out of the museum and climbed the small rise behind. To the west, a new panorama of mountains opened out, catching the light on their snow peaks. One of them, Tenzing had said, was Sagarmatha. From this angle it looked no higher than any other mountain. She could not, in fact, pick out which it was. I should be able to feel something, she thought. Some energy, some power, some great awakening. I thought for sure that if I could stand in sight of the Goddess Mother of the Universe, the Milk River below me, I would come alive again. But nothing is happening.

Still, the mountains were beautiful, in the warm gold glow of the late afternoon light. Below her, on the green grass, a white horse grazed peacefully. Maybe I'm trying too hard, she thought. Maybe I don't have to have the Great Spiritual Experience. If I let go, if I just allow myself to enjoy the beauty here, maybe a small camellia will blossom, if just for a moment. She sat down on the edge of her waterproof jacket and hugged her knees.

"It's beautiful, isn't it?" Howard said, appearing suddenly from around the building and plopping down beside her. "Do you know which one is Mount Everest? Tenzing said we could see it from here."

"Howard, I'm trying to meditate," Maya said. There, she had been direct with him at last. No reason to feel guilty just because he looked hurt and went off murmuring too many apologies and disturbing the air. So now I'd better, Maya thought. Meditate, that is. She folded her legs in lotus position, resting her hands, palms up, on her knees. Why does he irritate me so much? He's sweet enough, he's got a good heart; he just doesn't read the energy. Still, that's no reason to want to shoot the guy. Betty would have said that he represents some part of me I don't want to see. But really, he's exactly what I've been running from for twenty years. The kind of guy Betty would have liked me to marry.

No, that's not fair to her. Maya remembered when Betty's old school friends from Milwaukee had come for a visit, bringing their timid son. Leonard, that was his name. Debby and Maya had played prisoners of war with him, tying him up in an orange crate and hiding until he cried. His mother had to rescue him and they both got in trouble. Later, after Leonard and his parents had gone, Betty laughed.

"His father went to school with me," she told her daughters. "He was always asking me out on dates and I couldn't stand him. Do you mind? Do you mind that I didn't marry him? Maybe we'd all be together and living in Milwaukee in a big house on the lake."

Debby and Maya had both shouted no and made retching motions, and they'd laughed together. Oh, Betty, you had your wild side. How else did you end up with Joe Greenbaum? It's just that you would have liked me and Debby not to make your mistakes, to find men who would take care of us. Peter, that's who you'd have wanted me to be with, if he weren't Japanese. The alpha male, always marking his territory. You never understood why I couldn't stand men like that, why I needed not a provider but a hero, or failing that, an outlaw. I ran so hard from the Howards and Peters of the world I ran straight into the arms of the Rios. Who don't need to read the energy because they generate it themselves, but who aren't very good at taking care of anybody.

No, your daughters have not succeeded where you failed. We have not found men to take care of us.

Maya opened her eyes and watched the light play on the mountains, dancing from ice face to ice face, warming to a deeper gold as the sun dropped. She could look down the trail that led to Tengpoche and Kala Pattar, the trail that led up to base camp and the slopes of Chomolungma herself, or beyond, twisting and winding through country where tourists rarely go. Far down the trail, she could see a spot of green moving, someone walking alone, off into the wild. Maya pulled her camera out of her backpack and looked through the zoom lens. She recognized the girl from the café and the bridge. *She* wasn't plagued with Howards. No, she was off somewhere on her own, gathering power, as Maya should be. Yes, that was the problem with this trip, with her whole concept of it. She had lost her power—how could she expect to find it again on a guided tour?

Tenzing came out with the others. They all stood a little way off, giving her privacy. He was pointing to the mountains, to the small, insignificant-looking peak that was Sagarmatha, Chomolungma. Maya followed his finger. There it was, a mountain like any other mountain. If only she could get close enough to feel its immensity, to soak up power from its power. Goddess Mother of the Universe, I come to you with the ashes of my own mother on my back. I am one who seeks power, not to control but to know and heal and be, and every time in my life when I've gone seeking it I've abandoned somebody. My mother. Rio. Johanna. Chomolungma, Sagarmatha, where do I find power now that I'm growing too old for that? I'm not the Seer anymore, not the Virgin, unmated and free, I'm at the stage of life when I should be the Singer, the Mother, the Nurturer, she who creates and sustains and changes, when I should be getting done with mothering, moving on to Reaper. But I have no child of my own and my mother is dead and I no longer know if it was right, Sagarmatha, to leave her like I did, to hurt her like I did. At seventeen, I was so sure of everything. But now I'm almost middle-aged, and I'm not sure. I'm not sure at all.

10

June 1967

It's strange, Karla thought as she folded her clothes, how the same place could exist in different worlds of being and feeling, as if parallel universes truly lay side by side, provided with the same buildings and streets, furnished with the same bedspreads and blinds. Like school, which in the three weeks since their acid trip had become an alien place of vast hallways filled with dangers and disapproving faces. Or this room, her room, which had always been her refuge, a place of comfort, where she could listen to *Blonde on Blonde* over and over again on the old hi-fi or reread *Anne of Green Gables* for the tenth time, fondly imagining herself to be an orphan. But now everything faced her with an accusation: the white porcelain deer that decorated her dresser, her old Chatty Cathy doll on the bed with the peace sign pinned to her dress, the posters of Albert Einstein and Bob Dylan and Ho Chi Minh that gazed down on her from the ceiling. "You'll forget," they seemed to say. "You are the only one who remembers what you caught a glimpse of, and you won't be able to hold it. Soon you too will be lulled back into the easy sleep of ordinary life."

No, not me. Not like Johanna, who would no longer speak to Karla or meet her eye when they passed in the hallway at school or respond to the notes Karla slipped her in Frank Harvey's class. Harvey had shaken his head and gazed at them with surprised disappointment, like a hurt dog, when they returned after their three-day suspension. But he said nothing, for which Karla was extremely grateful. She had been lectured enough—by her mother, by her father long-distance from New York, by his lawyer friend who had managed to get the case against them dismissed, by Miss Darley and Miss Wright, who'd told the police only that they saw the girls looking disoriented and suspected that they had taken drugs.

On the day they returned to school, Miss Wright had called them into her office as gym class began. The office was a glass cubicle next to the equipment room, and Karla could hear the voices of girls calling out to one another behind her as she stared fixedly at the scenic calendar above Miss Wright's desk, wishing she were far away somewhere in the mountains. Johanna stood beside her, half a breath and a loud heartbeat away, but she turned her head to look at Karla. They were forbidden to speak to each other. That didn't surprise Karla. She'd expected that their mothers would order them to separate, but she hadn't expected Johanna to obey. It wasn't right to obey an unjust law—wasn't that what Martin Luther King had taught? And now Johanna had betrayed her.

"Look," Miss Wright said. "There's something I've got to explain to you." She paused and came out from behind her desk, perching on the edge and running her hand over her square-cut thatch of hair.

In the mountains, there you feel free. That was a line from a T. S. Eliot poem they'd studied in Harvey's class. Karla struggled not to squirm uncomfortably as Wright looked at them both for another long moment. She went on, in a lowered voice. "Miss Darley and I have lied for you. We are both honest people, and yet we've lied, for this reason only—because we know that if we told the truth, the punishment would be beyond all reasonable proportion. There are certain areas in which we have to stand together. And you don't have an easy road ahead of you if you go this route. Do you understand me?"

Karla and Johanna both nodded, although truthfully Karla didn't understand her at all.

"We've put ourselves out on a limb for you, and there's something I want you to promise me in return. That you will never again force this position on someone. Both for their sakes, and for yours, because there's no guarantee that someone else will make the same decision we did. Do you understand?"

Again they nodded, in synchrony as for some exotic rite.

"What you decide to do with yourselves is your own business. But do it with discretion. Not on the locker room floor. Is that clear?"

"Yes, Miss Wright."

"Thank you, Miss Wright."

Nevertheless, Karla couldn't help but feel that something was wrong. She was compromising some part of herself, capitulating to the fear. "Why not?" she wanted to ask. "Why not on the locker room floor, on the grass under the jacarandas, in the bright sun? What is so wrong, so horrible, about touch?" But she wasn't stoned, now, she was in her right mind, as her mother would say, and Johanna stood there shuttered and locked. Without her support, Karla could not break the silence.

She wanted to go away, leave the concrete and the rows of desks and the stifling boredom of her math class, and go, on and on without stopping, go to the mountains. Yes, that's what she'd do. She'd go. North, somewhere. Where she could find again what she'd known on the locker room floor and now could barely remember. Where she could live it.

"Let's run away," she had whispered to Johanna as they changed to go out onto the field and join the other girls. Johanna had turned her face away, as if she didn't hear her, and Karla repeated her suggestion.

"Karla, you are out of your mind," Johanna said. "Listen, we're not supposed to even be talking to each other."

"How can you say that?" Karla asked. There they were, in the same exact spot where a few days ago the world had broken open. "Don't you remember?"

"I remember," Johanna said grimly. "I remember it all." She slammed her locker shut and walked away from Karla, out to the field where lines of girls in white blouses and black shorts were doing sit-ups on the green grass. Karla followed, forlorn but not yet hopeless. Johanna would come around. After all, the bruise was still darkening on her cheek. It would heal. She was scared now, and guilty. She'd get over it. Anyway Karla couldn't abandon her, not while everyone else still looked sideways at them as they passed and whispered behind their backs. Tony Klein was a hero, with his arm in a sling, but Karla and Johanna made everyone uncomfortable. Even Joyce Levine licked her lips nervously when they came and sat down beside her, and Megan Ricci smiled at them but no longer invited them back to her place above the carousel. Not that they could have gone. They were both grounded until the end of school. No, Karla couldn't abandon Johanna now. She would give her until school let out, and then if she didn't change her mind, Karla would go alone.

Karla dragged a chair across the room and stood on top of it, rooting in the top of her closet. You have to choose, she imagined saying to Johanna. You can have comfort or you can have *that*. But, yes, already it was sliding away from Karla, too. She couldn't name it or define it but that was its nature, too, to slip between the fingers of the hand that closed around it. And she had to follow. She had to.

Karla grabbed the edge of her old flannel sleeping bag and pulled it down from the closet shelf. A box of letters tumbled down with it. "Damn," she swore, and began gathering them up again. Here were postcards from Joyce Levine the summer her family rented a cottage at Newport Beach, and a folded paper butterfly painted by Megan Ricci's artist boyfriend, and a stack of letters from Johanna's trip to visit her aunt in Memphis. "We're flying over the desert," she'd written. "Everything is yellow and brown and the land is full of peaks and ridges. It looks just exactly like swirly butter frosting. I wish you could see it. Now it's five minutes later, and the stewardess just brought me a Coke and a bag of peanuts. You can get all the soft drinks you want, and in a little while they'll serve us lunch. Everything is so beautiful from the air!"

Karla put the letter aside. She didn't have time to read it, to relive page by page those years when she and Johanna had been best friends.

Yet the act of folding the letter and replacing it in the box was painful. She was packing away her past and she might never retrieve it. That was okay. She couldn't carry the past with her where she was going. Still she was sad, sad. Sadness permeated her room like an odorless gas, hung in shreds from the handwoven Greek bags that decked her walls, fogged the features on the posters of Bob Dylan and Ho Chi Minh. She had to get out of there, leave sadness behind.

Again she balanced on the chair, replacing the box at the top of the closet. Let it stay there; let it rot. Now, which, of all her clothes, to take, when she would have to travel light? No more long closetful of dresses to change into when she chose. These clothes would become her, define her like a second skin. She got down, rolled up a Mexican peasant blouse, a blue work shirt, and a wool sweater and stuffed them into a duffel bag along with a poncho she had made herself from a light piece of paisley wool. She had worn that with Douglas the day they picnicked in Tapia Park and climbed the hill and made love under the live oak tree. The air had been full of sage and bay laurel. She was glad her first time had been out in the open, under a tree, even though she hadn't had an orgasm. She didn't think she had, anyway. Really, she wasn't sure, but Johanna had told her that if she had one, she'd know. It was unmistakable, Johanna said, smiling that just slightly superior smile of hers that always made Karla a little mad. Well, she was right. Karla knew that now. Thanks, Johanna, thanks for the memories.

Karla had loved Doug, loved his lean body and his fine, curly hair, and the smell of him, ached to press his long limbs against hers. But he had betrayed her, too, when his father made him break up with her. They were Catholic; his father didn't want Doug to marry a Jewish girl. She'd been indignant when he told her. "We're sixteen, we're not going to get married!" she'd said, but that wasn't the point, anyway. Doug had obeyed his father and she had lost all respect for him, bowing to a prejudice so unfair, so outmoded. Maybe she was doomed always to be betrayed by the ones she loved, just as her father had betrayed her mother, walked out on them all. Maybe she was doomed always to be wrong, somehow—too Jewish for Doug, too wild for Johanna, too weird for everyone else. Well, that was okay. She'd be alone, then. Fuck them all.

She added a handful of tampons, her birth control pills, a few pairs of underwear, her diary, and a couple of pens, a hairbrush and a toothbrush and her Tarot cards in the velvet bag she had made for them. In the pocket of her jeans, she had forty dollars, saved from baby-sitting jobs. She had wanted to buy a camera, but now she would live life instead of recording it.

What to wear? She changed into a clean pair of jeans, and over them she wore her favorite dress, a green-and-purple tunic. She added a pair of tights and a pair of sandals to her pack, but wore her sneakers.

Well, she was ready now. The last day of the semester was over. It was her birthday, too, and she'd thought maybe Johanna would say something, give her something, a card or a wink, even. Nobody had remembered except Betty, who left a card on the kitchen table when she left early to drop Debby at junior high before she went to work. The card depicted a blond teenager whirling in a dirndl skirt, her hair in a perfect flip, and a printed inscription: "From your loving mother: Happy birthday." Under it, Betty had written, "I hope next year's birthday will be a happier one. I cannot bring myself to give you a gift or offer you a celebration this year. I'm still too angry. But I have hopes that someday you will regain my trust, and I am still not sorry you were born. Love, Mom."

Karla had spent the morning at school writing and tearing up notes to her mother, until she finally achieved one she could keep. Now she wandered into the kitchen and placed her note on the table. "I'm sorry, Mom," it said. "I know this will hurt you but I've got to leave and go somewhere I can become what I believe in. I don't expect you to understand, but please trust that I'll be fine. Don't worry about me. I love you, and Debby, too. Karla."

Suddenly she wanted more than anything not to go, to sit at the table and make a cup of her mother's instant coffee and read the newspaper, to turn on the TV and watch the afternoon cartoons she had liked as a kid, to stay here where everything was dull and safe, safe, safe. Once she left, she might never have this everyday comfortableness again. She craved intensity but sometimes it could be too much. Home was like the white space on a page of poetry, the blankness that set off the meaning of the rest. The familiar things around her held their own kind of ordinary power: the dishes draining in the sink, the white clock that buzzed and rattled, the view of the neighbor's sycamore tree through the venetian blinds. Against their background, she defined herself. If she left them, abandoned them, betrayed them as she had been betrayed, who would she become? She would have to invent herself all over again. She would no longer be Karla-named-after-Karl-Marx Greenbaum.

In the driveway, a car gunned its engine. Karla watched through the window as Marian Weaver backed out of the drive, turned into the street, and drove away, heading toward the hospital where she was working the swing shift. Betty was at work. Debby was at the beach with her friends. The moment had come.

She went into the backyard and knocked at Johanna's window. After a minute, Johanna pushed the window open and leaned out.

"Karla, you know we're not supposed to do this. Aren't we in enough trouble?"

"Johanna, we've got to talk. Nobody's around. Nobody has to know. But I've got to talk to you or I'll lose my mind."

Johanna sighed.

"Come in."

Karla hoisted herself up on the window ledge and slid through. They sat on the floor in Johanna's room, out of the line of sight if anyone were there to see them.

"I'm leaving," Karla said. "I'm running away."

"Are you crazy?"

"No, I'm sane. Come with me."

"Come *with* you? What about my mother? What about your mother? How can you do that to her?"

"I'm not doing it *to* her, I'm doing it *for* her. Don't you understand?" Karla reached forward and took Johanna's hand. "Johanna, we had a breakthrough. It was real. Don't try to tell me that it wasn't. It's like a whole new possibility for the human race. But we've got to live it. We can't do that here. We've got to go somewhere where we'll be free to live it."

"What about high school?" Johanna asked, drawing her hand back and folding her arms. "We've still got a year to go."

"High school has nothing to do with it. How can you talk to me about high school when I'm talking about freedom?"

"How free are you going to be if you don't finish high school?"

Karla looked at Johanna's closed face, at her folded arms that seemed to barricade her soft parts. She tried again.

"Johanna, listen to me. Why can't we understand each other anymore? Can't you see that all that old stuff is fading away?"

Johanna shook her head sadly. "Girl, you sound like a Bob Dylan record. Where is your brain?"

Karla stood up and turned away from her. "I feel like we took the same trip and came out of it into different worlds."

"That's because we live in different worlds." Johanna rose and turned Karla around by the shoulder to face her. "Karla, we may have lived next door to each other since the fifth grade, but we are living in two different realities. I've tried not to realize that, but now that I see it it's crystal clear. You can afford to run off, break your mother's heart, blow your high school graduation. Fine. When you decide to drop back in, the door will be open. But I can't do that. I've got to live in this world the best I can, I've got to push that door open and stick my foot in the crack. That's what our—vision means to me. It's not a possible vision in this world. If we want to live it, we've got to remake the world."

Her words hurt Karla, but the intensity in her voice, the fixed brightness of her eyes, gave Karla hope. They were connecting again.

"Exactly! So come with me!" Karla said.

"But to do that, I've got to graduate. I can't afford to get busted out on the road somewhere. I can't afford not to get a scholarship to a good college. I can't afford to be branded as a dyke."

"What do you mean?"

"I mean what Wright meant, and what everyone else in school means when they turn their heads to the side and snicker every time one of us walks by."

"They think we're lesbians?"

Johanna nodded. "That's the generally accepted word for chicks that make it with other chicks."

"But that had nothing to do with it!" Maya flung herself down on Johanna's bed, then stood up again abruptly, as if suddenly afraid her gesture could be misinterpreted.

"Nothing to do with what?"

"I mean—what happened. It's not like . . . dressing up with socks in your pants and going to bars, or whatever they do. It was *us*. And now you're afraid."

"And you're not?" Johanna countered.

Karla took a deep breath. Above all, it was important to be honest here. "I'm afraid, but I've made up my mind never to let fear stop me again."

"Well, maybe I have more to be afraid of than you do."

They stood, face-to-face, close enough so that if Karla leaned forward, she could have seen her own reflection in Johanna's eyes. In the one-foot distance between them the dimensions warped, time and space turned inside out, and the laws that worked in one world did not apply in the other. Sad, sad, sad, Karla thought. But she couldn't change it.

"Well, I guess this is good-bye," she said at last.

"You're really going?"

"Yeah."

"You're going to kill your mama."

"Johanna, I can't believe you said that!"

"Well, it's true."

Karla shook her head. She didn't, wouldn't, think about it. Her mother's feelings were a trap she had to stay out of. Betty was Betty. Karla was Karla. She couldn't be responsible for her mother's life. "I'll write to you sometime. I'm changing my name. From now on I'm Maya. Like illusion. Maya J. Greenwood. That's what Greenbaum means, really—green tree. And the J is for you. So if you get a letter you'll know who it's from."

"Kar . . . Maya," Johanna reached out suddenly and grabbed her in a hug. They embraced, their eyes wet. "You be careful out there, you hear?"

"I will."

"Write to me. I'll worry about you."

"Don't worry. I'll be okay."

"Write to Johanna M. Weaver. The M will be for you."

Maya took a bus down Santa Monica Boulevard to the beach, walked down the ramp to the Pacific Coast Highway, and stuck out her thumb. She got a ride with two surfers who drove her to a turnoff just beyond Malibu.

She stood by the side of the road. The wind blew her hair back and it whipped around her face, smelling of the ocean just across the road. The white line of the highway seemed to stretch out to infinity, calling her to possibilities she could barely imagine. The sunlight slanted down in the gold of late afternoon. Far away she could see it reflected on the water. For one sharp moment, she wished desperately for Johanna, or somebody, to savor this moment with her. She was absolutely alone. But she was free.

Freedom was what she'd wanted. She settled in to savor the intoxication of liberty. She could follow any line she wished. She could give herself to the road and let the road sweep her away.

Her second ride was in a Volkswagen bus with two long-haired men and a smiling woman going to San Francisco. They smoked dope all the way up the coast. When they arrived, long after midnight, they offered to share the flat they were crashing in. The place consisted of two empty rooms in the Fillmore district, crawling with more cockroaches than Maya had ever seen in her relatively sheltered life. She slept outside, on the flat roof of the building next door.

The sun woke her. She stood up and stretched. From her perch on the roof, the city stretched out before her, white and gleaming in the mist-filtered light, seductive as a veiled dancer. The hills to the west rose like gold-crowned islands through a sea of fog. To the east, the spires of downtown hovered over the Bay, magical towers, fantasy palaces of elves and queens. Karla wanted to run out and enter the city, be enfolded in its embrace, give back in turn some spectacular act of love. Quietly, she rolled up her sleeping bag, picked up her bag, and tiptoed out without waking her benefactors.

She found herself on the downtown end of Haight Street. The crowded Victorian row houses seemed to loom over her, so different from the one-story ranch houses of her LA neighborhood. She liked them, just because they were different. It was an early Saturday morning. A few people were waiting at the bus stop. She asked directions to Haight-Ashbury, and headed west.

The fog lifted as the morning sun rose. After a mile or so, her arms got tired. She shifted her bag to the other shoulder and kept walking. The run-down houses of the Fillmore gradually gave way to rundown houses with psychedelic posters in the windows and doors painted in fantastic colors, bright orange, lime green. She rested for a while in Buena Vista Park, letting the growing strength of the sun warm her, then continued past the shops and cafés of the Haight. Most of the shops were closed, but through their windows she could see a cornucopia of fabulous objects: beads and bells, posters and tie-dyed skirts and T-shirts, books. She enjoyed looking and enjoyed even more the sensation of needing nothing, wanting nothing. She was complete in herself.

After a while, she stopped in a café, bought a cup of coffee, and sipped it slowly as she sat at a table in the sun, watching the street come to life. Four men stopped and spoke to her. One informed her that the Diggers would be serving free food in the Panhandle that afternoon, and gave her directions to the Haight Switchboard. Two asked her for spare change. She gave each of them a dime. One sat down and began to explain, at length, his theory that the universe was infinitely expanding, as was he, as was she, and how the eternally expanding space was a constant opening, like a huge cosmic orgasm, eternally unfolding, opening new space for new possibilities, and he could prove this but the scientists wouldn't listen to him. He had had the credentials but they had been taken away from him because of a long series of events that she began to find tedious, so she smiled enigmatically, stood up, and left.

The park at the end of Haight Street drew her. She walked down a path by a small pond, under a bridge, through a tunnel embellished with artificial stalagtites, through a stand of arching trees to a south-facing hillside dotted with long-haired people in bright-colored clothing. On a park bench, a battery of conga drummers provided a continuous beat against which a few flute players improvised, badly, but Maya didn't care. Some long-skirted women were whirling and dancing. She dropped her pack and joined them, laughing, feeling her body's joy in motion. Motion, she reflected, was very close to freedom. She would never have to sit still again.

After a time she began to feel a need to explore. She picked up her belongings, shouldered her bag, and walked on, west, always west, through winding paths and junglelike groves of tree ferns, on and on until she climbed a winding road that led to a small lake. In the center, an island rose. Farther down, she could see a bridge. She rested for a moment, sitting on her sleeping bag, looking down at her reflection in the water. Am I really here? she asked herself. Is this me? Karla? No, Maya. Maya, Maya, play of illusion like this face in the water that seems to be me but is only light. The Queen of Lies.

Her face rippled and dissolved as the prow of a rowboat drifted into view. A man stood up on the center strut, wielding his paddle like a long pole. His long blond hair flamed in the sun as he leaped gracefully ashore, dipped a finger into a pouch, and withdrew it coated with gold. Gently, he touched her forehead.

"You are a child of the sun," he said, taking her hand and holding the boat steady with his foot as he drew her aboard, tossing her bag in the back and pushing off with the paddle in one smooth motion. The boat was somewhat ungainly. He only had one paddle, but he managed it expertly, as he seated her in the prow and began rowing across to the island.

About halfway across, they heard shouts coming from behind them. The man threw back his head and laughed, as he paddled harder. His laugh held a wicked triumph and his hair flashed like a golden mane.

"I'm a pirate," he said, looking down at Maya. "Do you mind?"

She laughed back, wildly happy. They beached the boat; he jumped ashore, grabbing her bags and handing her on to the land.

"Come on," he said, shouldering her duffel bag. "Let's run for it."

They ran along a narrow path that circled the island, rising in a spiral up the hill. Maya's heart was pounding and her breathing was heavy. He seemed tireless, leading her up and up. Below them, they heard shouts and angry voices that seemed to be coming closer. They ran faster, on and on, until he motioned her into a small thicket of trees where they huddled together, trying to control their panting. As Maya's breath began to ease, he leaned toward her, touching again the spot on her forehead, then letting his finger trail softly down the bridge of her nose to linger between her lips. His eyes looked deeply into hers. They were blue, and big, and Maya sensed him reaching for her, reaching as she and Johanna had reached for each other. She let her tongue flick the end of his finger, and felt heat rush into her thighs and stomach and the lips of her vulva. He kissed her lightly, once on each eye, and then on the lips, a kiss that started gentle, tentative, and built in force and intensity until his arms were around her and they were clinging together, tongues twining like snakes behind their clamped lips. Wetness gushed from her as his hands traveled down over her shoulders to lift her tunic over her head and caress her breasts. He bowed his head and pressed his hands together in an act of worship before he bent to take her nipples in his mouth. His tongue sent little tendrils of electricity singing down her spine, and she unzipped his jeans as she wriggled out of her own, drawing him forth, rampant, magnificent. She wanted fire to be kindled deep inside her, wanted that wicked laugh to echo in her own depths, and then she was under him on the earth. The sun flashed through the tree branches and the gold crown of his hair. And only the tiniest, tiniest, most hidden part of her stayed separate enough to whisper, "See, Johanna, not a dyke!"

When it was over, they lay still together, still pulsing. He kissed her again, on the eyes.

"You are beautiful," he said. "What's your name?"

"Maya."

"Maya. Of course. What else could it possibly be? I saw you, sitting on the bank, so beautiful and so still, and I thought, 'This is not an ordinary woman. This is a goddess. How can I approach her? This is a woman who should only be approached over water, not by some mundane path on the earth. And then the boat came to hand. I took it as an omen."

"What's your name?"

"Rio. Rio Colorado. I named myself after a vision I had at the bottom of the Grand Canyon. Someday I'll tell you about it. Shall we spend the rest of our lives together?"

Maya smiled again, because she wasn't sure how to answer. She wasn't sure she wanted to spend the rest of her life with anybody, but she liked the question. She liked him. Like herself, he was following a vision. "We're spending this moment," she said.

"Who are you? Where do you come from? Are you crashing somewhere, or are you out on the street?"

"LA. I just got here, actually. Last night. I don't know where I'm crashing."

"That's easy, then. You can stay with me. I've got a van. But you mean this is your first day here? Your very first?"

"Yeah."

"Then we should make it special. I want to devote myself to making this a special day for you. A perfect day. A day you can remember when you're ninety years old, and look back and say, 'Yeah, that was a perfect day. A day of magic.' Are you hungry?"

"Yeah," Maya said, suddenly realizing how hungry she was.

"We'll put your stuff in the van, and go to Chinatown. You like Chinese food?"

"Yeah," Maya said again, feeling that she was scarcely being an overwhelming conversationalist. But that didn't seem to matter much to Rio.

"Then the first thing is to get out of here without getting busted."

"How do we do that?"

He winked at her. "Aren't you a witch? Can't you do some magic?"

She thought for a moment. "Sure." With her forefinger, she stirred their spilled juices into the dirt and made a pentacle like in the Tarot cards. She touched each of their eyelids lightly. "There. Now we're invisible."

And they were, or at least, unnoticed, as they went down the spiral path through the trees and over the bridge across the water, hand in hand under the misty sun of the day they had claimed together.

11

Night at Namche

Long time, Brothers, have you suffered the death of
a mother, for long the death of a father, for long the
death of a son, for long the death of a daughter, for
long the death of brothers and sisters, long time
have ye undergone the loss of your goods, long time
have you been afflicted with disease. And because
you have experienced the death of a mother, long
the death of a father, the death of a son, the death
of a daughter, the death of brothers and sisters, the
loss of goods, the pangs of disease, having been
united with the undesired and separated from the
desired, you have verily shed more tears upon this
long way—hastening from birth to death, from
death to birth—than all the waters that
are held in the Four Great Seas.

—THE WORD OF THE BUDDHA
THE WISDOM OF BUDDHISM

Maya had been more comfortable in her life. She had managed to secure a
spot on the long bench that ran along the side of Ang's main room, but
the bench was hard and the room felt crowded with people she didn't
know well or particularly like. She stretched out, wrapped in her sleeping bag, longing for someone she felt close to, someone she could really
talk to.

Debby had not arrived. She will come, Maya assured herself. Tomorrow, up at Tengpoche. I know she'll come. We can leave Betty's
ashes there, in sight of Sagarmatha.

She would write to Johanna. "Dear Jo, maybe life is redeemed if
even for a moment, all the boundaries and strictures fall away and the

clear light shines through. We had our moment young; we revealed it to
each other, and as you say, we've been finding and losing it ever since.
We're like clowns juggling fragments of a broken mirror along with cups
and plates and all the debris of daily life. What I wanted, though, was to
step into that moment, to reshape the world from the inside out. You
were wiser than me. You realized from the beginning that what we
needed to concentrate on was learning to throw and catch."

She had fled Johanna and run to Rio, and in the beginning he too
had opened the world for her. In spite of all their troubled years together,
all her resentment of him and grief for him, she remembered most clearly
how he seemed on that first morning, grinning at her from his stolen
boat, his hair flashing in the sun, an icon of freedom. Maybe it was best
just to remember him that way, not to meet again, not to see what the
years and the cages had done to him. Maybe as long as she held that
memory in her mind, some part of him that was eternally young and free
and joyous still existed. Could people do that for each other? If so, she
had better not go to Nevada, not answer his letters, not even read them,
maybe. Oh, what an excuse, what a perfect rationalization. Rio, I have cut
you off for seventeen years in order to preserve your soul unbound.

The lights were out, and everyone else was asleep, or trying to be.
Maya shifted on the bench and thought about going to the bathroom. The
outhouse was a long way away, through the crowded room, down the
hall, down the shaky ladder, through the byre of bedded-down *zopkios,*
out to the terrace, and then up a stone stairway that was hard to negotiate
even by day. She would wait a bit, until she was sure everyone was sound
asleep, and then pee on the grass that covered the narrow terrace.

In the meantime, she couldn't sleep. On the table beside her lay a
stack of letters and journal pages. She had sorted through them earlier in
the evening, while the one bulb that constituted Ang's electrical system
still gave some light. Johanna's diary was now interspersed with letters
Rio had written to his brother long ago. Maya would be able to read
through the story of her life, chronologically.

She hadn't understood why Rio's brother Steve had sent the letters
to her. He'd found them when he and his wife cleaned out the house
after Rio's mother died. Most of them were written to the eldest brother,
Jim. Evidently they'd been shipped home from Vietnam, along with Jim's
body and his other personal effects, and Rio's mother had never thrown
them away.

"I happened to see a review of your book," Steve had written her,
"when Laurie and I were trying to figure out what to do with all this
stuff. So I thought I'd send them to you and you could pass them on to
Richie. I mean, Rio. We don't have any contact with him, and I don't even
know where he's being held. As far as we're concerned, he might as well
be dead. Probably I should just burn these, but for some reason I can't

seem to bring myself to. Sorry if this is an inconvenience. Steve Connolly."

Now that she'd cleaned out her own mother's house, she could better imagine Steve's state of mind. She remembered wandering through the rooms, trying to bring herself to begin the work of sorting and packing. The still-intact house, the assemblage of books on shelves and clothes in drawers and pictures on the walls had seemed to be the last vestige of Betty, as if her mother's life had splintered into a thousand fragments, each still preserved in one of the objects she had regularly touched and used. To disassemble the house would be to kill her mother all over again.

Maya had tackled the job, fueling her energy each morning with a pot of black coffee, only to find herself immobilized, again and again, by decisions she couldn't make. What could she do with the six mismatched demitasse cups Betty had brought back from London? "I couldn't decide which pattern I liked best," she'd said, so instead of buying a set of china she'd bought one example of each. If Maya had a daughter, she could set the cups on a shelf and tell the story, and her child would come to know something of Betty at her best, her most adventurous, most humorous. But she had no child. How many things should she save on the off chance that she or Debby would someday produce offspring?

If only Debby had been there, to cry with her over Betty's mink coat. Joe had bought it for her in the early fifties when he was a rising young lawyer, before the blacklist. If she could have found a use for it, a home for it, she would have felt less as if she were desecrating a shrine as she removed it from its honored place in the hall closet. Could Debby wear it in Nepal? For Maya to wear it would be to ally herself publicly with an industry that had decimated the wildlife of six continents. She'd be denounced as soon as she set foot out the door. Maybe she could carry a sign: "These minks died in 1949, before the dawn of consciousness. This coat is recycled. I wear it not to support the fur industry but as proof that once upon a time my father did love my mother."

Maya had bundled up the coat and put it aside. But there were still stacks and piles and boxes of photos and mementos and papers. What do you do with your mother's graduate school transcripts or the program from your sister's first piano recital? Would Debby want them? Evidently Betty herself had faced the same issues, as Maya found her grandmother's certificate of graduation from night school and the plaque awarded to her by the Milwaukee Hadassah in 1963.

Yes, she could see why Steve might think that sending Rio's letters to her, care of her publisher, was a rational thing to do. In the end, Maya had put half her mother's things in storage and called Goodwill to come get the rest.

Maya had neither burned the letters nor read them nor sent them on. Instead she'd hidden them away in a drawer, where they might have remained until Rachel cleaned out the house after Maya's and Johanna's demise. She'd meant to send them, but to do that she would have had to answer Rio's letter, to tell him about Rachel or to lie by omission. And she had done neither.

Now here the letters were. She had brought them to read, to help her decide what to do, whether to go to Nevada or put him finally out of her mind. But to read them was to throw a stone into the still lake surface where his bright image was reflected, to stir up other memories that lurked in the depths. Not to mention the fact that technically, she was reading someone else's mail.

This is probably illegal, and it's definitely immoral, but I want to read them, she admitted to herself. I want to see Rio in three dimensions, and so get a round view of my own past. After all, Jim can't care—he's dead.

And Rio? What would he want?

How can I justify reading them? Can I say that his crimes abrogate his right to privacy? Even a Reagan-appointed Supreme Court wouldn't buy that. Do I have a right to read them in return for all the books of mine he says he's read? Not fair. Books are written for public consumption, after all, and these letters are private. Should I tell myself that he wants me to come and see him and this is what I need to do before I can decide?

No, let me just be honest. Right or wrong, I'm going to read them anyway. He can't stop me. He'll never even know, unless I tell him.

Rio's letters and Johanna's journal together would move her own memories off the flat surface of the past, give them the depth and dimension and perspective she needed. She reached for the small clip-on flashlight she kept in the side pocket of her pack, and turned it on. With a slight sense of guilt, she began to read.

12

Letter

James Patrick Connolly
Private First Class U.S.
Vietnam
June 15, 1967

Dear Jim,

How ya doin', bro? Still alive, and still with your manly faculties intact, I hope. And not committing more than your fair share of atrocities. Sometimes I wonder how it is we can still write to each other, but I guess blood is thicker than water. And the truth is, Jimbo, there's some things I really can only tell to you. Not because you aren't the world's worst flaming fascist asshole (say that fast three times), which you are, but I will say this for you, you always took me seriously. Even when we were kids, and I'd paddle around after you in my fat little pants. You might whop the shit out of me from time to time, but you never laughed at me.

Which is why I'm writing to you now, because I have something to tell you, something important. And you're the only one I can tell. I'm in love. Yes, that's the sad and sorry state of it. I'm a pitiful sight, man. I want to run around singing every corny stupid song out of every old movie you can think of. I want to buy her diamonds and emeralds and the finest quality, genuine grade-A Moroccan hash. (Not that I would ever really traffic in illegal substances, heh heh.) I want to write goddamned fucking poems.

Yes, me, your rotten little brother, that's who.

I'll tell you about her. Actually, I don't know much about her—I haven't asked her much. She just appeared, sitting on the banks of Stow Lake in Golden Gate Park. I saw her from across the water, and liked the look of her. Some dude in too-tight chinos was just helping this beehive-hair chick out of a rowboat near me, and something came over me. I leaped out of the bushes into the boat, shoved off, and before they knew what was happening, I was halfway across the lake, en route to my fair lady. Now, I don't want you to think I behaved badly. I told her straight out that I was a pirate. She seemed to like the idea. I rowed across to the island in the center of the lake. By that time, Chinos and Beehive were in hot pursuit, along with some official park sort of dude, so we beached the boat and made a run for it. She was game—I liked that about her. She didn't whine or whiffle, she just ran right alongside and we ducked into some bushes to wait out the heat, and then, as they say, we draw a curtain over the events that followed. All I can say is, while it was happening and when it was over, I knew that she was it for me. My lady, my mate, my woman, the one, Jim, just like we always used to dream. And I didn't even know her name.

So now she's living with me, in the van. Her name's Maya, by the way. I suppose you'll want to know what she looks like. She's medium tall, not short, and medium build. Well, maybe running a little to plumpness, but only where it does the most good, if you catch my drift. Anyway, you know I like 'em that way. She's got brown eyes that always look a little dreamy (or maybe we've just been stoned too much) and brown hair that starts to curl right from the top of her head and comes down in ripple after ripple, like a frozen waterfall, down almost to her shoulders. She claims it won't grow more than that, it just curls up into ringlets and winds itself into knots. She used to straighten it but I told her not to bother anymore. Her face is a little on the round side, with sweet, full lips. Unlike the type of chick you go for, she doesn't crap herself up with tons of stinking makeup. She doesn't need to.

We've been together for two days, practically every minute, and I've never been happier. I've been showing her the town, taking her out to eat, walking through the Japanese Gardens, hiking out by Land's End. And at night—well, I will have to leave that to your imagination. Except it's better. It's really true what they say, all the assholes. When you're in love, it's better.

Jim, Jim, I hope this happens to you before Charlie blows your ass sky-high. I never really thought it would happen to me.

Rio
alias Your Kid Brother,
Richie

13

Johanna Weaver's Diary

September 5, 1967

Dear Sheba:

Actually, I'm tired of calling you Sheba. It's a dumb name. Maybe it was okay when we were twelve years old, and Sheba was the only black queen I knew about. Except maybe Cleopatra—Uncle Marcus always said the Egyptians were black. But Cleopatra was a Greek, really—wasn't she? Oh well, that isn't the point, the point is I'm not twelve years old anymore. It was Karla's idea that we pretend our diaries were letters to girls that were holed up hiding from the Nazis, like Anne Frank. And we had to write to them all about ordinary life in the outside world, so that when they finally got out they could fit in, and if there were any Nazis around they wouldn't suspect anything. But I said I wanted mine to be a girl hiding from the slave hunters, on the Underground Railroad. A princess of an African tribe who'd been sold away and couldn't live in captivity. Karla said that wouldn't work—that slavery was over long ago, but so were the Nazis, I told her. And if we were making the whole thing up, what was the difference? She got all snooty and said the Nazis were contemporary history, and I told her I wasn't going to let her read my diary anyway as it was none of her business.

Oh, I just keep remembering more and more times with Karla and it makes me sad. I'm writing to you, Sheba, but who I want to write to, speak to, cuss out, and complain to isn't you, but Karla. Maya, maybe, but I don't know Maya, don't know who she's become since she went away. *She* doesn't write to me, and she knows where to find me. She doesn't write her mother or call, and Betty looks just awful. Her hair is full of gray streaks and her face is full of worry lines. She seems to yell more, too—I hear her screaming at Debby when the windows are open. Actually, she always did yell a lot, but now it's worse.

Mom is always going on about Karla, how thoughtless, how selfish she is. Last night at dinner she was complaining again. I guess it bothers her to see Betty like this. Maybe she's afraid I'll up and follow Karla, turn into her. Marian had made chili and cornbread for dinner, and we sat down to it together, with the table set and the milk in a pitcher and the napkins folded as neatly as if the queen were coming to dinner. That's what Mama always says. What Marian says. I've got to remember to call her that here because I'm not her baby girl anymore, even if it would hurt her to admit that. I'm a grown woman, even if I'm only seventeen. In most places in the world, I'd be long married and raising a pack of kids by now. By my age, Romeo and Juliet were already dead.

Marian and I are alike in some ways—we both like queens, or the idea of queens, we don't actually know any personally. But Marian likes the queen of England. God knows why. She likes to read about the royal family, and the Queen Mother's hats. Because they're so dull, she says, and stuffy, and different from growing up black in New Orleans, a "widow's" daughter.

"Poor Betty has aged ten years in the last month. After all she did for her, too, raising up those two girls all by herself," Marian was saying, while I pushed the food around on my plate and didn't say anything at all. Because the truth is, I miss Karla dreadfully. All summer long I've been a prisoner here, with everyone else away. Joyce Levine spent the summer in Hawaii with her mother and stepfather. Megan Ricci went to New York with her boyfriend. Tony was in Oregon, with his older brother. And I was stuck here, grounded for the whole summer, and Marian canceled our trip back to Louisiana and enrolled me in that stupid typing class. I hate typing.

"It won't hurt you to learn something practical," was what she said. "That way you can always get a job as a secretary."

I don't ever want a job as a secretary, and I would have said so but I knew she would just make some remark about how I'd better behave myself then, and apply myself to my studies. Yes, Mama, I'll be good, I'll study hard and go to college and never get in trouble again. No, it's definitely one of those times, as Karla would say, that you just have to get through. And Karla? Where the hell is she? Stark-ass naked on some sunny beach, or dead in the alley? I wish I knew.

Anyway, we were talking about Karla, or not talking, as the case may be. I wasn't, anyway, or eating much, either, and eventually Marian asked me if I was going to eat my chili or just torture it.

"I'm not hungry," I told her.

"Now I'm worried," Marian said. "I've never known adversity to put you off your feed, before. You know, child, I told you you were grounded all summer but maybe that was a bit harsh. I wouldn't object to you going out a bit with your friends. You've been a good girl this summer, Joanne."

I should have just left it at that, thanked her and held my peace. Why can't I learn to keep my big mouth shut? But instead, I told her that I don't have any friends, that they're all gone, like Karla.

"Some friend," Marian said. "Running off, leaving you here alone to face the music. Why don't you find some nice black friends? Some who would stick by you when things get tough. Surely there's some nice boys that you could go out with."

The truth is that the other black kids in school don't like me much. There aren't too many of them, mostly bussed in from South Central LA courtesy of Burt Lancaster's special program to send deserving Negroes to good white schools. They aren't in the honors track, except for Adam Kelly, who lives in Brentwood and his father is a doctor. They like him okay but that's because he's good at sports. Whenever *I* walk past the tables on the lower patio where they hang out, they turn away and make loud remarks about Oreo cookies. Black on the outside, white on the inside. You know. And nastier things. Bull dagger. Dyke. Or maybe I just imagine it. Fuck them anyway.

But I didn't want to get into all that with Marian. Still, I was in a pissy mood, so I said what I always say, "Why did you move us into a white neighborhood if you wanted me to have black friends?"

"Don't you sass me, young lady. You know perfectly well why we moved here, and what I hoped for you. What you nearly destroyed."

That's right, Mama. Twist the knife.

"The black kids don't like me. They think I'm stuck up."

"Well, perhaps you've given them reason to think that. Look in the mirror before you complain about someone else's dirty face."

Oh, Sheba, somewhere it's different from here. Somewhere every-body is dancing naked on the grass in the sunshine, and it doesn't matter what color they are or what grades they get or how love happens to take hold of them. Only that it does, from time to time. *That's* where Karla went, and I wish every day that I had gone with her.

But I really couldn't have done that to Marian. No matter how much she gets on my nerves, I still love her.

Anyway, today was our first day back at school. I felt a little nervous at first, when I went back behind the music bungalows where my friends, so called, when I have them, hang out. The last few weeks of school in June were so uncomfortable. I always felt before just as much a part of everything as anybody else. I mean, I didn't go around all the time think-ing, "I'm black, I'm different, how are people relating to me?" But then I started to notice things, or imagine them—the way the other kids look at me, or speak a beat too quick or a beat behind, as if they were crossing an invisible barrier and congratulating themselves, at the same time, for being willing to do it. Or the way they so carefully don't see me, my difference, my blackness, they don't mention it or talk about it, but sometimes when I come up on them they get suddenly quiet, as if they'd been saying something they wouldn't want me to hear. It seems to me that white people spend a lot of time not seeing. That's their first response to trouble. Shut the eyes, bury the head, hope it will go away. But what I know now, and what Marian tried to teach me, is that for us, survival depends on keeping your eyes open wide and your mind awake.

So, I went back to the lawn. Joyce Levine was sitting there, tan from Hawaii and tossing her sunstreaked hair. She hadn't called me when she got home, but now she jumped up and hugged me and made room for me to sit next to her. Tony Klein handed me the latest mimeographed issue of *The Other Side.* Joyce was chattering away about the lava in Hawaii, and what bad luck it was to carry pieces off the island. Tony was asking me to write for *The Other Side,* now that Karla was gone. The other kids who were hanging out moved over to make room for me, sometimes a bit too quickly, like they were trying to prove something. They offered me cookies out of their lunches and tried to get me to come to political meetings against the war. I felt like they needed me to justify something for them. But I was accepted again. In fact, it was weird—it was like nothing had ever happened at all. Here my whole life had turned around, my whole summer was ruined, Karla was gone, and none of that seemed to matter at all. It was just erased. Maybe teenage time is like dog time—you know, one year is worth seven. Something that happened back in the spring is like the ancient past.

So you see, Karla, you didn't have to run away. What you didn't count on was the power of just plain ordinariness. It creeps over everything and turns it normal. People get used to things. People forget.

And yet, in a funny way, I'm almost glad that Karla did run away. She's like the only thing that still is different, that still says, Yes, something important did happen to you. Maybe it didn't change the world, but it was real. Sometimes I think I'll go crazy from normality, from pretending, from being fine, just fine. Karla, Karla/Maya, were you crazy, ruthless, selfish, or were you right?

Later:
So there I was, in my room, writing in this diary at my desk, when I looked up. Betty was standing in my doorway.

"I thought you might like to know," Betty said, "that Karla called today. For my birthday."

I turned around to look at her, putting the diary down. "Oh, happy birthday, Mrs. Greenbaum," I said. I'd always called her Betty but since the Incident—I don't know, I felt a little funny with her. "Do you want to sit down?"

Betty came into the room and paced back and forth. She stared for a moment at my curtains, which in case I never bothered to describe them to you are dotted swiss, with ruffles. Marian sewed them for me when we first moved in, when I was nine, and I was so thrilled. She made me a bedspread to match, and every morning I'd arrange my collection of stuffed cats on the pillows. They had to go in a particular way, because some of them didn't get along with the others, and they might fight while I was gone if they were too close to each other. Anyway, I was so happy in my room—I thought it looked like something on the *Patty Duke Show* on TV. Now I'd like to change it all, drape the windows in red velvet or paint the walls black. Because the room and the curtains and the ruffles always seem to be reproaching me. See how good your Mama was to you—they say. You're still her baby girl. And Karla is gone for good, and taken your magic with her.

"No, I won't stay," Betty said. "I just wanted to let you know I'd heard from her."

I made noises like, "Thank you. That's kind of you. I worry about her."

"I know." Betty hesitated. Her skin was so pale, I could see the pulse in her throat and the color of her veins.

"How is Karla?" I asked. I thought she wanted me to say something.

"Alive," Betty said. "I guess that's something to be thankful for. She has some sort of boyfriend she's living with. She didn't say much else, except she asked about you. I told her to come home, that it's not too late for her to start school, for the fall. She said she doesn't want to go to school. I asked, what about her scholarship to Columbia? She can go there for free, you know, it's where her father teaches. She just laughed."

I didn't know what to say. Betty stood in the center of the room, looking awkward, with her hands hanging down at her sides as if she didn't know where to put them. Her feet were pointing one way, her body was trying to twist itself in another direction. I wished she would just sit down, or go.

"Can I get you anything?" I stood up. "Coffee, or a drink of water?"

"I'd like to talk to you," Betty admitted. "No, no I'm fine, I don't want anything."

Then we were both standing, facing each other, both of us with awkward hands and twisting feet and not knowing how we were supposed to behave.

"Please sit down," I said, and pulled the chair out from my desk for her. It's moments like that that make me glad Marian taught me manners. She perched on the chair edge, and I sat down on the end of my bed and tried to look encouraging.

"What went wrong?" Betty asked, looking away from me at my poster of Aretha Franklin on the far wall. "Why did she leave me?"

She paused and I could hear echoes of what she didn't say: Why did Joe leave me? Why does everybody leave me? What did I do to deserve to be alone?

"You have Debby," I said, and then I stopped, embarrassed because I realized I had answered her private thoughts.

Betty gave me a sharp look. "Debby is not the issue here. Karla is the issue. What went wrong with Karla? Was it her father? Was it me? Was it something I did, or said, or didn't say? You tell me, Johanna. You were her best friend. Was I so much worse than other mothers? There's plenty worse than I am, believe me, I see them in my office every day. But *their* kids don't run away. *Their* kids finish high school, for God's sake!"

"I know, Mrs. Greenbaum," I said. "I mean, I don't know, not really."

"Why are you suddenly calling me Mrs. Greenbaum, when you've called me Betty for years?"

"I thought you were mad at me."

"I was, but that doesn't make me a stranger. Was I too harsh with her? Was I supposed to applaud her taking drugs and getting arrested?"

"No, Betty," I said, feeling more and more uncomfortable. How did I get nominated to hold her hand? And what could I say without betraying Karla (the selfish bitch) or turning what happened to us into some cheap drug trip. It was more than that, much more, but already it was like a story I'd been told more than a live, real memory.

"Did I beat her? Abuse her? Did I ever so much as lay a hand on her in anger? All right, I yell, I admit it, but she never seemed daunted by it. She had a mouth, too—she gave as good as she got."

"Maybe it had nothing to do with you," I said slowly.

That made her mad. "How could it have nothing to do with me? I'm her mother!"

"Maybe she was just caught in the times."

"No, don't give me that, Johanna. I'm a psychologist, I know better. Kids don't run away, don't ruin their life, because of the times. The times are the times for everyone—but most of us still go on living a life. You do."

She was leaning forward, staring at me as if her eyes could peel my face. I had an urge to dive beneath the bedclothes and cover my head. But Betty was waiting for an answer.

"Karla's different from me. She's—logical. Once she sees something, she has to pursue it to the end, wherever that takes her. She doesn't like to compromise.''

"Explain her logic to me, would you please? I can't follow it.''

"I'm not sure I can. Explain her, I mean. Maybe if I really understood her myself, I'd be out there with her, on the road,'' I admitted. It was the first time I'd ever said as much out loud.

"I don't think so. I think you have too much common sense. And an instinct for self-preservation. I don't know what happened to hers. Maybe I coddled her too much, spoiled her. She was all puffed up with adolescent omnipotence, never willing to see any dangers or limits.''

"I think she saw the dangers. It's just that what looks like danger to her is what looks like safety and common sense to you.''

"What's that supposed to mean?''

"I think that to Karla, the worst danger seemed to be to sink into accepting things the way they are.''

"But what is so wrong with the way things are?'' Betty stood up and paced around the bedroom. "Karla never had to suffer, not like we did during the Depression! She had food on the table every day of her life, the nicest bedroom in the house, she went to a decent school. What was the matter?''

"The lies,'' I said, although anything I could name wouldn't really explain. "The war. Starvation. Prejudice. Murder.''

"But we fought all that!'' Betty said. "My God, her father was beaten in Mississippi, and we always supported civil rights.''

"But you lived in this world the way it was. So you accepted it. You talked against the bad stuff, but you lived lives like everybody else's. Comfortable lives—at least that's how Karla sees it. She doesn't want to do that.''

"Comfortable? My God, how much comfort did we have in the fifties, when Joe was blacklisted and couldn't get a job? How much comfort did I have when he walked out, leaving me with the kids to raise? I'm forty-seven years old, Johanna, I can't live in a commune. I'm entitled to a bit of comfort!''

"Of course you are,'' I said. "But Karla isn't interested in comfort. She wants to live without making any compromises.''

Was that true? I wondered. Was I just inventing excuses for Betty, or had I finally understood what Karla wanted? I felt guilty. I pushed her, I thought. I pushed us both over the edge, made us go as far as the acid could take us, and further still. Now I'm the one who compromises every day. But isn't that what life is about, unless you have the wealth and the power to make it be the way you want? Or unless you were willing to make terrible sacrifices.

And I'm not. I'm not willing. Is that sensibleness, or fear?

"It's sheer selfishness," Betty said, standing up again. "She's so much like her damned father. Oh, it's easy enough to be the great radical, when somebody else is paying the bills. Letting his law degree go to waste—he wouldn't compromise his politics, he said, enough to fit in to any firm this side of Cuba. Meanwhile he played at being working class, while I supported the family, waking up every night for the three A.M. feeding, while could he so much as change a diaper? What, the great Joe Greenbaum, get his hands dirty!" She stopped suddenly, and turned to me, looking young, somehow, and miserable. "I'm sorry, I shouldn't be burdening you with all of this."

"She did call," I said. "That's a good sign. Maybe she'll come home."

"I'm not sure I want her to," Betty said.

That was our conversation. So now I know that Karla is alive out there somewhere, that she's not completely dead to all family feeling. I wonder if she'll come home.

I wonder if *I* want her to.

Johanna

14

December 1967

When Maya and Rio had been together six months, she brought him home to her mother. By then they were veterans of their mutual campaigns in unbounded spaces. They had lain together beside the ocean, eye to eye, heart to heart, letting the tide wash over their feet, impervious to cold in the heat that passed between them on their rising and receding breath. Maya understood him; she opened herself to his visions and took them in and sheltered them. She was his luck, his Witch, his magic; she read cards for him that warned of sour deals and informers.

"I wouldn't do it," she would say. "The cards don't look good. See, there you are, the Knight of Wands, crossed by the Devil. Someone you shouldn't trust, someone who is not what he seems to be. And the Tower in the final outcome—disaster. Exposure. The false philosophers being thrown to the ground. It looks like a setup to me."

They had been reclining on the mattress in the back of Rio's van. Maya read cards by candlelight, aware that he liked to watch the warm glow of the flame flicker over her skin.

"It sounded too good to be true," he'd admitted. "A whole ki of Michoacán for a hundred bucks. I'll take a pass."

"Good," she said. "It doesn't smell right."

"You do, though," he said, reaching across the cards to stroke the wild, curly mass of her hair.

"How do you know? You can't smell me from way over there."

"I can. I'm like a wolf. Or do you want me to come closer?"

"You could," she said, brushing the cards into a pile and shuffling them back into the pack.

The van was their own private world, scented with incense from Nepal and bright with hangings from India, Morocco, Tibet. She was the priestess of his realm, the world he had created, small but mobile, free, safe. She made protection charms to hang on the rearview mirror, High John the Conqueror root soaked in patchouli she'd bought at a little botanica in the Mission. They parked by the Panhandle and took long walks in Golden Gate Park by moonlight, or took off at a moment's notice, up the coast, down the coast, away to Mount Shasta or the High Sierras. He bought her things that he said reminded him of her; colorful, beautiful, a little exotic—necklaces from China or embroidered dresses from Afghanistan or gypsy scarves. All his life, he told her, he'd known someone like her had to exist somewhere, someone who would love him and fly with him.

What she loved most about him, however, was not the gifts or the dope or even the sex. She loved the way he listened to her, intently, both eyes focused on her face, as if what she was saying was important to him.

"Stay with me," he'd whispered into her hair the first night she'd slept with him in the van, after they made love. She'd rolled over and propped herself up on her elbow.

"I'll stay with you as long as I can," she said. "As long as I can be true to what I've learned."

"What have you learned?" He'd rolled over to face her, and looked at her as if he really wanted to know.

"I've learned that most things that people think are important are lies. And what's true are just those few moments when you can break through the lies and really touch."

He held out his hand to her, palm facing her. She met his hand with her own, and he clasped it tight.

"We can do that," he said seriously. "We have that potential between us. I knew it as soon as I saw you, across the lake."

Maya nodded.

"We will do it. We'll never settle for less. Promise?"

"I promise," Maya said softly, feeling that she was making a holy vow.

He drew her close, rolling over on his back and slipping his arm under her shoulders. "When I was on my way out to California," he said, "I stopped at the Grand Canyon, and hiked down to the bottom. Have you ever been there?"

"When I was a kid, once, with my family. But only to the rim. We didn't go down."

"It's a mile down, through the most beautiful rocks you can imagine. I'd done a couple of hits of acid, and as I walked down that trail, I began to feel like I was walking through time. Time was frozen all around me, in the rocks, in all the layers of color. At the bottom, the river was flashing in the sun, singing its way over the stones. Then I understood."

"What?"

"What you understood, I think. That if you stay in the singing river, it'll carve through everything, even the hardest rock. And nothing else really matters. That's why I named myself Rio—it's Spanish for river. Rio Colorado."

He leaned over and kissed her on the mouth, gently. "I've never told anyone else about that before," he said. "I've never met anyone else who would have understood. We're lucky we've found each other. Let's never forget it. Let's never lose this."

"Never," Maya pledged. Yes, she had come to the right place, she had made the right choice. He filled the space Johanna had abandoned. He made up for everything. His hand started to travel down over her body, but she caught it and stopped it.

"Making love is holy," she told him. "For me, it's holy. It's the way we dive into the river. If you understand that, then we can stay together forever."

He lowered his head and kissed her vulva, letting his tongue caress her inner lips. "This is what I worship," he said softly. "This is my only god." He took her hand and moved it down to close over his swelling cock. "This is your god."

Slowly, tenderly, joyfully, they worshiped together.

In early December, he needed to go to LA to meet a contact who was supposed to have good-quality grass from over the border. The cards looked good, lots of pentacles and brimming cups, money and friend-ship, a good time. They drove down the coast together in the late fall sunshine, and she waited docilely in the van, reading Hermann Hesse's *Steppenwolf* while he conducted his negotiations. When the deal was done, and the bricks of grass stashed carefully inside the van, he asked if she wanted to stop and see her mother.

"I'm not sure," she admitted. "It could be an awful scene."

"I'll risk it," Rio said, smiling at her. "I'd risk more than that for you. And I suspect you'll regret it if we go back north without seeing her."

Maya didn't answer. She wanted to be an orphan, unparented, unencumbered, to have arisen out of sea foam or sprung from a fissure in a tree trunk or the head of some god. But he was right. Here they were, in LA, and she should at least stop and see Betty and Debby. From time to time, she felt wisps of guilt when she thought of her mother. She had called on Betty's birthday, and her voice had sounded old and bitter and flat. Yes, Maya owed her something—an afternoon at least, a day or so. She had changed enough in these last months. She was a new person now: Maya, not Karla any longer. She could afford to visit the past.

In the late afternoon, they arrived at her house, which sat on the corner of the block. Instead of a garage, Johanna's house shared the lot, facing the other street. Betty's car was not parked at the curb. She must still be at work.

The house looked smaller to Maya, a low, white bungalow, edged with juniper and agapanthus and a small front lawn. It was clean and neat and boring, not old, not new, not romantic like the gingerbread Victorians she had crashed in back in the Haight. As they stepped up onto the low front porch, Maya felt a sudden sense of panic, as if, once she crossed the threshold, she might suddenly turn back into Karla, who went to school dutifully and thought about her homework, and was afraid. Yes, already she was afraid, and maybe this was a bad idea. She took Rio's hand, ready to suggest they flee, but the door opened and Debby stared at her.

"Karla! What are you doing here?" Debby had an owlish face, big round glasses, and straight chestnut hair like Joe Greenbaum's, different from the mop of dark curls Maya inherited from Betty. Debby was still wearing her school clothes, what looked like a new outfit; a plaid jumper and a pink blouse underneath. Betty had always told them to change as soon as they got home from school, to save wear and tear on their good clothes. Usually Debby ignored her, and Maya had often nagged and bullied and threatened her until she did. Well, she wasn't going to get into that today.

"Visiting," Maya said, smiling. "How ya doin'?"

"Who's he?" Debby demanded.

"My old man." Maya winked at her. "His name's Rio. Rio, this is my sister, Debby. Don't you want to let us in?"

"I guess so."

"You're not very friendly."

"I'm mad at you," Debby said, but she stood away from the door so they could enter. "You ran off, and Betty's been yelling at me ever since."

Debby stared at Rio. He smiled at her, but she moved back. Maybe he frightened her, Maya thought. He'd grown his beard out and his hair hung down over his shoulders and he was shirtless under an afghan sheepskin vest. Maybe he smelled bad.

Maya was wearing one of her witch dresses, long and black and floaty, with a red paisley scarf tied around her hips. She tried to remember how cute Debby had once been, how they had played with their Barbie dolls together and wrestled on the floor. Reaching down, she grabbed her younger sister in a hug. Debby stood, passively, allowing herself to be caressed.

"Come on, Debs, lighten up," Maya said. "Hey, is there anything to eat in the kitchen? I'm starved."

They went into the kitchen, and Rio wandered into the living room.

"Maybe I'll make dinner," Maya said. "Have it ready for Mom when she comes home. Surprise her."

"What's the point?" Debby said. "It won't fix anything. She'll still scream at you."

"It might be nice for her," Maya said.

"Oh, suddenly you're *so* considerate."

Maya almost told her to fuck off, but she held it back. She wanted to try to get along.

"I'll make some coffee. You don't drink it yet, do you?"

"Black," she said. "I'm waiting for it to stunt my growth."

"Maybe it's backfired," Maya said, "I think you're as tall as I am now."

"Taller," Debby assured her. "I'm five feet, eight inches."

"Taller by an inch," Maya admitted, glad that they were no longer blatantly hostile. "But I stopped growing at your age. You won't be a giant."

Maya went to the sink and found it full of brown, greasy water.

"It's stopped up," Debby said.

"Damn!" Maya filled the kettle, careful not to overspill into the sink, and set it on the stove.

"Rio," she called from the kitchen. "Want some coffee?"

He came into the kitchen, where she was poking around the sink with a fork. Suddenly Maya desperately wanted everything to be perfect. She wanted her mother to come home and find the kitchen spotless, dinner prepared, all the hurts of the last year magically erased.

"What are you doing?" he asked.

"The sink's all stopped up," she said. "I wanted to make dinner for my mom, have it all ready and surprise her. But I can't get it to drain." Her voice sounded sharp; she was almost going to cry. He put an arm around her, holding his head to one side as if he were trying not to breathe in her face. Maya caught a whiff of something pungent and sharp. Alcohol. Some liqueur. Her mother had a bar in the living room, never touching the bottles for years on end.

"I've got some tools in the van," he said. "Probably just needs the trap cleared. I can fix it."

"You can?" Maya said. "I didn't know you could fix things."

"Hey, babe, I can do anything." He kissed her on the forehead, and went out.

He left a trail of alcohol fumes behind him. But why shouldn't he? Maya thought. Why not have a drink if he wants one? Why else did people keep liquor around for? Anyway, he must be feeling tense, too, as she was. It was just that she'd never known him to drink before, not more than a beer with Mexican food or pizza. Oh, well, it didn't matter.

She looked in the freezer. It was stocked with chicken and chuck steak and the cheaper cuts of beef, but in the back she found a package of lamb chops. She'd always liked lamb chops. There was lettuce in the refrigerator, and a couple of tomatoes, but no other fresh vegetables, so she took out a package of frozen green beans that came already seasoned in their own cream sauce in a plastic cooking pouch. Rio came back with his tools and plunged his hands unflinchingly into the greasy water backed up in the sink, while Debby left the room.

Maya poured herself a cup of instant coffee and made some for Debby, who came back into the kitchen dressed in her jeans and a purple-flowered T-shirt to stand, silent and still mildly hostile, observing Rio. Maya washed the lettuce in the bathroom sink and made a salad as water heated for the vegetables, and had the chops nicely broiling by the time she heard her mother's car drive up.

"Watch the lamb chops, would you?" she said to Debby, and went to open the door as Betty came up the walk, carrying a stack of case files.

"Mom," she said, as Betty saw her and stood still on the front porch. "I'm back. For a visit," she added swiftly, as she could see her mother's face start to take on a look of triumph. "Not for long. But I wanted to see you."

"So you're back," Betty said, still not moving. "I ought to throw you out of the house."

"Come on, Mom, don't be like that," Maya said. "Come in the house, I made supper. It's all ready."

Betty stepped forward. She looked tired, grayer, not just her hair, but her aura, as if some color had departed from her. She stood still, clutching her files, as Maya hugged her. She didn't return the hug, but she seemed to relax a little, to lose some inner guard.

"Let me set these down." She indicated the files, and put them on the hall table. "Now, let me look at you. You've lost weight. I wish I could. I eat more under stress."

"You look fine, Mom," Maya said. Actually she looked like someone who could grow old, someone who would someday die.

They went into the kitchen, where Rio's legs protruded from under the sink.

"What's going on here?" Betty asked.

"The sink was stopped up, and the faucet was leaking," Maya said. "This is my friend Rio. He offered to fix it."

"I meant to call the handyman to do it. I just haven't had time. Back-to-back appointments all day."

"Maya, hand me that wrench, would you?" Rio said from below the sink. She gave him the tool, and after a moment he emerged, and stood up.

"Sorry," he said. "I had the trap off and couldn't leave it like that. I'm Rio Colorado, Mrs. Greenbaum. I won't shake hands with you until I clean up a bit."

"What was wrong with the sink?" she asked, her tone still wary, not hostile but not friendly either.

"It just needed a new washer, and the trap cleaned out. Really, it was nothing."

"Well, thank you," Betty said grudgingly.

"Oh, no problem."

Betty turned to Maya. "Well, at least you didn't find a man like your father. Joe couldn't change a lightbulb."

In the awkward silence, Maya felt torn apart. She could feel her mother brimming full of anger, biting back a dozen hurtful things she would later say to Maya, and at the same time watching Rio, wanting to shake him open and find out if he were good enough for her daughter, wary of him as an outsider, a male intruder on their female bond. And Maya was part of Rio; but, yes, she was also part of her mother. They shared the same eyes, the same square jawline, and she knew her mother's history, how she had been hurt, and how she, Maya, had hurt her. Betty had reason to be on guard.

"Dinner's ready, Mom," Maya said. "Shall we eat?"

Betty shook her head. She was standing in the doorway to the dining room, and the light from the window cast harsh shadows on her face. "I'm not sure we can eat. I'm not sure I want to eat with you."

Maya went and got the bowl of salad from the counter, and placed it on the table as if she were staking a claim. "Look, Mom, I can understand that you're mad, but can't we just sit down to dinner? There'll be time later for you to give me the big lecture." She turned to check the chops in the broiler, and Betty grabbed her arm.

"You think you can just waltz in here after six months, cook dinner, and that makes everything all right again? After what I've been through?"

Maya jerked her hand away and opened her mouth to reply, but she felt Rio's steadying hand on her back.

"Excuse us, Mrs. Greenbaum," Rio said. "We didn't mean to upset you. We'll just go."

Betty grabbed at Maya's hand again and caught it, gripping her wrist. "Don't you dare walk out of here! I'm not telling you to leave—we have things to discuss. And I'm talking to you, Karla. Since when do you need your boyfriend to defend you?"

"I don't, Mom. But if you want to have a discussion, let's sit down and eat dinner, okay? At least let go of me so I can get these chops out of the broiler before they burn. I don't want to fight with you."

"That's a change." Betty dropped Maya's arm and turned to Rio. "She did nothing but fight with me since the day her father walked out the door, when she was seven. Subconsciously she blames me for his leaving."

"I do not!" Maya had turned off the broiler and opened the door;

now she banged it shut again. "Joe was a shit to you, I know that. If I blame anyone, I blame him!"

Betty shook her head. "You don't know what your subconscious thinks. Anyway, it's normal to feel that the parent you're left with drove the other one away. I know you can't help it."

"Jesus, Mom, do we have to have psychoanalysis right now? Can't we just eat?"

"Let's eat," Betty said. "But it doesn't mean that I forgive you."

"That's fine," Maya said. "It doesn't symbolize anything, this dinner. It's just dinner. A cigar is just a cigar. Okay?"

"Okay."

They called Debby and crowded around the table in the kitchen alcove. Maya served the frozen vegetables she'd steamed and the broiled lamb chops.

"I see you treat yourselves well," Betty said. "Chuck steak isn't good enough for you, no, it had to be lamb."

"It's delicious," Rio said quickly. "Thank you."

Betty turned to him. "So where are you from?"

"Pittsburgh. My dad works in the steel mills, there," he said, forestalling her next question.

"How nice."

Maya could imagine the picture forming behind her eyes, a big, blond, muscular brute, half-naked, spraying sweat as he drove a sledgehammer down on red-hot iron, behind him smoldering fires and vats of molten metal. *Goyish.* Definitely not Jewish.

"He's the shop steward," Rio said, "with the union."

"Rio, is that a Mexican name?"

"It's a name I gave myself. I liked it better than Richie."

"Oh." Yes, Maya could see her relax, just slightly, an almost imperceptible release of the tension around her eyes. "And when did you come to California?"

"I came out a couple of years ago, to go to Berkeley."

"Berkeley!" She perked up. Maya could almost see her prick her ears. "You must have had good grades."

"I dropped out after a year," he said. Her face fell again. "I figured if I just lived here and worked for a while, I could establish residency, and then go back without having to pay out-of-state tuition."

Maya looked at him sharply. Once again, her mother was doing it, finding out in five minutes of conversation things that she, Maya, hadn't learned in months of intimacy. She had never asked him why he came to California—where else would anyone want to go? She had never asked about his history or his plans. She didn't want him to exist in time and space, she wanted him to remain her magician, her secret, her pirate, for both of them to stay alive in the immortal present where there was no loss. Oh, it was a mistake to come here, a big mistake.

"How sensible," Betty said. "What were you majoring in?"

"I was trying to decide between sociology and political science." Maya scowled at her plate. Rio tried to catch her eye and smile, but she looked away. He was enjoying himself, she could tell. Probably it amused him that his magical Witch had a mother who was dying to find out how much money his father made, and a sister who sat quietly looking down at her plate, concealing the book on her lap, which she read throughout the conversation. "I wanted something as a good foundation for law school."

Maya dropped her fork and stared. Law school! He had to be kidding. Betty was looking more and more satisfied, and Rio waited until she glanced at Debby to wink at Maya.

"Debby, how many times have I told you not to read at the table! Put that book away, and participate in the conversation!"

Debby sighed, and closed the book. "I was just getting to the good part."

Betty turned back to Rio, a light smile on her lips. "Karla's father was a lawyer, you know. But he got caught up in the McCarthy era. You have to be careful, if you want to be admitted to the bar."

"Well, it's still a long way away," Rio said. "I have plenty of time to decide. Medicine appeals to me, too, or even psychology. I'd like a career that helps people."

Oh, the fucking con artist! He was putting her mother on, playing her up, and Maya could see her mother's eyes shining with visions of her daughter, the doctor/lawyer/psychoanalyst's wife, yes, she was a bit wild in her youth, but she met a wonderful guy who settled her down. And Rio was just feeding her, puffing her up, and what would happen to Betty when the crash came again? Why was he doing this? Wasn't it enough that Maya had hurt her once? Betty seemed so fragile, pitiable, with her ordinary hopes and dreams that were doomed to fail.

Suddenly she pitied her mother so much that she nearly choked on her bite of lamb. Yes, this was what had driven her out of the house in the first place: her mother's unbearable loneliness that permeated the house like an unseen toxin, all the more painful because Betty seemed unaware of it. She was bright and cheerful with her clients and her conferences and the peer groups she was always trotting off to. But Maya remembered those days after her father left, the string of Sundays when they would drive out to the valley, looking at houses for sale, all the new tract homes, each one just alike, with turquoise tile in the bathrooms and kitchens that opened out into the family room. Her mother had wanted a family room of her own. But even the cheap look-alike bungalows on their concrete slabs were beyond her means, and with the five thousand dollars Grandpa Stein had given her and her own small savings she bought this house in town, with the little house on the same lot she could rent out to help pay the mortgage. And so Johanna had moved into her life. But Maya still remembered the cool feel of the tile under her fingers, the smell of the new carpets in the model homes. When they got back to the apartment, Betty would kick off her shoes and let them have hot dogs on TV trays in front of the screen, watching old Shirley Temple movies. Debby had been too young to do more than fuss in the car and track dirt on the new carpets, straying from the plastic-lined paths laid out for them, but it was Maya who felt the need to make up somehow to Betty for—what? Something hollow at the core of their lives, something disappointed in her voice whenever the phone rang and it was not Joe coming back to them. I can't do it, Mom, she wanted to say. I can't be what you need. I can't justify your life. I can't live like you do, arranging your nice things as a bulwark against the hollow place. I stared it in the face too young, I've stared it down and gone through its core and found what lives on the other side. Don't you see, Mom, she wanted to say, if you stop pretending and defending and trying to make us into something your mother would have thought was okay, if you just let go and go down, you'll come out the other side. If only she could be a guide for Betty on that journey. But it was impossible. Her mother would never understand what she was talking about.

And so Betty was alone, with nobody to love her anymore but Debby, who was more interested, really, in her book, and Maya would be gone as she had to be gone, and what would happen to Betty when she got old? Who would look after her? Meanwhile Rio was going on and on about his career plans, and the two of them were painting a future for her that she didn't want, that wasn't her. No, nobody understood her. She couldn't take much more of this.

"Mom," she broke in, "isn't this enough of an interrogation? Have you decided yet whether you approve?"

Betty looked at her, the drawn look coming back to her mouth. "I'm just making conversation, Karla. Trying to get to know your boyfriend. Isn't that why you brought him here?"

"I brought him here to meet you, not to justify his existence," Maya said.

"Hey, it's cool," Rio said.

"Let's have a conversation, then," Betty said. "What would you like to discuss? How about your plans for school?"

"That would be a short discussion," Maya said. "I don't have any. Next topic?"

"I got an A on my math test," Debby said.

"That's nice, dear."

"Hey, great!" Rio said with hearty enthusiasm.

"I got the highest score in the whole class. Higher than Marty Friedman, the big fat pig who thinks he's so smart."

"That's enough, Debby."

"Well, he does. He's so stuck up! But I got higher grades than he did on the last two tests, and higher than Mickey Lane, and higher than—"

"That's enough, Debby," Betty said sharply. "We don't need to hear any more."

"Why not? I go to school, and I get good grades, too, and you don't even care! All you care about is her!"

"Debby!"

"Well, it's true!"

"Any more of that, and you can go to your room."

Debby jumped up, grabbed her book, and stalked out of the kitchen, slamming the door behind her.

Betty sighed. "She's at a difficult stage."

Rio nodded sagely, as if he personally had shepherded hundreds of subteens through awkward developmental phases. "Junior high is hell. Like war."

Betty turned back to Maya. "Are you going to see Johanna? She's been worried about you."

"I thought we weren't supposed to talk to each other."

"I think Johanna's levelheaded enough not to be corrupted by you, and her influence could only do you good."

"Thanks for your confidence in me."

"You know, you still could go back to school. No, now hear me out, Karla. You'd have to work hard, do a lot of makeup work, maybe take some summer school classes—"

"I'm not interested."

"But at least you'd have your diploma. I don't know, maybe you could still get into Columbia next fall."

"Mom!"

"It would be a bit dicey but I bet Joe could fix it."

"Mom, I don't want to go to Columbia."

"Maybe right now you don't, but think ahead a bit, Karla. Use your imagination. How are you going to feel next fall, when all your friends are back in school, going off to college—and you're left behind?"

"I won't be left behind. I'll be far ahead, in a different direction."

"Doing what? What do you imagine you can do without even a high school diploma? Being somebody's wife?"

"No."

"Then what? Living off your boyfriend, here? How long is he going to want you around if you don't do something with yourself? Think about it." She turned to Rio. "You're going back to college, you're going to want a wife with a degree. Somebody who can keep up with you, intellectually. You'll need one, if you want a career. You know when Joe was being interviewed for a position, before the blacklist, they had to interview me, too. A wife makes a difference."

"I'm not talking about being a wife," Maya said quickly to deflect her mother from Rio.

"Then what are you talking about?" Betty paused, but Maya didn't answer. First because she honestly couldn't say. She couldn't tell her mother that she only wanted to live true to one moment in her life, and that she knew with the same certainty with which she knew her own name, which had changed, that that was enough for a life's work. And second, she couldn't speak because she was suddenly burdened with unutterable sadness as she realized that Betty still thought of herself as Joe's wife, still preened from his importance.

"Where would I have been," Betty went on, "after Joe left us, if I hadn't had my social work degree?"

"Just stop it, Mom. Stop badgering me!"

"I have to badger you, badger some sense into you!"

"No, you don't! Just leave me alone, let me make my own decisions!"

"You aren't mature enough to make your own decisions. That's been my mistake—I've given you too much freedom! But that's over now." Betty set down her fork and pushed away her plate. "I'm ordering you to go back to school!"

Maya had finished her own lamb chop, and the meat sat heavily in her stomach, a dead lump of flesh. Perhaps she should become a vegetarian. "You can't order me around anymore!"

"I can and I will." Betty's voice rose. "You're still a minor! You leave here again, I'll get the police after you! Don't think I won't, just because I haven't yet. Do you want to get locked up again? Do you want your boyfriend charged with statutory rape?"

"Fuck you!" Maya jumped up from the table and pushed back her chair, screaming at Betty. "Do whatever the fuck you want. I don't care. You're not my mother, you've never known how to be a mother to me!" She turned and ran out of the room, slamming the front door behind her.

Maya lay on the mattress in the van, sobbing, as Rio came in, closing the sliding door behind him. He held her close and let her cry, without saying anything. That was why she loved him, she reminded herself, even if she was mad at him right now. She could cry with him and he would soothe her so patiently, as if he wouldn't mind sitting with her while she cried forever. She didn't know many people like that. Johanna, maybe. Betty tended to start yelling about how whatever was wrong was really Maya's fault. Maya had never cried with Tony, and when she cried because Doug was breaking up with her, he'd just gotten sheepish and nervous and had made an excuse to leave as soon as he could.

No, Rio was a prize, even if he still smelled faintly of alcohol.

When her sobs subsided, he patted her on the shoulder. "You just lie there," he said. "I'll drive us down to the beach. We can watch the sunset."

He parked the van close to the sand. Maya got up and joined him in the front seat.

"I wish I had a bottle of your mom's whiskey," he said, but instead he lit up a joint, and they passed it back and forth, smoking it down to nothing in long-held breaths that calmed Maya down. They sat for a long while, watching the sun do its nosedive into the indigo dark.

"She's a bitch," Maya said. "I hate her. Let's split, drive back up the coast tonight. I don't want to go back."

"She doesn't mean everything she says," Rio said. "Don't let her get to you."

"I wish we'd never come here."

"By the way," Rio said, after a long pause, "you never mentioned that you weren't eighteen yet."

"Does it make a difference?" Maya said fiercely because she felt guilty. No, she hadn't told him. They never talked about facts and dates, they talked about smoke and dreams. "Am I a different person, just because I was born in one year instead of another? Anyway, you never asked me."

"I did so. I asked you how old you were once, and you told me 'Several thousand years.' "

"Well, I am. I feel like it, anyway." She reached a hand across the gap that separated the bucket seats of the van, tentatively, hopefully. Rio took it and clasped it in his hand. "I'm sorry. I don't think she'll really make trouble for you."

"Nah, I'm not worried," Rio said, withdrawing his hand but only to light up another joint which he took from his shirt pocket. "She was just mouthing off." He inhaled, held his breath, and handed the joint to Maya. "You know how people fly off the handle," he said, letting a trickle of air escape his lungs. "Everybody does, everybody fights in families." He let out his breath with an explosive exhale. "You should meet my old man. Shit, when he'd get mad he'd throw us across the room, knock my mother's teeth out of her poor, bloody mouth. Until my brother Jim got big enough to stop him."

Maya had inhaled the smoke and let it sit in her lungs until the irritation grew too great, and it forced its way out.

"Betty doesn't hit," she said. "She's read too much psychology. She just yells. That's bad enough."

She handed the joint back to Rio, and he took another long hit before handing it back to her. She inhaled again and could feel herself relax.

"You know, your mother's house is nice," Rio said. "I looked around. It's full of all those books, literature and psychology. In my house all we had were back issues of the *Reader's Digest,* and maybe *Road and Track.* She's got all those nice souvenirs of her travels, cups and plates and little statues. And a whole cabinet full of liquor. I helped myself to a taste—hope that was okay. All the bottles were dusty. That was impressive."

"What do you mean?" Outside the van the sky darkened. Maya was ready to be held again and comforted, but the bucket seats kept them separate.

"My dad drinks anything he can get his hands on. No, sir, alcohol doesn't stay around James Matthew Connolly long enough to gather dust. He gets roaring, bellowing drunk . . . and then he's coming at you with his fists flying, slapping my mom across the face if she gets in the way. But your house is quiet, peaceful. I don't understand why you wanted to leave."

Maya sighed, wrapping her arms around her own body. If he didn't understand, she couldn't explain it to him.

His hand reached over, teased her arm loose. "Not that I'm complaining," he said, leaning over to kiss her neck. "Your mother's loss is my gain."

"You were bullshitting her," Maya complained. "All that crap about law school, for God's sake."

"Yeah, but she likes me. That'll make everything easier, for you, babe. I did it for you. Besides, how do you know it's bullshit? I might go to law school. Would that be so awful?"

"More likely to go to jail. More likely to need a lawyer than be one."

"Hey, babe, I'm smart. I did get good grades. I'm the first dude in the family to go to college, even if I did drop out. I could drop back in someday, if I wanted to. Make the old folks proud."

"Do you want to?" Maya asked, uneasy.

"I want you," Rio said firmly, stroking her hair. "I want you to be happy. I suspect you won't be if we don't go back to your mother's, give you a chance to make up."

The joint was reduced to embers. Rio put it out, studied the remains thoughtfully, then added them to a small envelope he kept in his pocket.

"You could be right," Maya admitted.

"She loves you," Rio said. "She's just afraid for you. So she's out of control. But what the fuck, you know? You can't expect her to understand. At least she doesn't throw the chairs around."

"I can't live in her fear."

"You don't have to—you've just got to visit it from time to time. Just like I call my folks every once in a while. Just like my brother Jim writes to me from Vietnam even though he thinks I'm hippy scum. It's family—you can't escape it."

They went back. Betty was in bed, watching Johnny Carson. Rio went into the living room and sampled the crème de menthe as Maya went in to her mother.

"I'm sorry we fought," Maya said, going over to the bed and hugging Betty, who looked profoundly relieved. "Let's not fight anymore, okay?"

"I thought you weren't coming back. I thought you were gone . . . forever, this time."

I thought you had abandoned me, like Joe, Maya heard echoing unsaid in the silence. She hugged her mother again.

"You're my mother. We're stuck with each other." I will never abandon you, not completely. I am tied to you by bonds nothing can break, she heard herself promising, and though she wanted to clamp her lips around that promise and sever it at its root, and though she spoke not a word of it, the promise was made.

And so I will never be wholly free, until you die.

15

Johanna Weaver's
Diary

December 4, 1967

Well, she's back. Who? Miss Supercool, Miss Hipper-Than-Thou, Miss I'm-So-Groovy-with-My-Stoner-Boyfriend—Maya, alias Karla Green-baum, that's who.

As you can probably tell, the visit is not a great success, so far. For one thing, I never get to spend any time with her alone, without the Incredible Hulk trailing around behind us. Oh, I suppose he's nice enough, if you like them big and blond and dumb. Karla never did be-fore—she always went for the skinny little intellectual types. But Rio, as he calls himself, follows her around with a look on his face like a drown-ing puppy who just sighted land. I suppose that's love.

They came over Wednesday afternoon, after I got home from school. Right away I felt bad. There I was in my little green skirt and my coordinated flowery blouse, carrying my biology textbook, and there she was in some floaty old lace evening dress that she must have picked up in a thrift store, ropes of colored beads, a paisley shawl tied around her hips, and her eyes in that half-closed snake stare that comes from smok-ing a little too much dope. She said she wanted the two most important people in her life to meet. I didn't believe her. What I mean, precisely, is that I didn't believe I was one of those two people. If I was, why didn't she write to me, or call me? Why didn't she come to me alone so we could really talk?

Anyway, they asked me to take a walk, and we strolled around the block. Really, what they wanted was for me to smoke dope with them, and I had to listen to Rio bullshit on about his primo grade-A buds of Michoacán until I wanted to vomit. I declined—not because I didn't want to smoke but because I knew Marian would ask what we did and I didn't want to lie to her. She always knows when I'm lying to her—and I have to live here.

Then, we couldn't seem to talk about anything.

"How's school?" she'd ask.

"Fine, school is fine."

"How's Joyce Levine?"

"Fine. She's fine."

I was looking around at the houses on our street, how clean and safe and dull they look, with their little lawns and the ferns and agapanthus that the Japanese or Mexican gardeners keep neat. Where have you been? I wanted to say. Is there some amazing exotic incredible place out there, and can we go to it?

"And Tony? Tony Klein?" she asked.

"Fine," I said. "He's still putting out the paper."

"Great. Glad he's carrying on."

"Nothing's changed," I told her. "It's as if nothing ever happened. You didn't have to leave."

"I had to. You know I had to."

You didn't have to leave for this—I wanted to say, meaning her boyfriend and her torn lace dress and her marijuana and her scene. I wanted to cry with disappointment, and that's what I couldn't say to her. I wanted her to have found some miracle, to tell me that somewhere we could go and find a circle of people who would welcome us home and recognize who we truly are and teach us how to love. Even if I hadn't found it, even if, yes, I had compromised and given in, I wanted someone to have found it. I wanted her to be my Harriet Tubman, to show me a pole star to follow, to lead me out of slavery into the promised land.

But Maya isn't leading anybody anywhere. All she's done is become the ultimate hippy cliché, with her lace and beads and buds. She might as well have stayed in school, made her mother happy. And now she's so stoned I can't talk to her. It's funny, I never noticed before, but it's like a glaze over her, like that stuff you put on furniture so hot drinks don't leave a mark. Nothing quite penetrates.

Later:

So, her boyfriend is one of those guys who likes to fix things. God knows we can use someone like that around here from time to time, with Uncle Marcus gone. Rio fixed Debby's ten-speed and gave Marian advice about the knock in her engine and opened windows that were stuck shut and shut windows that were stuck open. He seems to want to please. I guess I don't hate him. How can you hate a man who's changed your mother's spark plugs?

And Karla—I'm sorry, I've got to remember to call her Maya— Maya and I did talk. I feel better.

She came in early this morning. Marian was still asleep, and we went and sat out on the front step to talk, while Rio did some male mechanical thing to their van.

"We're leaving," Maya said. "Heading back up north. Betty's not happy but I don't think she'll call the state police, as long as I write her from time to time. Thank God for the last remnants of my dad's politics."

"Have a good trip," I said.

"Johanna, what's wrong between us? Do you hate me for running away?"

"Not for running away," I said, and then it all spilled out. "For not running farther. I hate you for settling for fantasyland."

Her mouth tightened. Sometimes I feel sorry for white girls— when they press their lips together they all but disappear.

"That's not fair," she said.

"When I look at you, I feel cheap. I feel like what happened to us was nothing but a stupid hippy game, an excuse for—I don't know. I don't know what to say about it."

"I don't hate you," she said. "I don't blame you . . . for what you've settled for."

"I haven't settled yet," I said. "I'm biding my time."

"Waiting for what? What do you think is going to come if we don't make it happen?"

"And is that what you think you're doing? Seems to me you're just tripping around having a fine old time."

"Johanna, I don't know how to make it happen." She stood up and paced around, waving her hands like an orchestra conductor. "Don't you understand? I'm not even sure I know what 'it' is, or how to talk about what we went through together. Every time I try, every time I try to name it or even think too much about it, I feel like I'm taking something holy and turning it into a greeting card. I hate words—they cheapen everything. Do you know what I mean?"

"Yes. I know."

"There's no map to the territory we tried to travel in." I knew what she meant and I was glad to hear her say it, but at the same time I couldn't help but think that she was posing just a bit, thinking how good she sounded.

"We're all just groping our way in the dark," she went on. "But we've got to stick together. I mean, we've got to at least stay in contact."

"You knew where I was, all this time. You could have written. Didn't you think I'd worry about you?"

She looked away from me, over at the neighbor's big sycamore tree across the street. "I was afraid. I was afraid Betty would find out where I was, and drag me back."

It was my turn to look away from her. "Sometimes I wish I'd gone with you."

That brought her back around, looking straight into my face, her eyes happy in a way that told me how much she'd wanted to hear me say that. As if she still needed me to justify what she'd done. "Do you?" she said. "Sometimes I wish I'd stayed home. Not very often, but once in a while. When Betty gets harping on my future. Maybe I will regret all of this—maybe I'll wish I finished school. I don't know. I only know that I can't go back now. I don't think I can ever go back. And that's scary, too." She sounded real now, not posing anymore.

"And I can't leave." I wanted to tell her about being a heart warrior, about how that means you have to do the hard stuff, and not shirk. But the words wouldn't come out of my mouth. Maybe I just didn't trust her enough.

"Can't you? Even for a bit? I don't mean quit school, I know you don't want to do that. But what about in the summer? Couldn't you come up, stay with us for a while?"

"I don't know if Marian would let me."

"Surely she couldn't grudge you one wild summer, before you start at the university."

"I'd like that," I admitted. God yes, I long for it, now—to be out of this house, free, with nobody's standards to live up to. Just for a time, a month. Oh, I'll probably have to work in the summer, save up money for the fall, but who knows? It's a nice dream. Maybe even a heart warrior gets a vacation every once in a while.

And then Rio was done with the van, and we were hugging good-bye, not kissing in front of him, or only the way ladies kiss at church, grazing cheeks, not touching lips. And then they were gone.

She says she'll write, but I don't believe her.

Johanna

16

Namche to Tengpoche

Today's hike takes us down to the banks of the
Dudh Kosi, then up the lower slopes of Khumbu,
its spires and rocks towering above us to a height of
19,000 feet. We gain and lose much elevation,
so be prepared to sweat!

—*MOUNTAIN CO-OP ADVENTURES*
BROCHURE

Small whitewashed stone huts lined the bank of the Dudh Kosi at the ford where the trail from Namche to Tengpoche crossed the river. Each small house held a prayer wheel, a cylindrical drum painted with bright-colored images of Buddhas and Bodhisattvas and Fearsome Deities. The running water of the stream caused the wheels to turn continuously, and each turn of the wheel sent another prayer into the void, lessened the aggregate weight of karma in the world, and hastened ultimate liberation. Hydraulic power harnessed for spiritual aims.

Maya had always believed that motion was akin to freedom, but as far as she could tell, to the Nepalis, sheer motion was itself a form of prayer. They built wheels spun by water and hung prayer flags to flap from roofs and strung them in lines from the peaks of the *stuppas* and set other wheels by the side of the road to be spun by passing travelers.

I should spin a few of those myself, she thought. I can use all the merit I can accumulate. Mea culpa, mea culpa. I can't go to confession here, and anyway they don't usually take Jewish Witches into the booth or let us take the holy wafer on our tongue—we might bite it, chew it, grind the holy body between our molars, God forbid—and during the Inquisition a lot of people were burned for allegedly doing just that—at any rate, there's no absolution for me.

How did the Yom Kippur prayers go? She was a bad Jew, she went to synagogue only during those times when Betty had dragged her back to Milwaukee to visit her grandparents for the High Holidays. For the sin I have sinned by reading Rio's letters, and for the sin I have sinned by not being good enough to my mother, and for the sin I have sinned by being less than Johanna hoped, less than I'd hoped, forgive me, absolve me, show me mercy. She could hear the chant wailing in her head.

The trekking group was sitting in a small clearing beside the stream, at the bottom of a gorge. All morning they had walked through a misty blue canyon, with high peaks looming above them. Sagarmatha was as yet unimpressive, but Ama Dablam, hung with a necklace of snow-fields, rose sharp and pointed as a child's drawing of a mountain. At times, clouds hid the summit, at other moments, they would part, re-vealing scooped-out bowls between the arms of the highest peaks, where ice-blue glaciers clung and blocks of packed snow hovered, ready to tumble down in an avalanche.

Now Maya sat in the sun as the kitchen boys prepared and served a lunch of fried eggs, fried potatoes, and fried meat. She was huddled against the side of the bank, too tired to stand up and walk over to where the food was being dished up. Her cough had seemed better in Namche, but today, as soon as they started up the hill to climb out of town, it had begun again. She was thoroughly sick of it. If only she could just sit, absorbing the healing rays of the sun, and not move all afternoon. But a climb lay ahead.

Jan was sketching down by the stream; Carolyn, Peter, and Howard were deep in conversation with Tenzing, over by the stone wall that enclosed the small green field. Maya felt relieved. She didn't really want to talk to any of them at the moment. Lonnie brought her plate over and sat down near Maya, who smiled at her weakly. She enjoyed Lonnie's wry cynicism and her humor but was weary of her thinly disguised curiosity about Maya's sexuality. She hadn't asked outright, but she wouldn't relax until she'd pinned Maya down.

"So, do you live alone?" she'd asked Maya over breakfast, her voice carefully casual.

"I live with a friend and her daughter," Maya had said, carefully not using the word *partner*. I'm just being perverse, she admitted to herself. The only reason I'm not telling her straight out is because she wants to know so badly.

"And why isn't your 'friend' on this trip with you?" Lonnie asked.

"Why should she be? We're not joined at the hip. She's just a friend."

"Oh, just a friend. I see."

"A close friend. A very close friend."

"Uh-huh," Lonnie had said, confused. Then Howard had joined them, ending the conversation.

Now Lonnie settled herself with her back against the low stone wall that bordered the clearing. "Aren't you eating?" she asked Maya. "The french fries are especially good."

"I'll eat in a minute, as soon as I get up the strength to walk over there," Maya said.

Before she could move, however, Tashi came over and handed her a plate of food. He was wearing a pair of wraparound sunglasses that completely hid his eyes, and a purple-and-turquoise sweat suit.

"You look tired," he said. "You must eat now, then much uphill."

"Oh, hurray," Maya said in a dull voice. "Cool shades, Tashi."

"Yes, very cool," Tashi agreed. "I look American?"

"One hundred percent red, white, and blue," Lonnie told him. "No one would ever guess you were a Sherpa, not a homeboy from East LA."

Pembila, who had walked with them that day, brought Maya a cup of hot tea. She pointed at Tashi, laughing. "He not Sherpa," she said. "He from Tibet."

"Tibet!" Lonnie turned to Tashi. "You been holding out on us, man. You never told us you were from Tibet!"

Tashi shook his head. "I am not from Tibet." He pronounced it tea-bet.

Pembila laughed. She was younger than Ang, in her mid-thirties, and when she smiled, crinkling her deep brown eyes into half-moons, she looked younger still, a girl-child teasing one of the big boys. "Tibet," she said. "Yes. Men from Tibet, not good chickie-chickie." Tashi looked outraged and Pembila covered her face to hide her mirth.

"Chickie-chickie?" Lonnie asked. "What's that?"

"Chickie-chickie." Pembila closed her left hand in a cylinder around her extended right forefinger, which she moved rapidly in and out, in an unmistakable and universal gesture.

"Ah, chickie-chickie!" Lonnie said. "The light dawns."

"Men from Tibet, very small," Pembila said. "Very short time, chickie-chickie." Now she was nearly doubled over with laughter.

"A slanderous statement if ever I heard one," Lonnie said. "Tashi, you going to let her get away with that? You aren't going to defend the manly honor of Tibet?"

"I am not from Tibet." Tashi stood up and adopted a pose of great dignity, although behind his shades he appeared to be laughing also. "I am a cowboy from Montana." He pronounced each syllable very carefully—Mon-tan-na.

He stalked off.

Tenzing walked over and Pembila gave the other two women a conspiratorial glance, and then slipped away.

"How do you feel?" he asked Maya. "How is your cough?"

"Okay," Maya said. "It's a cough."

"After lunch, we've got a long climb. Take it slow. Ang will stay with you."

"I'll be okay," Maya said. The attention, the solicitousness of the Sherpas embarrassed her. They seemed so kind, so eager to bear her burdens. She wasn't used to so much pampering. Betty had never been the kind of mother to hover around with tea trays and read stories when Maya was sick. Betty had a job to go to, and Maya's and Debby's illnesses angered her, as if they'd gotten sick on purpose just to make her life more difficult. Johanna, now, she had tried, brewing Maya herb tea and making up hot water bottles whenever she got the flu. But in their first years together, when Maya was just back from Mexico, trying to write but not yet making any money, she couldn't stand to have Johanna wait on her. She already depended too much on her, for a place to live, for groceries when the odd jobs she took fell through, for encouragement when the rejection letters came.

Maya had accepted her comfort, but when she was sick, she tended to push Johanna away, close her door and read herself to sleep, with some old Dorothy Sayers mystery she'd read five times before. And later, when the balance between them had shifted, when she might have welcomed some cosseting, the pattern was already set.

But that was the way of all relationships, wasn't it? A template somehow gets laid, and every change stems from the original design and reverts to it. The family template becomes the pattern for all the rest. Certainly Betty had believed that. Maya wasn't as sure. If she cast back in her own mind, as far as she could, back to when she was small and Joe had not yet gone away, she could remember only a vague sense of anxiety, an unease.

"Your mother wants to put me on the couch," she remembered her father saying. "What do you think of that?"

She closed her eyes in the warm sun, letting her food digest, letting the murmur of conversation around her become the background for her memories. She was watching her father shave and dress, as she often did in the early mornings while her mother brewed the coffee, made the toast, scrambled the eggs, and listened to the morning news on the radio. She was very small: The bathroom sink was at her eye level, and she had to tip her head up to see her father's face in the mirror. She had enjoyed watching him cover his chin with white lather; she loved the scraping sound of the razor on his beard. She didn't know what was so wrong with the couch, a solid, green divan that stood against the long wall of the living room, facing the TV. It was shabby, like most of their things, but comfortable. On Saturday mornings she and her father would curl up there and watch cartoons, while her mother made breakfast. He would tell her things about the way the world was.

"Those mice," he would say, "they're the workers. See how they're hungry? How they're forced to live in a hole in the wall? Why is that?"

"I don't know."

"Who keeps them there?"

"The cat?" she'd guess.

"Right. And who is the cat?"

"I don't know."

"The cat is the boss. Got that? And how does the cat control the mice?"

"I don't know."

"Think."

"He can eat them up."

"Right! Exactly!" When her father was pleased, his thick, black eyebrows shot apart, and while he didn't exactly smile, two deep curves outlined his mouth. His eyes were dark brown, like hers, and his skin was very pale. The shaved-off stubble of his beard showed on his cheeks. He smelled of cigarette smoke, an odor she liked because it was his smell. "The mice are afraid of the cat."

" 'Cause he has big teeth and he can eat them up," she said, knowing she had pleased him once, hoping it would work again.

"But who always wins?" he asked her, his brows diving back into their usual V.

She knew the answer to that one. "Mighty Mouse!"

Mighty Mouse could fly. He wore a cape and, although he was small, he could beat up the cats, punching them in the face while he remained suspended in air. Billy Jenkins said he could fly, too, but she was never sure if he meant fly like Mighty Mouse or fly a plane. Anyway, he would never show her because, he said, he had lost his flying license. She thought maybe he was lying, but she liked to make up stories for herself before she went to sleep in which she and Billy flew together, the billowing wind their highway.

"And why does Mighty Mouse win?"

"Because he has superpowers."

"And what makes them superpowers?"

"I don't know."

"I'll tell you." He always did tell her—that was the comforting thing about both her parents. They always told her things. "Mighty Mouse has superpowers because he's not afraid of the cat. He doesn't buy into the bullshit, right? He believes in the power of the mice—the little guy, the workers. And I'll tell you why else Mighty Mouse wins."

"Why, Joe?"

"Because he has history on his side," Joe would end, with satisfaction.

She was only five but she already knew a lot about history. And although she didn't know what her father meant by "the couch," she knew enough to shift her feet restlessly, afflicted with a deep sense of unease.

"Why does she want you on the couch?" she asked her father now.

A last bit of lather remained on the point of his chin, and he carefully scraped it off. Now the white foam was all gone.

She thought about the way the road disappeared when they drove in the car. It stretched ahead of them like a long triangle but they never caught up with the point. At night, the streetlights hung in a chain of glowing pearls. As they got closer each bead separated out and became distinct. She asked her mother how that happened. When Betty finally grasped what she was asking, she explained that the lights never were together in the first place. They only appeared to be.

"Isn't that fascinating!" she said to Joe. "She's really in a different mode of perception. It's like Piaget's experiments," and she had gone on talking in grown-up terms. Karla hunched away from her mother's encircling arms and stared out the window, trying to understand about the lights, and trying to understand why they were talking about her, Karla, as if she were somewhere else or had suddenly stopped being able to hear. They made her mad when they did that. Inside me, she was thinking, I'm just as much *me* as they are *them* inside them. The glowing chain of lights continued to recede, and the point where the two edges of the road came together also receded. She was filled with an anxious longing. She wished more than anything that she could grasp the lights in the beautiful string, before they began to come apart.

"She wants me to see a shrink," her father said as he washed his hands.

Karla was suddenly nervous. Something was coming apart.

"I like you big," she protested. "I like you the way you are."

"That's my baby girl," her father said.

"Don't let her shrink you. Promise!"

"I promise."

Together they went into the kitchen. Her mother had set the table, and she looked lonely all by herself.

"Where's Debby?" Karla asked.

"Shh," her mother whispered. "Don't wake her! For once she's not awake and screaming at six in the morning. Let her sleep."

"I helped Daddy shave," Karla said proudly. Betty said nothing at all, only something in her eyes changed, and suddenly Karla felt bad. Maybe she should have helped Betty set the table. Maybe she should have kept her company while Debby slept.

"A girl needs time alone with her daddy," Betty said. Suddenly she smiled at Karla and Joe, in the way she had of smiling as if she had arranged everything herself and planned it all to be the way it was. The thing that bothered Karla disappeared from her eyes, but her smile made Karla mad.

Joe snorted. "Watch it, Karla. You'll be getting an Oedipus complex. No—pardon me—an Electra complex."

"What's an electric complex?"

"It means you want to marry me and kill your mother."

"For God's sake, Joe!" Betty snapped. "What's wrong with you? Don't you have any sense at all?"

They yelled and screamed all through breakfast, but Debby didn't wake up. She was used to the noise. Karla ate her eggs and toast and wondered about words. Her parents fought all the time about words, so they must have some mysterious power that Karla couldn't quite understand. But she was determined to get that power for herself.

The door slammed. Her father was gone, off to work, leaving her mother with her lips pressed together as she cleared the table. Karla carefully picked up her plate and carried it to the sink.

"What's an electric complex?" she asked.

"Never mind."

"I don't want to kill you," Karla said.

"I know, baby." Betty pushed her hair back off her forehead. It fell in dark brown waves around her face. If Karla looked closely, she could see a wetness around her blue eyes that brought back the uneasy sense. She set down her plate and flung her arms around her mother's soft body. Betty was always worried about her weight, but Karla loved the plumpness of her round breasts, loved to curl up in the big rocker and feel her mother's body enfold her. Betty would sing her a song to make the fear go away.

> The wind won't hurt Karla
> And the sun won't hurt Karla
> And the moon and the stars
> Won't hurt Karla . . .

That was when Karla loved her best even though she thought the song was silly, because what she expected to hurt her wasn't in the sun or the moon or the wind, or anywhere she could name except maybe in the sound of a slamming door.

"What about a germ?" she would ask. Betty worried a lot about germs—that was why they had rules like washing your hands before you ate. Betty would purse her lips and try not to smile, but Karla knew she had said something clever and funny, so she always said it when her mother sang that song.

"Can I dry the silverware?"

"Here." Betty handed her a towel.

"What's an electric complex?"

"Don't nag."

"I'm not nagging. I want to know. Joe said I had one."

"Joe has no sense."

"Is it like a ray gun?" Maybe that was what he meant about killing Betty with it.

"No, it isn't like a ray gun. Just forget it."

"Maybe Miss Sperry knows." Miss Sperry was her kindergarten teacher, and her subtle threat. Betty always got nervous when Karla said she would ask Miss Sperry about things. It was part of the mysterious power of words. There were certain words Karla knew she wasn't supposed to say outside the house. Some of them were bad words—even though Joe said them all the time. Like "bullshit." It was okay for him but not for her, and that wasn't fair. But there were other words, mostly the ones she learned from her father. She wasn't supposed to talk about the workers or the bosses or the revolution, and she wasn't supposed to mention Marx, who was her father's friend, or someone who talked to Joe a lot, because Joe was always telling her things Marx said, and he had named her after him. The reason for silence was because of her father's enemy, whose name was McCarthy. McCarthy had made it so her father couldn't be a lawyer anymore, and they couldn't live in the big house Karla barely remembered. Now Joe worked in a warehouse and came home all dirty and sweaty, and they had a tiny apartment where her mother and father slept in the living room, on the green couch that folded out into a bed at night. Her mother was always afraid Karla would tell Miss Sperry something and then Miss Sperry would tell McCarthy and McCarthy would do something bad to Joe. Karla didn't think Miss Sperry would do that—because she was too nice, but Betty said she might not be able to help herself.

"Don't you go asking Miss Sperry about Electra complexes."

"Is it something about Marx?"

"No, it's not something about Marx."

"Then why can't I ask her? Is it something bad?"

"No, it's not something bad."

"Is it something Freud said?" Freud was her mother's friend, who told *her* things. Karla had never met either Freud or Marx, they never came to the house, but she thought if they ever did come at the same time it would just mean more fighting, because they didn't ever seem to agree.

"You're insatiable."

"What does that mean?"

"It means you're never satisfied. You just won't give up."

"I won't," Karla said. "So you might as well tell me."

Betty sighed. "It's a Freud thing. It means . . . that sometimes little girls feel close to their fathers in a special way. And maybe sometimes they wish their mothers weren't around so they could have their daddys all to themselves."

"Why is that electric?"

"It's not electric. Electra. She was a girl in ancient Greece, who . . . who felt that way, so they named it after her. When girls feel that way."

"I don't feel that way."

"You wouldn't know. It's all unconscious."

"What does that mean?"

"It means that you feel it, but you don't know that you feel it."

"I would know," Karla assured her.

Betty just laughed.

Lunch was over. Maya had drifted off into a light sleep while the kitchen boys cleaned up, and when she roused herself to hoist up her day pack, she still felt drowsy, almost dizzy. They started off, crossing the river on a small wooden bridge. Maya climbed slowly, stopping periodically to breathe and cough. Blue firs marched up the mountain with them, moss hung from the oaks, and the graceful, rose-gray branches of the birches waved high above, where big crows circled, yelling and cawing.

She was thinking about Betty. You were alone, she thought. Joe left, and I was never wholly yours. You were always in competition with someone—Joe, Johanna, Rio. But that's natural—I was your daughter, not your mate. Still she was feeling sad as she struggled up the hill. I hurt you, Betty. I'm sorry for that. At the time, it seemed I had to. Of course, it seems like that at seventeen and then twenty years later I can look back and see that nothing was really that clear. Maybe that's why the young and the middle-aged cannot meet. The young don't have the perspective, but the middle-aged gain it at the cost of that pure urgency.

But then nothing had really changed, even over twenty years, as far as Betty went. Maya was still always leaving her, up until the end, always going off somewhere because she had to. What did that mean, had to? Certainly Betty had never accepted it, at least not on her bad days, before the antidepressants kicked in. Maya remembered a conversation on one of her visits down to LA, after the cancer had been diagnosed.

"Is there anything more I can do for you before I go tomorrow?" Maya had asked. "The Changs have settled in, I'm sure they'll look after you really well. I bought groceries and that juice you wanted. Carola says she'll come by and give you a massage tomorrow. Not the heavy bodywork, she said, just a nice relaxing massage. What else can I do?"

"You could stay," her mother said in a weak voice. She was lying on her adjustable bed, with the back cranked up and the TV on so that the murmur of celebrity voices accompanied everything said in the room. Her hair had faded to white, and the skin on her face sagged as if it had lost the will to hold itself firm. She seemed fragile, pitiable.

"I wish I could, but I can't." Maya moved toward her, to stroke her hair or touch her face or make some other gesture of comfort, but her hand stayed by her side. No, they didn't have that kind of relationship; their closeness, such as it was, had not been physical since Maya ceased to be a lap-sized baby girl. "You know I've got to be in New York day after tomorrow."

"There's always something." Betty closed her eyes. "There's always something more important than me."

"I can't help it, this has been scheduled for months." Maya could hear her own voice getting sharp, defensive. She took a deep breath. "You're all right here. The Changs are very responsible. I can come back down next week if you need me to."

"No, no, I don't need you," Betty said, her face turned sideways on the pillow, her eyes still shut as if to close Maya out. "I've always had to take care of myself."

"You'll just sit here in the dark, right?" Maya tried to keep her tone light. Maybe she could tease Betty out of it, show her how childish she was being. "How many Jewish mothers does it take to change a lightbulb?"

"What are you talking about?"

Maya lost patience with her. "Betty, I swear I'll do everything I can for you. But you know you could be sick for a long time. I can't just drop everything and move in with you. I've got to make a living."

"Other people do," Betty said. "Look at Carola. She nursed her mother and her sister and then her father through cancer. She didn't let her career get in the way."

"I admire Carola." Maya took another deep breath. Betty was sick, and afraid, she knew that; she didn't want to end up yelling at her. "But I just don't think it would work for us. We'd wind up screaming at each other."

"Whose fault is that?"

"It's nobody's fault, it's just how it is, for better or worse. It's our dynamic."

"Dynamic, hell." Betty looked up now, seeming to acquire some new vitality from the argument. "It's you. You only care about your own sweet self. You always have. Just like your father."

"Oh, come on, Betty, don't get into that."

"You learned your lesson well from him. Walk away. Just walk away. If it's hard, if it's painful, if it's not all pleasure, just walk away."

"Betty, I'm not going to continue this conversation." Resolutely, Maya turned away. It was that or scream. Stay calm but firm, she told herself. Like the nice social worker from Senior Services suggested. "I'm going to make you some herb tea and some toast, and we can talk about something else."

"See, that's what I mean." Betty looked almost pleased, as if she had just convinced an invisible referee that Maya had made a foul. "You just cut me off."

And Maya had proved her right, walking out of the room, closing the door behind her, restraining herself from slamming it.

But really, she thought now, forcing herself to put one foot in front of the other, to hoist herself up the hill, one step at a time, really, I could have canceled New York, I could have cancelled everything if I'd known how soon she was going to die. But the doctors said another year or two, at least. Still, admit it—I knew. I looked at her, and I knew. I didn't want to know, and I knew.

Maybe if I had, maybe if I had totally devoted myself to her for a month, for two months, maybe she would finally have felt cared for. Maybe we could have been close then, without fighting anymore. I could have cared for her as she cared for me when I was a baby, and everything between us would have healed.

Sure. Maybe we would both have been taken bodily up to heaven with the other saints.

Maya paused for breath again. Another day, another uphill climb, she thought, as she began coughing once more. This is starting to get monotonous. Too much like life.

Anyway, Betty, I couldn't do it. I couldn't give you what you wanted, couldn't make up to you for all the abandonments. Couldn't even try. I'm sorry. All my successes, all that I've achieved, seem pointless measured against that failure. No wonder I've lost my power.

And Betty was right. Maya was running away again, doing it now. Leaving Johanna, trying to work out their relationship in absentia instead of staying with it and struggling face-to-face. As she had run from Rio for so many years, cutting him off, never answering his letter or making contact.

Well, I can't help it, she thought. I'm like those prayer wheels, I crave to be set in motion.

She stopped as another spasm of coughing took her. She dug into her pocket, desperately searching for a throat lozenge. Ang came up behind her, smiled, and lifted her day pack off her shoulders.

"I carry," he said.

She was reluctant to hand over her day pack. It was as if she could hear Betty's voice, triumphant. "See, even my ashes, light as they are, are too much for you."

But Ang, in his smiling, affable eagerness to help, was insistent. She unbuckled the day pack and gave it to him, and he motioned to her to hand him her camera. "I carry, too. Much uphill."

Without protesting, she handed him the camera. "I feel so stupid," she said. "I'm sorry I'm making extra work for you."

He smiled. "No work," he said. "Much uphill today. Go slow, you get better."

Oh, Betty, if only you could have come here, walked these trails, let the strong, kind Sherpas take care of you. Then you would have known nurturing. But Johanna was right, you were never the outdoors type. Still, you went snorkeling in Hawaii that time, you went to Scotland and drove on the wrong side of the road. You took me and Debby and Johanna to hear Paul Robeson sing when he came back to the States in the sixties. We were the only people there under the age of seventy. All the others were aging Jewish communists. You married Joe Greenbaum. No one could accuse you of lacking the spirit of adventure.

Maya followed Ang as he headed slowly up the path. A huge boulder carved with Buddhist inscriptions blocked their way.

"Mani stone," Ang said. "You know?"

"You're always supposed to keep them on your right when you pass, aren't you?" Maya said. Stephen Berznewski had said so.

"Good luck," Ang said. "Much merit." The path jogged left and humped over the edge of the boulder, and Maya hoisted herself up. It added uphill steps to the already long, steep hike, but what the hell, she needed all the merit she could acquire.

"We say clockwise," Maya said. "Sunwise. *Deosil.* In my tradition, too, we go sunwise to bring in good things, good karma—the opposite way to release things."

"What is your tradition?"

Maya paused for breath, then answered as they continued on. "I am a priestess of the Goddess."

"Ah. Which Goddess?"

Which Goddess indeed, Maya thought. I love this place! It's worth every drop of sweat to be here where a priestess of the Goddess is a perfectly natural, normal thing to be. The only question about it is, Which one? Artemis, wild and untamed? Or am I done with that? Hecate, crone of the crossroads? No, not yet. Gaea, generic Goddess of the earth? Or, if I were honest, would I say Persephone, she who causes her mother grief?

"The Goddess of Many Names," Maya said. "She is the Moon Goddess, but also the Earth Goddess too. Goddess of mountains. That's why I wanted to come here."

"Yes," Ang said. "You have come to the right place."

Yes, I have, I have come to the right place. I have a right to come to the place that is right for me. And I always came back, didn't I, Betty? I never completely abandoned you.

Anyway, she thought, as she climbed up and up the snaking path, her breath wheezing in her lungs and sweat dripping from her forehead, escape isn't such an easy route. It's damned hard work, just staying in motion, gaining a bit of ground. Besides, Betty, I could argue that you left me as much as I left you. More subtly, maybe—not that you weren't there, on the physical plane, not that you didn't work and sweat to pay the mortgage and feed us and send us to school, I give you credit for that. It's more than Joe did.

She paused, taking a drink from the water bottle that hung from her belt, wiping her forehead. I kind of like this, Betty, conversing with the dead. Finally I can get you to listen, without interrupting, without shouting me down. Don't you see how that's an abandonment, too— your unseeing of me, your unwillingness to look beyond your image of what I should be, and wasn't? Now you're telling me that I'm being unfair. Maybe so. I just want you to understand that you're not the only one who suffered. Don't you realize that when Joe left you, he left me as well? And he's not the only one. I am your daughter, really, truly. Whether it explains anything, whether it justifies anything or not, I want you just once to recognize that I, too, know what it's like to be abandoned.

17

August 1968

They lay naked on the beach, soaking up the sun like seals. Rio's skin and hair were the color of sand, and the same patterns played over the sand as over his skin, so that Maya could see they were made of the same substance, really, as the story went. Clay. Dirt. Beach sand. And Johanna, lying next to him, was more like the sweet dark soil of a garden, wet and gleaming after rain. This was important to understand, that the body was dirt. Not dirty, but earth.

Maya was happy. She was happy because Johanna had come back to her at last, on the first of August, appearing at the door of the basement apartment they'd sublet.

"I'm here for a vacation," she said. "Before I start college."

"Does my mother know? Does yours?"

"I have their blessing. I'm on a secret mission to save your soul."

They had abandoned the dreary flat, packed up the van, and headed for the coast. Rio knew a place to camp where the road pulled back and the abrupt Big Sur cliffs sloped gently down to a small lagoon. Maya was happy because somehow they had found the free place where they could lie together, they could touch, and talk, and the barriers were down again. Johanna was restored to her. This time nothing could spoil her happiness. Here were no cops and no concrete, only the pounding ocean and these birds leaving trails through her mind as they flew, wing after wing in the rhythmic air.

The sun darkened and the wind began to rise. On the western horizon, dark clouds began to pile up on top of each other. Cold fingers of wind walked over Maya's spine. The three of them sat up and reached for clothes.

"No," Maya said, taking Johanna's hand. "Don't try to shut it out yet. Let it touch you first. The cold."

"Sorry, I'm bred for the tropics," Johanna said, laughing. "I don't go for that Siberia shit."

"It's a rush," Rio said. "Dare you to jump in the ocean right now."

"You are a crazy man."

Maya leaped up and, before she could think, ran off and plunged into the waves. The water burned, and she shrieked. Rio was behind her, splashing water on her back, and she turned and splashed him, and then Johanna joined in, all of them laughing and shrieking and tumbling over each other in the shallows. Rain began to fall, lashing their already wet skin.

"What's our drug of choice for this storm?" Rio asked.

"Nothing," Maya said. "Let's do this one straight."

"How can we? We're not straight, are we?"

"I don't remember," Maya admitted, and they all laughed.

"Let's go up on top of the rock," she said. "Dare you. Double dare."

The rock was a small mountain of sandstone sculpted by the wind into the rough form of a whale. They climbed up the tail and over the rounded back. The wind bore down on them with so much force they couldn't stand but had to crawl forward on hands and knees. They were beyond feeling cold now. Their skin was numb, like a living skin of rock moving over rock, scoured by minute particles of sand in the air.

On the highest point, a small mound of stones made a natural seat. They crouched there, with the waves boiling and churning below them and the wind like a moving wall in their faces. Slowly Maya pulled herself to her feet. She could stand against the wind if she flung out her arms and leaned into it, trusting herself to its embrace. If the wind slackened for a moment, she would fall forward, into the pounding waves below. And that would be okay, really. The storm was calling her, promising her a cleaner ecstasy than the sweaty, grunting storms of human love. She opened her arms wider. Let the storm wash it all away, every part of her formed in an unnatural mold, all the secret fears. She was wild and pure, leaning into the wind, giving it her trust. The wind would hold her.

She heard a faint sound below her, like a plaintive bird cry. Johanna had her hands cupped around her mouth, calling to her.

"I'm going back," she said. "I can't take this anymore." She was shivering, and Rio slid an arm around her.

"Come on," he said. "Let's go get warm."

"Go," Maya yelled. "I'll come later."

"You crazy, girl," Johanna called back. "I'm not leaving you alone on this rock. You'll be trying to fly with the seagulls, next!"

"Maybe I can!" She spread her arms wide. The wind was so powerful. If she gave herself to it, if she became light, yes, who was to say she couldn't fly?

"Don't be an asshole!" Rio shouted. "Come on. Come with us. We want you."

She sighed and started down, angry that they couldn't follow her into the wind, that they were pulling her back from the brink of power.

But her anger dissolved when she saw how cold Johanna was. By the time they crawled down from the rock and made their way back to camp, Johanna's whole body was trembling. Their fire was drenched, and Rio looked at Maya in alarm.

"We've got to get Johanna warm," he said. "Get in the tent with her, and pile on all the sleeping bags. I'll try to build a fire."

There was dry wood under a tarp but no kindling. Maya huddled together with Johanna, feeling exhilaration turn back into cold. They shivered together. Rio gave up on the fire and joined them. Their skin felt like the wind congealed, icy, scoured, smooth. He rubbed Johanna's feet and Maya rubbed her hands and suddenly Johanna was crying. Maya knew that she wanted to melt, to dissolve into flesh and rock and sand.

"Don't cry," Maya murmured, kissing the tears as they stained her cheeks.

"I want this to be real," Johanna whispered. "I want to believe it could stand."

Maya embraced her and Rio wrapped his long arms around them both. "We are real," he murmured. "We will always love you."

They were kissing, and then the three of them were entwined, rubbing and kissing and warming each other's fish-cold flesh until the fires were kindled and they generated between them storm and wind and rain.

Maya lay half asleep, sandwiched between Rio and Johanna, deeply happy. Something was complete now, something that had started over a year ago when she and Johanna went searching together. This time no one would separate them. Here the blossom would have all the time in the world to unfold, to fruit.

Johanna spoke.

"I want to go home," she said.

Her words were like a lash across Maya's face. Stung, she sat up. "Why? Why don't you stay with us?"

Johanna sighed, as if she knew herself to be launched on a hopeless battle.

"Why don't you come home, Maya? Finish school. Straighten your life out again."

"Are you crazy?"

"I'm serious, Maya. You could start at City College, get your high school diploma by exam. Maybe next year we could be at UCLA together—or your daddy could get you into Columbia."

"You're joking."

"It'll be a tough year, probably. But otherwise what are you going to do for the rest of your life?"

"Johanna, you sound like my mother."

"Your mother might once in a while be right, you know."

"No, you can't! You can't do this again! You can't back away from it!" Maya turned to Johanna.

"Away from what?"

"This." She spread her hands, indicating the three of them huddled in the sunny tent, their sleeping bags still entwined. "Us. What happens for us, together. Last night."

"Last night was last night." Johanna looked away, refusing to meet Maya's eye. "I'm starting college next week."

"Oh, fuck college, Johanna! Is that how you want to live your life?"

"Is this how you want to live yours?"

"Yes."

Johanna sighed and propped herself up on her elbow. "Maya, this is a good way to spend a summer vacation. It is not a life."

Maya let her corner of the sleeping bag drop away from her, baring her naked breasts to the morning. "It's a life for me. It's a way of standing against all *that* life. The lie. That system's going to fall."

"Not without a long, hard push."

"That's what this is, Johanna!" Johanna's cool, quizzical eyes fed Maya's fire. "It's a way of tearing it down! By just living, living our freedom."

"How? Getting stoned on the beach? Dealing? Girl, that's not tearing anything down, that's just expanding the marketplace."

The argument woke Rio. He opened his eyes warily, as if warned by the tone of their voices that his peaceful nest of flesh was about to erupt. Grunting, he rolled out of bed, unzipped the tent, and stepped out into the cool morning air. He built a fire, feeding it crumpled paper and small sticks until it caught.

"There's this place we get to," Maya said to Johanna in a low voice, "where it all dissolves. And I know you go there too. But every time we come back from it, you run scared."

"I don't run scared." Now Johanna sat up, clutching the sleeping bag around her. "But maybe I understand some things you don't. We can't live there, Maya. We've got to live in the real world."

"*This* is the real world. College, your mother, all of that—that's not what's real. It's all ego. Posing. Trying to make yourself something to hide from the *place*."

"Bullshit, Maya." Johanna had heat in her own voice, now. "*Karla!* You cannot lie there and tell me my mama is not real! And talk about posing! You come down to LA flaunting your dope-dealer boyfriend in everybody's face, acting like Miss Cool. Acting like staying fucked up for a year gives you the right to be everybody's guru. Well, I got news for you. When it comes right down to it, you are a spoiled little white girl who wouldn't know reality if it whopped you upside the head.''

Maya flung off the last corner of the sleeping bag, jumped up, and ran out of the tent. She ran hard, down the path to the lagoon, and plunged into the cold water. The purity of her vision was gone; even in the water she couldn't regain it. Seeing herself through Johanna's eyes, she felt ugly. Under the water, her skin was blanched of its tan, fish-belly white. Was Johanna right about her? Was it all not a vision but a new and more elaborate pose? The question opened up a black space beneath her. If the water wasn't supporting her body, she felt she could fall and fall and fall.

When she returned later to the campsite, Rio had brewed coffee, and he and Johanna were eating scrambled eggs. He filled Maya's cup and handed her a plate, and the three of them sat together in an awkward silence.

"You two are mad," Rio said at last, just to be saying something. "But you'll get over it. Maya loves you, Johanna. You should hear the way she talked about you, all last year."

"I know," Johanna said. She was dressed in her jeans and a T-shirt and a sweatshirt, her hands cupped around the tin mug of coffee, as if she could not get warm enough. She jerked her head toward Maya, who squatted, naked, beside the fire. "But we're on two different roads, heading in different directions."

"Then let her be," Rio said, pushing the coffeepot on the metal grill over a hotter part of the fire. "Don't try to make her walk your road."

"She wants me to walk hers. But this is the end of the line for me, on this road. It's been a good trip, but I've got to go home."

"No sweat," Rio said. "We'll take you."

Maya refused to go.

"I've done LA. I've seen my mother. I want to stay here. If Johanna wants to go, fine. Let her."

Johanna had gone down to the beach for a last look at the water. Maya had dressed, finally, reluctantly. It seemed a concession. But the wind was cold. Still, maybe she should learn to endure cold, become cold, not shut it out with the rough wool of her long blue skirt, the warm flannel of the shirt she'd borrowed from Rio.

Rio, in his jeans and boots and the denim jacket she had embroidered for him, looked like a cowboy. Maya watched him toss his blond hair in the sun. Like a stallion, she thought. He was behaving like a man, today, insistent, protective, and she admired him for it even as she resisted it.

"We can't let her hitchhike alone all that way," Rio said patiently. "It's dangerous."

"Life is dangerous," Maya said. Then, aware of how she sounded, added, "We could take her to Monterey, put her on a bus."

"It's not that big a deal, Maya. We've got wheels. It's a few hours down, a few hours back."

"A day's drive each way, when we could be here." But she wasn't saying what she really meant. Which was, Don't go, don't desert me, don't leave me now that the wind has died and the sails are slack and I'm about to be swamped by the swell.

"If something happened to her, hitching, you'd never forgive yourself," Rio tried again.

"I've hitchhiked, plenty. Nothing ever happened to me."

"Well, I'd never forgive myself. Look, I'm going to take her. You can come, or you can stay," Rio said in a voice he rarely used, that sounded like somebody's dad laying down the law. He pulled the coffeepot off the grill, and poked at the embers with a stick.

"I'm staying."

It was their first serious fight. Maya felt that she was behaving badly, but she couldn't explain to Rio that she just could not bear the thought of eight hours together with Johanna in this mood that had come between them. She didn't want to explain; she wanted him to understand without words, the way she understood his looks and his touch and the smell of his skin. But he didn't. He didn't understand at all.

All right then, she would wait here, alone with the river and the rocks and the wind, with no one to hold her down. It would be good for her to be alone.

Rio tried, one more time. "Please, Maya, why don't you just come? I want you to come. I want us to be together."

She was wavering, and she might have given in, if he hadn't added, in a tone of annoyance, "It's not such a big deal."

"Fuck you," Maya said, and walked off.

As soon as she heard the van drive away, Maya regretted her stubbornness. She watched the van all along the curve of Highway 1 until it disappeared over the headland to the south, feeling a sense of foreboding. Something would happen; he would never return. She had eaten rampion or looked down to Camelot, violated some unknown taboo and brought a curse upon herself. She felt it. But that was ridiculous. I'm happy alone, she told herself firmly. The ocean was as beautiful, the rock as strong, the voices in the river as musical, whether the others were there or not.

She cleaned up the camp, did the breakfast dishes, hiked far upstream to explore bends of the river she had never seen before. When night came, she cooked some rice and watched the flames of the fire eat wood. The sky and the stars seemed vast and lonely. She was a small spark and it didn't seem to matter much whether or not she winked out. Yet because she was alone, she could almost but not quite hear something new in the dark, a voice that spoke only in solitude, whispering not of comforts but of challenges.

She awoke in the morning knowing that her challenge was to not spend the day anxiously waiting for Rio. She worked out a plan for herself. First she went to the top of the rock, to meditate on the wind. At noon, she lay out naked under the hot rays of the sun, to know fire. She spent the afternoon in the water, going from the moving stream to the still lagoon to the wild incoming tides of the ocean. After sunset, she spent a long time cradled in the roots of the huge cypress tree, smelling the earth.

She was not waiting.

She was not waiting as she built a fire, debating how much rice to cook. Surely he would eat on the road. She was not waiting as she watched the slow wheeling of the stars in the dark-moon sky, as she finally crawled into her sleeping bag and lay, open eyed, listening for the sound of wheels in the dark.

Maybe he had stayed an extra day down south. Maybe something had come up.

She was not waiting the next day, or the next. Not picturing accidents on the road, sudden death. Not turning over her Tarot cards, coming up over and over again with the Tower, the structure blasted by lightning, the world turned upside down. Not racked by storms of jealousy, imagining him settling down there with Johanna, accompanying her to classes. Not feeling herself abandoned. She was not afraid to be alone.

Nevertheless, Rio did not come.

On the fifth day of Maya's vigil, when the eggs were long gone and the rice was nearly done, the sheriff came, down the path from the top of the cliffs.

"You can't camp here," he said. "This is a private beach. You're going to have to move off."

"No one can own the beach," Maya said.

"Be that as it may, somebody does. You've got an hour to get going, or I'll arrest you for trespassing. Now, who else is camped down here?"

"Nobody. I'm alone."

"That's not safe, anyway. A young girl like you. Just last week we found a body, not five miles from here. Anything could happen to you."

He stood and smoked a cigarette while she rolled up her sleeping bag and struck the tent. It seemed to Maya as if some malevolent fate was dogging her. What was it she had done? Was it her ungenerosity to Johanna? Had Rio decided he didn't like her for it? But surely he could have told her, said good-bye, not just vanished. Or maybe that's what all men did, went off in answer to some unseen subpoena and sent a note home, Sorry, honey, I'm never coming back again. Love to the kids.

She had thought he was different. He had loved her, he had listened to her visions and told her his own. Between them, they had made magic. Surely, surely that was true.

But magic was notoriously elusive, ephemeral, easily destroyed with a wrong word. Oh God, why had she been such a bitch?

If she left, he'd never be able to come back. He wouldn't know where to find her. And where would she go? They'd given up their apartment, meaning to find a better place in the fall. She couldn't go back there. She wouldn't go home to Betty and Johanna, to say, Yes, you were right, as soon as it got tough and lonely I've come crawling back. No. But she would have to move on, at least for a while. The sheriff stubbed out his cigarette and regarded her impatiently. She continued to pack, as slowly as possible. She couldn't rid herself of the hope that Rio would miraculously appear, barreling down the highway at the last minute, screeching to a halt in a cloud of dust just as she stuck out her thumb for a ride.

Who came instead was a graduate student in a VW going to Berkeley. She took the ride as an omen. All the way up the coast, she kept checking the rearview mirror.

His name was Tom and he let her stay with him in a big wooden ramshackle house near Telegraph Avenue. He was somewhat comforting but he had a girlfriend, Katharine, who was coming back in a few days, and then Maya would have to clear out. Katharine was studying Russian and political science. She was twenty-six years old, had a closet full of ethnic dresses and a kitchen full of neat bottles of herbs labeled in her own caligraphy. Maya hated her, because she could have been her, in another life, and that life didn't look so bad from the vantage point of the street, where she hung out now, reading Tarot cards for a dollar or two for returning students and nervous tourists. Most of her possessions, all of her clothes and the special things Rio had bought her, were still in his van.

She became an expert at cadging places to crash, free meals from men she met in the Café Med and discarded after coffee, free showers by sneaking into the women's locker room at the university. On sunny afternoons, she'd spread out her Tarot cards in Sproul Plaza or a corner of Telegraph Avenue. When the rains began, she'd nurse a cappuccino through a long afternoon and wrestle with the temptation to give in and call home. She could have been starting classes, like the students who thronged the Med with intense discussions about Marcuse and McLuhan and Hermann Hesse. She could have been buying new clothes and getting her hair trimmed and building up her own barricade of distractions from the simple truth that everything good died.

What stopped her, really, was pride.

She couldn't face Johanna, even though some part of Maya seemed to be carrying on an endless conversation with her. On the days when the Med kicked her out and the weather turned cold and rainy, when nobody wanted their cards read and she wasn't sure where she was going to sleep, some little voice in the back of her mind was constantly whispering to Johanna—"See, not spoiled!"

She couldn't admit to her mother that her wonderful magician was, after all, a man like her father, who had abandoned her.

18

Letter

James Connolly, PFC
Vietnam
August 31, 1968

Dear Jim,

I assume you got the news by now, from the telegram we sent. I'm sorry you were out on maneuvers, we couldn't get word to you in time. I don't know if they would have given you leave, but it feels bad to me that you didn't even know. Shit, I almost didn't know myself. I'd been camping on the coast, with Maya and her girlfriend, Johanna. If I hadn't thought to call Roger, who takes my messages, when I was driving Johanna back to LA, I might not have found out for weeks. But he told me to call home right away, that they'd been trying to get me for two days. So I did, and got hold of Carl.

"It's Dad," he said. "He shot himself. In the car, out back by the garage."

I felt like someone had just socked me hard, right in the solar plexus, you know. Like I couldn't breathe for a moment, I couldn't think. All I could say was, "In the car?" like some kind of idiot. And then, "That bastard. That rotten stinking bastard."

Carl told me to come home, and I said I would. We were halfway down the coast, and now, this is the bad thing. Maya had stayed up where we were camping, and I didn't think I had time to go back for her—we were almost to LA by then. I figured I'd be back in a couple of days, she'd wait for me. Okay, maybe I figured in a way it would serve her right, to wait for a bit, because she'd really been kind of a bitch that morning, which is not like her. But I've been stuck here already for two days, it'll take me another couple just to get disentangled, and I'm starting to worry. I wish to God she had a telephone there.

But I'm getting ahead of myself. Johanna dropped me at the airport and I bought a ticket. Luckily I generally have a lot of cash on hand for reasons I won't go into in the U.S. Mail.

Carl picked me up and we went straight to the funeral home. I wasn't really dressed for the occasion but at least I was there. The minister was up on the pulpit talking about what a fine man Dad was, how he left four fine sons, one of whom was even now defending his country in far-off Vietnam, blah blah and bullshit. I wanted to stand up and scream. I wanted to yell, "Hey, that bastard never did nothing but knock us around, I hate his fucking cowardly guts. I'm glad he's dead!" But I just sat there and didn't say a word, for Mom's sake. She suffered enough while he was alive, I figured, why embarrass her now that he's finally dead?

Then we came back to the house. Carl and I drank up all his whiskey and a bottle of our own. I said he must have been desperate, to die with half a bottle of hard liquor left undrunk.

"We should finish it," Carl said. "It's our legacy."

"Our heritage, man," I agreed.

"Our goddamned inheritance," he said. "Hey, pass it over. Share the wealth."

Carl's grown, you know. He's just eighteen and bigger than you, with biceps bulging out of his undershirts. He works out.

He kept wanting to talk about Dad, how he used to take us fishing, all that sentimental crap, trying to make him out to be a father instead of a fall-down, smash-your-face drunk. I just kept saying, "Rot in hell, you bastard, rot in hell!"

"We used to take out the shotgun, go after woodchucks. Remember?" Carl kept saying. "Those were good times. Hey, we had some good times."

All I could remember was how I used to cry when we'd blow the heads off the poor little bloody fuckers, and Dad would laugh at me. You'd tell him to lay off. I remember that. I appreciate it, not that it did any good.

By that time, our heritage was gone. Yours too. It found a good home. We figured the least we could do for the old man was get righteously rip-roaring drunk, and we proceeded to do so.

That's why I didn't write you yesterday. My handwriting was a bit shaky, and I can't even begin to describe to you what my head felt like.

Mom is on my case, trying to get me to stay. She keeps whining about how she's all alone. You'd think she'd see it as an improvement, nobody to drink up her Social Security money and slap her across the mouth, but she actually seems to miss the old bastard. I told her Laurie and Steve would look after her.

"They've got each other. I'm all alone, now," she whined.

"Who did you ever have, Mom?" I asked her. "Dad treated you like shit."

"But he was somebody. Nobody knows what goes on between a woman and a man."

I swear to you, Jim, if I thought their marriage was an example of what goes on between a woman and a man, I'd turn faggot.

Anyway, I can't stay and look after Mom, not just because it would drive me crazy, but because Uncle Sam had a little notice for me that had been sitting here in the mail since last June, which Mom never bothered to send on. It seems that if I don't get my ass back in school I'll be joining you in the land of jungle rot. I was trying to explain this to her, when Carl comes in, banging the door behind him. Seems he'd gone downtown to the Recruitment Center and signed himself up for the Marines. Well, Mom went into hysterics, I was yelling at him for a prize fool and an idiot, not to mention a fascist. I know you won't agree but at least you've got to admit that the timing was pretty damn raw. Mom was crying about being alone, all alone, with all her babies gone off to war and her man dead, Carl was dead-ass drunk, and here's me, stuck in the middle, with four days to get back to Berkeley and signed up for classes, and Maya somewhere on the coast, alone, wondering what the fuck happened to me.

Sometimes I wonder how any of us managed to walk out of this house alive.

So it's three in the morning now, and I can't sleep. I'm worried about Maya, I'm worried about Mom, I'm worried about you over there with crotch rot and bullets flying, and Carl, that dumb idiot, and even Steve and Laurie—I worry that their faces will freeze in that look of pusillanimous disapproval they do so well. Tell me what to do, Jim. I've got to get out of here, don't I? I just can't take it anymore. There's a gray haze creeping out of the peeling paint on the ceiling. The TV is blaring day and night. I can't think straight. In another couple of days, I'll be punching holes in the walls.

Stay cool. That's what you'd say if you were here. I'm going to try to take your advice and get some sleep. At the moment, it's Maya who's worrying me the most. I've talked to her mother, I called Johanna and left them both the number here, in case she calls them. Wouldn't that be the first thing she'd do? There's a phone at the Big Sur Store not too far from where we were. She could hitchhike down there. I've got to believe that she'll trust me, that she'll know I wouldn't just run off and never come back. What we have together is so good, so strong. She's got to trust that. She's got to.

Well, I'm going to end and really try to sleep now. Tie one on for the old man, won't you—I guess we owe him that. Think of me when you're puking your guts out afterwards. And watch your back, bro. We've seen enough of Mr. Death for a while.

Take care,
Rio

19

Johanna Weaver's Journal

October 10, 1968

What am I going to do? What am I going to do? WHAT AM I GOING TO DO?

I've jumped off the bed fifteen times, until I'm black and blue. I called up Tony Klein, who was in town for the weekend, and got him to take me for a long, bumpy ride on his motorcycle. I've taken a million hot baths. Nothing helps.

God. I've just started classes. I was hoping to get a part-time job, save some money, live in the co-op next quarter.

I had to know. I had to know for sure, and I was afraid to go to student health, afraid—I don't know—of getting something on my record before I come to a decision. So I went downtown to the Free Clinic, last Monday. I told Marian I was going to study late in the library. They did a test, and today I called and got the results.

It's official. I'm pregnant.

Shit, shit, shit!

Oh, they were very helpful, and I'm sure if I want an abortion I can get one somewhere, somehow. I could take my savings and go down to Mexico. I could find someone to do it here—someone safe. It would cost, but if I work it right, Marian would never need to know.

That's what I should do. It's the sensible thing. I don't know why I can't bear the thought of it.

The thing is, it makes the most sense from the point of view of school and work and a career and keeping Marian proud of me. But then I start to hear Maya's voice.

"All that is just a game," she says. "It's posing. It's false. What's happening inside you is real. Somebody's there. Some of our magic is trying to incarnate."

The voice makes me mad. "Fuck off," I want to yell at her, "I owe nothing to you. It's you and your craziness that got me into this situation." Although I'm not completely sure that's true. It might have happened that last night, or it might have happened the next day, on the trip down. And I have no one to blame but myself for that, if I'm honest. Oh, sure, if Maya had been nice and made up and come with us, it wouldn't have happened. But how can I blame her, after what I said to her? And why was I so mad? Because deep inside I wanted so much to do exactly what she was begging me to do, to stay in the magic place where there aren't any barriers to love.

Well, there weren't any barriers to conception, either. So much for magic. I should have stayed on the pill, headaches, bloat & all. Whether or not I had a boyfriend.

Maybe I should blame AT&T. If Rio hadn't stopped to call the guy who gets his messages, he would never have known about his dad, and I wouldn't have felt so damn sorry for him. When I think of how he looked, coming back from that phone booth. His face scared me. It was kind of pus white, and he was walking kind of shaky like he might fall to pieces if he wasn't real careful. I knew something awful must have happened.

"What's wrong?" I asked him.

He started the engine without saying a word, and drove off as if seven devils were chasing him.

After a long, long time, he finally answered me.

"My dad is dead," he said, in this completely flat voice. "He shot himself."

I said something stupid. I mean, what can you say at a time like that? He didn't say a word, just drove like a demon. After he nearly crashed into the guard rail three or four times, I made him pull over. We stopped at a narrow overlook where below us the waves pounded against the shore. He looked like a small boy to me, all red in the face and trying not to cry. So I couldn't help myself, I had to try to comfort him. I reached over and put my arms around him, cradling his head against my shoulder. He needed to cry, but being a man, he didn't or maybe he couldn't. He just kept saying, "The bastard! The motherfucker!" over and over again.

"It's okay, Rio," I murmured. "It's gonna be okay." But I could tell that it wasn't. I could smell him, ocean wind and salt and woodsmoke still clinging to his hair. He smelled clean and I felt so bad for him. Maya should have been there. He needed her, or somebody permanent; all I was was a substitute. Still I stroked his back and soothed his hair, and then he was sliding his hands beneath my blouse, unbuttoning my jeans.

It shocked me at first—I mean, if Marian shot herself sex would be the last thing on my mind. But men are different. I thought, what the hell? He needs something to comfort him, this is something I can offer. So I let him. It was like being made love to by an animal, or a child. He needed me so much, his hands and mouth and skin were so hungry for comfort. No one ever needed me like that before, as if I alone could make the world all right again. I'm not sure it was all that sexy, but it touched me somewhere deep inside. I wanted to hold him and protect him and care for him. I almost felt like his mother. Which is maybe why I think it happened then. The mother part of me woke up and caught itself a seed.

You might say I let him use me. You might say, in fact, that I let him use me the way white men have always used black women. But it didn't feel like that at the time. It felt like a gift, a gift of love.

That's what I can't help but remember. One way or another, this child was conceived in love.

And now the mother part of me is wide awake and hungering. I want a child in my arms. I want it with an ache that goes against all common sense. I want to be sucked on, cried for. I want to be the sun and the moon and the stars to somebody.

What am I going to do?

Rio doesn't know. I don't think I'll tell him, whatever I decide. I saw him again, when he came to pick up the van. But of course, I didn't know then. We didn't do anything. He was in a tearing hurry to head back up the coast and find Maya, because he ended up staying in Pittsburgh a lot longer than he'd planned. He'd been phoning here every night, hoping she'd call, but she didn't. And he's been phoning here, and over to Betty's, ever since, because Miss Maya J. Greenwood alias Karla Greenbaum has once again dropped off the face of the earth. She wasn't there when he went back to our campsite by the lagoon. She did call a couple of their friends back in San Francisco, but they hadn't heard from Rio yet and she didn't call again. Still, at least it seems likely she's alive, not murdered and thrown behind a bush somewhere. So he keeps calling us, getting more and more frantic all the time.

I'm glad of that, in a way. I mean, I'm glad he really cares about her. Still, it's always Maya, Maya, Maya. He never says, "How ya doin', Johanna. Hey, want to come up for a long weekend, want me to come down and take you out dancing, thanks for the memories." I'm background to him, not foreground—one of Maya's accessories, like Barbie's friend Skipper. Not a person he can see.

If I decide to have an abortion, it's none of his business. If I decide to have the baby . . .

If I decide to have the baby, it'll be mine. Just mine. I'll need help, and I'm sure Marian will give it to me even if she wants to strangle me. But I don't need his help. My baby doesn't need a stoned, white hippy dope-dealer daddy, not at first, anyway. Maybe later, maybe someday, they'll meet—but not now.

Oh, God, what am I going to do?

Johanna

20

Tengpoche

Tengpoche Monastery is the spiritual heart of
Khumbu. At an elevation of 12,700 feet, its
spectacular setting includes views of Everest.

—*MOUNTAIN CO-OP ADVENTURES*
BROCHURE

Fog lay over the broad field by the monastery of Tengpoche. Maya lay in
her tent, her sleeping bag draped over her like a quilt, sipping her afternoon tea and munching on a biscuit that Tashi had brought her. She was
grateful to be done with the steep climb up the hill to the table of land
where the monastery stood, but she was ready to cry with disappointment. Debby had still not appeared, and Tenzing had assured Maya that
she couldn't be wandering anonymously in the misty field or quietly
hidden in a teahouse.

"When the doctor from Khunde comes, I will know," he said.

Maya had taken her hurt feelings to bed. Oh, Betty, now I know
exactly how you suffered. What can be so much more important to her
than me?

Now, for consolation, she spread Rio's letters and Johanna's journal pages about her knees. In her own journal she wrote:

Johanna,

I have to write to you even though I won't be able to send this
for another week, and if I mail it from Kathmandu, it probably won't
even reach you until after I get back. Because I understand now that
you are still challenging me, with these pages, still stripping yourself
before me as an offering, still trying to goad me to touch and be
saved. And maybe I do the same for you. We both resist, each in our

way. Perhaps because our moments of coming together have been much like trains crashing head on. Our lives get derailed.

And yet great gifts come to us. Rachel, for one.

Or maybe it's just inevitable that layers of evasion and accommodation build up in a life like plaque on teeth. Have I been naive not to realize that they must periodically be scraped away?

"Maya?" She heard Lonnie's voice outside the entrance to her tent. "You in there? You all right?"

"I'm fine." Somewhat reluctantly, she pulled herself up to her knees, scattering papers all around her, opened the zipper, and peered out. "I'm just enjoying a quiet moment of gratitude for being on the luxury tour. Someone else to pitch the tent, make the tea, carry the bags. It's almost sinful."

"It's the only way to go." Lonnie's dark curls were framed by her latest purchase, a stocking cap knitted of multicolored yak wool. It looked warm. "You want to come out, take a stroll around, check out the monastery?"

Maya debated. The tea had given her a new surge of energy, and she had to pee, anyway. Might as well get up, stop mooning about in the past. She should try to be a bit more sociable, make friends with some of the others in the group instead of just letting them irritate her. Lonnie was a good candidate to start with. "Sure."

The Sherpas had pitched a small tent above a deep hole they dug to accommodate the needs of the trekkers. Maya made her visit, and then she and Lonnie walked across the wide field dotted with camps of various-colored tents. There were several expeditions on their way up to Everest this spring, and the field was a stopping place for all of them, the traditional place to rest a day and acclimatize to the altitude. Through the fog moved figures dressed in the electric blues and purples and greens favored by the makers of outdoor gear. In the north corner of the field stood a massive ochre-painted shape, the monastery. Maya and Lonnie headed that way.

"Beautiful view," Lonnie commented, looking around at the dense mist that screened any glimpse of the mountains.

"So they say," Maya agreed.

"You believe them?"

Maya nodded. "It's an act of faith on my part."

"I say all the evidence isn't in yet."

The monastery of Tengpoche was a massive edifice of hand-cut stone, plastered over with saffron-colored stucco. It rose up a high two stories above a wide stone-paved courtyard, with a small third-story chamber crowned by a pagoda roof. Gray stone outbuildings flanked the

gompa itself and descended the slopes of the hill on terraces. The building was a work of fine craftsmanship, the wooden beams handcarved,
each doorframe and window fitted lovingly into the stuccoed stone walls.
But the roof, Maya noted, was of corrugated tin, as if energy and money
had run out at roof level. Or perhaps to the Sherpas of the thirties, when
the monastery was rebuilt, tin roofs were the leading edge high-tech
wonder of their time.

Maya and Lonnie walked the circle of its heavy stone walls, admir-
ing its solidity, the careful carving and fitting of the stone blocks visible at
its foundation. They made their way into a cloistered courtyard with a
stairway and balcony running along one side, and sat on the edge of the
low wooden steps that ran the length of the eastern wall.

"It's a beautiful place," Lonnie said, spreading the edge of her
jacket to cover her backside as she sat down. "It seems so old."

"It's not, though." Maya's own jacket wasn't quite long enough to
provide much insulation. She sat uncomfortably on its edge, feeling it put
a crease in her butt. "Stephen Berznewski says it was rebuilt in the
thirties, after an earthquake destroyed it."

"Really! I would have thought it was ancient. Guess it pays to read
the guidebook."

"Yes and no," Maya said. "I prefer the romance of thinking it's
been here for thousands of years. But really, it was only founded in the
early part of the century. Pangboche and Thami are much older."

A young monk in a bloodred robe walked across the courtyard,
mounted the steps, and disappeared behind a small door.

"I wonder what it's really like to live up here," Lonnie said. "To
devote yourself to meditating all the time. I wonder if they ever get
restless, long for the bright lights of Namche."

"I imagine they do. But I guess if they get restless enough, they can
leave. Still, it seems a good thing for men to do—meditating on the
mountain. Better than going off to war." She glanced at Lonnie, aware
that her ears were pricked to catch any nuance in Maya's mention of men
that might indicate how she really felt about women.

"Sure, sublimate that testosterone," Lonnie agreed. "Maybe we
should send all the men up to the mountain, let the women run the
world."

The sun was dimly warm on the stones and Maya soaked up what
warmth it offered, enjoying the hushed peace of the courtyard. "Sometimes I think I'd like to be a nun for a while," she mused. "Go somewhere and retreat from all the everyday hassles, just be able to
concentrate on the spirit. Maybe that's what I need. But I'm not very
good at accepting anyone else as my spiritual authority. I doubt that I
could handle the discipline."

"I doubt that I could handle the sanitary facilities," Lonnie said. "Or the cold ascetic cells, or the hard beds. I'd be a monk if I could have a sofa and central heating and a nice, comfy chair."

Maya laughed. "The pleasures of the flesh are high on your list of priorities, I see."

"Aren't they on yours?"

Maya found herself silent, staring at the wood plank wall of the low building across the courtyard, noting how its red paint had faded and weathered. She was thinking about being home with Johanna, cuddling together on her large bed watching "Lord Peter Wimsey" on PBS. When was that? Years ago, it must have been. Maya had wanted to switch the TV off, and they had argued.

"Talk to me," Maya had said. "Be with me."

"I'm here, aren't I? We're together, are we not?"

"Are we? Is this what we've come to? A mutual TV-watching support group?"

"You were the one who didn't want to go out."

"I did," Maya said. "I wanted to go to Lorraine's book party."

"Oh no!" Johanna rolled her eyes. "Not another one of those. I don't appreciate being on display as your tame black girlfriend."

"Jo!" Maya sat bolt upright. "That's not fair!"

"No? Remember the last party of Lorraine's you dragged me to."

"I thought you'd like to meet her, that you might have something to say to each other. She's a psychologist—you're a psychologist. She writes about young girls—you work with them."

"She never said a word to me all evening long. Instead, that bitch Brenda backed me into the corner all night to complain about black women taking over her organization. As if I'm supposed to answer for the race!"

"I didn't know she was going to be there, and I was surrounded by fifty women wanting me to tell them this and answer that. It was distracting. I didn't notice you needed rescuing, and frankly, you're a big girl. I expect you to be able to take care of yourself."

"That's it, exactly." Johanna nodded. "When we go out to those things, they're all over you, and I might just as well be the maid."

Maya lay back, defeated. "The ironic thing is," she said, "I wanted you there to give me moral support. Those women intimidate me. They're always quoting people I've never heard of and referring to books I've never read. I just thought that when the talk turned to the feminist critique of object relations theory, or some such thing, you'd be able to pick up the ball."

Johanna slid an arm under her shoulder. "Have you noticed how people almost always assume that you're the educated one in our couple?"

Maya sighed. "Maybe I should start introducing you as *Dr.* Weaver. 'Hello, Asshole, I'd like to introduce you to my childhood sweetheart and intermittent hot, sweet honey, Doctor Johanna Weaver, the noted educational psychologist. Dr. Weaver, meet Asshole.' What do you think?"

"I think this is nice and cozy, lying here like this. I'm glad we didn't go out. Sometimes we just get to relax."

Maya stared up at the ceiling. Yes, they were relaxed and cozy. Should she risk disturbing their peace?

She spoke lightly, half-joking. "But when do we get to smolder with passion, exploding in volcanic eruptions of heat and light?"

Johanna smiled. "Did you just make that up?"

"No," Maya admitted. "It was a line I was trying out this afternoon in the chapter I was writing. But I decided it was too clichéd."

"We're not clichéd," Johanna assured her. "We're special."

"Sure we are. I just can't help but think that if we'd been able to look ahead that morning on the locker room floor, and see us now, a cozy old couple tripping on late-night TV, we'd have been appalled."

"Maybe we would have been delighted . . . to know we'd still be together," Johanna countered.

Maya sighed.

"What?" Johanna asked.

"It's been too long since we've made love in a rainstorm."

"We're not teenagers anymore," Johanna said. "I for one could live quite comfortably without ever making love in a rainstorm again. It sounds so romantic, but your butt gets cold as hell."

"Well, I can't," Maya said. "I can't live contentedly when I feel we've settled for less."

"Less than what?" Johanna pulled away, and turned to look at her. "Less than nonstop intensity, every minute of the day. Girl, we haven't settled at all. *I* haven't. I'm out there fighting every day. I'm not going to trash myself because once in a while I want to relax at night. And you too. You've got responsibilities you didn't have at nineteen. You've got your writing. There's a world of people, and a season of rainstorms every year. But I don't think you can fuck them all and still have time and energy left to write your books."

"I write what I live," Maya said. "If I stop living, I'll stop writing."

Johanna shook her head. "Well, we haven't died just because we spend a night or two watching public television. Lighten up, girl!"

"I feel like some part of us has died," Maya whispered softly. She was hoping for a sympathetic response, for Johanna to soothe her and caress her and maybe even make love to her. Instead Johanna got out of bed.

"I can't talk about this anymore," she said. "We don't get anywhere with it. I'm going to make myself a bowl of Cheerios and a cup of herb tea." She left the room, closing the door behind her, leaving Maya staring at the blank TV screen.

"Aha, I see I've asked a touchy question," Lonnie said, breaking into Maya's reverie.

The silence of the place had grabbed Maya, gently closing her mouth with misty hands. Really there was no need to reply to every damn question somebody thought up.

"So," Lonnie asked, her voice carefully casual, "I've been wanting to ask you for days now—are you a dyke, or what?"

Pushy, pushy, Maya thought. At last she's come straight out with it. Lonnie was gazing at her with open and friendly curiosity, taking a breath to speak, to ask something else. She wouldn't give up. But there was no harm in her, nothing to justify Maya's desire to retreat deeper and deeper into silence.

"What," Maya said. "That's it exactly. I've been searching for a sexual identity, and now you've named it for me. I'm a what."

"Glad I could be of service." Lonnie bowed. "I sort of suspected as much."

"Why? Do I give off subtle signals that you recognize?"

"It's more the signals you don't give off. You never flash that Nancy Reagan male-adoration eye-batting smile, but you don't come off as a real dyke, either."

"How many years do you have to live with a woman before you qualify as a real dyke?"

"That depends." Lonnie stood up and paced about, hugging her arms to her chest for warmth. "Here's the checklist—five points for each correct answer. Do you have sex with this woman? Do you have sex with this woman exclusively? Do you have sex with women exclusively? Do you have fantasies about sex with women exclusively?"

"We have sex, but only intermittently," Maya admitted.

"Bingo. You qualify."

"What if I have fantasies about men?" Maya asked.

"Mezzo mezzo."

"Sex with men?"

"Oh, one of *those*." Lonnie raised her eyebrows. "Well, that doesn't necessarily disqualify you. Real dykes can sometimes have sex with men, as long as they retain a proper dread of bisexuals."

"Huh?" The stone steps were cold. Maya inched the bottom of her jacket farther under her butt. "I'm confused. If dykes can sleep with men, why are bisexuals so dreadful?"

"Because you can't build a sexual liberation movement on a morass of murky identity confusion. As soon as we admit, for one moment, that homosexuality might be less than a fixed, permanent condition, Pat Robertson and his boys will have us shipped off to Sexual Reorientation Camp. This way we have an excuse. 'I'm sorry, Senator Helms, I can't help it, it's inborn, a genetic defect, like any other disability, so please be nice to me.' "

Maya laughed and stood up. "It's too cold to sit," she said. "Let's walk around the building again."

"Okay."

Together they left the courtyard and paced slowly around the perimeter of the building. The fog enclosed them in a quiet, private world.

"Where's Jan?" Maya asked.

"We're taking some space," Lonnie said. "You know how that is."

"Oh yes, I know exactly how that is. I'm taking about ten thousand miles of it, myself."

"I see."

"But you and Jan seemed to be getting along so well. I mean, the energy between you two has been sizzling all week."

"Is it that obvious?" Lonnie stopped, and turned to face Maya.

"For those who have eyes to see." Lonnie looked alarmed, and Maya hastened to reassure her. "Not to everyone. Not to, say, the Sherpas, I'm sure—they wouldn't be expecting it. Or to Howard, for example. I'm sure he'd never notice a thing."

"Oh, Howard. He wouldn't notice if a rutting rhino cornered him in his own tent." Lonnie resumed walking forward.

"So what happened with you and Jan?" Maya asked, her voice carefully neutral, an imitation of her mother's voice in her interviewing mode. *If she can ask me probing questions, I can turn the tables on her.* Still, Maya hoped that she sounded supportive, not just nosey.

"We made the mistake of talking about the future." Lonnie sighed. "About what happens when the romantic interlude is over."

Maya shook her head sadly. "Oh, bad idea. Live for the moment, I always say."

"But one moment leads on to another, and eventually you have to decide, don't you? I do. I need to know whether I'm having a relationship, or just a shipboard romance."

"What do you want it to be?"

"I don't know." Lonnie hunched her down coat over her shoulders. "I'm *in* a relationship, back in Portland. It's boring."

Maya laughed. "That's pretty blunt."

"It's blunt, but it's true. Taylor and I have been together since law school. She works all the time. *I* work all the time. It's damn hard not to when you're trying to establish a practice. We live in the same house and hardly ever see each other, and when we do, we're exhausted. We can't even seem to coordinate our schedules to get away together."

"How does she feel about you going off with Jan?"

Lonnie shrugged. "The truth is, she thinks Jan and I are just good friends."

"I see."

They came to a corner of the building. Beyond, a hedge of dark junipers defined a slope. High above them, the mist parted for one moment, and Maya caught a glimpse of the gray flanks of a mountain where only clouds should be.

"I hate to hurt her," Lonnie said as they turned the corner to continue walking alongside the *gompa*'s outer wall. "And why should it, really?"

"There's no reason why it should," Maya said cautiously, thinking about her own and Johanna's experiments along the same lines. "But there's no denying that it often does. Infidelity, I mean."

"Ouch, do you have to call it that? Couldn't you please refer to it as, oh, expanding the parameters of our relationship? Yeah, that sounds good. How could that hurt anybody?"

"I have called it that, many times," Maya said. "Sometimes I've even believed it. For a while. Are you thinking about breaking up with—what was her name?"

"Taylor." Lonnie stopped again, looking up at the edge of mountain showing through the mist. "I don't know. I don't know. I've spent the last eight years building up a practice in Portland, I can't just throw it all over and move to New Mexico. And how can Jan be an up-and-coming New Mexico artist in Portland?" She turned to look at Maya again. "Sexually, we're great together, but geographically we're incompatible."

"That is a problem."

"Taylor *works* in my life. Whatever we have, or don't have." She looked away again. "I don't know, maybe I'm just not so romantic as I used to be. You get a bit older, you've got more of an investment in yourself. You aren't so eager to throw everything over and run off with a gorgeous stranger."

"Yeah." Maya shivered in the cold. She started walking again. "Anyway, no one considers that sort of thing romantic anymore. It's just neurotic, or some diseaselike addictive pattern you ought to recover from. Makes it damn hard to write novels."

"I can imagine." Lonnie trotted after her.

"But I don't want to recover from passion." Maya threw her arms open wide and jumped up on a nearby block of stone. "I want to jump up on a soapbox and proclaim to the world, 'Hey, people, wake up and admit that pleasure and passion in all their forms are holy!' "

"Bravo! Bravo!" Lonnie clapped her hands. "You've got my vote."

Maya jumped down. "And meanwhile, Johanna and I indulge in

storms of passion about as often as the moon eclipses the sun. Not never, but rarely. On the other hand, when it storms, it's thunder and lightning and pouring rain, with all the trimmings. For a while."

"And then life intervenes," Lonnie said. "That's the sensible way to look at it. I look at Jan, and the sensible me says, 'Enjoy it, honey, but don't take it seriously. Anyway, if you moved down to New Mexico, you'd end up just another happy, dull couple, keeping cats and making your visitors look at all your slides from Nepal.' But the unsensible me wonders sometimes. Why should my life be set in stone at thirty-four? If passion is holy, shouldn't it be worth throwing everything over?"

They rounded the corner, and the wall now blocked the wind.

"I've done that," Maya said, leaning against the stone wall that still held a bit of the sun's warmth. "Been there, done that, got the T-shirt."

"And? What does the T-shirt say?"

"It says: 'I leaped recklessly into the abyss, and now I lead guided tours to the gates of hell, for a percentage.' "

"That sounds awfully cynical."

"I'm only cynical about myself." The clouds were definitely shifting now, letting a low ray of sun sneak through to illuminate the mist with a golden glow. "I believe in what I'm teaching and doing. It's just that I started out with a life-shaking vision and ended up with a career." Maya fell silent. That's more than I ever intended to say to Lonnie, she thought. Possibly more than I ever intended to admit to myself.

"I don't think I've ever had a vision," Lonnie said. "I'm an attorney—not a visionary sort of gal."

"That's probably not true." Maya spoke sharply. "And if it is, be thankful. A real vision is a pain in the ass. It's something you have to serve for the rest of your life."

"Oh, I already have one of those," Lonnie said. "It's called the loans I took out to go to law school." The mist was pearly, glowing, now and then resolving itself into forms with golden edges. They watched as the faraway peaks teased them, revealing and concealing themselves moment by moment.

"I believe!" Lonnie said to the mist. "I do believe in mountains, I do, I do!"

Maya watched the clouds form and shift, remembering a ritual, one of the last she'd led before her mother died. She'd been invited months earlier to do a closing ceremony for a midwives' conference, and when the day came she'd thought about canceling. The midwives lived their lives in service to mothers, and her mother was dying and she had no child of her own. She had gone anyway because she had agreed to go, and part of her power lay in keeping her promises.

In the carpeted ballroom of the big hotel where the conference was held, she had turned down the lights and lit a candle and played her drum in a smooth, hypnotic beat. A story came to her and she told it to the midwives while she drummed, a story about being born into a world where women were free and the earth was healed. The hotel disappeared and soon they were all breathing the air of that world, feeling it on their skin as they ran free through the night under the moon in a place where nobody would harm them or hold them back. Her own grief had leaked through into the story, and roused the hidden grief of a hundred women. Even as they danced in the moonlight of the Otherworld, they remembered the cages and the assaults of this one and cried together, a hundred women wailing and sobbing and holding each other until grief changed to rage and rage to a roaring, thunderous dance of power. As Maya led them in and out of intricate spirals, the story became a chant:

> I am a wild woman,
> I am a loving woman,
> I am a healer,
> My soul will never die!

The chant rose and became a pure, wordless sound of power, the deep power that is backed by nothing but the movement of the moon and sun and the wash of the tides and the swelling of buds in the spring. With one voice, they sang that power and released it and brought it back to ground.

That's what I do, Maya thought. When I'm at my best, I can move the energy so that people feel the power shared and flowing and everything comes alive. But the magic really works only when they take the tools into their own hands.

Because the deep healing in that ritual hadn't come from the drumming or the trance or the story. It had happened as the women sat on the floor, letting the power drain back to earth. One woman had spoken to the group, asking for help for her son, who had a drug problem, and another had spoken and asked for energy for a mother she'd worked with whose baby had died, and then another spoke, and another, until one by one they poured their real pain into the pool of that hundred women. What healed them was nothing Maya did, not the chants she led or the story she told or the drumbeat she played. What healed was simply the opening to speak their pain and have it heard.

The very last woman who spoke was from high in the mountains of Chiapas, an *indígena* who wore the huipil of her village and her graying brown hair in two long braids. She spoke in the Spanish Maya remembered from her years in Mexico, and asked for healing for her sister, whose son was very ill, and who was accusing her of putting a curse on him, because she had seen her preparing the incense for a *limpieza,* a cleansing, and now was afraid she was a *bruja.* Witch, the interpreter translated the word, but Maya knew the subtle difference between *bruja* and *curandera,* sorceress and healer. She reminded Maya so much of the *curandera* she had known in Michoacán. Maya had begged to stay with her and learn from her, but Doña Elena had said no. "You must go home," she had told Maya, "you must find something of your own." But Maya couldn't go home then, because of Rio, not for years after.

Yet in the end she had found something of her own to give, to return to this woman as some small giving back for what she'd received in her wanderings. A simple gift, really, just the listening ears of a hundred women, many of whom had themselves been branded Witches, some of whom remembered in their deepest selves what it was to be burned. Something was completed: A circle was closed. The midwives had put the woman in the center and sung her name, Maria, and chanted for her protection and to give her power. And then Maya had asked for healing for herself, which she rarely did, and for her mother who was trying so hard to die. She'd sat in the center of the circle and let herself cry and cry as the women sang to her and held her.

From that day on, her mother had begun to let go. The relentless force that kept her tortured body breathing had begun to ease its grip, or perhaps Betty herself had begun to slip into the Otherworld, not all at once, but slowly, cautiously, as she used to enter a swimming pool, step by step, giving herself time to become accustomed to the feel of cold water on her ankles, knees, hips.

"What are you thinking about?" Lonnie's voice broke into her reverie.

Maya expelled a long breath. I can make the space. That's all. But they don't see that they do the work themselves.

"Contradictions," she said.

"Such as?"

"I know how to make an opening for power to flow," Maya said, not sure if Lonnie would understand any of what she was saying. "Really, that's all I know how to do. But the power isn't mine. I can teach people tools that help them make a space for it, but I don't create it. And people forget that. They identify it with me, and so instead of coming for the tools, they come back for the high. And I start to feel like a spiritual drug dealer."

Lonnie shrugged. "It's a legal high, isn't it? Maybe people need that. Didn't you say something like that yourself, when we were talking the other day?"

"But it's not just a high, when it works. When the power really moves, it can change your life. And that's terrifying. People think they want it, but do they really? Do you? Do I? Haven't we just been talking about that very question?''

"You mean you could do a ritual that would make me leave Taylor and go live with Jan?"

"No," Maya shook her head. "That's the point. I can't make you do anything. But on a real good day, if you were open, I could create the opportunity for you to touch something so deep it might make ordinary life unbearable."

"Whew," Lonnie whistled. "I thought only us lawyers could do that."

Maya smiled. "That's on a good day," she admitted. "The thing is, a lot of days aren't so good. Sometimes you open the space and nothing flows. And there you are, facing all these expectant people, wanting a life-changing moment to happen. I hate to disappoint people."

"So what do you do?"

"I perform. I know enough, now, to be able to fill the space with something. And what I don't understand is that even after the worst times, the times when I feel like I'm mouthing some words because nothing is really speaking to me, people will come up and tell me how much they got out of it, how they've been helped. Then I feel like a spiritual con artist."

"Why? If they got something out of it, then it worked, didn't it?"

"But is it real? Is it a real transformation, or a pseudoexperience, just enough to deflect them from pursuing what would be real, what would be theirs? Am I being honest?"

Lonnie pulled her cap off, shook out her hair, and replaced her hat. "Maybe you're taking too much on yourself. You can't decide what's real for somebody else. It seems to me that a change is a change."

"But a real vision, a real change, isn't *safe*," Maya said. "You don't pay a workshop fee for it, you pay with your life."

Lonnie shrugged. "How can you know what somebody else pays? Just because they don't go riding off to save France doesn't mean the change won't bring plenty of risks with it. You might not know what they are. You might not ever know. But that doesn't mean they won't be real."

The clouds had gathered back over the sun, and Maya shivered. "You're probably right. Don't think I haven't told myself the same thing. When I'm in the middle of it, when my passion is ripe for it, I don't have all these doubts. It's just that ever since my mother died, all I seem to feel is tired."

"Let's walk on," Lonnie suggested. "I'm cold."

They followed the wall of the building, continuing their circumambulation. They had walked around to the north wall of the monastery, which backed up against the woods and the sloping edge of the gorge. A big granite boulder loomed above them, incorporated into the wall.

"Look at that!" Maya said. "That's beautiful, how they incorporate the natural boulder into the stonework instead of blasting it away or going around it."

"Wait!" Lonnie said. "I can feel a metaphor approaching. It must be the presence of a real writer—I'm about to have a Genuinely Profound Insight. Something about passion being the rock and the stones are what we make of our lives . . . Help! Help me out!"

Maya laughed. "Don't strain yourself," she said.

"No, no, this is what I came to Nepal for. I want to get my money's worth out of the trip!"

"So is passion the boulder of life, or the wall?" Maya asked. "Is that the question?"

"No," Lonnie said, suddenly serious again. "The question is, how long does passion have to last to make it worth messing up your life for?"

They contemplated the boulder for a while, without speaking. Then they heard footsteps, and Pembila appeared from around the corner, a wide smile on her even-featured face. *"Namaste!"* she greeted them. "I looking for you."

"Debby?" Maya said hopefully. "Is my sister here?"

Pembila shook her head no and smiled kindly at Maya's look of disappointment. "She not come yet. But she will come. Don't worry."

"Ah, Pembila!" Lonnie said. "Maybe you can give us the Sherpa perspective. We were just discussing whether or not passion can last."

Pembila pursed her lips, then smiled again, obviously not understanding a word.

"Let me see, how to explain this," Lonnie said. She stepped closer to Pembila, and held up her right hand. "Man," she said. Pembila nodded. "Woman," she said, holding up her left. Pembila nodded again. "Married," Lonnie said, clasping them together.

"Yes, married."

"Very happy," Lonnie said, gesturing and smiling. "Very in love. Much chickie-chickie!"

"Yes, married, good chickie-chickie!" Pembila agreed. "If man good. Good to wife. Not hit, not shout. Make chickie-chickie. Make baby."

"Right. So, we have a man, a woman, married, happy, much chickie-chickie. Then, time passes. Much time. Still happy, still married, but not so much chickie-chickie?"

"Did anyone ever tell you," Maya asked, "that you have a real gift for communication?"

"It's why I went into the law," Lonnie said. "So—does that happen with Sherpa families?"

Pembila looked puzzled for a moment, and then her face broke into illumination. "Aha!" She drew close to them, almost conspiratorial. "Me, Ang—no chickie-chickie."

"No chickie-chickie?" Lonnie asked.

"No want baby. No chickie-chickie."

"I guess that answers that," Maya said.

"But Pembila, you know there's pills you can take, there's . . . lots of things, so you can have chickie-chickie and not have babies."

"I go to doctor, Khunde," Pembila said. She turned to Maya and smiled. "Sister doctor, Khunde. Then, chickie-chickie. Now, Tenzing say, you want go see Rinpoche?"

"Yes, I do," Maya said. "Very much."

"I'll take a pass," Lonnie said. "I've already had my quota of profundity today."

"Come," Pembila said to Maya. "This way."

Tenzing and Jan were waiting for her outside the entrance to the *gompa*. The others had already had their interview. After a short briefing by Tenzing, they were ushered in to the Rinpoche's study, a small stone room with one glass window facing out on the gorge of the Dudh Kosi River. Another young monk sat in a corner. Maya and Jan prostrated themselves three times as Tenzing had instructed them to do, kneeling down to touch their foreheads to the floor. The monk who accompanied them also bowed, and Maya admired his grace. Well, it was easier for him, she reflected. He had not turned his body into a living drapery pole hung with camera, water bottle, hanging wallet, and pack.

The Rinpoche sat close to them, on a low mattress behind a table piled with books, bottles, plates of candy, and jars full of pens. Around him were piles of rolled scrolls and scarves and boxes and bags, almost obscuring a high glass cabinet full of Buddhas and other holy figures. He had a kind, intelligent face, square and smooth-shaven, and he wore a pair of round black spectacles that gave him a scholarly look.

From her pack, Maya took out a white prayer scarf she had purchased beforehand in Kathmandu. She draped it over her two hands and held it out to him. He nodded, smiled, and took it from her, held it a moment, and handed it to the lama sitting nearby, who placed it in a pile against the wall.

The Rinpoche spoke in Sherpa to the young lama, who handed him an old honey jar from which he spooned a mixture of spices and small dark seeds and larger red seeds. Tenzing held out his hand and motioned to the others to do so. One by one, they each were given a palmful of seeds.

"What do we do with them?" Jan whispered to Tenzing.

"Eat them," he said, smiling, and they did. The seeds tasted of grain and cardamom and scents Maya could not identify.

The Rinpoche spoke again, and the young monk handed him a pile of red threads. He muttered some words over them and handed one to each of the visitors.

"For good luck," Tenzing said. "Do you have any questions for the Rinpoche?"

"I do," Jan said. "Tell him I want more than anything to be an artist, a good artist. I want my work to be filled with spirit, filled with the light. But I feel so earthbound. I can only draw what I see. What should I do?"

Now, if she'd asked me that question, Maya reflected, I would tell her, "Keep drawing, stop thinking. Your hands are wiser than your head." But I'm only a Witch, not a Great Spiritual Leader, and it could be argued that I am Not a Very Nice Person, either.

Maya observed the Rinpoche with interest as Tenzing translated for Jan. He seemed a kind, serene man, and in his presence she felt a sense of calm and peace. But nothing more. No great emotion, no overwhelming power. As a small child, Tenzing had told them, this man had picked out from a pile of clothing the robes of the old monk, Lama Gulu, who had been killed in the earthquake that destroyed Tengpoche in the thirties. He had recognized them as his own, cried until he was given the old Rinpoche's books and begging bowl, and thus proved that he was the latest reincarnation of a long line of masters, a man of power. But he seemed no more than a kindly, scholarly old gentleman.

"I paint," Jan went on. "I do some weaving and some crafts and sculpture. I'm starting to have some success in a small way. I've sold some things to a gallery—oh, why am I saying all this? I'm sure it doesn't mean anything to him. You don't have to translate all of that," she said to Tenzing. "Just say that something is missing. Somehow I feel like I'm not expressing my highest ideals. The things I do are pretty, but not profound."

I could ask him the same question, Maya thought. Am I changing lives, or just providing entertainment?

The Rinpoche was looking at Jan thoughtfully. "Go to the *gompa*," he said when she had finished. She waited expectantly for more, but that was all.

"Maya, would you like to ask something of the Rinpoche?" Tenzing said.

Maya was kneeling, her buttocks resting on her heels, and she shifted her weight off her feet, which were beginning to fall asleep. "Tell him I bring him greetings from those of us in the West who still worship the old Goddess and the Gods that are her consorts. Tell him we are a small people who have been persecuted for a long time and lied about, but now our religion is growing again. And that I am happy and honored to be here."

She waited while Tenzing translated. The Rinpoche looked at her curiously, and then spoke.

"He asks if your religion is Christian," Tenzing told her.

"No," she said, stung by the question. Christian! Hadn't he understood what she was saying? But of course not, probably to him all westerners were Christian by definition. Maybe "Christian" simply meant "religion of the round-eyes," and for all he knew, Goddess worshipers were simply another subsect, like Holy Rollers or Anabaptists. "Our religion is much older than Christianity. In fact, the Christians tried to wipe us out, branded us Witches, burned us at the stake. They still don't like us much."

She wriggled her legs out from under her as Tenzing translated, and the Rinpoche nodded. But did he really understand, or was he simply nodding, as people do, to be polite? she wondered, as she folded her legs up into a cross-legged sitting position. She seemed to take up a lot of space in this small room. If she squirmed around much more, she'd knock over the Rinpoche's pride and joy, a small electric heater hooked up to the new minihydro plant.

"Do you have a question for him?" Tenzing asked.

If only she could talk to him, one-on-one, without mediation or interference, if only they could chat, spiritual leader to spiritual leader, like. Hey, Rinpoche, have you ever felt burned out? she would ask. Does it ever happen that when people come and ask and ask and ask from you, that you feel dried up? Empty? Like you have nothing to give? What do you do, then? Do you ever go through the motions? Are you sitting there, bored, thinking, I'll just tell her to go to the *gompa,* now there's a harmless piece of advice, can't hurt and it might do some good?

Do the powers ever stop speaking to you?

But she couldn't ask him that. Not through Tenzing, anyway. No, she would have to explain herself before she could ask him anything worth asking, as she always had to explain herself. Her lifelong penalty for doing it different.

"Tell him during the times of persecution the lineage of our teachers was broken. Tell him we have lost our own elders. And so now, those of us who are called to be leaders have to take on great spiritual responsibility, sometimes very young. Ask if he has any words of guidance for me."

The Rinpoche gave her what she might have described in writing as a long, thoughtful look. But if I were being honest, Maya said to herself, I would say he looked bored. Deeply bored. But maybe that's just my assumption. Maybe he's just not fulfilling my expectations. He spoke to the young monk again and handed her a small plastic-coated card with a badly printed picture on it of the Green Tara. She held it in her hand and looked at it. Tara was as close as the Buddhists got to a Goddess, she knew. The figure had one foot extended; she was spirit moving into the world of form.

"He says he will pray for you," Tenzing said.

The interview was over. They prostrated themselves and left, to make way for the next group of seekers.

"We will go upstairs to the *gompa*," Tenzing said.

"Good," Jan said. "That's what he told me to do."

Maya was pondering the Rinpoche's message to her. Was she supposed to meditate on the Green Tara, or was the card merely a souvenir? Why had he said so little, not really answering her question at all? Did he mean that she was on the right path, that she didn't need any guidance, only a little boost from his prayers? Or did he mean that she was so far gone only divine intervention could help her? Or was he, indeed, simply bored?

Or had he answered on some deeper level, sent forth some emanation she hadn't been aware of? Was it some lack in her, that she didn't come away all starry eyed like the clumps of westerners she saw waiting on the steps? Maybe she just didn't get it, maybe it was a deficiency in her, like color blindness, or just a resistance to men in power. Where were the women, anyway? Didn't any nuns head up monasteries?

From the *gompa*, they could hear wonderful, promising sounds: drums and trumpets and the clash of bells. They went upstairs, removed their shoes again, prostrated, and entered.

The *gompa* was a whirl of color and sound and pattern. Every surface was painted with floral patterns and deities and Buddhas and nagas, with tonguelike shapes and swirls and wheels and tantric symbols. Hanging banners and tankas swayed gently in the air. Down the center were two rows of low tables, behind which sat monks, cross-legged, reading from texts and chanting in eerie, minor keys. They reminded Maya of the old men in her grandfather's synagogue, during those trips to Milwaukee for the High Holidays. She remembered being restless, chafing in a new starched pink dress as the service droned on. But here the droning was suddenly interrupted as all the monks picked up hand bells, the resonant bronze bells whose notes echoed through the hall with harmonics and overtones. They began to play, with a great ringing and crashing. The long trumpets came in, then a burst of percussion, drums, and cymbals. Then suddenly it stopped; the monks returned to their chanting.

Maya found a place by the wall where she could sit and listen and observe. The front wall was made of glass cabinets, their windows painted with great color and detail. In each sat a statue of Buddha or a Rinpoche or Tara, made of gold, silver, or bronze. On a side altar stood conical offerings made of barley and butter and sugar, decorated with flat, wheel-like forms like giant buttons in bright fluorescent colors.

Jan squatted next to Maya. They sat for a long time, letting the sound wash over them. Maya basked in the energy, the color, the play of form. I need to open, she thought. I need to let myself take in whatever is around me to take.

Maya glanced over at Jan and noticed she had tears in her eyes.

"The Rinpoche was right," she whispered to Maya. "He was so right. This is exactly what I needed."

At last Tenzing motioned to them, and they sidled out, reclaiming their shoes.

"Thank you," Maya said to him as they walked out. "Thank you for taking us."

"My pleasure." He smiled. "It is always good for me to see the Rinpoche."

"You haven't heard any word about my sister, have you?" Maya asked.

"Perhaps she will not come today," Tenzing said. "There was an accident in Khumjung this morning, I hear. A stone wall fell on the men building it. I think she is needed there."

Maya's face fell.

"Maybe she will come tomorrow," Tenzing said. "Yes, I am sure she will. And if not, then the next day we go to Khunde anyway, where the clinic is. Don't worry."

"I'm not worried, just a bit disappointed," Maya said. "I'd hoped we could be here at Tengpoche together." So that we could do a ritual for Betty, lay her ashes down in sight of the Goddess Mother of the Universe and in that one great gesture expiate all our sins, make up for all our failures and abandonments, and lay her spirit to rest.

"Maybe tomorrow," Tenzing said. "We will see." He said good-bye to them and went off to take care of some business of his own.

Maya and Jan walked back to the camp together. The sun had set, and the plateau was shrouded in the darkness of the mist, which concealed the stars. Only a glow in the east told them that the moon must be rising.

Jan sniffed. "I'm so glad we did that," she said in a soft, awed voice. "That was so powerful for me. Was it for you?"

"I don't know," Maya said, not wanting to blight Jan's experience with her own doubts. "I guess time will tell. But what happened for you?"

Jan sniffed and Maya fished a tissue out of her pocket to hand to her. "I sat there in the *gompa*," Jan said, "surrounded by all that color and sound and richness of detail, and I realized how much I hold myself back. In my art, in my life. I never want to give everything, never surrender myself completely. It's like I think that if I let out all the color and life and spirit in me, I'd lose it. But they don't think like that. They pull out all the stops, for everything, for odd little surfaces nobody will ever see. And it's so alive!''

"But I love what you do," Maya said. "Your work is graceful and subtle.''

"But it's not strong.''

"Its spareness is its strength.''

Jan shook her head. "It's not what it could be. Will be. This trip is going to change me.''

"Just promise me," Maya said, "that you won't start drawing rainbows and sunsets and Buddha figures surrounded by light. Keep drawing what you see.''

"But what I see is so limited compared to what I can imagine.''

"Not at all," Maya said. "It's just the opposite. What we can imagine is never as rich as what we can actually see.''

Lonnie, Carolyn, and Peter were gathered in the meal tent, where the kitchen boys had set out cups and thermoses of tea. Jan and Maya pulled up folding camp stools and joined them, grateful for the warmth and light.

"Do you have any Tylenol?" Howard asked, poking his head into the tent.

His face was mottled red and white, his eyes were ringed by lines of strain, his mouth frozen into a grimace.

"What's wrong?" Maya asked. "You look awful.''

"Just a headache," Howard said. "Probably the altitude." He coughed, a dry, rasping sound. "And I think I'm catching your cold.''

Carolyn and Peter exchanged worried glances. "Howard, those are symptoms of mountain sickness," Peter said. "Have you told Tenzing?''

"I'll be okay. I'll just take a couple of tablets and lie down. If someone can lend me a couple of Tylenol, aspirin . . . anything like that.''

"I have Tylenol with codeine, for emergencies, but I don't know if it's a good idea to take it if you might have altitude sickness," Lonnie said.

"Definitely not," Peter said. "Codeine depresses breathing.''

"I've got some regular Tylenol," Jan said. "I'll get it." She got up and left the tent.

Howard's whole aura was gray and cloudy. Maya felt an urge to work on him, to rub his head and shift his energy in the ways she had learned. It was like an itch, like the instinctive urge to straighten a crookedly hung picture. Sometimes she could heal. Not often—the *curandera* she had met in Mexico told her she did not have a great talent for it, but every now and then, when the impulse came to her, she wondered if the *curandera* might not have been wrong.

This was as good a place as any to try, she told herself, here in the middle of these mountains where magic was commonplace and everyone believed in miracles. And maybe this was the guru's answer, the next challenge set in her path.

But was it wise to encourage Howard in any way?

Still, she hated to see him looking miserable, missing his adventure. No, much as he irritated her when he was lively and well, she couldn't stand to see him weak and vulnerable. Suddenly she was flooded with pity, which she resisted. Howard, buck up, perk up, be strong again so I can scorn you and feel superior. Don't make me feel for you, don't make me imagine you carried down the mountain, sent home to admit to the guys back at LK that your one adventure ended in failure.

"Sit down, Howard," she said. "Sometimes I can cure a headache. I'll rub your neck a bit."

Eagerly, Howard took a seat, pulling a stool up beside Maya as she turned hers to face his back. Lonnie raised one eyebrow at Maya, and Maya gave just the suggestion of a shrug. She began to dig her fingers into the muscles at the base of Howard's neck. They were thick and ropy. For a deskbound computer whiz, he was quite well built.

"Ah, that feels good," Howard said happily.

"You're strong, Howard. Got a lot of muscle tone. You work out?"

"LK has a company gym. I try to get there at least three days a week."

"It shows."

"People die from altitude sickness," Peter was saying as he reached for a plate of cookies. "A few each year. It could be quite serious."

"Peter, you're so encouraging," Carolyn said.

"It's true. It's something to think about."

"Yeah, but it takes a few days, at least," Lonnie said, taking the plate from Peter and helping herself to a ginger snap. "You don't get a headache and then drop dead fifteen minutes later."

"I hope not!" Howard said fervently.

"Some people do," Peter countered. "I read it in the guidebook. When the runway was open at Syangboche, up at the Everest View Hotel, they had a number of incidents where people got off the plane and dropped dead. Pulmonary embolism."

"Peter, stop it," Carolyn said.

"Stop what? Those are facts. I'm not making up ghost stories to scare us all. I'm talking about reality, here."

Maya was beginning to feel her fingers grow warm. The pain, the thick miasma of subtle fluids collecting in Howard's brain, felt like gray dough collecting on her hands, and as discreetly as she could, she flicked it off, onto the ground. She ran her fingers through the energy collected around the crown of his head, not touching him, just combing through the subtle layers, grabbing the stuck energy, flicking it off. Howard shivered.

"Ooh," he said. "A chill ran up my spine."

"That's good," Maya said. "It means the energy is moving." And it was, she could feel it. Her hands were as warm as those packets of Instant Heat she had bought at the co-op.

If she could heal Howard, she wondered, why couldn't she always heal? Or if not always, at least with some consistency? And why did she feel this mixture of trepidation and reluctance? As if she were comforted by believing she had no power of this sort. Oh, she taught a hundred different exercises for learning to feel energy and sense it and name it and project it, and that was all right as a game, the Witch's party trick, feel an aura with a pendulum and make it spin—but on some deeper level, she hesitated. Her reluctance was like a thin film sliding between her and her power, the same screen that slipped between her and Johanna, walling away her passion.

But if she claimed this power, if she called herself a healer, she would have to answer Betty's charge: "What good is it to have a daughter who's a Witch if you can't do anything for me?"

"I'll try, Mom," Maya had offered, while thinking to herself, What good is it to have a daughter who's a doctor if she's off in Nepal when you need her? Why don't you ask that question?

But she had held her tongue, because her mother needed her support, not another fight about all the unresolved issues of their life together. They were in Betty's bedroom, shortly after the pain in her legs was diagnosed as bone cancer. Maya was perched on the edge of Betty's bed, while on TV Oprah interviewed women who assaulted their husbands. "Can we turn it off?"

"Go ahead. It's giving me a headache, anyway. All this pseudo-psychology, public confession stuff. Nothing but trash. I should have written my book, gone on those shows. What do you think? Do you think I could have been on Oprah Winfrey?"

"Who's to say?" Maya said cheerfully. "Who's to say you won't be."

"I won't be. I used to hope you'd be on, sometime. That's why I watch, really. I like to imagine you up there. But I don't suppose they interview Witches."

"Not in the way I want to be interviewed, not on Oprah, anyway," Maya said. "I don't want to be on with Dr. Hoodoo Voodoo, get you any man you want for nine hundred dollars, and the Witch Queen of New Orleans."

"What?"

"That was her last year's Halloween show. I'd like to be on with some serious feminist authors, but she doesn't seem to do those anymore. Anyway, lie down and relax, and I'll work on you." Maya picked up the remote and clicked off the TV.

Betty nestled down into her covers, and sighed. "Will this hurt?"

"No. Let me just move these covers back, to get to your leg. Can you lie on your side, so I can reach your spine? Is that comfortable for you? Good. Take some deep breaths. Now, I want you to imagine your leg feeling good again. There's no pain, you feel relaxed, at ease."

Betty was silent for a long moment, lying still, breathing quietly.

"I can't," she said finally. "I can't imagine it feeling good."

"Can you remember a time when it felt good?"

"No. I can't remember."

Maya let her hands travel over Betty's spine, down her thigh, feeling the energy like caked and throbbing mud. She began to work through it, raking it with her hands, breathing power into them. But she could only do so much alone. Betty had to be roused to help.

"What about when you were a kid?" Maya suggested. "You told me how you used to play kick the can, and your aunt Sadie would yell at you in Yiddish to stop."

"I was only ten when I got my period," Betty said. "She'd yell in Yiddish, 'Oy, Betty, stop running—you're a woman already!' Embarrassed the hell out of me."

"So how did you feel when you were running, before she'd start to yell at you?"

"I felt like I could fall."

Maya let out a long breath, trying to keep impatience out of her voice. "Betty, you're not helping. You've got to try."

"Try! I am trying! You want to know how I felt, I felt fat and awkward and clumsy and big as a house. That's how I felt."

Now Betty was sitting up, tense and angry, and Maya's hands had dropped away, losing whatever power they might have started to convey. This wasn't working. She must be patient with Betty. Maya took a long, deep breath herself.

"Okay. Let's try another tack. Just lie back down, relax again, take some more deep breaths. Good. Now, did you ever have a fantasy about your legs feeling good, feeling good in your body?"

"A fantasy? Yes, I used to imagine myself as a ballerina."

"Good, that's good." Maya let her hands travel over Betty's aura again, soothing and smoothing, trying to imagine Betty as slim and lithe—which she had never been. But she had been pretty, round faced, and plump in those early photos in the album, the little black-and-white ones taken before the war. How sad, really, that she had never loved her body, never felt strong and graceful and free. "Let yourself go into that fantasy now. See yourself dancing around, pirouetting, leaping high into the air and landing, as light as a feather. Breathe into that feeling. Let it fill you. Breathe it down into your leg, into your sore hip. Now, is there a color you can identify with that feeling?"

"Yes," Betty said in a soft voice. "I can see a color."

"What color?"

"White."

"White, that's good. What shade, what particular color of white?"

"Oh, a dirty white. Like a used tutu."

Howard let out little groans of satisfaction as Maya squeezed and pummeled his sturdy neck. She seemed to be having better results with him, but then, he wanted to be well. And Betty? It was hard to say. Surely she hadn't wanted to suffer like that, to die in so much pain. What she'd wanted was to be special and to be taken care of. Suddenly Maya was so sad she wanted to squat in a corner and cry. She removed her hands from Howard's neck, shook them out.

"You're done," she said.

"Thanks, that was great."

"Here's the Tylenol," Jan said, returning.

"Do you think I should take it?" Howard asked Maya.

She scooted her chair farther away from him. "Once there was a Zen master," she said, "who was asked what the secret of enlightenment was. And he said, 'Eat when you're hungry, sleep when you're tired.'"

"Huh?" Howard said.

"'And for a headache, take an aspirin,'" Lonnie chimed in. "'Or a Tylenol is equally good. And when you have menstrual cramps, try an Advil.'"

"Hopefully Howard doesn't," Peter said.

"You never know," Lonnie said. "Altitude does funny things."

Maya lay on her back in her sleeping bag. Dinner was over, she had peed outside in the cold and undressed in the warmth of her tent, and now she lay on her back, letting her go-to-bed coughing spasm subside. Really, her lungs seemed to be getting worse. They hurt now when she was lying down, not just when she was walking uphill. Maybe she should try out her curative powers on herself. Surely here, with the power of the great mountains around her, on this shelf of land impregnated with all those monastic prayers, she should be able to find some healing.

She sighed. Steadying her breathing, she began a slow descent into trance. Down, down, down a pillar of light, like Alice down the rabbit hole, down into that internal place she thought of as her place of power. In her mind's eye, she looked to the four directions. In the east, the coastal mountains rose in dry bands. To the south, they curved and held the small valley of her place in a bowl. To the west, the breakers of the Pacific rolled across a long, white shore. To the north, the beach stretched, beckoning. In the center, a small stream made a clear, still pool. Maya squatted by the pool, waiting. She enjoyed squatting in trance because in the physical world her tendons weren't long enough and she balanced precariously on her toes and fell over. The astral had many advantages over the physical. On the other hand, there were some real-life, physical experiences that could not be replaced by imagination. Sex, for one. Her teacher Sylvia had always sung the praises of astral sex, but Maya herself had always found it a rather abstracted flash of orgasm, more like being bombarded with a burst of light than. . . .

But she was losing focus. Concentrate. Look at the pool, at the clarity of the waters, and wait, wait for someone to come. Yes, there was a presence on the other side of the pool. A woman. An old woman. Perhaps it was the Crone, the Reaper herself, come to offer advice. Look up, now, slowly, slowly. The figure was robed in black, smoky black that curled and danced in wraithlike plumes around her. She was leaning on a stick. Now up, up to her face.

Which was covered in pancake makeup, slashed by a bloodred mouth drawn with too much lipstick, crowned by a blue-silver cap of hair sprayed into place. Like someone in a beauty parlor in lower Beverly Hills, not Rodeo Drive but something down around Pico Boulevard.

"Oh, for Goddess' sake, who are you?" Maya asked.

"I'm a beautician. What do you want?"

"Want? I want healing. I want wisdom. I want just a touch of exotica to justify dragging my tail up and down these mountains."

"What's the matter, you don't like my hairstyle?"

"Couldn't I have a monk? I don't ask for the Goddess, I don't ask for Tara or a devi or deva or even a Rinpoche, just a simple, low-level monk. Female, preferably. Other people get monks, Indians, shamans, enlightened masters. Why do I get a beautician? I don't need my hair done, I need my lungs reconstituted."

"Monks, shmonks. If it's not the Tibetans with you, it's the Celts or the Schmelts or the Hopi prophecies. You're a Jew, you know."

"So next you'll be telling me I need a good internist?"

The Beautician placed a hand on her hip and looked sternly at Maya.

"Do you or do you not have a bottle of penicillin tablets with you, for emergencies?"

"I do."

"So what kind of emergency are you waiting for? You're sick, you have medicine. Take it. Take it!"

Then she was gone. Sighing, Maya brought herself back out of trance and reached for her medical kit and her water bottle. She downed two pills. Then she flicked on her flashlight, and opened her journal.

Dear Rio,

  This is not a letter I will ever send. I just want to say, for the record, that you're not the only one who ever abandoned me. No, I've been dumped by better than you—by the great powers themselves, by the Goddess incarnate, discarnate and excarnate, whatever the hell that means. But I know what it means. It means that some essential part of myself has gone Missing in Action. I don't know why.

  Or maybe it's just not appearing in the forms I expect, or want to see.

  But it's not fair, really, to cast you as the Great Abandoner. You'd be the first to point that out to me. After all, who sent me a letter six years ago that I never answered?

  And what was it you said in your last letter? That my memory carries more weight for you than yours does for me? I'm not sure that's true. Sometimes it feels like your memory is a stone I've carried around my neck all these years, bowing me down.

  Sometimes it feels like your memory is a trampoline. I've jumped on it, tried to stomp it into the ground, but all that happens is I bounce off and fly.

  And sometimes it feels like your memory is a boomerang. Try as hard as I can to hurl it away, it keeps on coming back.

        Maya

21

October 1968

On a warm day in late October, maybe the last really warm day before winter, Maya had spread out her Tarot cards on the steps in front of Sproul Hall. Almost two months had passed since Rio abandoned her on the coast, and she was getting used to being without him. Most nights she stayed in a big communal house on Grove Street, where the living room was always full of wall-to-wall strangers, travelers, like her, making a small sojourn. Often someone would cook up a huge pot of rice and beans, enough to feed the multitudes. Other nights she would spend her small earnings on pizza or cheap Chinese food she bought on Telegraph Avenue. She dreamed of traveling, of heading north to Canada, or out to the country, or down to New Mexico. But she stayed, never quite giving up the forlorn hope that Rio would return. She was lonely, but that suited her. Somehow it seemed to her that she had always been lonely, had always, deep inside herself, been an orphan child with no home of her own. Now at last the outside corresponded to the inside. She felt strong, although when she contemplated the rains of winter, she found herself shivering. She would have to go somewhere. She would have to move on.

To amuse herself while waiting for customers, she pulled a card at random from the deck. The one that came to hand was the Knight of Wands, a card she'd always associated with Rio.

"Would you read for me?" someone asked. She looked up.

Rio stood looking down, planted on the sidewalk as if he were a natural feature of the neighborhood, something rooted as a tree that could never wander away and get lost. He had cut his hair so that it curled slightly around his collar. His beard had grown out, full and bushy, and he hadn't yet lost his summer tan. Maya was suddenly aware that she hadn't had a bath in three days, that her jeans were torn and ragged past the point of radical chic, that she didn't look good. She didn't know what to say to him. She wanted to throw herself into his arms and she wanted to scream at him. Instead, she shuffled the cards.

"What do you want to know?"

"I lost the woman I love," he said. "I want to know if she'll come back to me."

"Why did you leave her?" Maya asked, pulling a card and laying it down. It was the Death card.

"My father died," he said, squatting down beside her. "He killed himself. I found out suddenly, when I called home from LA. I had to go back to be with my mother, and I didn't have any way to let the woman I love know. I thought I'd only be gone for a few days. I thought she'd wait for me."

"Maybe she did," Maya said. "Why didn't you go back to her?" She laid out a second card. The Eight of Wands, reversed. Bad news, complications.

"Once I got home, I couldn't get away as quick as I thought. My mother wouldn't let me go—I thought she was going to have a seizure. My younger brother ran off and enlisted in the Marines. I called my lover's best friend in LA. I even called her mother. She didn't contact either of them. When I got back a week later, she was gone."

"Maybe the sheriff ran her off," Maya said, "and she couldn't stay any longer."

"Why didn't she contact any of our friends, in the city?"

"Maybe she did at first, and they hadn't heard from you. Maybe she didn't like feeling that she was trying to hunt you down. Maybe she thought you'd just gotten tired of her, and split."

"I can't believe she would think that," Rio said. "Do you?"

For an answer, she pulled another card. It was the Six of Cups, reversed, a childlike trust that was broken.

"Maybe she didn't know what to think."

"What do *you* think? Can she ever forgive me and come back to me?"

"Do you love her?"

"I love her," he said, taking her hand and then reaching across the cards to kiss her. "God, Maya, I've been so worried about you."

"Me too," she said. "I didn't know if you were alive or dead."

They clung together until the wind began to scatter the cards. She gathered them up and slipped them back into the velvet bag she had embroidered for them long ago, before she left home. On the top of the deck, she placed the Lovers.

Rio had returned to Maya, nevertheless she felt he had betrayed her in a fundamental way. He'd gone back to school. He had actually returned to Berkeley, to the poli-sci major he'd taken a leave of absence from two years back.

"Why?" she'd asked him. They were lying together on the big mattress he had placed underneath the sunny window of his one-room apartment in a converted garage behind a rambling old wooden house in the Berkeley flatlands. They'd made love until late in the night and again in the morning sun that poured hot and liquid over their naked bodies. Curled up in his arms, she was home. She felt sheltered, loved, protected. Yet in some subtler way, he had left her alone on the edge. "Why would you do that?"

"Why not? My old man's dead—that means the government'll give me Social Security money if I'm in school for the next couple of years. It beats working." Rio stretched languidly and smiled at her.

"Since when have you even considered working?"

He rolled over and propped himself on one elbow. "Maya, the street scene is getting heavy. It's not what it was a year ago, two years ago. There's smack coming in from Vietnam, and Mafia types running it. I want to get out while I still feel clean. This is a way. And besides, I have to do it to keep the draft board off my neck."

She couldn't argue with him, couldn't insist that he live his life to justify her own decisions. Still she felt that he had lied to her, not by anything he had said but by presenting himself in a certain light. Her working-class outlaw hero had a nearly straight-A record.

"You were serious, when I thought you were bullshitting my mother about law school!" she accused him. "You meant it!"

He reached over and stroked her hair. "Would that be so awful?" he asked. "Would you stop loving me if I went to law school? Maybe I could end up doing something good."

"Right. You'll be the great radical lawyer, battling injustice."

"Why not? There's a lot of shit in this world, Maya. You can only smoke so much of it. Some of it you've just got to fight any way you can. Like your dad does."

She moved away from him. "Don't. Don't do it. Don't turn into my father."

"Is he so awful?" Rio pulled his hand back. "Would you rather have me turn into *my* father?" The bitterness in his voice scared Maya.

"I'm sorry." She reached a hand over to him, but he rolled over and turned his back.

"I don't understand you, Maya. Don't you love me? Or are you just in love with some image of who you think I ought to be?"

"I do love you."

He shook his head against the pillow. "I don't think you do. I wouldn't care if *you* went to school. I'd love you if you weighed three hundred pounds or if you broke both legs and could never walk again."

"It's just that we swore we'd never buy into the lies."

He turned over onto his back. Maya could see his face again, but he looked up at the water stain on the ceiling, not at her. "I'm not buying into them."

"But you're playing the game."

"Yeah, but I know it's a game. That's the difference." Now he turned to look at her. "It's one thing for you to say you'll never play the game. Look at where you come from. But for me, I'd be the first person in my whole screwed-up family to play without striking out. Maybe I want to do that—just to prove I can."

"You don't have to prove anything to me." Maya reached out her hand to touch him, but he looked away again.

"I don't have to prove anything to anybody. But maybe I want to. Maybe I want to prove it to myself."

Still he took her hand and lay still, pressing it against his chest. After a moment he went on.

"Anyway, I'm playing a game right now. It's called Dope Dealer. I'm running a goddamned business, like any other business. Only it's getting uglier than most. Is that what you want me to be, a business-man?"

She didn't answer. She was no longer clear what she was arguing about. What she had devoted her life to was slippery. It kept changing, shape-shifting, just as she thought she'd finally grasped it. Perhaps what she was trying so hard to hold was only the shed skin of something that was already slithering away somewhere deeper in the wilderness. Maybe she should go back to school; maybe Johanna and her mother were right. She could have gone to Columbia, been part of the spring uprising, let Joe organize a Faculty Committee of Support in her defense. But when she pictured herself sitting at a desk, even one in the occupied office of the president, she felt trapped. No, she would continue to give herself to the street, and the road, and the wind. She would make revolution her own way.

Rio began to read. He brought home books from his classes on history, anthropology, mythology. They piled up in the one-room apartment, spilling off the shelves of simple boards balanced on bricks. When he finished his books, Maya picked them up and read them, to keep him company and have something to talk about. Often she went with him to class, feeling years older than the bright-faced young girls who flung their clean, long hair out of their eyes and asked ingenuous questions of the professors. Maya never asked questions—she felt too much the inter-loper, the illegal alien.

Rio continued to abandon her in subtle ways. Not so much by anything he did or said, but by his omissions. He wouldn't talk to her about his father's death. "That's over with, now." He no longer wanted to drop acid. Instead, he had begun to drink. Not much, a few beers after school, a couple of sixpacks on the weekends. Just enough so it became a liquid film that slid between them, keeping their skin a few millimeters apart. Funny, she thought, how marijuana and hash and acid had seemed to open something for them, not close it off, but she began to question even that. When they smoked together, he seemed to retreat into himself, going far away from her. She was smoking less herself, now that he was dealing only in small quantities, to a few trusted friends. Marijuana had changed, too. The new crop was stronger, harsher. It seemed to push the world away, instead of opening her to magic.

Something was wrong. Rio watched TV now. The nightly news brought them scenes of war, battles in the jungles and in the streets. Big-eyed children stared from the newspaper, holding out the ravaged flesh of a burned limb, lips stretched in soundless screams. Rio said they should have gone to Chicago for the Democratic convention—he called the time on the coast a waste. His brother Jim sent him letters from Vietnam filled with justifications and bravado. Rio spent long evenings writing him back, mailing leaflets from antiwar groups describing the torture practiced by the Americans. Tiger cages, pits where the prisoners could neither stand nor lie nor sit, napalm, defoliants eating the life of the jungle. Late at night, he kept the TV on, watching the news, beer in hand to ease the tension as he strained to read the features on the broken bodies of the American boys they were plucking from the ruined fields and shipping home in bags.

Somehow, during the dreamtime year since Maya had left home, the world had grown not more open, but harder-edged, uglier. Martin Luther King had been shot. She remembered watching the news footage of the March on Washington, curled up with Johanna in front of the Weavers' TV as Martin Luther King made his speech. "I have a dream." King's voice had thundered over the speakers, and Marian's eyes were misty as she told them, "This is a historical moment. Listen to the man, and don't you ever forget his words."

I haven't forgotten, Maya thought, and the struggle still goes on, but some phase of it was ended. The belief in the expanded possibilities of love was dead. Downed by a bullet on a Memphis balcony, murdered by the gun that shot Robert Kennedy at his own victory party, bloodied by the clubs of the Chicago police, teargassed, bombarded with napalm and white phosphorus and fragmentation bombs, defoliated by Agent Orange.

Could she stay as open to all this as she once had been to wind and water and rock? When she tried, she felt a pain that nothing seemed to ease, like the chemicals that clung to flesh and burned down to the bone. Yet the pain was mixed with her private pain, the ashes of her fear. That she had made a vast mistake with her life. That Rio would leave again.

That he would stop wanting her altogether. And what good did her pain and her sympathy do those whose skin and blood and muscle were really, at that very moment, burning?

An image from TV news was etched in her brain. A woman was on fire, running, mouth agape, flames dancing around her, a child burning in her arms. She seemed to haunt Maya, appearing on the street out of the corner of her eye, streaking through her dreams.

Two days after Nixon's inauguration, Rio received a phone call from his mother. His brother Jim's helicopter had been shot down in Vietnam. His body had been recovered, and the fragments were being shipped home to Pittsburgh.

"Jim's dead," he said to Maya, turning from the phone, and walking out of the door without another word. Half an hour later he returned, with a fifth of Scotch, sat down, and poured them each a glass full.

"We're going to have a wake," he said. "Drink up, babe."

"I'm sorry, Rio," Maya said. "I'm so sorry."

"Here's to Jim," Rio said, raising his glass, his eyes masked from her. "Another asshole victim of the American dream."

Maya raised her glass, and sipped, but whiskey tasted like paint thinner to her, and she set it down. She slid an arm around his shoulder.

"I'm sorry," she said again. "I'm sorry he's dead."

Rio downed a large swallow of the liquor, and then another. She could see the glaze settle over his features, and he seemed to sink away from her.

"The fuckers killed him," he said.

Then he drank some more.

Maya felt miserable. She felt bad for Rio's brother but also, as the liquor in the bottle diminished rapidly, she mostly felt afraid. She put her arm around his shoulder but she felt she was caressing a stone.

"I'm sorry," she said one more time, feeling stupid but not knowing what else to say.

"It's too much. First my dad, then Jim. Who's next, I want to know?"

She felt a little squirrelly sense of alarm deep in her stomach.

"Are you going to fly back to Pittsburgh?" she asked, trying to sound normal.

He turned to her, his eyes glazed on the surface but hot underneath, like nuclear fission viewed through a protective screen. She had never seen him look like that before.

"Fly-y-y!" he said, drawing the word out as if it had some deep, inner significance. "You think I can fly?"

"Rio, are you okay?"

"Fly, fly away."

He stood up suddenly, pushing away from her roughly. "Jim could fly," he said. "But the fuckers shot him down. Out of the sky—bye, bye!"

"Rio, you're scaring me!"

"Oh, I'm scaring you! No, sweet baby—I don't want to scare you. I want—dancing! Dancing for Jim! You dance with me?"

"Sure," Maya said, thinking maybe it would sober him up a little bit. She felt numb, somehow, as if what was happening was going on somewhere else, with someone else. Rio turned on the radio, which began to blast out rock and roll. He grabbed her in a clumsy ballroom grasp and swung her roughly around the room. Faster and faster they spun, banging into the walls and knocking cups off tables and books off the shelves.

"Please, be careful—you're hurting me." She was more than scared, now, she was terrified, as the room whirled around her and his eyes glowed like shaded spotlights. They seemed so big to her, she wanted to look away from them, and yet she couldn't seem to turn her face. She was hypnotized, like a rabbit before the oncoming lights of a car.

"No, no hurting! Dancing!" The radio was blaring a commercial but Rio was dancing to music he alone could hear. He slammed her roughly into the doorjamb that led to the bathroom and she broke away from him, crying.

"Don't cry, sweet baby! Dancing!"

"No, I don't want to. You're hurting me!"

"No, dancing!" Rio spun around by himself, slamming the back of his head roughly into the frame of the door.

"Who did that?" He turned suddenly, advancing on the door and into the bathroom, where he caught sight of his own reflection in the mirror. "Aha! You fucker! I knew I'd find you. Don't you look at me like that!"

He made a face at his reflection.

"Ugly fucker!" Rio snarled, and plunged his fist into the mirror. It shattered, sending streaks of light dancing over the walls and ceiling.

"Fuck you!" Rio cried and smashed it again. His fist was bleeding and he wiped the back of his hand across his mouth, smearing blood over his face, and then hit the broken shards with his bleeding hand and smashed them underfoot.

I should stop him, Maya was thinking. What's wrong with me? Why am I just standing here, letting him hurt himself? But she couldn't seem to move, or think of anything to do.

"Kill the fuckers!" Rio was roaring, flailing his arms and whirling around. He knocked into the rod that held the shower curtain, and it crashed to the floor. Turning again, he grabbed it like a lance, charging out of the bathroom trailing the plastic behind him, smeared with blood.

He charged into the room where Maya waited. She retreated to the corner, to the mattress that served as their bed. He's gone mad, she thought, and I'm huddling here, cowering from him, but the thought seemed unreal. He swung the pole, shattering the light fixture and knocking a pile of books off the dresser. Holding it over his head, he advanced on the telephone, bringing it down with a loud yell as he shattered the plastic casing. Because she did not know what else to do, Maya began to cry.

Rio heard her sobbing, dropped the pole, and came to her.

"You're crying," he said. "You're crying for Jim." He took her face in his hands, tenderly. She could feel them, slippery with blood, and as he stroked her cheek a shard of broken glass left a red trail.

She wasn't crying for Jim, she was crying for Rio, and herself, and the black bottomless void where she spun, suddenly, with nothing to hold to. He kissed the tears on her eyelids, and Maya began to shake as he put his arms around her. If he would only open his eyes and look at her with his sane soul looking out. If only her arms around his shoulders could soak up his pain. His hands were streaked with blood and shards of glass. When he touched her he left wounds, scratches, stains. "Don't cry," he said again and again, as she sobbed against his shoulder until the long night passed.

When Maya woke in the morning, Rio was lying next to her, stretched out straight on his back, his body rigid, his eyes fixed on the ceiling where he had knocked a hole the night before. She felt terrible. She ached from the inside out. Like napalm in reverse, she thought, burning from the bone outward, or as if she had swallowed the stuff and it had scorched an ash-filled hollow in her center. Around them was all the evidence of destruction, smears of blood, shards of glass, but he was still there, still alive. She turned to him and her fear dissolved and leaked away. He looked so miserable.

"I want to die," he said. She shared the sentiment, but nevertheless leaned over and kissed him. He turned his head away.

"It'll be all right, Rio," she said, although she had no reason to think it would.

"I'm just like my dad," he said. "Leave me. Go away."

"Rio, you're just hungover."

"No, I'm not. I'm telling you, I'm like my dad. The drunken fucking bastard."

"What are you talking about?"

"The smartest thing he ever did was to do himself in. Get away from me, Maya. Save yourself."

"Don't be stupid, Rio. I love you."

"Then you're a fool."

She couldn't lie there and feel this bad forever, so she got up, made coffee, swept up broken glass, scrubbed stains off the walls. Rio lay, unmoving. All she had to do, she thought, was to clean everything up, repair it, remove the evidence. Then they could go back to the way they were before. She scrubbed off bloodstains, rehung the rod to the shower curtain, and took a shower. She bundled up clothes and sheets and towels for the laundry. She made soup. All the while she was holding herself together, as if her self were an overcoat she clenched tightly to cover a gaping wound. Still he lay in silence.

The house was cleaner than it had been in weeks. She had thrown out the smashed telephone and the broken china. The room was filled with good smells, food cooking, the odor of nurture. Except for the holes in the plaster, and the empty mirror frames, nobody could tell that anything had happened. And so maybe it hadn't—or maybe it was just as easy to go on as if it hadn't, because even if it had, she thought, it was only once. And he was drunk. And his brother was dead. If he would only get up, stop lying there like that, like someone she didn't know, a stranger inhabiting a familiar body.

"Rio, please, eat something," she said, bringing a mug of soup over to the bed where he lay.

He shook his head. "Leave me alone."

"Please."

His eyes were fixed on the ceiling, away from her. "Maya, my dad spent his life getting raving drunk and knocking my mother and the rest of us around. Until Jim got big enough to beat the fucker up."

"I know." She was still holding the soup and she didn't know where to put it and she didn't know what to say, not really.

"I swore I'd never be like him. But I am. I can feel it in me, wanting to come out. Get away from me, Maya. Save yourself."

Maya put the soup down on the floor and turned to him, touching his face with her hand. "Rio, you didn't hurt me last night."

"You're a liar."

"No, I'm not!"

"Your face was bloody."

"That was just a scratch. More your blood than mine. You hurt yourself."

Rio closed his eyes, turning his head away from her hand. "It's only a matter of time."

Maya cradled his head, leaning down so he had to face her, even if he wouldn't open his eyes. But he must be able to feel her, feel the force of her love just as you can feel the sun through closed lids.

"Rio, you were drunk. I've never seen you drunk before, and I hope I never do again. It was terrifying. But you don't have to make a melodrama out of it."

His eyes popped open. "Is that what you think I'm doing?"

"Eat something. I made some rice and vegetables. Talk to me. Shouldn't you be calling your family? Are you going to go back for the funeral?"

Rio sighed, pulling free of her touch and rolling over on his side. "Not after what my uncle Joe said to me."

He was facing her now, and looking at her, and that was better, so much better. Yes, it was going to be all right. It really was. "What'd he say?" Maya asked.

"He said I was a stinking commie wimp who wasn't good enough to wipe Jim's ass—and various other things of that sort."

"You aren't going to let that stop you, are you?"

"I have a lot of respect for Jim. I didn't agree with him, but I respect him. I don't want to cause fighting and grief at his funeral." Slowly, he sat up. "And if I go back, I will. As soon as they start in on that patriotism shit, I will." He put his head in his hands. "God, Maya, I feel awful."

She put her arms around him and held him, enormously relieved because he was no longer talking about dying.

He clutched her, and she stroked his golden hair while he held her with lacerated hands. "Are you really going to stay with me?" he whispered.

"Of course."

"I've been so scared," he breathed. "So scared that you would go. Don't leave me, Maya."

"I won't leave you."

"I'll fight it, I really will. I'll never drink again, if you stay with me. I need you!"

"I will never leave you," she said, holding him and cherishing him. His words fed something in her, some deep spring of love that swelled and burst and overflowed, bathing them both in healing waters. "I love you, Rio."

"I love you, too."

The letter came five days later.

"Dear Richie," it began, because Jim always called Rio by his childhood name,

You know how all my life I've had these dreams about things, and then they would happen? Well, last night I dreamed my death. I feel like my luck is running out, bro. Maybe even by the time you get this, it'll have happened.

It's funny but I don't feel afraid. The dream wasn't bad—there was no pain in it, just colors, like the whole world blossoming into red, and noise, and then the light. And then—this is the funny part—I was sitting in the kitchen with Dad, and we had a six-pack of Coors on the table, and I said, "Dad, why did you do it to us?" and he just looked at me and said, "Drink up, Jim. You know you can only get this beer in the West."

Dreams are weird, man, but in case this one turns out to be true I want to say a couple of things to you. I need to tell you the truth about a couple of things. You know you always were my favorite brother, in spite of the trouble you caused, because pigheaded stubborn as you were, you had balls. Remember that time we stole Uncle Joe's car and got drunk in the graveyard? Jesus, we were crazy, crazy as our old man.

I always thought you would grow up to be something, to do something real. Christ, Richie, you were the smartest of any of us. And that's why I'm writing. Because I think I understand something now about what it means to be a man, something Dad couldn't teach us because he was too screwed up. And it's this. A real man puts his life on the line for something he believes in. That's why God gave us our lives, so we could put them behind something. Even a mistake. Women are here to bring life through, but men are meant to make that life mean something by being willing to lay it down. And that's all we have to do, really. We don't even have to be right.

It's funny isn't it, all those arguments we had about this war. Right now it doesn't even matter to me whether we were right or wrong to come over here, or whether we win or lose. Who was ever a bigger loser than Jesus?—and yet he understood this thing better than any of us and died to show us how to do it with style. You know I've never been real religious but I think I understand Him now. And if we lose this war, it'll be because the Viet Cong are the ones here who really know this better than we do, and have the guts to do it.

But like I said, that's not really what's at stake for me anymore. It's not the winning or the losing or the right or the wrong. It's just going down gracefully, without whining or sniveling. It's knowing who you are.

So I'm at peace. Don't cry for me, man. I would say right now I'm happier than I have ever been. I'm a man. I'm not afraid to die. I'm in a state of grace.

My only wish for you, little brother, is to find the same peace with yourself. I dare you to do it. Put yourself on the line, for something. I don't even care what it is—even if it's fighting against this same war I'm fighting for, as long as you believe in it. Even if you're wrong.

Good-bye, Richie. Pray for me, if you still believe in God. And if you don't, well, drain a six-pack of Coors, find some beautiful woman, and fuck her brains out for me.

I love you,
Jim

Tears were streaming out of Rio's eyes. Maya was relieved to see them; crying seemed to her such a sane thing to do. He handed her the letter, and she read it while he sat next to her, crying.

"What do you think?" he asked when she'd finished.

She didn't know what to say. Jim was dead, and she had never seen Rio cry like this before. How could she say, "There's a flaw in his reasoning"? How could she say, "These are the sentiments that will destroy the world"?

"I don't know, Rio," she said. "What do you think?"

"I think we need to stop this fucking war," he said.

They marched in demonstrations and went to meetings. Bulbs poked through the earth and bloomed, blossoms opened on the branches of fruit trees, and the hills to the east shone green from the rains of winter. Rio spent his days in classes and his nights at interminable meetings, listening to arguments Maya could not fathom and didn't want to try to follow. The students were striking in support of a program of Third World studies, and they were arguing about demands and tactics, how to word their leaflets, whether to provoke violence or avoid it. Rio seemed to enjoy the fights, tossing his blond hair and planting his feet in a wide stance.

"I know the working class in this country, man. I *am* working class, and I can tell you this, the working class is not impressed with a lot of fucking rhetoric. It's action they respect. You want to move this out of the university and out to the people, you got to act."

Because Maya wasn't in school or working, and had time, she was called on to run errands, type up position papers, drop copy at the printer's, make a hundred phone calls, post a thousand flyers on bulletin boards and telephone poles. On the street, now, she handed out leaflets and sold political buttons and papers. She set up tables at shopping centers and talked to women at supermarkets while their bored children pulled on their skirts and whined. She went downtown to the financial district and accosted office workers over lunch.

Actually, she was glad to have work to do. Just *being* no longer seemed enough of a justification. The street itself had changed. Artists who sold their crafts on Telegraph were taking classes at San Francisco State or moving to the country. People she saw every day were leaving, for Guatemala or India or Maui. The ones who stayed behind were, more and more, the wrecks, the burned-out speed freaks, the ones slightly on the edge of crazy. Was she one of them? Maya sometimes asked herself. Was she still chasing something that everyone else knew was only a hallucination?

Side by side with Rio, she faced down cops. The demonstrations seemed stylized as a dance. First movement: Dodge behind the Student Union building, heart pounding, sweat pouring down, as the cops pursued, clubs raised. Second movement: Crouch behind a bush as the heavy-footed officers pounded past. Third movement: Circle round to regroup behind them, resume chanting. And there was Rio—a gold flash in the middle of a sea of blue, wherever the action was hottest, the police most vicious. Late at night, when they got home, if they got home, she would kiss his wounds and they would make love, fiercely, while on the stereo the Stones played "Street Fighting Man." They'd found a new form of communion, slaking their rage in each other's bruised bodies, a small compensation for what was slipping away from them, that elusive thing that Maya had never been able to name. Now, without a name to evoke it, she could no longer conjure it up. In the magic-scented spring, when the roses opened and great loops of wisteria swayed gently, like a woman's hair, she walked down the street feeling old, overcome with nostalgia for something sweet that had already gone by.

She was walking by an empty lot near Telegraph Avenue one morning, on her way back from the printer's where she'd dropped off a leaflet Rio's friend Daniel had written. "Hey, Maya, come give us a hand," someone called out to her. It was Rob, one of the many thousands of people she knew from the street. She had read cards for him when he was trying to decide about switching his major from math to economics. Now he held a shovel. Nearby in the vacant lot where he stood, another long-haired man and a woman in a paisley skirt were digging.

"What's happening, man?" she asked.

"We're making a park. For the people, for us. And we've elected you," he smiled suggestively, "to dig this flower bed." He handed her a shovel.

Rob was one of the handsomest men Maya had ever seen. His black, wavy hair brushed his shoulders, and he had a flashing smile and a way of looking deeply into the eyes of any woman he stood near, parting his lips, and just nipping the tip of his tongue with his teeth that Maya found highly suggestive, even though she knew he had a girlfriend, a dance major named Liza whose slender grace Maya envied.

"Dig? Where?"

"Here," he said, indicating a plot of bare ground.

"You're really making a park, here?"

"We need a park." He winked at her. "The children need a park. The hippies need grass to lie on, not just to smoke. You need a park. The street fighters need a place for R and R. And the motherfuckers at the university need to learn a lesson. Once this was a block of homes. They bulldozed them down, for purposes of their own. So they need to be taught that they can't just go trashing people's homes and get away with it. You could say we've commandeered their property." He smiled again, a bad-boy grin. "Can you dig it?"

"I can dig it, man," she said, smiling back at him, and began.

She worked all that afternoon in a kind of euphoria. It had been a long time since she'd done anything so simply physical. The smell of the newly turned earth seemed to promise everything, the gestation of seeds, unimaginable fruitings and ripenings. Even the soreness in her muscles felt sweet. How long had it been since she built anything, made anything, created with her own hands?

She worked all that day and got home at dark to find Rio and Daniel sitting at the kitchen table, hammering out yet another leaflet on Rio's old manual typewriter. Daniel Wasserman was one of those tall, bony Jewish men who read voraciously and talked incessantly. With his beaked nose peeking out from under a wild explosion of wiry brown hair, he reminded her of an inquiring bird.

"Where've you been?" Rio asked. "We're hungry."

"We're making a park," Maya said eagerly. "It's wonderful—you should come and see it. All sorts of people were there today, not just freaks and politicos, but straight students and people from the neighborhood."

"A park for the children, how *gentle,*" Daniel said, blowing out a chain of perfect smoke rings. "People are dying in Vietnam, racist pigs are offing black brothers in the ghetto, and you're making a park."

"Fuck you," Maya said. She was furious, suddenly, and she stomped over to the back side of their room, which contained a stove and sink and refrigerator and a cupboard with a few dishes. She pulled out a pan and began filling it with water. "It's an action. It's a statement about property."

"Hey, don't get pissed," Daniel said, propping his cigarette on the edge of her favorite blue cereal bowl.

She hated when they messed up the dishes she ate from with their nasty ashes, but there was no point arguing about it. She just turned into a nag, when she got started. Better to fight about something important, like the park. "It's a better action than writing a thousand stupid position papers."

"It's a potential action," Daniel corrected her in a professorial tone. "A conflict in embryo. When the pigs try to run you out, it'll be an action. And I'll be the first to stand in line and get my head busted with you. You know that." He smiled, suddenly boyish, ingratiating.

Maya set the water on the back burner to boil. She checked the refrigerator. There wasn't much, but she pulled out an onion and a few carrots and started chopping.

"I heard about that park," Rio said, reaching over and taking a drag from Daniel's cigarette. "I was thinking of checkin' it out."

"What is an action, anyway?" Maya said, ignoring Daniel's smile, bringing her knife down again and again on the carrots. "You think an action's only real if it means fighting the cops. But doing something, making something—that can be an action, too."

"The purpose of action," Daniel said, reverting to his earlier tone, "is to make the contradictions in the system visible. If they leave you alone, you'll have a park, but not an action. If they bust you, well, then it gets interesting."

"So you're saying we can't win," Maya said.

"Oh no. I'm saying you can't lose."

Daniel and Rio came down to the park the next day, and over the following weeks even the most doctrinaire of the Berkeley politicos made at least a token attempt at planting a flower or seeding the grass. The flat patch of ruined land became transformed. Retired professors brought cuttings from their gardens. Young mothers, their babies asleep in strollers, stopped to help set out seedlings. Burned-out speed freaks knelt in the ground to hold steady a plank being hammered into place for a sandbox. Suddenly everyone seemed to be joining the movement, not a Party but a party to which everybody was invited, and came. And they all seemed beatified, even the ones Maya ordinarily disdained, those who played the game, the students who had chosen safety over freedom, the housewives and older women who lived conventional lives in outrageous times. The park was an intimation of some great goodness in people that only wanted an outlet, earth to till together, something to build. It was a small realized vision of what they were battling for, her lost magic popping up and blooming at her feet. Maybe a vision was not a luxury but a necessity, she thought. To make the vision real, to dare the dreamers to get their hands dirty—that was an action of another sort, one that did not need the benediction of repression to be real.

Rio was in his natural element. He built things and fixed things and solved problems that had solutions, unlike so many others. He helped install swings and a sandbox, and to raise and secure the giant letters someone had constructed, that spelled KNOW. When the park was nearing completion, Maya joined a group, including Rob and Liza, that cooked up huge vats of stew. Rio scavenged the supermarkets of Berkeley and Oakland for vegetables and potatoes, made contacts to pick up outdated milk and cheese that would otherwise be dumped, talked restaurants out of leftovers and bakeries out of day-old bread. The glaze receded from his eyes. When they made love, now, Maya imagined something being planted. Their skin smelled like earth and onions and flowers.

She found too, that in the park, the quality of her dreams and conversations changed. The nature of the work, and the sun, and the daily evidence of growth seemed to evoke discussions that were more, well, grounded than the flights of abstractions she continued to type for Daniel late into the night. Could the world really work this way? Would people work just for the joy of it, without being forced or coerced? What would it mean if they won? Could they transform the battleground into a garden?

She was sleeping, nestled in Rio's arms one morning in mid-May, when they heard a frantic pounding on their door. "The park!" someone in the street was yelling. "They're bulldozing People's Park!"

They threw on some clothes and ran out to the street, while the self-appointed town crier continued on his rounds, pounding on doors. Breathing hard, they covered the eight blocks up to Telegraph with amazing speed. Police were stationed on the street that ran beside the park. Behind the lines, they could hear the crunch of bulldozers and the voices of men shouting directions to each other. As the sun, implacably shining, climbed over the hills, they caught the glint of metal. The park was being fenced.

Maya stood, clutching Rio's hand, silent in a rage that went so deep there was no way to express it, hardly even to feel it. She wished, for the first time in all the battles, for a weapon. A grenade to blow the fence apart, a bomb to carry them all away. They'd murdered the park, all that work, all that hope; now they were enclosing its corpse in a cage. But they had not caged her, and they would never completely destroy the vision of the common garden, not if she herself had to become the weapon she hurled at them. Maybe before love could be lived, rage had to clear the way. Maybe rage itself was a state of grace.

"Now I know how the Vietnamese feel," a voice murmured at her elbow. Liza, Rob's girlfriend, her long blond hair hanging loose down her back, looked up at Maya through hazel eyes still heavy with sleep. Daniel's girlfriend, Edith, stood beside her. Edith had a nervous habit of grinding her teeth which made her jaw jump periodically. Her sallow skin was marked by acne scars, and in the harsh light of morning it covered the square bones of her face like a leather mask, framed by her blunt-cut, chestnut hair.

"No, you don't," Edith corrected her. "You haven't lost your

home, and your family, and your friends, and your crops. You haven't
been napalmed or shot.''

"Give them time," Rio said. "Just give them time."

By noon, a huge crowd had gathered in Sproul Plaza for an emergency
rally. Maya stood crushed between Rio and Daniel. Everything seemed
amplified, larger than life and at the same time slower and faster, rever-
berating like the beating wings of crows, shimmering in the heat waves
of rage.

"The whole fucking world is here," Daniel murmured. "Not just
your usual freaks and radicals, but the clean-cut, work-within-the-system
types from the business school. What is youth coming to?"

"Let's take the park!" the speaker cried, and the crowd yelled and
surged forward, spilling out onto Telegraph Avenue. Maya was pressed,
crushed in a wave of moving bodies, herself and yet not herself, caught
up in the chanting and the yelling and the pounding feet. She cried out in
her own voice, and it became part of the one united voice that for all its
roughness still rang with a high overtone of love.

The march moved out down the street. Behind her, the tinkling of
breaking glass portended all that was shattering around them: dreams
and hopes and falsities, all structures of control.

The police met them in the street, more police than she had ever
seen massed together, the regular Berkeley cops and special sheriff's
deputies called the Blue Meanies after their bright blue jumpsuits.

"Take the park!" Rio was shouting. He grabbed her hand and they
dashed around a clump of slower demonstrators. Ahead of them, a single
cop was clubbing a young woman who had her hands raised to protect
her head. Blood was streaming down her face. Rio jumped between them
and started wrestling the cop for his club.

"Run!" he yelled to the woman who stood up and walked slowly
off, sobbing. Another cop ran in and swung his club at Rio. Much to her
own surprise, Maya grabbed for it. It came loose in her hand and before
she could think, she was running, twisting, turning, dodging, with the
two cops chasing her. Her heart was pounding so hard she thought her
body would split open. She could hardly breathe but she didn't dare
slacken her pace. Suddenly it occurred to her to throw the club away.
She tossed it wildly to one side and heard it shatter a window.

"Nice shot," someone yelled. "You got the bank!"

She dove into a tight crowd of demonstrators, wriggled through to
come out on the other side with her pursuers still trapped across the
street. Breathing heavily, she continued to put distance between herself
and them. Someone had opened a fire hydrant and the water had gushed
out into the street. She waded through it, splashing some on her face.

The acrid smell of tear gas was beginning to seep through the street. She dipped her bandanna into the water and tied it over her mouth and nose. Masked, veiled, she turned to head back and look for Rio.

Across the street, a Blue Meany raised a shotgun and fired into the crowd.

At first Maya simply stood, frozen. This can't be happening, she thought. It's not happening. I didn't see it happen. Then a woman screamed, and she began to hear other shots behind her and around her.

"They're firing on people!" someone screamed. "Run!"

But Maya didn't know where to run. She felt as if time were suspended; she moved slowly through a viscous medium. Oh, they had talked about this, fantasized about it, even: the moment that ultimately had to come, when repression would escalate to outright war. But they had never really expected their government to fire on its own citizens.

Suddenly all of Daniel's arguments made sense. Yes, the park had been more important than they knew, if these were the lengths they would go to to crush it. Yes, if it was worth killing for, it was worth dying for. She understood Jim now, and Rio's fury, and her own. She was going to die, then, today, very likely, and that was okay. It was, as the Indians said, a good day to die, although really she would prefer to take a few cops with her. But she would die with dignity, gracefully, not running away, not screaming in fright, but walking, slowly and steadily, against the panicking surge of the crowd, back toward the park. Toward her goal, toward her vision.

She walked, slowly, in a calm trance where nothing mattered very much, and the noise and shouting and panic seemed far away. She slid between bodies pressing in the opposite direction. Police rushed past her, hot in pursuit of some fleeing runner; she walked calmly on. She turned a corner and found herself at the park, alone except for a young cop guarding the newly erected fence. The demonstrators had gone and the cops had gone after them. From down the street, shouts and cries could be heard, but they were distant. Her mask had slipped down from her face, but the tear gas had cleared and she could breathe. Still in her strange, silent calm, she walked toward the lone policeman. She half expected him to fire on her but he only yelled, nervously.

"Get out of here! This area is restricted! I order you to turn around and leave, now."

Instead she walked up to him, getting closer, until she could look him in the eye. Behind him stood the fence; behind the fence, the wasteland, the mud and sticks and debris of their visions.

"Stand back," he said. "I don't want to have to shoot you."

He was young, not as young as she was but not much older, and his eyes were a sort of blue gray that deepened to colorless shadows. She was looking into his eyes, trying to understand how he could be *him* and she could be herself, trying to fathom what separated them. What made him willing to kill her? For if she could understand that, she thought, if she could make the contact across the gap as she had done once with Johanna or with Rio, if she could reach her enemy with the heart, then wouldn't everything transform?

Just for one moment, for an instant, when she looked into his eyes she thought she was looking into a mirror. She couldn't remember if her own eyes were blue or brown. She knew him, down to his soul, and she knew that he was afraid, as she was afraid. They were the same, and they recognized each other. Her being reached out to encompass him, and he, clutching his rifle, holding the power of life and death over her, encompassed her. Maybe this possibility was always present, Maya thought, to remember who we really are, to stand unprotected at the barriers. Maybe we can take hands and turn, and he will lay down his gun. We'll walk in peace together back through the embattled streets, and let the garden bloom. But then his eyes went opaque. The moment passed, and the light was gone.

"Shame on you," Maya said. "Shame, shame, shame!"

She turned and walked away, back toward the street. After a long while, she found herself on one of the quiet side streets off Telegraph. Her eyes were streaming from tear gas and she wasn't sure where she was. She'd thought she was going to die, but she was still alive, even though on the street the cops were still shooting people. Rio, she thought, and felt a sharp stab of fear. He would be in front, wherever the danger was worst. Would she ever see him again?

"Maya! You okay?" Daniel came running up behind her, and suddenly she was desperately glad to see him. She actually grabbed for him and hugged him, clinging fiercely as he patted her, saying soothingly, "Hey, it's okay. It's gonna be okay."

He wasn't so bad, she thought, unable to let go.

"You hurt?" he asked.

She shook her head no.

"C'mon," he said, extricating himself at last. "Let's go back to your pad. Rio and I agreed we'd meet there. There's nothing more we can do on the street right now, except get ourselves an ass full of buckshot."

"You saw Rio?" Maya said. "He's alive?"

"He was half an hour ago. They're only shooting birdshot and buckshot—it can hurt like hell but it doesn't generally kill you."

"I didn't know," Maya said.

They collected at the apartment, Maya and Daniel, Liza and Edith. Edith had brewed up coffee and Liza was boiling up water for rice and stewed vegetables. The news blared from the TV. Governor Reagan had called out the National Guard. Troops were converging, armed with rifles and bayonets. Maya lay on the bed but kept jumping up, thinking she heard footsteps, to peer anxiously out the front door.

"He'll be all right. Relax," Daniel said. "Don't worry about old Rio."

"I can't help it," Maya said, but at that moment the door opened and Rio walked in, followed by Rob. Maya leaped up and grabbed Rio, and he swung her around, bent her over his arm, and kissed her. He was exuberant; there was so much vitality leaking from his pores that her eyes stung with it, like with gas. She wanted to pull him down on top of her and make love right there, in the midst of them all.

"Street fightin' mama!" Rio said. "You okay? Those pigs didn't get you?"

"Not me," Maya said, suddenly happy again, even though there was a bitter-edged tang to her joy, like the chemical aftertaste in cheap wine. "I'm too quick."

"You saved my neck, love of my life. Shit, man, that was a rough scene out there. They were fuckin' shooting people."

"It was definitely an action," Daniel conceded.

By midnight, the streets were full of National Guardsmen. Rob and Liza lived across campus; Daniel and Edith in the city. Suddenly these familiar distances were transformed into a danger zone, a risky border crossing. Maya pulled out sheets and sleeping bags and made beds for them all.

They slept little and talked much. Perhaps because Maya was still in a state of shock, everything Daniel said suddenly seemed reasonable, inevitable. Or maybe he had been right all along, ahead of her, and she just hadn't been able to see it.

"The movement has to enter a new phase," Daniel said now, stretched out on the Salvation Army sofa that took up one wall of the room. "We've got to get serious. We can't expect they're going to go on letting us live our normal lives, protesting on weekends and holidays. The time has come to take some bigger risks."

"Like what?" Rio asked.

"Like organizing effectively," Daniel said. "Nothing scares them more than that. We need smaller groups that can move in the streets and stay mobile, like little cells. The big organizations are unwieldy."

"It's all the infighting," Rob said. He was perched on one of the kitchen chairs, rolling a joint at the table. "The Leninists and the Trots and the Maoists and the ordinary assholes who don't give a flying fuck about ideologies. They're never going to get free of it."

"The big organizations are always going to be under pressure, from the factions. They're always going to be infiltrated," Daniel said.

"It's destroying the movement," Edith said. "We should be building something, not tearing ourselves apart." She was sitting on the floor, leaning up against the couch, letting Daniel's hand graze her head. It could have been a sexy gesture, but Edith seemed oblivious.

Rob licked the paper seam on his joint, lit it up, and inhaled deeply. Rio watched him closely, and when Rob set it down, Rio got up to bring it over to where he and Maya had been sitting together on the mattress that formed their double bed, their backs supported by the wall.

"We were building something, in the park," Maya was saying. "The pigs tore that apart."

"That's the other part of it," Daniel said. "What we've got to face up to. Peaceful change is all very well—but today proves that no matter how nonviolent we are, they're going to use violence against us."

"Violence is the American way," Rob said. He stood up and saluted, his voice taking on the stentorian tones of the patriotic films shown in high school citizenship classes. "From the genocide of the Indians to the enslavement of the Africans, from the Haymarket Massacre to the bombing of Hanoi, violence has always been this country's strength in times of war and refuge in times of peace."

"So what are you saying?" Edith asked. "That we should give up on nonviolence?"

"No, no, no!" Daniel said. "We can't give up. But we can't be naive either. We were unprepared, today. Deep in our hearts, we just couldn't believe they'd shoot into a crowd of American kids. But they did. We can't ever forget that. We can't let them take us by surprise again."

"But we can't let them stop us," Maya said. "We've got to go ahead and keep on trying to build things, like the park."

"Of course," Daniel agreed. "But now we know beyond a doubt that everything we try to build is something we're going to have to fight for. Otherwise the system will just tear it down. We've got to learn to defend ourselves."

"How?" Rob asked. "Take arms against a sea of troubles, and by opposing, end them?"

"Come again?" Liza said. Maya watched her warily. She was leaning up against their mattress, and it seemed to Maya she nestled unnecessarily close to Rio. He inhaled from the joint, looked from Maya to Liza, as if unsure what to do, and then handed it down to Liza on the floor, giving Maya an apologetic grin.

"Only as a very last resort," Daniel said. "Still, it's not illegal to own a few guns, and know how to use them. Not yet, anyway. And they might be a deterrent to the pigs, in a situation like today."

"Are you sure of that?" Edith said. "Wouldn't they just be an incentive to aim better?"

"People aren't going to lie down and get their heads beat forever,"

Rob said. "Look what happened to the civil rights movement, after King got killed. They're talking self-defense now, not nonviolence."

"We're not the Black Panthers," Liza said, in the small half voice that held in the smoke she'd inhaled. Rio reached down and took the joint back from her, inhaled again, and then passed it to Maya with a slightly sheepish smile.

"But we should be supporting them," Edith said. "They're the vanguard of the real revolution."

Rio expelled his breath with a cough. "You think we should support them by killing a few cops? It'd make a good slogan—Off an officer for Huey!"

"That's not what I'm saying," Daniel said sharply. "There's a lot of ways to support the revolutionary forces in this country, short of picking up a gun. We could have demonstrations in the white suburbs when the ghettos are rioting, divide the police forces. We could sit in at the media. But I don't buy all this liberal moralizing about the Panthers, either, all this crying for the good old days when Martin Luther King made the darkies be nice to white folks. The brothers are living in a war zone. The ghettos are a police state. How can we blame people for fighting back in that situation?"

"I don't blame them," Rio said, his voice serious. "But, just to be honest here, I don't know if I'm ready to join them. Today, when they started shooting at people, man, I have to admit I was scared shitless."

"Me too," Maya said softly.

"We all were," Daniel said. "But don't you see, that's what today proves to us—that if we, even we, the privileged, reach for our true aims and desires, the state has no choice but to suppress us brutally. And we, therefore, if we want to achieve our desires, have no choice but to move from resistance to revolution."

"How do we do that?" Rob asked. "That's the question, isn't it?"

"We've got to organize," Edith said.

"And educate ourselves," Daniel agreed. "We need a strategy, not just a series of emotional outbursts. We've got to build coalitions. When change comes, it's going to come from East Oakland and the Fillmore and Hunter's Point. Revolutions are made by the desperate."

"Well then, what on earth makes you think they're going to be made by us?" Liza asked. "We're not desperate. We're white middle-class college students."

"Not all of us," Maya said. The joint was getting small. She offered it to Edith, who waved it away. Rio took it back again.

"We have a role to play, the intelligentsia," Daniel said. "Because of our class privilege, it's like we're standing on higher ground. So we can see a little further than those who've got their faces down in the mud."

"That's awfully elitist," Edith said.

Rio shook his head. "Not anymore. They won't let us be elite, anymore, not if we stand up for what we believe in. That's what today proves to me. That we can die, doing this. We can die for our most innocent dreams."

"I'm willing to die," Edith said. "But I feel I have a responsibility to live, for the revolution."

One man, James Rector, did die of buckshot wounds received that night. Another man, an artist named Alan Blanchard, was blinded by birdshot. Rector was a nonstudent, the papers said, as if that somehow made his death acceptable. Being a nonstudent was a condition Maya shared, which she only now understood could become, at any moment, terminal.

Therefore it must be important, she thought. Her refusal to go to school, to do what was acceptable and safe and expected, allied her with the victims of the clubs and the bombs. She had taken a radical stance, made her life an act of revolution.

Sooner or later, Rio would join her again. Already his grades were slipping. How could he study when the streets were ablaze? Law school had not been mentioned for a long time.

He would join her again. They would be together on the edge, visionary outlaws, fighting the lies and building the dreams. They would rise together or go down together, ablaze with love and rage, searing a path for change to follow.

22

Letter

Mrs. Jeanette Connolly
1443 River Road
Pittsburgh, PA
June 4, 1969

Dear Mom,

How's the weather? I hear you're having a heat wave back there. Here it's nice and cool. June can be foggy.

I wish I could come back for the summer vacation, but there's just too much on my plate here at school. I'm going to take the summer quarter, get some more credits I need. With all the disturbance here in the spring, I didn't do quite as well as I'd hoped to. Steve and Laurie'll look out for you, I'm sure.

No, I don't hear much from Carl. Jim used to write to me, regular, but Carl and I don't seem to communicate all that well. I hope he's okay, and that you aren't worrying about him too much. I know it's hard for you.

Mom, I've just got to say something about what you wrote in your last letter. It's this. If something is wrong, it's wrong. The fact that Jim died for it—this war, I mean, the fact that Carl might die for it—doesn't make it right. In fact it makes it all the more wrong, if you ask me.

I'm not betraying Jim's memory to say that the war is wrong. I said the same thing to him when he was alive. If he'd listened to me, he'd still be here. All right, maybe that's unfair. But it's true. Carl, too. Nobody told him to go enlist in the Marines. In fact I recall you yourself were pretty goddamned mad about it at the time.

I can't bring Jim back by telling a lie. I can't keep Carl safe by pretending to agree with something that stinks in every direction. I'm sorry if that hurts you, I'm sorry if Steve doesn't want me in his house— and by the way, that's the real reason I don't come back much, I don't want to cause a lot of fighting for you. But I can't lie. I can't condone the liars, either. I've got to try to stop this war. Isn't that what you do, when something is rotten? Try to end it? Isn't that how you tried to bring us up?

What does the priest at St. Catherine's say? You know a lot of clergy are against the war. Look at the Berrigan brothers.

Anyway, enough of that. I'm fine, my girlfriend is fine, and hey— luck of the draw, my lottery number is bottom of the bin, so it looks like Uncle Sam won't be trying to ship *my* rear end overseas, for the moment, anyway.

You take care of yourself, now. Tell Laurie congratulations—so we're going to have a new little Connolly in a few months. Let's hope he, she, or it doesn't take after the rest of the family.

Just joking,
Rio (Richie)

23

Johanna Weaver's Journal

June 15, 1969

Yes, it's finally happened. I am a mother now. Mother of a beautiful, sweet, precious little girl. I named her Rachel, after Grandma, and Roberta, after Daddy. Rachel Roberta Weaver. A nice, solid name. Nothing to make fun of in it.

She's beautiful, beautiful, beautiful! Nine pounds, two ounces, which is big for a newborn but still tiny, with the most perfect little fingers and toes and long eyelashes and lots of dark, curly hair. And she does the most amazing things! She yawns, she cries, she sucks and sleeps and thrashes her little arms and legs around. Marian laughs at me. "You'd think no baby was ever born before in the whole history of the universe!" But she's just as proud and happy as I am.

It wasn't easy. I haven't been writing here very much these last months, partly because I had too much schoolwork and I was so tired all the time, and partly because I just didn't want to put down on paper what I was going through since I broke the news to Marian. We were sitting at our dining room table, eating the Hula Lula pizza we'd brought home from Shakey's, and I thought she'd choke on a bite of ham.

"You're what?" she said to me.

"I'm pregnant."

"Oh, Lord have mercy!"

"I'm sorry."

"Sorry! Joanne, I thought you'd grown some sense, if not some morals in the last year. With all I've sweated and saved and sacrificed for you, child, what possesses you to go and mess up your life?"

"I don't know, Mama."

"How did it happen?"

"The usual way," I said.

"Don't get smart with me."

I didn't mean to make her mad—not any madder than she was bound to be anyway—so I backed off real quick. "I'm not getting smart, Mama. I need your help."

Then she looked at me with that look of mother-sympathy that made me want to cry, and she looked like she might start to cry, but she just said in a real low voice, "What are you going to do?"

I took a deep breath. Here it comes.

"I want to have the baby, and keep it, and raise it. Will you help me?"

"You haven't thought about . . . alternatives?" she said in an even lower voice.

"I've thought about every alternative I can imagine. I don't want to have an abortion, Mama. Don't ask me why. I know it would make everything much easier. But I just can't make up my mind to do it. Besides, I kind of thought you wouldn't want me to."

"The church part of me is glad to hear you say that," Marian admitted. "I'm glad to hear you still have a conscience, some sense of right and wrong. The sensible part of me wonders why you couldn't have developed that conscience *before* you got yourself into this situation."

"It would have been better," I agreed. "But it's too late, now. Now I just have to deal with what is."

"What about the baby's father? Have you told him? Would he marry you?"

That was the question I'd been dreading. But there was nothing to do but answer it straight on. "I wouldn't marry him. No, I haven't told him and I don't plan to."

"Who is he? You've hardly been out on a date with anyone since you started school."

"He's nobody you know," I said, which was sort of true. Marian had met Rio but she didn't truly know him. I had thought long and hard about what to tell her, and decided that I just couldn't tell her I'd been to bed with Maya's boyfriend. So I gave her the truth with a few omissions. "He was somebody I met this summer, when I was staying with M—with Karla."

"Karla! I knew I should never, never have let you go up there."

"It's not her fault." No, it certainly wasn't.

"Did you love him?" Marian asked in a softer voice that made me want to cry. I wished, for her sake, for my sake, that I had loved Rio, instead of merely pitying him.

"Maybe I thought I did, at first. But then I found out he was using drugs." Okay, I admit that if that wasn't a lie in the fabric it was in the ruffles and fringes, but what could I do? Anyway, it worked.

"Drugs! What drugs?"

"Marijuana, mostly. Nothing that would harm the baby. But I don't trust him. That's why I don't want him to know."

"Oh, Lord. Joanne, Joanne, what are we going to do? I did so want for you to get an education." She was looking so distressed that I just couldn't bear it.

"I will, Mama," I said quickly. "I'll stay in school until the baby's born. With luck, I'll finish out this year. And then, see, if you'll help me, I'll manage somehow next year. I could take a lighter schedule, get some extra baby-sitting—I've got the Social Security and VA money from Daddy's pension, and I'll live here instead of moving into the dorms. We'll manage."

"But you could have done so many things! I wanted you to go places, see things, travel! I pictured you going out to college dances, and . . . I don't know. As pretty as you are . . . having boyfriends, lots of them. What kind of boyfriend is going to want you with a baby?"

"The kind who likes kids, I guess," I said. But I felt sad, Sheba, because I knew what she was saying is that she'd wanted me to have everything she never had, and had wanted for herself. And I had taken that away from her. But of course I couldn't admit that, I had to take an attitude about it. "Mama, it's 1968. We're not living in Ozzie-and-Harriet land anymore. If I didn't have a baby, I wouldn't be going to dances, I'd be going to demonstrations, probably getting arrested again and beaten up and teargassed. Who knows? Maybe this is the best thing that ever happened to me."

She just shook her head. "It's hard to raise a child alone, Joanne. You don't know what you're getting yourself into."

"You raised me alone, and I came out all right."

"I don't know about that." She pushed away her pizza plate and began to cry. "I would never have married your daddy if I'd known he was going to die. My mother raised me all alone, and Marcus too. I saw her struggle. You don't know how the kids used to whisper about us, the things they'd say. I would never have had you if I'd known I was going to be left alone."

"But are you sorry you have me now?"

"Yes. Yes, I am. I'm sorry you were ever born!"

"You don't mean that, Mama."

"No, you're right. I don't mean it. I just wanted everything to be different for you."

I went over to her chair and bent down and hugged her. "It will be different, Mama. Not ideal, maybe, but different." I paused for a moment, and then played my last card. "I could give it up for adoption."

She sat bolt upright and pushed me away. "Oh no! No, you can't do that! I don't trust what they do with black babies."

"Sell them for parts?" I suggested. "Grind them up for dog food?"

"Nothing would surprise me. No, Joanne, if you're going to have this baby, then we owe it a good home and good upbringing. I won't hear otherwise."

"Okay. Oh, Mama, if you help me, I promise you, I'll never get in trouble again. I'll finish school, I'll get a Ph.D., I'll make you proud of me." I was babbling by then, and Marian pulled me down to her and cradled my head in her arms, and we had a good cry together.

But then it was months and months of swinging back and forth between her getting mad all the time and getting overly solicitous of my well-being.

"Joanne, you put those groceries down. Don't you carry that heavy bag!"

"Mama, I can carry it better than you, with your high blood pressure. Don't you know I'm descended from those old slave women who worked in the fields up until the baby was due, lay down, gave birth, and got right back up to pick some mo' cotton?"

"I believe it's the Chinese women you're thinking of, or at least what they say about them." She'd take the bag out of my arms and carry it herself. "And you are not descended from the Chinese."

Meanwhile, I grew larger and larger. I progressed from throwing up in the morning, before Survey of World Literature, to throwing up in the afternoon, usually in the middle of Psychology 1. And then I stopped throwing up and just grew and grew and grew. I grew out of my jeans and out of my dresses and out of Marian's muumuus. I grew out of the desks at school and had to sit in a straight-backed chair and write on a clipboard. The bigger I got, the more sleep I seemed to need. This last quarter I tried to schedule only morning classes, so I could nap in the afternoon. I had one elective—art history, and that was a mistake. Mostly the professor showed slides. As soon as the lights went out, my chin went down to my chest and it was all I could do not to snore. The only thing that kept me awake, most of the time, was the fact that I had to pee about every fifteen minutes. I dropped out of the Black Students Union because I kept falling asleep in meetings. By the end, I tell you, I was really ready for that child to come out.

But there were good things about being pregnant, don't get me wrong. Actually, I loved it. I loved feeling like inside me was this wonderful secret—not secret for long! you might say. I loved feeling that I was creating somebody, all by myself. When she'd kick or turn, I felt such a thrill. Sometimes Marian would put a hand on my belly and feel the child move, and it was like everything linked up, she and I and what I came to call the line of women behind us. I could feel them all there, stretching down the ages, back to Africa and beyond, passing one to another their life and hope and power and sheer grit for survival. And now I was part of that line, another link in the chain, passing my birthright on to what I was always sure would be my daughter. And Marian and I were the same. She had done this, too—passed the gift on to me. And while sometimes I felt sorry that I wasn't doing this whole number ten years from now, with a nice respectable husband to feel the baby kick and bring me special things to eat, most times I felt like some ancient, ancient part of me recognized that it was all right. That it was good for a mother and daughter to be together in this, because it was our stake in the future that was growing inside me. Something changed between us. I was no longer her little girl—I was another woman in the line.

All this while, I didn't hear from Maya. Rio stopped calling after he found her in Berkeley and they got back together. Occasionally Betty would give her news of me. I don't know if she told Maya about the baby or not. I kind of wondered if she would, and if Rio would put two and two together. But I'm not sure the boy can count that high.

Anyway, Friday I finished my last final, and Monday I woke up in a pool of water. My bag of waters had broken, early. Mama was just home from her shift at the hospital and she got me up and walked me around. The pains came on, stronger than anything I could have imagined, even though I did take a few of those Lamaze classes where they try to teach you to breathe. I might have wanted to do a home birth but Marian would never hear of it, even though her own mother was a midwife.

"We've progressed since then," she'd say. "That's what science and hospitals are for."

She might have said different if she'd realized how it was going to be. At least she might have insisted on my going to Kaiser, where she works and everybody knows her. But I wanted to go to UCLA, because that's where my student health insurance is. And Marian agreed—maybe because deep in her heart she didn't want all her friends at work watching while her unmarried daughter had a baby out of wedlock.

We went up to UCLA about noon, when the pains were coming every few minutes. And the thing is, that almost all the doctors and nurses and office workers at that hospital are white. And there I was, a college student, granted, but still a black teenage mother giving birth to an illegitimate child. And they made us feel it. Yes, ma'am. From the moment we walked in and they let us sit and sit and sit in the admissions room before they got around to processing our paperwork, and the way they asked me again and again if I was really a student at the university and called to verify my student health card. Meanwhile I thought I was going to die. They say women forget the pain of childbirth so let me set it down here before it fades—Ow! Oh, God, did it hurt. These hot waves of cramps, rolling over me, again and again and again. And I just wanted to let myself go under, and meanwhile they were asking me a million times what drugs I'd taken during my pregnancy, and not believing me when I said I hadn't taken any, not even an aspirin. Which was true, because even before I hadn't been smoking a lot and the very thought of anything stronger made me want to vomit even more than I was already. But they kept saying, "We just have to know. It's not going to get you in trouble, but we have to be prepared for any possible consequences to the baby." And I could hardly concentrate on what they were saying, except that Marian was getting madder and madder, and finally I thought she was going to throttle this young blond creep behind the desk.

"I am a nurse!" she kept saying. "Who is your supervisor? If you don't stop harassing my daughter and get her some medical attention, I'm going to report you."

Then they finally admitted me and took me upstairs to a room on the maternity ward. I don't remember a lot of it. I was just in this world of pain where it felt like my body was trying to tear itself open, but I do remember that every stage along the way we had to wait and wait and wait—for someone to bring me a hospital gown, for someone to shave me, for someone to come and examine me and give me pain medication. All the while Marian was crooning to me, "Oh Joanne, Joanne, my baby, it's gonna be all right, it's okay, baby." And then turning and yelling, "Where is the doctor? Where is the nurse? My daughter is having a baby—she needs medical attention!"

And then when the doctor finally did come, he checked me, sticking his big, red beefy fingers up my you know what, and then called for the nurses to come wheel me into the delivery room. And I could hear him saying to the nurse, "That's the way these people are—just pop 'em right out, like sausages."

He wasn't my regular doctor, who was not on call that morning. I'd never seen him before. They wheeled me into this room full of bright lights and green-coated men, and I didn't even realize until too late that they hadn't let Marian come with me. I was all alone and my body was ripping apart and suddenly I was scared, so scared. The nurses grabbed my hands and strapped them down to the table.

"Why are you doing that?" I asked, but then another pain came and they were telling me to push.

"So you don't hurt yourself," they said, and I didn't understand what they thought I'd do to myself—grab a scalpel and rip open my own jugular vein? rise from the bed and attack the doctor? But they said it was standard procedure and I guess it is. Sometimes anesthetic makes people do funny things and I was fuzzy from the pills they'd given me, but by the time they got around to examining me and getting me into the room, it was too late for the saddle block I was supposed to get. Then the doctor came at me again, with a knife, and he cut me. It's what they do to keep you from tearing. But with the drugs and the pain I was a little out of my mind, and suddenly I was a young slave woman, tied down to be raped; I was an animal strapped for slaughter, I was the whole line of women, back and back, who had been sold and raped and butchered. I began to scream. I would have kicked that doctor in the face if they hadn't strapped down my feet. And then suddenly I felt a pain and a stretching like nothing that had come before, and this one nurse who was kind of sympathetic was telling me to push, push. I felt a great, deep strength come over me. The whole line of women were holding me in their arms; I could lean back against them and feel their support. And my body was strong, strong, stronger than any warrior's body. It didn't matter what they did to me; no one could take away that strength. Life itself was pushing through me. Then I felt the baby come out, the head first, and then the whole body slid free, and I wanted to reach for her, but I couldn't move my hands.

They snatched her away. I guess they were smacking her backside because I could hear her cry. Something squirted from my breasts. But the doctor and the nurses were weighing her and poking her and examining every last bit of her, and I flipped out again. I was back in slavery days, and they'd tied me up and snatched my baby away and they were going to sell her away from me before I ever had a chance to hold her, and I started to yell and howl and scream like nobody in that hospital had ever heard before. I swear, Sheba, if I weren't strapped down I would have jumped up, trailing blood and cord and placenta and all, and throttled that doctor.

But then the nice nurse kept telling me to calm down, calm down, I'd see my baby in a minute, and finally they brought her to me, all wrapped in a little pink blanket, and they loosed my hands and I held her in my arms. Sheba, it made up for everything in the whole world.

Then they finally gave me some more medication, a bit after the fact, if you ask me, but it made me very sleepy and they took her away again. I knew she didn't want to go—I could feel it. When I woke up I was in another room, all clean, with Marian crooning over me, and then they brought her back again for an hour, to nurse, and we had time to look her over and examine every perfect detail. You should have seen Marian's face. She looked so proud and pleased, I almost cried. She was holding me and I was holding Rachel and suddenly I understood my mother; I knew exactly how she felt and why she'd been the way she had with me. Because when I looked down at my daughter it came to me that I didn't want her to go through what I've been through. She's so beautiful and precious and pure, right now, untouched yet by any of the meanness in the world.

I'm willing to be a warrior myself but I don't want her to have to be one. I want everything to come to her, easy and with grace; I want her to have ruffled curtains and stuffed cats and parties and dances—I want her to be a dancer, a poet, president! Queen! Empress of the universe!

Oh, Sheba, nothing's too good for Miss Rachel Roberta Weaver. Yes, Sheba, I understood Marian completely, and I knew she could feel that I did. And I had to laugh at myself. I just had to laugh.

We were happy, Sheba. And now I've been home with Rachel for a whole day already, and I have her all to myself. I can hold her any time I want to, feed her whenever she cries, gaze at her milky eyes for hours if I want to.

Wow, I've written a lot. She's sleeping, still. I'm going to stop writing, and sleep myself until she wakes up.

Johanna, mother of Rachel

24

Pangboche

On your rest day, an enjoyable four-and-one-half-
hour hike to the monastery of Pangboche will help
your lungs to acclimatize. Great views from this
gompa high on the mountainside!

—*MOUNTAIN CO-OP ADVENTURES*
BROCHURE

Maya shivered. She sat beside the hearth of the small *bhatti* in
Pangboche, stretching out her hands to the small fire. The heat of the
flames only seemed to redden her skin without transferring any warmth
to the rest of her body, and she was so tired she wanted to cry. She could
have spent the day lying peacefully in her tent at Tengpoche, reading and
sleeping and trying to heal her lungs. But she'd awakened in a burst of
optimism. The penicillin was working; the heavy, fiery feeling in her
lungs was gone. She could breathe again. How could she stay behind and
miss one of the oldest *gompas* on their route?

No, she was filled with emotions she couldn't identify, brought on
by Johanna's last entry, and she needed time to sort them out. Easier
done on the move than huddled against the cold in her tent, where
Howard might come calling, where she'd inevitably spend the day waiting for Debby, setting herself up for another disappointment. Let Debby
come and wait for her.

So she'd gone on the hike with Ang and Tenzing. Carolyn, Peter,
and Lonnie had come, too, but Jan had gone off by herself to draw.
Howard had stayed in camp to nurse his headache.

For the first part of the hike, the level stretch along the riverbank
that led through cool, dripping forests of junipers and rhododendrons,
Maya was near tears. But for what? And why? Her own memories played

against the pages of journals and letters like water pushing against stones, trying to rearrange the past.

The stubborn rhododendrons surrounded her, their green buds closed tight. They wouldn't bloom for weeks yet, and that made her sad. To come all this way, to pass through these forests, to see the bud and know that she would never see the blossom. Was she crying for blooms she could never behold? Or because she would never feel what Johanna had felt, holding Rachel in her arms for the first time, never thrill to the milky smell of her own newborn? Not unless she did something about the matter, made some radical change in her life, took action. Was that her pain? That she could no longer take refuge in unreflecting action, that she had passed the point in life—and history—when a woman could get knocked up as easily as she took a nap. Was that at the root of her restlessness with Johanna?

I could have a baby if I wanted to, she told herself. But I would have to *decide,* to say, "I want this and I will do A, B, C, and D to make it happen," find a donor or go to a sperm bank and track my menstruations and take my temperature every day and Goddess knows what all else. Getting knocked up would have to be a conscious, a self-conscious act. And I'm not good at that. What I'm best at, still, is getting lost in the moment, even if I have to create the moment to get lost in. But how do you do that with a woman partner? Or without a partner in the age of AIDS?

They crossed the river on the iron suspension bridge that spanned the Dudh Kosi. She paused for a moment, looking down at the white-blue foaming waters, thinking about Rio. The singing river, he had called their moments of magic. I shouldn't have been so careful, she thought, I should have had your baby when I had the chance. But no, what a mess that would have been, on the run with a kid. Anyway, in those days, she didn't want a baby. She'd wanted to gestate a revolution, birth a whole new world.

As they started the uphill climb on the other side, Maya's cough returned. The day grew cold, dreary. Twisted black beeches made grim patterns against the cold, gray sky. Even when the mist began to lift, revealing the ice-blue glaciers of sharp-peaked Ama Dablam, the pale sun didn't shed any warmth. She stopped thinking about anything except the effort required to wheeze her way up the trail. Ang came up behind her and, with a smile, took her day pack to carry. She didn't argue. She had given up her fantasy of making a pilgrimage up these mountains with her mother's ashes on her back. Let Ang carry them. It was enough work to convey her own living flesh up these trails.

It's not a Beautician I need, she told herself, it's a Higher Personal Trainer. By the time she reached the *gompa,* the monastery, an ochre-colored two-story building crowned with a red tile roof in the center of the small village of stone houses perched on walled terraces, her shirt was soaked through with sweat. Nevertheless, she had dutifully removed her heavy hiking boots in the entry hall and prostrated herself on the ground three times, as Ang smiled his approval. She would demonstrate respect for every custom they could come up with if it killed her. And it might, she thought, prowling around the interior of the *gompa* in her stocking feet, with the cold seeping up from the stone floor and making her legs ache.

She felt cold all the way through, as if her body had forgotten how to generate heat, and no external source could penetrate. A hot bath, she thought to herself, I'd give my whole store of accumulated merit for one right now. I'd sell my soul to the devil just for a chance at those fires of hell.

Still there were so many fascinating things to look at in the dim hall that she couldn't bring herself to put her shoes back on and go. Light filtered through the open doorway. The afternoon was dark and she had to look hard to pick out the details of the delicately painted images that covered every surface. The walls were painted with Buddhas and Bodhisattvas, the beams were carved and painted with leaves and whorls and spirals, the benches that lined the walls were decorated with designs and hundreds of painted mandalas hung from the rafters, waving gently in the air. On one of the benches lay a collection of instruments, bronze handbells and long trumpets made of bone decorated with silver. In a corner, a monk sat, cross-legged on a bench, chanting from one of the narrow loose-leafed books of sacred texts. His red robe, his shaved head, his still posture, created a sense of rapt concentration in the dark room.

Candles lined the altars. Ang encouraged Maya to light one. She nodded—anything that might possibly warm the place up, even to an immeasurably small degree, seemed a good idea. She took one of the low yellow candles, lit it from the flame of one already burning on the altar, and placed it next to its sister. I should make a prayer, she thought, but for what? A baby? No, I'm not ready to pray for a baby yet. For my sister to come to me, care about me, love me? Better to stick to something more basic.

"Please, spirits, don't let me die of pneumonia." She murmured the heartfelt prayer under her breath. But then something seemed to move in the cold air, as if a larger presence entered and filled the room, and suddenly she was standing before the altar with tears welling up in her eyes. The chanting of the monk reverberated in the hall; from time to time he picked up one of the bronze bells and rang it, its sweet overtones singing like moving water between stones. The sound echoed every moment of grace she'd had in her life, led her back to the cold wind on the coast, to the locker room floor. Yes, she thought, looking at the candle's pale flame. Yes, that's it. But as soon as her mind formed words the singing moment abandoned her. The monk's low voice droned, leaving her with nothing she could name or hold, only a sudden urge to take her mother's ashes out of the backpack, to cease carrying them, to give them to the monk and ask him to take them for her, to be a guide for Betty wherever she was. She actually began to move toward the bench where Ang had set her pack. As she stepped away from the candle, the spell was broken. The cold burned through her wool socks, and she remembered she was bringing her mother's ashes to Debby. She still had something to complete; the time had not yet come to let them go.

Besides, Betty wouldn't have liked it here. She liked Los Angeles, sun and palm trees, shirtsleeves in February. She'd hated the cold, had moved from Milwaukee to escape it.

Tenzing was speaking in a low voice to the others, who were gathered in the corner near the entranceway, examining the wall paintings, which Tenzing said showed the life of Padmasambhava, who brought Buddhism to Tibet. Maya walked over to them instead.

"There used to be a yeti skull in this *gompa*," Tenzing was saying. "But it was stolen."

"Stolen? Why would anybody want to steal a yeti skull?" Carolyn asked.

"Probably some damn tourist," Peter suggested. "Thought it would make a great souvenir."

"Yeti skull," Ang sniffed. "I have seen. Goat skull, no yeti." He smiled.

"Oh, Ang, you cynic," Lonnie said. "Don't spoil the dream. I want to go home and say that I was in a monastery with a yeti skull."

"So who's stopping you?" Peter asked. "You can say whatever you want. Who the hell is going to check?"

"Ah, but I want to believe it," Lonnie said.

Tenzing motioned to them to go. Maya had laced up her hiking boots again, grateful for their thick soles. He steered them across the terraced fields to the teahouse. Maya entered, eager for warmth and shelter, but the air inside its stone walls seemed no warmer than the air outside. She sat down with the others, waiting for tea, in the main room which held several small tables for eating and long benches for sleeping. The walls were decorated with pictures from old issues of the *National Geographic,* mountain posters, and a rather incongruous map of the growth of civilization in the Near East. There were also photographs of famous visitors, notably Jimmy, Rosalynn, and Amy Carter, on their way up to Kala Pattar. The picture depressed Maya because the Carters had been years older than she was, heading up to higher altitudes, looking cheerful and fit while she felt like lying down and letting dogs walk over her. What was wrong with her? She was so exhausted she couldn't imagine going on to Kala Pattar at eighteen thousand feet. And she hadn't even been president, a job to tax one's strength if ever there was one.

By then her teeth were chattering audibly. Ang took her by the hand, motioning to her to get up, and led her into the kitchen to sit by the hearth, a low mud-and-stone stove where juniper branches were burning. Shelves on the wall across from the window held dishes, pots and pans, rows of the ubiquitous cheap Chinese thermos bottles, packages of cookies and bottles of Coke—the stores of the little eating place. Maya eyed them hungrily.

The small room was lit by one window set into the wide stone wall. Pictures from a western fashion magazine lined the window niche. Maya wondered what the simple dresses and blouses meant to the Sherpa woman who had hung the pictures. Were they some sort of dream ideal? Did she just find the shapes and colors pretty? Or perhaps she intuitively understood that these things were the true religious icons of the West, and put them up much as Maya enjoyed the calendar of Tibetan mandalas that hung in her own bathroom, something exotic to look at, from another world.

She watched the two Sherpa women, mother and daughter, as they chatted and laughed while they prepared a simple lunch for the trekkers. The women wore the traditional long skirts and multicolored striped aprons and headscarfs. They seemed completely at ease with each other, comfortable working together, doing what needed to be done. Had she and Betty ever been like that? Long, long ago, maybe. Maya could remember making a seder back in Milwaukee, for Baba, Betty's mother, the year she'd had the heart attack and couldn't do it for herself. Maya had been ten, so proud of the matzo balls she made herself, so superior to baby Debby, who could be trusted to do only simple tasks like setting the table or putting out bowls of cut-up parsley to be dipped in the salt water. But then Maya had dug deep into the cupboards and come up with a pan to put the matzo balls in, and Betty had screamed at her when she discovered what she'd done because the pan wasn't kosher for Pesach, and Maya had screamed back at her, How was I supposed to know? It's not like we do the kosher bit at home, Mom. And then Baba, hearing the screaming from her sickbed, got all worked up, yelling at Betty that she wasn't going to eat a bite of the dinner, no, not one bite, she didn't trust it, and, Oy vehs mier, you're going to give me a heart attack all over again. Yes, there had been moments, but they hadn't lasted.

The older Sherpani presented Maya with a cup of hot tea, and she accepted with a grateful smile, cupping her hands around the tin cup for warmth, breathing in the steam, sipping the hot liquid. She could feel it leave a trail of warmth through the cold regions of her interior. Yes, another cup or two and she might begin to thaw.

Next to the hearth was a huge jug that contained hot water, and the daughter filled a thermos from it and took it out to the main room where the others waited. The mother began dishing out rice and lentils and dumplings that had been warming on the hearth, filling plates that the daughter, returning from the other room, carried out. The mother handed a plate to Maya, with a smile, and gave her a fork and spoon to eat with. The hot food tasted good and added to the slowly growing pool of warmth in Maya's center.

She and Johanna, now, they worked together with that same ease. One of them making a salad while the other boiled noodles for pasta; one of them stirring a sauce as the other chopped broccoli to steam. One of them painting the wall while the other followed to paint the trim; one of them digging the garden while the other planted the seedlings, and all the while talking with that same comfort and familiarity. Gossiping about Jo's work or Rachel's latest exploit at school. Yes, there was a feel to their life together like that of a comfortable old shirt, knit of the threads of the everyday. As Lonnie would say, they *worked* in each other's lives. Maybe Maya didn't sufficiently appreciate that.

Maya was starting to feel if not warm at least less cold, when a group of young trekkers entered, laughing and talking, unloading the heavy packs they carried by themselves in the main room of the teahouse and then joining her around the hearth to warm their hands. The small room was filled with young, strong bodies and laughing voices in a mix of accents, stomping their feet, peeling off jackets, and crowding close to the hearth, blocking the heat. But they're cold, she told herself, fresh from outside, and I've had undisputed possession for almost twenty minutes now. Reluctantly, she moved back to give them more room, retreating to the window seat.

"Oh, God, what a walk," said a blond woman in a German accent. "I am so hungry! I am going to order a yak steak, a yak burger, and yak stew!"

"I'm going to order up a plate of chips all round. I hope they have plenty of potatoes," said her companion, a tall young man in a green down vest. "I nearly cried last night when they ran out of *dhal bhaat*."

"Good thing you had those PowerBars," said a second young woman, who sat on the edge of the hearth untying her hiking boots and removing her striped socks. "We'd never have made it down from Kala Pattar."

"Oh, my aching head," said the blond woman. "I don't even want to think about Kala Pattar. You know, really I think I prefer the Annapurnas. The scenery is quite as beautiful but the trails are not so high."

She, too, removed her shoes and socks. The kitchen rapidly began to smell like a locker room. But, Maya told herself, I should be the last person in the world to complain about that, given that a locker room was the site of my spiritual awakening. That's my mistake: looking for power in the mountains when I was evidently meant to meditate to the sounds of banging metal doors and the incense of sweaty underwear.

"But the teahouses are even worse crowded than here," said the woman with the striped socks.

The young man had returned from the other room, followed by the older Sherpani, who with a polite smile attempted to maneuver around her own hearth, which was now blocked by bodies and garlanded by shoes and socks.

"They say Manaslu is the place to be," he commented. "They say it's like Khumbu was twenty years ago. Not ruined yet."

The Sherpani, observing her hearth, was looking distressed, speaking rapidly and excitedly in Sherpa. The young trekkers ignored her. Another young woman entered, standing in the doorway. Maya looked up and caught her eye. It was the girl in the green sweater.

"I hear Bhutan is good. Hard to get into, though. You need a special visa. Or you can get someone to guide you over the border, maybe," the German woman was saying.

"Or maybe not," said the woman with the striped socks. "I don't know, I think I've had enough of the mountains. I met a bloke in Kathmandu who told me about a beach in Thailand where you can live for practically nothing on seafood and tropical fruit. Sun and water—that's for me."

"Please," said the Sherpani, helplessly gesturing at the hearth.

"Let the lady through," said the man. "Come on, Elaine, how can we eat if she can't get over there to cook?"

"I'm just warming my hands. Give me one more minute."

"It's not that," said the girl in the green sweater. Her eyes were gray and level, Maya noted, her thin, heart-shaped face so young it looked not quite finished yet, a rough sketch of what it would be someday when all the lines were filled in. Her voice was young, too, so light and soft it could almost have been a child's voice, except that she spoke with a calm authority that quieted the room. "You've got to take away your shoes and socks. The hearth is sacred here. You're insulting it."

Maya looked up at her and smiled, feeling a rush of pride, as if the girl somehow belonged to her.

"Oh, give me a break," Elaine said. "My socks are soaking wet . . . I just need to dry them. Surely she can understand that!"

"It's not a matter of understanding," said the girl, in her sure, quiet voice. "What's sacred is sacred. It's not negotiable." She looked around for allies and caught Maya's eye.

I'll support her, Maya thought. I'll back her up, and then we'll talk, and this time I won't say anything stupid.

"She's right, you know," Maya said. "We're guests of these people. We've got to respect their traditions."

"Ah balls," the young man grumbled. "A silly superstition to have in a country with so bloody many ways of getting your feet wet. I swear the Nepalis excel in thinking up ways to make an already difficult life more uncomfortable than it has to be." But he stooped and picked up his shoes and socks. "Elaine? Ursula? Shall I grab yours, too?"

The blond Ursula gave Maya a nasty look, but she picked up her stockings and shoes and brushed roughly past the girl in the green sweater who still stood in the doorway.

"I've got clean socks in my pack," she said, and went into the other room.

The other two followed.

The Sherpani smiled with relief. Maya stood up, intending to go into the other room and leave the kitchen free, but the Sherpani shook her head and gestured for her to sit back down. Gratefully, she did so, and the girl in the green sweater joined her on the window ledge.

"We've met before, on the way to Namche," Maya said. "My name is Maya. What's your name?"

"Claire," she said.

The Sherpani handed Claire a steaming cup of hot *chiyaa*, and took Maya's cup and refilled it. They sat, drinking together, in a silence Maya wanted to break but didn't know how. What is it I want from her? she wondered. A blessing? A benediction? Do I need my own younger self to tell me that I haven't compromised or given in, that I really am okay?

Their silence faded into the silence of the village, the distilled essence of a loneliness Maya was familiar with, the quiet that descended in late afternoon, when everyone was away at work, and only she was at home, trying to write. A peaceful, poignant silence, with the light beginning to fail and time running out. In a moment, they would have finished their tea. An opportunity would be lost.

"How is your trip going?" Maya asked. A scarcely original comment, but there it was.

"Good."

The girl seemed part of the silence, she seemed in her quiet to hold treasures revealed only by small shafts of sunlight through parchment windows. But maybe I'm reading all that into it. Maybe she's just shy.

"Where are you going, today?"

Claire smiled, the self-contained, mysterious half smile of an archaic Greek Kore. "I don't know. Maybe nowhere. Maybe I'll just stay here, study with the monks at the *gompa*."

"Can you do that? I didn't know they took on westerners."

Claire shrugged. "I don't know that they don't. But I might go back to Tengpoche, although I don't like it so much there. It's too crowded, too many trekkers. Or over to Thami."

"It's good to be so free when you're young," Maya said, because she felt compelled to offer the girl something. "When you get older, life gets more . . . complicated."

"It doesn't have to," Claire said decisively, as if it were a credo she claimed for herself.

"I believed that once," Maya said. "But the complications have a way of sneaking up on you." Suddenly Maya wanted to take her by the shoulders and warn her, advise her, sit her down and pour out everything she'd learned in twenty years. Look, look, this is how life is and how it should be, I have traveled your road, I have inflicted myself on *curanderas* and healers and shamans all over the Third World. I know how to gather power and I know how it feels when it drains out of you and leaks away downhill. Listen to me, let me make it easy for you. I don't want you to have to go through what I've been through.

So that's what I feel for her, Maya thought. Not sexual lust, but mother lust. I'm twenty years older than she is—old enough. I want to be somebody's mother, have someone to follow me, to pass things on to.

"You have to be vigilant," Claire said. Maya was struck by the word she used. Vigilant. Like *vigil.* And it was impossible to think *vigil* without thinking *lonely,* just as it was impossible to say *chainsaw,* for example, without thinking *Texas* and *massacre.* Was the girl lonely? And was that what she herself needed, a dose of good old-fashioned loneliness, to wake her up and make her appreciate the warmth of Johanna's kitchen?

"But if you're too vigilant," Maya said, "if you're too committed to your own freedom, then you can never commit to anyone else or anything. It can be an empty way to live."

"The lamas say that emptiness is form, form is emptiness," Claire countered. "The complications are all illusions. Once you break through the veil, emptiness is all there is."

There was a tone in her voice, under the calm and the quiet, just a soft hint Maya caught of something plaintive, as if she was trying to convince herself of something.

She *is* lonely, Maya thought. She needs a mother or a lover or a best friend, and instead of admitting it and going out to find one, she's convinced herself that loneliness is a spiritual path.

Well, I know how that's done.

"Yes, but they also say you're supposed to live a life first." Maya spoke lightly, but she had a sense of having joined a battle that was already underway inside the girl. "Have sex, have kids, have whatever was the sixth-century equivalent of a career. Then you have something to

renounce. You don't go off and find enlightenment at seventeen, generally.''

"Eighteen," said the girl. "A lot of the young men do go to the
monasteries at eighteen. Some go even younger, when they're children.
They live a totally spiritual life."

"Ah," Maya said, "but maybe you and I were born in women's
bodies in the West precisely so we could struggle with all the contradictions of murky, messy, ordinary life."

The girl sighed. "That's what everybody says. That's how everybody justifies it. And so it keeps going on."

But I should be saying that, Maya almost protested. I should be
eighteen and screaming about purity. Why do I suddenly want to talk this
girl into going home, and going to college, and going out on dates? Is this
my maternal instinct descending in the worst possible way? In a moment
I'll be repeating Betty's lines.

The girl was a messenger. But what was the message? Have I not
been vigilant enough, have I allowed my purity to be complicated by
work and Jo and commitments and all the anxieties of daily life? Or have I
been too vigilant, cutting off the complications that could have fed me,
like a child of my own? Like Rio. Why am I so sure I know what's right for
her, when I don't know what's right for me?

"Maybe you'll be the one," Maya said. "Maybe you'll be the one to
do it, break through it all, and stay free. I thought I would be, once—but I
turned out to be someone else."

"I have to try," Claire said. "That's all I know."

"Que le vaya bien," Maya said.

"That's Spanish, isn't it? What does it mean?"

"May it go well with you."

Maya thought about their conversation all the way back to Tengpoche.
Going downhill, she could keep up with the others without wheezing
and coughing as they clambered down the terraced hillsides. I should
have warned her, Maya thought. I should have told her that there's a
power in disconnection, in formlessness, that can get out of hand. I've
seen it happen, seen the hippies drift down to Panahachel looking for
enlightenment, settling for cheap dope. I shouldn't have let her go. She
needs someone to guide her, or maybe I just need somebody to mother,
someone to let me feel that I can join what Johanna calls the line of
women, those ancestors stretching back into the past, those yet to come
stretching down into the future. But I'm the broken link, out of line,
motherless, childless. Adrift with no holdfast to earth, like a kite cut loose
from its string.

Of course I have Rachel, she told herself. I've learned to braid her hair—well enough to get what Johanna always said were passing marks for a white girl—I've watched over her homework and her softball games and attended her dance performances and made her practice her piano and chauffeured her around.

But I didn't carry her in my womb, birth her, forge that connection of blood and milk and bone.

Was that so important? Or was she perhaps feeling Betty's spirit breathe on the nape of her neck, whispering, "Baby. Grandchildren. Don't let my line die away!"

Well then, she would just have a baby. Plenty of women did it alone.

They were crossing the suspension bridge, and for a moment she stopped to look down at the blue pools of the Dudh Kosi and the frothing foam that swirled and danced white around their edges.

If I were a different sort of person, she mused, I could get myself knocked up by one of the Sherpas. I don't think AIDS is a problem here, not yet. Tashi, maybe, he's young and virile. I could have a lovely little Sherpa baby, sweet and brown and at home at high altitudes.

But no, the kid would climb up every damn thing in sight, and I'd never be able to catch it.

Baby lust, she thought as she walked on. Now the path began to climb again, but gently. She fell back behind the others, but that suited her. She didn't want to talk, she wanted to think.

Was that what was happening? Why she was suddenly so restless, so discontented in her relationship with Johanna? She had seen it happen before—two seemingly perfectly happy women, devoted to each other, reaching that age where the alarm on the biological clock begins to ring, and suddenly one or the other ends up with a man. Sometimes only to break up painfully a few years down the road, with teams of lawyers fighting expensive custody battles.

Betty, you wanted a grandchild so badly. And neither I nor Debby was about to give you one. Did your desire break loose like a free-floating miasma when you died, and insert itself into me?

Is it a ghost I can exorcize? Or a spirit I might welcome? Or does it mean simply that I wasn't enough for you, as I am?

They had come to the place along the trail where a series of small, stone huts housed the gold- and red- and green- and blue-painted prayer wheels, cylindrical drums that could be turned by pushing on the spokes that protruded from their base. Ahead of her, Maya could see that Ang spun each wheel as he passed, and when she reached the hut, she did the same. Never pass up a chance to gain merit, that was her philosophy. She watched the wheel spin round, its forms and colors blurring, still thinking about her mother. It seemed like the good times between them were like the blurred spinning of the wheel. Something moved, changed, was let loose, and for a short time she'd had merit in her mother's eyes. But then the wheel would slow and stop, and the old hard-edged patterns would reappear, unchanged.

Before the wheel could stop, Maya pulled on the spoke and spun it again. The trick was to stay in motion, that was the thing. Motion was akin to freedom. Both brought merit, erased sin, challenged gravity itself. Both offered escape from ghosts and miasmas.

She spun and spun the wheel, while the others walked on far out of sight, spinning to lose herself in the colors and the patterns and the blurred speed. Enough merit, enough motion, enough freedom, and she would escape the complications and the memories, spin herself back to the simple purity of vision. She would be like Claire, eighteen again; she would turn back time.

And on this round, she would not make the same mistakes.

25

November 1969

"This is my daughter Karla, the activist." Betty's hand rested on Maya's shoulder, and there was a note in her voice that approximated pride. The touch, the tone, made Maya happy but wary. She might grow accustomed to being approved of, and then what would happen when the real conditions of her life made themselves evident?

They were marching with her sister, Debby, and a small contingent of her mother's friends who'd come up from LA for the November Mobilization. The women were smiling, their gray hair reflecting the sun. Debby's eyes followed Maya admiringly as she greeted friends and conferred with monitors about details of the route. For Maya had become an organizer. Not a leader, not someone who argued points of theory in late-night meetings, but one of the legions of mostly women who helped out in the office, typed letters, made phone calls, and arranged places for out-of-town demonstrators to stay.

It was part of the strategy of the Home Front, as Daniel had named the collective they formed after People's Park. She and Rio, Daniel and Edith, Rob and Liza, had met throughout the summer, ostensibly for strategy sessions and mutual education. Really they had long potluck brunches, smoked dope, and argued endlessly about how to end the war.

In August, they'd gone off to camp together for ten days, up in the High Sierras. A skill-building session, Daniel had called it. They'd had a serious debate at one of their brunches about whether or not to bring a couple of rifles, practice target shooting.

"We should prepare ourselves for all contingencies," Daniel had said.

"I'm not ready for that one," Liza had said. "I just can't see myself in the Revolutionary Rifle Brigade."

"If you were in Vietnam, you wouldn't have the luxury of choice," Edith said. "You'd have to defend yourself."

"But I'm not in Vietnam," Liza said, pouring maple syrup in a delicate stream over her plate of pancakes. "I'm a dance major at Cal. Parading around with a rifle won't change that."

"I'm only saying that we need to develop a broad range of skills," Daniel said. "I hope we'll never have to use guns, that it won't come to that. But if we ever do need them, we should be able to use them. Then we can make a real choice. If we decide to be nonviolent, it'll be a political decision, not because we don't know a butt from a muzzle."

"Yeah, think how embarrassing," Rob said with a wink. "There you are, the Panthers and the pigs, shooting it out on the barricades, the brother in front of you takes a bullet in the heart, bam, pow! The revolutionary sister by his side picks up his fallen rifle, hands it to you—a solemn trust. And you say, 'Oh, by the way, how do you work this thing?' "

"Can't you ever take anything seriously, Rob?" Edith frowned at him. "Someday what we decide here could mean life or death to someone."

"I do take it seriously," Rob said. "I just think we might be taking *ourselves* a bit too seriously."

"But if we don't take ourselves seriously, who will?" Edith asked. "It might be good for us all to learn to shoot. Teach us the discipline that comes from handling real power."

"I know how to shoot," Rio said. "I know all about guns, shit, I grew up with them. Hunting woodchucks and rabbits. And I hate it. I hate killing things."

"We're talking about self-defense, not killing," Daniel said.

"I used to cry when the little woodchucks died, and my dad and my brothers all used to stand around and laugh at me."

"Then you can teach us," Daniel said.

Rio shook his head. "Not on this trip. For one thing, we don't have any rifles . . . and they're expensive. And for another thing, it's not hunting season. You can't go tromping around the woods with guns in the summertime."

"Rio's right," Rob said. "If we decide we actually need to know how to use a gun, we should go up to the rifle range some Sunday, shoot clay pigeons."

Daniel shook his head. "Too much chance of being observed and remembered."

"Oh, come on, Daniel," Maya said. "Do you really think anyone's that interested in us?"

"As soon as we start taking effective action, they will be. We've got to expect that, train ourselves to deal with it by behaving from the beginning as if it were true. As Edith said, we've got to take ourselves seriously."

"Well, I do," Rio said. "I take it real seriously that we've got to end the war. Seriously and personally. My brother is dead—that's serious. My kid brother is over there right now. If I have to die to end this war, hey, that's okay. I'm willing. But I remember how it felt, looking down at the goddamned bloody little woodchucks with their heads blown off. I don't know if I'm willing to kill."

A long silence followed his statement.

"Me neither," Maya said at last in a small voice, wanting to support him somehow, knowing what it cost him to talk about his brother. "I don't want to kill anyone."

"I'm not talking about killing anyone," Daniel said. "God knows, I don't want to kill people. I don't even want to hurt anyone, if it can be avoided. But we've got to recognize that ultimately, we might not be able to avoid it. We're up against a system of institutionalized violence, and it's not going to hand over power just because we ask it nicely."

Again the group fell silent. Maya rose and began clearing off the table, and the discussion shifted to the menu for the trip.

They backpacked to a high alpine lake and practiced fire building, signaling, and finding their way cross-country with map and compass. Maya wasn't sure why these skills were necessary to stop the war, but she enjoyed the trip thoroughly. At night, over the fire, they'd have long political discussions. Should they work with the Moratorium in the fall, the group planning a full day of activities to stop the war? A low-risk general strike for liberals, Daniel called it. Should they work with the group planning the big November Mobilization, the next in the series of giant marches to which thousands returned every spring and fall, regular as migrating birds? Should they remain independent, take their own actions, intensify the struggle on their own terms, whatever those were? Above them the sky was plastered with too many stars. By day the sky was extraordinarily blue, mirrored by hidden lakes they discovered high up on ledges of gray-specked, sun-warmed granite. "If this wasn't nature," Daniel complained, "it would be in bad taste. Overdone."

Now Maya marched down Geary Street behind the banner of Women Strike for Peace, in the company of women in polyester pantsuits and flat-heeled shoes, who were pushing strollers or displaying pictures of their grandsons and smiling and waving at the crowds who lined the streets. They were teachers and mothers and social workers, all of them except for Maya embedded in ordinary life. They were not considering laying down those lives to stop the war they opposed. When they tired of singing "Ain't Gonna Study War No More," they talked about their jobs, about which was the most authentic restaurant in Chinatown, about taking the ferry to Sausalito and where to eat on Fisherman's Wharf, about their sons in graduate school and their daughters who were married and how the priest in their local parish had come out against the war. Maya began to feel a strange sense of dislocation, as if the march had transformed itself without her knowledge into a suburban picnic, part of a packaged tour. What was she doing there? The woman who ran flaming through the evening news, where was she? Who remembered her? Would Mrs. Kohls stanch her wounds with coffee from her thermos? Could her baby ride in the stroller with Mrs. Irving's daughter, its blackened, flaking skin shaded by the umbrellas they raised against gusts of rain?

Her mother turned to her and smiled. "This is a beautiful thing, this march. I'm proud that you had a hand in organizing it."

Betty had aged, Maya noticed. New lines surrounded her eyes, and her brown hair was streaked with gray. Her skin was soft and pale and lightly freckled. She wore blue polyester pants with an elastic band at the waist, and a red-and-white flowered blouse. Suddenly Maya was overwhelmed with tenderness for her. She wanted to gather her mother up in her arms and hold her as if Betty were the child, and keep her from ever being hurt again. Yet she suspected that she herself would go on hurting her. Because where, after all, did her loyalty lie? To her mother's softfleshed arms? To the woman on fire?

"I love you, Mom," Maya said. "I'm really glad you came up, and Debby, too. I'm so happy we can march together, like this."

Betty's eyes filled with tears. She slipped her arm around Maya's shoulder, and her other arm around Debby's waist, and walked on, a proud woman supported by her daughters. And if we could only stay like this, Maya thought, and not speak, and not ruin it . . . She opened her mouth and began to sing.

> "I'm going to lay down my sword and shield,
> Down by the riverside . . .
> Down by the riverside . . . ."

The women's voices rose with the song, and the music swelled around them and carried them like the river they sang of, laced with filaments of love. For the first time in a long time, Maya realized, she was happy. Her mother loved her again. The people were rising. Even the ordinary people, the ones who weren't brave or hip or willing to die— maybe even *they* would stop the war.

But the route was a long one, and they couldn't sing forever. Mrs. Kohls passed her bottomless thermos around, and Maya drank gratefully the brew that was strong and milky and sweet.

"Did you know that Johanna had a baby?" Betty said.

"What? You're kidding!"

"No, it's true. Last June. It's been a rough year for her."

"Did she drop out of school?"

"No, she's hanging in there. Marian's helping her out. She lives at home and Marian works night shift, sleeps in the morning, watches the kid in the afternoon. I guess in the morning Johanna takes the kid to class. What a life some people have!"

"I can't believe it!" I can't believe she didn't tell me about it, Maya thought, that she would let her anger continue to be a barricade between us. How was it possible to touch so deeply and end so separately?

"Don't count on me to do the same for you," Betty warned.

"I'm not planning to get pregnant, Mom. Don't worry. Before I have kids I want to make the world a fit place to bring them up." Or go down trying, she added silently to herself, an outcome she actually thought was more likely.

"Let's hope that happy day arrives before menopause," her mother said.

The march continued up a hill, and they were silent as they struggled up. The older women slowed down, and Maya took a sign and carried it for a woman who was breathing heavily. Finally they crested the hill. At the top, they turned for a moment to see the long, long line behind them—thousands of people filling the streets, stretching back to the Bay, a ribbon of color cleaving the city.

As they started down, Betty spoke again. "So, do you ever think about going back to school?" she asked in a voice so carefully casual that it made Maya's ears ache.

"I need to stay free right now, to be able to devote my full time to this work. We've got to end this war, Betty. There's so much in this country that's wrong, that we've got to change."

"I can't argue with that. I'm here, aren't I? But how can you be prepared to make changes if you don't have an education?"

"Mom, what they teach in the university is how to prevent change, not how to make it. I'm getting my education, on the streets."

"Oh, God, give me a break!"

"It's true!"

"Karla, I'm talking about your life, not your rhetoric. What kind of a life are you making for yourself? Even your boyfriend's in school. Is he going to want a wife who doesn't even have a high school diploma?"

Her mother's arm was withdrawn, and Maya pulled away, wrapping herself in her own silence.

"Well, is he? Answer me that!"

"I can't possibly answer that, Mom. It's just—you and I think in such totally different terms that I can't even begin to talk to you."

"Try. I don't see how you can change the world if you can't even explain your ideas to your own mother."

Maya stole a glance at Debby, hoping for an ally. But her sister's face was carefully composed, neutral, shuttered. How could she tell her mother what she really believed? Could she say, Mom, we are living in the last days? This is all going to crumble, and I've pledged myself to help bring it down. I'll be surprised if I ever see twenty-one.

"Look, Mom, I don't want to fight with you today. Can't we just say that this is a historic moment, and I want to be part of it?"

"But all over the country, *college students* are part of it." Betty's voice rose to a near squeal. "And when the moment passes, they'll still have something. An education. A degree. A future." She stopped walking for a moment, drew a deep breath, and slid her arm around Maya's shoulder. "Karla, listen to me, this is something you only learn by living through it, but these things pass. A movement is like a mood—you're in it, and then you're out of it, but life goes on."

Maya slid out of her mother's embrace and resumed their uphill walk. "Can't we talk about something else? Like you, Debby. How's Harding High?"

"It's okay," Debby said. "I've been pretty busy this semester, because I've got a dual major, in science and languages. That way when I get to be a doctor, I can travel all over the world."

"That's great, Debby," Maya said, avoiding her mother's eye.

Debby gulped in a breath, glanced from her sister to her mother and back again. "Don't you want to be anything, Karla? I mean, do you just want to do this all of your life?"

"I am something, Debby. I'm me." Debby was young. She could still be salvaged if only Maya could reach her. "That's enough. Because what I want is so much bigger than any single thing I could be."

"What do you want?"

"I want everything to change. I want a different world to be in."

Much to her surprise, her mother's arm slid back across her shoulders. "I just ache for you," Betty said. "I wish I could give you a different world. I wish I could make things easy for you."

Maya didn't pull away. She allowed herself to be drawn close. If only she could give in, let her mother shelter her again, be a child for a while. But that time had passed. She would have to continue to fight. "I'm not asking you to make things easy, Mom. Just let me go through them in my own way."

"Well," Betty said. "I hadn't noticed that I've had much success in stopping you."

•   •   •

Maya sent a note back with them for Johanna.

> Dear Johanna,
>
> I heard about your baby. I guess I should say congratulations, even though I'm sure it isn't easy going to school and having a baby, too.
>
> I hope you're not still mad at me. I'm certainly not mad at you. I guess I've learned a lot and I understand now how the racism of this unjust system has always divided us. It's not really surprising that you saw that before I did. I just want you to know that I'm devoting my life to work against the oppression of your people and other Third World people, like in Vietnam. I would like to be your ally in some way.
>
> Love,
> Maya J.

This letter did not satisfy her. It sounded stiff, like something written by committee, not by her. She sent it anyway. The problem was, she could no longer simply write a letter from Maya J. to Johanna M., because she was too conscious of writing a letter from a White Person to a Black Person. It seemed to be yet another time when they could not communicate. She didn't really expect an answer, and she did not receive one.

Maya rubbed her hands together and stomped her feet, which had turned to numb stumps. She'd been standing all day in the cold outside Macy's on Union Square, holding a papier-mâché dove with an opening for coins. Christmas was less than a week away. Down the street the Salvation Army rang their bell and sang doleful carols. Around her were gathered the other members of the Home Front. They were handing out balloons that said PEACE ON EARTH: STOP THE WAR IN VIETNAM.

"Would you like a balloon, little boy?" asked Daniel, who was dressed as Santa Claus, in a red plush suit covered with political buttons. He made a skinny, beaky, but outgoing Saint Nick.

Rio was manning the helium tank, along with Rob.

"Isn't that nice," said the boy's mother, who was wearing a dark fur coat and spike heels. "Say thank you to Santa. . . . Wait a minute! What is this?" as she caught sight of the message emblazoned on the balloons.

"Peace," Edith said, placing a leaflet in the woman's hand. "Do you know how many children have been killed in Vietnam this year?"

"Joey, give that balloon back!"

"I don't want to!"

She yanked the string out of his hand, and he began to cry as she dragged him away.

"You should be ashamed of yourselves," the woman shouted. "Using children for your propaganda."

"Think of the children in Vietnam," Edith called after her. "Think about their Christmas!"

Edith knew all the facts and statistics about Vietnam, how many had died, how many tons of bombs had been dropped, how exactly napalm and white phosphorus affected human skin. She never failed to remember to shout them out. Maya felt inadequate in the face of her determination.

"Hey you, there! Get away from there! You're not allowed around here!" The store security guard, a husky man with a ruddy face, emerged from the main entrance and accosted Daniel.

"Ho, ho, ho!" Daniel said jovially.

"I'll ho you!"

"Merry Christmas," Rob said, handing a balloon to a little girl. "Peace on earth."

"This is wonderful work you're doing," a young woman said. "Come on, Jessica. Merry Christmas."

"Why is that man hurting Santa?" Jessica asked. The security guard had grabbed Daniel's wrist and was trying to strong-arm him away from the store entrance. The child began to cry.

"Leave Santa alone!" the woman said. "You're scaring the children." A crowd was forming, and Edith was busy reciting facts and handing out leaflets. Maya held the dove, smiled, and said, "Happy holidays! Would you care to make a contribution to peace?"

The detective dropped Daniel's arm but made a call into his walkie-talkie. Rio was madly filling balloons with helium. Rob handed them out to children and anyone else who would take them. The crowd grew, yelling encouragement and screaming accusations at them, until the police came.

"You are ordered to disperse," the officer said. "This is an illegal gathering."

"Now, Officer," Daniel said, "does that show the Christmas spirit?"

"Peace on earth," Rio said, handing the second cop a balloon. The man dropped the string and the balloon wafted up into the sky.

"Peace on earth, stop the war in Vietnam," Maya said, grabbing a handful of balloons and distributing them quickly to a knot of children who were gathered near Santa.

"You're under arrest," the first cop said to Santa.

The children began crying and screaming, as did most of their mothers. "You can't arrest Santa Claus in front of my kid!"

"That man is a travesty! Arrest him now!"

Daniel, smiling, sat down. Edith, following suit, joined him. Across the street, Liza, their lookout, waved an arm to show she was there. Rob grabbed the helium tank and attempted to back quietly away with it, but another squad car had pulled up and he was blocked by two other cops. Sirens were wailing and children were wailing. Maya and Rio sat down with the others, linking arms in a chain and singing:

> You better watch out
> You better all shout
> Too many have died
> And that is why
> Santa Claus wants out of
> Vietnam!

Maya felt excitement but no fear as the club under her arm wrenched her free from Rio's grip. With a thud, another club landed on her back. She heard the crack of clubs hitting the others, and she tried to reach back to protect the base of her neck but her hand was grabbed and her arm wrenched behind her and twisted.

"Let's go, sister," she heard.

They sang the second verse somewhat raggedly as the cops dragged them away.

> He knows who you've been beating,
> He knows the heads you break,
> He knows what napalm does to kids,
> So get out for goodness' sake!

"We need to do more," Edith said. After they were released on bail, they'd gone back to the flat in San Francisco on Capp Street where Edith and Daniel lived. They were sitting in the small living room that opened off the kitchen. Rob was stretched out on a couch with no springs. Daniel had taken the most comfortable seat, on an easy chair that had lost its legs. Edith perched on the arm. "Somehow everybody needs to do more. We need to be more committed."

"But committed how? And to what?" Rio asked. He was sitting on one of the kitchen chairs turned the wrong way around, his legs draped over the sides, his arms folded across its back.

"Committed to ending the war."

"Right. But how? That's the question."

"And not just ending the war," Daniel said, gesturing with his lit cigarette, "but changing the system that makes war possible. Inevitable."

He had taken off his Santa Claus hat but still wore the red coat with the white cotton trim.

"You tell me how to do it," Liza said, "and I'll do just about anything. But frankly, I don't see anything we've done so far being very effective." She was seated on the floor, stretching as they talked, showing off her long legs in their black dancer's tights.

"Look at the way public opinion has turned around in the last two years," Daniel said. "Now the war is a subject of national debate."

"Big fucking deal," Rio said. "They're debating how to kill more gooks and fewer American boys, get the heat off their necks back home."

"A million people marching in the streets haven't stopped the war," Edith said, fanning the smoke that wafted toward her from Daniel's cigarette. "Hundreds of arrests, thousands of demonstrations, countless letters and teach-ins and protest songs, and the war goes on. The Moratorium didn't stop it and the November Mobe didn't stop it. SDS has pretty much broken up. The only faction with any guts is the Weathermen. At least they're taking action."

"We can't act until we educate ourselves," Daniel said. "We've got to determine what our own positions are. Action alone isn't enough, it requires timing and strategy and an overall revolutionary program."

"What have we been doing for the last six months?" Rio said. "We've read so many goddamned books, we ought to get course credit."

"There's more to study. We've barely dipped into Marx."

"Oh no," Maya said. She was standing in the kitchen, waiting for water to boil so she could make coffee for them all. "I'm willing to die for the revolution, but I'm not willing to die of boredom trying to understand *Das Kapital*."

"But to be cadre, you've got to understand *Das Kapital*," Daniel said. "You've got to be able to analyze the contradictions and know what you're fighting for."

"Great, you explain it to me," Maya said. "I understand things by being outside, in the wind, or on the street. Not through books."

"Maya, why do you sell your own intellect short? You're not really just this stupid mystical chick who can't think, you know. You've got a brain in your head, it wouldn't hurt you to use it." Daniel gestured again with his cigarette, knocking ash onto the white collar of Santa's suit.

"Fuck you!" Maya turned her back on him and applied herself to the coffee.

"Oh, our happy little collective is starting off already with peace and harmony and fellowship," Liza said. "Kiss and make up, kids."

"Maya, you were rude," Edith said. "But Daniel, you were patronizing."

"I'm sorry, all right. It's just that this anti-intellectual bent in the movement really gets to me. What's wrong with using your mind?"

"Nothing," Maya said over her shoulder as she poured water through the ground coffee in the paper towel they used as a filter. "It's just that there's more than one way to use it." How could she explain that she didn't want an ideology or a structure for her thoughts, that she was following something intuitive as a scent, as a feeling in her own body that rose up in the presence of freedom? Her critique of what was wrong was not something she could put into a ten-point program. It was a sense of enclosure, a recognition of the deadening of life, that seemed to be generated by structures of thought. Yet maybe they were necessary, maybe the unfenced freedom she craved was, in truth, not a practical basis for a life. Or not enough. Because now, she realized, she wanted more than freedom. For the sake of the woman on fire, she wanted her freedom to mean something.

"I don't want to get trapped in abstractions," she said finally.

"Nobody's arguing with that," Daniel said. "Ideology should be a foundation, not a cage."

"So what are we going to do?" Liza asked.

"In the long run or the short run?" Daniel asked.

"Oh, the long run is clear enough," Rio said. "In the long run, we smash the state. In the short run, I say we go back downtown tomorrow . . . maybe try Powell and Market."

"But I want to be Santa Claus this time," Rob said from the couch where he lay prone, his eyes closed.

"You! Whoever heard of a Mexican-Italian Santa?" Daniel asked.

"Whoever heard of a Jewish Santa?" Rob countered, raising his head.

"Jesus was a Jew—why shouldn't Santa Claus be, too?" Daniel asked.

"I move that in keeping with our commitment to the democratic process, we rotate the position of Santa Claus," Edith said. Maya turned around to look at her sharply. If anyone else had said that, it would have been a joke. But Edith was quite serious.

"All right!" Rob said, grinning. "*Adelante!* The Santa Claus brigade!"

"I don't know," Daniel muttered. "Sounds suspiciously Red to me."

The day the Home Front received arms to take up in the struggle, Rio shot every clock in the house. Ironically enough, the arms, in the form of two hunting rifles, a shotgun, and a pistol, were Jim's posthumous gifts, sent to Rio by his mother when she cleared out the boys' old bedroom so her widowed sister could move in.

Maya had come in from the street, back to their converted garage, her hands chapped with chill from setting out cards for strangers, her feet aching. Rio was sitting on the couch, his legs propped up on the old telephone spool they used as a coffee table, where a fifth of Scotch reposed next to the remains of a six-pack of Heinekens. He grinned up at her, blearily. Beside him, a cardboard carton lay partially unpacked.

He picked up a shiny black pistol in his right hand, aimed it at her head, and said, playfully, "Bang bang!"

"What the fuck is that?" Maya asked. "Put it away!"

"Time is dead," he said with exaggerated solemnity, swiveling slowly to aim at the kitchen clock. He pulled the trigger, and the shot seemed to tear Maya apart. She screamed as the clock shattered into pieces.

"Rio, you're out of your mind!"

"Out of my mind, she says!" He gestured to an invisible audience. "The problem with you is you don't understand time. New time. You're clinging to the old times, but now it's a good time."

"Please, Rio!" Maya said, trying to walk slowly, calmly toward him, trying not to panic because somebody she didn't recognize seemed to be looking out of his eyes.

"Time, time, time . . ." he began to sing, reaching over and taking a swig of Scotch out of the bottle.

"Please, please!"

"We're gonna have a good time. Come to me, baby. Come here."

She went because she didn't want to antagonize him, and because she thought maybe she could calm him, and because she was afraid and wanted to cling to him even though he himself was what she was afraid of. She slid next to him on the couch, hoping to grab the gun. Instead he wrapped his arms around her, pointing the gun at her breast.

"What time is it now, boys and girls?" He winked at her.

"No, Rio. Please, it's not funny!"

"Time to struggle, time to win." He stared at her fixedly, and then turned suddenly and pumped a series of shots into the clock on top of the TV.

"Good time . . . good time . . ." He began laughing. He looked at her accusingly, and so to placate him she laughed with him.

"This is the beginning of the revolution," he said, and laughed harder as he reached again for the Scotch.

"Please, Rio, don't drink any more. Okay? For me, baby? Please, put the gun away," Maya crooned, wondering just for a moment who she had become.

"Seize the time," he said, and passed out.

26

Johanna Weaver's
Journal

January 10, 1970

Well, my New Year's resolution was to answer Maya's letter, but ten days have gone by and I haven't written a word. So I guess I'm not going to. Really, it's hard to know what to say to her. At first I was just going to tear the damn thing up. She made me mad! Maya, you asshole, I wanted to say, what have they done to you in Berkeley? Turned you into a pole-up-the-ass ideologue? Lord, how dreary. How dreadfully sad.

Then, I got mad all over again. Child, you talk about racism but this letter is the most racist thing I've ever known you to do, with all of our fights and struggles. Where the hell did I go for you? How did I turn from a person into an abstraction, a Black Person? Ain't I a woman? Aren't I still the girl whose kinky hair you nearly pulled out as we screamed together at the Beatles on the *Ed Sullivan Show*? Didn't we once, twice, touch—heart to heart, hand to hand?

But I couldn't write that letter, either. Because when I sat back and looked in the mirror, I had to admit that my own face had some dirt on it, too. I had to admit that I was the one who first dragged race into our friendship, screaming at her that morning that she was a spoiled little *white* girl. Lord, Lord, if I'd known how much trouble that one word would cause, I would have held my tongue. But then I wouldn't have Rachel, would I?

Maya, I would write if I could, racism is real. Injustice is real. But what divides us is simply guilt. Yours, because for some reason you feel obligated to take upon your shoulders all the sins of the white race—although in point of fact while my people were being shipped from Africa, yours were dodging around Eastern Europe somewhere getting skewered by Cossacks and barbecued by the Inquisition. Maybe you just haven't really figured out yet that you're Jewish. Granted, you have privilege—didn't I try to tell you that? But don't let it go to your head. There's a price you pay.

And then there's my guilt, which is simpler and more personal. That I fucked your boyfriend behind your back and now I have his baby. And I don't want him to know. I don't want to share her, except a bit with Marian. She's mine. She's sits up now, and eats solid food, and I swear to God she has a special grunt that means "Mama" and another for "cookie" and she understands half of what I say. Her eyes follow me all around the room with this old, wise expression in them, as if she knows far, far more than I do about what's coming.

But I can't write that to Maya, either. The bold, mean truth is this—that I can't get close to her again without telling her who Rachel's father is, and I'm not willing to do that.

I can't answer her letter.

Johanna

27

Night at Tengpoche

The Monastery of Tengpoche is the spiritual heart
of Khumbu. Although not ancient, it is the home of
many works of art and irreplaceable manuscripts.
Here the Sherpa people keep their treasures.

—MOUNTAIN CO-OP ADVENTURES
BROCHURE

"The yeti like to imitate human beings," Tenzing said with his small, teasing smile. "They will see people digging and planting fields by day, and at night they will try to do the same, and end by destroying them. For this reason the village people do not like them."

They were sitting in the dining tent in the field by Tengpoche, finishing their dinner of cauliflower fritters, fried potatoes, lentils, and rice. The warm glow of a kerosene lamp chased away the dark, and, with a solid quotient of fat inside her, Maya felt warmer than she had all day. The warmth and the calories almost made up for her disappointment that Debby had still not appeared.

"You can certainly see why," Lonnie said, wiping her mouth on the back of her bandanna. "Like an infestation of King Kong gophers."

"In one village," Tenzing went on, "the people dug a big pit and went inside it. There they drank water and made believe they were fighting with wooden knives. Then they left the pit, and that night they put real knives inside, and bottles of alcohol. The yetis all got drunk, and they slaughtered each other. Only one escaped, a pregnant female who couldn't take part in the fight."

"How sad!" Jan said. "How terribly, awfully sad. Think how she must have felt, with all her people dead."

"Actually, it sounds like my neighborhood on a Saturday night," Maya observed, wondering if she dared have a second helping of fritters.

What would the Higher Personal Trainer say? Oh, to hell with it, she deserved a little comfort. She'd hoped, she really had, that Debby would join them here, on this high plateau where they could have left Betty's ashes in sight of Chomolungma. She would have to let go of that fantasy. Debby had seen to that. Of course, to be fair, Debby didn't know that Maya had brought their mother's ashes, that she had hoped for a full-moon night like this, with the mountains shining in the distance like gods.

She didn't know because Maya hadn't told her, had only sent the barest bones of a message. What we don't say divides us, Maya reflected. Secrets carve Grand Canyons of separation through relationships. Look at Jo and me—separated by the secret of Rachel. And the same secret kept me from reaching out to Rio, from answering the letter he sent. Or was the secret just a pretext for maintaining a silence I didn't really want to break? Not so much because of what he'd done, but because of who I'd let myself become, when I was with him?

And who did I become for Johanna, keeping her secret from him?

The conversation went on around her, and Maya tried to focus on it, because she didn't like the direction her thoughts were heading in.

"Tell us another story," Carolyn was saying to Tenzing. "Another yeti story."

"There was a yak herder," Tenzing said, "who used to rub butter on his skin, as a lotion. The yeti watched him. He left out lots and lots of yak butter for the yeti, and when the yeti had rubbed it into his skin, he caught fire. He ran and ran, until he found his friend. 'Where shall I go? Where shall I go?' he asked, and his friend said, 'To the river.' But the yeti heard, 'To the forest,' and so he ran under the trees and burned the forest down, killing himself and his friend."

"Why do I get the feeling these yeti stories are the Polack jokes of Sherpaland?" Peter mused.

"That's sad, too," Jan said. "Aren't there any cheerful stories about the yeti?"

"Perhaps the existential quality of yetihood is not a happy one," Lonnie suggested.

"There aren't a lot of cheery stories about vampires or goblins, for that matter," Peter observed.

"But the yeti seem different. I don't know, I always think of them as being so close to human," Jan said.

"That's what I mean," Lonnie said. "The existential quality of being human is not so damn happy, when you think about it."

I had wanted to tell Rachel the truth, Maya was thinking. I almost did, the night she asked me. Maybe I should have, but the timing seemed wrong. Jo and I had been together—what?—three or four years by then, since I'd come back from Mexico. Already we'd been arguing about where our passion had gone.

"Maybe regularity spoils it for us," Jo had said. "I'm a daughter of Oshun. I can't be a one-woman dog."

Oshun was the Yoruba Goddess of love, and Jo had recently started studying with Nimba, a friend of Maya's who was a Lucumi priestess. Jo and Maya had gone together to a *bimbe,* letting the wild drums and the rhythmic movements of the dance carry them into trance. Afterward, while they were eating stewed chicken and okra and couscous and greens, Maya had noticed Johanna deep in conversation with one of the drummers, a handsome well-muscled man with wild dreadlocks and glossy dark skin who turned out to be a professor of anthropology at Cal by day.

"You mean you want to go out with that drummer," Maya said accusingly.

"Luis? Maybe. Would that be so awful? Would you mind?"

"Mind? I don't know." Maybe I will, she thought, but maybe we've grown too familiar to each other, too entwined. Maybe I need some breathing space, too. "You'd be sure to be safe, wouldn't you?"

"Maya, I'm not talking about sleeping with the guy, just going out to dinner."

"Oh, you've got a date already made?"

"Tentatively. I told him I had to check my calendar."

"You didn't tell him you had to check with your girlfriend?"

"No, I didn't. I hardly know the guy. Besides, we've been over and over this issue before. My private life is my own business. I don't have to proclaim it to everybody in the world." She faced Maya, her voice defensive. "I've said this before, and I'll say it again—I have to work in the whole black community, not just the women's auxiliary. Our strongest support in Hunter's Point comes from the churches—and they are not gay friendly. The good I can do lesbians by coming out doesn't outweigh the harm it would do to the kids I'm trying to work with."

"How about proclaiming it to someone you're about to let in to your private life?"

"If we get involved, of course I'll tell him. But all we're doing is going out to dinner."

In the end, Johanna had gone on her date, and Maya had stayed home with Rachel, helping her with her math homework and rereading the manuscript of *From the Mountain,* trying to discern why it had received yet another rejection notice. She wasn't thinking about Johanna and Luis. She wasn't jealous. If anything, she was feeling a whisper of relief. The flat seemed more open, the kitchen, where she sat next to Rachel at the small, wooden table, seemed more spacious.

"You've known my mom for a long time, haven't you?" Rachel said abruptly, looking up from her paper and pencil. Her hair hung down in two long braids, and her eyes measured Maya as if she were assessing something.

"Since we were girls. Just about as old as you are now." Maya studied Rachel's paper, reading upside down. Mrs. Eller, 5th Grade, Fraction Worksheet, it said. Rachel's tone was too carefully casual, always a sign that she was about to say something of grave importance.

"So you must have known my daddy, too."

Maya was silent. She picked up her cup of tea and sipped it slowly. Here it was, at last, the moment she had always known would come someday, the moment that she and Johanna had never agreed on how to handle.

"I knew him," she said at last.

"What's the big mystery about him?"

"What do you mean?"

"Why won't Mom ever talk about him? And her voice gets all funny. We don't have any pictures or anything—not like Grandma Marian does of Mama's daddy."

If I lie to her, Maya thought, she will never trust me again. If I tell her the truth, what will Johanna say? Especially tonight. She'll never believe I didn't do it out of jealousy and spite.

"I'm not a baby," Rachel proclaimed in answer to Maya's silence. "And I think somebody should tell me the truth."

She's right, Maya thought. But I can't be the one.

"Why don't you ask your mother?"

"I have, a million times. She just says, 'He died in the war,' and changes the subject."

Maya sat silent, twisting her fingers, not meeting Rachel's eye.

"Tell me! I want to know!"

"It's not my place to tell you," she said finally. "It's your mother's place."

"But she won't, and you know!"

"I'm sorry."

"If you're sorry, then tell me about him. Whose dad was he, anyway?"

"I think you have a right to know," Maya said. "But I'm not your mother."

"I thought you were my friend," Rachel said.

Damn you, Johanna, Maya thought. Damn you to hell for putting me into this position.

"Anyway, I know they were never really married," Rachel said.

"How do you know that?"

"Because my last name is Weaver, same as my mom's."

"That doesn't mean anything," Maya countered. "Lots of feminists give their kids their mother's name. Why should the woman's name die out?"

"So they were really married? Where's the wedding pictures?"

"Don't try to manipulate me," Maya said. "I told you, you need to ask your mother. I don't agree with her, but it's her right to decide what to tell you."

"What about me? What about my rights? You don't care about me." Rachel flung her book down and ran out of the room.

Oh, Goddess, Johanna! How did I get between the two of you? And what do I say to her?—I love you, but your mother is my lover, my best friend, my sole emotional and major financial support right now. My keeper.

Maya stood up and followed Rachel into her room. The girl lay on her bed, crying.

"I do care about you," Maya said, stroking her back gently.

"No, you don't!"

"Oh, sweetie, don't cry. I am sorry." Don't hate me. Don't blame me. "I tell you what, I'll talk to your mother for you. I'll try to persuade her."

Rachel rolled over on her back and stared up at the ceiling. "I don't care what you do," she said. "I hate you."

"Come on, honey, don't say that. Come on, let's go back in the kitchen. I'll make you some hot chocolate, and I'll help you with your math problems."

But Rachel's face had closed, in the way a child's face can close. As soon pry open a clenched fist.

By the time Johanna had come home, Rachel was sound asleep in her bed. Maya waited up, drinking too many cups of herb tea and failing to concentrate on her manuscript. Finally she heard the door open, and the murmur of voices down below. Johanna clambered up the stairs. Maya was relieved to see that Luis did not follow.

"How was your date?" Maya asked.

"Oh, Maya, what can I tell you?" Johanna slung her purse across the back of the chair, sat down, and took off her high-heeled shoes. "It was interesting. You know, just to dress up and go out with somebody different, go to dinner at one of those places you read about in Herb Caen but never get to see. Where they serve you five stuffed mushrooms on an endive and it tastes better than anything you've ever put in your mouth before. How was your evening? Were you okay?"

"Fine." Maya stared at her teacup.

"I did tell him about you," Johanna said.

"Oh, you did. Does that mean you're *involved*?"

"It means I think he's a nice guy and I trust him. Dammit, Maya, can't you understand that sometimes I might need to sort some things out with someone who also knows the black community from the inside? Do you think I'm always comfortable with the contradictions?"

Maya shook her head. "No. I know how hard it is for you."

"You think I'm a coward."

"No, I don't."

"I'm not a coward. I've never shied away from doing something because it was difficult. It's just that I've got to decide for myself what makes sense. What's right."

"That's fine." Maya looked up. "Really, Johanna, I'm fine about whatever you choose to say to the world, or not. But there is something else."

"What?"

"Rachel. She asked me about her father."

"Oh, she did." Johanna's voice was low, suspicious.

"I told her to ask you. We had a fight about it. And I felt like shit. Dammit, Johanna, it's time to tell her the truth."

"She's too young."

"She's asking! That tells me she's old enough to know."

"She's only ten."

"Ten going on forty. She's very mature for her age."

"Not as mature as she seems."

"But she's asking!" Maya's voice rose, and Johanna turned to meet her eye. "I hate having to lie to her and evade her. How can she ever trust me?"

"I see." Johanna nodded. "This isn't about her, it's about you. You want me to tell her about her father in order to relieve *your* discomfort."

"No, I don't. I want you to tell her in order to relieve *her* uncertainty. And because she has a right to know."

Johanna stood up. "I should have known. I should have known you'd have to get back at me somehow for going out with Luis."

"That's not the issue."

"I think it is. I don't think this is about Rachel at all. It's about your jealousy."

"That's bullshit!" Maya banged her cup down on the table and looked up at her.

"Maybe. But then can you please explain to me why you have to raise this subject tonight, of all nights? You want to punish me."

"She *asked* me tonight, that's why," Maya said sharply.

"Just out of the blue—with no little hints or cues from you?"

"I told you, she asked me." Maya took a deep breath, and spoke again more calmly. "Honestly, Jo, I didn't put her up to it. But I don't want to be in that position again. I can't go on lying to her!"

"Now you're accusing me of lying!"

"I'm just saying—"

"She's my daughter!" Johanna said in a voice that allowed no argument or compromise. "Not yours! This is a decision I should make for her, not you. You have no right to take it away from me!"

They stared at each other, eye to eye, glaring angrily. Nothing here is mine, Maya thought. It's all on sufferance from Johanna, and that's all right, until I cross her. Just because we haven't clashed before doesn't mean that this barrier hasn't been there. No wonder the waters don't rise for us. I have got to get out, to make a change. To give it all up before it closes in on me.

Johanna's face softened.

"I'm sorry," she said. "I didn't mean that like it sounded."

"You did mean it," Maya said. "It's okay, it's true. Rachel is yours." She stood up and turned to walk out the door, and Johanna put out a hand to hold her back.

"But she's not all mine." Johanna's hand on her arm was a plea. Forgive me, it said, love me anyway. How could Maya pull away from that? "Please, Maya, this is one thing I've got to do myself. And I will. When the time is right, I will. You've got to trust me."

"Maybe the right time is when she asks," Maya said, not pulling away but not letting herself be drawn close, embraced.

"Maybe. I'll think about it."

"Will you?"

"I will."

She did think about it, Maya admitted to herself. She thought and she thought. Eventually, Rachel stopped asking.

The kitchen boys brought in steaming pots of tea and bowls of canned peaches, and began clearing away the dinner plates. Rachel had stopped asking, but she never stopped wanting to know. The secret was always there, between her and Maya, a barrier they never did cross.

"At least the weather has cleared up," Carolyn was saying. "That's a happy thought. We'll have a great view of the mountains, tomorrow."

"Just when we're leaving," Lonnie grumbled.

"The moon is really beautiful tonight," Jan said. She turned to Maya. "It's full. Don't you think it's a good night for a ritual?"

"I guess so," Maya said reluctantly. She wasn't in the mood to dance in the moonlight. I have no child, she told herself again. Rachel was never mine. My own mother is nothing but a bag of ashes in my pack, and my sister hasn't bothered to come see me. We can't do the ritual I imagined together; we can't lay Betty to rest in sight of the

Goddess Mother of the Universe. So why do anything at all? The dining tent was warm—why should she freeze to death trying to dredge up the dregs of her power, and risk exposing her lacks and her pain?

Damn Debby anyway, the selfish bitch. But that was unfair. If Maya had told her how important it was to her to meet here . . . but no. Maya had had a reason for not telling her. Debby was just as likely to be resistant as sympathetic. She hadn't wanted to argue with her by cable; she'd wanted to present her with a fait accompli. Here I am—sister, ashes, moonlight, holy mountain—all the pieces in place. What do you say, sis?

Well, hell. Debby or no Debby, the moon was still full and shining on Chomolungma. Maybe she should stop feeling like a petulant two-year-old, and behave like a priestess, forget disappointment and her ashes, and dance for herself.

"After we finish our tea, we'll go out and dance for the moon," Maya said. "Anyone who wants to can come."

"Not just women?" Carolyn asked.

"No, men too. If you want to."

"Thanks," Peter said, yawning. "But I think it's bed for me."

In the end, only the four women walked out together to the edge of the plateau, away from the groups of tents and the lanterns and the voices, onto an open patch of ground. Maya carried her day pack, with her mother's ashes and the small hand drum she had brought. She gave Jan a bowl of milk she'd borrowed from the kitchen boys to use for an offering. She chose a flat piece of ground and set up a simple altar: just the bowl of milk, and her candle lantern on the bare ground. The night was clear in patches. At moments, the moon would shine down on them, illuminating the snow and the tents and the rims of the high mountains with her silver glow. Maya would hold her breath, as if to suck in the beauty of the night. Then the clouds would swirl back across her face, turning the night to a deep blue-velvet.

"Shall we begin?" Maya asked a little hesitantly. She could still feel her reluctance, like a speed bump in the road she would have to make herself get over. From the low bank behind them, she heard a soft cough. She turned to find Ila, their yak driver, squatting on the ground, with Tashi behind him.

Ila grinned shyly. Of all the Sherpas, he was the only one who ever looked unkempt, his hair not quite combed, his face covered with the heavy shadow of a beard he shaved irregularly. He reminded Maya of a Himalayan version of Humphrey Bogart in *The Treasure of the Sierra Madre*. But he had a small, sweet smile, and a low, beautiful voice. Every morning he crooned Buddhist chants as he made up the round, sticky balls of some substance that yaks adored, for their daily treat.

"Possible looking for me?" he said. Maya stared at him blankly.

"Possible looking for me?" he repeated. Suddenly she understood. "You want to watch!"

He nodded.

"Of course you can watch." Ordinarily she would have said no. Ritual was not a performance to be observed. But here, in this place where everyone had so generously allowed her to observe their ceremonies, how could she exclude him? "You can join, if you want to."

"I, join?" he laughed.

"You, join. If you want to." Behind him Tashi stood back a few paces, giggling. "Tashi, too. Anyone."

Tashi moved forward. "We can join?"

"Sure. In fact, it'd be great if you want to translate for Ila."

Tashi lay on his back and laughed quietly to himself, but he stood up and joined the others as Maya formed them into a circle.

"It's okay, isn't it . . . for us to do our own ritual here?" Maya asked Tashi. "I mean, do we need to get permission from the Rinpoche or anything?"

"No, here is okay. In the *gompa,* no." He dissolved in giggles again, apparently at the very thought.

"What do we do?" Carolyn asked.

"Take hands," Maya said. "Breathe together, feel your feet on the earth."

She led them through a short meditation, directing them to feel their connection with the ground.

"Breathe deep and imagine yourself as a tree that can take root here. Let your breath sink down through your roots into the earth."

She could feel her energy begin to shift. Yes, the earth here held power, the crust so thick, miles of it beneath her feet. She could feel it pulsing up, pressing against her soles. All she needed to do was let it in.

"Draw the power of the earth up," she said. "Let it fill you." But the words remained only words. The soles of her hiking boots remained a barrier between her feet and the ground.

"In my tradition," she explained to Tashi, "we always begin by acknowledging the four directions. So, maybe tonight we should name them as the sacred mountains that surround us. Sagarmatha. Ama Dablam. Help me, Tashi . . . what are the others?"

Tashi was murmuring to Ila, evidently translating because Ila looked up and said helpfully, "Lhotse. Nuptse."

"Thank you. Blessed be. Sacred mountains, powers of the earth, winds that sweep over these peaks, sun that warms the air—we wish!

Waters of the Dudh Kosi and all the sacred rivers, be with us. Lend us your strength.'' She waited while Tashi translated for Ila, who nodded in approval.

Then she stood for a moment, wondering what to do. A ritual could be ecstasy, energy, intimacy. At best, all three. But it needed a purpose, a focus, a story to bring it together. Without her mother to lay to rest, what were they doing, here under the the hide-and-seek moon?

They were all looking at her, expectantly.

''Ila,'' she said, ''would you like to offer a prayer?'' Tashi translated, and Ila shook his head, shyly.

''Then let's sing to the moon Goddess,'' Maya said. She took out the small hand drum she had brought in her duffel bag and began to play, singing a simple chant that Tashi interpreted.

After a moment, the others joined in.

> ''She changes everything she touches,
> And everything she touches, changes.''

Yes, that's how she used to do it, before her power had deserted her. She would begin to drum, a soft beat, breathing in time to the motions her fingers made on the drumskin, letting it whisper, letting it move. Then she would open her mouth and let the words come out, words that took people places, told them the stories that they needed to hear. Until the words and the images and the drumbeat and the breath drew them all together, the separate people becoming one breathing being that traveled together, that fought demons and sang to Goddesses, that cried and exulted in a voice that built and built until power was generated and formed and released.

But now the drumbeat sounded dead. Thud, thud, thud. When she stood still to let power fill her, she remained empty. The night surrounded her with beauty, but the words that came were rote words, things memorized or invented long ago, the shed exoskeletons of past moments of power.

''Goddess of change, help us through the changes we face,'' Maya said when the singing had stopped.

''Let's be quiet for a moment, and meditate on the moon and the night and the mountains,'' Maya said, to buy herself some time to think. ''Let's listen deep, to hear what they have to say to us.''

She listened, hoping for a voice or at least an intuition that would tell her what to do. All she could hear was her mother's petulant voice.

''I wasn't good enough for you. Oh no. You had to go out and invent yourself the great Mother Goddess.''

''I didn't invent the Goddess, Betty,'' Maya said. ''She's been around since long before either of us.''

"You were disappointed in my maternal omnipotence when your father left us. You had to replace me with a powerful mother figure."

No, no, she was never meant to leave the ashes here. That wouldn't be the story this ritual would tell. Time to fall back on something tried and true.

"The full moon is the time of culmination and fulfillment," Maya said. "Let's each name what we hope will be fulfilled in the coming month."

"My work," Jan said immediately. Maya lifted the bowl of milk and handed it to her.

"Pour out a few drops, for an offering," she said.

Jan did, and Maya motioned to her to pass the bowl to Lonnie, on her left.

"This is for the blossoming of passion," Lonnie said, spilling some milk on the ground.

Ila stood beside her, and he looked up at Maya questioningly as Lonnie handed him the bowl.

"I am to do?" he asked.

"Can you explain?" Maya said to Tashi, who spoke rapidly to Ila.

Ila smiled, and poured out some of the milk, speaking at length in Sherpa.

"He says he makes a prayer for the things we are planting now, the potatoes and the barley, and for the good health of all the animals and of all of us," Tashi translated.

Maybe the story is as simple as that, Maya thought. Witches from the West and Sherpas from the East have come together to worship the moon in the shadow of the Goddess Mother of the Universe. Maybe whether or not I feel a rush of power is not the issue here. I have fulfilled my function simply by making this happen.

"Now you take the bowl, and make a wish," Maya told Tashi.

He did, laughing to himself and looking somewhat embarrassed.

"I wish," he said with a dramatic flourish, "for a motorcycle!" He poured out a good measure of milk onto the ground. Carolyn reached out and took the bowl away from him.

"Leave some for the rest of us," she said. She held the bowl up and looked at it thoughtfully. "I wish for a child," she said finally, and poured the liquid onto the ground.

Maya took the bowl. Maybe that's what I should ask for, she thought. For all that Carolyn is married, professional, and slim, she could be a messenger for me, too. But I'm not ready.

"I wish for peace for my mother's spirit," she said, and poured out the last few drops of milk.

Now they should chant and dance and raise power, but Maya wasn't sure she was up to it. Instead she began a quiet chant.

"We are the power in everyone
We are the dance of the moon and sun."

They sang softly, and the moon came out behind the clouds, painting silver edges on the mountains. This place is so beautiful, Maya thought. The ritual is superfluous. The others will all remember this night as luminous, magical. It's only me, with my expectations, who will think of it as a disappointment. That's my flaw. If I could let go of how I expect the energy to move, I could bask in the silver, quiet power that is here, now, and be content.

They fell silent, again.

"Touch the earth," Maya said, "to give her some of the power we've raised."

They knelt and squatted, with their hands on the ground. The Sherpas followed suit, Ila with his encouraging smile, Tashi still giggling.

"Now, let's just each say something we're grateful for in the last month," Maya said. It was a good way to end. Never prolong a ritual in the cold, that was one of her mottos, although truthfully she felt warmer now than she had sitting by the fire in Pangboche. "I'll start. I'm grateful to be here, in this beautiful and sacred space, and grateful for the warmth and friendship of the Sherpa people."

Tashi translated, and Ila spoke out of turn.

"He says he is grateful for your group which is so friendly and kind," Tashi interpreted. "He says that he hopes you will come back many times to our country."

One by one, the others spoke of their gratitude, following Maya's lead in praising the land and the people of Khumbu. Tashi's giggles finally overcame him when his turn came around. Lonnie asked Ila to sing them a song, and after a long consultation, he and Tashi sang together and the others hummed along.

"Blessed be," Maya said. She thanked the Goddess and the directions and the elements and the sacred mountains, and the ritual was done.

I feel better, she thought to herself as she gathered her things. Ila insisted on taking the bowl back to the kitchen, and she didn't argue. Suddenly she was very tired. But she felt a sense of peace, as if the silver night had infiltrated the gray spaces inside her. She would crawl into her tent, and sleep soundly under the moon.

Maya lay in her tent, her journal open before her, thinking about writing by flashlight, or reading more of Johanna's journal, or even one of Rio's letters. Her sleeping bag was warm, and maybe she should just drift off to sleep.

"Hello?" a voice called softly. "Maya, can I talk to you for a moment? It's Howard."

The peace the ritual had filled her with evaporated. Damn. She was tempted to tell him just to go away, but against her better judgment, she sat up and partially unzipped her tent flap, enough to peer out. His face filled the opening, and her flashlight illuminated the blond thatch of hair, the wide eyes, the slight trembling of his lower lip.

"What is it?" Maya asked.

"Uh, I just wanted to thank you, for the massage, yesterday. My head feels a lot better."

"I'm glad, Howard."

"And, uh . . ." he hesitated.

Oh, Goddess, she'd let herself in for this. She knew it. She should never have succumbed to her impulse to be kind to him.

"Well, you're alone, and I'm alone," he went on. "I wondered if you wanted company?"

There was a time in her life, she realized, when she would have said yes out of pure pity. Give the man an adventure, something to tell the boys back at LK. Be the magical Witch who would teach his fumbling hands to unlock the secrets of the universe. But she had outgrown that, thank the Goddess. Oh, men would never know how often they were pity-fucked. She thought of Johanna and Rio. But that was different, wasn't it?

"Howard," she said patiently, "when I rubbed your neck yesterday, I really just wanted to help your headache. It wasn't meant as a come-on."

"Oh," he said, looking disappointed and a bit confused.

"You're a nice guy, but I'm tired. I'm going to sleep now. Good night," she said firmly, and zipped up the tent again. After a moment, she heard him walk away.

There was a time, she admitted to herself, when she would have said yes just because she hated to reject anybody. It was one of her failures. She should be outraged, furious at being seen as a sex object, not lying here in the dark feeling sad for him, feeling his disappointment. Let him feel his own disappointment, dammit! Let him pick on someone his own age.

On the other hand, if baby lust was really at the core of her troubles, maybe she had just thrown away a perfectly good chance to get knocked up. He'd never have to know. He wasn't the type to have AIDS—although of course you couldn't ever be sure. On the other hand, he *was* the type to be cautious. She might have had to argue him out of using a condom, and that could be difficult. And if she failed, she might have put herself through a mildly unpleasant experience for nothing.

On the other hand, if she'd succeeded, she could have had a nice little blond baby, bright, good at math, and under her guidance, not quite so awkward. But no, that wouldn't work. If she couldn't stomach the idea of Howard for herself, how could he be good enough to be the Father of Her Baby?

Who was good enough? God himself, maybe. Or possibly Bruce Springsteen. Wasn't he breaking up with his wife because she didn't want to have a child? Maybe she should write him a letter, send him a copy of one of her books. "Dear Bruce, I'm a great fan of yours and I wonder if you would mind sending me a teaspoonful of semen, packed in ice."

If only there were a Famous Rock Stars Sperm Bank! She could have one by Bruce, a boy, of course, kind of rough and ready and good at fixing cars—Goddess knows, that would come in handy! And then maybe one by Peter Gabriel, a girl, sensitive and musical. And just to round things off and for old times' sake, a pair of frizzy-haired Jewish twins with whiny voices by Bob Dylan.

Damn Howard, she'd been winding down to sleep and now she was wide awake. She took out her journal, switched on the clip-on light that illuminated the pages, and began to write.

> Jealousy. Is that what it comes down to? The real thing that separates me and Johanna. Not of Luis or Raymond or Lillian or any of Jo's other lovers, but of Rachel. Her child. *Her* child. Sure, she's always shared her with me, I've been part of her life since she was six years old, I was possibly there at her conception, but still, that point always comes, doesn't it, those crucial moments when the decision has to be made—How late should she stay up? How much allowance should she get? Should we tell her the truth about her father? We discuss . . . but she decides. I've been her consultant, not her partner.
>
> Or am I rationalizing, trying to justify what's probably just a biological clamoring of my genes, wanting to preserve themselves, wanting to be passed down? Or my mother's ghost, riding my back, still trying to get me to fulfill her dreams?

Eventually she slept. In her dreams, she was pursued by a giant, clumsy figure, trailing flame behind him.

28

January 1970

Maya didn't want to live with the Home Front Collective but she thought it would be good for Rio. His drinking was slowly, steadily increasing. In a big, communal house, filled with people, he would have to keep it under control. He had dropped out of school, but somehow she found herself feeling more distressed than vindicated. She wanted him to realize his dreams, whatever they might be. She loved him, and felt his disappointment perhaps more keenly than he did. But he never spoke to her about his decision, just announced it one day when he came home and then proceeded to down a six-pack. Now he took construction jobs, coming home sweaty, beer on his breath. Yes, it would be better to live with other people. Somewhere deep down where she didn't have to look at it, the thought was there that if he had another one of what she called his episodes, she would not be alone to cope with it.

The house on Capp Street was an old Victorian divided into flats. Daniel and Edith, joined by Rob and Liza, rented the bottom floor, a series of rooms strung out along a dark hallway. Maya and Rio took the smallest and darkest, with a window looking out on a light well. They shared it with a desk and an electric typewriter, which took up most of the available space and meant that at any moment of the day or night, someone was likely to walk in on them. They weren't supposed to care. The living room was filled with broken-down chairs and couches, and reeked of tobacco smoke from the meetings that seemed to be eternally in progress. The kitchen was a dark alcove separated by a counter from the living room. Behind the stove hung a poster of Che Guevara, emblazoned with his statement: "At the risk of seeming ridiculous, let me say that the true revolutionary is motivated by great feelings of love." The poster was spattered with grease: *Love* was almost unreadable.

Maya hated the airless, claustrophobic flat. She hated the endless meetings, the political discussions that accompanied even the simplest decisions. But Rio drank less and laughed more. Of all of them, he was the only one who could unplug a clogged toilet, change the oil in a car, or build a platform for a rally that would not collapse. They needed him, and he liked feeling useful.

"How can you change the world when you can't even change a washer on a leaky faucet?" he was often heard to mutter.

"How can you clean up injustice when you can't clean up your own dirty dishes?" Maya might counter, but they were still able to laugh together, then.

"How can you stop the war when you can't stop the toilet from running?"

"How can you make revolution when you can't make the bed?"

"Make love, not the bed!" Rio would cry, and grab her and carry her off.

In reality, they never made the bed, which was only a mattress on the floor. Occasionally Maya would brush crumbs and ashes out of the sheets, and at intervals, bundle them off to the Laundromat. Maya made coffee, endless pots of it, emptied ashtrays, and washed the stacked dishes when they ran out of clean ones. Edith occasionally helped her. Liza was generally too busy, running off to a dance class or a meeting, and the men complained that housework was a bourgeois fixation, and laughed at her.

The war went on. In December, Black Panther leader Fred Hampton had been shot in bed by the cops. In March, the newspapers were full of the explosion in the Greenwich Village town house that killed three of the Weather Underground. Maya was horrified but, on some other level, shamed. It seemed as if the dead were the ones who were taking the real action, who were committed in a way she claimed to be but hadn't yet acted on. She was surrounded, however unwillingly, by the protective bubble of her whiteness, her middle-classness—there was no suffering to which she could lay claim. Oh, the holocaust, but that was past, done with. The Panthers spoke at rallies, attended by bodyguards, draped with ammunition and holding machine guns, their legs in a wide, easy stance, their hands folded over their chests, berets cocked at an angle. They seemed to represent something that made all her pain unreal, the empty posturing of a spoiled white girl, as Johanna had called her. As if the only way to make herself real, to make her own suffering valid, was to do things that were more and more difficult, until she could finally commit some act so extreme, and sacrifice so much that she would be vindicated. Yet what could she ever do, what act could she take, that could be matched against the pain of the woman on fire?

At these times, she wished deeply for Johanna, not even so much to talk to, but for her presence, her touch. The letter she'd written had received no response, as was fitting, Maya thought. When she reconsidered its contents, her cheeks burned from shame. She thought about writing another but never did.

The meetings of the Home Front centered more and more on questions of tactics. Demonstrations, marches, street theater—they'd done them all, and still the war went on. Had the moment for armed struggle come? Rio's guns were locked away in the basement, at Maya's and Liza's insistence. Was it time to take them out? Every day there were bomb scares in public buildings, explosions in draft boards or recruiting stations. Someone was acting. Shouldn't they be doing the same?

"We're not doing enough. We're not risking enough," Edith said. They were meeting in the Home Front living room. She was seated on the couch under the window, next to Daniel, who rested one hand on her thigh while the other curled around a cigarette. Liza was down on the floor, stretching, with Rob in a chair behind her. Rio paced the kitchen with a beer in his hand, and Maya watched it all from a chair placed strategically far from the cigarette smoke, which gave her a headache, along with the endless discussions that seemed to circle around and around the same points.

"But what should we be doing?" Rob said.

"We need to keep educating ourselves," Daniel said. "Our analysis is unclear."

"That's all we ever fuckin' do, is educate ourselves," Rio complained. Maya listened to him sharply, alert for the slightest beginning of a slur in his voice. "What about stopping the fuckin' war?"

"Is it absolutely necessary to use the word 'fuck' as an adjective fifteen times in every sentence?" Liza complained.

"Fuck yes!" Rio said. "That's the fuckin' way fuckin' real people fuckin' talk, man. People who aren't fuckin' college students. You got a problem with it?" Maya listened anxiously, but he was humorous, half making fun of himself, not over the edge, yet. How many beers were left of the night's six-pack? she wondered.

"If we go back to what Lenin said in *What Is to Be Done,*" Daniel began, but Maya interrupted him.

"Boring!"

"Please, Maya," Edith said, "we're trying to have a serious discussion here."

"I am serious. Marx and Lenin and Trotsky and all of them, they're dead. They're dead old men. What do they know about trying to stop the war?"

"Are we just trying to stop the war, or are we trying to make a revolution?" Rob asked.

"That's why we need a clear analysis," Daniel said. "Because frankly I think events are proving that we cannot stop the war without a revolution. War is inherent in this system. It's the fruit on the tree of capitalism. We have to cut down the tree to prevent the fruit from growing.''

"I think we agree on that part of the analysis, Daniel," Edith said. "What we don't agree on is what to use for an ax."

Rio finished his beer, set it down on the table, and went to the refrigerator. God, Maya thought, it's going to be one of those nights. But if I say anything, he'll just get mad.

"We use ourselves, man," Rio said. "We are the ax."

"But how?"

"We all ought to read the Weathermen position paper. We can't critique it unless we've read it," Daniel said.

"We can't read it," Maya said. "I can't read it, because it's totally unreadable. The only good part of it is the title: 'You Don't Need a Weatherman to Know Which Way the Wind Blows,' and they took that from Bob Dylan. I'd rather just listen to the album."

Edith sighed. She and Daniel exchanged long-suffering glances. "Your problem, Maya, is you lack focus. Why don't you get a job? Just hanging out on the street is counterproductive at this point."

"Why don't you work in a factory," Daniel suggested, "if you don't want to go back to school. Go to the School of Life. Maybe you could organize the workers."

"I don't want to work in a factory," Maya said. "I would hate it."

"Most people in the world have to do things they hate," Edith said, chewing the inside of her cheeks.

"Yeah, and I don't want to be one of them," Maya said.

Daniel looked at her sadly. "Do you understand how privileged your attitude is?"

"*You're* not working in a factory—you're in graduate school. You're doing what you want to do," Maya countered.

"What I want to do! What do you know about what I want?" Daniel stood up and paced the room.

Maya looked at him in surprise, because just for a moment there was something in his voice she had never heard before, an intensity of emotion as if he were about to confess his most secret dreams and desires. For the first time, she considered whether he might want something from her. "What, then?" she asked mildly.

"I'll tell you what I want. I want to write a goddamned brilliant thesis on the economic factors driving the Cold War, and get a fellowship to study at the Sorbonne, in Paris, and drink Pernod in the afternoons at a little café on the Left Bank with beautiful women dressed in black, and in the summer, I want to wander in the Pyrenees." He flung himself onto the couch, and his voice dropped. "I want to teach at a university, in a way that challenges every assumption that someone walks in with. I want to have kids. I want to live the life I was raised to live. And if there wasn't a goddamned, bloodsucking war on, or if I were the kind of person who could ignore it, pretend I don't smell the stench from the gas ovens down the road, I'd do just that. But I'm not, and I can't, and neither are you, any of you, or you wouldn't be here. So we don't get to do what we want. We've got to do what has to be done, whether we want to or not.''

"But what is it that has to be done?'' Rob said quietly. ''That's what I don't understand. Because what we're doing isn't working.''

Daniel was still focused on Maya. "If you were doing what you truly wanted, if you were really following a dream, I'd be behind you all the way. But as far as I can see, you aren't doing jack shit with your life. So you might as well make yourself useful.''

I am, Maya wanted to cry. I am staying loyal to my vision at all costs! But she could never explain that to Daniel. And was it even true? Maybe he was right, and she was simply lost.

"Oh, lay off her,'' Rio snapped. "Why the fuck should she go work in a factory? She's not going to do shit there anyway, man. I come from the working class, okay? Union, they understand. Revolution, no.''

"But it's our job to educate them,'' Edith said.

"Educate them to what? That they should be eager to go off, get shot in the fuckin' street? Come off it, Edith. Let's just stop the war, and leave the working class alone.'' He tipped his head back and drained most of the bottle of beer.

He had defended her, and Maya was grateful. He was so real and fierce compared to the rest of them, tied up in their intellectual knots. How many beers were left, anyway? Would he be too wasted after the meeting for sex?

"But we can't make a revolution without the working class,'' Daniel said, almost hopelessly.

"Can't live with 'em, can't live without 'em,'' Rob said, winking at Maya. "Like the ladies.''

Maya stood up and went to the refrigerator. There were two beers left. Enough to put him firmly over the edge. She pulled one out and reached for the bottle opener. Rio was watching her, quizzically.

"I'm thirsty!'' she said to him. "Do you mind?''

"Hey, drink up, babe,'' he said expansively. "We're a collective, we share everything. Smash private property. Smash the state.''

"There's one more,'' she said. "Anybody else want it?''

"Sure, let me have it,'' Rob said, giving her his you-and-I-have-a-secret smile. With profound relief, she handed it over. Now Rio would be okay. And when this interminable meeting was over . . .

When it was over, she and Rio sat in their tiny airless room, legs stretched out on the mattress, backs propped against the wall. He had wanted to go out for more beer but she had persuaded him to share a joint instead. Maya felt loose, relaxed, as if her body could sink into the wall. The room looked gray to her, and she felt trapped in it, with nothing to look at, no color to take her traveling outside its boundaries. But Rio was next to her and he was warm and alive and beautiful, all the colors of the living world playing in his skin.

"I understand Daniel," he was saying. "Don't let him get to you like that. See, the thing is, he never had anyone teach him how to do anything real. To him, books *are* what's real."

"I can understand him," Maya said, "but he has to understand me, too. I want to learn from life, not from books. I don't want to read Lenin or Mao or Bernardine Dohrn. I don't want to read Marx."

"Marx is a poet," Rio said.

"Yeah, for about one paragraph out of every fifty pages. And the rest is boring. *Boring!*"

"Maybe I can liven it up for you," he said, slipping her T-shirt over her head. He licked her left nipple. "That's the thesis," he said, and then kissed the nipple on her right breast. "And that's the antithesis." He unsnapped her jeans and pushed them down over her hips, nuzzling her navel. "And here's the synthesis." Slowly, he worked his way down to the curls of her pubic hair, letting his tongue caress her clitoris. She looked down to meet his eyes over the mound of her belly, and he raised his head and grinned. "The hoarded stores of capital," he said, sliding out of his own jeans and bringing his face up to kiss her as he placed her hand down on his root. "Can you feel it—the potent power of the proletariat?"

"I feel it," she said, laughing.

"But do you really feel it?"

"I really feel it," she said, rubbing up against him.

"Feel it," he murmured. "Do you feel what's happening to it?"

"Yes," she whispered.

"It's rising. The proletariat is rising."

Now that Telegraph Avenue was a long bus ride away, Maya no longer regularly read cards there. Instead she got jobs cleaning houses or doing temporary office work. Of the two sorts of work, she preferred cleaning as it left her mind free. In an office, forced to concentrate on typing other people's letters and reports, she felt trapped.

"Bank of America! Whew!" Daniel whistled when she reported at dinner on her newest temp job. "That could be useful! Maybe you could pick up some inside information."

"I doubt it," Maya said, wearily twirling her fork to pick up strands of spaghetti. She'd worked all day and then come home to make dinner, because nobody else had bothered. "I'm only typing labels for their filing system."

"You'd be surprised what you can learn from file labels," Daniel said. "Look at how they reconstitute medieval economics from old church account books."

"It's mostly just names of employees, for their health insurance records," Maya said.

"Names could be useful."

"How?" Rob asked. "You think we should take a few secretaries hostage? Threaten to wipe out the typing pool if they don't stop financing the war?"

"That's just it," Daniel said. "I don't know what might be useful, and what might not. I don't know what we're going to have to do, in the end."

Rob nodded. Rio looked at Daniel thoughtfully. "What are you saying?"

"Nothing seems to be working," Daniel said. He looked at Edith, a quick glance as if to confirm some conversation they'd had before.

"We've been over and over this ground," Edith said. "Eventually we've got to stop studying and do something."

"We've been doing something," Maya said. "Lots of somethings. We spend our whole lives marching and organizing and talking to housewives at the shopping center."

"We've been making gestures," Daniel said. "Doing things to make ourselves feel noble and good. Manipulating symbols. But we haven't stopped the war."

"At least we've tried," Rob said. "When our grandchildren, if we have them, ask us, 'What did you do in the anti-war, Daddy?' we'll have something to tell them."

"That's what I mean," Daniel said. "We've been doing what lets us look ourselves in the mirror in the morning, and that's fine, as far as it goes. But what good is it to the Vietnamese or the poor shmucks we send over there to do our killing for us, if it doesn't work? Aren't we just indulging in a more refined form of selfishness, if we shy away from doing what might work, but might not feel so moral and pure?"

"What do you have in mind?" Rob asked.

"I've thought about this a lot," Edith said, glancing at Daniel. "Personally, I'm not willing to harm another human being, even to stop the war. I couldn't do that. But I'm willing to take action against property. I don't consider that violent."

"What property? Where?" Rio asked.

"That's what we should be analyzing," she said. "What to target, and when, and how—so that we're sure nobody gets hurt. Because nothing else we've done seems to be working."

Daniel set down his fork. "A hundred thousand people marching peacefully don't get nearly the reaction of one small bomb scare at a draft board."

Liza looked alarmed. "I don't know anything about bombs," she said.

"You can learn," Edith said. "We can all learn whatever we have to learn to bring this system down. The question is, are we willing to do what it takes? Or are we too scared?" She looked around, challenging them all. No one answered her.

I am scared, Maya thought. In Edith's eyes she seemed to see a reflection of the woman on fire. I once swore that I would never let fear stop me again. But she pushed her plate aside, no longer hungry. Ahead of her somewhere, something seemed to be coming apart, like strings of beautiful lights dissolving. Or maybe they were converging, outlining paths she couldn't foresee and wouldn't have chosen for herself.

In May, Nixon invaded Cambodia. Maya dutifully marched and chanted and dodged cops, trying to take heart in the sheer scale of the outrage. After the National Guard shot four students at Kent State, universities all over the country went on strike. Yet somehow she mostly felt tired. I've done this before, she thought. Some hope had flowered, spilled its seeds, and died.

She was losing faith. But I can't give up, she told herself. I can't just go back to school and forget the war and try to be normal. Because it isn't the war, it's the heart, the beating flowering open heart. Someone had to keep faith with it, live for it, speak for it.

Rio and Daniel and Edith and Rob began holding secret meetings from which she and Liza were excluded.

"It's not that we don't trust you," Daniel said. "But the less you know, the less you can accidentally give away."

Maya had been angry, but Rio had soothed her. "Aw, calm down," he said. "You don't want to be at those meetings, anyway. Mostly it's Edith and Daniel talking for hours about which is worse, the company that makes napalm or the bank that loans them money. I think it's their form of foreplay. The only reason they let me come in on it is that if we ever do anything practical, they'll need me."

She was always half waiting to hear on the news that some building she'd worked in had been blown up, with one of the leaflets she'd typed slightly reworded to justify the act. But nothing ever happened. In fact, she thought, in spite of the rhetoric that floated around the house, the copies of Mao's little Red Book kept in the bathroom for reading on the john, the anguished debates, she firmly expected that nothing ever actually would happen. And that was okay by her; in fact, it was preferable. The thought of Rio planting a bomb in the Presidio or commanding an attack on a major media outlet seemed unreal. The thought of Daniel doing the same was positively ludicrous. He was a man clearly born to write abstruse articles in academic Marxist journals.

More and more, he reminded her of her own father. But her father, at least, was working class, or really, in his own childhood, downright poor. He had actually worked in factories, during the years when he'd been blacklisted from teaching or practicing law. At times she found herself wishing she could show him the collective, hear his critique of them, talk to him heart-to-heart about her own doubts and fears. She had written to him; he had her address. He wrote about as often as he ever had, which is to say, sometimes a card on her birthday, which she suspected was prompted by Betty. Sometimes he dashed off a polemic on the current political scene, something she suspected was written more to organize his thoughts than to communicate to her. When she responded, with a long, thoughtful answer, he never replied.

She arrived home one afternoon to hear a familiar voice thundering out from the living room.

"But you can't just adapt Fanon to America's domestic politics. An anticolonialist rebellion is a different animal from a Marxist revolution."

It was her father. She hadn't seen him in the flesh for years, not since the winter before she ran away, but she knew his voice immediately, and the sound of it, thundering down the hallway, resonant with his love of debate, made her feel suddenly sheltered and complete, as if all the meandering pathways of her life had suddenly converged.

She paused in the doorway for a moment to observe the scene. He and Daniel faced each other across the crate that served as a coffee table. Rio, sitting somewhat apart, was nursing a beer, and Edith was chopping vegetables in the kitchen. There were beer bottles on the floor, and Joe and Daniel were deep in argument. Joe's hair, she noted, was quite white now, and he ran his hand through it until it stood up like the ruff of an angry cat. He and Daniel were indeed similar, as if they had come off the same production line, Daniel the younger, thinner model of what Joe had become.

Something about the scene was primally male—they could have been two giant gorillas squaring off and beating their breasts, making challenging noises with their mouths. Rio watched, slightly amused. It was a battle being fought on turf that was not his own. Every now and then he stretched his arm, made a fist, and twisted it to ease the tendons that she knew had begun to strain him occasionally when he did too much hammering. The movement made his biceps contract and bulge.

Suddenly the scene struck her the way things sometimes did on acid, as a parody of itself. Couldn't the players see what script they were enacting?

"Hi, Dad," she said.

He stood up and grabbed her in a fierce hug. "Karla! Let me take a look at you." He held her out at arm's length. "Too skinny, girl. What's the matter? Isn't the revolution feeding you?"

"What are you doing here?"

"I came out for a conference of the National Lawyer's Guild. Thought I'd surprise you."

"You never told us your father was Joe Greenbaum," Daniel said. "The famous radical lawyer."

"You never asked," Maya said.

"Daniel and, uh, Rio, were telling me about your group," Joe said.

"Oh, good," Maya said.

"I'm just not clear," Joe said, sitting back down and settling into the couch, with Maya perched a little awkwardly beside him, "on your ideology. You call yourselves a Marxist-Leninist collective, but that can cover a multitude of sins. I don't know what it means to you, what you believe in."

"We believe in action," Rio said. "People need an example. They got to see that action can be taken that can seriously harm the war machine."

"What do you mean, seriously harm?" Joe asked. "Do you believe that anything you or I or the entire Weathernut Underground, all twenty of them, can do is going to seriously harm the war machine in this country? Do you have any conception of what you're up against?"

"In the last year, there've been over five hundred political bombings," Daniel said. "Sure, each one is a small act in itself, but all together they're something to contend with."

"Like an attack of mosquitoes," Rio said, his lips stretched over his teeth in a grin, "sucking the blood from the belly of the beast."

"Well, this beast is armed with DDT," Joe said. "Any bugs make trouble—and zip. They're wiped out."

"But don't you understand, Joe," Edith said, leaning forward, gesturing with the vegetable knife. "These actions are unstoppable because they're decentralized. There's no central leadership controlling it all to get wiped out. Not even the Weathermen. It's lots of small groups, little circles, collectives, independent of each other but linked because they're taking action, and each one can become a foco, like a little motor that drives the engine of revolution."

"Like the Little Engine that Could," Rio said. "I think I can, I think I can, I think I can, I think I . . . ."

"Cool it, Rio," Daniel said.

"Choo choo!"

Joe looked sharply at him, and Maya quickly spoke up to divert his attention.

"Did you ever fill a glass with sugar water, Dad? And then drop a string into it? Overnight, the crystals form on the string. That's how we see action—something for people to crystallize around."

"They're not going to crystallize around violence," Joe said. "Not in this country."

"We're not talking about violence, necessarily," Daniel said. "We're just not rejecting it out of hand. As you yourself said, we're up against the greatest constellation of force ever assembled in the world. We can't afford to reject any options."

"I strongly suggest you do reject that one," Joe said. "I'm not a pacifist. I went to Spain in '38. I fought in the World War. I know there comes a moment when you've got to pick up the gun. But that time is not now. I'm a realist. In this country right now, the violence that's crept into the movement is alienating the very people we need to reach."

"I don't know if that's true, Joe," Daniel said. "It seems to me that in this country, people don't take you seriously unless you're willing to fight for what you believe in. We've still got the frontier mentality. Unless you stand there with a gun in your hand, metaphorically speaking, you're just pissing into the wind as far as the American people go."

"And anyway, what are we calling violent?" Edith said. "Damaging property that's being used to help kill people? Calling the cops names, or tossing a few rocks? Pouring blood on draft files? Really, all the violence you can possibly attribute to the movement, even the very few deaths, doesn't match up to one single foray into a Vietnamese village, let alone something like a bombing raid or a My Lai."

"But that's not how the American people perceive it," Joe said. "It's their minds you've got to change."

"Sometimes you need to alienate people in order to change them," Rob said brightly. "It's the leftist version of destroying the village in order to save it."

Edith glowered at him.

"We don't go with the liberal position that you tell people only what they want to hear, in ways they feel comfortable with," Daniel carried on. "How the hell can that ever change anyone?"

"But you don't want to close off dialogue, either," Joe said. "The New Left has done far too much of that."

"Choo choo!" Rio said.

"Of course not," Edith said quickly. "Joe, would you like to stay for dinner? I'm putting on some rice, and there's plenty of vegetables."

"Actually, I was hoping to take my daughter out to dinner," Joe said, sinking back into the chair.

Maya gave a quick glance at Rio, who stood up silently, went into the kitchen, and emerged with another beer. She watched him, attempting to read by the glaze in his eyes and the slightest of shuffles in his walk, just what was his state of sobriety. Would he be charming . . . or belligerent?

"Rio?" she asked hesitantly.

"We got a meeting," he said. She couldn't read the tone of his voice. Was he hurt? Angry? He flashed white teeth at Joe. "Probably you'd like some time alone with your daughter, Mr. Greenbaum," he said.

Was he being genuine? Or was his politeness ever so slightly ironical, mocking? He winked at her and she knew that he was drunk, not enough to have an episode, but enough to cause trouble. Better to get her father out of there.

"Yeah, that'd be cool, Dad," she said.

She put on the skirt and sweater she wore to work in offices downtown, pulled on pink tights to wear under her sandals, which were only somewhat battered, and twisted her shaggy hair into a bun. She looked far from elegant, but no place would actually throw her out. Her father took her downtown to Chinatown, to a restaurant with intricately carved wooden booths and curtains that pulled across, giving the illusion of privacy. She couldn't recall ever going out to dinner alone with him before. When he'd visited them in LA, he'd taken her and Debby both, usually to the local pizza parlor or Bob's Big Boy.

They ordered a variety of dishes to share, shrimp and chicken and barbecued pork, a feast of things Maya rarely saw anymore. It seemed like extreme indulgence; she wondered for a moment how a man as political as her father could justify the expenditure on this meal, which would have kept her and Rio in food for a week. And yet, it was really only a modest Chinese restaurant, just down the street from the place Rio had taken her the night he pirated her away from Stow Lake. They used to eat in Chinatown often, laughing over the odd names of dishes on the menu. What has happened to me? she thought suddenly. And Rio . . . when did we sacrifice our capacity for pleasure?

They were sipping the fragrant jasmine tea. Maya didn't know how to break the silence because what she wanted to ask was something like, Tell me what will really change the world. At last Joe spoke.

"Did you hear Debby's going to be a foreign exchange student? She's going to Madrid for a year of high school."

"Really? That's great. No, I haven't talked to Betty for a few weeks."

"She's a good kid, Debby. Wants to be a doctor."

"I know. She always did. Even when we were little, that was her favorite game. I always had to be the patient, and she'd give me pills."

Their dinner arrived, and they were taken up with ladling out rice and sharing portions of the dishes, tasting and comparing. The food was good and Maya was happy on an animal level, just to taste spices and seasonings and concentrated protein after the everlasting meals of rice and veggies, punctuated by the occasional pizza. Silence fell again. Maya was sure Joe was looking at her, wondering how he could have a daughter who was such a misfit, a dropout failure, when her younger sister was so brilliant and good. But if I could only really talk to him, Maya thought, heart-to-heart, through all those layers of judgments and expectations, if he could see me and what I've become . . .

But what had she become? Or where had she gone, that girl who could stand naked, arms uplifted into the screaming wind?

Finally Joe spoke again. "Listen, Karla, why don't you go back to school? It wouldn't kill you. And it doesn't have to be Columbia. Look, next fall is my sabbatical year. I'm going to teach at the U. of Washington, in Seattle. You'd like Seattle, it's a nice town. You could live with me, and your tuition'd be covered for the first year."

"Sounds like you've got it all planned out, Dad." She looked down at her plate, contemplating a shrimp balanced precariously between her two chopsticks, not meeting his eyes. The problem was, she was tempted. It would be, in a way, a relief. Leave it all behind—the ratty flat and their ratty room and their ratty, ragged love, the strain of trying to convince herself that she really was following something when the trail seemed long cold. She could be a student, somewhere else, and wash her hair every day so it shone when she tossed it in the breeze.

"My life is pledged to the revolution," she said, not because she believed it but because she wanted to see how he'd react.

"Bullshit, Karla! Jesus H. Christ, don't feed me that crap! Me, of all people! Even Angela Davis got a goddamned Ph.D!" He gestured with his chopsticks as if they were spears, and minute drops of oyster sauce went flying over the table. "If you want to serve the revolution, educate yourself so you have something to serve it with."

"I didn't finish high school, Dad, remember? How can I go to college?"

"Take a test. I'm telling you, I can fix it for you. You're a bright kid. I've talked to the admissions counselor. You've just got to make up your mind to want to do it. If you want it, it's possible. I'll make it possible for you."

"I don't need you to make my possibilities, Joe."

"That's where you're wrong. You do need me, whether or not you think you do. Because frankly, Karla, from what I can see, all you're making for yourself is a big mess."

"Thanks a lot, Joe. That's a real vote of confidence."

"Karla, listen to me. That house . . . those people, they're like kids playing with gunpowder. What do they know about the real world?

Believe me, I've seen plenty of people who want to make a revolution. I've spent a lifetime at it. More than thirty years since I went to Spain, and I was in the Party before that." He gestured with his chopsticks, scattering rice on his plate. "It's not an easy thing to do, I can tell you that. If it was, we would have done it already. The effort takes a big toll. It takes a lot out of you, to sustain. After a while you get a sense for who's going to make it and who's going to self-destruct along the way."

"I'll bear that in mind." She was angry now. Funny, she had wanted his opinion of the Front, of her life, but not this way. What she wanted was that he and she, seeing each other, could then together look at her life, and she could lean on his history, so as not to have to reinvent it for herself. But he was blind to her.

"Look, if you were driving in a car and I saw you get on the freeway in the wrong direction, wouldn't I try to warn you? Stop you? And wouldn't you thank me for it?" His eyes were wide, brown, appealing. She almost felt sorry for him. He was her father, after all. With all the failings between them, he still wanted to love her, shelter her, protect her. But then his voice turned dictatorial again. "I swear to you, Karla, if God himself existed, he'd be standing right beside me holding up a big red freeway sign that said TURN BACK! YOU ARE GOING THE WRONG WAY!"

"Are you done insulting me?"

"I'm not insulting you, for God's sake. I just want to help you!"

"I don't need your help."

"Look, I'm sorry. I don't want to ride you. Just think about it. Promise me you'll just consider it."

"I'll think about it," Maya said. Joe reached his hand across the table and clasped hers. His grip was strong and warm and solid, and so tight that it hurt.

"If you can't keep him from drinking, what use are you?"

Edith's eyes were cold as she challenged Maya. They were alone in the kitchen for once, and Maya, as usual, was cleaning up after everybody else.

Rio had been drinking heavily again, going out to bars with Randy and T-Bone, two of the guys he met on his construction job. They were good contacts, he claimed—they might have access to explosives. Maya did not trust them. They made her nervous, swilling beer on the battered couch, their eyes hooded, their expressions hidden behind thick beards. She suspected they encouraged Rio to experiment with more powerful drugs than alchohol and pot—speed, maybe, or downers. Sometimes he seemed overly animated, talking too fast, his eyes too bright. At other times he slept so deeply she could hardly rouse him. She worried; nevertheless she did not want to discuss the problem with Edith.

"For one thing, I keep this place from being buried in the collective garbage."

"Why don't you leave it? How are the men ever going to learn to be responsible if you take care of it all the time?"

"The men around here could trip over live rats and not notice them," Maya said patiently. "How about you giving me a hand with these dishes?"

"You are expendable," Edith said, but she did grab a dish towel. "I don't mean that in an insulting way. I'm expendable, too. But Rio is not. He has skills we can't do without."

"I've tried to keep him from drinking. It just makes him mad."

"He's not happy with you," Edith said. "I wonder how much you're really willing to sacrifice."

"What do you mean?"

"If he were happier with someone else, if that kept him better able to function for the revolution, would you let him go?"

"What are you talking about? You?"

"I'm not talking about anything," Edith said. "I'm just questioning."

What about me? Maya wanted to ask. Do I exist just to service Rio, to be the sharpening stone for his ax? The question scared her. If she answered it honestly, what would she have left? She continued washing the dishes, ignoring Edith's droning complaints about the way the student strike was losing energy over the summer.

The question is, she thought as she let the dirty water drain from the sink before she tackled the big greasy frying pan, the question is, in time of war, how much of a life does anyone have a right to?

What kind of a personal life was available to the woman on fire? Was anyone urging her to go back to school, in Seattle?

But how do we ever get out of this mess without a vision of some other possibility? Marx had a system, a plan to make things change. She'd never had a plan, but it seemed to her that she had had a vision once, a glimpse, at least, of something else. But maybe not. Maybe she'd only had a series of inchoate feelings in the spray of the ocean wind.

Maybe she should listen to her father, after all. Seattle might not be bad. And yet she couldn't leave Rio. She loved him. They were bound together. No, she would have to try to protect him from himself.

If only she had someone she could talk to! Someone who wouldn't try to make her be or do anything, but would listen, with just the right mixture of sympathy and detachment. She ached for Johanna, for all those long afternoons when they would come home from school, fling themselves down on her bedroom rug, and talk talk talk. Never again. And she had no friend like Johanna here. Edith was no candidate. And Liza—Liza had frailties of her own, the worst of which, from Maya's point of view, was seducing every good-looking man who walked through the door. Which was maybe only a fair return for Rob's adventures with the women he brought home from rallies and rescued from cops, each one younger and prettier than the last. But it was finding Liza cuddled up to Rio in their bed one afternoon when Maya came home unexpectedly that clarified the intention behind Edith's little talk. I've been set up for this, Maya thought, and she was mad.

"Honey, I hate to see your face get all stoney like that." Rio grinned up at her, but her expression remained unchanged.

Liza arose with a smooth, dancer's grace. "Perhaps I'd best leave you two for a minute." She left the room.

Rio stood up, and put his hand on Maya's shoulder. She shrugged it off.

"Do we have to be bourgeois about this?" he asked. "Can't you accept freedom?"

Maya stood, silent, too hurt to know what to say. And humiliated, yes, that was what she felt. Because she'd thought he would always love only her, and that was stupid. Yes, bourgeois, romantic, stupid, stupid.

"I love you," Rio said. "Don't cry."

He kissed the tears out from under her eyelids.

Rob was gone for the night, off with someone he'd met in his Spanish class. Rio and Liza were closeted in her bed, with the door closed and occasional moans issuing through the wall. Maya was releasing her emotions by cleaning, scouring the stove and tossing out all the old containers of moldy food from the refrigerator, stripping the counters of their accumulation of old coffee cups, stained leaflets, papers, and crumbs, moving the table and chairs to scrub beneath them. Edith was staying over in the East Bay after a late class, and Daniel was reading in the living room, his feet up on the coffee table, absently tapping his cigarette on an ashtray precariously full.

"If you knock over that ashtray," Maya said, emerging from the kitchen with a bucket of dirty water, "I will dump this water all over your head."

"Hey, take it easy," Daniel said. He looked down at the ashtray, carried it gingerly into the kitchen, and deposited the butts in the garbage. "Is that better? Do you feel more secure now?"

"Now you've made footprints all over my nice clean floor!"

"For God's sake, Maya, what is this? A Spic and Span commercial? I'm trying to get some work done."

"So am I!" She headed back to the kitchen, brandishing a rag, but he stopped her and put an arm around her.

"Is something the matter?"

She shook his arm off. "Let's just say I'm not in the best god-damned mood tonight."

He slid his arm back around her shoulder and jerked his head toward the bedroom. "Them?"

"I don't want to talk about it right now."

"Now, Maya, you know the old saying: 'Don't get hurt, get revenge.' "

"What do you mean?"

"I mean why should you suffer through this alone when we could smash monogamy together? I've always been attracted to you, you know."

He stood there staring at her, blinking, his blue eyes slightly watery, his hair going in five different directions. She wasn't attracted to him. There were times when he irritated her so strongly that she could happily have gunned him down with one of the rifles locked in the basement, and yet there was something dear about him—his brilliance coupled with his awkwardness, maybe. She couldn't hate him. No, they were comrades, working together for the same goals.

"You want me to fuck you out of revenge?" she countered. "You want me to use you?"

"Not revenge, exactly," Daniel said. "Call it . . . symmetry."

"What about Edith?"

"Edith and I don't have that kind of relationship anymore. Not for a while, now. She says she wants to conserve her energy for the cause." Daniel gave her a wry smile. "The truth is, the woman should have been a nun. It's what my mother always warned me about, you know. 'Don't get mixed up with the goyim, my son,' she would say, 'they are very strange. Find yourself a nice Jewish girl.' "

He grinned at her, and suddenly she was laughing. Why not fuck him, anyway? He wanted it, and what did it really matter to her? It would be a lesson for Rio, too. Hadn't she fucked men she knew less well, shared nothing with? Although not for a while. It had been a long while since she had gone to bed with anyone except Rio. Well, maybe it was time for that to change.

"Go brush your teeth," she said to him.

In bed, she found herself surprised by his gentleness, his attentiveness. He stroked and petted her with endless patience, alert to every cue, every change in her breathing. He was a humble lover, willing to give all, expecting nothing. She could lie back and float away and allow herself to be pleasured; except that each time she began to drift, Rio's face would intrude. She would find herself remembering his hot urgency, the feeling of being swept away by a raw, animal power. Meanwhile Daniel continued to make love carefully, Talmudically, as if she were a text he was dissecting, lingering over the mystical value of each sacred vowel.

When at last they were done, he cradled her in his arm and lay with his face nuzzled into her neck, reluctant to draw apart. It had been a long time since she and Rio had lingered together like that. Suddenly she was struck by a sense of deep familiarity, as if she and Daniel had been together a thousand times before, as if they had always been meant for each other. He was her predestined mate, the nice Jewish boy fate had picked out for her. They were meant to marry and breed and create the family she had never had. On holidays they would gather and he would argue happily with her father while she and Betty served the food to their large brood of children who were all the smartest kids in their class. After many years together they would retire to Florida.

She sat up abruptly. "We can't do this," she said.

"What's wrong?" Daniel asked. "Did I do something wrong? Weren't you satisfied?"

She shook her head. "It's not that. That was fine. Wonderful. No, it's us. Look at us!"

"We look pretty good to me," Daniel said. "A bit pale, perhaps, but we live in a fog zone."

"No, don't you see—this is what they want from us. You and me, to be together. You'll finish your dissertation and I'll go back to school and we'll have nice Jewish children and live in the suburbs of some small town where you'll be the local radical at the state university. We can't do this!"

He reached over and took her hand and squeezed it tightly.

"You feel it," Maya said softly. "You feel it too. Maybe it's what you want, deep inside, but it's not what I want."

"Maya," he began, and then paused. His voice surprised her. It seemed to come from somewhere deep inside his chest, as if everything she'd ever heard him say before had emerged from some superficial layer, and now at last she was hearing his true self speak. "Maya," he started over, "we aren't going to live that long. Not if we believe what we say we believe. Not if we do what has to be done. You know that, don't you?"

She did, she had often said so, but truthfully the thought of dying seemed unreal to her. He reached up with his free hand and lightly traced the line of her cheek, as if he were memorizing the shape of her face, trying to hold her in his mind and make her immortal.

"That's why Edith gave this up," he whispered softly. "She said it was too painful for her, to feel so alive. But I'm not like that. I want to live all I can, as long as I can."

She drew in a breath, wanting to say something to him that would offer assent if not comfort. But he pulled away.

"God, listen to me," he said, his voice resuming its usual half-mocking tone. "I sound just like a hero out of Hemingway. *For Whom the Bell Tolls.* You ever read that book? Nah, of course not, I forgot. You don't *read,* you sniff the wind."

"I do so read," Maya said. "I read Hemingway in high school."

"I thought you dropped out of high school."

"Before I dropped out. Mr. Harvey, fourth period, World Lit. 'Even if these three days are all we ever have, they can be a lifetime for us.' Something like that."

Daniel thumped lightly on Maya's skull. "A brain! I knew she had a brain. Why does she try to hide it?"

"I don't try to hide it. I just use it in my own way." Maya pushed his hand away. "You know, my father fought in that war. He went to Spain. And he came back, and he's still alive."

"What are you saying?"

"We might survive, that's all."

"We might," Daniel admitted. His voice dropped, becoming serious again. "But it's better not to hope for it, not to think about it. Because if we do, we'll start to make our decisions based on what will help us survive, not on what needs to be done."

"Would that be so bad?" Maya asked.

"Not if you want your happy little life in the suburbs, no. But if you want to remake the world, then yes. The ax that chops the tree is going to get blunted."

"Couldn't we just plant something new, and wait for the tree to fall?"

"We tried that," Daniel said. "Remember the park?"

"How could you do it?" Rio had glowered at her over breakfast, refused to speak to her all day, ignored her throughout dinner, and sulked through their evening meeting. Now, at the end of the night, he followed her into their room and closed the door behind him.

"You were the one who wanted to smash monogamy!" Maya said.

"I do! I just don't understand why you had to do it with Daniel, of all people."

"How can you say that? You fucked Liza."

"That's different."

"What the fuck do you mean, that's different? How is it different?"

"Look, I don't object to you fucking him, if you want to fuck him. But I don't believe you really do. I think you just wanted to get even with me. It's like sexual snooker around here. Some chick fucks Rob so Liza fucks me so you fuck Daniel so Edith goes to the library."

"Well, who started it?" Maya asked.

"Who started it? Jesus, you sound like a six-year-old!"

"It's not your fucking her I care about," Maya said, almost convinced that she told the truth, "it's the way you did it. You never discussed it with me, first. You weren't honest with me."

"I never lied to you."

"You did! You lied by not telling me it was going on!"

"It wasn't. . . . It just happened. Okay? That's the truth. Look, Maya, I love you. Does that mean I can't have feelings for Liza, too? Don't you think I have enough love to go around?"

"No. You don't. We hardly ever see each other, when we do half the time you're drunk or wasted or so preoccupied with some shit you can't talk about—"

"Just lay off me, okay? Goddammit, Maya, you really can be a bitch! Just understand this—you cannot fucking control me! I'm not your private property, I'm not your possession, I'm not your little boy—"

"Oh, fuck you!"

"Fuck you! Fuck you! That's your fucking answer to everything! Great! Well, don't fuck me, fuck Daniel! Fuck Rob, fuck any asshole on the street you can find that'll hold still long enough. Just don't come fucking crying to me!"

He stomped out of the room, slamming the door. Maya flung herself down on the bed and cried. At first she cried with one ear half cocked, hoping he'd come back and be sweet and stroke her hair and dry her tears on his shirt. Later she just cried, desolate. Much, much later, when the black rectangle of their window had turned a shadowy, dark gray, he returned, stinking of sweat and liquor. Without undressing, he lay down next to her, throwing his arm over her shoulders, and began to snore. His heavy arm pinned her down, but she decided to interpret its weight as comfort, and at last she slept.

Rob had a stormy fight with Edith and moved out of the house. He was leaving town for the summer, anyway, going to Fresno to organize farm workers. Maya avoided Daniel's approaches, ignored his hints, and stuck close to Rio. For Liza also moved out. She claimed she wanted to be back in the East Bay. Rio and Maya moved into Liza's old room, which was marginally lighter but quite a bit bigger. Now, Maya thought, things have to get better again. She found Indian print bedspreads in a free box, and hung them on the walls of their room. She covered the window with old bits of lace she bought in a second-hand store, and hung her earrings on a ribbon she pinned to the door. The room seemed festive, to her, full of the color and beauty she hungered for.

The summer passed, and they never once went to the mountains.

Fall came, and classes resumed at all the universities that had gone on strike the previous spring. It seemed that students couldn't sustain an action over the summer. How could they sustain a revolution, then? Maybe Americans just weren't made of revolutionary material, or were too indoctrinated by TV, or were, perhaps, not desperate enough. Or just frightened. Frightened of the great abyss of freedom that yawned at their feet. Frightened of being left without something, an education, a degree, if they dreamed too deep. Frightened of committing themselves to something that might indeed be only a mood and would pass.

As she herself was frightened. Maybe there was nothing, really, that she could do for the woman on fire. Rio seemed remote, almost always separate from her, somehow, just busy enough, or plastered enough, to keep from really touching. And yet still there was so often a sweetness between them—after they'd yelled and stormed and screamed, and she was beginning to touch that hollow place where what he said, and Johanna and her mother and her own fears said, were right, and she really was mistaken and stubborn and worthless, then he would touch her, just a hand, maybe, on her cheek or stroke her hair.

"I'm sorry, baby," he would whisper. "I know I'm being a shit to you. You deserve better than me."

"But I love you," she would murmur back.

"Someday I'll make it up to you. If we come through all of this alive. I swear it."

She believed him. Their love was all she had left of the magic, and no matter how rarely they touched, when they did she was still filled with honey gold. She loved his lips, full and demanding, on hers, his body pressed against her in the night, big and warm, enfolding her own with a feeling of shelter. No, how could she give it up? Yet in the background, now, she was conscious of Daniel, watching them, biding his time, as if deep inside he knew that she was ultimately doomed to come to him, or someone like him. No, Rio was if nothing else her talisman, warding off her fate.

"I don't know what to say about myself," Maya said. "I mean, I don't know what kind of experience of oppression to talk about."

She was sitting in a circle of women, sprawled on the floor of Leona Burke's apartment. Leona was a dark-haired woman with wide, staring eyes, whom Maya knew from the old Moratorium Committee. Now she was organizing the East Bay Women's Center and had offered to facilitate this first meeting of a new consciousness-raising group. Liza had suggested Maya and she go together. They had met downtown on the street one morning when Maya was hurrying to a job she was late for.

"Look," Liza said, "I'm sorry about me and Rio. I'm sorry we let a man get in the way of our solidarity as women."

Oh, God, Maya thought, another crusade, another cause. Spare me. "That's cool."

"I don't want to lose contact now that I'm out of the flat. Our friendship is important to me."

"Oh?"

"Really, Maya. Have you joined a consciousness-raising group yet? There's a new one starting Tuesday night. Why don't we go together."

"I'm not sure."

"I promise you, you don't have to read a thing."

Maya was dubious but let herself be persuaded. And now she sat in this circle, expected to open up and share her most intimate life experiences with these strangers and with Liza, whom she couldn't help but view as a dubious ally at best, if not an open enemy.

"I don't really think I am oppressed," Maya went on.

"Are you kidding, Maya?" Liza interrupted. "You are one of the most oppressed people I know."

"How can you say that?"

"Look at you. You never finished high school and you're cleaning other people's houses for a living, or else you do shitwork in corporate offices in order to help Daniel with his research. Your diet resembles the cuisine of the kwashiorkor belt. You live in a little rathole of a room with a dude who drinks too much and fucks other women. You clean up after the men, type their leaflets, cook the food, wash the dishes, empty the goddamned ashtrays, practically wipe the assholes of the assholes. No woman in the world, even the Third World, would envy you for a moment."

"You should talk about Rio fucking other women," Maya said bitterly.

"I'm sorry about that. What can I say? My consciousness wasn't raised yet. He wasn't even a very good fuck."

"What do you mean? Rio's a *great* fuck!" Maya said, outraged but at the same time uneasy. Isn't he? she wondered. Is there something wrong with me that I think he is? Is there something I don't know?

"I don't really want to listen to a lot of discussion about the sexual prowess of straight women's boyfriends," Leona said. "That's not what we're here for."

"We're getting out of process," said Mary. "We're supposed to be letting Maya talk without interrupting her."

Maya gulped some air and went on. "Even if you're right, Liza, even if my life is as fucked up as you say it is, that doesn't make me oppressed. I have choices."

"What good is having choices if you've been conditioned to be unable to make choices?" Liza demanded.

"What good is having a process if we don't stick to it?" Leona said. "Stop interrupting her."

"Everything I am is what I've chosen to be. So I have no one to blame but myself." She sat in silence, unwilling to speak. The other women seemed to be a court assembled to pass judgment on her life, and she wanted to conceal it from them. "I don't have anything to say."

"You get your ten minutes, whether you choose to use them or not," Leona said. "If you don't want to talk, that's okay. We'll just sit here in silence."

"Let somebody else go," Maya said.

"That's not the process," Leona said.

"Maybe you could tell us how you came to make the choices in your life," Ilene said gently. "Liza's made me curious. Like, why did you drop out of school?"

"My best friend Johanna and I dropped acid together. We were trying to become enlightened." She hesitated. The story was hard to tell without diminishing it. The bare words skated over the surface and left out so much. But she continued. "We were pretty stoned, and we ended up stark naked on the locker room floor—touching. Until the gym teachers found us."

The women waited in a silence alive as a crouching cat. "So they kicked you out for being a dyke," Donna whispered. She cradled a cigarette in her too-thin fingers and gave a forced smile as she lifted it to her lips.

"Not exactly," Maya said. "They did call the police on us, and we got busted, but in the end they tried to cover for us. They didn't kick me out of school. But there was such a huge . . . gap . . . between the way I felt and the way everybody else reacted that I knew I didn't belong in their system ever again. I know it's the worst sort of cliché to talk about love, but we felt it. We really did. And there didn't seem to be any place for what we felt." Because even the word *love* wasn't big enough, she thought. What we glimpsed was what love might lead to.

The silence that greeted her words was comforting, as if they were being deeply and slowly digested. In the silence, she could consider her own story in a new light. "We can't let them make us think we were wrong," she had said to Johanna, but had she ever really believed she and Johanna were right? Believed it enough to be angry instead of ashamed?

Believed it enough to believe also that her own wild love was something
to fight for, as she had fought so hard for so long for others?

Donna drew in a deep draft of smoke and exhaled it slowly. "My
story is somewhat similar. My best friend Lucia and I got caught doing it
up on the meadow near our boarding school. Only in my case they sent
me to a psychiatrist. The psychiatrist started delving into all the deep-
seated reasons why something might have gone wrong with me, that I
would be attracted to women, not men. I got depressed. So we had more
sessions, one a day. I got really depressed. So he put me into a hospital,
on a locked ward. Then, let me tell you, I was pretty suicidal. So they
gave me shock treatments. Then I had trouble remembering things or
focusing on what was going on. So then they gave me drugs, and the
drugs made me really crazy. And then I met Mary, on the ward. And we
fell in love." She turned and smiled at Mary, who reached out with her
own plump, brown hand and patted Donna's shoulder. "And here we
are, just trying to survive."

They were linked, the six of them, in the silence.

"Why?" Maya asked. "What is so dangerous about love? Why do
they have to destroy it?"

"Love is political," Leona said. "Our own lives are political. We
need to get angry for ourselves, not just for other people. We need to
fight for ourselves. Our rage is a form of love."

My rage is old and tired and stale, Maya thought. But what if it were
rage for me? What if I myself were the woman on fire?

When she got home, at midnight, the sink was full of dishes and cigarette
ashes, the floor full of beer bottles. Rio was out somewhere. Daniel
smiled at her suggestively and said casually, "Glad you're home. I was
getting hungry."

"It's midnight. You haven't eaten yet?"

"I was waiting for you."

"Why? So you wouldn't have to fry your own egg?"

"Oh fuck, Maya, don't tell me you're going to start spouting all that
women's liberation dreck. Here we are, the privileged white women of
America—no more guilt for us, oh no. At last we have an oppression to
call our own."

"Fuck you, Daniel."

"That's the best idea you've had yet!"

"I mean it!"

"Come on, Maya, be nice to me. I'm wiped. I've been working
hard all day and all night."

She felt like a bug being slowly wrapped with spider silk. A phrase, a thread. Sticky, softly confining. She would start thinking about how brave he was, how ready to die, and feel sorry for him.

"No," she said, "I won't let you suck me into this. Cook your own dinner."

"Rio's out for the night," Daniel said.

"What does that have to do with anything?" she said, but she knew it did. Yes, part of her wanted to taste again the sweet, painful familiarity of his body. She would let him restore to her something she'd never really had, knowing all the while that fate intended soon to take it away.

"I got a Hemingway anthology from the library," he said. "We could have an intellectual evening, the two of us. Reading together."

Maya sighed, and gave in. "Once . . . and then never again. Okay?"

"Why? Are you afraid you might get to like it?"

"Once," she said again. How could she explain to him how familiar he felt to her. You are of my own kind, she thought. We are kin. Too close, too inbred. You are too much like my father, and already you have promised to abandon me.

"Johanna? It's Maya." Maya's hand trembled as it clasped the receiver of the telephone, waiting through the long pause that followed her announcement of her name. At last Johanna spoke.

"Maya? My *ally*, Maya? I'm surprised to hear from you. I thought you were too busy working against the oppression of *my people*."

"I'm sorry about that stupid letter." Maya hurried to say as much as she could before Johanna changed her mind and hung up. "I'm sorry I ever wrote it. But I just have to talk to you. To be in contact. I can't let us go into this silence."

There was silence on the other end of the line. Again Maya waited for a long, long moment.

"Johanna, are you there? Won't you talk to me? I mean really, I'm sorry about our fight, about the letter, about everything. Can't we forget the stupid letter, pretend I never sent it?"

"Hell no, child," Johanna said at last. "You never gonna live that down."

"Oh, Johanna, it's so good to talk to you. Just to hear your voice."

"Yes, it is good. Oh, Maya, girl, I do miss you."

"Do you? Do you really?"

"Yes, crazy as you are, I do. How's the revolution?"

"Not so good. It's beginning to seem to me that I never learned to be an ally to myself. Does that make sense?"

"First sense I've heard you make in years. How's Rio?"

"Fine." Maya paused. "No, he's not fine. There's no point in talking to you after all this time if I'm just going to lie and pretend things. He drinks too much and screws other women."

Another silence. "I'm sorry to hear that," Johanna said. "Not surprised, but sorry."

"He's a man," Maya said. "Maybe that's all we can expect from them."

"Maybe. Sure seems that way sometimes."

"How are you? How's the baby? What's her name?"

"Her name is Rachel, after my grandmother. Oh, Maya, I wish you could see her. I mean, I won't tell you it hasn't been hard, but it's worth it. There's no feeling like it in the world."

"How'd you decide to go ahead and have her?" Maya asked.

Johanna waited before answering. "Well," she said lightly, at last, "I'd always wanted to have a baby someday, and I thought, what better time to have a baby than when you're pregnant?"

Maya laughed. "There's a logic there."

"I'm moving up to Berkeley next year, in the fall. Transferring. I gotta get out of here! You can imagine what it's like, with my mama and all. I mean, she's been good to me. She's really stood behind me. But sooner or later I've got to stand on my own. I've got to breathe some different air."

"God, it'd be good to have you up here. To be able to see you all the time. If I don't go away. My dad wants me to go back to school. He says he can get me in where he'll be next year, in Seattle."

"You gonna do it?"

"I'm thinking about it." It was the first time Maya had admitted, even to herself, that this was true.

"Well, you know you're gonna have to do it eventually, so why not get it over with?"

"You think?"

"You got to live in this world, sister."

"I guess that's true."

She was giving Rio one last chance. Maybe they could still find the magic they'd once made together. At least they would look for it, they agreed, in the mountains, just the two of them, going away not for training or map-reading practice or any larger purpose than just to be together. The June sky was a deep blue and the open windows of the van let the hot winds of the Central Valley whip through their hair. The van climbed up and up through the foothills, the slow, steady slope of the western Sierras. They would have a whole week together, maybe more. He would have no booze or other women to distract him, to keep them from finding the sweet place. Yes, everything was going to be all right, after all. No matter that he was silent now, brooding, withdrawn into himself. She would have all the time she needed to bring him out again.

As the foothills began to turn into mountains, forested with tall pines and studded with resorts, the freeway became an ordinary highway. Rio pulled off on a turnoff where a weathered, sprawling log building sported a sign that said PINEWOODS TAVERN.

"Rio," Maya said, trying hard to keep her voice neutral, controlled, "you promised you wouldn't drink on this trip."

"I'm not going to drink. Jesus Christ, are you my fucking keeper? I want to go to the goddamned john."

"If you get drunk in there," she said, "I'll leave you. I really will this time."

"Oh, for Christ's sake, Maya. You really know how to piss me off." He stomped off, turning his back to her. She watched him go up the two steps to the wooden porch that ringed the saloon, push open the door, and slam it behind him.

She waited.

"I don't have to worry yet," she thought. "I have five minutes, ten minutes." And then, "What am I going to do?"

When fifteen minutes had passed, she knew he was not coming out until he got drunk. And I can't bear it, she thought. She couldn't bear the crashing disappointment, or the waiting, wondering whether to go in and confront him and risk making him mad, or to pace the dusty parking lot, fantasizing about riding off with some other man in some other car. She wanted to be rescued, but he had always been her rescuer, and who would save her from him? No, she would have to save herself this time.

She could go in there, drag him out, make him go. But no, she couldn't do that, not again. God, she wished he would just come out, tell her some excuse, even some lie, so that she could evade this once again. So she could once again believe it could all work out, they could be all right together. Okay, she would wait five more minutes. And if he came, they could forget this . . . incident. Soon they'd be up in the mountains, where there wouldn't be any booze. And if he didn't come, she would . . . she would wait five minutes more.

But when fifteen more minutes had come and gone, and she had walked all around the parking lot again, counted a hundred cars going by on the highway, and then a hundred more, she opened the door and took out her backpack. Slowly, she divided their food, filling her pack with supplies for several days, all the while thinking that he would surely come and stop her. But at last, she finished. Still he did not emerge. She closed the pack, closed the door. She thought of one more thing— another water bottle. Still hoping, still waiting, she opened the door, opened her pack, repacked again, all the while feeling as if she were watching herself perform underwater, with all sounds muffled and something stifling her breath.

Was she really going to do it? If she didn't think, if she just picked up her pack and stood by the side of the highway and stuck out her thumb, surely he would come back before she got a ride. Surely. Because, she told herself as she walked to the roadside and waited, because it didn't make sense for love to end like this, all that sweetness. No, it didn't make sense not to know the touch of his hand on her cheek, not to think that his eyes wouldn't look into hers, see how badly he had hurt her, and change. Surely he would come.

A car stopped before he came. All the long way up the mountain, she kept looking out the back window, expecting to see him following in the van.

But no one followed behind her.

She asked the driver to let her out at the top of the pass. She knew a trailhead that began there. Shouldering her pack, she started walking. All the while she was calm. Tears dripped from her eyes, but she concentrated on moving, one foot following the other. This moment, this trail, this footstep was all she had to get through. Although she knew the chances of his following her were slim, she couldn't help listening behind her. The trail went up the side of a mountain and through meadows that astounded her with their sky-embracing beauty, past lakes cradled in granite, so clear and blue she could hardly bear to look at them. She was panting and sweating and so she didn't have to think, as the trail crested a pass and began to descend down to a lake that lay cupped in a bowl of rock like a teardrop in a rough hand. The sun had long since set, and she raced the darkness down to a sheltered spot where she could pitch the tent, unroll her sleeping bag, crawl inside, and cry.

She cried for a long, long time, maybe the whole night. She hadn't realized she could cry like that, as if her insides would come out with her sobs, as if she would never stop. At dawn, she slept long enough to dream that he had come after her and found her. He lay beside her cradling her head in his arm, and opened to her and told her all his pain. They wept together, their tears making one salt stream. The dream was as sweet as their first night together, but when she woke, she was alone.

29

Letter

James Patrick Connolly
Somewhere in Hell, probably
August 15, 1971

Dear Jim,

Why am I writing to you? You're dead, and I'm drunk. Not as drunk as I'd like to be, not dead drunk, hardy har har. Drunk enough so my hand is shaking and nobody will ever be able to read this. Which is for the best. I'm writing to you, Jim, because I expect to be joining you soon. I'm ready. I long to join you. The truth is, man, I'm writing to you because there's nobody else. No-goddamned-body else.

Maya has disappeared. No word, no sign. My fault. My fucking fault. But hers, too, goddammit. She should have known not to badger me like that. She should have known not to take me seriously. Or maybe I should have taken her seriously when she threatened to leave. Shit. But she'd said it a hundred times before. How could I believe her? We belonged to each other, man. I knew it, from the first moment I saw her across the lake. From the first time I touched her. I felt at home with her. I felt like you do when you open a door after a day hunting woodchucks in January, with the snow biting into your neck and your feet nearly frozen and you open the door and the house is warm and smells like coffee.

I trusted her, goddammit! She told me whatever I did, she'd always be there for me. She told me she'd never leave me.

So yeah, all right, Jimbo you moldering corpse, I tested her. Hell, I'm young, man, I need room to maneuver. I can't just fuck one woman for the rest of my life, no matter how much I love her.

Anyway, she's gone, and it's my own fault. I just had to stop in the tavern. It was the sky. So blue, man, as we got higher into the mountains. So cold and blue and clean. I needed something to take the edge off, tone the brightness down. Just one drink, I thought, in that bar. Just one. But the stuffing was coming out of the torn red plastic on the barstools, and the waitress had her lipstick smeared a little too far above her upper lip. God, how that made me sad.

So one thing led to another. I was mad at Maya, for hassling me. Fuck her, I thought. Let her wait a bit. Let her wait.

Oh, God, Jim—why was I born stupid?

You know all those old stories, about a man who marries a fairy wife. He's in love with her, he's happy, but there's one thing he's not supposed to do or say, and he always does it or says it, and then she goes and never comes back.

I feel like that man, Jim. But I don't know what the thing was. I don't know what it was.

When I first came out of the bar, I thought she'd just gone to take a leak or something, buy something in the store. I waited. She didn't come back. Then I thought she was trying to pay me back. I got madder and madder. But finally I looked in the van and noticed her pack was gone. The food was divided. Then I realized she'd really split.

I must have driven up and down that highway a hundred times. I didn't know where she went. All afternoon, back and forth, up and down—I was like a crazy man. Finally the thought came to me that for sure she'd gone back to the city. Right—she wouldn't go off into the mountains alone. She'd go home, complain to our friends, bitch to her women's group. I drove back so fast it's lucky the state police didn't run me in. But she wasn't there.

Daniel and Edith were having some kind of meeting with Randy and T-Bone, the two guys I brought into the group because they work for a company that sometimes does some blasting. Ah shit—I shouldn't be writing this down but hell, I'm going to tear this letter up as soon as I get it all out of me. Anyway, they're willing but not too bright. Randy is big and blond, T-Bone is little and scrawny and dark. They're okay, I guess— at least they are the genuine working-class article. Daniel was pontificating away and they were sitting there, either stoned or bored to death, or both, and Edith was chewing her cheeks and the ashtrays had spilled all over the floor and the whole goddamned house stank. I couldn't take it. I've had it, Jim, with talk talk talk and refining our fucking ideologies. The movement's gone to shit. Cambodia made it look like it was happening but that was over a year ago and nothing much has happened since. Even the Weathermen—pardon me, the Weather Underground—has sort of drizzled away. And meanwhile the war goes on. While I'm here flipping out because my girlfriend's left me, while Daniel is running his mouth and Edith is chewing hers, while we wallow in this shithole full of our own goddamned garbage, the war goes on. Guys like you are being blown into little pieces of spoiled meat. Other guys like you are gunning down children and taking their mothers out into the bush and nailing them before they blow their heads off.

I couldn't take it. I got mad—I yelled and screamed at them all, don't ask me what the fuck I said. I threw some chairs around. Yeah, it was a scene worthy of our old man.

Daniel and Edith were yelling back at me but T-Bone just took me aside, out into the hall. "Calm down," he said to me. "If you're so fucking sick of talk, do something. Go ahead, Randy and me'll back you up. These people, man, they'll talk themselves to death. Maybe the way to get them off their asses is to show them."

"Maybe you're right," I said. I felt calm, happy. Yeah, he was right. To hell with all this strategy and consensus. Nothing was stopping me from doing whatever I wanted to do. I went down to the basement, where we keep the stuff T-Bone got us. I started to try to put something together, just to see if I could, you know. But it was too much for me, in my state of extreme fucked-uppedness, which was much more fucked up than I am now, even. That's delicate, precision work. You got to be damn careful or you blow your own ass sky-high. Which at the time I didn't give a shit about but still I guess I've got an instinct for self-preservation.

Edith came down while I was working.

"What do you think you're doing?" she asked.

"Taking action," I said. "I've had enough bullshit."

"You are bullshit," Edith said. "Put that stuff down, goddammit. Don't you realize how dangerous it is? Get the fuck out of here, Rio. You're drunk and irresponsible."

My arm moved, Jim. It flew through the air towards her face. The fist attached to the arm would have knocked some teeth out if it had connected. She ducked away from me. Then I ran. I had to get out of there. Because our old man had nearly got me. I could feel him, hanging on my shoulders; I could smell his whiskey breath. If I didn't do something, something pure and drastic and clean, I was going to turn right into him.

I drove the van downtown. I pulled off on a little side street, siphoned some gas out of the tank, and filled a Pepsi bottle. I soaked a rag in it and stuffed it in the top.

The whole time I felt like I was stone cold sober. Everything was so clear, Jim, clear and distant, as if I were looking at the world through the wrong end of a telescope, and it was far, far away. I felt good. I felt like I was where I was supposed to be, doing what I had to do. Now I understand your last letter. I understand what you mean about putting your life on the line. My own doesn't mean much but it felt good to be willing to lay it down, to be taking some real action, no matter how small.

I locked up the van and hid the bottle under my coat. I could feel it, cold against my heart, which was beating so hard I could almost hear it knocking against the bottle. So even though my mind was calm, my body was scared shitless. Over on Market Street was the Army Recruitment

Center. We'd checked them out before as a possible target—they didn't have a night watchman or security guard. I walked over there. On the way, I picked up a loose brick I found in an empty lot, where a drunk was curled up, wrapped in newspapers. For a moment, I stood and looked at him. He could have been me. I could be him, stinking of my own turds, crashed out among the broken glass. But he looked so peaceful, almost innocent, like in his sleep he'd turned back into a child. It came to me that maybe we all have that innocence in us still, somewhere. Even me. We move out of it into misery and sin, but it's there, waiting for us, waiting to claim us as soon as we let it. Then I wasn't afraid anymore. No, I was calm and peaceful as I walked over to Market Street.

I looked around. By then it was so late even the bums had deserted the street. The recruitment center had a big plate-glass window full of posters. UNCLE SAM WANTS YOU! Not me. No, Jim, they got you but not me. I threw a brick through the window, smashing Uncle Sam. The noise, the crash, and the tinkle, like falling water, sounded good to me. Clean. I took the bottle out from my coat, struck a match, and lit the rag. Before I had a chance to think, I threw it through the window. Then I walked away.

After a moment I heard a rumble, and then a roar. I let myself take one glance back. It was beautiful, Jim, the orange flames rising into the black night, the smoke like spirits dancing under the streetlights. Beautiful and powerful, more powerful than you or me. Clean, hot flame.

Then I made myself walk slowly back to the van. Not running, not hurrying, even though by then the fear kicked back in. I wanted to stop and shit in every vacant lot, or sit down so my legs could hold me. I was sure the pigs would be there in a minute, my hands were trembling, feeling the cuffs already around my wrists. I don't mind dying, Jim, but I don't think I could stand being locked up. That really scares me.

But no cops came. I made it back to the van, started the engine. God, did it sound loud! I was sure everyone for a mile around would hear it. But nobody came to their window and shouted. By then I could hear sirens on Market Street, but there were none where I was so I drove off, heading south down to Harrison Street and back out to the Mission. It was four in the morning when I got home, but Daniel was still up, smoking and reading and making notes.

"Better put that down," I said, "and start working on our leaflet. Study time is over, man. Action time is here."

"What the hell are you talking about?" he asked, and I told him.

He just sat there and looked at me, Jim, with those sad, watery eyes of his, and then I realized that he'd started to cry. He was sitting on the couch, letting his cigarette drip ash on the floor, and quietly weeping.

"This isn't the way it was supposed to be," he said, shaking his head. "This isn't the way it was supposed to be."

Oh fuck, Jim, what is?

I left him crying alone and went to bed. I lay down and tried to sleep, but suddenly I felt cold. I wanted Maya to be there, to roll up against me and keep me warm. But she was gone, and I was shivering and couldn't stop. It hit me then that I could have killed somebody. It hit me then, Jim, that I'm just what I never wanted to be, a chip off the old block, crazy drunk and mean and dangerous.

So we can't escape. No matter what we do or don't do, we can't escape what he did to us, what he passed to us in our blood. But I intend to put it to use, O my dead and rotting and wasted brother. I'll go down, I know that, but I won't go down easy. I intend to put it to use.

I don't know how you'll ever get this letter. We'll see if I'm drunk enough to mail it.

Rio

30

The Fire Sermon

All things, O Bhikkus, are on fire.
The eye, O Bhikkus, is on fire; forms are on fire;
eye-consciousness is on fire; impressions received
by the eye are on fire; and whatever sensation,
pleasant, unpleasant or indifferent, originates in
dependence on impressions received by the eye,
that also is on fire.

—THE FIRE SERMON
THE WISDOM OF BUDDHISM

Maya was dreaming of smoke and noise and voices shouting. Rio was throwing a Molotov cocktail at a yeti in flames who was chasing a woman on fire around and around through the woods. The woods were burning, and the smoke was making Maya cough and choke. Soon she would be burning, too, her lungs seared, her skin scorched and flaking. And then there would be no pain that outweighed hers, no dimension of suffering she would not know.

She woke up coughing, hearing Tenzing's voice calling her. "Wake up. Wake up, Maya, and dress quickly. The *gompa* is on fire!"

Her small tent was stifling, smoky enough to make breathing difficult for her already irritated lungs. She sat up and held her head in her hands for a moment. Her head was heavy and hurt, and she couldn't think what to do.

Air. She must have air. She unzipped the door flap to let in a blast of cold wind, carrying the tang of smoke. She fought down a sense of panic, a feeling she was trapped in the small tent, that smoke would rush in and suffocate her and she wouldn't be able to get out. Movement, that was the thing. Groping in the dark, she found her pile sweatpants, her long undershirt and sweater and the heavy wool socks she'd hiked in to

Pangboche and back. One by one, she put everything on, just stuffing her feet into her boots without bothering with the laces. Grabbing her jacket and cap, she pushed her way out of the tent.

Outside, the air moved more freely, heavy smoke alternating with gusts of cold wind. She was still having trouble breathing, but the sense of panic lessened. At least here she could move.

She squatted down to lace up her boots. The wind had blown away the fog, and the full moon shone down on immense peaks, their snowy tops and icy flanks glowing blue white. A red glow came from the *gompa,* and black smoke poured from its roof and windows, billowing up in the silver night like an evil prayer.

Tenzing had finished waking the other group members. They stood together, watching the destruction in a dull, sleep-ridden horror. Lonnie and Jan held hands. Howard stood far away from Maya and would not meet her eye. Just as well, she thought. She tried to flash him a small, cool smile, a smile that would say, "I will still be friendly and polite to you since we are trapped in this group together, but don't ask for more." She suspected that all she achieved was a grimace that got lost in the dark.

"Can we help in any way?" Peter asked.

"You could help in the lines," Tenzing said. "But stay far back. Do not endanger yourselves."

Several lines of people stretched away from the *gompa* to the open field. At their head, Maya could dimly see figures darting in and out of the smoke. They were monks, saving what treasures they could. In each line, people were passing books and tankas and artifacts back, hand to hand, to be piled up and covered with tarps safely away from the fire.

Maya shivered. The cold of the night, the fear in her dream, and the reality of the burning *gompa* left her feeling dislocated, not sure if she was awake or asleep. She stared in fascination at the fire. At first she saw mostly smoke, a pall of it pouring out of the windows and roof of the monastery. Then Maya saw the flames, darting out the windows and flickering deep inside. The flames rose and danced as the monks ran in and out. She held her breath, waiting for the figures that disappeared into the haze to reappear again.

She hated waiting without being able to do anything. Peter and Lonnie had joined the lines, and she, too, walked over to the shortest of them, helping to move the precious objects that could be salvaged from the holocaust. On her left stood one of the kitchen boys whose name she had never learned but who greeted her with a warm smile. On her right stood one of the lean blond explorers from the Danish expedition, a man who, for all she knew, would shortly be venturing up the cols and cums of Sagarmatha herself. But here in the line, all distinctions of class and fitness fell away. They were all equals.

Maya's spot was well back from the fire, and mostly she stood, with her partners, watching and waiting as people dashed back and forth. A few monks ran forward, their red robes whipped about them by the wind, to toss buckets of water on the flames. The effort seemed more in the nature of an offering than a serious attempt to quench the fire. The water made an ineffectual splash, devoured in an instant by the roaring mouth of flame. Here the elements raged unchecked, unmediated. Fire was fire, water was water, givers of life, takers of lives.

"This is terrible," said the Danish climber in good, almost accentless English. "To think that there is nothing more we can do!"

He was tall and godlike in a Greek Apollo sort of way. How strong he must be, how fit, what an incredible cardiovascular system he must have!

"No fire department here," Maya said. "No water pumps and hydrants and helicopters."

"Helicopters," he said. "If only they could bring in some helicopters. Scoop up water from the lakes and drop it on the fire. But of course it is impossible at night."

"Tricky enough to fly by day," Maya agreed. "It's a mixed blessing, all right, living so close to the elements. They have a tendency to become . . . elemental."

And by the way, she imagined saying, would you like to have a child? You seem to have good genetic potential. The Danes, she had heard, were extremely open-minded about a lot of things. Why not try?

"There are benefits to modern civilization," the Potential Father of Her Child agreed. "Up here one understands why we went to the trouble to invent technology."

The truth was, Maya admitted to herself, that she was not the kind of person who could make a suggestion like that in cold blood. No, she was far too demure, ladylike, shy. Or at any rate, sensitive to the energy, unlike certain people, Howard for one. That was the advantage of the sperm bank, she supposed, something anonymous, impersonal. If only there were one for famous climbers. Or even not-famous climbers. On the other hand, was it really wise to produce a child who would always be able to outrun you?

She was just about to ask the climber his name, when someone hailed him from across the way, and giving her a brief smile, he left the line and walked off. Maya moved forward to close the gap, but nothing was coming down the line at the moment. She felt superfluous and, quite unreasonably, abandoned.

Tears blurred her eyes. For a moment, she felt responsible for the burning of the *gompa,* as if she had carried fire with her on her back, unleashed it by reading Rio's letter.

Don't be stupid, she told herself. None of it is your fault. Not this fire, not the others. I had a right to leave him. My fault was in staying with him as long as I did. Plenty of women leave their boyfriends, and most of them don't go burn down the draft board.

Still the residue of his pain stayed with her. I wanted to hurt him, she admitted, and I did. But I didn't want seventeen years of revenge.

I shouldn't have read the letters. For that matter, how had that last letter survived? Why hadn't he torn it up, as anyone with any sense would have done? Had he really been drunk enough to mail it? And then how had it come back to his mother, to be found by Carl and sent on to her?

I was wrong to read his letters. Still, at least I know how much he loved me, in his own warped way. As I loved him. What does that mean now, after all these years and silences, except that we were able to cause each other pain?

Should I go see him? Is that the path back to reclaim my power? And if so, do I tell him about Rachel? And risk my relationship with Johanna?

She could imagine Johanna's recriminations. No wonder their passion faltered. Their love was riddled with secrets and lies of omission, like wood rot in a supporting beam.

"This is awful!" Lonnie came up behind Maya and stood next to her, filling the climber's empty place. Maya moved back a few feet again. "What are we going to tell the folks back home? We came to the spiritual center of all Khumbu, and as soon as we arrived, it burned down!"

"You think it was our influence?" Maya asked. She was joking, but she couldn't completely rid herself of traces of irrational guilt.

"They're saying that it was the electric heater in the lama's study. It tipped over, and shorted out. Is that ironic, or what?"

"It reeks of symbolism," Maya agreed. "Technology comes to Khumbu, only to destroy the spiritual heart of the country."

"Yeah," Lonnie said. "Kind of makes you think."

"I wonder what the Rinpoche thinks."

"He's over there." Lonnie gestured with her chin at a knot of monks. In the midst of them, Maya could see the Rinpoche. He was not a tall man. When the monks crowded around him, he all but disappeared. Then they moved away, and Maya caught a glimpse of his face. He stood quietly, rapt in stillness, watching the flames. What was he thinking about? Maya wondered. Was this the greatest tragedy of his life, or just another lesson in impermanence?

She thought about her own home, all the things that were her daily ground and background; her favorite mug, just the size and shape and thickness that she liked; her old oak desk with its copious drawers that she'd bought at Busvan; her bed with the deep purple Egyptian cotton sheets; the collection of clay and stone and painted wood Goddesses that filled her bedroom altar and spilled out to cover the tops of bookcases, dressers, cabinets; the stained-glass moon she'd given Johanna that hung in the living room and fractured the afternoon light. They seemed so permanent, like features of nature, eternal in their very ordinariness. And yet, between one breath and the next, a wire could spark, a candle topple, and they could be gone.

All her life she had been at war with the ordinary, the everyday, but now she realized how strongly it had captured her allegiance and her heart. She cherished the memory of each separate simple thing in her own house. The faucet whose leaking washer they had just replaced, miracle deliverer of water; the wool blanket she'd bought in Ireland that hung on the arm of the couch; the collection of pictures Rachel had drawn over the years that Johanna had framed and hung in the hall. Dear Goddess, let them continue. May they be preserved in an impermanent world.

"Here we go," Lonnie said. A flood of objects was suddenly coming down the line. Sacred books, the long, thin Tibetan texts with their loose folios of paper, tankas of painted silk, statues dressed in colorful robes, like doll clothes. Turn, swing, grasp, turn, release. Like a dance. She was still half-asleep, and everything still seemed . . . not exactly unreal, but caught in that state the *curandera* she'd met in Mexico used to talk about, where reality was not so fixed and you could sometimes shift between them, the Good Reality and the Bad. El Mundo Bueno and El Mundo Malo, she had called them. Or you could slip into one or the other, and get stuck. Rio, now, he had fallen into the Bad Reality years ago, and never come out. Well, this was El Mundo Malo, for sure, and as far as she could see, it had progressed altogether too far to be shifted back into the reality she'd gone to sleep in just a few hours ago. Now, that time seemed to exist in some other eternity. She had been eternally cold, her back had ached for centuries, eons, while between her hands passed sacred texts and priceless tankas, all the treasures and debris of a spiritual life. A carved bone trumpet and a wool hat. A gilded Buddha and a pile of red wool robes that needed to be laundered. A bronze hand bell and a stack of aluminum pots. The material signs of impermanence, the debris of mysticism. Hah, she thought, They're no different than me— just a bunch of Pagans. We're all junk collectors.

The monks had given up their attempts to douse the flames with buckets of water. Like the lama, they stood and watched, while the brave few continued to dash into the smoke to save what they could. Maya was remembering the painted *gompa,* the vivid world of saffron and rust red and viridian and indigo blue she had seen just yesterday afternoon. She could imagine how it would be inside, the bright colors blackening from smoke, and then the bright flame licking the walls, eating the wood down to the stone. Where were they now, the painted lineages of

Rinpoches, the peaceful and wrathful deities? Released to the air? Liberated? Or simply gone?

The tongues of flame became great roaring banners, waving and dancing like red prayer flags from the windows, leaping for the roof. The Rinpoche called out, and one of the older monks restrained the boldest youngster who was about to make another foray into the burning building. He stepped back, his head drooping, and they all moved away as the flames reached higher through an open hole in the roof.

A last statue came down the line, and Maya held it for a moment. A bronze Tara, her face delicate and self-contained, her right foot extended, the symbol of her readiness to enter the material world. Where were you, tonight? Maya wanted to ask. Were you preoccupied, looking after events elsewhere? Or is it too utterly simple to think that the great powers of manifestation and dissolution are concerned about the same things we are?

The smoke poured out, the flames leaped and crept and rose and devoured, blackening the stones and roaring over the roof beams until with a great, thundering crash, the roof fell in.

Lonnie reached for Maya's hand and gripped it tight. The line moved back, dissolving into scattered groups who simply stood and watched the tiger devour its prey.

Tenzing came by and motioned to them to join their fellow trekkers where they had gathered, close to their own kitchen tent.

"It is over," Tenzing said sadly. "We can do no more. Best to try to sleep for an hour or two. I will have the kitchen boys wake us late."

"I don't think I can sleep," Carolyn said.

"Try. We have a long walk tomorrow, and you will need your rest."

On the way back to her tent, Maya saw the Rinpoche again. He stood still in the center of a cluster of monks who were talking at a rapid pace. Over his red robe he wore a down jacket. Other monks were running around, putting tarpaulins over the piles of ritual objects and scriptures that dotted the field like a new range of hills. He was looking at the ruins of the monastery as they smoldered red and black under the moonlight. Maybe Maya was imagining it, but his face looked utterly serene, as if he simply accepted the loss of his home, another do-si-do in the dance of impermanence. First there is a *gompa,* then there is no *gompa,* then there is. Was he remembering his other lives? Thinking, Well, hey. It's better than the time the whole place crashed down on me in the earthquake and buried me in the ruins. Or was he able simply to gaze upon what is, with no screens in the way, no comparisons to what was, no chatter of blame or self-blame or regret.

If so, she could learn from him.

31

Summer Passing to
Autumn, 1971

Maya awoke alone. She had made camp beside a lake cradled in a shallow bowl of the Sierras. The narrow ledge that rimmed the east side of the lake hung suspended high above a deep canyon. Far below, a green river carved its way down to the sea.

The light woke her. Not the sun itself, that would take hours to climb the ridges and filter through the tall pines that sheltered her, but the change of the air from indigo to pearl gray. She lay still for a moment, waiting for the ache of loneliness to shudder through her. It came, as it had every morning for the past week since she'd left Rio. But not as sharply, not as deep or long-lasting as during those first few days, when she'd hurt all over with the pain of his absence. She'd lain awake, night after night, listening for the crunch of footsteps on scree, hoping he would follow and find her. Surely their magic was strong enough to overcome time and distance and all that separated them. Surely he would come.

But he didn't come. The everyday had captured him and eroded their magic away.

Now even her pain, her last connection to him, was diminishing. Mourning it, she rose from her sleeping bag, crawled out of her tent, and stood naked in the dawn, letting the cool wind caress her flesh that longed for touch. Long ago, on the coast, she had imagined the wind as her lover, but now she wanted simply to feel it as it was. The wind was real and constant. The smell of the pines, and the woodsmoke smell of her banked fire which she now blew back into flame, the sound of the stream pouring down over rocks to fill the lake, the intensity of the blue sky; all of them were real. She had been living in a fog of abstractions. Now she had emerged again into the real world, a world that went about its business asking nothing from her, needing nothing. She was not required to fix it or save it or change it or do anything but simply be in it, a sojourner, a guest. Perhaps one day, if she stayed long enough, she might step through the screen that still kept her separate, and belong.

She rose and walked to the edge of the lake. The water was cold, fresh from the ice fields high in the scree above her. Some days she entered slowly, walking in step by step, savoring each new sensation of cold on skin as she gradually submerged. Today she plunged in, a shallow, awkward dive that propelled her forward. She swam for a few moments, the cold so intense that she could hardly breathe, hardly make her arms and legs keep moving. Where her head emerged from the water, the cold made an aching ring around her neck. But that, too, was something like the mountain, that she didn't have to change or fix. She had a cold neck, and later she would have a warm neck. And if she stopped calling the sensation cold it became simply information, neither pleasant nor unpleasant, just intense. The word *cold* shut the experience off.

She splashed back to the shallows and knelt over the small fire she had built. If she did not think "warm," as she rubbed herself vigorously with her towel, then cold and warm became nothing more than different sorts of fire tingling on her skin. She was alive, alive, alive.

She considered breakfast. Her food was almost gone. She would eat last night's leftover rice and save the last of her oatmeal. When her food ran out, she would have to go home. Wouldn't she?

But where was home? Back to Rio, and Capp Street? When she thought about him, she shivered in spite of the fire's warmth. Their life together seemed covered with a thin gray film. When she looked back on herself, she appeared half-asleep, numb, under a dull spell. Here on the mountain, she could see in color again.

If only Rio had followed her up here, maybe the lake would have cleansed him, too. But he hadn't. He wouldn't. That was real. He had made another choice.

If she went back, would he have realized his mistake? Would he have missed her, longed for her as she longed for him, wanted her, reformed for her?

She wanted to believe he had changed. She yearned to believe, but deep inside she knew the answer was no. No, he hadn't changed, or if he had, it was for the worse. Life offered you certain crossroads, and once past them, paths diverged. There was no turning back, no retracing your steps. She hated to believe she and Rio had passed such a point, that their mutual magic was truly, irrevocably gone. Suddenly Maya was crying, holding her bowl of cold brown rice and nestling close to the fire. No, she didn't want their love to be over, she wanted him there beside the fire with her, warm and alive and glowing as he had been when they were first together, his beard golden, his eyes kind.

He wasn't there. That was the point she kept coming back to, the thing that was real. What she wanted and what she wished and what might have been were as much abstractions as all of Marxist-Leninist theory rolled together. What was real was the blue silent loneliness of this lake-sky mountain place, where she had broken out of the spell and was free once again.

Where to go, then? To Daniel? If Rio could not be salvaged, should she give in to fate, letting Daniel's slow, careful lovemaking bind them together? She shuddered. He would wrap her up in threads of words and suck her dry.

Back to her mother, in LA? That would be falling into another spell, older and deeper even than the ensorcellment of Rio and revolution. If she went home, Betty would assume Maya was admitting that she been wrong all along.

And maybe I have been, Maya thought, but *right* and *wrong* are abstractions, too. Why should I let her judge me just when I'm breaking free from judging *cold* and *warm, hungry* and *full*? No, no, no. I am what I am, like Popeye the Sailor Man, and that's all what I am, as the lake is the lake, is something for which *lake* is only an approximation, a description that makes you look at your mental picture of *lake* and cuts you off from the thing itself.

If she stayed here long enough, she could unlearn words. Because who she was, eating her cold rice, squatting on the earth and letting her hair dry in the sun with the scent of woodsmoke on it, was a person tracking something that had no words. She didn't know where she was going and she couldn't define or describe what she was following. She knew only that she was devoted to it, whatever the hell it was.

She sighed. No, Betty never would, never could, understand that. She had no sympathy with formless journeys or mystic quests. Really, I don't myself, Maya thought. Words like that, any words, any names at all for it, sound vomitously pompous and dumb.

Anyway, none of the names would be accurate. She had found her holy grail, long ago, on the locker room floor with Johanna—she just couldn't exactly remember what it was or figure out how to fit it into the same world as the wisteria and the woman on fire.

Definitions were traps. She should avoid them, avoid situations that would force her to use them. Betty's judgments, even Betty's worried love, were not what she needed. How could she go home and say, "Mom, I'm no different than I was when I left four years ago, and I'm not going to change. I'm not going to school. I'm not going to look for a job. I just want to wander around the world and be free. Ah, but you say, I haven't made any progress in all these years. But if I have no destination, then there's nothing to make progress towards."

No, Betty would have her enrolled in social work school or something like it before Maya could protest twice, and this time maybe Maya wouldn't have the nerve and stamina to resist.

Her dad, then? "Hi, Joe, I've decided to take you up on your offer, go back to school in Seattle." Joe would be easier to deal with because once he'd arranged her life, he'd probably leave her alone. But then how would Betty feel? Maya would have abandoned her again, thrown her over for Joe, the betrayer, let him succeed in fixing her where Betty had failed. Was that fair? Was that right? Hadn't she praised Betty to the women in the consciousness-raising group for supporting Debby and her alone all those years after Joe walked out, for being responsible as women always were while the men ran off to be free? How could she ally herself with Joe, now?

No, it was all too much. What she needed to do was to continue to wander, without map or compass, to climb up the streambed to the high scree above, to discover the springs that were the source of the lake.

The rice was finished; tonight she would cook the last of her remaining supply. What was more serious, even, was that she had come to the end of her instant coffee. But she wanted to stay. Maybe she would learn to live without drugs—caffeine included. Drugs were screens, too, even more than words. Maybe she needed to learn to be hungry. With all the Front's frantic identification with the Third World, with all their voluntary or not-so-voluntary poverty, she had never gone hungry—not in the sense of wanting food and not being able to get it, day after day, not like most of the children in the world felt all the time.

She would stay. If hunger were what she needed to learn, she would learn hunger, although the thought did not appeal to her. If she needed to learn cold, she would be cold. If loneliness was the lesson, well, she was all alone here. Other campers had appeared on what she'd guessed was the weekend in the outside world. They hadn't bothered her, and she wouldn't have to speak to them, except that she could beg their leftover food when they were about to pack out. She wouldn't starve. But she would speak as little as possible. Mostly, she would try to stop speaking to herself, to stop naming and describing and limiting and open her mouth to taste what was really there. She would stay, until winter came or she knew where to go, whichever came first.

She survived on handouts of rice and beans and packages of freeze-dried dinners. She boiled up pine needles for tea, ate berries where she found them. The less she spoke, the more she felt drawn to look, to see, to wake in the morning and stare at the lake, drinking with her eyes before she plunged into the water. The more she looked, the more there was to see: the shifting light on the water, the sunset glow over the river canyon, the small variations in color that came with the play of shadows. She hiked far down the river canyon to watch the stream grow, tumbling over boulders and feeding the roots of trees; she climbed up the granite outcropping above the lake, high up into hidden meadows on the far slopes of the mountains to find the blue-green ice-melt tarns where streams began. And so each day she wandered, looking at stones and leaves and the play of light on moving water, staring with the blank, open gaze of an infant in a new world.

On a good day she could hold the purity of dissolution, let the sun pour golden through her veins, and know that the tracery of pine boughs against the sky and the wind's cold caress on her bare back were simply patterns in the tapestry woven by the shuttle of her breath. She could follow that rhythm out and hear the moon's backbeat against the measured turning of night to day, could feel her own bare footfall on rock, on sand, on bark-becoming-earth as she herself was becoming earth, slowly.

Each night she made her way back down the rocks to her campsite at the water's edge, gathered downed wood, blew the banked embers of her campfire into renewed life. She warmed her hands, watching the red glow flicker on her palms, almost surprised to see them remain human in form. She felt like an animal: wordless, needing no divisions between her being and the life of the mountain.

On a day lost in time, when the sun shone but the bite of a cold winter had already crept into the night wind, and the rainstorms of summer had already begun to threaten snow, she lay on a granite boulder, sunning herself like a lizard or a cat, enjoying the fleeting warmth. In a moment she would begin her daily round. Follow the shore of the lake and climb the granite ledge on the opposite side, to stand with her face buried in the bark of the lone pine that stood atop the rocks. The bark was rough and scented like pineapple, and whenever she breathed the aromatic scent, she felt as if she were breathing the scent of a lover. The land became an erotic presence that awoke each day to reach out and enfold her. The trees, the streams, the boulders, all were alive, reaching and calling to her, asking for her to be their witness, to perceive them as they changed in the changing light, to admire and praise and adore them.

From the lone pine she would continue up the mountain, scrambling from boulder to boulder, following the course of the stream that fed the lake. High up on the shoulders of the mountains were clearings rimmed with fir and pine, and higher still was a small hidden meadow where wildflowers bloomed on the edge of winter. Nestled under the sharp-rimmed bowl of the highest ridge, a clear pool was fed by the still unmelted snows that lingered on the scree.

There she would pause for a long time, occasionally dipping her hands to drink, but mostly simply looking, gazing into the pool as if she were gazing into Rio's eyes, or the eyes of a better lover, one who would gaze back and be her perfect mirror. That love, that mirroring, she understood at last, was what she had always searched for and desired, was what all original religion stemmed from. The speech of the gods was the speech of the land. But even to say so, to use those words, was to intrude a false language. For "the land" was not a thing separate from her; they were not two separate beings in the tenuous connection called relationship. She had become part of this land/sky/tree/lake/changing-light thing that was also her. She had stopped telling herself a story about being separate and allowed herself to know that she was as much an expression of the earth as any tree or rock.

The land was always calling out for lovers, for witnesses. She had answered, and become its servant. She served by looking with open attention at the trees, at the wildflowers, at the clarity of the pool. Simply by perceiving, she gave something back.

We are not a mistake, she thought. We have a purpose we are meant to fulfill. Mostly she tried not to think, but to exist as a blank, open-eyed stare. The more she let go of human speech, the more she could love-talk with the land itself, could feel the trees quickening to consciousness under her touch. She had found her work—talking the trees awake.

The trees spoke to her. The trees, the pool, the soft hint of snow to come on the breath of the wind; that day they all spoke to her, not in words but in images/memories of storms and ice and snow piling itself high, high above her head. You cannot survive, she translated. Winter is coming. You must go.

When she thought about leaving the mountain, she felt an ache in her bones, deep as the pain she had felt leaving Rio. But she would obey. She knew better than to argue with trees and rocks and wind. She knew not to outstay her welcome.

"But where do I go? What do I do?" she asked the pool that mirrored her own eyes back to her.

"Wake things up," she heard, forming the words for herself because words, she now understood, were containers in which she could hold and carry what she would have to leave. "In the mountains, wake the mountain. Among your people, wake the mountain that sleeps inside your people. Speak with the mountain's voice. Be our eyes and ears."

Clouds formed over the pass, hiding the sun. She hiked down to her campsite, and packed up as the snow began to fall.

32

Tengpoche to
Khumjung

Let us live happily, though we call nothing our
own. Let us be like gods, feeding on love.

—THE DHAMMAPADA
THE WISDOM OF BUDDHISM

"Namaste."

The soft voice of the youngest kitchen boy penetrated Maya's restless sleep. After the fire died out, she had lain down in her tent, but
everything smelled of smoke and it made her cough. She couldn't catch
her breath. For a long time, she lay awake, panting, panicky, wondering
why the penicillin wasn't helping, knowing she needed to rest. Finally
she had willed herself to think of mountains, to evoke the memories of
that summer she had spent alone. The memories had lulled her to sleep
for an hour or two. Now she awoke tasting fire in the back of her throat.

"Namaste," the kitchen boy said again. Groaning, she unzipped
her tent and accepted the hot cup of tea and the wash water he'd
brought her. She sat up and slowly sipped the hot brew, waiting for the
caffeine to take hold. If only she could sleep and sleep and sleep, preferably in her own bed back home in their small, sunny bedroom. Johanna
was right, she thought. We should have taken a Caribbean cruise together. I could be lying out on the sundeck right now, not facing another
day of hauling myself up mountains and trudging through old, stale memories.

She drank the tea slowly, reluctant to open her tent, to face the
smoldering ruins of the monastery. If she stayed here, enclosed in her
own plastic bubble, she could pretend for one more moment that everything was unchanged, that she could open the door and walk through the

painted *gompa* hall and beg the monks to let her stay there, yes, and the girl in the green sweater, too. Together they would sit at the feet of the Rinpoche and seek enlightenment. Maya would shave her head, take a vow of celibacy, and return home in about twenty years.

Her wash water would be getting cold. Time to get up and seize the day, as they say. Quickly, she washed and dressed and packed up. Today they would hike up to Khunde, where Debby's clinic was. Tonight, for sure, she would finally see her sister.

She stepped out of the tent and caught her breath. The sky had cleared. She stood in a bowl surrounded by mountains, stark and massive, crowned with ice fields that gleamed blue and white, etched with ridges so sharp they seemed to cut the air. They towered above the plateau and the ruined *gompa*, beautiful beyond the scale of human judgment.

Once she had known how to talk to mountains, how to enter them and become them and caress them. If she could do that here, if she could become lover to the Goddess Mother, would her power return? But these mountains were of a whole other order. They dwarfed the Sierras, made the Rockies look like pimples. She was not sure she could rise to their dimensions. They called for a love so vast it would turn her inside out.

The group ate a breakfast in near silence. Everyone looked sleepy, even the indefatigable Tenzing was bleary-eyed and swollen faced. Maya finished her oatmeal quickly and took her tea outside the tent so she could stare up at the mountains. Lhotse, Nuptse, Sagarmatha. They stood, radiating a presence, a consciousness—neither benevolent nor malevolent, but simply of a different order than hers. The mountains didn't care if she coughed or if Lonnie and Jan ended up together or if she and Johanna broke up. They weren't distressed that Rio had ruined his life. No, and they didn't care if she went to Nevada or reached Nirvana. Or did they? Was there some deeper level, some plane upon which the consciousness of mountains responded to death and waste and pain? Was there a compassion embedded in the very rocks, so that they offered their beauty in compensation for human loss?

She was close to a revelation, although she couldn't help feeling that she was about to discover something she already knew. If she could have stayed there for another hour, even twenty minutes, she might have had a breakthrough. But it was time to go. Already the monks were up and about, picking through the cooling ruins of the *gompa*. They would have much work to do, and the trekkers, Tenzing said, would only be in the way. Shouldering her day pack, she followed the group down the path she had climbed so laboriously only two days before.

The way down, as always, was easy. But when they crossed the river and started on the uphill stretch of trail that led back toward Namche and then up to Khumjung, Maya found herself lagging behind. She moved slowly, her feet dragging, her lungs aching in the cold air. She was tired, tired of her memories, tired of the walk, tired of mustering up all the energy she could to take one more step uphill, and then another, and another.

Why did I come on this trip? she berated herself. I'm not who I was seventeen years ago, able to hike for days on a few handfuls of rice, able to glory in cold without ever snivelling. Now I'm fat and weak and sick and out of shape. I'm no longer fit to be a lover of mountains. That's for the young and slim, for the possessors of quads of steel and perfect cardiovascular systems and ragged green sweaters, who aren't carrying the baggage of their imperfect loves, who aren't milked dry by other people's hungers. Oh, dammit, dammit, why do I have to spoil this for myself?

Ang came by, smiling, and took her pack again. Ila passed her with the yaks. No matter how slowly Maya walked, one of the Sherpas would stay behind her and watch out for her, and never complain or ridicule her. But she felt bad. The path was like an endless torture that went on for eternity. I can't do it, she thought. I can't go on. What would happen if she were to sit down in the middle of the trail and cry? Would they carry her? Would they continue to be gracious, smiling, accepting, or would they resent the hell out of her, having to lug some beefy, spoiled American woman up this trail where she had no right to be?

She wanted to cry. She tried to look away from Pembila, who smiled at her sweetly because if anyone was kind to her she knew she'd burst into tears. And that wasn't right, there was nothing really wrong, she was just tired and sweaty and sick. If only she weren't sick, she might not be so tired. If only she weren't so tired, she might not feel so sick.

Goddess! It was a damn good thing she hadn't run off into the mountains with the girl in the green sweater; she could never keep up. She couldn't even keep up with the packaged tour. No wonder the great powers weren't singing to her. No wonder the Rinpoche thought she needed praying for.

She remembered the look on his face as he watched his monastery burn. The same flat, neutral gaze with which he had regarded her. What if it wasn't boredom, but the open-eyed infant stare with which she'd once regarded the mountains? Had the Rinpoche learned to drop the screens of words and judgments that kept him from being the world's lover? Had he offered her the same clear mirror as her mountain pool?

She sighed. The path continued up, with no relief, no level stretch in sight, and she really couldn't sit down on the trail and cry. She had to go on. There was no choice. She had put herself into this situation and now she would have to walk out of it.

All right. Here she was in Buddha land. Why not try the Buddha path? Accept what the Rinpoche had shown her. Remember what she already knew, and let go. Let her body be, with its limitations and imperfections, its wheezing lungs and its extra pounds of flesh. Stop trying to carve it and chisel it and make it into something it isn't, and love it like a pine, like a boulder. Stop blaming herself for being sick and slow and heavy. Let go of the words *sick* and *slow* and the weight of all they conveyed, and just feel the workings of her muscles against the rock. Stop wishing the uphill were downhill; stop telling herself a story about what she should feel, and let be.

She stopped. Just for a moment, she let herself breathe in the clean, thin air. She was surrounded by incredible beauty, white crowns on the blue forms of mountains so high they appeared just where you'd expect only birds or stars to be. For that one moment, she was present in the beauty, no longer wishing she were somewhere else, home in Johanna's arms or curled up on the sofa with a nice cup of tea. The path was still steep, her breath still rasping, her body still slow and terribly tired, she was still worried about what to say to Debby and what Debby would say to her, but somehow none of that was between her and the mountains any longer. She was released from a glass cage full of clamoring, chattering noise, into a world where she could feel the air on her skin and hear the bell-like tones of silence. Light danced off the glaciers to caress her eyes, and she opened, letting herself be emptied, disemboweled, a conduit for wave after wave of love deep enough to match the mountains.

And the mountains met her love with love. She was their beloved and their cherished child; she was living rock and a skinless organ of rapture.

Then the moment passed, and she resumed walking her slow climb up the stony path beside an old riverbank. She was still breathing heavily as she moved through the forests of gnarled rhododendrons, watching the mountains come and go through the clouds. But now the river sang and the day was luminous.

So this is what they mean by ego loss, she thought. Not losing the self, not dropping into some formless void, but getting the hell out of your own way so you can see and feel and touch what is. I knew that. I knew it at seventeen and I found it again on the mountain, and now here. It's really very simple, and it's the most difficult thing in the world to do.

I can be the mountains' lover after all, she thought. I can train the compassion of the rocks on my own history and look at my life with this same luminous vision.

What I see is the one thing I most truly know: that when you are present in the world, everything comes alive to meet you. Sleepers awaken; the dead revive. Johanna and I found that out when we touched on the locker room floor, and we've been finding and losing it ever since. When we are present with each other, we kindle passion. When we are absent, passion dies.

Well, hot damn, Maya thought, I've done it at last. A Genuine
Spiritual Insight, as Lonnie would say. Maybe I should share it with her.
Hey, Lonnie, this is what I've figured out. Passion has nothing to do with
monogomy, or the lack thereof. No, passion is evoked by consciousness,
blighted by self-consciousness, by the stories we tell to define ourselves.

I should write that down in my journal. Either it's the supreme
insight of my life, or it's like the things you come up with on acid that
seem so brilliant at the time but sound banal or incomprehensible the
next day. We'll see.

Or maybe she should write to Johanna.

Dear Johanna, I've made the most marvelous discovery about our
relationship—there is nothing wrong with it. It is what it is, a treasure, a
jewel, rich and tangy and complicated and yes, not everything at every
moment to each of us, but I've let that separate me from what is between
us, the touch of the heart that has never failed, wild and beautiful as these
rising peaks.

At last the path crested the ridge and came out on a vista of brown
terraced fields that gave way to paths lined by the rock walls of the twin
villages. They walked through a broad valley of stone-lined terraces in a
bowl of dark ridges, now covered by clouds once again. Maya could
hardly make her feet move, but she walked contentedly at her slow pace.
Everything delighted her: the changing light, the long walls of carved
prayer stones, the kids playing and singing in the school yard. Everything
seemed to fall together in a kind of perfection that included her.

They made camp in a field beside a small white *stuppa*. The trekkers were served tea in a nearby *bhatti* while the kitchen boys set up the
tents. The stone lodge seemed colder than the air outside, and Maya
huddled around the small spot of warmth her cup provided, and thought
about her sister.

She was here. Debby's clinic was just up the hill in the village
somewhere. Maya would see her at last. Debby would have no more
excuses to postpone the encounter. And now Maya was ready. Their
meeting would be the first test of her newfound serenity. Could she stop
describing their relationship by its history and be present for Debby,
could she gaze open-eyed without judgment or expectations on who her
sister was today?

Ang entered the room and came over to where Maya sat, a little
apart from the others, with her journal open as an excuse not to talk.

"You want go see sister?" he asked.

"Yes. Can you take me, or tell me how to find the clinic?"

"You rest," Ang said. "You very tired. Tent is up. Rest one hour, I
work. Then we go see sister."

"Thanks, Ang." Yes, that would be good. A little rest first, so as not to face Debby in a state of complete exhaustion. Maya gathered up her journal and went out to her tent. Yes, truly the thought of walking even a hundred feet uphill seemed impossible.

It was still early, even though the sky was cloudy and dark. She would crawl into her sleeping bag and warm up. Maybe she would nap for a bit, or just lie and think, or finish reading Johanna's journal. Yes, that would be good. Get a bit of practice in, before she encountered Debby, in training this new awareness, this soft peace that permeated everything, on her own past.

33

Johanna Weaver's
Journal

November 4, 1971

Oh God, oh God, oh God. It's been a long time since I've written in here, but tonight I have to write or go insane. For the first time in my life, I wish I had a bottle of whiskey or vodka, something to bring on oblivion. Just to get through the night. If I could wake up tomorrow and know, I could deal. But wondering, not knowing, picturing gruesome horrors in my imagination . . . I can't take it. Damn damn damn them both, damn them all! Damn that fool white boy and his guns and bombs and damn Maya's father for filling her head with rhetoric from the day of her birth and damn her for not seeing through the both of them. Damn the goddamned FBI! Where the hell were they? Why weren't they on the job? Why didn't they stop them?

Maybe I'd better start from the beginning. This morning I tuned in to the news on KPFA while I was fixing Rachel's breakfast. They had the report, the beginning of it, anyway. How someone bombed the Bank of America last night, and credit was claimed by the Home Front Collective. At first I didn't pay it much attention—somebody's always bombing something or other, these days. But they went on with the story. Apparently the bomb was planted in the women's bathroom. They had called in a warning but the timing was off, or the bomb went off too soon, and a woman security guard—a black woman—went in there to go to the john, and it killed her. Jesus, I said to myself, isn't that the way it always goes? A bunch of white kids playing at revolution, no doubt, and whose blood is shed? The black woman's. Some poor woman, three kids, the radio said she had, and no father in the picture; she was working to support them. Yes, I could identify with her. Poor sister. One is hard enough to care for.

So I was thinking these thoughts while I made Rachel eat her cereal and drink her milk, which she didn't want to do because she wanted chocolate milk, which I wouldn't give to her. I don't want her to

"Maya has sense," I defended her. "It just doesn't add up to the same kind of sense you and I recognize."

"Oh God. Oh God, Johanna, what's going to happen?"

"I don't know. Debby, she's still my friend, whatever she's done. If she needs help, I want to try and help her."

It sounded like Debby was crying on the other end of the phone. I waited for a moment.

"Don't cry," I said. "Maybe I'm wrong. Maybe it isn't them. Maybe Maya was somewhere else. Oh, Jesus, Debby, now I'm sorry I called you. I should never have gotten you so upset."

Finally she quieted. "No, no, I'm glad you called. It's better to be prepared, whatever happens. Poor Mom. This is going to kill her."

"Don't tell her. Don't tell her until we're sure. Promise? You'll only worry her sick, maybe for nothing."

"What can I do? I've got to tell somebody. I've got to watch the news!"

"You could call your father," I suggested.

"My father? What good would that do?"

"He's been through similar situations, I bet. He might have some ideas of what to do."

"There's nothing we can do," Debby said. "We don't even know where she is. We might never know."

"Tell Sarah, then," I said. "She's still your best friend, isn't she? Tony Klein's kid sister?"

"Yeah.

"Go over to her house, watch the news over there. Leave your mother a note, make up some excuse. You have to study together for a surprise quiz. She needs tutoring in algebra. Stay the night, if you can— unless, unless . . ."

"Right. Don't say it."

"I won't. Oh, and see if you can get Tony's number. He's up here somewhere but I haven't run into him, yet. Maybe he's in the phone book, I'll look. But call me from their house, if you want to talk. Not yours. It's just possible that they might tap your phone."

"Okay."

"I'll call you later there. I still know the number, it's permanently engraved in my memory cells."

"Sarah has her own private phone. Call me on her number—then you can call as late as you want."

I grabbed a pencil and wrote down the number she dictated. "Got it. I'll call you. And, Debby . . . I'm sorry. I'm really sorry."

"It's not your fault," she said, and hung up.

But I couldn't help feeling that it was my fault. If I had stuck with Maya, if I had reached out to her, if I hadn't fucked her boyfriend behind her back and gotten myself knocked up and then kept it a secret from her, if I had let her stand by me, this wouldn't have happened. I know it wouldn't have happened.

But then it was time to pick up Rachel, and to listen to her scream and yell and throw herself down on the ground when I tried to put her raincoat on. I don't know what it is with her. She actually likes the school, I believe, and the teachers say she plays with the other kids and enjoys herself all day, but as soon as I arrive she loses it. I guess she has to punish me for leaving her, for taking her away from Grandma. And I can never explain to her that I had to go, I had to leave to save my life. Not because Marian was mean or critical or anything but my staunch support, but because if I didn't start to walk alone, I was going to wind up crippled. We were too close, Marian and I. I began to forget who I am.

Which is a warrior. A warrior of the heart.

Which is not the same thing at all, Maya, you asshole, as tossing bombs around.

I walked home with Rachel in the rain. That's one thing I love about Berkeley, everything is so compact. We can walk from the apartment to Rachel's school in fifteen minutes, and campus is only a few blocks away. Of course she had to jump in every puddle on the way. On any other day, that walk would have been pure pleasure, watching her jump and play, enjoying her delight in her new yellow boots, in the way the water splashes up when her feet land, in the sound and the clear light and the wetness of it. But today I was crazy to get home and turn on the news. Still, I didn't feel I could hurry her. Poor kid, we get little enough time together. So I let her play and search for snails in the ivy of the big house on the corner, and generally dawdle around. When we got back she was hungry, of course. I just boiled her up a hot dog for dinner. I don't like to do it—it can't be all that nutritious—but it's quick, and I steamed some frozen vegetables. I didn't make a salad. It's useless with her, anyway, she won't eat salad.

I turned on the TV while we were eating, which I also don't generally do. Rachel of course wanted to watch cartoons, but I told her I had to watch a grown-up thing and anyway, there weren't any cartoons on. Which was a lie, and she knew it, because as soon as my back was turned for a minute she switched channels and there was Bullwinkle the moose. She yelled when I turned it back and I yelled back and then I had to make her go to her room for a few minutes. While she was there, the story came on again. I didn't even notice her creep back out, but I think she sensed that I was upset because she was quiet, climbing onto my lap and sucking her thumb while I watched.

There were about fifteen police cars all lined up outside an old falling-down place in the Mission district, over in the city. The commentator was saying that the police had received a hot tip from an informer earlier that day that led them to the flat, where they expected to arrest the members of the Home Front Collective. When they arrived, they claimed, they were met by gunfire. Who knows if that's true? The cops like to come in blazing and then explain, after the fact, that they were fired on first. At any rate, one officer had been wounded and now was in critical condition in San Francisco General's Trauma Unit. They cordoned off the area and were now attempting to clear out the house by firing canisters of tear gas in through the windows.

I wanted to go down there. I sat there holding Rachel and watching the scene on TV, all reduced to black and white, the night and the cop cars and the issues, staring at that run-down old house, no different from a thousand others in San Francisco. A false-front Victorian, two stories high above a garage, a big bay window next to the front door on the first floor, two bay windows above. It needed painting and there was a big hole in one window where the cops had lobbed the tear gas. But nobody had come out.

Everyone was waiting. I tried to imagine what it was like inside. Were they panicked? Were they resigned to their fate? Were they hoping to cop a plea bargain in the end, or were they hoping to die?

If I could be there, talk to her . . . But I had nobody to leave Rachel with, and I couldn't bring her down into that danger. And anyway, what could I say? Live, Maya, live in a cage for the rest of your life, if need be, but don't die so that I don't have to live with you forever on my conscience, forever guilty that I pulled away from you, that I wasn't honest with you. That dark window, the shattered glass, had the cold, ominous look of deep water, like the Bay in a storm when you're driving over the bridge and you look down and wonder what it would be like to fall. I wanted to toss my own message through. To say, Rio, I have your child, and you will die without ever having seen her. My fault. My fault.

Then suddenly there was a loud noise, a burst of gunfire from inside the house, and everyone on the street took cover. The cops returned fire, shattering the rest of the windows with their machine guns. No one came out.

Were they dead in there? Was she lying on the floor, blood dripping out of her mouth? Oh, God, I should be there. I should be with her.

The phone rang. Rachel ran and grabbed it before I could haul myself up from the couch. I've never lost all the weight I put on with the pregnancy. She said hello, but I snatched it out of her hand and she began to cry, so I could hardly hear the voice on the other end.

"Quiet!" I told her. "You know I don't like you to answer the phone. Now hush, so Mommy can talk, or go to your room." I put on my most stern face, and she subsided into quiet sobs.

"Johanna? Is that you?"

"It's me. Debby?"

"I called to give you Tony's number. Do you have a pencil?"

"Just a minute." I grabbed a pencil and wrote the number on the back of the gas bill that I hadn't paid yet. "Thanks. I'll call him later."

"Are you watching the news?"

"I am. Are you okay?"

"Yeah. No. I'm at Sarah Klein's. Johanna, I'm scared. They're going to kill her. They're going to kill my sister."

"Don't think like that, Debby. She may not even be in there."

I could still see the TV, because the phone was in the ell of the living-dining room. At that moment, a picture of Rio flashed on the screen.

They must have taken it at some demonstration, it had the grainy look of a photo snapped by an undercover cop. His head was thrown back and his hair was long and flying, his lips parted, and there was a look on his face of triumph, a warrior's look, battle joy. Yes, crazy as he was, he was a warrior too. No wonder we had come together to produce a child between us who would be—what? Someone strong willed and brave.

"Update," said the commentator. "NBC news has just received an exclusive report identifying three of the suspected members of the Home Front Collective. On screen is Richard 'Rio' Connolly, twenty-four years old, a former Berkeley student."

Rio, I wished I could tell him, you have done one good thing.

Then the picture was gone, and they were showing people I didn't recognize and naming names I had never heard.

"Did you see that?" Debby asked. I was still holding the phone frozen to my ear. "It *is* them, Johanna. It is!"

"They didn't show Maya's picture," I said. "Maybe she didn't go back to them. Maybe she's not there. I'm sure she's not there."

I lied. I wasn't sure at all.

The TV cameras focused on the house again. We heard another rattling burst of gunfire. And then, as if the bullets had ignited something deep inside the dark void of the house, we could hear a rumble. It was low, at first, like disaster clearing its throat before it strikes, and then a sudden loud clap and roar and the whole house exploded into flames.

"Stand back," the police were shouting to the crowd, and, "Come out with your hands up!" they yelled over their bullhorns at the house. But nobody came out.

Nobody came out.

"Debby," I said. "Debby, are you all right?" It seemed for a moment as if we had both been there, able to feel the shock wave, nostrils burning from the smoke. But I was across the Bay and she was five hundred miles away in LA, sobbing her heart out on the telephone.

"No. I've got to get off, Johanna, I can't stand it. I can't stand it!" She hung up the phone.

Then I was alone, watching the inferno, tears streaming down my cheeks. But not alone, because Rachel came up and gave me a hug. I squatted down to hold her, and she patted me on the back, offering comfort. That made me cry more. She was so tiny and so sweet, and she didn't even know that I was watching her father burn alive.

The commentators were commentating and pontificating and speculating on whether or not anyone could possibly be left alive. I wanted to watch the fire, in silence, to mourn them in dignity, but Rachel was starting to ask questions about the fire and I didn't want to frighten her. Oh, God, sometimes it's hard being a mother, you're not your own woman for a moment, even a moment of grief. But it's good, too. I shut the TV off and ran her bath and calmed myself with the simple, everyday duties of washing her and helping her dry off and dressing her in her bunny pajamas and reading her a story. Tonight the ordinary acts of nurture seemed heroic, acts of a heart warrior defying death.

And then she was in bed. I put on her nightlight and tiptoed out to let her sleep.

And so I write, and wait. For a phone call. For the eleven o'clock news. For the flames to die down, and the corpses to be identified.

Oh, God, if Maya by some miracle gets out of this alive, I will never lie to her again. I will keep no more secrets.

I wait. I wait.

Johanna

34

November 1971

Maya stood by the side of the road. The light snowfall that had begun while she was packing up had turned to a freezing rain that poured down over her face and plastered her hair to her neck. She was trying to hold within her the purity of the cold mountain springs, trying to hold to it on the dark edge of the highway. Cars sped by leaving trails of light. She reached out her hand, her thumb up, her fingers curled as if to grasp the light that streamed through and slipped away from her. Cold in the mountains was not the same as cold on the highway. She began to wonder if she was really strong enough to bring the heart of the mountain back into the world.

A car stopped. For a moment she stared, then she ran to open the door to the backseat and jumped in.

A young man with long sandy hair was driving, and his girlfriend sat next to him in the front. Maya was assaulted by smell and sound. The radio was playing loud rock music, and the young woman was sucking on a joint. The smoke made Maya's head spin as they sped off into the rain.

"Thanks," Maya said, after a moment, remembering that she should say something.

"It's cool," the man said. "Where you going?"

She thought for a moment, realizing that she didn't know the answer.

"The city," she said, finally.

"Cool," the man said again. "We're going to Berkeley."

"Close enough. Thanks," Maya said. She was unused to talking. Her words felt clotted.

The woman turned and offered her the joint. "Want to smoke some weed?"

Maya shook her head. "Thanks anyway."

The woman shrugged and turned the radio up louder, too loud for conversation.

The car sped down the mountains in the rain and the dark. Maya, huddled in her wet clothes, felt cold turn to chill. She shivered. Already

she missed the clear air and the wide sky. Here she was enclosed in a
stinking metal box, cramped together with two strangers and feeling
alone become *lonely*. The voice was telling her to hold, not the air and
the sky themselves but what they brought to her and said to her. But the
chill was creeping down. In her pack she had a dry sweater and a ragged
skirt. She wriggled out of her wet things and put on her dry clothes. The
chill receded. She would learn, once again, to allow herself to be sheltered.

After a time, the music and the raucous-voiced advertisements
faded to a murmur she could ignore. Motion soothed her. She grieved for
her lost mountain, but some part of her was glad to be moving again,
following her inner lodestone back into the world. She slept.

A voice on the radio woke her. Something caught her ear—some
familiar phrase, or name, reaching out of some faraway past place of
memory. She pulled herself back to consciousness to listen.

". . . and more on that firefight in the Mission district of San
Francisco. Police sources have identified the building at 352 Capp Street
as the headquarters of the notorious terrorist group the Home Front. At
least three people died tonight when bullets apparently ignited a store of
plastic explosives. Identification of the bodies has not been established.
The Home Front has claimed responsibility for a rash of political bombings over the last year, most notably, yesterday's explosion in the Bank of
America building that killed a security guard and injured . . ."

She couldn't hear anymore. She was seeing a charred body in the
wreck of the old house where they had loved and fought so many times.
When the voice said "bodies" it meant that they must be dead, Daniel
with his carefully concealed heart, Edith with her guilt. And Rio. One of
the bodies must be his, his sweet skin covered with downy blond hair,
now black, charred, smoking. She was going to be sick.

He was dead. Dead. The word was like a cold fog inside her and
she tried to feel for him but there was nothing but a clammy blankness.

I shouldn't have left him, she thought. I knew if I left him, he'd die.
Then she pushed the thought away.

I loved him, she thought instead. She cried silently, hoping the
strangers in the front seat would not turn around and offer her sympathy
or ask questions. She remembered days on the coast, following Rio upstream, both of them naked as they clambered from rock to rock. She
remembered the soft grass of the meadow as they made love, under their
bodies the sweet clover smell of alyssum, around their heads the drone of
bees. For that brief time, the honey-gold touch of the heart had rested on
them like one of those same furred bees, but they couldn't hold it. As she
had never been able to hold it, as she was losing, now, with every rolling
turn of the wheels, the clarity of her lake, her pool.

But that was her challenge, to hold the mountain, to hold what was far too big for her. Or to lose it and find it, again and again, until the losing and the finding itself became the on-off pulse of a beating heart.

And what was she going to do now? Because in the back of her mind all along had been the idea that she would go back to him. Back to the house on Capp Street, back to the complications and temptations that would test the clarity of the mountain, brew its pure waters into a bittersweet intoxicant. Oh, God, what had she done? What had she done?

They dropped her on Telegraph Avenue. The rain was still falling heavily and the street was gloomy, the display windows dark and the doors all closed. She had no money and no place to go, and what she wanted more than anything was to hitch a ride across the Bay and wail over the smoldering ashes. Oh, God, if only she had a radio, a TV, something to give her the news. The wet night was so different from the cleansing rain of the mountains. She had to be careful; she knew that. She must stay calm, maintain just as if she were stoned on acid, keep herself hovering above the abyss of loss in a small, clear space where she could think out what to do. Survival, she must dedicate herself to survival.

Who could she go to? One of her friends from her old women's group? Leona? Donna? They would take her in, shelter her, hide her if necessary, but they wouldn't understand her grief. They'd never known Rio in the good times, when he was still her magician, her pirate, her golden sun king.

Halfway down the block, she came to a phone booth. Maya stopped.

There was only one person she wanted, one who might share her grief as they had shared the source of it that night in the storm. Johanna. She had said that she was transferring up to Berkeley in the fall. By now, school had started. She must be here.

Maya dug into the side pockets of her pack where, months ago, she had stashed the few coins she'd had in her pocket when she left Rio. She put a dime into the phone and dialed information, asking for a number for a Johanna Weaver.

"I have a Johanna M. Weaver on Carleton," the operator said.

"And the address?"

"Twenty-two thirty-three, apartment four."

Carleton was just around the corner, only a few blocks away. Maya was flooded with contradictory emotions, relief, fear, sorrow, hope. Maybe Johanna hated her, wouldn't want her around. But no, they had talked on the phone, they had said they were still friends. She would take Maya in. She would.

Suddenly she was aware of how tired she was, and cold, and hungry. She was a wild animal trapped in a hostile place; she needed a refuge, a safe place where she could curl up and cry. Please, God, she murmured, or not God but the true Gods I have named for myself, please wind and rain and sun and rock, let Johanna comfort me, take me in.

She was starting to shiver from the cold. The elements were too strong for her here. She couldn't meet their power on these asphalt streets, couldn't rise to them with her heart heavy with grief. She wanted to be inside, out of the wind. She began to walk.

On a street of gracious old wooden houses, Johanna's apartment building was a stucco box with all the charm of a Motel 6. It had been built in the early sixties, a rectangular structure with four doors on the lower level and four above, linked by a narrow balcony with a metal rail. Johanna's door was the third on the bottom level. Maya stood in front of it for a long while. Someone was home. She could see the blue light of a TV screen playing on the curtains. If she never knocked, she could never be turned away, driven back into the cold. She could always believe that Johanna *would* have welcomed her, sheltered her.

She took a deep breath, stepped forward, and rang the bell.

Someone moved inside. Feet moved across the floor, the door opened a crack, still held by a chain. Maya heard someone gasp, and then the door closed again.

But Johanna was only sliding the chain off. The next moment, the door was flung open, two brown hands reached for Maya and pulled her inside, and warm arms were flung around her.

"Maya!" she said, crying. "Maya, Maya, Maya!"

Maya had hoped for a welcome, but she was unprepared for the fierceness with which Johanna hugged her. Tears were streaming down Johanna's cheeks, her hands stroking Maya's wet hair. Her touch brought back the pool, the mountain. Her touch restored Maya to life.

Johanna buried her head against Maya's shoulder, sobbing.

"Johanna, it's okay, it's okay," Maya crooned to her. Her arms clasped Johanna's warm body, offering comfort. "It's all right."

After a long moment, they pulled apart and stepped back to look at each other.

"I thought you were dead," Johanna said.

"Me? Not me. I'm not the one who's dead. Why did you think that?"

"Weren't you with Rio?"

"Not for . . . months," Maya said. The words were hard to find. She was accustomed to time measured in sunrise and moonrise and the seasons of cold and rain, not as something to be measured and counted and accounted for.

"Where the hell have you been, then?" Johanna asked, scrutinizing Maya's sun-browned cheeks and wind-roughened hair.

"I've been on the mountain. Alone."

On the television, firemen were dousing flames, while charred bodies, wrapped in sheets, were carried out on stretchers.

"So you weren't with them? You weren't in the house?"

Maya shook her head, unable to tear her eyes away from the television set. She had longed for news but now the images hurt her eyes, burned themselves indelibly into her memory. Was this the last she would ever see of Rio, a shapeless form under a white sheet on the late news? Was Daniel in one of those body bags, his blue eyes charred to lumps of coal?

"You weren't there," Johanna said, more to herself than to Maya, as if she needed to reassure herself that it was true. "You really weren't there."

The voices on the television were predicting bad weather. They were done with the Home Front, done with Rio and Daniel and Edith. They were old news now. Johanna walked over and switched the set off.

"What mountain?" she asked.

It was so hard to talk, hard to formulate answers to questions that seemed to come from another world. The mountain with the blue lake, Maya wanted to say. The mountain with the pine smell, granite wind, hint-of-coming-rain air, the mountain of thunderstorms, the sun-on-wildflowers mountain—or to say none of these, because all of them were abstractions, descriptions, that had nothing to do with the real except to trick people into thinking they understood when they didn't.

"Are you okay?" Johanna asked.

Maya shook her head. She stood with her arms wrapped around herself, shivering. Everything that had ever warmed her had just burned to the ground.

"You heard?" Johanna said softly. "You heard what happened?"

Maya nodded. Now her shivering turned to shaking. She was a walking earthquake; she was going to come to pieces right there in Johanna's living room.

Johanna came over and put her arms around Maya. She held her in a tight grip, as if she were literally holding her together.

"Go ahead and cry," Johanna said. "It's okay. I'm here."

But it wasn't okay and Maya couldn't cry. She could hardly breathe, as if each indrawing of air to her lungs was another betrayal of the dead. She should have been with them. How could they be dead and she still be alive?

"You're wet," Johanna said, her voice suddenly practical. "I'm going to run you a nice, hot bath, and then heat you up some soup. Okay?"

"I should go down there," Maya said in a low voice. "I should be with them."

"Maya, honey, there's no place to go. It's all over. It was over hours ago. The late news is just a repeat, you know that."

"I should be with them," Maya said again. "I should be dead, too."

"Don't you say that!"

Johanna's sharp voice jolted her. Maya gasped, taking a long, deep breath, and began to cry.

"Oh Maya, child, I don't want to hear you talk like that. You just get out of those wet things, before you catch your death of cold."

"I loved him," Maya said. "I hate his guts, but I loved him so much! Oh God, oh hell!" She was no longer even sure whom she was talking about, Rio or Daniel or all of them together, or simply herself.

Johanna let her cry for a long time, and then led her into the bathroom, drew the bath, laced the water with pine-scented salts, and undressed Maya like a child while the tub filled. She made Maya lie down in the hot, fragrant water and soak up its warmth, while she sat on the edge of the tub, holding Maya's hand.

The warmth of the water was a comfort Maya could not feel she deserved. The pine scent brought back her mountain. Oh, she should never have left them alone, any of them, all of them—but having done so she should have stayed on the mountain, learned to melt snow with her body heat, never have come down.

"Come on now," Johanna said at last. "We'll dry you off, feed you up a bit. You're too skinny, girl."

She helped Maya out of the tub, rubbed her down with a towel. She's bringing me back to life, Maya thought. She's calling me back from the wild and anchoring me into the human world. And I don't want to come. But I have no choice.

"So you weren't with them," Johanna said, rubbing the towel on Maya's legs as if reassuring herself of Maya's solidity. "You weren't involved in the bombing?"

"I split in the summer," Maya said. That was the word, the name for the green meadow, warming, wildflower time. If it was important to Johanna that she be able to talk in time-words, she would have to try. "Rio and I were going up to the mountains. We had a fight, and I went alone."

"Thank God for that," Johanna said. "Now lift your feet, one at a time. That's right. I'm pretty good at this, don't you think? I've been practicing."

"Practicing?" Maya asked as Johanna rubbed her feet.

"Remember I'm a mom, now."

"Oh, right." Maya had, in fact, forgotten. She couldn't think of Johanna as somebody's mother. She has a whole life separate from me, Maya thought. Years and years, and separate ties of blood. She doesn't belong to me anymore. And everyone who does is dead.

"Come on, put this bathrobe on," Johanna coaxed. "Want to see the baby?"

"The baby? Oh, of course, the baby."

Johanna put her arm around Maya's shoulder and put her finger to her own lips. "Shh," she said, as she steered her to the door of the bedroom and opened it quietly. Maya looked in to see a small figure curled up on a low bed. The child looked like she was two or three years old. Her left arm was flung over a stuffed bear Maya remembered from Johanna's childhood, and something in the look of her face, the structure of the bones or the curve of her brow, reminded Maya of the last night she slept with Rio. She'd looked down at him, his eyelids fluttering like the child's did now with the scenes of some secret dream, and wondered how he could give himself up to the wholehearted innocence of sleep. The child had milk-chocolate skin and a cloud of dark hair.

Johanna closed the door.

"She's beautiful," Maya said.

"She's Rio's daughter."

Maya began shaking again as soon as the warmth of the tub subsided. She didn't want soup; she wanted to fast, to rend her garments and tear her hair. To eat something now, she felt, would be a mockery of the dead. But under Johanna's weary gaze, she forced herself to eat.

Johanna opened up the studio couch in the living room and made the bed. She tucked Maya in and climbed in next to her, sitting up against the back. "There's no other place to sleep," she explained, a slight note of apology in her voice. "I gave the bedroom to the baby."

"The baby," Maya said. Using words still felt like putting on clothes after running naked in the wind. "Rio's baby."

"I'm sorry," Johanna whispered. "I should have told you all about it long ago. Tonight, when I thought you were dead, I swore that if you turned up alive I would never lie to you again."

"Why? Why did you have to lie?"

Johanna turned her head away from Maya, looking in the direction of Rachel's door. "I felt guilty. And ashamed, I guess. He was your boyfriend."

"What did that matter?"

"I was afraid it would. Mostly, I was afraid. I didn't really know Rio very well, and he struck me as the kind of guy who could get out of control. It seemed safer, less messy, having her just be mine." Johanna sat silent for a long moment, and then went on. "I was mad, too . . . at him. I'd given him comfort, and then afterwards, he acted like it had never happened. The only times he ever contacted me were to ask if I'd heard from you."

"And me? Why didn't you tell me?"

"I couldn't tell you without telling him, could I?"

"I guess not."

"I'm sorry now," Johanna whispered. "So sorry. It doesn't seem fair that he should have died without ever knowing her."

Maya was feeling numb again. The reality of Rio's death had ebbed away. In a moment it would wash over her again, choking and drowning her, but for the moment she lay high and dry. She was thinking about time and the worlds it created and how they changed and shifted without warning. Just this morning she'd awakened in a mountain world, in which the cold wind whipping down the high passes and the first flurries of snow told her, in an unmistakable voice, that the time had come to leave. In that world, her world, Rio still existed and his child did not. Now that had changed. She couldn't get used to it.

"When did it happen?" Maya asked.

Johanna waited for a long moment, before she answered. "In the storm that night, or the next day. When we went down to LA."

"Oh. You mean . . ."

"He was so torn up when he found out about his dad. I'm sorry."

Maya was silent, trying to digest this piece of information. Johanna seemed to expect it to mean something to her, to matter that she'd made love with Rio twice instead of once. Maya felt like a fairy creature dragged in from the wild, unused to human ways or company. What should it mean? Should she be angry or jealous? Maybe she would have been before, certainly the Maya who had lived with Rio was jealous enough. But now? Now what could it conceivably matter that the lump under the white sheet had taken pleasure with Johanna? Except that he left a seed, some spark of himself, with her. If Maya was jealous, she was jealous of that—that he lived on through Johanna, not her. That Johanna had incarnated the best of him, how he was on the coast, young and clean and free.

"Do you mind?" Johanna asked.

Maya shook her head. "Not now."

"I should have told you long ago. I shouldn't have tried to keep it a secret. It divided us."

Words were layers, but layers were what Maya needed, some padding between her and the raw and terrible grief. She asked another question. "When did you know?"

"Not for a while. I started UCLA. Right about midterm time, the signs became unmistakable."

"That must have been hard."

"It wasn't easy. Oh, at first I thought about getting an abortion. *That* wasn't too easy then, but it would have been possible. But, it was strange, Maya. It was like I kept hearing this voice inside me. She was talking to me, saying, 'I'm here for a reason, Mama. I have a purpose to fulfill.' And I just couldn't do it. I tried to tell her, 'Look, I'm here for a reason, too. And your purpose is going to make my purpose pretty damn hard to carry out. Can't you wait awhile?' But she was adamant. Still is a child with a strong will.

"So I thought, well, hell, at least let me get through the first year of college, and then when the baby comes, I'll just see if I can handle it. Maybe it'll take me longer, but I'll do it."

"What did your mother say?"

"You can imagine. She had some words to say to me. But when she calmed down, and when I told her I didn't intend to drop out of school if I could help it, she decided to help me out. And Rachel helped out. She delayed her entrance three weeks past her due date, so she was born the week after final exams. On your birthday, in fact—the thirteenth of June, 1969. That gave me the summer off to take care of her and kind of get used to her. Then when school started in the fall, I just took her to class. People were bringing their dogs to class in those days. I figured, why couldn't I bring my baby? Nobody was going to be allergic to her."

"And now you're up here?"

"I'm finishing up here, and then, hopefully, going on to graduate school. In psychology, if I get in."

Johanna spoke simply and plainly, but Maya heard the nuances ring in the way she had learned to hear in the silence of the mountain. She heard Johanna's pride and she heard also, not exactly a criticism of herself, but an awareness of contrast. What did she have to show for her own life that could compare to the solid reality of a college degree and a child? The charred corpse of a love, and the clear waters of solitude.

"You've done well," Maya said.

"I did what was in front of me."

"I tried," Maya said slowly, as if she was making a confession. "I tried to hold what we had. And then everything got fucked up. So I went to the mountain, and there it was. But now . . ."

She stopped. Suddenly she was shivering again, on the edge of tears. The world had come apart and put itself back together inside out. How could Rio be dead? How could he not be raging, storming, glowering, laughing, ready to make love? How could he have come alive in this unforeseen way, through Johanna, not through her?

Johanna reached out her hand and stroked Maya's hair.

"He may not be dead, you know," she said. "They didn't say who the bodies were. It's bad luck to mourn him yet."

Rio. He was like a physical presence there in the room with them. Maya wondered if she sensed his ghost or only the consolidation of memory. Her eyes were wet and her face was wet. She touched her own cheek. Tears. That was the word for it. There were names for what she felt. She could call it pain or grief or sorrow. But words were flat things, nothing like this well of emptiness and loss that echoed inside her and made her very bones ache.

"I couldn't stay with him," Maya said in a whisper. "I couldn't change him. I tried."

"I'm sure you did."

"If I hadn't left, he would still be alive."

Johanna shook her head. "More likely you'd be dead."

I should be, Maya thought. The dead were pulling her, calling to her. They were her true family, her destiny.

As if she heard the unspoken words, Johanna slid down and put her arms around Maya. Johanna's body was warm, alive. Her body sang of life, a counterpoint to the call of the dead. Maya remembered the last time they'd touched—that very night on the coast, when Johanna was the one who'd needed warmth. She and Rio had placed her between them. He should be here now, on her other side. But when she reached out for him, she touched a cold, clammy miasma. Daniel's ghost, looking up at her with blue glass eyes, saying, "Maya, we aren't going to live that long. We aren't going to live."

I have betrayed you, Daniel, Maya thought. I have not kept our pact.

"So you were in the mountains all summer?" Johanna asked. "Who were you with?"

"I was alone," Maya said. Johanna waited, wanting facts, information, words, words, words. Maya sighed. "I got a ride, after I left Rio. They dropped me off by a trailhead and I started walking. I walked all day and camped and found a place I wanted to be. A lake, high up on the Pacific Crest Trail. I just stayed there. People gave me food. Backpackers, who brought too much in and didn't want to carry it out. I felt like if I stayed there long enough, I could understand something—something like we were trying to get to together once. Remember?"

"I remember," Johanna said. "But it seems long ago and far away."

"We've lost it," Maya whispered. "It's all dead and gone and buried now. We'll never find it again." She began to cry, great racking sobs that shook her body and choked off her breath. Johanna's arms cradled her inside a warm circle. Johanna's voice crooned; her hands stroked Maya's hair. But the dead were caressing her, too. Cold fingers traced patterns on her spine; cold breath stole into her mouth, slid between her choking sobs, insinuated itself into her breast. Safer, cleaner to let them in, she thought. Let it be like the last act of a tragedy—all the players wiped off the stage. Only the magic circle of Johanna's arms held back the dead. Without her warmth, they would snatch Maya away.

"What we found can never be lost," Johanna murmured. "It's always there, waiting for us."

I need to choose, Maya thought. Either to join them, the ghosts, or to come to life again.

"Do you believe that?" she asked. "Do you really believe it?"

"More than anything else in the world," Johanna said, her voice low, vibrant, as if she was making a pledge.

"I've lived on it, for years I've lived on that one moment," Maya said. "But now I can hardly remember it."

"Lie still," Johanna said, stroking Maya's cheek. "Lie still, and we'll remember together."

Maya buried her face in Johanna's breast, trying to crawl closer, to merge with her warmth. Suddenly she was filled with a desperate desire to live. If they could touch, once again, even for a moment, the cold ghosts would be driven away. If she could enter into one more blossoming, she would have the strength to face the coming charred morning.

"Please," she whispered to Johanna. "Please."

Johanna kissed her, tentatively, almost maternally, on the top of her head.

"Yes," Maya murmured. "Yes."

Johanna raised Maya's face to hers, and kissed her lips.

Bring me to life, Maya wanted to beg. She had turned to stone, and Johanna was a Goddess whose hands conveyed living fire. Everywhere her fingers touched, breasts, thighs, belly, stone warmed to soil, forests grew, birds began to fly.

"Touch me everywhere," Maya whispered, and Johanna complied. Her hands shaped mountains, smoothed canyons, and entered into the deepest caverns, bringing dormant springs to life, making the healing waters flow.

Later, they lay still, their bodies pressed together, their arms around each other.

"I would like to shelter you," Johanna whispered. "I'm sorry I ever called you spoiled, all those years ago. I wish more than anything that I could keep you safe, and spoil you."

"I wish you could," Maya said. "I would like to stay here with you, forever, just as we are now."

"But we can't," Johanna said. "Oh Maya, honey, I'm afraid for you. They're not going to let this lie. As soon as the ashes cool, they'll be rounding up everyone who ever was connected with them."

"Sshh," Maya said. "I don't want to think about that now. I don't want to be afraid."

"But Maya . . ." Johanna began.

Maya put her finger on Johanna's lips, silencing her. "Every time we get to this place, something happens to make us afraid. But I won't be. Not now. In the morning, then I'll figure out what to do. But now let's just stay here, be here, sleep here. Then we'll be strong. Then we'll have something to live on for years and years and years."

"You are a crazy child," Johanna said. "But I'll help you all I can."

The morning brought a resurrection. "Rio Connolly Arrested!" the headlines screamed. "Terrorist Cell Destroyed!"

Maya sat looking at the paper, her hands shaking. They had found him passed out in the front seat of his van, drunk. He was alive, although his face on the front page looked as if he wished he were dead. Two cops were leading him away in handcuffs, a newsprint icon of retribution.

She felt numb. Under the frozen crust that held her together, a mantle of pain churned and boiled underground. Somewhere deep, deep below, she sensed a core, like the red heart of a blossom. The night before, she had touched it; someday she would delve deep and live once again by its rhythms. But for now, she must tread carefully on the surface, as if walking on a thin crust of newly spilled lava. One crack, one breakthrough, and she would be burned alive.

She shuddered. Better not to think about burning, or entertain images of fire.

Maya was sitting at the kitchen table in the linoleum-paved alcove off the living room that faced the narrow kitchen. Johanna stood by the stove, frying bacon and eggs. Coffee was brewing on the back burner. The ordinary, everyday smells seemed to call back something of the self Maya had been for twenty-one years before the summer in the mountains. A self for whom words were familiar tools, and Johanna's presence was utterly natural, ordinary. A self that could sit and talk as if she were still fifteen years old on a Friday morning, as if there had never been that last fight on the coast, and the long silence after, as if her life did not lie smoldering in ruins.

"He'll hate being in jail," Maya said.

"Better than being dead."

"Not for him. It'll just be a long, slow death." As it would be for me, Maya thought. Might be. She felt a little clutch in her chest.

"I feel bad for him," Johanna said. "But it's you I'm worried about right now. What are you going to do?"

"I don't know." She couldn't tear her eyes away from his picture. His head was down, his face barely visible, his hands cuffed behind his back. Would he ever be free again?

"Well, it's morning now, girl. Time we began to figure it out, before they come after you."

They, who were they? Couldn't she say to them, I am not the same person I was when I was with him? I have changed, and all of that history seems to belong to somebody else. Except for the pain. Then the mud-slide of loss hit again. If only Rio were still free, she wouldn't care what he did, who he fucked, how much he drank. Oh Gods of lake and moun-tain, why couldn't he have another chance?

Johanna turned a strip of bacon over. "How involved were you?" she asked. "How much do you know?"

"I was never in the middle of the action," Maya said slowly. "I never knew what was really going on, never made cadre, as they used to say."

"You knew a lot of people? People you could identify?"

"Sure." Unfold your arms, Maya wanted to say. Hold me, touch me again, keep me safe from the realm of abstractions like the law and the cops. But the cops would be real enough if they came after her. Jail would be real, too. She would die there, locked away from the sun and the wind.

Johanna sighed. "You're in trouble."

Maya felt Johanna's love surround her and she felt her fear, like a whiff of smog on the wind. She knew, suddenly, that to survive, she could not afford to be afraid. Fear would suck her down, consume her. She must shut it away, stay on the dry, encrusted surface, not think too much, not picture herself locked away, not let herself see the image of Rio's caged, defeated eyes.

"I know," she said.

"Maybe I can help," Johanna said. "I'd hate to see you locked up to pay for Rio's sins."

She set the bacon on a pile of paper towels to drain, and broke eggs into a blue bowl. Maya sat with her head in her hands. Rio was alive, but she couldn't go to him, soothe him, hold him. He would never again run free and naked in a storm on the coast. Outside the window, which looked out on the wall of the building next door, rain pounded down. The other bodies had been identified. One was a local derelict whom Maya vaguely remembered used to take shelter on their back porch from time to time. Poor man, he'd picked the wrong night this time. One was Daniel. They would never succumb together to the seductions of ordi-nary life. He would never argue with her again, never make slow, careful love, never again reveal the sweet heart he kept wrapped in words, words, words. We were the opposites who should have mated, Maya thought. He'll never finish his dissertation, now, never sit flicking ashes on the floor, dirtying the coffee cups, holding forth on his theories. But no, she couldn't really believe it. Something had gone wrong with the world, but surely the script would be rewritten.

The third body was Edith's. Had she finally done enough, given enough? She had succeeded where Maya had failed, and become the woman on fire.

The bedroom door opened, and a small brown girl came running out.

"Sleepyhead." Johanna smiled and picked Rachel up, giving her a big hug. "Come and meet my friend Maya. Maya, this is Rachel."

Rachel observed Maya critically for a long moment, and then wriggled out of her mother's arms and climbed up into Maya's lap. Her body was soft and warm and alive, and Maya held her tightly, as if she were grasping a lifeline. Rachel squirmed and slid down, disappearing into her room, only to emerge a moment later clutching a doll. She tugged at Maya's sleeve, her eyes wide and proud, reminding Maya, yes, of Rio in their early days together, when he'd bring her some new gift or exotic offering. Maybe she was reading that in—really, Rachel looked like Johanna most of all, with her rounded cheeks and the generous sculpture of her mouth.

"Dolly!" Rachel said, adding something indistinguishable.

"What's she saying?" Maya asked.

"Harriet Tubman," Johanna said. "The doll's name is Harriet Tubman."

Maya found herself holding a black Barbie doll. "She's, uh, beautiful."

"Be gentle," Rachel said, holding the doll up for Maya to kiss, and then snatching it away and trotting back to the bedroom with it.

"You can't isolate them from the culture," Johanna said, beating the eggs with a fork. "You've got to reinterpret it for them."

"What do you think I should do?" Maya asked. "Run away? Turn myself in? If they're really after me, I can't stay here. I wouldn't want to get you in trouble."

Before Johanna could answer, something soft was thrust into Maya's hands.

"Bear. Pooh bear," Rachel said.

"He's lovely."

"Poo-poo bear!" Rachel said, laughing and running off again.

"Eat," Johanna said, setting down a plate of bacon and eggs. "Rachel, you come get your breakfast."

Maya ate. The dead would forgive her, and for the living, she would need strength. She had forgotten how hungry she was. She had eaten little in days. Rachel appeared lugging a big stuffed duck. Her mother sent her sternly back to leave it in the bedroom.

"Does the paper say what he's charged with?" Johanna asked.

Maya looked down at the newspaper. Words, little blots of ink on newsprint that meant the end of lives. "Everything," she said sadly. "Everything from illegal possession of firearms to second-degree murder. A woman was killed in that last bombing."

"I know."

"A black woman. God. The cops are claiming that the Front was shooting back at them. Something caught fire, blew up. I wonder how he escaped?"

Rachel came back, sat quietly down at her place, and began to eat.

"Who knew you were with the Front?" Johanna asked. "Anyone who'd volunteer the information to the Feds?"

"I don't know. Everyone knew, I guess. I mean, it was no secret. People on the old Moratorium Committee, my women's group, my father. *He'd* never talk to the Feds, but who can say what everybody else would do?"

"Well then," Johanna said, "we can assume the Feds already know. Those groups are bound to be infiltrated. Most likely your group was, too."

"We were so small," Maya said. "And so careful. We knew each other so well." Except for Randy and T-Bone, she thought to herself. What happened to them? Where were they when the massacre happened? But it was no use speculating about them, now. It was herself she had to worry about. She pushed her plate aside. "I don't want to go to jail. I'd die there. I don't want to be used to drive the nails into Rio's coffin, either."

"Could you be?"

"I guess so. I know enough for that."

"Seems to me you can handle this one of two ways," Johanna said. "You can go out and hire yourself a hotshot political lawyer. Maybe your father knows somebody. Or you can disappear. Get out of town, go away for a while."

"Don't go away," Rachel said. "I like you."

Maya smiled. "I like you too."

"Are you eating that egg, or just messing with it?" Johanna asked Rachel. "Clear your place, child, and go get your shoes and socks on." Rachel pushed her chair back and ran off to the bedroom.

"I wish it was summer," Maya said. "I'd just go back to the mountains. But the snows are coming."

"I think you'd do best to go somewhere. Don't you have any contacts with the underground?"

Maya shook her head. "I don't want to hang out with those people, spend the next ten years listening to arguments about my class analysis. It was only for Rio's sake that I ever put up with it." Each time she spoke, she added a new layer of personality. But she could put them on and take them off now, she thought. She was no longer trapped in them. She would no longer mistake the covering for the core. "I don't think I need to go underground. If I'm not on the scene for a while, I'll get passed over. After Rio's been tried, and they've made sure everyone else is either dead or in jail, what I know won't matter anymore. If I hook up with the underground, I'll just end up knowing more stuff that could hurt more people for longer, and I'll never get free of it all.''

Rachel appeared, carrying her coat and a small red bag. Johanna stood up.

"I've got to take her to school. We're late. Listen, I'll be back this afternoon. You just sit tight here. I'll talk to some people for you."

Rachel offered her cheek to Maya for a kiss. "Bye," she said.

"Bye," Maya said. "I'll see you again. And when I do, I'll tell you a story."

"There's food in the refrigerator, make yourself at home," Johanna said. "You rest up, you hear? And don't you touch those dishes. I'll do them when I get home."

Johanna's apartment was spare, but ordered. A boxlike living room held a couch, one big chair, and a small TV. The furniture was covered with bright African print cloth, and swaths of the same patterns provided wall decoration. Books stood on shelves made of bricks and boards, and a wicker basket held Rachel's toys. There were no luxuries visible, but the room felt cared for. It felt like a haven.

Maya cleaned the kitchen and made the bed and washed out the things from her pack that needed cleaning. The more she kept her hands busy, the less she had to think. She turned the radio to the all-news station, but it continued to report the facts she already knew. Nevertheless she needed to hear them over and over again, to make them real to herself. Johanna's books intrigued her but she couldn't concentrate. She took a long bath, then put a record on the stereo, Bob Dylan's *Blonde on Blonde.* Lying on the sofa with her eyes closed, she listened, over and over again, to "Sad Eyed Lady of the Lowlands."

Johanna returned around three o'clock, with cartons of take-out Chinese food, three hundred dollars in cash, and a birth certificate for a Margaret Anne Bradley.

"You're set," she said. "One of your old friends came through."

"Who?"

"Good old Tony Klein. He's up here now, and he's some big honcho in radical politics. At least he seems to know some useful people. He sends his love."

"That was quick."

"Efficiency is my middle name." Johanna winked. She set the food down on the kitchen table, got spoons from the drawer, and began dishing rice and cashew chicken onto plates. "Actually, you can thank Tony's nameless friends. They're prepared for emergencies. I suppose if that's your line of work, you have to be. When you've got to disappear, you've got to do it fast—can't sit around for a week or two waiting for the paperwork to come through.''

Maya looked down at her plateful of food in dismay. It was too much, Johanna had done too much. "But, Johanna, I can't take your money. I'm sure you need it . . . with the baby and all.''

"Girlfriend, this is not my money. This is the Harding High Alumni Support-Your-Local-Terrorist Fund." Johanna pulled up a chair and began to eat.

"Come again?''

"It's out of my bank account, but I'm collecting checks to cover it. Tony offered, and he called Joyce Levine—she's at Brandeis. And Debby's got some savings. She thinks maybe your dad might pay her back." Johanna gestured at Maya's plate. "Eat up, girl. You're going to need your strength. Unfortunately, I'm afraid you'd better clear out of here ASAP. Tony says the Feds are all over Berkeley, interrogating everyone who was ever remotely near the Front.''

"So Debby knows I'm safe? That's good. I wouldn't want Betty to lose her mind." Maya took a spoonful of food. Yes, she should eat while she could.

"I called her last night, after you fell asleep. At her friend Sarah's. She stayed the night there. Apparently Betty never knew anything about it—she doesn't listen to the evening news.''

"She reads the morning paper, though. She'll hear about Rio.''

"And Debby'll be able to tell her what's going on. Your father, too. You don't need to worry about them.''

Maya found tears welling up in her eyes. "Johanna, you're a wonder. I don't know how to begin to thank you.''

"Don't.'' Johanna stood up, went over, and put a hand on Maya's shoulder. "You'd do the same for me. We're best friends, aren't we?''

"Are we still?''

"I've never found anyone crazy enough to replace you, yet. I only wish you could stay here for a while.''

"Where should I go?'' Maya asked. Suddenly the world seemed a great gray void. What would she do? She would drop into oblivion and never be heard from again.

"Away. Don't tell me where.'' Johanna squatted down and took Maya's hands. "But write when the heat's off, okay? I don't want you to disappear out of my life for good. I don't want to worry all the time about what's happening to you.''

Maya stood, raising Johanna up with her. They put their arms around each other and hugged for a long moment, their foreheads touching, breathing each other's scent.

"I've just found you again,'' Maya said. "I hate to lose you so quickly." I don't want to go away, she cried silently. I'm afraid. I'm alone. But she would go, now, before Johanna went to fetch Rachel from school, before she could lose her nerve. The memory of the blossoming night would sustain her. The road would carry her, once again.

"We'll never lose each other," Johanna said. "I know that now. We are each other's karma."

"You must have done something pretty bad in your last lifetime, then." Maya smiled.

"Not bad enough to deserve to lose you," Johanna said. "You take care of yourself."

35

Khunde

This mind of yours is inseparable luminosity and
emptiness in the form of a great mass of light;
it has no birth or death, therefore it is
the Buddha of Immortal Light. To recognize this
is all that is necessary.

—THE GREAT LIBERATION THROUGH
HEARING THE BARDO
THE TIBETAN BOOK OF THE DEAD

The clinic lay on the edge of town, just where the broad, flat fields began
to rise on the slopes of the mountain. The Sherpa-style building was long
and low, with a tin roof. Maya followed Ang up the narrow lanes. She'd
had a nap after their arrival, but she was still tired, worn by the weight of
her memories as much as by the effort of the walk. The short climb was
an effort.

"Thanks for showing me the way," she said to Ang as he led her up
the hill.

"No problem. I must come anyway, for medicine." He patted his
stomach, smiling. "Ulcer."

"Ulcer! Ang, you don't mean to tell me that you have an ulcer!"

He nodded sadly.

"There go all my illusions about the healthful, stress-free life of the
mountains!"

"When my daughter die, very sad," he said. "Stomach go bad.
Doctor help very much."

"I'm sorry."

He nodded again, silently accepting her sympathy as they walked
on.

"And I'm so sorry about Tengpoche," Maya said, puffing slightly as they climbed a stone stairway. "What a horrible tragedy! Will they re-build, do you think?"

"Oh yes," Ang said. "But much time, much money needed."

"Maybe we could make some kind of contribution," she suggested. "I'll talk to the others about it."

"This group, very good people."

"I'd like to do it."

They continued on. She was glad of his company. Now that her meeting with Debby was near, she felt apprehensive. She hadn't seen Debby for so long—and the last time they'd been together, they'd fought. What about? Oh yes, Joe's memorial.

Maya had flown down to LA when she heard the news that Joe had died, keeling over in the middle of a lecture with a massive heart attack. She told her mother that she had to meet with an agent about a possible consulting job on a film. The agent was Megan Ricci from Harding High, now one of the minor movers and shakers of the industry. If need be, she would back up Maya's story, because in reality she had gone down only to be with Betty, to comfort her wordlessly so that Betty wouldn't have to admit she needed comfort, that she was mourning a man who had abandoned her thirty years before.

She arrived to find her mother glorying in grief. Debby had been home, for once, making her preparations for Nepal, studying tapes of the Sherpa language, muttering phrases as she shopped and packed. Betty had talked incessantly about Joe, how attractive he'd been when he was young, how dynamic, how much he'd adored his baby daughters. She was talking about another Joe altogether from the one Maya remembered, that distant figure who sent them copies of his books, but no checks. Finally Betty lay down on her bed and wept, then roused herself to exhort her daughters to grieve, to let it out, to go ahead and have a good cry.

"I can't cry," Debby had said. "How can I cry? I barely even knew the bastard!"

"Debby! The man was your father, for God's sake. He wasn't a perfect father, by any means, but it's still a loss!"

They were sitting in Betty's bedroom, with the TV on, Oprah interviewing young wives of older men. Maya switched it off.

"It's no loss to me," Debby said. Betty was propped up on her bed, leaning against the pillows, with Debby perched at the foot of it. Maya came and sat down beside her mother.

"Don't say that. It isn't true." Betty turned to look at Maya. "What about you? Are you going to tell me Joe's death isn't a loss for you?"

"It's a loss, Mom. I feel it," Maya said. Debby glared at her. "But of course, I'm older. He was around more of my life. He was more of a father to me."

The truth was, the loss was abstract, she so rarely saw Joe or heard from him. But yes, she could feel the pain of knowing that she would never see him again, that now he never could come rescue her, come transform their lives with his magic male presence.

"There's going to be a memorial for him, a week from now," Betty said. "At Columbia. I'm going. And you two, also."

"Do you think that's a good idea?" Maya started to say reasonably when Debby jumped in.

"I'm not going. No way. And neither are you, if you have any sense."

"I'm his wife," Betty said. "I belong there. It wouldn't be complete without me."

No, Maya wanted to scream, don't say that, I can't bear to have you think that, but she said nothing.

"You were his wife thirty years ago," Debby said harshly. "He's had three others since then, the last one so young she wasn't even born when he walked out on you. Jesus Christ, Mom, she's younger than we are! Why should you go? You don't owe him a damn thing."

"He's part of my life," Betty said. "He's the father of my children."

"You'll be humiliated. I refuse to go and watch."

"Oh, shut up," Maya said to her. She didn't know which was worse—her mother's growing tendency to wrap herself in a Joe Greenbaum fantasyland, or Debby's harshness.

"Why should I shut up? I'm only telling the truth."

"You're just upset. Your father is dead," Betty said in her most soothing therapist voice. But suddenly she looked old to Maya, her face round with extra flesh, her jowls hanging heavy, the lines and creases all too evident on her skin. She was aged and fragile. Maya wanted more than anything for her not to hurt. "So you're projecting your pain onto me."

Debby was relentless. "I am not! I'm not upset because my father is dead. I'm upset because you're out of touch with reality."

"Oh, Debby, stop it," Maya said.

"It's true! Dammit, Betty, you've got to stop thinking of yourself and Joe in the same little circle. You are not together with him. You, Joe, not together. He walked out on us all thirty years ago and I refuse to enshrine his memory!"

"Oh, you shut up!" Betty said. "You think you're so smart, Miss Doctor. What do you know about it? You don't know a goddamned thing!" She lashed out with the back of her hand, missing Debby and accidentally hitting Maya in the face.

"Ow, that hurt!"

"Oh, get out of here, both of you!"

"Me, what have I done?" Maya said. "I was supporting you!"

"The hell you were. I know the two of you—always ganging up on me. I know how you think. Well, let me tell you this. I belong at Joe's memorial. I'm the mother of his children, pair of brats that you are, and I belong there! I was cheated out of thirty years with him, but I'm not letting anyone cheat me out of that!"

They fled into the kitchen. Searching for comfort, they found an archaic bottle of Manischewitz wine in the cupboard above the refrigerator, and opened it.

"She'll calm down," Debby said, pouring Maya a generous glassful.

Maya took the glass Debby handed her and sat down. "Why do you have to bait her like that?"

"I just want her to see, just once, what she's doing," Debby said, joining Maya at the table. "Why couldn't she get over him, get married again, like everybody else's mom? What's wrong with her?"

"I don't know, but you won't cure it by rubbing her face in it. She's getting old, Debby. She's almost seventy. She's not going to change."

"Well, I'm not going to any Joe Greenbaum memorial. I'm not going to stand up and pretend to be his darling, dutiful daughter. Or maybe I should go. Get up and give a speech about how he never sent her any child support. In this day and age he'd be thrown in jail!"

Maya sipped the sweet, cloying liquid. "Look, you're mad at him. I'm mad at him, too. But why take it out on Betty?"

"Because she's a fool. A self-deluded old fool. And I can't stand it, Karla." Debby's eyes held tears. "She drives me crazy!"

Maya reached across the table to pat Debby's hand. "She drives me crazy, too, all right. But she's our mother. She didn't run out on us. We've got to support her."

"Fine." Debby drew her hand away. "You support her. You're the one who always ran out on her before—I'm the one who got to stay home and live in the mess. Well, I'm done with that. I'm going, now, and it's your turn to prop her up if that's what you want to do. But I can't stand it. I really can't stand it."

Maya went with Betty to the memorial. Debby stayed behind. Betty looked dignified in her black suit, but old, and all the comfort and attention went to Mrs. Joe Greenbaum number four, a twenty-nine-year-old graduate student who had simpered at Betty through her copious tears.

"Joe's first wife, how kind of you to come. Why, it's like history coming alive!"

All of Joe's colleagues had said nice things about him, and while Maya was impressed and gratified to learn what a stalwart and honored place he'd held among the intelligentsia of the left, and how his legal scholarship had revised the accepted opinion on this and that, she found herself nursing a pain in the gut that, while undoubtedly psychosomatic, still hurt like hell. The worst of it was watching Betty enjoying herself, in the midst of her grief. Once again she was bathed in Joe's reflected glory.

"I'm part of his history," she murmured proudly to Maya.

If Debby had been there, she would have screamed at Betty that the comment was an insult, not a compliment. If Maya had been younger and more optimistic, she would have cried to Betty that she was an important person in her own right, that she didn't need Joe's glory to make her someone. Instead she kept silent, smiling politely at Mrs. Joe Greenbaum numbers two, three, and four, letting Betty enjoy what she evidently experienced as her hour of triumph. Maya went home, Debby flew off to Kathmandu and trekked up to Khumbu. Six months later Betty was diagnosed with cancer.

A light burned in the back of the clinic. Ang knocked on the door.

Maybe we'll connect this time, Maya thought. She took a deep breath. If I can open to her as if she were a mountain, if I can be her witness and her mirror, not her judge, then maybe she'll meet me. We can be present for each other, talk and hold and comfort each other like true sisters. After all, we're both orphans now, with no mother to cling to, no daughters, no other female line but us.

She would hold that thought. No matter what Debby said or did, she would reserve judgment and keep her temper and show her love.

A slight Sherpani in a bright striped apron opened the door. She and Ang conversed rapidly for a moment, and then Ang turned to Maya.

"So sorry," he said. "Your sister gone."

"Gone?"

"Not so far," he said. "Wait. She bringing message."

The woman had disappeared into the house, then emerged holding an envelope, which she handed to Maya. Maya opened it and read:

"Dear Karla—Maya, I mean, I'll never get used to calling you that. Anyway, I'm so sorry but I've got to go handle an emergency situation a day's walk from here—a possible outbreak of typhoid. It's very serious and I can't delay. But I know your schedule. I will meet you in Thami and camp with you that night and walk back to Namche with you the next day. I'm sorry things have worked out so that we don't have much time together, but you know how it is. I hope you're enjoying Khumbu. Love, Debby."

I should have known, Maya thought. Damn her, anyway! She doesn't want to meet me. She's just evading me. How the hell can I practice Buddha-like acceptance if she won't even show up for me to practice on!

"Bad news?" Ang said anxiously, looking at her face.

Maya sighed. "She says she'll meet us tomorrow. I'm just disappointed."

"Yes, very sad," Ang agreed. "You look forward so to see your sister."

"That's right," Maya said. But deep inside she also felt a slight quiver of relief. Maybe tomorrow she wouldn't be so tired. Maybe tomorrow would be a better day to meet, less contentious, more auspicious for connection.

She forced a smile for Ang. "We'll meet tomorrow. It'll be okay."

"Now we go back," Ang said. "Eat dinner. You very tired, good to sleep tonight, resting good. Tomorrow we go Thami, not so hard. Easy. Then you meet sister."

Maya thanked the woman who had given her Debby's letter, bowing her head and saying *"namaste"* as Ang slipped her a couple of rupiahs. They headed back down the hill to the camp.

While dinner was being prepared, Maya walked out to the edge of the field where they were camped. A low stone wall overlooked the white *stuppa* on the edge of the village. Under the deep, glowing, saturated blue of the twilight sky, the building shone softly. She picked her way over the loose stones of the wall, intending to sit and contemplate the silence, when she noticed a still figure already perched on the wall.

Maya recognized Pembila and smiled at her. Pembila smiled back, but suddenly Maya noticed tears on the other woman's cheeks.

"Pembila, what's wrong? Are you okay? Can I help?"

Pembila shook her head.

"Isn't there anything I can do?" Maya asked. She had never seen the Sherpa woman be anything but smiling, gracious, laughing, and teasing. I should leave her, Maya thought. Maybe I'm humiliating her, intruding on her private tears. But maybe she needs comfort, a shoulder to cry on. What do I do? Do I put my arms around her or go away?

Uncertain, she sat down next to Pembila and took her hand. If I feel her withdraw, she thought, I'll leave. "I'm sorry you feel sad," Maya said.

Pembila squeezed her hand tightly. "One year ago, daughter die," she said softly. "Now very sad."

"I am so sorry," Maya said. She didn't know how to offer more. There was no consolation for such a loss. But Pembila clung to her hand, seeming to take comfort from her quiet presence. Maya breathed softly, as if she were holding something precious that a sigh or a sudden movement could disturb. They sat together, two grieving women holding hands, as the light faded and the sky grew dark.

36

December 1971

"And if you close the mouth of the milk carton right away," Mrs. Porter said, "it will keep the cockroaches out."

Maya complied, as she did with all the old woman's commands and requests. She poured the gray water from washing the floor into the toilet before scrubbing the bowl. She mixed, as instructed, just one tablespoon of bleach into a gallon of water before scrubbing the shower curtain. She boiled Mrs. Porter's egg for exactly two and a half minutes, and served it in the right bowl with the right teaspoon, with just a dash of salt.

"The girl I had before you, she always had to argue about every little thing," Mrs. Porter went on. "I don't see that it's too much to ask, at my age, to have things done my way. If you don't want to live with roaches, you've got to keep on top of them. You can't throw your garbage every which way, like those people downstairs. This building is full of people who live no better than pigs. I try to tell them, but they don't listen to me."

She was a frail old woman, fretful and often in pain from the arthritis that twisted her hands into claws and kept her confined to her bed or wheelchair. When the elevator was working in the old brick building on West 116th Street, she would go for a daily outing in the afternoon, while Maya cleaned. More often, when the elevator jammed or the weather was bad, she would stay in and supervise. Her hair was white and fine, and her light brows angled up over her wide blue eyes, giving her face a look of perpetual outrage. Each afternoon Maya helped her warm a special medicinal wax and embed her hands and bony arms in it. The wax sucked away some of the pain, and later, when they freed her arms from the cocoon, they would emerge wrinkled and translucent as if her skin itself were only another sort of waxen coating.

The tiny apartment was permeated with an air of sadness and loneliness and restricted life. Mrs. Porter lived on her small disability grant, which barely stretched to pay for rent and food. She sent Maya to the store with precise instructions about which brand of margarine to buy to save a few cents, and which size box of cereal, and how many carrots and potatoes. Fresh fruit was purchased once a week. If Maya slipped up, purchasing perhaps an extra apple or two because they looked good, Mrs. Porter would cry in frustration and real fear.

The state gave her twenty-five dollars a week to spend on an assistant, someone to clean and shop and cook for her. For this Maya was supposed to work two hours a day, Monday through Friday. It wasn't a great job, but it suited Maya, or Maggie, as she called herself now. She didn't have to provide evidence of a high school diploma or a Social Security Number. She was housesitting the apartment of a mathematics grad student at Columbia who'd put up a notice on a bulletin board asking for someone who would water his plants and feed his cat while he was away settling the estate of his recently deceased father. He had a living room, a bedroom, and a tiny kitchen coated with grease that faced an air shaft. Maya had systematically scrubbed the kitchen as soon as the student was gone. In spite of her rigorous cleaning, the cockroaches remained.

Mrs. Porter was lonely because nobody liked her, and nobody liked her because she was old and fussy and complained all the time. Maya was lonely because she was trying to hold the solitude of the mountains in the middle of Manhattan, and because she was waiting. Waiting to grow comfortably into this new person that she was/wasn't, Margaret Anne Bradley. Waiting for a driver's license and a passport, waiting for Rio's trial, or for winter to turn to spring, waiting for snowmelt in the high passes of the mountains.

"What I don't understand," Mrs. Porter said to her one day, "is why a young girl like yourself doesn't make something of yourself. Not that I'm complaining. It's hard to get good help. For some reason, they all quit on me. But you, you should be doing something better than this."

"I want to be a writer," Maya said. "Maybe someday I'll be successful."

Actually this was another of her many lies. She didn't want to be a writer; she still mistrusted words, used them miserly, as if each were a concession to forces she regretted having to acknowledge. But she had discovered, in her first days in New York, that she had to be something in order to forestall questions. She had come to New York because the first bus leaving the Greyhound station was going there. It seemed big enough to disappear into, and the only person she knew there was her father, who was away on his sabbatical, teaching in Seattle. She aspired only to being anonymous. Everyone else in New York, it seemed, wanted to be someone of importance: an actor, an artist, a poet. Maya could not imagine herself as an artist; even her mother had never discerned the slightest signs of talent in her paintings. Actors and dancers were forever taking classes and trying out for parts. She had neither the money nor the inclination for either. But writers were solitary creatures. The fact that she had no work to show was no hindrance; New York was full of aspiring writers who never produced anything.

When she wasn't working for Mrs. Porter, Maya roamed the streets, trying to watch the constant parade of people as if it were a stream roaring down the slopes of a mountain. Her years in the Front had at least taught her how to live on virtually nothing. For breakfast she ate yogurt. For lunch and dinner, she cooked up pots of beans and lentil soup. To save bus and subway fares, she walked wherever she could, uptown to the Cloisters or across the park to the Metropolitan Museum, where she looked intently at ancient sculptures and medieval paintings, trying to discover what the artists had known. She sat in on history and music and art lectures at Columbia, the big classes with hundreds of students where she could fade anonymously into the back rows. "Guess what, Joe?" she imagined writing. "I'm at Columbia after all!"

She meditated in Central Park, trying to convince herself that her vision remained intact, that she hadn't after all become a kind of ghost, trapped in a netherworld in which her real life was indefinitely suspended. There were moments when she found herself deliberately brushing against people on the street, or knocking into a young man as they left a classroom, just to touch somebody for a moment, to know that she was still real. She felt like a thief, a touch thief, stealing little moments of contact.

The dead haunted her. She would glimpse Daniel in the hunched shoulders of a man walking down Broadway, and catch her breath until she could see his face turn into a stranger's. Or she would hear a tone in a woman's voice behind her in line for groceries, and wheel around, expecting to see Edith's worried face. Often she would catch sight of her own reflection in a window, her face gaunt under a mane of untrimmed brown hair, her chapped hands shoved into the pockets of the worn cloth coat with a fake fur collar she'd bought at a thrift store for five dollars, and the thought would come to her that somewhere in her life she'd made a wrong turn. She could have been one of the students she sat beside in the classes she stole into. She could have been there by right, making good grades, wearing leather gloves and elegant boots and a fashionable winter coat. Her lover could have been lean and confident, a skier who would take her away for weekends on the slopes, a scholar who would argue points of medieval history with her over steaming cappuccino, an artist who would throw wild, fashionable parties in his loft—anyone, anything, but a man in a cage who might have been better off with the fire-cleansed dead. Yes, the thought of Rio locked away haunted her worse than the ghosts of Edith and Daniel. She could do nothing for him; she couldn't even write to him without endangering herself. So she waited, trying, as a meditation, as a spiritual discipline, to put him out of her mind.

As December moved toward Christmas, the crowds got thicker, noisier, and more cheerful. Maya felt her loneliness more acutely, as did Mrs. Porter, who took to complaining incessantly that nobody had invited her for Christmas dinner.

"You'd think at the church, there'd be somebody," she said, "or one of the neighbors. But people are selfish nowadays. They don't think about anyone else. Turn that broom the other way. If you shift it around from time to time it wears more evenly."

On Christmas Eve day, however, she appeared more cheerful. "My neighbor Sylvia upstairs invited me for dinner," she said. "Isn't that nice? But I have a favor to ask you. I don't want to interfere with your day, but would you be willing to stop by if the elevator isn't working and help Sylvia's boyfriend get me up the stairs? It's only one flight."

"Sure," Maya said. In reality, she had no plans for the day, except to take herself out for squid at one of the local Cuban-Chinese restaurants with the few dollars she had saved. The thought of eating dinner in a restaurant alone was not greatly alluring, but the thought of a bowl of lentil soup in her empty apartment was even worse.

The elevator, as usual, wasn't working. At noon, Maya arrived and helped Eric, a robust man in his early sixties, maneuver Mrs. Porter and her chair up the stairs. They were ushered into an apartment as tiny as the one downstairs, but completely overrun by books. Shelves of books covered every wall, and stacks of them were piled on chairs and under tables. The room smelled of dust and something more pungent, like incense, along with the rich, meaty smell of roasting turkey.

Sylvia proved to be a silver-haired woman of great stature, also well into her sixties, with a long face, intelligent gray eyes, and a slightly ironic smile. Her white hair was pinned up in braids that circled her head like a wreath. She spoke with a British accent, welcoming them, and inviting Maya to partake of eggnog.

"I should be going," Maya said, but the drink looked so appealing, frothy and thick in a big crystal punch bowl, that she allowed herself to be persuaded to try a cup. The eggnog was sweet and rich and mildly intoxicating, like everything in life Maya missed.

"Can you stay for turkey?" Sylvia asked. "There's plenty, and we'd be delighted to have you."

She wanted to say no, because she wanted to have someplace better to go than this cramped room full of old people. In her mind she was picturing a room with high ceilings and ornate moldings where slim people in fashionable clothes sipped champagne. And there would be someone there, a man like her, somewhat out of place and oddly dressed, but more real in his Levi's than all the others in their tailored suits. He would look into her eyes, and take her hand, and say, "Let's get out of here, you and me. Let's get away from these phonies. I want to know you, I want to make love to you, I want us to spend the rest of our lives together. . . ."

Stop it! she told herself firmly, because the man in her imagination was looking moment by moment more like Rio. Suddenly she was feeling his loss, like a hole in her heart. Where was he today? Did they serve turkey at Christmas in prison? Probably, so why the hell shouldn't she have some? Frankly, she was hungry. For the moment she had lost her mountain, the peace, the still-water calm. So, trapped between the cravings of the body and the promptings of pride, why not eat?

"I'd be happy to join you," Maya said, and made herself helpful, clearing places to sit from among the books with fascinating titles. *The White Goddess, The Secret Teachings of All Ages, Mothers and Amazons, The Greater Key of Solomon, Tarot Revealed.* Evidently, Sylvia's tastes leaned toward the occult. They sat down to feast on turkey and stuffing and sweet potatoes, while Mrs. Porter chattered on with complaints about the building's super, who never fixed anything, and Eric winked at Maya as he carved.

"Tell us about yourself, Maggie," Sylvia said somewhat abruptly, as Mrs. Porter was about to launch off into a new attack on the downstairs neighbors.

"There's nothing much to tell," Maya said. "I work for Mrs. Porter. I'm new in town."

"Maggie's a writer," Mrs. Porter said. "Someday she'll be famous."

"A writer!" Sylvia and Eric exchanged glances. "Now, if that isn't synchronicity at work. I was just saying to Eric that what I need is a writer to collaborate with me. And here she is. Are you looking for work?"

"Uh, well, I'm not sure I'm a very good writer. Yet. I mean, I'm sort of just beginning. Learning," Maya said awkwardly.

Sylvia looked her over, the older woman's eyes slightly unfocused, as if she were seeing something beyond Maya's physical presence. "I have an intuition about this," she said. "I felt something as soon as you walked through the door. I could be wrong, but I suspect we're meant to do something together. Anyway, I'm sure you're a very good writer. You can always spot the bad ones—they memorize their own poems and recite them at any opportunity. Seriously, I do need someone to collaborate with, and I can pay you, too. Four, maybe five dollars an hour."

Four dollars an hour might mean unheard of luxuries—fresh apples every day. Eggs. Woolen gloves. Subway tokens down to the Village. But did she have the right to deceive this woman who was feeding her and had welcomed her so graciously? On the other hand, maybe she could do the job, whatever it was. She had been good at writing in high school. Hadn't Frank Harvey predicted a career for her? Xeroxed her essays? Hadn't she written all those articles for Tony's underground paper?

"Tell me what you want," Maya said.

Again Sylvia and Eric exchanged glances. "It's just some . . . memoirs I'm trying to put in order," Sylvia said. "But we'll talk after dinner. We shouldn't spoil a meal with business."

Instead, Eric told amusing stories about his experiences driving a taxicab in the city, and they discussed politics. The war in Vietnam was sputtering along, perhaps even winding down. Maya could not feel any sense of personal triumph. It seemed to be ending in spite of, rather than because of, their efforts.

After dinner, after Mrs. Porter had begun to doze off and been carried downstairs, the other three settled down to talk.

"This is a confidential project," Sylvia said. "It requires someone discreet. Can you keep a secret?"

"That I can do," Maya said.

"What I'm working on is a book of rituals. Eric and I, we practice the Old Religion."

"Which old religion?"

"The one that goes back before Christianity. Pagan, you could call it. We worship the Goddess."

"What goddess?"

"She who is birth, growth, death, and regeneration."

The words settled in the room and prickled at the nape of Maya's neck. Her ears rang. There was something here for her.

"I don't know anything about her," Maya said. "But I'd be willing to learn."

They loaded her up with books and leftover turkey, and sent her home to read. She felt grateful; the food would keep her for days, and the books would keep the edge off her loneliness. And so she spent Christmas night reading voraciously in her apartment. She hadn't read much in a long time. For all the years in the Front, she'd felt she could only justify not reading Marx by not reading much of anything at all. But here, alone in the city, she'd gone through the stash of mysteries and science fiction in the mathematician's apartment, feeling all the time as if she were reverting to a drug, something to take her away from herself.

Now, however, she was ready to read differently, to take in new ideas, to absorb information. Living in a place where the mind ruled the body, where nature was the abstraction and human thought was what was real, she would learn to move once more in the realm of thought. She'd been good at it once; she might be good at it still.

She plowed through the first book, something by a man named

Gerald Gardner called *Witchcraft Today,* which had been published in the early fifties. He claimed to have discovered, in the New Forest in the south of England, a group practicing an ancient tradition that went back before the Norman Conquest. His type of Witchcraft was not devil worship, as the church tried to paint it, but the worship of nature, and the training of the mind and intuition. As Maya read, she grew more and more excited. For years, she'd called herself a Witch without really knowing what the word meant. She'd read Tarot cards and made protection charms for Rio, but now she began to see herself as part of a long tradition as rich in its dimensions as any other system. The Old Religion, according to the books, was the ancient knowledge that celebrated life and its cycles of renewal. Through centuries of persecution, the secret teachings had survived. That was a myth, she recognized, but she wanted to believe it. Whether or not the history could be verified, the teachings rang true. They gave names to the wordless experiences she'd had on the mountain.

She had always been wary of descriptions. She had struggled so hard to do away with words, to let go of frames that diminished what was real. But now she began to feel a need for some container in which to pour the power she'd evoked. Without a way to hold them and carry them, visions dissolved and their power leached away. Could words be used not as a box to confine what was real but as a cauldron in which experience could simmer and brew?

She read on. *The White Goddess* was harder going, due to Robert Graves's annoying habit of making references to things she didn't know and books she hadn't read. If she'd stayed in school, if she'd gone to college the way her mother had wanted her to, she might know who the Carians and the Mosynoechians were, but she didn't. Still, there were ideas, names, images, that rang inside her with the sound of water dropping onto granite in the silence of the mountains. She had made her own names for the powers, but maybe she wasn't the only one to have ever encountered the Seer or the Singer or the Reaper.

"I don't know if I'll really be much help to you," Maya told Sylvia when she returned the books. They were sitting at a round wooden table at the one window in the living room that caught the sun, drinking tea, English style, with a dash of milk, another small luxury for Maya. The asceticism of poverty was, paradoxically, making her rich. The world was now full of small attainable indulgences. "I never went to college. I don't know if I really can write."

"Well, let's try and we'll see," Sylvia said. "Don't worry. If it doesn't work out, I'll tell you."

"I'd like to try, anyway. More than that, Sylvia. I read those books—or started them, at least. They're fascinating. I want to learn more. I want to be trained. I never knew any of this existed, but in a funny way, I think I am a Witch."

"Quite likely," Sylvia said. "You have the look of it."

"What look?"

"Something about the face . . . and the aura. That's the energy body that surrounds your physical body. I see a pentacle in yours. That's how I recognized that you were one of us."

"A pentacle?"

"This sign of the Goddess, the four sacred elements, plus the fifth, which is spirit and commands them all, in the circle of the full moon. I see blue water and green trees. A mountain?"

"I spent the summer in the mountains." Maya found herself telling Sylvia things she had never shared with anybody, even Johanna. How the silence had seemed to call out a deeper silence within herself, until in the core of the soundless space she began to hear voices that were not so much words or sounds but a sense of presence and knowing. The mountain seemed far away from this stuffy, cramped apartment with sirens blaring in the streets outside and horns bleating and loud voices shouting at each other, yet the intensity of Sylvia's shrouded eyes as she listened was a link between the worlds.

"Well, you've done very well on your own," she said at last, when Maya had finished. "You've established your contacts, as we say. Generally that's very advanced work. You must have some past lives as a priestess. Later you'll learn to remember them. But you should be trained. It's like ballet, in a way. You can't just do the fancy leaps without the basic barre work, or you end up with the psychic equivalent of strained ligaments. And really, this will work out perfectly, because what I want to write is sort of a basic psychic training manual. We can formulate each exercise as you progress through it. When shall we begin?"

"Today, after I finish with Mrs. Porter?"

"Right-oh."

"But I don't want you to pay me," Maya said. She had wrestled deeply with her conscience, and after a sigh for the lost possibilities of eggs and butter and bagels and cheese, had found the terms upon which she could live with her own lies. "It'll be a trade. My help for your training."

Sylvia looked at her steadily for a long time, and finally nodded. "Fair enough."

Maya's days settled into a new pattern. Now she went to Mrs. Porter in the mornings and spent the afternoons with Sylvia, practicing meditations and exercises and then searching for the best words to convey their effects on paper. She learned the breathing from down in her diaphragm that brought relaxation and opened the psychic centers. She learned how to ground, how to establish her contact with the earth, sending roots of energy down, through the concrete and asphalt and the underground systems of subways and sewer pipes to find earth energies. She learned about the elements of earth, air, water, and fire, how to make contact with each, how to call forth its particular energies and protective powers.

For so many years, she had refused to submit herself to any sort of formal instruction. At times the discipline chafed. Leave me alone, she wanted to say, let me experience what I do on my own, don't define it for me. But she kept on, mostly because she enjoyed Sylvia's company, the calm, good-humored, no-nonsense presence that made the occult jargon bearable.

"Words," Sylvia would say, "are only a convenience, like currency, that allow us to trade hints of the Wordless back and forth. Always remember that the real mysteries cannot be told. Not because we're forbidden to tell them, but because they cannot be expressed in speech."

Sylvia fed her lunch, over Maya's protests, and provided high tea at the end of each working session. Over sandwiches and biscuits she would tell stories of magical islands of women where the ancient priestesses once were trained, of circles called covens gathering to raise power to turn back Hitler's invasions, of prophecies of the return of the old ways. Her tradition, she said, came from Scotland, from the old, indigenous race of the little people they called Faeries, who were not flitty things with wings but a real, if undersized, group of tribes: the Picts, pixies, known for their magic and their matriarchal form of organization. She told of the raising of the standing stones, sung into place with music. And she told stories of the Burning Times, the times of persecution, when those who were accused of Witchcraft were raped and hideously tortured and then burned alive, and the Craft itself went underground.

"Eventually, you'll meet some of the others," Sylvia said. "And when you do, remember the first rule of etiquette is never to identify someone else as a Witch. Never blow anybody's cover, as you Americans say. Leave it to them to identify themselves."

The discussion contributed to Maya's growing uneasiness and sense of guilt over her own secrets. How much did Sylvia know? she wondered, as the older woman taught her to read the subtle energies of the body, first with her fingertips, later to see them with her eyes as cool flickering lights and colors of indescribable shades. What could she read of Maya's life, when together they could time-travel back into the parallel lives that Sylvia insisted were not so much past as omnipresent, since all time existed as one? That thought did not please Maya, who preferred to think of certain chapters of her past as closed.

Out of guilt, Maya began, on her free evenings, to attend readings and sit in on poetry workshops. At least, she thought, I can learn what other people think good writing is.

What other people thought was good writing proved to be obscure to Maya. The poems that received praise were pastiches of images that never quite coalesced into a meaning she could identify. She sat in the back, in her threadbare jeans and thrift store sweaters, feeling intimidated.

One night she found herself talking to a woman who had read a poem that Maya liked, because it was clear and vivid and spoke to a subject she knew well—the breakdown of love. The woman invited her to join a women's writing group that was forming.

She went to the first meeting because it was down the block from where she was staying, and she was feeling especially lonely that night. The jury was being selected for Rio's trial, and the papers were full of the story. She had watched the evening news, seen his picture with his face gaunt and bruised and his eyes haunted. There was nothing she could do for him, no way even to make contact except, perhaps, by the etheric routes that Sylvia was teaching her. Maybe he could feel her concern; maybe not. She switched off the TV and went out.

There were six women already gathered in the living room of the apartment when Maya arrived. Immediately, she felt out of place. Probably none of them were rich, but they all wore tailored trousers or jeans just worn enough to be fashionable, high boots of soft leather and sweaters that were handknit out of real cotton or wool, not covered with little pills of acrylic fuzz, like hers. They were chatting about grants they'd applied for and their teaching schedules for the quarter and whom to contact at *Ms.* magazine. Maya quietly helped herself to a plateful of cheese and crackers, trying not to look obviously hungry and wondering if it was too late to slip away.

"Let's get started," said Christina, the woman who'd invited Maya. To Maya's horror, she realized that before the women began reading their work, they intended to go around the circle and give each woman a chance to talk about her life. The last thing in the world she wanted to talk about was her life. Really, she would rather have discussed the labor theory of value.

She forced herself to listen to the other women as they went around. All of them seemed to be graduate students or teachers or assistant editors at publishing houses. Their problems seemed so rational and sane and respectable: how to get their work taken seriously, how to beat the odds against women and get promoted, how to discipline themselves to work. And what could she say? I'm the maid for a cranky old woman and I'm upset now because my lover, former lover, I should say, is going to be sent up for a long, long time and I miss him terribly even though I hate his bloody guts. That was the truth, and she could feel tears swimming into her eyes, which she fought down, because she was not going to cry here, not going to drip her salt tears on the suede boots of these women and then have to lie about why she was crying. When it came right down to it, she was a bad liar. She wasn't suited for this role, heroine of the underground. She should have listened to Johanna, finished high school, gone to college at Columbia, and married someone like Daniel should have been. Then she would never have gotten mixed up with Rio and she would belong in this room with these women, and her own problems would be nice and containable, too.

When her turn came, she decided to tell them as much of the truth as she could.

"I'm new in New York," she said. "I don't know too many people here. I'm not a student, or anything. I guess right now the main thing in my life is learning about the Goddess."

Much to her surprise, this elicited a chorus of questions that she tried to answer. She told them that before the religions based on books and Gods and male power had triumphed, there had been a time when women had power and respect, when people worshiped a Goddess of birth and growth and life.

"But what's the evidence for it?" Christina asked.

"Oh, I don't care about the evidence," said a red-haired slender woman who wove tapestries. "I want to believe it. We all want to believe it—that there was something different once. Tell me the symbols of the Goddess, I want to weave something."

"She is the Weaver, in one of her aspects," Maya said. "She's earth and air and fire and water, and the three phases of the moon. She's the sacred tree and the cat and the bird, the five-petalled flower and the passage of time. She's the stone and the star and the buds that open into leaves that change color and drop from the trees to return to earth and fertilize the ground."

Something began to happen as she spoke. She stopped feeling like the poor little match girl and began to feel power running through her once again, as if by speaking the words, *moon, stone, star,* she invoked someone—the Singer, who danced off her tongue into the center of the room, laughing.

"And how are you learning about this?" asked Carol, the tiny dark-haired woman who worked at Doubleday.

She told them about Sylvia, and then they got really excited.

"Would she come here, do you think? Would she teach us? Would she speak to us?"

"I don't know," Maya said. "I can ask her."

Afterward, they went out to eat at one of the dim, fashionable restaurants that had sprung up in the neighborhood. Maya ordered tea, which she sat nursing while the others ate salads and linguini and spa-ghetti with clam sauce. "I'm not hungry," she claimed. It was another lie.

"Are you really not hungry, or are you just broke?" Carol asked. "Because I've got plenty of cash. I can loan you some."

"I'm not hungry," Maya repeated stubbornly. It would take her weeks to pay back the five or ten bucks that the meal would cost, and she made up her mind never to go out with these women again. Yet here she was in New York, and while the mountain had taught her something about silence, the city's lessons seemed to have something to do with conversation. Maybe she needed to learn that, too.

"Connolly Enters Guilty Plea," trumpeted the morning headlines. She spent a precious dime to buy a paper on her way to work, but she didn't have a chance to read the article until she finished with Mrs. Porter and went up to Sylvia's apartment for lunch. She spread the paper out on the table. There would be no trial. He had pled guilty to all the charges, from illegal possession of firearms to second-degree murder. Sentencing was scheduled for the following week. Rio had made no statement to the judge or to the press. The photo showed his hands covering his face. Behind his fingers, Maya thought she could discern his desolation. More than anything, she wanted to cry. But Sylvia was watching her intently.

"What's so fascinating in the paper?" she asked.

Maya sighed. How long, she wondered, could she go on lying to this woman who could read images in her energy field and ferret out her past lives? What made her think she could conceal this life?

"What's wrong, dear?"

Maya began to cry. The old woman sat down and put her arms around her. Maya could smell incense clinging to her clothes. The scent wrapped around her and yet also seemed to suffocate her. She longed for the clean fresh wind off the ocean or the dry wind that came rattling over the granite ridges of the high passes, for Johanna's comforting touch or even the sheltering arms of her own mother, who probably hated her by now. She was crying for the Rio who had stood with her on the rocky shelf of the coast, their arms outstretched, leaning into the wind. There was something good in him that shouldn't have been wasted. He should have had a just war to fight, or a real revolution. She should have been able to save him.

"What's wrong?" Sylvia asked again.

"I'm a liar," Maya said finally. "I'm not who you think I am. My name isn't Maggie Bradley, its Maya Greenbaum. And that man," she pointed to the paper, "is my lover. Was."

"Goodness," Sylvia said. "I knew you'd been sitting on something, but this is a fair treat."

"Do you hate me?"

"Don't be ridiculous. But now I'm madly curious to hear the story."

Maya told her all of it.

"Do you love him?" Sylvia asked when she was finished.

"I guess I do. I keep trying not to."

"Never try not to love. The Goddess is love—even the kind that rips your heart out. Maybe especially that kind," she added thoughtfully. "It always has something to teach us."

"Well, I wish I knew what I was supposed to learn from this."

"Why, it's obvious. It brought you to the mountain, and it brought you here."

"And Rio? Does he have something to learn, too?" Maya asked, looking down at the grainy newspaper photo, all she would ever have of him.

"The Goddess is the great teacher, but her teaching methods sometimes leave a lot to be desired in human terms. Her scale of measure is so different from ours. She thinks in eons, millennia. A few years are nothing to her. But whatever lessons are his, either he'll learn or he won't. You can't do it for him."

"And the dead? What do they learn?"

"We don't know."

"They were friends of mine, too," Maya said. "Daniel was my lover, once or twice."

"Have you mourned them? Have you made your peace with them?"

"I've been too busy just surviving."

"We'll talk to them, at the dark of the moon."

At the dark of the moon, the court gave Rio twenty-five years to life. Maya walked down Broadway, repeating it to herself like a mantra. Twenty-five to life. Twenty-five plus twenty-two—she would be forty-seven years old when he got out, and he would be nearly fifty. Fifty. It seemed like a lifetime gone but then there were lives gone to be paid for, the security guard who had supported three kids on her own, shrill Edith and brilliant Daniel and the unknown bum on the stairs, gone and dead and charred. She lit candles for them, spoke to their spirits, or at least said words into empty air. She wasn't sure which. Look, spirits, if I had any part in your death, anything I did or didn't do, I'm sorry. Dear Daniel, if I have let you down by surviving, if I have been less than you expected or given less than was demanded by the times, forgive me. She didn't sense much response, even though she was beginning to see the living as lights, globes of color that danced and played in patterns and images that told her stories. But these dead remained silent, cold. She could more easily feel Rio, or imagine that she felt him, withdrawn and miserable. Life. It seemed like a long, long time.

Sylvia was quite taken with the idea of attending the women's group, and went with Maya the following week. She brought one of her meditations to read out loud, and Maya, feeling that there was only one way she could redeem her false position, had actually written a poem to share. It was, perhaps, an unwise poem to read out loud, since it was about Rio, but the writing had relieved her feelings in a surprising way, and when she read it, the others praised its emotional power without quite grasping the literal nature of the imagery.

> *A summer of immersions*
> *daily in clear spring water*
> *cannot wash away the stink*
> *of booze, piss, blood.*
> *You shot the clock*
> *for target practice*
> *shattered every mirror in the house*
> *with your bare hands*
> *shouting*
> *Kill the images! Smash the spectacle!*
> *It all erupted*
> *accidentally, as things do erupt*
> *the casualties were unplanned*
> *murders, yes,*
> *but not premeditated.*

• • •

"He could be out in ten or fifteen years," Eric assured her. The thought was small comfort. Ten or fifteen years was still a long, long time. They were cleaning out Sylvia's back bedroom so that Maya could move in. The mathematics student was returning and Sylvia had offered her a place to stay. The book was progressing nicely. Each week they tried out a new meditation on the women's group. Carol knew of an editor who might be interested in the manuscript. They had sent out an outline and a sample chapter. Maya discovered, to her surprise, that she had made herself a life.

Her room was tiny, but it had a window that actually opened and looked out on the street. A single mattress took up most of the floor space. She covered the walls with poems, and postcards of her favorite paintings and faraway places, places she would like to be. She read Tarot cards for people she met through her women's group, adding to her cash. She was saving for the moment when she would move on again, back to the mountain, across a border somewhere. In the meantime, she made tea in the morning for Sylvia, brought her breakfast in bed, because she enjoyed pampering the older woman. She cleaned Mrs. Porter's house. She wrote.

"I am not unhappy," she wrote Johanna in a letter she was afraid to mail.

> Although I miss you—but I have missed you for years, ever since we had that fight on the coast, and before. Funny how our moments of connection have always been so much briefer than our separations, and yet in some way you are a part of me I am never without, my sister, my mirror, my love. And I miss him, Goddess help me. Maybe not so much him-who-he-was, but the promise of sweetness that was never fulfilled. That's what hurts the most. I can't let go of what I never had.
>
> Anyway, I am learning something about form, and structure, and discipline. About time, I suppose you might say. I wanted to believe that the purity of the vision was enough. But even saying that puts a form on something that of its very nature has no form, and so becomes a lie. I don't know. Maybe you've been right all along, that we can't live these things in their purity in this world, or speak of them in the English language. Is there a language that can truly describe the mysteries?
>
> Sylvia says we all share in what she calls the group mind. And to change that mind, what you bring in must not be too different from what the mind already believes, or it will simply be rejected. But if you join with the mind of the group and move it a little bit one way, and then a little more, and a little more, you can take it anywhere. It's like leading a pack of Girl Scouts through the woods. If you want them to follow you, you can only be a little ways ahead, or they lose sight of where you are. But the danger, of course, is that the closer you stay to them, the more you begin to walk and talk and think like they do, and you can easily forget where you are going.
>
> I don't know. I never wanted to lead anyone, or have anybody follow me. I just wanted to live something. And now I feel like I'm walking down a road, but I don't know my own destination.

•   •   •

They finished the manuscript on the first of April.

"An auspicious day," Sylvia said.

"Let's hope so."

"April Fools'. The Fool is the Trickster, you know, just another aspect of the God."

Eric brought over a bottle of champagne, and they drank a toast. "To *The Star in the Wheel*," he said. "Like the pentagram inside the circle, for which it is named, may it bring abundance and blessings and protection."

"Blessed be," Maya and Sylvia answered.

The next day Maya, grateful at last for the typing practice she'd gotten in all the office jobs she'd hated, sat down to type the finished manuscript. After a week of solid work, she finished. When she handed the original to Sylvia along with the copies she had made at the shop down the street, they both sensed the ending of something. Mid-April, Maya reminded herself, was still winter in the high mountains. But there were other mountains and coastlines and blooming deserts. New York had begun to feel like a cage.

"You didn't put your name on it," Sylvia said, looking at the title page.

"I can't use my real name, and I don't want to put an alias on it," Maya said. "It wouldn't be good magic."

"It's not fair, though," Sylvia said. "You should get credit for your work."

"It's your work," Maya said. "Your ideas, your knowledge, your exercises."

"But your language and your images add so much to it. Really, Maya, it's beautifully written. And I don't feel honest passing off your work as my own. Why don't you use a pen name? That's a fine old tradition."

Maya shook her head. "I have too many names already. I can hardly keep track of them as it is. In a funny way, it feels right to be a ghost writer. That's a fine old tradition, too."

Sylvia said she'd have one of Eric's lawyer friends draw up a simple contract, assuring Maya a percentage of any profits from the book.

"Of course if you disappear, it'll be hard to collect," Sylvia warned.

"I don't want to disappear. But I've got to get out of New York. And I won't be back next winter. My father'll be back here again, at Columbia, and that's a little too close for comfort. They might be watching him. I'm safer if he doesn't run into me, or know where I am."

"You'll have to write to us, then. Stay in touch."

"I will."

"And you'll have to return between Yule and New Year's, so we can initiate you. I'd do it now, but really one is supposed to wait at least a year and a day from when you begin to study. How convenient that you started on a memorable day like Christmas."

"Sylvia, you're too good to me." Maya took the older woman's hand.

"I'm even better than you realize, because I'm also going to give you some traveling money," she said, reaching into her pocket and slipping an envelope into Maya's hand. "Consider it an advance. Anyway, I don't want to think of you hitchhiking around alone. Take a Greyhound."

"Okay, Sylvia, it's a deal."

37

Letter

March 1, 1988

Dear Maya,

If you've read this far, you'll be almost to the end of the journal selections I picked out for you. Actually, rereading them myself has been quite an experience. We have a history together, girlfriend. To me, that's worth something. I hope it is to you.

Don't get me wrong. I'm not trying to beg you or pressure you. I'm just laying my cards on the table. I don't want to lose what we have. Even if it's not perfect, it's rich.

Oh, Maya, I don't want to communicate like this, putting down words on the page because we've lost the ability to be together. I'd rather lie next to you and murmur my memories into the nape of your neck—but we don't seem to be doing much of that these days. Anyway, I'm not ready to share with you much of the recent years of my journal. But I've enclosed some odds and ends you might find interesting—some of your letters to me.

Don't worry if you lose them. They're all copies. Just in case somebody wants to publish your collected correspondence someday, I'm keeping the originals.

When you get back, we'll talk.

Love,
Johanna

38

Letter

Jan. 15, 1973
St. Martin, Uruapan
Michoacán, Mexico

Dear Johanna,

It was good to hear from you and get the pictures. Rachel is certainly getting big! And it's so wonderful to be able to write regularly.

Mexico has been a real refuge for me, even though I haven't succeeded in what I came here to do, which was to find a traditional healer to work with. But maybe I've learned something, after all.

The problem wasn't in finding the person I wanted to learn from. No, *curanderas* are thick on the ground here, but when I met Doña Elena, I knew she was the one. Some friends I made at the hostel in Mexico City turned me on to her—we all came down here to get a reading and as soon as she looked at me she told me that I had too many names and too many selves and that I carried a black weight of sorrow on my back. (My Spanish has gotten to be quite fluent—Mrs. Martinez back at Harding High would be proud!) Anyway, she sent us all off to the market in Uruapan to buy white flowers and candles and cornmeal and salt, and when we got back she performed a *limpieza,* a cleansing, on me, basically a kind of auric bath with all of the above and lots of scented oils that come in spray cans, named things like Seven African Powers, Change Your Luck, Love Come to Me. Although really what I most need is probably Law Away. Maybe I should keep some of that around—wouldn't it be handy? The police come knocking at your door in the middle of the night, and you just give them a few squirts—kind of like Raid for cops—and zip, they're gone.

Anyway, there I was in her altar room, which is just a square, windowless house of cement blocks with a tin roof and dirt floor, looking at her altar, a carved wooden Virgin in a glass box with a gold frame surrounded by plastic roses, buckets of fresh and fading flowers, blinking Christmas lights, the top covered with a terry cloth towel. She was stroking my back with the white flowers and murmuring incantations and suddenly I knew that I wanted to stay there, in that crowded courtyard of block houses with the pigs and chickens rooting underfoot, and be her apprentice.

When we were all done, I asked her. She gave me a long, hard look, picked up my hands and stared at my palms, and then shook her head.

"Your power is not in your hands," she said.

"But I can learn!" I protested. "I won't be a burden to you. I'm willing to sleep on the floor, and help with all the work. I can scrub and clean and I don't even mind cleaning up after the pigs."

Again, she shook her head. "It would be of no use. I can teach you to gather the herbs, to prepare the teas and the oils, but they will not work. You are not a healer."

I wanted to protest, to stay and argue with her, but I sensed that wouldn't be the way. But I also couldn't give up. So I found a place to stay, not in her village but in the town about five miles up the road. It's not exactly a place with a lot of tourist accommodations—just a dirty, dusty, ugly little town of cement block buildings in a dry landscape. There is a cheap hotel of sorts that caters to local travelers, so for two bucks a night I rented a dark, cell-like room with a lumpy bed and an indescribably filthy toilet, more like a hole in the floor, across the court- yard. It's a bit like paying to be in jail, except that I can walk out, which is a big difference. A big difference. I think a lot about our friend, and where he must be. And it makes me sad, Johanna. All the *limpiezas* in the world can't take that sorrow away.

Anyway, for a week I've stayed here and eaten from stalls in the market (and yes, that means I'm visiting that awful toilet a lot, but such is life in the Third World), and then walking the five miles down the road to see Doña Elena. I've had four card readings and three *limpiezas* and watched her perform many healings—because this is how it works here. The healer has no private waiting room, and you don't generally come to see her alone, but with most of your family along for moral support. Your mother, your daughter, a couple of cousins, whatever. And then you sit and wait while she deals with whoever is there before you—and who- ever comes after gets to hear all your most intimate problems. You could say that I've learned a lot just by observing how people band together and support each other. Of course, they also drive each other nuts, hire *brujas* to put curses on each other, fight. But there's no shame in having a problem—no slinking around to go secretly visit your shrink on your lunch hour, no need to pretend. Because everyone has problems here. Everyone is poor, everyone gets sick and the nearest health clinic is far away. Disasters are a part of daily life.

So I learn, just sitting in that dark room waiting my turn for a reading, walking the dusty road afterward, learning how to time my arrival so that I'm not there first and have an excuse to wait. I've grown so familiar that the locals stop their pickup trucks now and give me a ride, just as they would for any of the villagers. Often I don't have to walk back to town, I travel in style, standing up in the back of the pickup, clutching the metal rail while the truck leaps and bucks up the dirt road, and the bundle of peppers an old woman is bringing to market whacks me in the face.

I had hoped my perseverence might impress Doña Elena, that she might relent and take me on. I would have been content just to keep coming and visiting her every day. But yesterday she wouldn't take my money, wouldn't read the cards or do anything for me.

"What do you want?" she snapped at me. "You have asked me to teach you and I have said no. Why do you keep coming back?"

"Perhaps you will change your mind?" I said.

"I will never change. You are not a healer and there is nothing for you here. Why do you not go home? Your mother is crying for you."

"I can't go home," I admitted. "I had some problems . . . because of a man I loved." While it is not uncommon to have problems with the law here, for a woman to be on the run is rather unheard of. But troubles with a man—that everyone can understand. The various members of three extended families all waiting to come after me nodded and sighed in empathy.

"But you cannot stay here. There is nothing here for you. This is not where you will gather power."

"Where should I go?"

"You must find what is yours. Not what is mine." She stopped then, for a minute, as if she were receiving some communication. "Follow your name," she said finally, "until you can go home."

So, I guess that's what I'll do. But which name? They call me Margarita, like the drink. Or Maggie? Is it time yet to say I ain't gonna work on Maggie's farm no more? Margaret? Karla? Maya?

Maya, probably. Since, anyway, I'm due for a trip to the Yucatán. Sylvia's book has made a bit of money and she and Eric are going to take a vacation. I'll meet them for a few days so that she can finally do my initiation ritual. I'm long overdue, she says, but as you know I've never felt safe about going back to New York, now that my dad is back there.

And, sorry as I am to leave the *curandera,* I will not be sorry at all to leave the little hotel and the awful toilet. Although I'm sure it won't be the last of those I'll encounter. In fact, I won't mind at all joining Sylvia and Eric for a few days of tourist luxury. They've reserved a room at their hotel for me, right on the beach.

I hope graduate school is not too taxing. Are you still glad you decided to stay at Cal? That world seems so far away from me now. Most likely you and my mother were right, I should have gone back to school long ago. But now I probably never will. Still, I'm getting an education of another sort. You can tell Betty that for me, if you write to her. I don't feel safe writing her myself. If they're still on the lookout for contacts of the Front, watching her mail would be such an obvious thing to do. But I hope she's not really crying for me. Tell her she doesn't need to. I'm fine, really. Just fine.

Sometimes I would give anything just to have you here, to sit down and have a long, long talk about psychology, and magic, and who we are, and what we're doing here in the world. Someday it'll happen. I'll be able to come back home, or maybe you'll come here. How is Rachel adjusting to kindergarten this semester? Are the fruit trees in blossom yet?

I pulled a card for us. It came up Strength, the woman holding the jaws of the lion. She's wreathed in roses: they form a figure eight, the sign of infinity. Karma.

You haven't lost me yet. One of these days, like an old bone you thought you'd buried, I'll turn up.

Love,
Maya

39

Letter

May 4, 1973
Santiago Atitlán
Guatemala

Dear Johanna,

I'm sorry I haven't written in a while. I've been on the move. I'm in Guatemala, now, up here in the highlands to escape the heat. This town is perched on the edge of what must be the most beautiful lake in the world, an old volcanic crater filled with blue, blue water, and cone-like peaks rising at its edge. The people here still wear their traditional dress. The women wear beautifully embroidered shirts called huipils, and each town has a different traditional design and colors. The men wear bright embroidered trousers and cowboy hats. Out on the lake, you can see the fishermen standing in their little wooden boats, hauling in their nets while the waves rise and fall so that the boat disappears in the troughs and the men appear to be walking on water.

I had a great time with Sylvia and Eric. We rented a car in Merida and Eric drove us over some pretty awful dirt roads to tour the Mayan sites in the Yucatán—Chichén Itzá and Tulum. I enclose postcards. We stayed in a small, simple hotel (but with good plumbing and a clean bathroom!) on the beach just north of Tulum. It's still quite wild there, and not very developed, so at night we had the whole long beach to ourselves. The air was warm, the moon was full, and the ceremony was powerful. I wish I could write you details, but I'm not supposed to talk about it. All I can say is that it felt like a confirmation as much as an initiation—or a bit like the scene in the *Wizard of Oz* when the Wizard tells the Cowardly Lion the only difference between him and a hero is that a hero has a medal. Now I've received my testimonial, I can see that I've had many initiations since our moment on the locker room floor.

Sylvia is getting older, and it's hard for her to walk very far. Still, she has amazing energy. We were up and on the go almost every minute of the day—swimming or touring or pursuing leads to the local *curanderas.* The manager of the hotel we stayed in gave us directions to a woman named Doña Isabel, a tiny old crone who lives in a small house in the jungle. Sylvia was just thrilled to go and have a reading from her, and with me translating, managed to talk shop with her, Witch to Witch.

Here's what Doña Isabel taught us:

There are two worlds, she says, or maybe it would be more accurate to call them two realities, the Good Reality and the Bad Reality, *El Mundo Bueno y El Mundo Malo.* If we're lucky, we live on the Good Reality like walking on the thin skin over boiled milk. It's always possible to break through and drown.

In the Good Reality, the rains come when they are due, the police do not notice you as you walk by, the speeding car passes before your face, missing you. But in the Bad Reality, drought kills the crops and the cattle, the police pick you out of the crowd to check your papers, the car smashes into you head-on.

To take a risk, especially a big risk, is like shouting at *El Mundo Malo,* "Come and get me, sucker!" It is like sticking out your tongue and making a face at God.

And yet it is necessary to take risks in order to live.

To be a Witch, a *bruja,* Doña Isabel says, is to have the power to shift from one reality to another, to grab hold of the ice (shifting metaphors on you here) and hoist oneself out of the freezing water, or (let's be honest here) to know how to push someone else through the crust (that sort of magic being, however, karmically inadvisable). She herself is not a *bruja* but a *curandera,* a healer.

"You are not a healer," she told me, confirming Doña Elena's diagnosis. "But it is just possible that this may be your talent—to move between worlds, to change one for the other."

"How do you do it?" I asked.

"I am not a *bruja.* How can I tell you? I know only this, that there are two things you need. It is necessary to acquire power. And it is necessary to refuse the Bad Reality, to refuse to accept your fate."

"But isn't that madness—to refuse to accept reality?"

"Madness is the sorcery of the powerless. It does no good to refuse reality unless you can change it. But it also does no good to acquire power if you fear to challenge *El Mundo Malo.*"

I'm still thinking about this. It seems to me I have been challenging the Bad Reality all my life, with varying degrees of success.

"If reality can be changed," I said, "why all around us are people living on dust?"

"Because they have no power. If they should refuse to accept this world, where would they gather the power to change it? Could all the *brujas* in the Yucatán, assuming they could put aside their differences and quarrels and work together, could they change this government? And if they could, is that going to change the dust to gold, or corn, or anything useful?''

"Maybe," I said, wondering how Marx would have liked her theory.

"I say this to you: Stay clear of those who live in *El Mundo Malo*. Especially the men. They have a great attraction for you, because they call to that part of you that is a changer. You want to save them. But you do not yet have power, and they will pull you down."

Well, Johanna, I couldn't argue with that.

Anyway, after Sylvia and Eric went home I made my way by bus and boat and thumb down to Guatemala, visiting as many of the Mayan sites as I could get to—and most of them are damn hard to get to! Tell Rachel I saw a real, live toucan in the jungle near Tikal, and heard the howler monkeys in the dawn. And now I'm here for a while, in this beautiful place, where the living is cheap and I have endless time to walk and swim and think and write in my journal.

And having said all that, I'll say one more thing. I want to come home! Oh, Jo, I miss you, I ache for you, and more than that, I'm tired of wandering and looking at the edges of other people's lives. I want to take root somewhere, to work hard at something, to wake up in the morning and know that the people I see that day are people I'll see the next day and the next, for weeks, months, years. Here I mostly hang out with other tourists, the young travelers who are seeing the world on almost no money, who know the hip places to go and sometimes the most interesting things to see. In a way, I'm doing just what they're doing. If I'd gone to school and graduated, I might have taken a year or two to do exactly this. But I didn't, and there's a big difference between them and me.

They can go home, and I can't.

I'm sorry—I don't mean to sound self-pitying here. Really I'm fine, still learning a lot, still having a great time.

But do keep checking with Tony for me. I'm sorry he doesn't think it's wise for me to come back yet. If that changes, let me know. You can write to me c/o American Express, Antigua. Mail is relatively reliable there—here, it's impossible.

Love to Rachel, Tony, Debby, and Betty, if you hear from them. And your mom, too. I miss them all. Tell Debby I'm real sorry I couldn't be at her graduation.

Love,
Maya

40

January 1976

She had bathed in the sacred pool of Palenque, walked the battlements of Tulum and the processional way of Chichén Itzá, seen dawn at Tikal and sunset over Lake Atitlán, spent days alone in the rain forests of Chiapas and nights awake on the beaches of the Yucatán. But it was at an ordinary bus stop in the middle of Mexico City that Maya had her vision, on an ordinary street whose sole grace was that as she lifted her eyes to the horizon on that extraordinarily clear day, she could see in the distance the outlines of the great volcanoes, Popocatépetl, the Prince of the Mountain, and Ixtacihuatl, La Mujer Dormida, the Woman Who Sleeps.

The street was full of fumes from passing traffic that stung her eyes. She closed them for a moment, and when she opened them, a woman was sitting beside her. She was small and brown, dressed in the colorful huipil of the Mayas and a woven skirt, with a striped shawl thrown over her shoulders. Maya smiled.

"Buenos días," she said.

"Buenos días," the woman replied. *"Adónde vas?"*

Maya was a little surprised to be asked where she was going. Usually people wanted to know where she was from. But she answered politely, in Spanish, that she was going to the American Express office to look for mail.

"No," the woman said to her, "that is not what I desire to know. I want to know, where are you going?"

Startled, Maya looked at her more closely. She was round bodied, neither old nor young, her clear brown eyes in her oval face looking slightly amused. Now Maya noticed that the shawl was wrapped and tied to carry something on her back. She seemed solid, real, not a vision or an apparition but a woman like Maya who could pay money to a driver and take up space in a seat on a bus.

"Adónde vas?" the woman asked again.

Maya considered for a long, hard moment. "I don't know," she admitted. "Something is complete for me here, but I don't know what comes next."

"How can you travel when you don't know your destination?"

"I don't know. I just do."

"What do you follow?"

"Something. A scent on the wind. A hint that one way or another is right."

The woman turned and gestured toward the horizon. "Look," she said. "Do you see La Mujer Dormida?"

"Yes."

"In your country, also, she sleeps, sí?"

"Sí," Maya said. "Where I come from, there is a mountain that the Indians called Tamalpais, which means in their language the 'Sleeping Lady.' "

"It's the same. She has been sleeping for a long, long time. But now you must return to that land. Because she is going to awaken. She is going to give birth."

They were speaking in Spanish and to say "give birth" the woman used the phrase *dar a luz,* literally "give to light." Maya looked at the mountain and suddenly it seemed to move, pulsing like a living belly filled with a great hot living light, not cool and white but red like womb blood and life and the full moon on the horizon.

"You must go home," the woman said. "Your work is there, now. Your work is to be a midwife of what is to come."

"How do I do that?"

"Let the skills you have learned as the Seer and the power you have gathered teach you how to become the Singer."

"What do you mean?" Maya asked, feeling a cold ripple up her spine, because the woman had used her own private names for powers, names she had never told anyone, not even Sylvia.

"You have come here, like the others from your land, looking, looking, looking. That is good, that is where power begins. But looking cannot go on forever. It must change; it must develop into giving or it will become merely taking."

Maya nodded, but she felt a strange sense of vertigo. Had she fallen into another reality, like the *curandera* used to talk about? Or was this woman simply crazy, some paranoid Mexican nationalist accosting tourists on the street?

"Go home," the woman said. "Go back where you came from. To become the Singer, you must sing power up from your own land."

"I am afraid to go back to my country," Maya admitted. "I had some trouble with the police."

"Don't be afraid. There is no danger to you from the police, now."

"How do you know?"

"I see what forces gather around you, and what pursues you. It is time for you to return."

"But how do I become the Singer? What does that mean?"

"It is easy," she said. *"Cuenta el cuento. Canta la canción."*

Tell the story. Sing the song. "But what story?" Maya asked. "What song?"

"Here," the woman said, "I will give you something to help you. But if you take it, you must carry it. You cannot put it down."

She undid the knot that tied her shawl, and handed the bundle to Maya. Maya's arms enfolded something that felt alive, like a tiny baby or an animal, and her heart was flooded with love, as if she had been born to cherish this tiny thing that she could not as yet see. And yet it was also heavy in her arms, so that they ached with the weight of it.

"Here, I am going to help you. I am going to show you how to carry it," the woman said. "Carry it on your back, like this." And she showed Maya how to drape the shawl so that the burden hung between her shoulder blades, and how to tie it in a knot in front.

Just as the knot was tied, the bus arrived. Maya turned to thank the woman, but no one was there behind her. Without thinking, she found herself paying the fare, getting on the bus, taking a seat toward the back. She leaned gingerly against the seat so as not to crush the thing she carried behind her, but she met no resistance until her back itself touched the seat. She reached behind her, but her hand encountered nothing. She was wrapped in an empty, dusty shawl, and the weight settled into her own heart, and dropped down into her womb.

41

Johanna Weaver's Journal

February 11, 1976

It started off as one of those days. First, I had my little conference with Ms. Evans, after I was done counseling my last student for the day.

I was trying to be patient with her, trying to speak in a low, controlled voice. "I'm just saying that it's not the worst outcome for a healthy woman to give birth to a healthy child. Even if she's young. Even if she's young and poor. Even if she's young and poor and black." Don't show your emotion, girl, I said to myself. Keep that rage in your fingertips, okay to pick at the chipping polish on your nails, if you must, but keep it out of your voice, off your face.

"Even if there's no responsible father in the picture?" Ms. Evans said.

This is war, I told myself. You cannot be self-indulgent. Don't say anything that she can use against you. Don't sound like a man hater. "A good father is a wonderful thing. Nevertheless, single motherhood doesn't have to be viewed as among the world's great tragedies."

"Then you'd encourage them? That's not what we're here for, Miss Weaver." Ms. Evans's blue eyes were frosty behind her glasses. Her nails were perfect red shells. She patted a straying strand of her gray hair firmly back into its sprayed silver helmet, and favored me with a smile, a stretching of her thin lips.

She hates me. I hate her. But in war, you do what you have to do. Smile. Show some teeth. "No, I'm not talking about encouraging teenage pregnancy. I'm merely suggesting a few programs aimed at practical and emotional support to mediate the most detrimental aspects of the situation and ensure the best outcome for mother, child, and society." Take that, bitch. I went on. "Certainly our primary goal should be to prevent the situation from developing. But once a young woman gets pregnant, and makes the decision to keep the child, and bear in mind that we cannot, by law, counsel her to have an abortion, our goal should be to keep the girl in school and give her the knowledge, skills, and help she needs to raise a child who can realize its full potential."

"But your programs imply tacit support for unwed motherhood. Why, it would be like saying to these girls that we think they've made a rational, responsible choice."

"Well, Ms. Evans, I do believe we might get further with the girls if we treated them as adults who have made the choice that seems most reasonable to them, given their options and circumstances."

"But they're completely irresponsible! They're not making decisions, they're acting like—like animals!" She gave me the old reptile stare from her beady blue eyes.

"Then maybe it's up to us to teach them responsibility. The punitive approach isn't working, Ms. Evans. Let's stop ghettoizing them and humiliating them and see if we can't bring them a little further into society, instead of casting them out." That's the note, girl. Passion. Commitment. Do not call her a racist until she says something really stupid in front of witnesses.

Ms. Evans looked down at her desk, moved a paper from the back of a pile to the front of a pile, and aligned the stack carefully. "Exactly what is it that you want to do?"

"I want to hold an assembly and talk to the students about the problem. I want to enlist their help, to form a mutual aid group for every single mother in the school. To help out with baby-sitting so she can study. To raise money for clothes and collect toys and help solve problems that arise. I want to offer special classes in child care and development . . . for all the students. Right here at the high school level, which is where they most need it."

Miss Evans looked alarmed. "There's no budget for that!"

"It won't require a budget. The child development I'll teach myself, as part of my regular hours. I'll put together a three-, four-day unit that I can teach in the homerooms. The child-rearing component will be taught by those who know it best—community people. Mothers and fathers and grannies and aunties. We'll get them involved in the school, and they'll be role models for the kids."

"Don't you think this'll just romanticize pregnancy for the girls? They'll get all this coddling and attention for it."

"That's why the practical component. Once the ones who aren't pregnant have changed a few diapers and sat out a few crying spells, I believe a lot of the romance will be gone. That's where we get our deterrent effect."

She shuffled her papers again. I almost felt sorry for her. She wanted so badly to have a good reason to say no. I wasn't giving her any.

"What do you want from me?"

"I want your support, as the principal of this school, Ms. Evans."
Show teeth. Wait a beat. Two. "I need to know that you're with me on
this."

"It means a lot of extra work. You'll have to do it."

"I want to do it." Wait a beat. "I need to do it. It'll work out well
for me, as research data for my doctoral thesis." Was that a mistake?
Admitting my self-interest?

"Aha." Ms. Evans smiled again, and this time I detected a glint of
something warmer than hatred, although perhaps calling it friendliness
would be an overstatement. "I understand."

You understand nothing, bitch. War. Show those teeth again. "If
this works, we might publish something on it. The school could come in
for some positive attention."

"Positive attention is never unwelcome," Ms. Evans said. "I suppose we might as well give this a try. But remember, no budget."

Us darkies jes' love to work for free, ma'am. Brings back memories
of those carefree slavery days. "Of course. I appreciate your backing, Ms.
Evans."

"We'll see."

The interview had kept me late and that meant I would barely
make it to Rachel's after-school care in time, so I would have to shop for
dinner with the child in tow, hungry and fretful. What should I make?
Maybe we should just stop off for Kentucky Fried Chicken. Not too
healthy, but hell. Or burritos. Weren't they the perfect meal? Combining
all four food groups—protein, starch, and if we added sour cream and
guacamole, we'd have dairy and green vegetable. And then I might have
time to read Rachel a story before I had to run off and teach my evening
class at San Francisco State.

With all my talk about the righteousness of single motherhood, I
had to admit that my own life had a relentless quality. There was never
enough time, money, rest. Oh, it was better now that Rachel was in
school and I was done with my own course work. It would get better,
yet. Better and better and better.

I was late arriving at the Happy Valley Child Care Center, and
Rachel with her new digital watch that Marian gave her for Christmas
knew exactly how late.

"I've been ready to go since five o'clock, and now it's five twenty-
two and thirty-eight seconds," she informed me. "Thirty-nine. Forty."

"I'm sorry, baby. I had to talk to the principal, and you know how
she is."

"Was she mean to you?"

"I talked her around. You got your lunch pail?"

"I told you, I've been ready for the last twenty-three minutes and
ten seconds."

"I've got Rachel. Thanks, Cindy," I shouted down the hall as we left.

Cut to the scene where the harried mother and fretful child arrive at their doorstep. I was trying to balance the burritos on one arm and my books on the other while inserting the key into the lock of our front door, and I could hear the phone ringing. The door swung open and one of the burritos slid out of its bag and splattered on the steps.

"Shit!" I must confess to exclaiming.

"That's a bad word, Mama," Rachel said, squeezing by me and dashing for the phone as I tried to gather up what I could of the food.

I clumped heavily up the stairs, breathing hard as I juggled parcels. Still haven't lost that weight, and it's been what? Almost eight years, now. Still keep saying I'm going to exercise, but when do I have the time, tell me? I dumped the parcels on the table, grabbed a rag, and headed back down the steps to clean up.

"It's Mrs. Samuels," Rachel yelled down the hall. "She says she can't baby-sit tonight. She's got the stomach flu."

"Double shit!"

"Mama!"

Not only relentless, I thought as I swiped at the mess of meat and sour cream on the steps. Out of control. Now I would have to take Rachel with me to class, which was hard on everyone, and unfair. What else can go wrong? I wondered. Really, it would be nice just to sit on this step and cry. Or sleep.

I closed my eyes for a moment.

When I opened them, she was standing before me, tanned, smiling, dressed in a highly colored, heavily embroidered poncho-thing and shifting a heavy bundle off her back.

"Maya?"

"I'm back. Glad to see me?"

I stood up, laughing, and flung my arms around her. "Girl! I can hardly believe it!"

"Can I stay with you?" she asked.

"No other option will be entertained!"

We stood for a moment, just looking at each other. Maya looked so thin, lithe and light and free. By comparison, I felt weighty, solid, burdened.

"You lookin' good," I told her. "Lean, mean, and tan."

"It's so good to see you," she said. I could hear the air between us hum and crackle and buzz.

I led her up the steps into the flat.

It'd been over four years since we'd seen each other. But I felt like she'd just walked out the door that morning. With us, it's always the same. Our friendship exists somewhere in some other dimension, outside of time.

I had her put her things in the small room in front that we used for guests, and called Rachel over to come and meet her auntie Maya. I could see Maya looking the child over, Rachel's two neat braids hanging down her back, her plaid skirt, her red sweater for once still relatively clean, and Rio's own smile flashing out from her sweet milk-chocolate skin. Aside from her coloring, the girl doesn't look much like me. A judgment, I suppose, but an improvement nevertheless.

"Hello," Rachel said politely, looking like the model child. I beamed proudly.

"Hello," Maya said. "Last time I saw you, you were just a baby. How old are you now? Seven? Eight?"

"Six and a half."

"Four years, then." Maya shook her head. "It's hard to believe I've been gone so long. I'm sure you don't remember me, from before. But I remember you. In fact, I believe I owe you a story."

"I like stories." Rachel smiled, and I knew they were going to be friends, which was good. Sometimes Rachel just takes against somebody for no reason I can see, and then there's hell to pay.

Meanwhile, the clock was still ticking and class would soon be starting and none of us were fed.

"You must be hungry," I said. "What do I have that I can fix you quick? Damn, I wish I didn't have to teach tonight! I can't bear to run off and leave you. You eat eggs? Rachel, girl, you eat that good burrito. We've got to leave in fifteen minutes." I was babbling along nervously because I hated like hell to run out on Maya five minutes after she'd arrived, and because I was halfway afraid she'd disappear again if I left her alone. "It's one of those days—the baby-sitter canceled, I dropped the dinner on the steps . . ."

"You sit down," Maya said. "Relax. I'm not a guest, remember? I'm your old partner in crime. And I'm not going anywhere for a long while."

"Is that a promise?" I asked her seriously.

"It's a warning. I'm sick of traveling. I'm sick of running away and hiding. I want to settle down and settle in and become who I am again. Why don't you eat the burrito and let me cook something for Rachel and me while you teach? And then when you're back, we can have a good, long talk."

"I can't take advantage of you like that," I said, but it was mere formality, something Marian would have wanted me to say. I knew that I could and would. And also, if she was watching Rachel, she wouldn't run off somewhere before I came home. I mean, Maya might be flighty, but she'd never leave a six-year-old on her own.

"Why not?" Maya asked. "I intend to take advantage of you. Besides, I'll love it."

"All right. You win."

Then I dashed for the door, ate the burrito in the car—which meant that my coat took on a glaze of bean juice and avocado—and made it to class only five minutes late. And now they're all in small groups processing their reactions to last week's reading, while I catch up on this journal.

Whoops—their fifteen minutes are up. Got to go.

Johanna

42

February 1976

"Let me tell you the story," Maya said, "about the woman who became a mountain." She had fed Rachel, supervised her homework, watched the girl's favorite TV program with her, all the while feeling split, both strange and normal. Here was this child who was a stranger, and yet Maya felt that she had known her all her life, that they were linked on a cellular level as if she had indeed been part of the child's conception. In Rachel's wide-set eyes she saw Rio's lost innocence, and in her clear, milk-chocolate skin, Johanna's girlhood, and in her cleverness she heard something of her own voice.

"The woman lived a long, long time ago, in a land where women were powerful and free. Men too, for that matter. And the people worshiped their Mother the Earth, and the Rain God, and the Snake."

"I like snakes," Rachel said. "They're my favorite of the reptiles, except for dinosaurs, but they're extinct."

"Me too. They're very magical animals. Do you know why?"

"Because they have no legs?"

"Yes, and they shed their skins. So they seem to be dead, but they come alive again. So they represent rebirth."

"Like recarnation?" Rachel asked.

"Reincarnation. Right. You know a lot of big words for someone only six years old."

"I'm smart," Rachel said. "And Mama explains things to me."

"I'm sure she does," Maya said, longing to squeeze the child and hold her close. She restrained herself. She doesn't know me well, yet, Maya thought. I'd better go slow.

"I told Mama that when you die, you come back as another person. That's what I believe. And she said it was called recarnation. Is that what you believe?"

"More or less." It was strange to be speaking English, sometimes she had to stop for a moment to find the words she wanted.

"Do you think you could come back as an animal?"

"I don't see why not. The Hindus believe you can."

"What about a really big animal? Like an elephant, or a whale? Does that take more than one person to make it?"

"That's a beautiful thought," Maya said. "Maybe if you love a lot of people when you're alive, you all come back together as a whale."

"Or a mountain," Rachel said. "Or something really big, anyway. Go on with the story, please."

"This woman, in our story, was the daughter of Earth Mother and Rain God, and she was the leader of the people. She could run faster than anybody, and sing beautiful songs, and weave headdresses of feathers. Whenever people were unhappy, she had good advice for them. And everyone lived well.

"Until the day War God was born. He leaped up fully grown and armed from Earth Mother's belly, after she'd accidentally swallowed some feathers. All the people thought he was so handsome, tall and strong and his spear was so shiny. He dazzled them. They followed him off to war and learned to kill other people and take their things, and Earth Mother's Daughter was very sad.

"She tried to talk to the people, and warn them, but they laughed at her and then they got mad at her. 'Kill her! Kill her!' War God cried. And she ran away.

"She ran and she ran and she ran, until she couldn't run any farther. She was helped by Rain God's son, Cloud, who was also unhappy with the new ways. He was a gentle soul, and he didn't like to rumble and thunder and drop spears of lightning on people. He always said it gave him indigestion. No, he liked to rain a soft, gentle rain that soaked into the earth and fed the plants and the trees.

"So he ran away with Earth Mother's Daughter. Finally, darkness fell. They were so tired, they lay down on the ground. Cloud wept and his tears soaked the earth and woke the spirit of Earth Mother herself. She listened to their sad tale, and finally she spoke.

" 'This is a bad time,' Earth Mother said. 'The people have gone on a bad road. But until they come to the end of it, they won't believe you when you tell them it leads nowhere good. They'll only kill you, too. You must wait for them to reach the end of this road. You must wait for a change of heart.'

" 'How shall we wait?' Earth Mother's Daughter asked. 'They are hunting for us, and they'll kill us.'

" 'Come into me,' said Earth Mother. 'I'll hide you and protect you, until the time comes when the people have a change of heart.'

"And so they slept in the arms of Earth Mother, and when morning came, the woman had become a mountain, with her friend Cloud draped about her head. And so she waits until the people have a change of heart."

"That's a weird story," Rachel said. "But I like it."

"Me too."

"Will you tell me another story tomorrow?"

"Of course. I'll tell you a story every day, as long as I stay here."

"How long will you stay here?" Rachel asked, her eyes beginning to close in sleep.

"Until I do what I've come to do."

"What's that?"

"To waken Earth Mother's Daughter," Maya said.

"So what are your plans?" Johanna asked. They were on their second glass of wine, sitting at the small table crowded into a corner of the kitchen.

Maya looked at Johanna, drinking her in. It was hard to believe she was home at last, that she could stay there and see Johanna every day, and get to know Rachel, and not be packing up and moving on in the morning.

"Don't laugh," Maya said, "but I want to write. I guess Sylvia gave me a taste for it."

"How's her book doing?"

"Not bad. Quite well, actually, in a small way. She makes three or four thousand a year from it, and insists on giving me half. So I've got a bit of money saved up . . . I didn't spend much in Mexico."

"That's great!" When Johanna smiled, her eyes crinkled up and there were the faintest lines around the edges. She was a bit rounder than she'd been four years ago—or maybe not. It was hard to remember—that time together had been so brief. When Maya pictured her in her mind, she saw the Johanna of their high school days. But this Johanna was mature, sophisticated in her red suit with her hair in a neatly trimmed Afro.

"I want to write about what I learned on the mountain, maybe. And in Mexico. I don't know. I have to recover from culture shock first."

"And you're not worried about the legal stuff? From Rio?"

"The *bruja*—that means Witch, or maybe sorceress—she told me not to worry. So, I won't worry."

"I haven't talked to Tony Klein in a long time," Johanna said. "He's become a hotshot radical lawyer, in Berkeley. Give him a call tomorrow. He'll know what you need to do."

"Good old Tony Klein."

"Joyce Levine is a psychotherapist in Boston."

Maya smiled. "I guess you've all done well, all the old crowd. Except for me. And Rio."

"You're not done yet," Johanna said.

"And Rio?"

Johanna was silent for a moment. Then she looked up at Maya. "Are you in contact with him?"

"No. I don't even know what prison he's in. I suppose I could find out."

"Are you going to?"

"I don't think so. I guess I still feel that making contact with him might be pushing my luck. Anyway, it all seems long ago and far away." Was that true? Maya asked herself. Or was she still trying to push it away? "There's not much left of that love but the consequences."

From the relief in Johanna's face, Maya could tell she'd given the right answer.

"Does Rachel know?" Maya asked. "About her father?"

Johanna shook her head. "I didn't see any reason to tell her. She thinks her daddy died in the Vietnam War."

"Well, in a way that's true," Maya said. "Still, do you think it's wise, to raise her on a lie? Won't she resent it when she finds out?"

"You gonna tell her?" Johanna asked.

Maya took a long sip of wine, feeling Johanna's tension rise as she waited for an answer. "Not unless you want me to."

"I'll tell her, someday, when she's old enough to understand." Johanna's voice was higher in tone, slightly defensive. "Now it would only burden her."

"Does it make you wonder, about your own dad?" Maya asked. "How do you know he really died in Korea?"

"I got money from the Veterans Administration to go to school. My mama had scrapbooks of pictures of him. Wedding pictures. Barbecue-with-the-family pictures," Johanna snapped, and then fell silent. Her eyes traveled around the walls of the kitchen, as if searching for nonexistent evidence. "Oh. Okay. I see what you're driving at."

"She's a very smart kid, you know. I wouldn't wait forever."

Johanna stared thoughtfully into the bowl of her wineglass. "When she gets her blood, I'll tell her then. You gonna stick around that long?"

"I don't know. I think that I'd like to," Maya said hesitantly. The thought of staying anywhere for more than a few weeks was both appealing and frightening. "I hope to. If you want me to."

"I do. I need somebody, Maya. It's getting hard, going it all alone."

"I know." Maya slid her hand across the table, to rest on Johanna's fingers where they curled around the stem of her glass. The fingers were delicate and smooth, and as their hands touched, Maya's whole body became one beating heart.

"Yes," Maya said.

"Yes, what?"

"You know what."

"I know," Johanna said slowly. "But . . ."

"But what?" Maya asked, drawing her hand away.

"Think of our track record," Johanna said with a small, forced smile. "Every time we do, some catastrophe follows. Cops, gym teachers, suicides, more cops."

"Maybe we can break the pattern." Maya smiled. Then her eyes grew serious. "Or maybe you don't want to. That's okay. We'll still be friends."

"We'll always be friends," Johanna said. "We'll always be lovers, in the deepest sense of the word. And it scares the hell out of me."

"Why?"

"We've made love exactly three times," Johanna said, reaching out and taking Maya's hand again. A warm glow moved up through Maya's fingers, through her arm, down into the core of her body where it kindled fire. "And each time brought me a great gift bought at a high, high price. The first time blew the world apart for us both and taught me what I had to be."

"What is that?"

"The phrase I use for it is heart warrior. Warrior of the heart."

"I like that," Maya said, clasping her free hand over Johanna's, so that she could cradle warmth between her palms. "It fits you. It sounds good in Spanish, too. *Guerrilla del corazón.* And the second time?"

"The second time brought me Rachel."

Maya pressed Johanna's hand between hers. "And the third?"

"The third time, I found you and lost you at the same moment."

"I'm not going away this time," Maya promised.

Johanna looked down at the table.

"Are you afraid of that?" Maya asked.

"Maybe," Johanna admitted. "I'm a mom, and a teacher, and a graduate student. I've got a dissertation to write. I'm not sure I can handle having my world blown apart on a daily basis."

"If we do it daily," Maya said, "or even, say, biweekly, maybe we'll get used to it. It won't be such a life-shattering experience."

"And what if it's meant to be?" Johanna asked. "What if it's meant to be rare and magical and out of the ordinary, not something dragged down by everybody's prejudices and politics and all the grind of everyday life? What if I don't want to proclaim myself a lesbian and join the Women's Center?"

"Is that what's bothering you?" Maya let Johanna go.

"To be absolutely honest, that's part of it."

"I see." Maya tipped her chair back and balanced against the wall. "You're a mom and a graduate student and a pillar of society. I guess it's easier for me. I'm just a hippie, a high school dropout, a revolutionary, and a fugitive—so why not a lesbian, too?"

"You're not black," Johanna said. "The black community doesn't take well to lesbians. And that's where my work is, Maya. It's not that I'm afraid of what people will say. It's do I have the right to indulge my desires if that will destroy my usefulness?"

Maya set her chair down firmly on its four legs, and leaned forward. "You forget I've heard those arguments before. That's what we said, over and over again, in the Front. Do we have a right to a personal life in times of war? Poor dead Edith, and Daniel—he always felt doomed. I never knew how to argue with them, but something always felt wrong to me. What use can we possibly be if we don't live out fully who we are? What kind of world can half people make?"

"I don't want to define myself," Johanna said. "I do like men, you know. I find them attractive."

"We both do," Maya said. "Sometimes even the same one."

"Are you mad about that?"

"No."

They sat together in a long silence.

Johanna reached out and again took Maya's hand. "So what are we left with?" she asked.

"A powerful love for each other," Maya whispered. "One that we can't confine or define or fit into any categories . . . because we found it when we went looking to break all the boundaries down."

"I'm scared," Johanna said softly, "but I am a heart warrior. I won't let fear stop me."

"No?"

"What do you want?"

Maya clung to Johanna's hand, soaking in her electric touch. "Our first time was fire, our second, in that rainstorm, water. The third was earth and this time . . ."

"What would this time be?" Johanna murmured.

"I want this time to be like birds caressing each other with delicate wings, like eagles mating in freefall, clenched in each other's talons, turning spirals as they drop to earth."

❀

___

43

Khunde to Thami

Travel west along the traditional trade route to
Tibet. At the end of the day, we reach the
monastery of Thami, one of the oldest in the
region, seeming to grow out of the rocks of the
mountain. A gentle, constant upgrade,
with the last hour rather steep.

—*MOUNTAIN CO-OP ADVENTURES*
BROCHURE

Maya awoke to the low growl of Tibetan horns. At first they sounded like
a motor warming up or an errant small plane, but it was still too dark for
any plane to venture into these mountains. Tashi, who brought her tea,
grinned at her when she asked what the sound was.

"A ceremony," he said. "Someone has died in the village, probably."

She listened to the low, low harmonies as she drank her morning
tea. The horns seemed to be played in pairs, one rising for a moment,
producing a sound more recognizable as music, a call or a warning to evil
spirits, "Depart! Depart!" Then it dropped back to join its brother in the
deep realms of the abyss, humming a low, resonant growl, as if the earth
herself were trying to sing.

And she is, Maya thought. This is how the earth gives herself a
voice here, growing the horns and the trumpet bones and the lips to play
them, feeding them from herself so that every atom and molecule of their
bodies is of her grass, her barley, her potato fields.

Suddenly, leaning up against the wall of the tent, her lower body
lying on the earth, she had a deep intimation of what it would be like to
really belong here in these mountains, to eat nothing that wasn't grown
in these fields or grazed on these meadows, sanctified by prayer and

sweat. She saw the stone walls raising themselves to shelter the small plots of land and the stone houses growing up to shelter the people, the *gompas* erecting their tiered roofs and painting their mandalas and hanging their tankas and prayer flags, not as things done by the people upon the earth or to the earth, but as the earth's own form of self-expression, so that the food and the shelter and the chanting and the prayers of the people were all one seamless fabric of relationship. Or were, once. Now the seams, perhaps, were fraying a bit. And here I am, she thought, a foreign logo trying to embroider itself into the brocade, without truly understanding it. Sipping this tea, which I didn't make for myself, or grow. Which was grown on land with which I have no relationship.

In fact, almost everything I've ever eaten in my life, aside from the few herbs and lettuces we grow in the backyard, comes from land I have no relationship with. That seems obscene, somehow. Like constantly having sex without any personal involvement. Worse, even. Food is a much more intimate penetration.

Maya set down her empty cup. Maybe that's why so many of us have cancer, she thought. It's not the additives, it's the disconnection they represent. But what do we do about it? We can't all go back and become farmers.

The high horns began chasing each other up and down a scale of minor, dissonant notes. Where do I belong? she wondered. With Johanna? We've always felt we belonged together. That's why we've stayed together for twelve years, never quite losing the magic although, as she feared, certainly the everyday wore us down. But we stuck it out, through my rise from penniless outlaw to published author, through our experiments in nonmonogamy, through all our arguments, in good times and bad. We've been together so long we are each partly the expression of the other, as these horns are the expression of the rising and falling of these trails.

But now Maya was feeling the gaps, the disconnections. All those years of exile, she thought. I blamed Rio, and so I colluded with Johanna to exile him, never contacting him even when it would have been safe, because of her secret. Oh, I warned her, I advised her to be honest with Rachel, but I kept silent.

At Rachel's first blood ceremony, they'd sat her in the center of a candlelit circle of seven women dressed in red. They bathed her in spring water laced with waters collected for a year by all their traveling friends, from Brigid's holy well in Ireland and the Niger River and the Nile. They clothed the girl in a red cape Maya had made for her, and placed red roses in her hand.

"Now you are a woman," they told her, as she sat in the center of their sacred circle. "Ask us anything you like about being a woman, and we will try to answer you honestly."

"Tell me about my father," she said to Johanna. Johanna reluctantly told her that her father had tried to stop the Vietnam war by using violent means, that he had bombed the Bank of America building, and accidentally killed a woman. Rachel's eyes were big in the dark room, and Maya could see the candle flames reflected in their depths. Then Johanna had lied. She told Rachel that her father was dead.

What could I have done? Maya wondered. Should I have risen up in the sacred circle and accused her of lying? Should I have told Rachel myself, later?

They had fought, of course, behind the closed door of the bedroom after all the women had gone and Rachel was asleep.

"You're afraid of a rival," Maya had accused Johanna. "You're trying to hoard her love."

"I'm trying to protect her," Johanna said. "All right, it isn't true that he's dead, but in another sense it is. The Rio we knew is dead."

"That's sophistry!"

"Look, Maya." Johanna took Maya's hands. They were standing in the dark next to the bed, and Maya could barely see Jo's face. "You've told me about what Rio was like, those last few years when you lived with him. You said yourself that he was an alcoholic, that he was crazy drunk and out of control. Every day, I work with dozens of young girls who have been raped and tortured with incest and abused by their drunken fathers and uncles and stepfathers. If she knows he's alive, she'll want to contact him. How can I risk it?"

"He's in prison," Maya said. "He can scarcely molest her from there."

"All the more reason to protect her," Johanna insisted. "Do you really think a dozen years in prison has improved his character?"

Maya was silent. Her hands felt limp in Johanna's grasp.

"Look at us," Johanna went on, squeezing Maya's hands tighter. "My father was dead, and I had a great relationship with him. I talked to him at night when I said my prayers, I always felt his love and support. Maybe they were imaginary, but that didn't matter. Your father was alive, and he was a constant source of disappointment to you."

"But that was real," Maya said, pulling away and sitting down on the bed. "Better a real disappointment than an unreal fantasy."

"I don't agree," Johanna said. "A positive fantasy is a hell of a lot better than an abusive reality. Haven't you read the studies about how many creative women grew up without fathers?"

"I haven't read any studies, about anything," Maya said. "You know that. I just say that you shouldn't have lied. We were in sacred space, inside the circle, and you should have told her the truth."

I could have fought her then, Maya thought. I could have left her. I could leave her now, uproot myself from my ground, smash the mirror and open up a wide, wide space that anything might fill. I could be free.

The thought made her cold. She opened the door of her tent and looked out on a field frosted with snow.

Snow teased the trekking group all morning, falling in swirls and eddies and then retreating as they walked over open boulder-strewn land, wide vistas that reminded Maya of the open meadows of the Sierras, red-brown earth and scrub bushes and high peaks under the lowering clouds. The trail descended into a fir-lined canyon where they could see down the blue horizon of trails and mountains unfolding and beckoning—the "highway," the ancient trade route, to Tibet. Maya's long johns and down vest couldn't keep the cold wind from sneaking through every layer of protection she could devise. But at least the trail was mostly downhill or level, and she could breathe in the fresh, pungent air. Maybe the penicillin was finally working.

After lunch, the weather got worse and the trail began to climb through a rugged blue gorge over the wide gravel bed of a fierce, small river. The sides of the canyon rose, bare and black and rocky as the clouds closed in, and the snow flurries turned to a steady wet sleet.

Finally the trail took a steep dip down to the river, crossed a bridge beside rock walls graced with paintings of Tara and Guru Rinpoche. Maya looked down to where the white-blue waters had carved and sculpted the gray rock into undulated forms and holes that looked like bones. Water had soaked through her hiking boots and her feet were cold stones. Across the river, the trail rose in sharp switchbacks up the side of the mountain.

I get it, Goddess, she said to the water, the rock, the rising canyon walls. This is a test. Yesterday I had the Big Revelation about acceptance, so today you want to find out has she really got it? Can she hold on to it when the going gets rough? You couldn't give me one day just to bask in it, oh no, not you.

Well hey, no problem. She turned and started back up the trail. Her cold feet ached, but that was just a sensation. If she didn't shrink from the cold, didn't pull away from it, didn't think ahead to a nice cup of tea inside a warm shelter—hah, that was a laugh; she doubted such a thing existed in all of Khumbu—if she just let herself be with the steepness of the trail and her cough, which had returned, and the icy sleet, which shut off all views of the mountain . . .

Give me a break, Sagarmatha, Chomolungma, whatever you want to call yourself. What you don't seem to understand is that I'm trying to do Acceptance 101 and this is like the midterm from the graduate seminar.

Still she climbed, feeding herself on shadowy silhouettes of trees or glimpses of the stream, which came closer and closer to the trail as the gorge opened out into sloping fields. They followed the low stone walls past a few houses, crossed the stream on stepping stones, and finally reached their camp, a field beside a teahouse standing alone under the shoulder of the mountain.

Tenzing was waiting for her as she passed through the small gap in the stone wall that opened into the field.

"Come inside and get warm," he said. "The kitchen boys will put up your tents."

"I have to find my sister," Maya told him.

"I think she will find you," he said, smiling, and she took him at his word and followed him into the *bhatti*.

To call the *bhatti* warm would have been a gross exaggeration, but it was slightly less cold than the outside air and considerably drier. Maya changed into her pile sweatpants and a dry wool sweater and socks. She was just settling down to warm her hands around a cup of hot tea, when the door opened. A woman walked in, dressed in traditional Sherpa garb, the headscarf, the long jumper, the striped aprons tied front and back. The Nikes on her feet looked incongruous. Her eyes scanned the room and for a long moment Maya didn't recognize her. Then their eyes met. They stared at each other for a moment, then rushed forward and hugged each other.

They hugged for a long moment, tightly, as if by pressing close enough, they could erase all the gaps that had ever separated them.

"Debby!" Maya said, pulling back at last. Debby's chestnut bangs fell straight to her forehead under her headscarf, and her big, round glasses gave her the same earnest, owlish look she'd had as a child. "I was beginning to think I'd hike all through Sherpaland without ever catching a glimpse of you."

Debby pulled back from Maya's embrace.

"Tell me about Mom," she said. Her voice dropped. "She's dead, isn't she?"

"You never did get my letter?"

Debby shook her head. "No. But I knew, when I got the message from the trekking company. You wouldn't be coming here if she were still alive."

Debby's voice was sad, but it carried an undertone of accusation. Maya stepped back.

"I couldn't put it in a cable," she said. "It was too abrupt. Mom dead, stop. That wasn't how I wanted you to find out. So I wrote. But you didn't get it?"

"I knew anyway."

"I'm sorry. But I didn't really want to just write you a letter. I wanted to be able to hold you, comfort you."

Debby shook her head. "Don't try to mother me now, Karla. Maya . . . whatever. It's too late for that. Just because Mom is dead doesn't mean that you inherit her place."

"I'm not trying to take her place," Maya said.

They stood for a moment in awkward silence with each other.

"Come and meet the rest of the group," Maya said finally. They joined the others around a large table where tea was being served. Tenzing, Ang, and the other Sherpas were old acquaintances of one of only two doctors within a day's walk of Namche, and Debby spoke to them in a mix of English and Sherpa with a friendly camaraderie. The Americans received her with warm curiosity.

"How long have you practiced up here?" Carolyn asked.

"Almost two years," Debby said.

"I'm interested in the mental health issues in these villages," Peter said. "Are there many psychoses?"

Debby smiled. "Up here, sanity and insanity are in a whole different context. The community takes care of most of the needs we take to psychotherapists. The lamas and the traditional healers take care of most of the rest."

"But you must see some true psychosis," Peter insisted. "It exists in every culture."

"When we do, it's seen in the old way, as possession by evil spirits. They mostly treat it with prayer and magic. And frankly, that seems to work as well as most western medicine in those cases." Debby changed the subject. "You were all up at Tengpoche when it burned, I hear. Tell me about it."

"It was terrible," Carolyn said. "I've never felt so helpless."

Peter launched into a long description of the night's events, Lonnie interrupted him, and the others chimed in. Maya sat and listened, growing impatient. She wanted her sister for herself.

Howard was sitting quietly, a little apart from the others. He caught Maya's eye and gave her a shy half smile. She tried to return it with a kindly, amicable nod, one that would convey a friendly but neutral regard. Really, she didn't want to hurt his feelings or blight his trip. She wanted him to have the wildest, safest, cleanest adventure he possibly could. His smile deepened in return. Quickly Maya looked away and interrupted the others.

"I was thinking," she said, "that we should all contribute some money and make a donation toward the rebuilding of the *gompa.*"

"Yes, we were thinking the same," Peter said. "That's a good idea."

They launched into a new discussion, and Maya interrupted again.

"You know, Debby and I have barely had a chance to talk. Do you mind if I take her away?"

Carolyn beamed. "Of course you want to talk," she said. Debby and Maya picked up their cups and plates of cookies, and migrated to a small table in the far corner.

Debby spoke to the Sherpani who ran the teahouse, and she brought them a fresh pot of tea and a pile of flat bread. The Sherpani went on and on for a while in her own language, evidently describing some symptom or problem, for Debby listened thoughtfully and now and then made a comment in a professional tone. Debby belongs here, Maya realized suddenly. She's not grown from these mountains any more than I am, the medicine she offers has no more connection with this land than imported canned fruit, but somehow she has come to take root here.

At last the woman disappeared back into her kitchen, and Maya and Debby could talk.

"You look great," Maya said, trying to strike a light note. Let us connect first, before we descend into the heavy company of death. "Lean and tan!" Oh, Goddess, listen to me. Why do women always have to begin this way, assuring each other we look good? A ritual of connection, like dogs politely lifting their tails for a sniff. "I didn't expect you'd be wearing the local dress."

"They make people feel more comfortable," Debby said. "The clothes, I mean. And you look lean and mean yourself."

"Now you're lying," Maya said. "No one can look slender in pile sweatpants." She turned her head aside and coughed for a moment, and Debby fixed a professional eye on her, worried.

"You don't sound so good, though. How long have you had that cough?"

"Since I caught cold on the airplane coming over here. It just doesn't get any better."

"No, it won't, up at this altitude. Nothing heals easily up here, especially not lungs. The air is so dry. But are you sure you don't have a touch of mountain sickness? That can be quite serious, you know."

"I know. But I don't have any other symptoms. And it seems to be getting slightly better. I don't know, at this point, I'm so used to it that if I stopped coughing I wouldn't know who I was."

Debby looked unconvinced. "You could probably use a good, long rest. You don't take care of yourself."

"You sound like Betty when you say that."

"Sometimes Betty was right." Debby's eyes began to cloud over with tears. Maya reached out a hand across the table. Yes, this was what she had wanted, to be with Debby, to comfort her, to connect. But Debby pushed Maya's hand away. "You should have let me know, Karla. You should have told me she was dying."

Maya sighed. So this was how it was going to be. As it always was, always had been, between her and Debby, between her and Betty. They would grope toward each other and miss and land blows instead of soft comforting touches.

"She was dying for a year and a half." Maya tried to keep her voice calm, neutral. I'm not making judgments, just stating facts. "You knew she had cancer. You never came home."

"Cancer can mean years. I was trying to come home. It just takes a while to arrange things here. I can't just go off and leave these people."

Maya sat, her lips closed, letting the steam from her teacup surround her face like a cloud, a veil.

"What is it?" Debby said. "Go ahead, spit it out. I can take it."

Is this really why I came? Maya asked herself. Not to comfort, but to confront? J'accuse, j'accuse, Debby. I was there for her at the end, and you weren't.

"Well?" Debby was waiting.

"In a year and a half, you could have found someone to relieve you. Of all people, the Sherpas would understand that you needed to go comfort your dying mother."

As soon as she'd said the words, Maya regretted them. Debby just looked at her, her gaze level behind the round lenses that reflected Maya's own face back at her. Looking at Debby was like looking into a mirror, the mirror that had always shown her what she could have been, should have been, what she could never live up to. The good sister. She was always the bad one. But the bad one had been with Betty at the end.

"This is my life," Debby said, finally. "I chose it. It's lived in out-of-the-way places, where I'm really needed. That's what I want. I don't want to do nose jobs on Wilshire Boulevard. I want to help the people who need it most. There's a price, like there is for anything. I suppose you and Mom paid a part of that price. Chalk it up as your contribution to the Third World."

"Look, I'm sorry I said that." Tentatively, Maya reached her hand forward again, but at Debby's look, she withdrew it. "It's not that I want to make you feel guilty."

"You're just trying your damndest to."

"Let's say the spirit of Betty took possession of me for a moment there." Maya ventured a momentary smile.

"What are you laughing at?"

"I was thinking that yesterday afternoon I thought I'd reached a kind of enlightenment. But there's nothing like your own family to knock the Buddha-like serenity clean out of you."

Debby looked at her, and suddenly a small hint of a smile played around the edges of her mouth.

"I'm sorry, Karla—Maya. I know you did your best for her. I know it was a strain on you."

Now Debby reached her hand across the table, and Maya took it. So that's how it is, she thought. We can connect if I let her mother me, if I let her be the one to step into Betty's shoes. Well, why not?

"Sometimes I wish I'd done more," Maya admitted. "Sometimes I feel like hell that I didn't drop my life and move down there to look after her."

"I know. But she would have driven you crazy."

"And that's the tragedy of Betty."

"That's the tragedy of life," Debby said. "But I am sorry, too. Sorry, sorry, sorry. I'll be sorry the rest of my life that I didn't get to say good-bye to her. Was it . . . hard at the end?"

"At the very end, it was peaceful," Maya said. "I felt her go, and suddenly the room was filled with a great sense of peace. And relief. Up until then, it was hell. It's amazing how torturously the body tries to stay alive. Still breathing, when there's no point to it anymore."

"I know."

"I guess you do. I washed her body, after she died. The nurse let me. I blessed every part of her. Her hair was still falling out, from the radiation. Pubic hair, too. It was so hard not to get hair stuck all over her. I still think of that."

"I suppose you had the funeral already?"

"It has to be within a day, by Jewish law. You know that."

Debby nodded. "Not that Jewish law ever meant a whole hell of a lot to Betty."

"Well, what could I do? I couldn't keep her in cold storage for a month or two while we rooted you out of the Himalayas."

"No, of course not," Debby conceded. "Well, how was it? Was it a nice funeral?"

"I taped it for you. All the second cousins came, and a lot of her colleagues. People said beautiful things." She reached into her day pack and brought out a gift-wrapped cassette, handing it to Debby as a peace offering.

"Thanks." Debby held the cassette in her hand, unwrapping it and looking at it as if it were something that could sting. "Where did you bury her?"

"She didn't want to be buried, tradition or no tradition. I had her cremated."

Debby nodded. "That's better. I hated thinking of her in one of

those Forest Lawn–type places in LA. What did you do with the ashes?''
She tucked the cassette into a pouch in her apron.

''Nothing, yet. I thought we could do something together.''

Debby fell silent.

''What?'' Maya asked. ''What is it?''

''I might stay on,'' she said. ''Now that Betty's dead, there's no
reason for me to go back just yet. I might stay on another year.''

She looked up at Maya, a swift glance as if she expected anger or
recriminations, but Maya just shrugged.

''That makes sense. Why not?''

''I mean, I miss you. I wanted to see you, but now you're here.''

''For a couple of days.''

''Come back. Now that you know the way, drop in anytime.''

They laughed. Yes, when we smile, when she throws her head
back like that, then we look alike, Maya thought. We are sisters.

''So anyway, I guess you should just go ahead and do whatever
with the ashes. I mean, I appreciate your thinking of me, and all
that . . .''

''Actually,'' Maya said, ''I have the ashes here.''

''You have what?''

''I brought them with me.''

''Why in the name of the seven Buddhas would you do that?''

''Because you couldn't come to the funeral. Because I'm so goddamned psychic that somewhere deep down I knew you wouldn't be
back any time soon.''

''But, Maya, she doesn't belong up here!'' Debby raised her hands
in frustration. ''She's not a Sherpa!''

''Neither are you, but you're here.''

''That's not the same. And not forever, either.''

''Long enough,'' Maya said, and immediately wished she hadn't.
''I'm sorry, I don't know what the hell is wrong with me.''

''I know exactly what's wrong with you. You're mad. You're mad
because in your mind, you're supposed to be the one who gets to go off
and do exciting things and have adventures and disappear into God
knows where, and I'm the one who's supposed to be stuck taking care of
Mom. And for once it worked out the other way around.''

Was that true? Maya wondered. Was she resentful of Debby for not
fulfilling her good sister role, and leaving Maya free? It could be true. She
would have to examine it in a moment of reflective calm, if such a
moment ever came. Right now all she felt was a kind of numb sting, and
an urge to lash back and protect herself. It was a sensation, an energy
state that felt deeply familiar. In half an hour together, she and Debby had
reproduced exactly what Betty and Joe had generated between them,
what had driven them apart.

We are our parents' daughters. She almost said it out loud, but instead she said simply, "I don't want to fight with you, Debby. I'm sorry. I don't want to make you feel bad."

Debby's face had a puffy look, as if she were trying hard not to cry. "I can't believe you brought her ashes up here. In what? An urn, on yak back? A box?"

"A plastic bag, if you must know. That's how they came from the crematorium."

Debby shuddered. "Why not just ship her corpse? We could chop it up and feed it to the vultures, like the Tibetans do. I would have thought you of all people would have a sense of what belongs and what doesn't belong! I should have been there at the end, not you!"

I'm not going to say it, Maya thought. I'm not going to say, And whose fault is it, that you weren't?

Maya took a deep breath, and tried to speak in a calm, detached tone, without entirely succeeding.

"Maybe you're right, maybe you should have been there instead of me. Maybe Betty would have preferred it that way, I don't know. But you weren't. I had to make the decisions. So, fine, tell me where she belongs, and I'll take her there. Mount Zion, in the Holy Land? Russia? LA, out in some smoggy cemetery in the valley where you and I will never go to visit? Should I have sprinkled her in the patio of her house, and then sold it? Should I bury her in my backyard? Tell me what I should have done with Mom!"

"Why didn't you ask her what she wanted done?"

"I did! Dozens of times! She wouldn't say. All she said was she didn't want to be buried. No, that's not true. What she actually said was, 'If I can't be buried next to Joe, I don't want to be buried anywhere.' "

"Oh, God, she didn't really say that, did she?"

"She did."

Debby looked up at Maya, and shook her head. "She never got over him, did she?"

"She got worse at the end. She'd cry and cry and cry about how he betrayed her."

"Oh, God."

They could look at each other again, now, linked by a mixture of pity and embarrassment familiar to them both.

"I probably should have just scattered her ashes in New York Harbor, like Joe's, so they could mingle together at the bottom of the sea," Maya said. "That's what she would really have wanted, although she couldn't bring herself to say so. And I couldn't bring myself to do it."

"No. No, you couldn't do that." Debby reached her hand forward, and Maya took it. They sat, holding hands, united at last.

"We are going to walk up to the *gompa*." Tenzing came over to their table and broke the silence between them. "The rain has stopped. Will you come?"

Debby looked at Maya. "The *gompa*'s very beautiful," she said. "You shouldn't miss it."

"Don't tell me," Maya said to Tenzing. "It's all uphill, I bet?"

He nodded, smiling. "But coming back, it will be all downhill."

The rain had not so much stopped as turned itself into a powdery snow that blew sideways at them as they climbed. Snow covered the trees with a fine white outline, made white streaks on the sticks of wood a young Sherpa boy was carrying down the mountain, glazed the backs of the yaks that passed them. As they walked up the path, looming shapes appeared suddenly out of the gray, and as they got closer, took on form and definition, becoming a prayer wall, a bent tree, a stone gate.

Maya was back to her snaillike crawl, breathing laboriously and stopping periodically to cough. Debby took the climb easily, not even breathing hard, but she stayed beside Maya, looking worried.

"Maybe we would have done better to stay at the *bhatti*," she said. "You really sound like you could use a good rest."

"You know me," Maya said, stopping for a moment. "I hate to miss anything. Besides, the trek is almost over. I'll have plenty of time to rest when I get home."

"You'll never grow up," Debby said.

"I hope not," Maya said fervently. She was still trying to practice her discipline of acceptance. If she could let Debby be, as she could let be her own slowness, her cough, then their relationship would seem to her as beautiful as a piece of old marble, colored with many veins and flaws and imperfections, rich and strong.

They rounded a bend, to find that the clouds had parted to reveal a shaft of sunlight and a glimpse of the high mountains across the gorge. Pembila, Lonnie, Jan, and Carolyn sat on a stone wall looking at the view and resting, as Maya and Debby came up to them. The men had all gone on ahead, and Maya was relieved to see that Howard was nowhere around. His presence made Maya anxious, as if by rejecting him she had committed some wrong that would lay her open to retribution.

I'm not obligated to sleep with every man who asks me, she told herself firmly. After twenty years of feminism, surely I shouldn't still have to convince myself.

No, that's not what's bugging me. Maybe in some deep, hidden realm of my subconscious, I feel that by rejecting Howard, basically decent, stable, responsible Howard, I leave myself open to Rio.

Maya set down her day pack and joined the women on the wall. The change in breathing triggered a new round of coughing. She avoided Debby's eye.

"So, are you happy working here?" Carolyn asked Debby.

"I love it," Debby said fervently. "It's the most fascinating place I've ever been . . . and I'm needed every day."

"That must be satisfying," Carolyn said.

"But don't you get lonely?" Jan asked. She was sitting close to Lonnie. They were not quite touching, and once again Maya could almost feel the air between them growing warm.

"Not so far. You can't get too lonely in a village. When the Sherpa people take you in, you've got instant family."

Pembila had been listening intently, and at this she smiled.

"Not lonely," she said to Debby. "You stay Khumbu, we find you Sherpa husband."

She smiled at Maya. Once again, Pembila was her usual, cheerful self, showing no traces of sadness. Only an extra warmth in her smile acknowledged the evening she and Maya had sat and mourned together.

"He better be young and good looking," Debby said. "No old geezers for me."

"How about one of the kitchen boys?" Maya suggested. "They're really good cooks."

"Too young," Debby objected. "I'm not a cradle robber."

"Tashi, then."

"Tashi, he good for doctor, maybe." Pembila turned to Lonnie, a teasing smile on her face. "Better for you."

"Me! He's a bit young for me, don't you think?"

"Young man, better," Pembila said.

"Ah, maybe that's what I need, a trophy husband," Lonnie said. "That would certainly resolve my relationship dilemmas. But Pembila, you told me Tashi was Tibetan, and they're not good for chickie-chickie. If I'm going to get married, I want some good chickie-chickie out of the deal."

At that moment, Tashi came up the trail whistling. Debby grinned at him.

"Hey, Tashi, Pembila's trying to marry you off."

He stopped, his eyes growing round with mock alarm. "I cannot marry," he said.

"Why not?" Lonnie asked.

"I have wife and children," he proclaimed. "Many, many children."

"I guess they marry you off young in Tibet," Lonnie said.

"Not in Tibet. I have wife and children in Mon-ta-na."

"On the cattle ranch? With your horse."

"Not horse," Tashi said. "Motorcycle."

"Tashi have big nose," Pembila said. "Big nose, big . . ." She pointed suggestively at Tashi's crotch and winked. "Good for chickie-chickie."

Tashi blushed.

"Pembila, you're incorrigible," Debby said. She turned to the rest of them. "This is not a typical conversation with a Sherpani. I just want you all to know that. Mostly the women here are quite reserved about sex."

"Noted," Lonnie said.

"You marry her," Pembila said to Tashi, pointing at Lonnie. "She much woman." Pembila squeezed Lonnie's breast playfully. "Need young, strong man."

Tashi fled up the gorge.

"Now you've chased him away," Lonnie complained.

Then the clouds closed overhead, and the sun disappeared. They stood up to resume the climb.

"Not long," Pembila said. Once again they trudged upward through the mist. They passed through a small gatehouse with mandalas painted on the ceiling. When they emerged, the wind had died and the snow drifted down in big flakes. Above them they could see the old stone buildings of the monastery nestled into the hills. They continued up, terrace after terrace, Debby cruising easily up at the front with Pembila, talking in Sherpa, Maya following slowly behind. The others disappeared, leaving her to crest the final terrace by herself.

As she did, she looked up to the wall that edged the flat piece of land upon which the *gompa* stood. Something moved along the wall, flapped a wing, and suddenly a big pheasant appeared, standing out like a gaudy circus in the winter-barren landscape of brown and white. The bird had a green crest above a red face, red and green neck rings, and a plump body of royal blue and iridescent peacock, with a golden tail. It looked like one of the bright wall paintings come alive.

Maya stood still, her breath indrawn. As she watched, a whole flock followed their leader onto the wall, the males preening and strutting before the drab, brown females. One flew down, spreading his golden tail, passing not far from her, and she felt as if he had showered her with gold, as if the land had given her a sign that she was passing her tests, that she was wanted and welcome after all. She hugged herself, shivering with gratitude and cold.

The cold finally drove Maya into the *gompa* hall, although the temperature indoors was not significantly warmer than outdoors. By some dispensation they were allowed to keep their shoes on, and Maya was grateful. All the trekkers and Debby were gathered around Ang, who was telling them that the monastery was very old, maybe a thousand years old. He had studied there himself as a young man. It was so dark inside they could barely see, but Tenzing and Ang had flashlights that they played over the mandalas and tankas and hidden recesses of the walls, illuminating mysteries.

The walls were lined with cubbyholes. In each, a long, narrow Tibetan text was shelved, only its end showing, draped with silk. On benches stood big conch shells and long Tibetan horns, ornamented with silver. From the rafters hung round drums, their edges carved and painted red. Tankas hung from the crossbeams, framed in colorful silk, and on the back wall were paintings of Buddhas and aspects of Tara dancing. On the other walls were images of Rinpoches and full Buddha lineages, painted wood sculptures in niches, and yet other Buddhas painted in ecstatic union with their consorts. Maya looked at everything, trying to witness the *gompa* as she had witnessed the mountain, seeing every painted curve and hue as the land revealing and expressing itself in color and form. She had wondered about the colors before, at so much brightness and pattern emerging out of this land of green and brown and blue, but now that she had seen the pheasants, she understood that Nature herself was the most profligate colorist around these parts.

At the front altar, a young lama was preparing and lighting butter lamps before a statue of the Buddha. Maya made a donation, dropping a few rupiahs into the box provided, and lit a lamp. Out of the corner of her eye, she noticed Debby do the same. Maya was saying a silent prayer for Betty, and she wondered if Debby was also. We should be praying together, she thought. We should do something.

Small, square windows revealed that outside the daylight was fading. Snow was blowing around the portals of the *gompa.* Suddenly Maya was filled with anxiety. If they didn't do something now, they never would. The ritual would never happen.

She stepped over to where her sister stood contemplating a fierce deity with red eyes and a toothed mouth in the center of his stomach.

"Debby, come with me, now," she said softly. "Let's do something for Mom, up here."

"Do what for her?" Debby whispered.

"A ritual. A good-bye."

"Why here?"

"Because we *are* here. And it's a holy place. And this is the only night we have together, outside of Namche. It's strange, I must have been here in these mountains too long, but I've started to think of Namche as the big city."

"You do something, if you want to," Debby said.

"But the point is to do it together."

"The point for you, maybe. But for me, it doesn't mean anything."

"What do you mean, it doesn't mean anything?"

Their voices had risen and the young lama was looking at them curiously. Debby took Maya's arm and steered her toward the alcove at the entrance to the *gompa*.

"Look, Maya," she said. "I didn't ask you to come here. Ritual is your thing, not mine. And certainly not Mom's."

"But you weren't at the funeral. You never said good-bye to her."

"I'm sorry, okay? I already said I was sorry! For God's sake, are you never going to stop blaming me for that? It's not as if I don't feel bad enough already! But I can't do anything about it now."

Maya took a deep breath. "I'm not blaming you. I'm offering you . . . offering you a chance to do something now. To make an end. An honoring of the end."

"But that's your need, not mine!"

"So? So is it a crime for me to have a need?"

"No, just don't assume that it's my responsibility to fulfill it."

"I'm asking you to share it with me."

"There's sharing, and there's forcing."

"Nobody's forcing you to do a goddamn thing!"

They stood, glaring at each other, eye to eye. Then Debby turned away. She wasn't going to give in, Maya realized. And there's nothing I can do. I can't make her want to do a ritual for Mom. I can't force her to love me, forgive me for the past.

This was another moment of walking up the mountain, another thing she would just have to accept. She and Debby weren't going to connect. They would never do the ritual together that she had imagined. She'd come for nothing. She had carried her mother's ashes—or not carried them, more accurately—all the way up here for nothing. Well, there was something Zen about that. She had brought them up and she would bring them down. If she were an enlightened master, she would laugh.

But she wasn't enlightened and she wanted to cry. She could feel tears welling up. She didn't want to cry in the alcove of the *gompa,* with all the other trekkers gathering around and Howard staring down the back of her neck. Silently she grabbed her day pack, with her mother's ashes inside, and slipped out.

A path led up the mountain from behind the building, and she followed it up. The snow was blowing around her, turning to sleet that stung her face as she headed into the wind. Just a little way. Soon it would be dark, and Tenzing and Ang would be alarmed if they realized she had gone off alone. She would have to get back quickly. Anyway, she wanted to get back quickly. She was scared. The loneliness of the mountain, the cold, the sleet, the gloom, all made her feel alone, alone, alone.

She really wanted to be back inside somewhere safe, with a fire and a cup of hot tea, and company.

But she had spent her whole life both resisting and craving safety and comfort, hadn't she? And always, when she left them behind, when she went to the edge, she found something. Now she would do what she should have done in the first place—go alone to the heights, unguarded, unsheltered. The mountain had reached for her, shown her its colors. She should be unafraid.

Darkness would soon fall. She would have to hurry. These trails were no place to be wandering alone at night, in a snowfall softening to rain. She climbed uphill, as fast as she could make her tired body go.

This wasn't the way I wanted it, Betty. I wanted a ritual for you that had grandeur, style, not a hurried scattering into the face of the storm. But this is how it is.

She stopped to catch her breath. Here, here is as good as anywhere, since I can't see anything in this rain. I could be anywhere, at the end of the world. Or on the main village path to the outhouse, for all I know. Is this really right, Betty?

Just then the drizzle changed to a torrent. The rain came down in sheets. Maya ducked her head and ran up the path, or what she thought was the path. She could no longer see where she was going, only feel that she continued to move upward, her feet slipping on the muddy ground. If she were smart, she would turn around and go back to the *gompa,* but she found herself reluctant to give up. But this was no longer mystical, this running upward into the dark, this was stupidity of the first order, the kind of thing tourists do who don't know the mountains and get themselves killed.

She stopped. Maybe the rain was telling her that this was not the time or the place to leave Betty's ashes. She would turn around and go down. Debby was right, it was time to grow up. The only thing was, she wasn't exactly sure which way she'd come up. There didn't seem to be a trail under her feet. Still, she had come up and the *gompa* definitely lay in the direction of down. All she had to do was follow her feet, and let them take her there.

She began walking. The mountain had shown her its colors; surely it would guide her now. And, as Tenzing would agree, it was easier to walk down than up. She'd be back in no time at all, only she had to be careful to keep her feet from sliding out from under her. Her socks were wet inside her boots and she could feel a blister starting on one heel. Her pile sweatpants were soaked through. If she stopped moving, she knew, she'd be very, very cold.

When she had scrambled down about as far as she'd come up, she stopped for a moment. The rain was still heavy as she tried to peer through it. Surely she should be able to see the lights in the *gompa,* those butter lamps the lama had so piously lit. The lamp of her own offering. But there was nothing ahead of her but dark.

Well, no matter. Probably the rain was too heavy. If she continued, just a little farther . . .

But a little farther, and a little farther still, brought no change. Maybe her sense of distance and proportion was confused, maybe she just hadn't gone down far enough yet. But what if she went too far down? What if she was heading down the wrong side of the ridge, away from the *gompa* and the village? She could die of hypothermia before anyone found her.

Now stop that, she told herself. Don't panic, that's the first rule. What to do when you're lost in the mountains? Stop, everyone said, and wait for rescue. Surely Ang and Tenzing would come looking for her. But if she stopped, she would freeze. No, she would climb back twenty paces, veering slightly to the left, and then climb down again, making a zigzag pattern around the side of the hill, until she found something—a path, a hut, a stone wall. Surely in this inhabited land she would find some marker to guide her. And she would call, as she went.

"Ang! Tenzing!" The rain lashed her face and threw her voice back at her. She climbed up twenty paces, then veered down another twenty, only to climb back up again, heading always to her left. Which was all very well, as long as the *gompa* wasn't to her right. Don't think about that, she was sure, almost sure, that if she had veered away from the path, it was toward the right. So she had to be going the right way, now. Anyway, it was a fifty-fifty chance. Don't think about being lost all night, don't think about Sagarmatha handing you the postgraduate course in acceptance, also known as Death 101. Just think about being in the Good Reality, where you could come sauntering back into the *gompa* hall, heh heh, just stepped out for a moment, got caught in the rain . . .

"Ang! Tenzing!" Nothing. Nothing but darkness, and silence. Maya had been tired to start with, but now she was starting to feel exhausted, as she continued her zigzag course up and down the mountain. Surely she couldn't have come this far, could she? And how long could she keep this up? Maybe she had passed the trail already and missed it? Oh, Goddess, if she didn't die of exposure soon she was going to drive herself mad. But she couldn't die out here. Debby would never forgive herself, and anyway dying wasn't her thing. It was what Betty did. She had never wanted to do what Betty did.

But she had been there with Betty. She had murmured and crooned and stroked her hand, and talked her down, feeling her mother sinking. Down and down, she had said, into water, into a deep pool, let yourself drift and float and dissolve, until there is nothing left but essence, but who you are. Yes, now Betty was going where Maya had always wanted to lead her, into the spirit depths where everyone she had ever loved awaited her. Now at the end of her life she could let Maya guide her, let Maya be the strong one, the one in charge. As if her mother, in dying, had finally come into the world Maya had inhabited all of her life, finally come to where Maya had a gift she could give her.

"Would you like to say a prayer? The Shemah?" Maya had asked. Betty nodded.

"I'll say it with you. Which would you like, the old one, or one of the new, feminist versions?"

"The old one," Betty whispered.

They said it together, the first prayer a child learns, the last prayer said while dying.

Shemah, Yisroel, Adonai Elohenu Adonai echod.
Hear, O Israel, the Lord our God, the Lord is One.

The words echoed with the whispers of ancestors, Zaydeh Stein with his prayer shawl and tefillin strapped around his arm, murmuring prayers morning and evening, Baba Stein teaching it to Debby, the words that played on the lips of the martyrs of the holocaust, echoed in the gas chambers, burst from the charred lips of the victims of the same Inquisition that had burned the Witches. Maya could relinquish her mother into the ancestors' care, and yet she could not herself say even this simplest, most basic of prayers and wholly believe it. No, she could not call God Lord, or even God, or One, except as a pomegranate is one whole of many seeds, as an organism is one creature of many cells. Listen, people, what we call the sacred has many forms and infinite variety! Listen, friends, you are Goddess, thou art that, *tat tvam asi.* Sisters and brothers, every tongue that speaks its own truth names a new God!

But her mother was dying, and it was too late for theology. Maya was seized with a terrible anxiety. There was something she needed to know, something only Betty could tell her, but she couldn't think what it was. Your mother's maiden name, Mom, your favorite color, what food you liked best. What did you cook—I can't remember, except for that awful dish with the frozen french cut green beans and the frozen onion rings and the mushroom soup. You thought it was my favorite because I liked it when I was ten, and you made it for me every time I came home, and I never told you I'd outgrown it, that I laughed at it. You see, you see, with all I did, how I protected you? And suddenly Maya was holding her mother's hand and sobbing, tears running down her cheeks, and Betty turned to her and asked, "Why are you crying?"

"Because you're dying, Mom."

"You're crying for you, not for me."

A doctor strode into the room, young and blond and snapping with efficiency.

"Mrs. Greenbaum, I'm told you've refused the antibiotics. Do you understand that without them we can't treat your lung infection?" He rattled on, a long list of technical terms and dire possibilities.

Betty turned to Maya. "What's he saying?"

"He's saying that if you don't take the antibiotics, you'll die sooner."

"Good. That's what I want." Then she turned to the doctor, thoughtfully. "Tell me, how will I know when I'm dead?"

The doctor stopped speaking for a moment, taken aback. Probably no one has ever asked him that, before, Maya thought. Good one, Mom. Oh, if only you could still embarrass me by quizzing him on where he went to school and why he chose medicine and how he got along with his father. If only you would get up and yell at me, one more time.

"Uh, you won't know," the doctor said. "You'll be unconscious."

"I'll tell you, Mom," Maya said. Betty turned and looked at her.

"How will I know?"

"You'll stop breathing. Your heart will stop. Your spirit will leave your body."

"Do you believe in spirits?" Betty asked, closing her eyes.

"I do. I believe that when you die, you aren't completely gone. That something of you continues, and joins the others, the ones you've loved before, the ancestors. They'll help you."

"They didn't help me before," Betty said.

"When?"

"In the waterfall."

"What waterfall?"

"You know. The waterfall of antiquity."

What had Betty meant? Maya wondered. Where had she been, where had she gone? Where was she now, when Maya needed her, her own tears mingling with the rain? Oh, Betty, I'm sorry. Maybe in the end it's you I need to accept, with all your strengths and flaws, with all the ways you loved me and tried to control me and drove me nuts.

I wanted to lay you to rest somewhere beautiful, spectacular, I wanted to find the highest mountain, the Goddess Mother of the Universe herself, I wanted to give you something, Betty, to give you in death what I could never give you in life—what you could never receive. A glimpse, a taste, a hint of the place I've always been moving toward, reaching for. I wanted to lay you to rest here, in the arms of the mountain, in the sweet singing river, I wanted you to be cradled in a pink flower just about to bud. So that at last you would understand me.

But instead, I seem to be about to lay myself to rest. How stupid. How unutterably stupid.

Just at that moment, the rain let up slightly. A low gleam of the twilight sun lit the mountain, and just up ahead, Maya could see a small structure. She ran for it, ducking under the roof of an arched gateway, to stand in the center of a square, open pavilion, just a roof and no walls, enough to keep the rain off, enough to assure her that she was not wholly and forever lost. Thank you, Goddess; thank you, Mom. I am most likely not going to die now—although I'm not out of the woods, or more accurately, the rain, yet. The relief was so great that she wanted to laugh. This was one of the gateways to the *gompa,* and all she had to do was follow the path it stood upon, up or down. If she only knew which. If she could only remember the details of the lower gate they had passed through—or see this one clearly.

The rain seemed to be lessening slightly. She would walk up, and if she didn't soon come to the terraces and stone walls of the *gompa,* turn around and walk down. That would be better than going down and having to turn around and walk up.

She stepped out of the shelter and began walking up the path. She heard a muffled sound, like footsteps walking down the path toward her.

"Ang? Tenzing?" she called.

"Hello!" A woman's voice came back to her.

"Debby?" Had her sister come to look for her, ready to make up their fight, maybe, to do the ritual after all?

The woman who came toward her, materializing out of the mist and rain, was not Debby but the girl in the green sweater, Claire.

At the moment, she was not wearing a green sweater but a long, navy-blue anorak. She walked out of the storm like someone arriving from another world, but when she spoke, her voice was human.

"Thank goodness," she said when she saw Maya. "I thought I was lost."

"I am lost," Maya admitted. "There's a gateway just behind me, but I don't know if it's below or above the *gompa.*"

"It's got to be above," Claire said. "There's nothing farther up, but mountain. I've just come from there."

Just then a flash of lightning lit the sky, and the rain began pouring down again.

"Come on," Maya said, grabbing her hand, and together they ran to shelter.

They huddled in the center of the pavilion. "I missed the trail up above," Claire said. "I finally found a path, but I wasn't sure if it was the right one or not."

"I know," Maya said. "Same thing happened to me. It's scary."

"You look cold." Maya was shivering. Her pile sweatpants were surprisingly warm, though wet, but the water had soaked through her Gore-Tex jacket and drenched her sweatshirt underneath.

"I wish I was wearing my wool sweater," Maya said, "but I'm not."

"I've got a dry sweater in my rucksack. Wait a minute."

Claire took off her pack, rummaged within, and produced a long-sleeve shirt and the torn green sweater.

"It's not the cleanest," she said.

"I don't care. Thanks." Maya quickly shed her own dripping clothes and squeezed into Claire's, which hugged her more ample figure tightly. The rain beat down fiercely all around them, but under their shelter they were in their own safe world.

"Should we run for it?" Maya suggested. "It'll be dark, soon."

"Let's wait a few minutes. Maybe it'll lighten up."

"A few minutes," Maya agreed. "After that, we'll run for it."

"What are you doing out here alone?" Claire asked. "I thought you were with the trekking group."

"I was sulking," Maya admitted. "I had a fight with my sister—she's the doctor over at Khunde, and she met us here. So I ran out for a moment, to have a good cry, and the rest is history. Or I was, almost." She was so happy to be found, not lost, to be alive, not following her mother into death. She felt entirely at ease with Claire, as if they had moved through the mist and met somewhere beyond time and space, where none of the ordinary rules applied and nothing needed to be proved to anyone. "What are you doing, lost on the mountain?"

"I came here to join the *gompa*. But they wouldn't have me. So I went for a hike, to get over it."

"Oh, I'm sorry. I guess I'm sorry—maybe I'm not. Why wouldn't they have you?"

"They said I should go home and learn from my own people."

"Oh. Well, that's probably good advice."

"But why? Why me? They take on other westerners."

"Maybe they see another destiny for you. They're good at that, I hear."

"Anyway, I went up the mountain to try to figure out what to do next. That's always how I decide. I listen, and hear what calls to me."

"You're wise, if you've learned to do that at your age," Maya said. "Well, at any age, really," she added, afraid that she sounded patronizing.

"But nothing calls to me," Claire said plaintively. "All I got was wet."

"The same thing happened to me once," Maya told her. "I wanted to study with a *curandera*. A wise woman. She read cards and did healings for people, did rituals for them to help them get what they wanted. Funny, she was a lot like my mother, in that way—the one you'd come to with your problems, the one who would sort it all out. Not me, I could never take my problems to my mother, not after I was about ten years old. But other people did. She was a therapist. A sort of *curandera*, in our western terms. But anyway, the *curandera* in Mexico told me to go home. 'This is not your tradition,' she said. 'These are not your people. This land is not your land. You must find what is yours.' It took me years to take her advice. But of course I was afraid to go home.''

"Why?"

"That's a long story."

"Was she right?"

"Right? Yes, I suppose she was, in the end. I could have learned from her. Then I could have brought the knowledge home and translated it into something it wasn't. Another credential, you know, something else to list on the résumé, to put in the bio—'studied with *curandera* in Mexico.' I would have used her, without meaning to, taken something that was hers and turned it into something else, with all the best intentions in the world.''

"But I don't want a bio," Claire said. "I don't want credentials. I'd swear never to tell anyone where I learned what I learned, or how, or when. I just wanted to be with them."

"But it still wouldn't be real. It wouldn't be honest."

"Why?"

"Because this isn't where you belong—where I belong. We're just passing through. And if you did belong here, you wouldn't be studying at this monastery. Women don't. You might be at the nunnery over by Tengpoche." She thought about Pembila, sitting still as an offering on the stone wall by the *stuppa*. "You might be married and pregnant and learning detachment by watching half your children die."

"But where do I belong? I've been a traveler all my life. I'm as much at home here as anywhere."

"Well, maybe that's our problem," Maya said. "All of us in the so-called modern world. Not a one of us really belongs anywhere in the way these people do. We don't eat from the earth we live on or give anything back to it or listen to what it says. We aren't very good at being the hands the earth uses to shape herself. I mean, I love San Francisco, but I don't belong to it, my body wasn't formed of its food and water, my songs and my writings don't emerge from my relationship with it. None of us knows where we are or where to go or even where to bury our ancestors. That's my problem."

"What's your problem?"

The rain had closed around them like a moving wall. Maybe I have died, Maya thought suddenly. Who would tell me? How would I know? This could be death's way station, the gateway between the worlds.

"I brought my mother's ashes here," Maya said, as if she were speaking not to Claire but to the guardian of the gate, as if she were called to confess her failures and all the unfulfilled quests of her life. "So that my sister and I could scatter them together. But she didn't want to."

"Why not?"

"She resists ritual. She resists me. I couldn't persuade her."

"What will you do with them, now?"

Maya stood silent for a moment, watching the impenetrable rain. If she were to spin around in this place beyond time, she would lose all sense of up and down. She put a hand out, to feel the post that supported the gateway, to steady herself.

"I was going to scatter them on the mountain. But then the rain came, and I got lost." Yes, the light was fading. Claire was a dark figure, a shape in the mist. She could be anyone. She could be a peasant woman in a striped shawl who had long ago given Maya something to carry on her back.

"Will you help me?" Maya asked, not sure whom she was speaking to. "Will you help me scatter my mother's ashes, here on this holy ground?"

"Is this the right place? The right time? Are you sure?"

Yes, Maya thought. Here, in the gateway between the worlds, I will let Betty go, into this wild maelstrom of lightning and wind and drenching rain, scatter her to the storm, let her fertilize these fields. Here was as good as anywhere, and if not now, when?

"I'm sure," Maya said.

She slipped her own small pack off, reached in and pulled out the cloth sack in which she had packed the plastic bag she'd received from the crematorium. Now that the moment had come, she found herself somewhat reluctant to open it, to reach her hand in and touch the ash and chunks of bone that had once been her mother. To scatter the ashes would be to make death final. She and Debby would stand alone then, with no one between them and death, no longer young, no longer immortal.

And that's why I must do it, she told herself, drawing the plastic bag up and looking out into the rain.

"Let's ground," she said. "Breathe together, feel your deep connection to the earth, to the air, to the fire, to the water. Listen to the voice of the storm. . . ."

Maya listened. The wind whistled and shuddered, the rain beat down. She might be dead but she felt alive, electric, ecstatic, as if the rain that drenched her had caressed her, claimed her. She sucked in a long deep breath, opened her mouth to chant, but instead was seized with a long, racking cough.

Well that's that, she thought. Now I know I'm not dead, at least. I cough, therefore I live.

When her coughing subsided, she stood and listened to the rain, waiting for a sign, a confirmation that what she was about to do was right. She waited for a long moment, and then waited again. Nowhere in the wind or the storm or the mountain did she hear anything that called for Betty.

She sighed. "This isn't working," she admitted to the girl. "It's not right. My mother doesn't belong here, any more than you or I do."

Claire simply nodded. Maya closed up the plastic bag. As she slipped it back into her day pack, she felt something else and drew it out. It was an old, frayed letter; the letter from Rio she'd received many years ago and never answered.

"What are you going to do with her?" Claire asked.

Was the letter a sign? Maya wondered. Was it telling her something? She replaced it carefully, deep in her pack beneath her mother's ashes, where the rain would not reach it.

"I don't know," she said to Claire. "Maybe I'll put her in an urn, on the mantel. Maybe I'll have to carry her around for years and years, like an albatross, until the right place reveals itself."

Claire shook her head. "I don't think that's a good idea."

"What do you think?"

"I think you have to ask the right question. You always have to ask the right question, in order to get an answer."

"And what do you think the right question is?" Maya still had the sensation of speaking not to the girl but to some great force of life and death beyond her, someone who had guarded a threshold and meted out fate. "Where does Betty belong?"

"No," Claire said. "The question is, 'What do you have to do, to lay your mother to rest?'"

Maya shivered. A small ball of electric fire leaped up her spine.

What do I have to do? Maya repeated to herself. To lay my mother, my sister, my history, my past to rest, to move on? This is what I came here for—to stand between the worlds in this half shelter in the middle of a storm, having nearly died, and have this child ask me that question. And now I can go home, carrying my ashes and my unanswered letters and my journals and my sister's ire, not knowing the answer, maybe, but knowing at least what the question is.

"Thank you," Maya said. "Thank you for asking me that."

"What do you have to do?" Claire said again. "Where do you have to go, to lay your mother to rest?"

And then suddenly Maya knew.

To lay her mother to rest was to lay to rest her own history, to be present to all of it as she could sometimes be present to Johanna, to the mountains.

And that means, most of all, to be present to myself. Oh, Jo, you came to realize how the secret between us separated us from each other. Why couldn't you see that the secret we kept together made us evade ourselves?

"Nevada," Maya said. Claire looked up at her, surprised. "I have to go to Nevada. There's somebody I have to see there, and I can't lay my mother to rest until I do."

"Well, there you are, then."

The rain slackened for a moment, and the sky lightened, just slightly, but enough so that Claire's features resolved into the mortal face of a very young woman who was alive and vulnerable and alone.

"And you? What do you have to do, to go home?" Maya asked her.

"I have to make a home," Claire said. "I don't have one."

"Well, there *you* are, then. That's your challenge—that's what you do next."

"It sounds so banal."

"It's not," Maya said. "We are very much alike, you know. It's taken me thirty-eight years to realize that there's as much power in the everyday as in all the *gompas* of the Himalayas."

"What do you mean?"

"I mean whatever you have to do to make a home for yourself will be exactly what is hardest for you, and what you most need to do to grow. Maybe for you, staying here and meditating would be easy. In some ways, it would be for me. But going back to the States and renting an apartment or moving in with a bunch of people you have to relate to— that could be a killer spiritual test. If you stay present. If you stay aware. Take me, for example. I can love any mountain with the depth of the Goddess herself. I know that now. But put me in the same room with my sister, and compassion withers away. So I have something to work on."

Her voice dropped as the noise of the rain softened and finally eased.

"It's lightened up," Claire said.

"Let's run for it."

Claire shook her head. "I think I'll stay here just a bit longer. I'll meditate on what you said."

"But it's getting dark!"

"I'm staying with a family, just behind the *gompa*. I know where I am now. I won't get lost."

"What about your sweater?" Maya said, starting to peel it off.

"Keep it," Claire said. "It's an old one, anyway. Look, the rain's stopped. You better run."

Maya nodded. She would leave Claire in the gateway between the worlds, without saying good-bye. Skidding and sliding, she ran down the path toward the flickering lights of butter lamps in the *gompa*.

44

Letter

Lexington Honor Farm
April 27, 1983

Dear Maya,

   You'll probably be surprised and maybe not all that happy to hear from me, and I couldn't say as I'd blame you. Maybe I shouldn't be writing to you at all. But you can, you know, at any moment pick this up and throw it into the garbage, which is maybe where it belongs. No, I take that back. I'm trying really hard not to trash myself, mostly because it gets in the way of what I need to do, which is to make amends as far as I can. I don't want to beg for your sympathy or your comfort, so if I slide into asking from time to time, please ignore me. Because I don't honestly know if I'll have the guts to reread this letter before I send it, so it may be kind of raw.

   Get to the point, boy. I read your book, *From the Mountain.* The guy who lent it to me, Dave Ryan, was in here for several years for pouring blood on draft board files and now he's back for hammering on the nose cones of missiles. I'm sure he didn't realize I knew you, he just liked the book. So do I. I wanted to say that to you. You've done something good, something to be proud of.

   And I want to say this to you—that I'm sorry. I'm sorry that I hurt you. I'm sorry that I wasn't there to stand beside you when you needed me, that you had to go through so much alone. I know this doesn't change anything, maybe you don't even want to hear it, but there it is. Anyway, it's true.

   Maya, I'm an alcoholic. I can admit that now. Ten years ago I couldn't. If I could have, everything would have been different, but of course there's no use going back over that now. That's not a pleasant thing to have to admit. I hate thinking about how much that stands at the core of everything I did or didn't do. Because it's not even the drinking that I'm talking about, but what it stood for in me. My own failures of courage. The ways I tried to slide away from pain. The ways I slid away from you.

You know, whenever we touched, I used to feel safe, at peace, at home. From the first moment I saw you, across Stow Lake, from the very first time we made love, under the trees, I felt like wherever, whoever I was or became, you would be there to greet me. And I had come to trust that, that great echoing sweet sound that passed through our bodies when we were together. I trusted it, and it scared the hell out of me, I guess because I'd never felt it before. So I had to violate it.

I'm sorry, now. I'm sorry I wasn't strong enough to accept the gift that you were, that we were together. But it was too much for me. There were times when just your touch seemed to strip away the flesh from my bones. Well, I was young and dumb, and, as you maybe remember, we all thought we were about to die.

I tell you this not for justification but maybe to gain some clarity, for both of us. I've made a lot of big mistakes in my life, but that is the one I most regret right now, the one that maybe the others stemmed from—my failure to love.

The first few years in here were pretty bad. It's hard to be an alcoholic in the joint. You—no, I—I lived from binge to binge, for whatever I could bribe or cheat or manipulate that would get me high. I did things I can hardly bear to remember, but I won't burden you with them. Funny, I can barely even remember my own trial. Or non-trial, as it turned out, just a migraine blur, where men in good suits made deals with my life. All I could think about was that I wanted to die, and I wanted a drink.

I got in a lot of trouble those first years, a lot of fights, got thrown in the hole quite a bit. One time I was locked up in solitary for sixty days. I thought I was going to go crazy, from the silence. Not just the silence outside me, which I could get used to. What got me was the silence inside. After a while, when I tried to talk to people inside my head, they weren't there. Or I'd see them, and they'd turn away. Jim turned his back on me. You walked off. My mother just covered her face with her hands.

I was about as close to rock bottom as it's possible to get. I had to do something or I was going to break in a way that would be worse than dying. Because up until then I still felt, no matter what I'd done or how bad it got, that somewhere in me was still a core of—of what? Heart? Ideals? Something I had once been willing to put my life behind. But like wet soap in the shower, that part of me was slipping away fast.

I started to think about something Dave Ryan said once, after he'd done a stretch in solitary. He said when there was nobody else to talk to, he talked to God. I was desperate enough to talk to the devil if I could have summoned him up, but I didn't believe in God. I'd slept through a lot of AA meetings trying to make points toward parole, and I was ready to admit that I was a drunk, at least to myself, but there was no Higher Power I felt the least bit of confidence in.

In fact, that core of me, that still-maybe-redeemable part, was tied to my being a Marxist and a materialist and a revolutionary. Or let's say that I did what I did in the Home Front out of the conviction that we had to act for ourselves, that we couldn't depend on some god or some abstraction to fix life for us, that we had to shape history with our own hands. And in spite of how it turned out, I still believed—maybe I should say believe—in our motivations.

Which is not to excuse our errors. We hadn't yet understood that the end doesn't justify the means—that in fact there often is no end beyond the means, so you better be damn careful in choosing them.

I have to live with the choices I made. The dead are dead. They're beyond the reach of my excuses or amends. But I still have to live my life. I know that now. I still have to do what I *can* do.

So I had no one to pray to, no one to talk to. In fact, I couldn't remember having a spiritual experience that wasn't based on some drug or another, and even though as you know we had some pretty cosmic acid trips, I just couldn't see basing my spiritual life on a drug-induced hallucination. Not if I was serious about changing. And you know, Maya, this may sound funny to you but that threw me into a deeper level of despair than I had ever felt. It was like someone tapped that unbreakable part of me with a hammer and I split along the lines of my flaws.

I just lay down on the floor (they didn't give you a bed there, just a mattress) and I don't know how long I lay there. I was remembering those times on the coast with you and Johanna but mostly I just remembered the wind, what it felt like blowing on my face and scrunching my eyes against it and tasting salt on my beard, and the smell of the wet earth and the look of the sky without any walls around it. And then I remembered the storm—you know that time when we were going to drop acid, and the storm was coming in, and you said, "No, let's see how it feels to do this one straight." You made us take off our clothes and we climbed up on Whale Rock and stood there above the ocean while the black clouds rolled in. God, was I cold! I thought I was going to die. But then after a while the cold changed, stopped being *cold* and became something else. My whole skin was electric. The waves were leaping and thundering below us, and the rain broke and came down in silver sheets, like wet light. I felt so clean, afterwards.

And it came to me that even if I didn't have a Higher Power, I could maybe have a Place of Power. Even if I couldn't believe in a loving, kindly, person sort of god, I could believe in the rock and the wind and the rain. And maybe, if I remembered them strongly enough, if I imagined them strongly enough, I could feel a taste of that cleanness again.

So that's what I did. I lay there and I imagined myself back on

Whale Rock. I hungered for that cleanness with everything still alive in me, because I thought that if I could make it real, even in my imagination, if I could feel a hint of what the storm had brought, I could turn my life over to it.

After a time, I began to smell the spray. This cell had boarded-up windows, and they only turned the light on for a few hours each day, so most of the time I lay in the dark. But there was a crack of light where one of the metal grates over the window didn't quite fit right, and so during the day a little ray of sunlight would seep in. And that sunlight began to seem like a hand reaching out to me. I could touch it and feel warm. I could (this may sound crazy) open my mouth and taste it. The light tasted sweet like honey and it tasted like that cleanness on the rock. And, Maya, that was enough. Just that one ray of sun, and when it was gone, the memory of it. I felt redeemed. Not forgiven, exactly—I no longer needed to be forgiven, even by myself. The sun and the rock and wind and water didn't care what I had done. They didn't care about me, personally. They just reached and rained because that was their nature. All I had to do was stretch out my hand to them. They were always there, offering.

Why I'm telling you all of this is to thank you, to let you know what a gift you have given me. When I read your book, I realized you had found something similar up there on the mountain. Maybe that's not so surprising, since we started from the same place.

And in case this letter is misleading, you should know that things are really a lot better now. They began to turn around for me after that time. That was, what—five years ago? It still seemed like I had an endless amount of time to do, like I was going to be in here forever. But I was determined not to dodge the pain anymore. When I let myself really hurt, for where I was, and what I was, and what I had wasted, then I found that for the first time in years there was something I wanted that was within my reach. I wanted to go outside. That was all. Just to see the sky again, even if there were walls that surrounded it. And I knew I could. I would have to behave myself, to earn back my exercise privilege, but I could do that now. I had my own purpose to sustain me. Before, every time I gave in, every time I obeyed an order, I felt that stone core of myself being chipped away. I could feel it getting smaller and smaller. And the thing is, Maya, in prison that's what it comes down to, every minute. Obey, or disobey. And you just can't disobey all the time. Nobody can. Maybe Gandhi, but not too many others.

Yeah, I've been reading Gandhi. Don't laugh. Some of the men here that come out of the peace resistance started a little study group. Actually, my life right now is pretty good. I work doing construction and plumbing on the grounds, so I get outside a lot. I've been moved into the Honor Farm. I have some friends. There's some Native Americans here and once a month one of their elders comes in to do a sweat. They let me come sometimes, thanks to my Cherokee great-grandma. Probably my life doesn't sound like much to you but to me, it's a big improvement. I'll be out in three or four years, which is still a long time but not an endless time.

Don't answer this if you don't want to. Probably you're happy with someone else now, and this is all ancient history. I hope so. But I needed to say this all to you. I hope you don't mind. Do you know what happened to Johanna? I would like to write to her, too.

Please don't take it wrong if I sign this,

Love,
Rio

45

Thami to Namche

If thou art told that to become Arhan, thou hast to
cease to love all beings—tell them that they lie.
If thou art taught that sin is born of action and bliss
of absolute inaction, tell them that they err.

—THE VOICE OF THE SILENCE
THE WISDOM OF BUDDHISM

"I've been thinking about it," Debby said, sitting up in her sleeping bag
in the tent she and Maya had shared, and cradling her morning tea in her
hands. "The prayer we should say for Mom is the Jewish prayer—the one
you say for the dead."

Maya turned her own head to look at her sister. Caffeine, she
thought, taking a long sip from her own cup. I need caffeine to deal with
this, if not something stronger.

"It's a good thing I'm a writer," she said to Debby. "Not to mention a psychic. I've developed an ear for subtext. Because have you
noticed in our family nobody ever apologizes straight out? You'd have a
fight with Betty, yell and scream and hang up on the telephone, and she'd
never admit that she was wrong. Never, never, never. But the next day
she'd call you up and talk about how she went to the theater with Lenore
Kapfenberg and give you the whole plot of the play and a rundown on all
the actors and by the end of the conversation she'd be insisting on
treating you to tickets when the play came to San Francisco."

"What are you saying?"

"I'm just trying to clarify for myself what *you're* saying. Do you
mean to imply—just as a wild guess—that maybe you're sorry you've
been such a bitch to me when I came all this way to see you and sorry
that you yelled at me in front of the trekking group and told me that I
shouldn't be let out without a keeper just because I got caught in the

rainstorm, and that I might just possibly be right about us doing something together for Betty?''

"And if I was?''

"Then I would make some cheerful comment about some totally irrelevant subject which wouldn't say outright but might imply that I admit bringing Betty's ashes up here was a way of not manipulating exactly, but trying to create a situation you couldn't get out of.''

Debby smiled. "You didn't happen to bring a Jewish prayer book, did you?''

"To tell you the truth, it never occurred to me.'' Maya sipped her hot tea slowly. "But now that you've made the suggestion, I think I agree. Yes, that feels right. We should say Kaddish. The only problem is, how? We don't know the words, and we don't have the book.''

"I don't imagine anyone else in the group would have one.''

"I doubt it,'' Maya said. "Lonnie's Jewish, but she doesn't strike me as the devout type. But I'll ask her.''

"What if she doesn't have one?''

"We'll make up our own Kaddish,'' Maya said. "What I know about the Kaddish is that it says nothing at all about death. It's all about praising God.''

Debby shook her head. "I'm not that much into praising God. I'd rather do it in Hebrew, so I don't have to worry about what it means.''

"Well, we could praise life,'' Maya suggested. "Praise the mountains, praise the rivers, praise the arcane workings of human physiology—whatever turns you on.''

"Let's hope we can find the Hebrew,'' Debby said.

"I believe it's Aramaic,'' Maya said. "I remember reading that somewhere.''

"Whatever.'' She reached out to Maya, and they clasped hands, sipping their tea in the dawn.

This is your ritual, Betty, Maya thought. No beautiful chants, no rich colors, no incense or Tibetan horns. Just the simple ceremony of your two daughters trying and failing to connect, arguing and bitching in a dance of our own, failing and trying and once in a while succeeding. My offering to you, Mom, is simply my pledge that I will never give up. I will go on reaching for her, and so ally myself with the wind and the rocks and the rain.

She was thinking about Rio's letter. Maybe he's right, she thought. Maybe this world is a thigh bone trumpet, a temple horn through which compassion calls. When we respond, miracles happen.

She squeezed Debby's hand. "I've been so frustrated,'' Debby said softly. "I wanted to have more time with you. When I heard you were coming, I got so excited, even though I knew that it meant that Mom was dead. But there was so much I wanted to show you."

"I would never have guessed," Maya said dryly.

"I didn't invent the emergencies. They really happened."

"I thought you were avoiding me."

"No."

They sat together in silence, holding hands, until Maya's ass began to hurt and she shifted her position.

"Are you happy, Maya?" Debby asked softly. "You know, living with Johanna and writing and all? Are you doing what you really want to do?"

"I don't know," Maya admitted. "I think so. But since Mom died, I haven't felt so sure. Everything seems to have gone flat. But I think so. I think I'm doing what I'm meant to be doing. Happiness isn't so much in the circumstances, but how you meet them, anyway."

"I suppose that's true."

"And you? Are you happy?"

"I'm happy in my work. I'm happy being here."

"You aren't lonely?"

"Sometimes. I'd like to have a partner. I'd like to have a child. But I don't suppose I will. I'm not very good at getting coupled up."

"One of us ought to," Maya said. "Have a child, that is. Lay Betty's ghost to rest. Give her pictures of a grandchild she can show in heaven."

"Do you want to?"

"I'm thinking about it. A lot, since I've been up here. I'm at that age when the biological clock begins to tick like a time bomb."

"How does Johanna feel about it?"

"We haven't talked about it." Actually, Maya admitted to herself, she hadn't really considered the question. What did that mean? That subconsciously, she was seeing her future as separate from Johanna's—or that what she really wanted was merely a baby fantasy, not something that would throw her lifestyle, relationships, and living accommodations into question. Didn't someone market a video baby? Like the video fishtank, no feeding, no messy cleaning, just turn it on and watch the kid play, gurgle, and grow. "Rachel's in college already. I don't think Jo really wants to start all over again."

"I guess not. But wouldn't she be supportive if you wanted to?"

"She'd feel that she should be. But I'm not sure I want to put her in that position. Anyway, we've got other things to work out first."

"Well, you'd be a good mother," Debby said.

"Really?" Maya said, surprised. "I wouldn't have expected you to think so."

"Why not?"

"I thought you thought I was one of the world's major weird people."

Debby propped herself up on one elbow. "Honestly, Maya, sometimes I feel you have me cast as a character in a movie I'm not actually in. You know?"

"No. I thought you had *me* cast in a wrong movie."

They laughed.

"We haven't been very good at really seeing each other," Maya said.

"I know," Debby admitted. "I guess we inherit that from Betty. She always had us cast in supporting roles in her own drama. She never could understand that we had movies of our own."

"That's why it was so hard to be with her," Maya said quietly. "Why I couldn't move down there. Why you didn't come home."

"I know. It was a mistake," Debby admitted. "I should have come. But I know why I made it. Still I'm sad. Sad that she's dead, sad that she was so lonely while she was alive. But that's why I didn't want to do a ritual with you. I didn't want to just be an extra in your movie."

"I was thinking more that we'd be costars."

"Saying the Kaddish together, we can. Doing your ritual, I'm nothing but a walk-on part."

The morning's hike retraced their route along the canyon, and then climbed up to Namche. The sun was warm. Maya wore Claire's green sweater, and tied her own jacket onto her day pack. For the first time on the trek, she felt strong, waving away the eager Sherpas who offered to carry her pack. In spite of her drenching the day before, she was hardly coughing at all.

Maybe I'm finally getting in shape, now that the trek's nearly over, Maya thought. If I ever do this again, I swear I'll join a gym first. But that's the saddest part, for me, about how hard it's been. I probably won't want to do it again.

Still, she was enjoying the simple sensation of walking, feeling her muscles strong and springy. She wasn't as strong as Peter, maybe, or as swift as Jan or Carolyn, who were all far ahead of her, striding rapidly along. But fit enough that she felt she could walk forever, down the ancient trade route to Tibet and up to China, over the high slopes of Chomolungma, out to the moon and the far reaches of the stars or, at least, to be realistic, the nearer planets, Venus or Mercury. Maybe the trek would prove to be like childbirth—she'd forget the pain and remember only the moments of ecstasy. Or maybe her body was just like an old warhorse, quickening its pace as it heads home to the stable.

At first, Debby walked beside her, pointing out trails she had taken and huts she'd visited to set a broken bone or deliver a baby. After a while she drifted ahead to chat with Ang and Pembila. Maya walked alone, still thinking about Rio's letter.

I should have written him, she admitted to herself. Sure, Tony warned me not to, said it might stir up new investigations, get them interested in me. But I could have found a way. I meant to. I never said to myself, no, I'm not going to answer him, I'm going to cut him off. I carried the letter in my purse for years, always believing that on the next plane ride, or when I finished the next chapter, or when the holidays were over, I would write. But I never did. I was always too tired, or packing for the next trip, or behind on starting the next chapter.

Something always stopped me. I couldn't answer that letter unless I answered it honestly. And I couldn't do that without telling him about Rachel.

The truth is, both Johanna and I would have been more comfortable if he had died with the others. We could have said Kaddish for him, praised what there was to praise in his life, raged and mourned and talked about him openly. He would have been our mutual romantic tragedy, and we would have been oh so comfortable in our assurance that we were better, saner, stronger than he was. Dead, he could have been anything we wanted him to be. But alive, he was always a small danger, a continual secret that we had to bury, lest he turn up and turn into something we didn't expect and couldn't cope with.

So what do I do now? Dig him up and take my chances? Or let him lie?

Thinking about the Kaddish reminded her of her problem. Lonnie was walking slowly, not far ahead, and Maya hurried to catch up.

"Hey, Lonnie," Maya asked as she came up beside her. "Do you happen to know the Hebrew prayer for the dead? We want to say Kaddish for our mother. But we don't have the book and we don't know the prayer."

"I bet Howard knows it," Lonnie said.

"Howard?" Oh Goddess, was she going to have to turn to him for help? "With those Nordic good looks? I didn't know he was Jewish."

"Half," Lonnie said. "But he's into it. Goes to a Jewish Renewal group in Palo Alto. He told me all about it."

"How awkward," Maya said.

"Awkward? Why?" Lonnie stopped on the trail and regarded Maya shrewdly. "Don't tell me, let me guess. He made a pass at you, and you turned him down."

"You got it," Maya said.

"Were you rude to him? Insulting?"

"No, I was quite polite."

"I wouldn't let it bother you," Lonnie said, resuming her walk.

"Guys like Howard, they get used to being rejected. It just rolls right off their backs."

"Well, I'll ask him," Maya said. The trail was wide enough for her and Lonnie to walk side by side, and she matched Lonnie's easy pace. "How are you and Jan doing? Have you come to any decision about what you're going to do?"

"Yeah, we've decided to do the Annapurna trek next year together. In the meantime, we'll go home and think some more. Maybe I'll try to come to one of your rituals this year—let you turn my life inside out. You got any plans to come to Portland?"

"I think I've got something on the schedule for Seattle," Maya admitted.

"Close enough."

When the group reached Namche, they settled their things in Ang's house, staked out their sleeping spaces, and had their tea. Maya had seated herself on a small stool across from Howard, who had claimed the far corner of the long bench. Debby sat beside him. As they nibbled the last of the cookies, Maya made herself speak up.

"Can I ask you a favor, Howard?"

"A favor? Sure." He looked surprised, and so pleased to be asked that Maya almost felt guilty.

"Lonnie mentioned to me that you're Jewish."

"Half. My mother never converted. My father sent me to Hebrew school and all that—to be bar mitzvahed. But I always felt a little like, you know, like I wasn't quite the genuine article." Howard chattered on nervously. "It goes through the mother, you know—Jewishness. If she's Jewish, you're Jewish. If she's not, you're not. But I always feel like I am."

He wants to please, Maya thought. He wants to be what I want him to be. He's trying to mold himself into what he imagines I want. And not quite succeeding. How sad.

That's why human beings were harder to love than mountains, she thought. People were always constructing themselves, using each other as blueprints and foils and mirrors. Mountains were just mountains, high or low, craggy or rounded, forested or bare. They formed themselves not in relationship to some ideal but in response to real things: the shifting of the earth's plates, the pressure of molten rock, the action of wind and rain and running water.

"It's the last holdover from matriarchy, the mother thing," Maya said. "But really, if you feel you're Jewish, you're more Jewish than most of us, I say." Now she was trying to buttress him, to atone for her pity by making him feel better about himself.

"Well, the Reform groups now, some of them say it doesn't matter which parent was Jewish," Howard said. "I like that idea."

"I was wondering," Maya interjected. "Do you happen to have a prayer book with you?"

"A prayer book? No. I never thought about bringing one. What do you want with a prayer book?"

"We want to say Kaddish for our mother."

"The Kaddish? I know that by heart. I said it almost every day for a year after my father died."

"You do?" Maya said, delighted. "Oh, that's wonderful! Howard, you've saved us."

"But to say the Kaddish, you need a minyan," Howard said, distressed. "That's ten Jews. It used to be ten Jewish men, but nowadays, they count women."

"How enlightened," Debby said.

"Only the ultra-Orthodox still stick to the rule about men," Howard said. "But we don't have ten Jews here."

"We've got four," Maya said. "Us three and Lonnie. Isn't that close enough?"

"It's not a matter of percentages," Howard said. "Ten is supposed to be ten."

"Oh, come on, Howard," Debby said impatiently. "Would God really mind?"

"That's not the point." A vertical line appeared in the center of Howard's brow, and suddenly Maya could see how worry would sculpt his face when he got old. "The point is that the Kaddish is a prayer that's supposed to be said in community. It's not an individual prayer."

"What do you mean?" Maya asked.

"The Kaddish is about the community rising up in praise of God and life, in the face of death," Howard said. "That's what gives support to the mourners and holds the fabric of life together when death has ruptured it. Without the community, the prayer is meaningless. It's just a bunch of empty words."

Maya looked at him, amazed. His eyes were shining and his nervousness and awkwardness were gone. He's forgotten himself, she thought, and so for the first time his true self is showing through, authentic and solid as a mountain.

Yes, mountains were easy to love. They didn't have to define themselves against the valleys or the plains or the hills, or worry about how they appeared. They didn't need to lower some other mountain in order to raise themselves.

And she? Hadn't she been using Howard, for the whole trip, as her foil? Casting him as the nerd, the wimp, the timid one, so that she could stand out against him as courageous and wild and free. So that she had not, until this moment, allowed herself to catch even a glimpse of who he truly was.

Had she not used Rio the same way?

"Howard, you surprise me," Maya said. "I had no idea you were such a theologian."

He smiled a bit sheepishly. "We've got a great rabbi in Palo Alto. Judith Pizer, her name is. After my father died, I joined a study group. We went over the Kaddish in detail."

"I hear what you're saying, Howard," Debby said. "But this is the only chance Maya and I have to say this prayer together, maybe for years. Can't we make an exception, this one time?"

Debby glanced at Maya and met her eye. Not a word nor a wink passed between them, and yet Maya knew that they both felt their connection, their common purpose. And that is all I ever really wanted from her, Maya realized. Simply to be linked, moving toward the same end, small or large. I thought we had to do a ritual, but really we could have cooked a dinner or planted a field. How ironic that Howard should be the instrument of our connection.

"But why would you want to do something for your mother that essentially is meaningless?" Howard asked.

"Because it wouldn't be meaningless," Maya said. She paused for a moment. The more they talked about the Kaddish, the more strongly she felt that saying the prayer was the right and perfect ritual for Betty. But how did she turn that intuition into a reasoned argument? "The meaning would change," she began slowly. Howard and Debby looked at her, waiting. "The prayer would become an offering to our ancestors."

"That sounds more pagan than Jewish," Howard objected.

"I *am* a Pagan," Maya said, "but hear me out. You talk about repairing ruptures. Well here we are, me and Debby, rupture incarnate. I'm a priestess of the Goddess, she's a . . . what? What are you, Debby? An atheist?"

"Not exactly. Sort of a semi-Buddhist agnostic, I guess I'd say."

Maya smiled. "Our mother herself believed more in Freud than in God."

"Not in recent years," Debby interjected. "Give her some credit. She'd moved on to the post-Freudians."

"Whatever," Maya went on. "Our father was a Communist. Our family is either dead or scattered, but here we are together, in Nepal, of all places. And the point is, how do we make peace with our ancestors? In the Goddess tradition, death doesn't rupture the community. The community continues on, beyond death. So that if we have four living Jews here, we've got forty thousand spirits, or more. We'd be saying the prayer as a way of coming home to them."

When she said the words "coming home," Maya suddenly thought about Claire. I should have gotten her address, she thought, or invited her to visit in San Francisco. I'll never know whether she makes a home for herself or not.

And me? My way home to myself, to whatever Jo and I can be to each other, seems to be making a detour through Nevada. Maybe I need to let the Kaddish bring me home to my ancestors so they can teach me how to wander in the desert.

"It still doesn't sound right to me," Howard said. "But what the hay—it's your funeral." Then he blushed. "Oh, I'm so sorry, I didn't mean it that way. God! What a stupid remark!"

Maya and Debby laughed.

"Don't apologize," Maya said. "You're right. It is our funeral. And that's good."

They stood on the terrace outside of Ang's house: Maya and Debby, Howard and Lonnie. From the door of the byre, Ila and the *zopkios* watched respectfully. The sun was setting behind the mountains, and the air glowed. Streaks of rose and gold lit up the sky.

"Yiskadol v yiskadash shemay rabah . . ."

Howard stood in front of the women, uncomfortable in his role as rabbi, not quite knowing what to do with his hands as he slowly spoke the words of the prayer for the others to repeat.

"V'almah di vrah cheruteh—v'amlich malchuteh . . ."

The ancient words rang out from the ledge, floating above Namche.

This isn't what I imagined, Maya thought. This isn't the fantasy ritual I had dreamed up for Betty. I still carry her ashes on my back and will carry them down as I carried them up, until I can lay them to rest for good.

But as she looked at her sister, crooning the ancient words, Debby appeared suddenly radiant as Tara stepping into the world of form, her eyes alight, her whole body pregnant with illumination. Lonnie, beside her, glowed with the holy passion of the Dakini, and Howard became transformed, his awkwardness the grace of the holy clown. Maya wanted to raise her hands and dance, to spin in circles, crying out a new mantra: Debby, Howard, Lonnie! shouting to heaven and earth that here before her eyes was Buddha, Goddess incarnate. You, you are the Perfect One, she wanted to say to them all, to gather in Ila and Tenzing and Jan and Carolyn and Peter, to send out thought waves to Johanna at home and Rio in Nevada, asking forgiveness for how she had not seen and seen them. Praise Pembila and Tashi! Exalted be Ang! Hosannas to the stolid *zopkios* in their stalls! You are all more, so much more than I have allowed myself to know, you are crevices and canyons and folds where living waters flow and forests are born, you are each Goddess Mother of your own universe, and I have only let myself glimpse picture postcards in the bazaar. But now, now I know. Betty, I have gathered a chorus of gods to offer you prayer.

The desert was waiting for her. She would come down from the mountain to walk its spare sand plains. The revelations she brought with her were not of the order that could be carved on stone tablets or proclaimed to the multitudes. They were more like the well of sweet water that was said to follow Miriam the prophetess wherever she went. As she wandered, she would be sustained.

She held Debby's hand, murmuring the sonorous words while the rock arms of the mountains cradled them both. The sky floated banners of color like prayer flags loosed on the wind, and forty thousand spirits danced above the town.

46

Letter

Nevada Test Site
March 4, 1988

Dear Maya,

You probably won't get this letter until you get back from your trip. I hope it was a good one. Maybe I shouldn't be writing to you again. I don't want to intrude on your privacy. It's only that after I wrote you last week, I realized how much I hadn't told you. And since I'm asking you to come here, I feel like I owe you all of the truth.

The problem is, the truth is hard to tell. Oh, I can give you facts, I can even emote on cue. It's a trick I have—maybe we all have, a kind of emotional sleight-of-hand—distracting your audience by exposing your pain. But what you show is the pain you can bear to show, the story you've told so many times that its edges are worn smooth and it no longer cuts you as you roll over it. So that honesty becomes an illusion of honesty, and you keep the real stuff down inside, where even *you* don't see it anymore.

I don't want to do that with you. I don't want to lie to you.

But I may. That's a warning.

What I have to write you about is what really happened to me in these last years, and how I got here. When I wrote you from prison I was in a good space; I had come to a kind of acceptance of things. I've had my ups and downs since then. You know, it's hard when you undertake to change yourself in some fundamental way. At first there's this rush of energy, a kind of euphoria, but you get worn down and ground down by the day to day. The regular bullshit of living would be enough to deal with when you're outside, but when you're inside—prison, that is— you've got the added stress of being locked up and watched and searched and ordered around and generally humiliated fifteen times a day. Not to mention the strain of constantly watching your back to make sure some- body doesn't stick a knife into it. I hung in there, not always high but steady on my feet, if you know what I mean, and about three years ago I was released.

You probably have an image in your mind of what that's like—a grainy old film where a guy walks out of the gates of the state prison, in a suit that doesn't fit too well, and the warden shakes his hand and says, "Good luck, son." Well, it's not like that. I was in a halfway house for a couple of months, where you're free to go out and look for work during the day, but there's a curfew at night. You room in a dorm with a bunch of guys, and all and all it's a little like boot camp—without the exercise. In New York City, the house was, down in Brooklyn, and not the best part of it either.

From the moment I walked out of those prison grounds, I wanted one thing and one thing only, a drink. That was my image of freedom—to be able to walk into a bar, sit down, say, "Gimme a Dos Equis." Just a beer, nothing hard. Maybe if I could have gone to the mountains, or out to the clean beaches of the West, I would have thought of freedom in some other terms. But the beaches of Brooklyn were covered with garbage and used syringes and the waves were sullen and oily.

I didn't drink. I was afraid of what it would lead to. But, God, how I wanted to! Like a nun for Jesus, like Mao for revolution, like a baby for his mama's breast—that was how I longed for a drink. A desire so intense, I kept thinking, it should be focused on something meaningful and deep. Conversing with the burning bush, climbing Everest, freeing India, changing the world. Ah . . . but I had tried that, and look what it led to. Maybe I was less dangerous fixated on my battle with the bottle.

I didn't drink, but I didn't find a job, either. Funny how it looks on a résumé, you know—1971–1985 Arlington Federal Prison. I'm joking, of course. I was mostly looking for construction jobs. They don't ask for a résumé but they do want to know where you got your training and what your references are. I got some day labor jobs, but that was about it.

Still, I was going to make it. I saved my money at the halfway house. I had a little put away from prison. They only pay a few cents an hour but over fourteen years it adds up. I didn't have anybody to go to. Not you, certainly, and all of our old friends were either dead or disappeared or had long ago written me off. And if they hadn't, I wouldn't have trusted them. Like Groucho Marx used to say—I wouldn't want to join any club that would have me as a member. My family had written me off, too, so I was on my own.

For fourteen years, everything was decided for me. When to get up, what to eat, when to go to bed. The goddamned coffee already has sugar in it when they serve it to you. There's not a lot of room for choice.

Suddenly, there you are, out on the street, facing the void. Everything seems too big, too wide open, the lights too glary, the noises too confusing. You're not used to it. You wake up and the day stretches ahead of you endlessly, and you don't know how to chop it up into manageable pieces. You don't have a job to go to or a soul that cares about you except for your parole officer, and you won't see him again for three months, if you're lucky. You don't even have a dog to walk.

The worst of it is, you keep thinking, "I'm a free man, I'm supposed to be happy. This is what I looked forward to for fourteen years." But you don't feel free, you feel like you've fallen into some kind of vacuum, a nonlife, where none of your actions count. Like you're a ghost, and your hands pass right through everything you try to grasp. I could feel the rage begin to build. Like we felt about the war, you remember— that sense that we could shout and march and rampage through the streets forever, and it wouldn't matter. Nobody was listening. Nothing was going to change. And so you get driven on to do the next thing, the more extreme thing, until you do the thing you can't take back. And then, they're listening all right, they've been watching every move you made for years, they play back transcripts of your telephone calls and enter your brother's letters into evidence.

But I'm getting bitter, and that's dangerous, now as it was then. My old temptation—blame somebody else for all the fuckups, blame the government, blame you for leaving me, blame anybody so as not to have to say, yes, I accept it, my own hands did the deed that put me here.

I kept fighting. I kept trying to fight my way back to that clean place, with the wind and the rain and the rock. I graduated from the halfway house into a cheap room in a skid row hotel but then they closed the place, and I couldn't find another room I could afford. I was sleeping on the streets, and they were rock-hard, all right, but there in the middle of Brooklyn the wind is just bitter and the rain is full of smoke and grit. So time went on. I was still getting some laborer's jobs, less and less as I got dirtier, but then one day I was helping this guy carry a cast-iron bathtub up three flights of steps, and the asshole dropped it. The thing barreled down and knocked me over. Well, I was lucky I didn't get crushed to death, or break anything, but I twisted my ankle pretty bad and so I couldn't work at all for a while.

That did me in. I'm not proud about this next bit, Maya, but I swore I'd write you an honest letter, and so I will. The guy I'd been working for took me down to the county hospital, and paid me off with twenty-five bucks. They wrapped up my ankle so I could hobble around, and I went out and bought a pint of vodka. There's a big old spreading oak tree out in Prospect Park. I sat myself down under it with my back to its trunk, and I drank myself into oblivion. And Maya, I have to tell you that oblivion's a pretty sweet place. Nothing hurts, there. No ghosts, no memories, no regrets.

I liked oblivion so much that when I finished that bottle I went out and bought another. When I ran out of money, I made myself a cardboard sign that said WOUNDED VET—PLEASE HELP and sat on a concrete divider in the middle of the street until I collected enough money to get drunk again. Hell, I figured, I'm as much a casualty of Vietnam as anyone who ever put on a uniform and shot at Charlie for Uncle Sam.

I was happy, Maya. I remember thinking, "Pretty soon, winter'll be coming, and I'll lie down in the snow and be dead." Permanent oblivion. No more begging and scraping for spare change to pay for it. No more awkward intervals of consciousness and fear. And then, "Why wait? Why wait for winter?"

By then that oak tree had begun to seem like my mother. Not my real mother, God help her, whining and beaten down, but like the mother everybody wishes they'd had, big and sheltering and kind. She slowed the wind down and kept the rain off my back, and I found myself talking to her. I can't say as she said a whole lot in reply, but after a while I began to feel like she did answer me. When I was really, really drunk, she'd answer in words, with a rubbery talking mouth like in a Disney cartoon. When I was not quite so drunk, the conversation was more like an answer I could feel deep inside me somewhere.

Maybe you think I'm working up to an alco-mystic vision, but what the oak tree told me was very practical. She said, "Never commit suicide on an empty stomach."

Now there was a piece of advice for you. It made me feel like a little whining kid being put in his place by Mom, and it reminded me that I hadn't eaten in a long time. When you're into serious drinking, food is a low priority.

I knew then that I had to make a choice—live or die. Dying seemed preferable but somehow wrong. Maybe because of Jim. He was always the good brother, the model boy. Dying was just another thing he got to do that I wasn't worthy of. Or more—he didn't want to die. For me to die was to cheapen his death. Or worse. I thought about my dad, blowing his brains out in the car behind our house. My whole life, the one thing I was always most afraid of was turning into him. And now here I was, my father's son, dead drunk and thinking about suicide.

I stood right up and walked down to the St. Francis Mission and waited in line for a dinner of rice and beans and let them pray over me and give me a bed for the night, and a shower, and a few clean clothes. I often think about that walk over there, the way I was, filthy and stinking and weaving back and forth, a piece of human garbage, you would say if you'd seen me. Yet there I was, walking, slow and desperate, back into life. Which is just to say that I always try to remember that you never know where anybody is going, or coming from. Somebody who seems past all hope may be right at the point of turning.

Bad as that time was, I don't regret it, because it taught me so much I need to know in the work I do now. Which is feeding people.

What happened was, I stayed at the St. Francis Mission for a few days, until I got over the worst of the hangover-multiplied-a-thousand-times—I hope you can't even imagine what *that* was like. As I sobered up a bit, and felt better, the prayers began to get to me. There was another shelter over at the Acts of Mercy House, run by a group of radical Catholics connected with the Peace movement. I remembered Dave Ryan, the activist who made friends with me in jail. He'd been with them before he broke away to form his own group. I stayed with them for a while and started going back to AA meetings there, and helping out in the kitchen, and after a bit, they offered me a job, as assistant cook and general handyman. It didn't pay much, but it came with a room in their community house and plenty of friendly company. They were religious, but not pious—if you follow me—in a way I felt comfortable with. So that's what I did, until just this summer, when my parole was finally up.

The work was good for me, and I was good for the work. I've come to see that there are some gifts I've received from my life, fucked up as a lot of it has been. One is that I can talk to anybody. I don't judge anybody, because I've been there. Further down than there, even. And another one is, that I can be honest—as I'm trying to be with you. I don't have any pretense to keep up. I don't have any face left to save.

And so in the end, I am free.

One of the conditions of my parole was that I stay away from political groups and demonstrations. Last summer, when my parole finally ended, I decided to take off from the soup kitchen for a year and travel with this group called Grains of Truth, that specializes in feeding large numbers of people at political actions. We're kind of a motley crew—there's me, there's Marge, a great older woman who took off after her husband died and decided to work for peace, there's Lissa, who's twenty-two and a bit of a lost soul, and there's Herb, an old guy who fought against Franco in the Lincoln Brigade and now spends all his time fighting the government, in spite of the fact that he's got a dicey heart. We pick up more of a crew when we need them, and we know how to feed several hundred people on less money than you can imagine, even out in the middle of the desert with no running water, making sure nobody gets sick. Which is a skill worth having.

So now you know how I got to Nevada. I hope it doesn't scare you off, because I sure would like for you to come—not just for political reasons, but because, to go on being honest, I would like to see you, to talk over old times, as they say. I feel I've earned the right to want that, if maybe not the right to get it.

But no, this is still only partway honest. I read it over and it sounds so cold, so matter-of-fact, compared to what I feel. Bear with me, Maya love, if you haven't thrown this out, if you're reading it at all, bear with me, please. It's taken me too many awful years to be able to say these two words, "I hurt," and I can't say them plain and unvarnished more than once a page or so. Please help me out. Help me not to lie. Tune your ears to the channel of those two words, and you'll hear them, like a ghost voice on the radio, a low buzz under everything else I say.

Everything in me is fighting not to say them, to keep my cool, to pretend that what you decide doesn't really matter all that much to me. I guess I was wrong when I said I have no face left to save.

What I would say, if I were honest, is that I feel like you and I got interrupted in the middle of a conversation seventeen years ago. All right, call it an argument. A fight. But it's like I got cut off in the middle of a sentence, before I could finish what I was saying. I never got to say good-bye.

I know that you did love me once, and now I can look at you leaving and see it as an act of love. At the time I was just as bewildered as an abandoned dog. I never got the chance—I wasn't capable of telling you how much I did love you. I couldn't admit that I needed you. I thought what I needed was anything else—freedom, some other woman to fuck, a drink.

So I drove you away. Somehow you disappeared, transformed yourself into a vacuum, nothingness, a void in the air.

I can't bear the vacuum any longer, Maya. I can't stand the holes, the empty spaces, the silences in my past. I know that I have no right to ask you for anything but I am asking you for help. Until I speak to you, until I finish that sentence, I can't move on. I can never completely heal.

The one thing that gives me the nerve to ask you to help me is that I believe that conversation is still unfinished for you, too. None of us can really get away with cutting off the past. I believe that I'm not just asking for but offering some healing.

And in case I'm not clear, all I want to do is talk to you, face-to-face, just for a little while.

There's more, Maya. This is not the total story, but it's as much as I can tell—not as honest as I'd like to be, but as honest as I can be. I have to stop. I'm sorry. Or maybe I'm not. Now I'm rambling. I'm going to end this letter now, and mail it before I lose my nerve.

Rio

47

Nevada

In April of 1988, thousands of concerned citizens
from all over the United States will converge on the
Nevada Test Site to express their opposition to
nuclear war. In this critical election year,
it is more vital than ever to take a stand.
Join us in the desert for two weeks of actions to stop
the Department of Defense from carrying out
its planned series of belowground nuclear tests.
Raise your voice for peace!

—*COMMITTEE TO BAN NUCLEAR
TESTING FLYER*

The gates of doom were being stormed by an army of ragged clowns, masked magicians, and dreadlocked drummers. Maya's head hurt. She stood in front of the main gate of the Nevada Test Site, surrounded by a crowd wearing animal masks, bird feathers, ancestral images made of painted plaster gauze. The noise of the drums was deafening, what Maya thought of as hippie drumming—lively, on the beat, but unfocused—a good-natured din. Her own drum, an hourglass-shaped metal *doumbek,* was locked in the trunk of her car. She felt no urge to play, only a desire to set up her tent and lie down somewhere.

The last few days had involved so much motion, so many flights through so many time zones, that she'd moved beyond jet lag and come unstuck in time. Her body no longer knew when to wake or when to sleep or when to expect the sun to rise.

But she couldn't sleep until she saw Rio. He was the culmination of her journey, the destiny of all her frenetic motion. So where is he? she thought. How frustrating, to come ten thousand miles and then not find him.

She had looked for him at the camp, in the large kitchen tent set up by Grains of Truth. A helpful young woman with a shaved head had directed her down to the roadside by the main gate, where Grains was dispensing hot soup and coffee from a small table. But Rio wasn't there either, and the young man in the blue mohawk who was volunteering seemed to have no idea where he was.

"Check back later," he suggested. "Marge'll be back in half an hour or so. She'll probably know where he's gone."

Maybe this is my doom, Maya thought, to go through fire and water to meet people who aren't there when I finally arrive. But he's got to be around here somewhere. Patience. I'll see him soon enough.

Maybe this is just another of the Goddess's little challenges. I pledged to myself that I would remember what I learned in Nepal. I have to not think of Rio as my summit, my rest stop, my cup of tea at my final destination, but just walk up this mountain and be where I am.

"Maya!" A young woman danced up out of the crowd and flung her arms around Maya, gripping her in a fierce hug. "You came! You came after all!"

"Alix!" Maya was delighted to find someone she knew even slightly. Alix had come to several of the rituals she led, and Maya had always been drawn to her. She was in her early twenties, called herself an anarchist, had a black rose tatooed on her left shoulder, five rings in each ear and one in her nose. Her blond hair was cropped short in front and hung down in a dyed red tail behind, and her eyes were level and challenging, conveying the impression that regardless of relative height, she neither looked up to nor down on anyone.

"I asked the committee to invite you, but nobody knew whether you would really come," Alix said.

"I didn't know for sure, myself, until—Goddess, was it only a few days ago? It seems like decades ago, in another world."

"You were in Nepal, I heard."

"That's right."

Maya felt Alix's openhearted warmth and clung to her for a moment, feeling welcomed and wanted. She suspected that she might need to draw on her friendship. Yes, she admitted to herself, she was scared to talk to Rio, afraid of his rightful anger. She needed a home base.

"It's so cool that you're here!" Alix took her hand and led her to the open land alongside the road, where the crowd was thinner and the noise not so overpowering. "Good, now we can hear each other. Come and meet my affinity group, Circle A."

A small knot of people were standing together, and Alix introduced Maya around. "This is my friend Maya," Alix announced. "Let's see, this is Laura, Hazel, Ben, Kathy, Tommy, and Roger, our resident anthropologist."

"Out here on the desert, all the natives are assigned a resident anthropologist," Tommy said. He smiled at Maya, his tight, blond curls and wide blue eyes giving him a look of almost angelic innocence. "It comes with the territory."

"Are you really an anthropologist?" Maya asked Roger, a tall, dark-haired man wearing a crown of stag's horns. "Perhaps you can explain the meaning of the colorful local customs. Like the masks, for example."

"Sociologist. I'm doing a doctoral dissertation on the Peace movement," he said. "And they represent all the life that is threatened by nuclear war. But I've met you before. You wouldn't remember, but I heard you speak last year when I was back in Boston."

"Now I recognize you," Hazel said. "You're Maya Greenwood. I was at a reading you did. I love your books." She was small and blond, with big glasses and a round body, and looked up at Maya shyly through a crown of feathers.

Maya felt embarrassed. She had come here for a very private encounter with her past, yet as soon as she announced her name, she became again a public figure. Granted, she was only semifamous, hardly a household word, but in certain communities such as this one, she was well-enough known that announcing herself to be Maya Greenwood made her immediately accountable to crowds of strangers.

She could see the ways Alix and her friends began to adjust and present themselves to her. Hazel was looking up at her eagerly and Alix was beaming proudly, taking credit for having produced this prize. Ben brightened; Roger was suddenly interested in her. Laura looked shy, and Kathy seemed slightly embarrassed, as if she had never heard of Maya and felt she should have. The change was subtle, so slight that had she not become sensitized she would never have noticed it.

She felt a sharp stab of panic. This is what's wrong with me, she realized. This is why I could never keep a group together, why they always felt like I was dominating them. Not because of anything I did, but because as soon as I said my name, I became the star of the movie. And I couldn't see it, because of course I *am* the star of my own movie, as we all are.

But I don't want that now. I can't encounter Rio, make peace with my history, if I feel like I'm under a spotlight of attention. I want the cover of darkness, shadows, anonymity.

"Can't I be Maggie, for a while?" she asked. "I feel like being anonymous."

"Hey, it's a fine old tradition," Ben said. "A nom de guerre. But why?"

"It must get hard, having people recognize you all the time, and gush over you," Hazel said. "I withdraw my comment."

"What, now you don't like her books?" Ben asked. He was tall, lanky, with bright red hair partly concealed under a bear mask he wore pushed back on his head. His face was pale and freckled and he seemed to be about Maya's age. "I do, and I'm not ashamed to admit it."

"We were hoping, if you came, you'd lead a ritual," Laura said. A yellow-beaked raven mask crowned her dark hair, which was cut in a boyish fashion, nearly shaved at the back but long in front.

"I'm here to support the action," Maya said, "but I'm also here for personal reasons. I need some space for a few days, to sort them out."

Tommy gestured at the wide desert plain, the low hills on the horizon, the blue, unbroken sky. "You've come to the right place, then. Space is what we've got."

"I might not want to live up to myself, for a while . . . if that makes sense." Maya felt the need to explain. "I might need room to just be an asshole."

"Can we adopt her?" Alix asked the group, and they all smiled warmly.

"Hey, she said the magic word." Tommy grinned. "Circle A for Asshole. Welcome aboard."

"You can camp with us," Alix told Maya. "Maybe we'll even do an action."

"Anything you want," Tommy said. "Nonviolence training, block-ade strategies, rundowns on the effects of low-level radiation, or local gossip—just consider us your own private action emporium." He handed her an open bag of M&M's. "Begin with this, the official candy of the Circle A affinity group. Tastes good, travels well, won't melt in your pocket, and provides that extra burst of energy you need when the Feds are on your tail."

The drums up at the front gate grew louder.

"Something's happening," Alix said. "Let's go see."

Circle A moved up into the thick of the crowd, and Maya followed.

In front of the double gates, drummers and dancers were massed by the cattle guard of metal bars set across a trench in the road. Behind stood a line of police and Wackenhut Security Guards from the private company that Ben said guarded all federal facilities. Farther down the road, behind the demonstrators, three police cars were pulled up along the curb, and a sheriff leaned against the door of one of them, talking into a walkie-talkie.

Maya found herself oddly disappointed by the ordinariness of it all. She had expected something more, a feeling of doom and dread like the Gates of Mordor, a view of blasted, ruined earth. But Ground Zero, where the bombs were detonated, was twenty-five miles away. Here all they could see on the far horizon were the lights of Mercury, the test site's company town.

Drums pounded, dancers gyrated, but nothing else seemed to be happening. Maya scanned the crowd but saw no sign of Rio. Would she recognize him? Maya wondered. What did he look like now? Was he weathered, beaten down, did his face show the marks of someone who had lived too long in hard places, slept too many nights unsheltered? Was his hair gray? Or was he, perish the thought, bald? I know we're not young anymore, we're both getting into middle age, she admitted. But the thought of a bald Rio was almost too much to bear.

Suddenly she felt the full weight of her exhaustion. I haven't really stopped since Nepal, she thought. Two full days on planes getting back, a highly charged interlude with Johanna, another airplane, another intensely emotional conversation, another airplane . . . Goddess! It was a wonder she was still on her feet. I feel like I'm on the last hurdle of a long race, she thought, chasing after or facing up to a series of uncomfortable encounters. Like a strange treasure hunt. First clue, find your sister in Nepal. Second, sit down across the kitchen table from Johanna on your return, and tell her that you realized some things on the trip.

"What?" Johanna had asked, her eyes wary. She had done her hair in a new style, with dozens of braided extensions looped up and behind, so that she looked regal, and Maya thought she had never looked so beautiful. She herself wanted nothing more than to sleep, but she knew this conversation had to be faced. Rio's letter had awaited her in the pile of mail on her desk. She had sat down and read it straight through while Johanna was out looking for a safe parking place for the car. Now she was determined to be at least as honest as he was.

"For one, that I love you."

Johanna smiled. "Had to go all the way to Nepal to figure that out? I never doubted it. But . . . ? I hear a *but* in your voice."

"But I can only stay with you under two conditions."

"What are they?"

"That you tell Rachel about Rio. And that I tell Rio about Rachel."

Johanna leaned back in her chair and closed her eyes. "What brought this on?"

"We've been lying, Johanna. Lying to her, and lying to him with our silence." She wished that Johanna would look at her, meet her eye. "I can't live with you if you require that of me."

Johanna sat up. "I don't call it lying. I call it discretion."

"Call it what you like. I can't go on doing it. I haven't written to him for seventeen years because I didn't know what to say to him without telling him about her. Just like you didn't talk to me. . . . Remember? You gave me those journal pages to read, Jo. Don't tell me you didn't expect me to come to this decision."

Jo was silent.

"Or was that why you gave me your journal? You wanted me to force your hand. Consciously or unconsciously."

The teakettle whistled. Johanna got up, took a teapot down from the shelf, rinsed it with hot water from the tap, and made a pot of tea. She set the pot on the table, brought mugs from the cupboard, got the milk out of the refrigerator, and set out spoons. Only when everything was carefully arranged and the tea sat steeping in front of them did she look at Maya and say, "I read those pages before I gave them to you. There was something that jumped out at me—something I said about Marian. How she was holding on to a lie because she was afraid of losing a love."

"I remember that."

"Do you think we're doomed to turn into our parents?" Johanna asked.

Maya reached out and took Johanna's hand.

"I don't think we're doomed at all. Except to keep on groping for that thing we keep on losing."

Johanna had tears in her eyes, but she smiled. "And can we keep on doing that together?"

"There's no one I'd rather have as a groping partner," Maya said.

"I'm afraid," Johanna admitted. "I know we have to tell them both, but I'm scared. That's hard for a tough old warrior like me to admit. I'd much rather feel self-righteous."

"Don't be afraid," Maya reassured her. "I've heard from him, Jo. He's changed. He's been through a lot, but he's grown, too. He'd never do anything to hurt her."

Johanna shook her head. "He might not mean to hurt her, but she could still be hurt. Still, it's not him I'm afraid of anymore. Now I'm more afraid of losing her."

Maya squeezed her hand. "Jojo, you silly bear, you're not going to lose her. She loves you!"

"She'll be furious at me, for lying to her."

"No doubt. She'll be mad as hell at both of us. But we just have to have faith that she'll forgive us."

"You think so?"

"Of course she will. Look at all the stuff we forgave our mothers for."

"I just wanted to protect her," Johanna said, pouring out the tea. "I didn't want her to grow up in an intimate relationship with someone I didn't trust. Is that so wrong?"

"Yes, it was wrong," Maya said. "Understandable, forgivable, but wrong." Wasn't it? she wondered. What would it have been like for Rachel, writing letters to her father in prison, being taken to see him, maybe—meeting him for the first time in some visiting room surrounded by the other cons, or in one of those horrible booths, separated by a sheet of glass, talking by telephone. Or later, having him turn up drunk and filthy, asking for money. Of course, maybe if he'd known he had a daughter, maybe if he'd been able to come to them after he got out of prison, he wouldn't have ended up drunk and on the street. Who could say? They might have taken him in and still he could have smashed all the furniture and broken Rachel's heart.

"Anyway, right or wrong, that isn't the issue now," Maya said. "That's done. What we have to look at is what we do now. I'm going to Nevada, Jo. To the action there, that they've invited me to. Rio's there. He wrote to me. I'm going to see him, and I'm not going to lie to him."

"No, you have to tell him," Johanna said. "But I will ask you for something."

"What?"

"I want you to talk to Rachel before you tell him. She deserves that."

"She does," Maya agreed. "Shouldn't you be the one to tell her?"

Johanna sighed. "I should be. You're right—I just wish you would. But I suppose that's not fair."

"I'll be right beside you," Maya said. "But how do we tell her? Over the telephone? She won't be home until the beginning of June."

"I guess we'll just have to call her before you go to Nevada."

But instead, Maya had called the airlines and cashed in some of her frequent flyer miles. She had slept for a few hours, then woke at five in the morning, her inner clock responding to some misset alarm. Johanna groaned, rolled over, and flung an arm over Maya. They nuzzled together. Maya bathed in the sweet familiarity of her scent, her touch. Johanna opened her eyes and smiled at Maya, reaching up to stroke her hair. They kissed. Their hands, their lips, found each other. Traveling over the curves and mounds and rises of Johanna's body, Maya's hands retraced her journey. Together they climbed the mountain, lingering on its peaks while colors and spirits danced for them. They opened their arms to the avalanche, and let it bury them alive under soft, wet snow.

Then she had packed frantically for a few hours and napped until it was time for Johanna to drive her back to the airport to catch the red-eye to Boston.

"I've done every hard thing in life that ever came up for me to do," Johanna said softly as they hugged good-bye in the lounge. "I had Rachel, I kept her and raised her on my own. I fought my way through school and now I fight every day for the kids in this city. Am I so awful, can I be such a coward, for letting let you do this one?"

"I'm willing to do it for you," Maya said. "Consider it a love-gift, an offering."

Rachel had met her, as they'd arranged, at the gate. They found a small table in the only airport cafeteria open so early in the morning. Maya drank black coffee, hoping it would wake her up, and Rachel joined her. The girl had Johanna's eyes and Rio's cheekbones and a slim elegance that was all her own. Her hair was pulled back from her crown, flying loose in a wild cloud behind her. She wore a gray tunic over black wool leggings, and her nails were painted bloodred.

Maya began slowly. "This is something I should have told you a long time ago. It's about your father. I wanted to but . . ." But your mother wouldn't let me. No, that wasn't fair. "But I didn't. I'm sorry for that."

"Sorry for what?"

"Your father isn't dead. He's alive."

"What?" Rachel set down her coffee cup and stared at Maya.

"Your father is alive."

"Alive! You mean he's been alive all this time?"

Maya had an idiot urge to giggle nervously or say something stupid. No, he was dead but he's been revived. She restrained herself and simply nodded.

"But Mom told me he was dead! That he was shot by the cops in some sixties firefight."

"He wasn't shot," Maya said. "He was arrested . . . and in prison for fourteen years. But he's alive."

"You're saying she lied to me!" Rachel gripped the edge of the table. "She told me he was dead!"

Maya reached for her hand but Rachel pulled back. "She was trying to protect you."

"But I talked to him! Every Halloween, I used to light candles for him. I talked to his spirit all the time!"

Maya said nothing. What was there to say? She sipped her coffee, a bitter brew.

"And you knew?" Rachel's voice dropped, so that the words seemed to hiss out of her. "You were in contact with him, all that time, and you never told me?"

Maya shook her head. "I wasn't in contact with him. I was afraid to be." She took a deep breath. "You see, he was my boyfriend, actually, more than Johanna's. We shared him, you could say. You know how it was in the sixties—we shared everything. But I was with him, with his group, when they were first talking about the bombing stuff. I got out before it got real, but when they caught him, I had to go away. So that I couldn't be forced into a position where I would have to testify against him. When I came back, I was afraid to contact him."

"For fourteen years? You were afraid, for fourteen years?" Rachel's eyes accused her, and Maya couldn't meet them. "You just let him rot in prison, all that time, and never even tried to go see him?"

"No."

"Did you write to him, at least?"

Maya shook her head. "He wrote to me, once, but I never answered."

"You wrote that whole book about your life and never even actually wrote to *him*?"

"It was wrong," Maya admitted. "Maybe everyone has one place in their life where they sin or fail, one moment when they don't live up to who they are. Rio was mine. I'm sorry for it, now."

"But it wasn't just one moment. It was years and years and years." Rachel looked young and vulnerable. Maya longed to reach for her, to hold her, but she was wrapped in her anger, untouchable.

"I can't defend myself," Maya said. "All I can say is, I'm going to see him now. He doesn't know about you. Johanna would never tell him. That's part of why I didn't write. I couldn't figure out what to say to him without telling him about you."

"You should have told him," Rachel said. "What was he going to do—demand custody?"

"I'm going to tell him now. I hope you don't mind."

"Mind? What is there to mind? That I exist?"

"That I tell him about you, now. I'm not exactly asking for your permission—because I intend to tell him. But I'd like you to feel you have some say in the matter."

"What say?" Rachel stared out at the corridor, which was beginning to fill up with passengers heading out to the gates for early flights. "First you don't tell him or me anything, for nineteen years, and now you're going to, whatever I say. And anyway, it's not a 'say'—it's a reality. *I'm* a reality. You and Mom, you think you can make up reality and make it the way you want it to be or think it should be, but you can't. I exist, and if he's my father, he has a right to know about it. I have a right to know about him. And you and Mom have violated those rights."

"We wanted to protect you," Maya said in a small voice.

"From what?" Rachel turned to Maya again, her voice rising. "Did you think it would be such a big disgrace, having a father in prison, so much worse than not having a father at all? When I already had a mother who was a dyke and a Witch—you never worried about protecting me from that! Or did you think he'd break out of jail and come and molest me? Was he that dangerous?"

People were looking at them curiously. Maya spoke in a low voice. "No. It's just . . . well, Johanna put it this way. She didn't want you to grow up in a relationship with someone she didn't trust."

"So, she should have thought of that before she went to bed with him, and used a condom." Rachel settled back in her chair with a thump.

Maya tried out a small smile. "We didn't use them in the good old days. We didn't have to worry about AIDS yet."

"Anyway, was it better to let me grow up having a relationship

with a ghost that didn't even exist? I've never felt so incredibly humiliated!'' Rachel had tears in her eyes and again Maya wanted to reach for
her, but she didn't dare.

"I'm sorry."

They stared for a long moment at the passing parade of people.
Maya finished her coffee and went and got a second cup. Her stomach
would protest, later, but right now she desperately needed energy, even
false energy. She sat down again, and Rachel spoke in a softer voice.

"What's he like?"

The coffee was too hot to drink. Maya blew on it to cool it. What to
tell her? "He's still political. He's been out of prison for a couple of years.
Right now he's in Nevada, at the test site. He works with a group that
feeds people at political actions, and helps the homeless. I got a letter
from him, recently. That's why I'm going." For a moment, she debated
showing Rachel the letters. But no, that would be the ultimate unfairness.
He should have the right to present himself to his daughter in whatever
way he chose, to make his own mistakes, to paint whatever face he liked.
"I can't say much more than that. I haven't seen him in seventeen years.
But if it's okay with you, I'll ask him to write to you. He writes great
letters. Or call you, if you'd rather."

"Whatever," Rachel said. "I mean, either one. You can give him
my number. But what's he *like*?"

"I don't know what he's like right now. When he was young, he
was tall and blond and beautiful. Irish in background, with a bit of something else—Cherokee, I think he said once. His name is Rio, Rio Connolly. Did your mother tell you that? Richard, actually, he took the Rio
part himself." She sipped the coffee, burned her tongue, and set the cup
down. "I loved him, then. He was wild and loving and magical, *and* he
was an asshole who screwed around with my girlfriends and drank too
much. Not so different from any other asshole."

"Maybe I should write to him," Rachel said. "You could take him a
note."

"Sure."

"What should I say?" Suddenly she looked like a child, shy and
uncertain.

"Whatever you want to say."

Rachel thought for a long moment, then took out a pen and scribbled something onto a page Maya tore out of her journal. From her
wallet, she extracted a picture. "Here, give this to him. It's one of my
high school graduation pictures—an extra. I wish I had a picture of him."

"I'll try to get you one. You don't hate me?"

Rachel shook her head. "I don't hate you. Or Mom. But I'm mad."

"You've got a right to be. But try to remember, Jo always tried to
do what was best for you," Maya said, realizing she sounded like every

adult in the world. "That sounds lame, and I guess it's partly true, and partly that she did what she thought was best for her. But she *was* acting out of love for you."

"A love that can't be honest isn't worth very much."

"She loved you as best she could. We both did. We always will. And that love isn't perfect, Rachel. We both have faults. But it's something to hang on to, while we learn."

They stood, and Rachel allowed Maya to hug her good-bye.

Maya's feet hurt from standing. At the cattle guard, the drummers and dancers had begun a pulsing, wordless chant. The crowd filled the road, and Maya wormed her way out to the edge where she could keep the Grains of Truth table in view. The same blue-haired young man continued to dish out soup.

"Are you hungry?" Alix asked, coming up behind her with Tommy and noting the direction of her gaze.

"The plain but nourishing cuisine of Grains of Truth is renowned among action aficionados everywhere for its subtle insouciance and its fart potential," Tommy proclaimed.

"Shut up, Tommy," Alix said.

Maya sighed. "I'm looking for somebody," she confided, then stopped. Should she ask them for help? Why not? Yet actually saying his name out loud felt like exposing a raw secret she had long kept safe in the privacy of her mind. "An old friend—someone I came here to see."

"Who?" Alix asked. "Maybe we know this person."

Maya took a long breath. To name him was to make him real. He would exist outside the realm of memory, no longer a ghost but a man of solid flesh that others might also see.

"Do you know a man named Rio?" she asked. "He's with Grains of Truth."

"Rio, sure," Tommy said. "Everybody knows Rio."

"We should look for him back at the campsite, at the kitchen tent," Alix said.

"I did. They said he was down here. But the guy at their table hadn't seen him. He said to ask Marge, but she isn't there."

"I just saw her," Alix said. "Up by the cattle guard. Follow me."

Alix squeezed through the crowd, moving toward the front where the lines of police and security guards and the crowd of demonstrators met face to face. Tommy and Maya followed her. In Maya's exhausted state, she perceived the mass of people as pure energy, raw and diffused. Waves of power began to build and swirl and move as the crowd chanted. If that power could be focused, as it would be in ritual, some great change might be born here. She was tempted to try, and the impulse surprised her. I must be recovering, she thought. I can think about doing ritual without that awful, dead feeling creeping in.

The chant rose around her, imposing a chord on the chaos of the crowd. She joined in, attempting to ground, to make contact with the earth. Earth energy rose up through her feet and emerged through her throat.

Then the mood shifted, as from the back of the crowd a loud voice bellowed a different sort of chant:

"One, two, three, four,
Nobody wins in a nuclear war!"

A chorus of voices took up the chant. Maya tried to join in, but when she opened her mouth, all that came out was a cough. Damn, she'd thought she was finally getting over it.

"Hey, Marge!" Alix called, hailing a gray-haired, grandmotherly woman in her sixties who was peering anxiously across the cattle guard into the fenced off holding pens on the other side, where a few demonstrators who had been arrested earlier paced back and forth. "We're looking for Rio. Have you seen him?"

"He went with Herb, over to Duncan's teepee," she said. "They're planning to hike into Mercury, and they wanted to get a permit."

Tommy explained to Maya. "Everyone who does an action in the back country gets a permit from the Western Shoshone Nation. All of this is really their land."

"Marge, this is May—uh—Maggie, Rio's old friend," Alix said.

"Rio's friend!" Marge said. "Oh, he'll be so happy to see you! He was hoping so much that you would come." Her warm face clouded. "Maybe you can talk them out of doing this action. Or at least go with them. Alix, I'm worried."

"Why?"

"Herb's health is not good," Marge said. "He shouldn't be doing an action at all. But that stubborn son of a . . ." She shook her head. "That stubborn old man. He just can't admit he's no longer the fighting tiger of the Lincoln Brigade. He had his heart set on going with the Ground Zero team. Trained for it all year—he wanted to prove a man of his age could do it, I think. Anyway, Ruth at the medical tent wouldn't let him go. He was so disappointed, I thought his heart might literally break, right there on the spot. So finally, Rio promised he'd hike into Mercury with him tonight." She took Alix's arm. "And that's another thing. I don't like Rio doing an action." She glanced at Maya, as if unsure how much to reveal. "You know his history?"

Maya nodded. I am his history, she wanted to say.

"He'll probably be just fine," Marge went on. "They're not even technically arresting people, just 'detaining' us. So they don't check fingerprints or worry too much about IDs. But I have a bad feeling. Still, I couldn't talk Rio out of it. You know how he feels about Herb."

Alix looked at Tommy. "Got plans for the evening? Maybe Circle A should go in with them. That way, if something happens to Herb, there'd be someone to go for help."

Tommy nodded. "They shouldn't go alone."

"Come on," Alix said. "Let's go find them." They said good-bye to Marge and headed off toward a cluster of teepees pitched a few hundred yards down the road.

"I have a question," Maya said, a little breathless at Alix's brisk pace. "Why Mercury?"

"I hear there's a coffee shop there," Tommy remarked.

Maya ignored him. "I mean, I understand people hiking into Ground Zero to try to get in the way of the tests. I can see how that would be effective. And I understand blockading the workers at the main gate. But why Mercury? What's that supposed to prove?"

"It proves we can get through their security," Tommy said. "We can draw some heat away from the teams hiking into Ground Zero. And if we get to town, we can always talk to the workers, try to persuade them that what they're doing is wrong."

"Has anyone, anywhere in the history of the world, ever really been persuaded to throw over their whole life by talking to a demonstrator?" Maya asked.

"Once," Tommy said. "January fourteenth, 1947, during the Salt March, Mahatma Gandhi persuaded one British officer to feel mildly guilty as he bonked someone on the head. Later the officer left his post and devoted himself to praying for the poor. Ever since then, we've been hoping for a repeat."

"Really?"

"No, not really," Alix said. "Don't listen to him. He doesn't even have the dates right."

"Seriously, I have seen people change," Tommy said. "Once at Vandenburg one of the military police threw down his rifle and joined us. It can happen."

"We don't know what will be effective," Alix said, slowing down a bit as she noticed Maya scurrying to keep up. "Maybe nothing we do will keep them from blowing up the world. But we can't give up before we even try. We've got to believe it's possible to succeed. That's why I'm here."

"I guess I'm just the sort of person who feels guilty," Maya said, "if I don't do it all. If I don't try for Ground Zero, even if it's beyond me. If I don't make it up to Kala Pattar, even when I'm barely able to get up the hill where I am. I had a friend once who would have said we're just making gestures to let ourselves feel noble and pure.''

"We aren't doing enough, we aren't risking enough," she heard Edith's spirit voice whisper. And then Daniel, murmuring in her ear, "It's better not to hope—because if we do, we'll make our choices based on what will help us survive, not what needs to be done."

But they were dead. That thinking led to death. Was that the necessary price for stopping wars, saving the world? Certainly it had a simple logic of its own. But maybe in order to truly defend the mountain, the desert, the woman on fire, you *had* to hope, had to choose life with all its murky complexities and limitations. Wasn't that what she'd coughed her way across the Himalayas to find out?

"Not all of us can make Ground Zero," Tommy said. "Some of us have to walk to Mercury just because it's brightly lit and right in front of us. It's what we can do."

"You're here, that's what counts," Alix said.

"As for me," Tommy said, "I'm here because the Holiday Inn was overbooked."

Down the road, coming toward them, Maya could see two figures walking. They came closer, the slanting afternoon sun making halos of their hair.

"There they are!" Alix said. She waved at them and sped up again.
Rio.

Images flashed on her inner eyelids. Rio poling toward her in a rowboat on a lake in Golden Gate Park. His face on the TV news as they led him away to prison. The wind whipping through his hair on the beach. His eyes glazed and drunk. Who would he be? The man who wrote her the letters or the man who put his fist through mirrors?

As Maya drew closer, she could see that his hair was gray. Otherwise, from a distance at least, he could still be her pirate, her outlaw hero, dressed in faded blue jeans and an old flannel shirt. Now she could make out his features. He was weathered and sunburned, his face thinner than she remembered and carved into gullies and canyons. A stranger who could be any derelict off the street. And yet he was deeply familiar, like the back of her own hand, which also surprised her, these days, with its lines and wrinkles.

How will I look to him? she wondered. Older? Fatter? They drew closer. He caught sight of her, and for one long moment his face lit up with a child's pure joy.

"Maya! You came!"

He moved toward her, and then stopped, suddenly shy, his hands half rising as if he wanted to hug her and was afraid to try. What do we do? she wondered. Do I embrace him or shake his hand or fall on my knees to make my confession?

There was too much to say. He had been too long an icon in her mind—as she must have been for him. It was almost embarrassing that they both really existed.

"I came," she said simply.

"Herb, this is my friend Maya, the one I told you about," Rio said to the older man next to him. "Maya, this is Herb."

Herb reached out and shook her hand. "I've heard a lot about you," he said. He had a shock of white hair over a lined, pink face that seemed reddened less by the sun than by some congestion of blood within him, and he seemed to Maya to be breathing a bit heavily. But his handshake was steady and firm.

"Hey, Herb, we want in on your action," Alix said. "What do you say?"

He narrowed his eyes and looked at her suspiciously. "Has Marge been talking to you? That woman thinks she's my mother!"

"Yeah," Tommy said. "She told us there's a bowling alley in Mercury. We thought we could blockade the lanes and issue our demands. Stop nuclear testing, or we'll strike!"

Alix groaned. Rio was stealing glances at Maya and then quickly looking away, as if she might see too much if she caught his eye.

"Oh, all right," Herb said. "The more the merrier, after all."

"Can we talk?" Maya asked Rio. "It's like you said in your letter—we have a conversation to finish."

Rio nodded. He turned to Herb. "We can leave a little later, can't we? You understand."

"You two go talk," Herb said. "I'll get my gear ready."

"We'll go round up the usual suspects," Tommy said. "Meet you in an hour back by the Grains of Truth table."

Maya and Rio walked out onto the desert. "There's a nice rock we can sit on, over there," he said. "Unless you want shade. If you do, we'll have to head back to camp—or maybe find a spot by the teepees."

"It's okay," Maya said. "The sun is low."

He led her to a group of boulders in a small hollow. "Here you are. You couldn't ask for a nicer sofa." He perched on a high rock.

"The cushions could use a bit of padding," Maya said, sitting down on a level rock. "But the decor is lovely. Sort of a desert theme."

"Watch out for the cholla," Rio pointed at a cactus close to her thigh. "The spines are fierce, and they've got little barbs on them, so it hurts like hell to pull them out."

Maya shifted her leg away. They sat for a moment, just looking at each other, until Maya had to turn away from the intensity of his gaze.

"You look great," he said at last. "Wonderful. You look just like I remember you—only you've got a more sophisticated haircut."

Maya smiled. "You're a liar. But thanks anyway."

"Thanks for coming."

They fell silent. After a long while, he spoke again. "I wanted you to come, so bad. I've imagined this conversation a thousand times. And now that you're here, I don't know how to begin."

Maya took a deep breath. I have to do it, she thought. I have to say what I've come here to say, no matter what it costs.

"I'll begin," Maya said. Yes, she would start with the smaller confession, work her way up to the big one. "Rio, I read your letters. Not just the ones you sent me, but your old ones. The ones you wrote to your brother Jim. I know I shouldn't have, but I did."

"You can read my letters, Maya. It's okay. I don't even know what's in them anymore. But I don't have anything to hide from you."

"There was one that you wrote," she said, "the night after I left you. You were kind of drunk, and you were writing to Jim, even though he was dead, about the draft board . . ."

"For God's sake, you better burn that one!" He sat bolt upright. "I must have been shit-faced drunk. I don't even remember it."

"Anyway, what I wanted to say is, I didn't realize until I read it how much I'd hurt you."

"I deserved it. I treated you like shit."

"Well, I'm sorry anyway."

"No, I'm the one who's sorry."

They were getting into an argument, she realized with some amusement. "Hey, it's not a competition. Let me have my part, and you can have the rest, okay?"

"Fair enough." He smiled at her ruefully. "You know how I am, Maya. When I decide to do guilt, I like to do it all the way."

"Well, you can't. You're not the worst person in the world, Rio, any more than you're the best."

"I was an asshole."

"You were twenty-four years old, and I was twenty-one. Who's not an asshole at that age?"

He didn't answer. Maya's butt hurt and her head ached from jetlag and lack of sleep. "Rio?"

His voice was low. "If I'd had more sense, I would have followed you when you split. I tried, you know. I went up and down that highway for hours. Never did make it to wherever it was we were going. I kept picturing you, raped or beat up, left for dead by the side of the road."

"I wasn't brave enough to face you," Maya said. "If I had tried to say good-bye, I would never have had the strength to go. All I could do was leave."

"It's okay. In the end, I was glad you walked out. Really glad. Even though it hurt at the time."

"At the time, you seemed sort of impervious to pain."

"Well, I'm not." He closed his eyes for a moment, as if shielding something from her view. What would it cost me, she thought, to reach out and take his hand? What would it commit me to?

He gave his head a small shake, blinked his eyes, and smiled at her, a gesture she suddenly remembered. The familiarity of it made her shiver.

"Enough of that," he said. "Tell me about yourself. What's your life like, nowadays?"

Maya thought for a moment.

"I'm lucky, I guess. I do what I want to do, and get paid for it. Paid well, actually. I write, and I travel quite a bit, giving lectures and workshops in ritual and magic."

"That's great, Maya!"

"Not too bad for a high school dropout. I can't complain."

"Are you happy?" he asked quietly.

"Happy enough. I don't know. Sometimes I question what I do."

"Why?"

She was silent for a moment, wondering how to answer. "What I know, I had to go to the edge to find," she said finally. "I've always thought my work was to bring the magic back into the world, the everyday. To open people's eyes and ears to hear the voices of the land, to listen to what's around us. Like you said in your letter, long ago—to know that the wind and the rain and the rock are reaching for us. I believe we have to learn to reach back, or we'll die. We're dying now.

"And yet when the magic comes into the everyday, it changes. When you live a comfortable life, the purity of your vision can get murky. But I'm almost forty years old, and I like my comforts. I can't live on the edge all the time. Does that make sense? I can visit it, I can be a tourist there, but where I live is somewhere else."

Rio wrapped his arms around his chest. "I used to think like that. I used to think I had to be a hero. It nearly killed me."

"What are you saying?"

"I'm not sure I totally understand what you're talking about. But it seems to me that if magic, or anything, is really any good to us, it's got to be good in ordinary life. Wasn't that really the mistake we all made— what Edith and Daniel really died of? All this going to the edge stuff—is it killing you?"

Maya looked at him, balanced above her like a boulder she could climb. "You know," she said slowly, "now I realize how right you were. You are exactly the one person I've most needed to talk to."

Rio smiled. "Sometimes I wonder if anyone else remembers them. Oh, their families, I'm sure, but for the rest of the world, we're all just footnotes in some comprehensive history of the sixties. But every year, when Christmas comes around, I think I see Daniel in that Santa Claus suit.''

''Me too. Maybe that's part of my problem with comfort—Edith's ghost whispering in my ear.''

''Don't knock comfort. I've been without it, and I've learned to appreciate it.''

''I have too,'' she admitted.

He was silent for a long moment. ''They shouldn't be dead,'' he said abruptly. ''What a waste. What a fucking waste.''

She heard a trace of the old, angry Rio in his voice. ''Daniel always believed he would die,'' she said softly. ''I think he knew, somewhere deep down.''

''Oh, every asshole and his brother thought they were going to die on the barricades,'' Rio said. ''And you know what? Most of them didn't. I didn't care much whether I lived or died, after you left—at least I didn't think I did, until I really had to face the question. But Daniel wanted to live.''

We are talking about the dead, Maya thought. I could take his hand now. We could finally comfort each other. But then I would still have to tell him about the living.

''I was insanely jealous of Daniel, did you know that?'' Rio said. ''When you were sleeping with him. I know it seems like the worst macho double standard, considering what I was doing. But I was so afraid he would take you away from me. It seemed like the two of you belonged together. He was a lot like your father, you know? That Jewish, intellectual, political type. I was afraid you'd wake up one day and want to be with somebody smarter than me.''

''I felt that, sometimes, with him,'' Maya admitted. ''It scared the hell out of me. I don't know why, now. Now it doesn't seem the worst fate in the world, to grow up and marry and lead a political, scholarly life. But I wouldn't have left you for him.''

''It would have just about served me right if you had.'' He turned away from her, staring off at the distant hills.

''I loved you, Rio.'' There, she had said it now, whatever it meant to him. Would that confession buy her absolution for her long silence?

''Be careful,'' he warned her. ''You could get into trouble, saying things like that. Because to you, you're talking about twenty years ago. But I've stared down time too long. It doesn't exist for me in the same way. I might think you're talking about five minutes ago, or even now.''

She could hear in his voice how much in this moment he wanted her love. I can't hurt him again, she thought. Our lives are twined together, and when I tell him about Rachel, we'll be bound irrevocably until the end of our lives. I must be very careful what I say.

"I did love you," she repeated. "Even when I walked away."

He was silent, withdrawn back into himself. "I wish I'd been able to love you better," he said at last. "That I didn't have to push you away. That's what hurts. Nothing really hurts unless you know you deserve it."

"I tried to come back to you. In the fall. I came down from the mountain and heard about the explosion on the radio. We thought you were dead, me and Johanna. And then the next morning, when you got busted, I went underground. I didn't ever want to have to testify against you." She offered him up her sacrifice.

"I didn't know if you were alive or dead, Maya. For years, until Dave Ryan gave me that book. In the bad times, it seemed that if you were alive, you would surely write to me, if only to tell me how fucked up I'd been."

"I was afraid to." Maya paused. That was part of the truth, but he deserved all of it. "First I was afraid, and then, I don't know. I just didn't."

"Was it hard on you?" he asked. "Being on the run? Did you hate me?"

"Sometimes," she admitted. "Sometimes I was poor and afraid and terribly lonely. And sometimes I was playing to an invisible audience, enjoying displaying my pain. I was furious at you, and I missed you at the same time. I don't know. There were a lot of things I couldn't do—go back to school, for one. Poor Betty. But I don't know if I would have done them, anyway."

"I bet you would have."

"Maybe. Maybe not. Who can say if my life would really have been better if I had? If I were a therapist, now, like Betty? The truth is, those years on the run were just another way of walking to Mercury."

"What do you mean?"

"I mean I did what I *could* do, and I went toward what was in front of me. That's what made me who I am. Those years made me a Witch, and a writer. They gave me my power, such as it is."

The last shreds of a long-carried burden began to fall away as she said the words. Yes, she thought, I used him to define myself. I can choose to resent him, or I can let it go and travel weightless, unhindered.

"I made my own choices, Rio. I made my own history, and mostly I'm proud of it," she said. "I was angry at you for a long, long time, but no more."

He reached out then, as if he were daring a leap into space, and took her hand.

"Maybe we can just start all over again, do you think? I forgive you, you forgive me, clean slate."

"I don't know if we can start over," she said, warning him gently. "But we can start where we are."

"That's what I mean." He started to move his hand away, but she held on to it. "Are you with someone?" he asked after a moment. "Are you married?"

Maya shook her head. "Not that comfortable. No, I live with Johanna. We bought a house together, in San Francisco. But I wouldn't call us married."

"Really? I'm glad for you," he said after a moment, in a suddenly flat voice, dropping her hand as if he were relinquishing something. She felt unreasonably guilty. "You're happy?"

"Happy enough. We like to say we're carrying on an open, bisexual, long-running affair, conducted one night at a time."

He was silent. "Rio," she began, and then stopped. What did she want to say to him? Pursue me, persuade me, don't give up. You are my lost passion. Or? Go away, go away, you are a danger and a diversion and you will mess up my life if I let you in?

"Don't be kind to me," he said. "I don't have any illusions about what we might be to each other after all this time. Some things are gone forever. But we have a history together that nobody else shares. I just needed to see you, to talk to you, maybe remember the ghosts that everyone else has forgotten."

"I know."

He shifted on his rock. Behind him shadows walked over the mountains. Soon it would be night, and she still would not have said what she needed to say.

"So how is Johanna?" he asked after a moment.

"Impressive. She's got a long string of advanced degrees, and works as a high-level consultant to the school district. She's an educational psychologist."

"Good for her." He was still looking off at the hills, watching the light change. "It's the two of you? Didn't she have a kid, or something?"

Here it comes, Maya thought. Goddess help me.

"Rachel's away at college. That's Johanna's daughter," she said in a carefully casual tone.

"In college already?" Rio said.

Closer and closer. Was she going to circle around it forever, or was she going to tell him?

"Harvard premed."

He was so innocent, so unsuspicious. How would he feel when he knew?

"Really? Well, Johanna was always smart," Rio said.

"I know." She hesitated for one last moment, cherishing the comfort and the closeness they felt. But the time had come to tell the truth. "Rio, do you remember the night of the storm, on the coast?"

"I sure do."

"You remember what the three of us did?"

"Of course I do." His voice was low. "I've lived on that memory, for years at a time. I haven't forgotten a single raindrop or a gust of wind."

"Rio, she's yours," Maya blurted out, feeling tender and scared.

"What?"

"Johanna's daughter. She's your daughter, too. From the storm."

"Oh." He stared as if the words he heard made no sense to him. "Would you say that again?"

"You are the father of Johanna's kid."

For a long moment he sat still, looking disoriented, as if Maya had suddenly assured him he were somebody else.

"Are you sure?" he asked.

"She looks just like you," Maya said. "Dark, of course, but with your bone structure and eyes and mouth."

"And she's . . . okay? Not . . . crazy?"

"Not drunk, not depressed, not nuts. She's fine."

Then he got mad. "Why the hell didn't somebody tell me?"

She didn't know how to answer. Could she say, "Because Johanna didn't really know you or trust you? Because of my memory of your fist through the wall?" Could she say, "You were the instrument we used, without knowing it, to produce a child between us?"

"Don't answer," he said bitterly. "I know the answer. You decided that having me as a father was worse than having nobody." He turned away from Maya, staring off at the retreating sun, then turned to face her, his face flushed and red. "Maybe I can understand how you might think that. But I don't accept it. No, goddammit, I don't accept it at all!"

She reached toward him, but he folded his hands under his arms, as if to remove any remote possibility of contact with her, and hugged himself. Yes, he was really, really angry now.

"Well, I've got to hand it to you, Maya. You really did it all the way. No half measures, you went for complete annihilation. The government just locked me up, but you and Johanna, you wiped out my whole existence."

His eyes were filling with tears that he fought back. Maya noticed that her own eyes were wet.

"I'm sorry, Rio."

"You didn't know what I might have done or not done, and you didn't even give me a chance to find out. Or her. There are men in prison who have kids, you know. You don't stop being a human being. They write them letters, send them cards on their birthdays, talk to them on the phone. Some of them have done a lot worse things than I have, but their kids don't write them off." He stood up, shivering with rage and sorrow. "I just don't get it. What did I ever do to you, or Johanna, to make you think that my love would be worse than nothing?"

There was nothing Maya could say to that, but she had to say something.

"We thought maybe you didn't have any love to give."

"And who the hell gave you the right to make that judgment?"

His anger felt hot, explosive, volcanic, like something rising and rising, about to spew out and destroy. She remembered that anger, she recognized it and instinctively started to shrink away.

She shivered. He loomed over her, watching her flinch. Then he turned his back on her and walked away.

"Rio!" She jumped up and started to follow him but he waved her away.

"Get out of here! Leave me the fuck alone!"

His voice was breaking, and he was trying hard not to cry. She stood and watched him disappear toward the camp.

48

Back Country

Solidarity is the way we attempt to protect every
member of our movement. We do not allow
individuals to be targeted or singled out. We stand
behind each other, even when we must make
sacrifices to do so.

—NEVADA TEST SITE ACTION
HANDBOOK

The vast sky pressed the land flat around them. Against the unbounded
moonlight, the hills stood out in silhouette. Maya and Circle A clustered
together in a low hollow of ground on the edge of the camp. Across the
road, on the test site land, they could see the bright searchlights of the
main gate. Herb had joined their huddle, wearing a baseball cap and
carrying an old Boy Scout rucksack on his back. On the north horizon,
Mercury itself was a string of jewels, beckoning.

Rio had not appeared. Maya had waited a long time by the rocks,
hoping that he might forgive her enough to come back and talk. Finally
she had given up her vigil. Not knowing what else to do, she had gone
back to the blockade to meet her friends.

"The trick is," Ben was saying, "not to get arrested until we get to
Mercury. We'll head down for a mile or so on this side of the road, the
legal side, and then look for the culvert. That's where Mike told me they
went across, but it's also where we really have to watch out. The Wackenhuts patrol along the road and along the base of the foothills in their
jeeps. Other groups have had a hard time getting through."

On Alix's instructions, Maya had given her car keys, ID, and money
to Roger, who was not going to go with them to Mercury but would pick
them up when they were released. She had stuffed her jacket and extra
water bottle into her day pack and followed Alix to this meeting on the

edge of camp, all the while feeling miserable and scanning the crowd for Rio. This is how he must have felt when I left him by the highway, she thought. Goddess, if only I could apologize again, make it better, explain. But he had become an absence, a void.

"What about the infrared?" Hazel asked.

"It's not too effective unless they bring out a helicopter. And large groups show up on it best. We'll split up . . . but stay within earshot of each other. Anything goes wrong, you need help in any way, let out an owl call. Like this." Ben hooted three times in a high-pitched voice.

"Are there owls in the desert?" Laura asked.

"Duncan, the Shoshone medicine man, told me there used to be." Hazel adjusted the strap on her pack. "There used to be a lot of birds. Every spring they'd do a seed-scattering ceremony, and the birds would come back. But now they're all gone."

Maya's eyes began to fill with tears for the lost birds. Stop it, she told herself firmly. You are not allowed to burst into tears just because you're jet-lagged and you hurt Rio terribly and you can't make up to him for Rachel's childhood no matter what you do now. She had put on Claire's old green sweater for luck, and she stood with her arms wrapped around herself, shivering not from cold but a sense of colliding worlds. What's happening? she thought. Where is he? How can I be standing here talking about how to evade infrared? Is this what I have to do to make amends to Rio? Is this what I have to do to lay my mother to rest?

"If you do get busted, try to let the rest of us know," Alix said, "make a lot of noise. But don't be obvious, don't let the Wackenhuts know you're signaling. Just sing something at the top of your lungs— 'Ain't Gonna Study War No More,' something like that. And noncooperate, if you can. Try to keep them occupied."

"Noncooperate?" Maya suddenly realized that she should be paying attention. "What do you mean?"

"I mean don't do what they say—not in a belligerent way, but just quietly and respectfully decline. Don't walk if they ask you to, go limp and make them carry you."

"Or drag you through the cholla," Hazel said. "Personally, I prefer to go limp on softer ground."

"What happens if you get arrested?" Maya asked. "They really don't put you in jail?"

"They haven't, so far," Laura told her. "They release us because they can't afford to keep us. But that doesn't mean they won't, someday. You can never predict one hundred percent what they'll do."

Alix looked distressed. "You're really supposed to take nonviolence training before you do an action. But there isn't time. Have you ever taken one?"

"I had violence training in the sixties." Maya smiled. "But I think I can control myself from running amok and attacking the Wackenhuts with my Swiss army knife."

"It isn't just that." Alix shook her head. "You'd have gotten all the legal information, too."

"Well, she didn't," Tommy snapped. "It's okay. Why are we anarchists, anyway, if we can't break a rule now and then?"

"Are we ready to go?" Ben asked. "Let's do a quick check. Everybody have extra water? If you end up out there after daybreak, you can dehydrate very quickly."

"Ben's very good with supplies," Tommy told Maya. "Ever since the time he and Hazel invaded Cape Canaveral by rubber raft . . . and forgot the paddles."

One by one they nodded their heads.

"Let's go, then," Ben said.

"Where's Rio?" Alix asked.

"He's not coming," Herb announced. "I just talked to him, a few minutes ago. There's no need for him, now that the rest of you volunteered to go with me. And it's more dangerous for him."

Not coming! What should I do? Maya wondered. Should I abandon the group, stay here and look for him? Maybe after he cools down, we can talk.

"Let's do a circle of protection before we leave," Alix suggested.

"Know any good spells for invisibility?" Tommy asked Maya.

"What?"

"Would you lead us in a grounding?" Hazel asked.

No, Maya wanted to cry out. I can't ground when I don't know what I should do and barely know where I am. Should I stay, or go with them? Maybe I should leave him alone for a day or two, give him some space. Or maybe it's already too late.

They were all looking at her eagerly, with expectant eyes, except for Herb who seemed somewhat bemused.

"You lead a grounding," she told Alix. "I'll make an offering, to give something back to the land."

"What should we offer?" Laura asked.

The momentum of the group was carrying her along. Should she resist it? Or should she make an offering, not just for the action, but for her and Rio and Rachel and all of them, the living and the dead? She considered. I don't know this place, she thought, I haven't been here long enough even to learn it as a tourist. I don't know how this land grows its voice or cries from its wounds, what colors it paints with, what gifts it requires.

"Water," she said. "In a dry land like this, water is a good thing to offer. We can pour a little out each time we stop along the way, and ask the spirits to protect us."

"I like that," Hazel agreed. "That feels right."

"We don't have extra water to waste," Ben objected.

"We only need a few drops," Maya said. "And we won't be wasting it. The fact that it's precious to us, that our lives depend on it, is what makes it a true offering."

They stepped closer, nestled their bodies together, and began breathing deeply.

"Feel yourself like a desert plant," Alix murmured, "and feel your roots going down through the soil and the dust, even the radioactive dust, feeling the power of the land to regenerate itself. . . ."

"And you feel the waters under the earth," Laura went on, so smoothly that it seemed the meditation was still being guided by one voice, which simply moved from mouth to mouth. "And you're a thirsty plant looking for water. . . ."

I guess I am doing this action, Maya thought. Rio or no Rio. Maybe it's better this way—it might be easier for him to get over the raw hurt if I'm not there.

"And you bring the power up," Ben continued, "up into your body, your feet and legs, your sexual places and your belly and your heart, and it warms you and protects you and strengthens you for this action, and it comes into your arms and hands and your throat, and out the top of your head. . . ."

"And it surrounds you and encloses you," Maya added. "It's a shield around you, and you see how it takes on the form of the sky and the plants and the rocks and the stars, like a cloak of protection, so that anyone looking at you looks right through you. And you mold a little of that fire into eyes and ears and whiskers like cat whiskers, wards to hang on the edge of your aura to warn you if any danger is around."

They were silent for a moment. What she was describing for them was, she knew, a real and somewhat complex magical operation. She didn't know the extent of their training or skill. But the metaphor will work on some level, she thought, as she set her own wards and called in her own spirit power, which stirred within her like the roots of a seed coming alive after a cold winter.

"Powers of the east." Hazel turned to face the direction as she spoke, and they all turned with her. "Powers of air and wind, I call you to bring us clarity and vision and awareness tonight. Help us see clearly in the dark."

"Powers of the south," Tommy said, turning again. "You fiery ones, courage and passion and rage, let the life fire run strong in us, stronger than the fires of destruction."

I don't have to anchor this circle, she thought. I can stand with the others, on the rim, and so leave space in the center for power to come through.

"You waters of the west," Laura went on. "Help us bring the waters of life and healing to this land."

"Spirits of the north, earth spirits," Alix completed the circle. "Guard our bodies out there, protect us and help us heal the earth."

Maya looked around the circle. In the moonlight, they were grave and beautiful as the hills around them. They had dropped their banter and their cool facade and stood with faces bared to the spirits, and in that moment she loved them dearly as mountains. Let go, she thought. If I can, just for a moment, remember what I've learned and drop my guilt and my sorrow, then this action can become a Kaddish, a making holy, a prayer that can only be done in community.

She spun a circle around them, silently calling the Seer and the Singer and the Reaper, feeling them come, the chill up her spine, the rush of power that sent a shudder through her shoulders.

"Earth Mother, Desert Mother, Spider," she said out loud, "you who have so many names, you who are the makers of life known to the people of these dry desert lands, weave and spin for us tonight. Spin the thread of our journey out over the land, spin us into the web of life weavers, healers, spin out a new fate for this land and its people, spin out a new fate for the earth."

"Mercury, you old God of thieves," Ben said, "protect us on our way to your town."

They were silent for a moment. Maya felt power gather around them, swirling like mist in the moon's clear light. The desert was illuminated, a poem of sculptured forms.

"It's beautiful here!" she murmured. The land was beginning to speak.

"Ah well," Tommy said. "If you like Mother Nature, in Nevada you can see her naked."

As they started up the slight rise, Rio came walking up behind them.

"Rio!" Maya cried.

He stood a little apart from the group, not greeting Maya nor looking at her.

"I thought you weren't coming," Herb said.

"I changed my mind." His voice was hard, flat, a convict's voice.

"Rio," Ben said, "there's been rumors floating around camp, that the Feds have targeted the Grains—and that could mean you in particular. Maybe you should sit this one out."

"I don't give a fuck about rumors."

"I usually don't myself," Ben said. "But I think this one may have some truth behind it."

Rio shook his head. "I'm not going to live that way, Ben. Fuck it. There's no point to it, anyway. Skulking in the bushes and trying to play it safe. That never protected me from anything." He turned to Herb. "I promised you we'd walk to Mercury tonight, and I intend to keep my promise."

Herb looked distressed. "I don't want to be responsible for your putting yourself in danger."

"You're not responsible, Herb. I am. I hereby absolve you of all responsibility. Okay? Now can we go?"

"I'm not sure we ought to." Alix's voice was concerned. "Rio, just think for a minute . . . what happens if they single you out?"

"That'll be my problem."

"But we'll all end up doing solidarity actions for you. So it's our decision, too."

"I'm not asking you to do a goddamned thing for me, except stay the fuck out of my business."

Alix fell silent, looking hurt.

Ben shook his head. "Well, if that's the way you want it, we can't stop you. With any luck they won't ask you for ID, and you'll slide through."

"I don't like our process around this," Hazel said, distressed.

"Leave it," Tommy advised her, looking at Rio's brooding form. "Just let it go."

"Now, how are we going to form up these teams?" Ben said quickly.

Alix shrugged, and began explaining to Maya. "Usually, we do separate women's teams and men's teams, because when we get arrested—"

"You mean *detained*," Tommy broke in.

"Whatever, anyway, eventually they separate the women and the men, so that way you can be sure to have company. But if you want to go with Rio, Maya—"

"No," Rio said sharply. "I'm going with Herb."

There was an awkward silence while the group exchanged puzzled glances. Maya looked down at the sand, pockmarked into little hollows of darkness as the light faded. I should bow out of the action, she thought, and let him go on without me. But dammit, I'm not going to! I'm not going to let it end like this.

"Pardon me for asking," Laura said, "but if you two by any chance need some mediation—"

"We don't," Rio cut her off. "We need to have one conversation maybe every fifteen or twenty years, and we've just had one, thank you. Now can we get the fuck on our way to Mercury?"

"Rio, if you're upset about something, it's really not a good time to do an action," Alix cautioned.

"I'm not upset."

"You look upset. You sound upset," Hazel countered.

"It's a guy thing," Tommy explained. "That time of month, you know."

"That's right, Tommy," Rio said coldly. "I'm on my moon, okay? I'm bleeding. Now can we stop trying to fix me and get on with what we're here to do?"

"Tommy and I will go with you and Herb," Ben suggested.

"Four of us together . . . that's too many," Herb objected. "We'll be a big target for the infrared."

"But Herb, the whole point of us doing this action is so that if something happens to you, there'll be people to stay with you and people to go get help," Alix pointed out. "It's worth sacrificing a little cover for that."

"I don't need to be coddled." Herb looked at Rio for support.

But Rio shook his head. "She's right."

Ben let out a long sigh. "Why don't you women split into two teams?"

"Can I go with you?" Hazel asked Maya, a little shyly.

"Sure," Maya said.

"Then Laura and I will go together," Alix said. *Vámonos.*

The desert was a wide, flat expanse, but under Maya's feet it became a patchwork of gullies and washes, of infinite small pockets of variation, hard sand and patches of broken rocks, soft dust and clear mud flats. They skirted cholla cactus with their dangerous, almost invisible needles, and tall yucca, their sharp, spiny leaves radiating out from crowns held up like proud heads on ragged stalks. Slight dips and rises in the ground concealed the faraway lights of cars, revealing them suddenly, great burning eyes that sent the teams scurrying into the shadows to crouch, hearts pounding, afraid of surveillance even while they still stood on the legal side of the road.

Maya found herself up at the front, with Ben and Tommy. All that hiking in Nepal, she thought, I guess it payed off after all. I'm in pretty good shape. Not even coughing much tonight, so far. Rio followed far behind, going at Herb's slow pace. I can do nothing, now, Maya thought, but wait. This is my penance, my discipline. Wait and stay close, hoping for the energy to shift, trying to accept what is—this moonlit night in which we are walking to Mercury together.

They stopped to let the others catch up.

"That's the culvert over there," Tommy said. "Where we usually cross."

"Why don't you guys take the culvert," Alix suggested. "We'll go a bit farther down the road. I'm worried that they'll be watching the culvert mouth, and six of us going through would be pushing our luck."

"If you hear a copter, get close to a big cactus. It helps confuse the infrared," Ben said.

"Cuddle up to a yucca?" Alix said brightly.

"Our theme song." Tommy winked at Maya. "Come on, boys and girls, you know it brings us luck."

They all chimed in,

"Cuddle up to a yucca, cuddle up.
When you have to duck-a, always cuddle up."

Maya recognized the tune from the seat-belt safety campaign of her childhood. Alix reached out to squeeze Maya's hand. They're afraid, Maya thought. Even if they've done this a hundred times, they're still scared.

They all finished together:

"Just embrace the spines,
To conceal your crimes,
Cuddle up to a yucca, always cuddle, cuddle up."

"Watch your silhouette," Ben went on, "and when you're in doubt, freeze. Movement is easy to spot, but if you hold still you're surprisingly hard to see. And Hazel—watch your glasses. They can reflect light from miles away. Good luck!"

"Wait." Alix opened her canteen, poured out a few drops of water. "For the healing of all wounds, and for the healing of this land."

"Blessed be," they chorused.

"Here." Ben handed Maya a folded piece of paper. "I forgot to give this to you."

"What is it?"

"It's your permit from the Shoshone. And I'd just love to make a test case out of it in court."

"Thanks." Maya put the paper in her pocket. I still don't know this land, she thought. I still have not eaten its fruits or tasted its poisoned waters or heard its song. But at least I have permission to be here. Written permission, at that.

"I have to pee," Hazel said.

"You always do, in the middle of every action!" Laura complained.

"There's more than one way of offering water."

•   •   •

The men split off to make a separate foray onto the land. Maya watched Rio duck into the culvert. She had to stop herself from crying out and begging him not to go yet, to talk with her first, forgive her. He was disappearing into the underworld; he might be sucked into its depths and never emerge again. She would have destroyed him with her secret, and be left with silence and her unburied dead.

The women huddled in a gully by the roadbed.

"Let's stay together at least until we cross the road," Hazel said.

"We should look for another culvert," Laura said.

"I'm not sure," Alix said. "What if they have all the culverts staked out? Maybe we'd be just as safe crossing the road."

"That's what I think," Maya said. "I think we should just do it." She felt hollow inside. Something of her had gone with Rio into the forbidden territory over the line, and she wanted to follow as quickly as possible.

"All together?"

"Two by two," Laura said.

"I want to go first," Alix said.

"That's cool," Hazel said. "Maya and I'll watch you. If there's trouble on the other side, run back across, or yell. Otherwise, we'll follow."

The two women headed off. Maya crouched, watching, as they dashed across the road. There was silence.

"How long should we wait?" Maya asked Hazel.

"You won't believe this, but I have to pee again. I guess I'm nervous."

"Might as well do it while we're still legal."

In fact, she herself had to pee, which she did, still crouching in the gully. Hazel finished; they buttoned up their pants and left, walking stooped over to hide their silhouettes. A low gully and a barbed-wire fence edged the road. They slipped off their packs, passed them through the wire, and held the strands apart for each other as they crawled through.

"Flat!" Hazel whispered. They lay down as a truck passed, its headlights sweeping across the landscape in a wide wedge. Then it was gone.

"Look!" Maya said. To the west, on test site land, the lights of a jeep made their way at the base of the foothills. A searchlight played in an arc around it.

"What do we do? The others are already over there."

"Go now," Maya said, "while it's still far away, before it has a chance to turn around."

She grabbed her pack and looked up the road. It was dark and silent. "Now!"

Her heart was pounding as she ran. Her hiking boots seemed to be lead weights on her feet, and she could hardly breathe, as if she were suddenly back in the Himalayas where the oxygen was thin. Fear, that's what's wrong with me, she thought, and forced herself on. The Bad Reality is reaching out its tendrils to grab me, keep me separated from Rio so that terrible things can happen. Her legs felt weak. A stretch of land separated the two wide roadbeds, and she forced herself across it.

Then she was across the road, with Hazel right behind her. Another barbed-wire fence blocked their way. Quickly they tossed their packs over and held the strands apart for each other. Grabbing their packs again, they dashed across a dirt jeep road and up a slight rise into the shadow of a yucca.

"Let's get farther from the road," she heard Alix whisper, and they ran on another fifteen feet until they heard the sound of an engine behind them.

"Get down!" Alix whispered.

Only one large cactus stood nearby. The four of them threw themselves into its shadow, crouched on top of their gear and each other. They could hear the grinding of the jeep's engine, getting closer.

"What should we do?" Laura whispered.

"Run for it?" Hazel said. "Maya, you go!"

"I can't. Alix is lying on my pack." She didn't know what to do. Run or hide? The jeep came closer and closer.

"Hold still," Alix whispered. "Don't move."

They lay in absolute silence. Maya felt as if her skin were a thin bag holding her pounding heart. She made her breath soft, light. She was crouched on something spiny, but didn't dare to move.

The jeep came closer, and then, with dread, they heard the engine stop. A door slammed.

Go away, Maya thought. Please, Goddess, just let them go away. She felt exposed, silly, lying with her face in the dust and nothing over her but half a shadow. Footsteps came closer and closer.

They've got to see us, she thought. This is stupid, hiding like this. We should rise and face them, accept our fate. But she lay still, trying to reweave the magical cloak of protection, forcing herself to imagine them all invisible, blending into the stars and the rocks, not disturbing even with their energy the patterns of the desert.

She was going to cough. The need possessed her, tickling the back of her throat, burning in her lungs. Oh, Goddess, she was going to give them all away.

She held her breath, bit her lips, bit her tongue. The footsteps came closer still. The guard was chewing gum; she could hear it cracking in his jaws, and feel his breath in her aura. Her hair stood on end.

Think about the mountain, she told herself. Remember what it was like to stand on its steep side, coughing like I want to do now. If I could only recapture what I felt then, I could make this moment perfect, whatever happens. What is the story I am telling myself that makes me so afraid?

The footsteps turned and walked back.

Still hardly daring to breathe, they heard the door of the jeep slam again, and the engine start up. They lay still for a long time, until they could no longer hear the grinding of the motor. Cautiously, they rose. The jeep was once again far down to the west, on the slopes of the mountains.

Maya took a long drink of water and received a throat lozenge from Laura, who gave her a handful to keep in her pocket.

"Let's get out of here before they come back," Alix said.

"Wait," Maya said. She unscrewed the cap on her canteen and poured out a few drops of water. "For all those who are hiding tonight." She rose up with a dizzy sense of hope. They had slipped the clutches of El Mundo Malo. The desert had sheltered them, taken them in. Maybe they would yet be given another chance.

They headed north, toward the lights of Mercury, moving from yucca to yucca, kneeling in the shadows when they heard the engine of the jeep returning, moving on swiftly once it was gone. After a few hundred yards, they decided the two teams should separate.

"There's another jeep road ahead of us that curves off from the foothills to link up with the road from the main gate. Watch out for it," Alix warned. "Good luck."

"Safe journey," Hazel said. They waited while the other two disappeared into the shadows of the night.

"I have to pee again," Hazel said.

"Are you all right?"

"Just nerves, I guess. I feel like a dog."

"Think of it as marking our territory," Maya said, pouring a little water as she waited for Hazel.

To walk in the desert in the moonlight was to find a rhythm that responded to brush and cactus, not a straight path but a zigzag dodging from yucca to yucca, stepping over a cactus here and sidestepping mesquite there, a rising and falling dance from knoll to gully, stone to dust. The lights of Mercury were hidden by a rise in the ground. The town was a glow on the horizon, in competition with the sailing moon. Behind the glow, dark hills made a solid barrier against the stars.

They walked for a long time, stopping often to listen for engines or footsteps, scanning the shadows for traces of motion. Maya found the rush of adrenaline beginning to wear off. She walked in trance, letting the place speak to her, listening only to the silence of the night.

"Down," Hazel whispered. They crouched together under another yucca, this one with three large stalks. "I saw something, over there."

Maya looked where she pointed. At first she saw nothing but the silhouettes of desert plants against the glow of the sky. The moon was a yellow smear on the west horizon, about to set. Which meant, she thought, that they didn't have all that much time. Full moon was three or four days away, so it would set roughly three or four hours before sunrise. But the sky would grow light at least an hour before the sun came up. . . .

She focused her eyes, sharply, startled. Something was moving out there. She watched a clump of yuccas. On its eastern edge was a tall silhouette that could have been a plant . . . or a person. In the dim light, the figure appeared to be moving, bending and swaying, performing a dance. Or perhaps it was a tree, swaying in the wind. But there were no trees on the desert and no wind was blowing and the sturdy yucca would not bend to any breeze. Nothing else was moving.

She shivered. Thin lines seemed to reach upward from the figure, like antennae. Was it a Wackenhut out there with a walkie-talkie, spying on them? Whatever it was moved with an eerie grace, like something unearthly. As she watched, other figures joined the first, or emerged from the first, she couldn't tell which. A whole platoon of Wackenhuts were dancing a secret midnight polka, or a clump of yuccas were swaying and mirroring each other's movements, or a circle of the ancestors were joining hands to lift something high above them. Or was she merely seeing the swirling energy patterns of the night, or responding to some defect of her own eyes? For when she tried to focus, everything was still, but then as she looked again, she saw movement, delicate and rhythmic and unreal.

"What could it be?" Maya whispered.

"Security. With a radio?" Hazel saw it, too. Whatever Maya was seeing was more than a trick of her eyes or imagination.

"I don't think so." The silent figures swayed, and the night became alive. Faces seemed to loom about her. She began to see fantastic creatures, great horned human heads, wings that ended in hands. She saw a woman running in the dark, surrounded by a fiery glow, and a tall, lean figure who seemed to be gesturing with a cigarette in a way that seemed familiar. In the center, a group of figures appeared to be raising a banner or a high pole topped by prayer flags, doing work together, making something holy. Ghosts. A call split the darkness, a yip yip yip ending in a howl. The spirits of night whirled in their dance.

"Coyote," Hazel whispered.

Maya poured water. All her senses were extended. Through her ran the life of the pack and the spiny yucca life and the cactus needle and the dry mesquite bush. Boundaries and edges disappeared, and everything ran together, life pouring into life, her own life feeding on this powerful place, and giving back water and breath. She didn't know this place, but she had learned to listen. She belonged nowhere, and anywhere could become her home.

She had come to Nevada to repair the fabric of her life. Nuclear bombs had been an abstraction to her; suddenly they became real. She could feel the rupture, the glaring disruption of the lights and the fences and the bombs dropped into the earth heart, like a pain in her gut, like a great, bleeding wound. More than her fate or Rio's fate hung in the balance, for to hallow this land was to ally herself with wind and rock and rain, with the perfection of the moon and the vast sweep of the hills and the howl of the pack against powers that would destroy the earth.

She wanted to cry for the beauty and the brokenness. Opening her canteen, she poured out a silver stream of water with a prayer. "May we make holy this land."

Could they muster that much power? Could they even redeem one life? Maybe all that could ever be redeemed was the moment in which, burdened by the relics of imperfect acts of love, they hid from spirits dancing in the dark and listened to coyotes howl. Yet if all time was truly one, then this moment encompassed all. She heard the hissing breath of forty thousand ancestors, whispering soft words.

"To heal what is broken you need the power of what is broken, which is different from the power of what is perfect. What is perfected reaches its peak and passes away. Only what is broken endures."

She touched the earth.

From where the spirits had gathered, they suddenly heard a loud, human cry. Three owl calls rang through the night.

"Herb!" Hazel whispered. "Something's happened to him!"

In the distance, the pack of coyotes raised a howl.

"Let's go!"

They moved cautiously but swiftly toward the east, through a land mired with spirits. Maya became aware of a movement in the night, as if one of the spirits had cut loose from the pack to dance ahead of them. It seemed to her as if it turned its head, looking back at them, like a dog beckoning them to follow.

She grabbed Hazel's arm. "This way," she said. "Follow it."

"Follow what?"

"You don't see it?"

"What are you talking about?"

Maybe it was a trick of her own eyes, Maya thought, or a mild hallucination brought on by lack of sleep. But something was beckoning her in the night.

"Follow me," she said.

She herself was following a trick of the moonlight, a silent call that sometimes felt clear as a bell and sometimes disappeared, or the scent of a blossom only half remembered. Well, I've had plenty of practice, she told herself. She blinked, and the ghost turned into Santa Claus, a lanky, beak-nosed Santa driving a sleigh full of reindeer across the desert sand, rising into the air above a tall clump of yuccas.

"Over there," Maya whispered. "Come on."

They were sitting in a low hollow of ground, surrounded by the tall, spiny yuccas. Herb was stretched out on the ground, his head cradled in Rio's lap. Tommy and Ben were crouched beside him.

Maya knelt down beside Rio. Tears were streaming down his cheeks.

"Herb?" Hazel whispered, squatting at her side. "Is he okay?"

Rio shook his head. "I'm afraid. I'm afraid he's dying."

Hazel stood and let out three owl calls. "Laura's a nurse. She'll know what to do."

"I'm such an asshole," Rio whispered. "I should have listened to Marge."

Maya opened her canteen, poured out a few drops for the spirits. Hazel stood up and hooted again.

Maya leaned over Herb. His breathing was rasping and irregular, and he didn't seem aware of her presence. Already he was slipping into another world.

"He was doing fine," Rio said. "Slow, but not too bad. Then suddenly he yelled and clutched his left side and fell over." He sounded wretched, and Hazel patted his shoulder to comfort him. "I should never have let him do this."

"It's done, now," she said. "There's no use worrying about what would have happened. You did what he wanted."

"It looked like he had a stroke," Tommy said. "Or maybe a heart attack. Don't any of us know CPR?"

"I'm a lawyer," Ben said. "I don't know anything."

"He's breathing," Hazel said. "Isn't CPR for when you stop breathing?"

"Or when your heart stops," Tommy said.

"Well, his heart is beating. Maybe he'll be all right," Hazel said hopefully.

Maya listened to Herb's irregular breath. In the moonlight, she could see him surrounded by shreds and tatters of clouds, as if his spirit were a fragile cloth being torn as something pulled it free from his body. She thought about power. She and Rio had sought it together. At times they had believed in the kind that comes out of the barrel of a gun, but in the end they had both learned to seek only the upwelling power that comes from the land and the spirits and the patterns of things. Her only magic was her willingness to hear the speech of the land and respond.

That may or may not be power, she thought, but it's all I've got. But what good is it in a situation like this? What I need right now is just a little of the Witch's traditional power to tweak fate, to bend events, to change the Bad Reality for the Good.

Hazel stood up and hooted again.

"We could carry him," Tommy suggested.

"We'd be a pretty obvious target for the Wackenhuts," Ben said.

"Good, then they'd bust us and *they'd* have to carry him," Tommy said.

"If we're going to do that, we could just stay right here and make noise to attract them." Hazel stood up.

"Don't!" Ben grabbed her arm.

"I'm just going to do another owl call, for Alix and Laura." She hooted.

If only I were a healer, Maya thought. If only the *curandera* had let me study with her, pick up what knowledge I could. If only I truly had an army of spirits at my command, *naguales,* fetches, familiars.

"We could go for help," Ben suggested. "Head back to camp and get someone from the medical team."

Hazel let out another owl call. "Where are Alix and Laura?"

Tommy shook his head. "We'd save time by carrying him out. If we get the medics, that's what they'll have to do, and still under the noses of the Wackenhuts."

"So let's get the Wackenhuts, then," Hazel pleaded.

"And what makes you think that the Wackenhuts are little angels of mercy?" Rio asked. "They're more likely to beat him up and stick him in some locked room alone."

"They wouldn't do that," Hazel said. "They're human beings."

"They're cops," Rio told her. "Cops do that. They are doing that right now, in every prison in America." He cradled Herb's head and stroked his hair. "I don't want to put him through that kind of ordeal. Let him stay out here, where he's free."

"Let's carry him out," Ben said. "As soon as Alix and Laura get here. We'll take shifts."

Far off in the distance, they heard the sound of high voices singing. "Ain't gonna study war no more, ain't gonna study war no more . . ."

"Hell!" Hazel said. "Laura had the medical kit."

"I don't think it would have helped us much, anyway," Ben said quietly. "He needs a hospital, not an aspirin."

Spirits of this land, Maya cried out silently. I know how to listen to you, a little bit, but I don't know how to call you. I don't know your names or your language or your voices, but I am here anyway to ask for your help.

"Shh," Tommy said. "Is that an engine?"

The desert was still as an indrawn breath. Shadows flickered, and the moonlight shimmered in waves. The hair rose at the nape of her neck, and little rushes of power ran up her spine. A pulsing play of shadows and half-seen forms surrounded her. A web of energies rose from the land and carried her with them as emotions arose in her: anger and rage and pain, pain, pain. Somewhere an act of transformation occurred, earth was ripped from earth and changed. Fire, blasting, violation, a ripping tear in the fabric of life, that went on and on, until she was on fire from within, burning from the womb out to the bone. A fine dust of poison settled on her skin, and she began to die.

"I want to stand with you." She wanted to cry out to the land as she had once cried to Johanna, but she stood on two legs, kin to the spoilers. Her life was filled with futile gestures and superficial offerings. She could walk to Mercury and walk away, but the land remained, in its torment. Where could the land go to escape what came crashing into it? Why did she think she could find power in this tortured place? If such power existed, why had it allowed this land to be spoiled?

"I don't hear anything," Ben said.

"We've got to get help for Herb," Hazel said. "If the Wackenhuts are coming, let's go now."

Ben turned to Rio. "You get out of here first. You can't get busted with a dying man right now. You don't need that kind of attention on you."

"I don't want to leave him," Rio said. "He's my friend. I'll take my chances."

Birds were gathering in the desert, hovering over Herb's still form, circling, waiting. The ghost birds of species long extinct; golden-tailed, bright-colored pheasants; beaky-nosed, chain-smoking, cheek-chewing birds. They had come to take Herb's life away, and she had nothing to offer them in his place.

"You don't understand," Ben said. "They're out for you, man. I've been trying to tell you, I heard it from Tony in the DA's office. Someone in the Justice Department wants your head, on a platter."

Her mother's ashes, she realized, were still in the bottom of her pack. Maybe this was why she had carried them so long, why she couldn't leave them in Nepal. We come of a desert people, she thought. Maybe this is where she belongs, the offering that can redeem Herb's life.

"I can't worry about that," Rio said. "If they want to get me, they'll get me. I want to stay with Herb."

"You don't have to deliver your ass up to them, tied with a bow," Tommy argued. "Make them work for it."

I offer you my ancestors, Maya said to the spirits. I will give you the most precious thing I carry, my mother's bones. Let us be in the Good Reality, let Herb wake up from his nap refreshed, let Rio escape, let the land be healed.

All around her was a great silence. The only voice she heard was Betty's, in her mind.

"So what is this? First you drag me up and down the Himalayas, trying to lose me on the mountaintop, and now you're trying to dump me in the world's most polluted desert. What am I to you, anyway? *Your* mother, *your* ashes, *your* most precious possession! What about me? Talk about abstractions, you've made me into the great abstraction of all times. I've got news for you—I'm not just Mother with a capital *M*. I'm Betty Stein Greenbaum. What about what I want?"

"Don't do it, man," Tommy begged Rio. "Don't make a grand heroic gesture that'll fuck up the rest of your life."

"Death was good enough for me," Betty complained. "Why should some guy you don't even know escape?"

Oh, Maya was a poor excuse for a shaman, unable to bury her own mother let alone command the great forces of life and death.

Now at last Rio turned to look at her. His face was gray in the moonlight, and his voice seemed to come from the bowels of the underworld itself. He spoke as if the others had receded to the far hills and she alone could hear him.

"Do you know where I was when they gunned down Edith and Daniel? I was in a bar, getting drunk."

Herb lay dying before them, and Maya could not reach for him, could not even take his hand.

"I watched them die on TV."

In the silence, they could all hear the distant thrum of an engine.

I can't absolve him, she thought. Only the birds with their green and golden wings can fan us free of our mistakes.

"So did I," she said at last. "So did I. But you've paid for that already, if you ever can. This is different. Ben is right."

"No." Rio looked at her with the eyes she remembered from a grainy picture in a newspaper where he had shielded them from the light. "Don't you see? I've missed my whole life. Every important moment, either I've fucked up or I wasn't there. I wasn't with Edith and Daniel at the end. I didn't even know when my kid was born." He was crying, now, tears like the autumn rains on granite ledges. "This is the way I get a second chance, a chance to do it right."

No, Maya wanted to cry. I don't see. Was this another lesson in acceptance? His spiritual lesson to learn? She remembered the face of the Rinpoche, watching his *gompa* burn. Maybe this was Rio's conflagration, the way the universe had of breaking him so that he would endure.

But everything within her rebelled. No, she thought. Some things are not acceptable. The woman on fire. The burning of the earth. Rio going back to jail. They're not abstractions, they're not images or stories I tell myself about myself. They are as real as any mountain, and they hurt. They hurt. I believe they even injure the earth herself.

Where do I find the power to become a healer for those wounds?

"Maybe that matters more than what happens to me. Maybe that matters more than anything," Rio whispered.

Was that the sound of an engine, or the thrumming of wings?

"It seems like that now," Tommy warned, "but it'll wear off, that noble feeling. Usually I find it happens about the third day in jail."

"While we're arguing, he's dying." Hazel was crying as she stroked Herb's head. "Please don't die!"

Rio turned to her. "Maybe that isn't the worst thing that could happen. Maybe this is how he wants to go, out in the desert, trying to walk to Mercury."

"It's a selfish way to do it," Ben said grimly.

Rio shrugged. "When do you get to be selfish, if not when you're dying?"

Yes, something was coming toward them, Maya realized, winged and wild and thrumming with light, and suddenly Betty was smiling at her, holding out her arms and comforting her as she had long ago when Maya was a baby and Joe had loved them both. "Don't be afraid," Betty murmured. "There's nothing to fear."

Maya looked up at Rio, tears in her eyes. "Be with him, then. Tell him that you love him, tell him it's okay to let go."

Rio looked down at Herb's head, cradled in his lap. "Don't be afraid, Herb," he whispered so softly that Maya could hardly hear him. "It's okay. It's okay. Oh shit, Herb. What am I going to do without you? I never even got to tell you what she told me today. Oh God, Herb, what am I going to do?"

"We love you, Herb," Hazel whispered through tears. "We love you."

They crouched around him in the sand, crooning to him and weeping while the desert pulsed and thrummed and sobbed around them. Above them the sky began to lighten. Searchlights approached. Herb gave a long, rasping breath. Suddenly his body was shaken by a deep spasm. He arched, convulsed, and let out a moaning, strangled cry. Maya smelled shit and blood. The sky opened like a blossom and filled with birds, their feathers colored like the premonition of dawn to come, their wings beating the air into a clean, cold wind that blew unobstructed from the sea.

"I love you," Rio was crying now, the full hard tears of a winter storm. "You were better to me than my own dad. You trusted me when nobody else would."

A whirlwind of ghost birds spiraled out to the disappearing stars. They heard bird cries, and jingle bells, and Herb was gone.

For one long heartbeat, they all sat still. Herb lay in perfect peace. The night seemed to be generating light from within.

We should say a prayer, Maya thought. What kind of Kaddish do we say for him? I don't even know what his religion was.

She opened her canteen and poured water. Suddenly she realized that the throbbing in the air was no longer spirit wings but a jeep rapidly approaching.

"Now go," Ben ordered Rio. "Maya, make him go. Go with him. We'll deal with the Wackenhuts. Herb's gone . . . you can't do anything more for him."

"I want to wash him," Rio said firmly. "I don't want them to find him like this."

"We'll wash him," Hazel said.

"I was his friend."

"Then hurry," Ben urged. He and Tommy dug a small hole while Rio gently and tenderly cleaned Herb with toilet paper and water from Hazel's bottle, as if he were anointing him with sacred offerings, his touch a benediction. Watching him, Maya could see the father he might have been, how he would have bathed Rachel carefully and powdered her small bottom and held her tiny hand. He would never have the chance, now.

Tommy and Ben took the soiled tissue and quickly buried it.

"Good-bye, Herb," Rio whispered, holding Herb's face in his hands. "Good journey."

"Hurry," Ben said. The sound of the engine had grown louder.

Rio rose slowly.

"Go!" Ben urged. Now they could hear the crackle of walkie-talkies. "Don't crucify yourself to be his honor guard. Try to make it back to camp without getting popped."

"It's too late," Rio said. "It'll be daylight in half an hour."

"Then go to Mercury," Tommy suggested. "Yeah, that's a better strategy. Do what you planned in the first place, a simple action like everybody else. They'll be so distracted by this scene, you'll probably slide through."

"Just don't give them your real name," Ben pleaded. "Please, for the sake of the unborn grandchildren of the entire legal team. You don't have ID on you, do you? Either of you?"

"No. But I don't like lying. It makes it worse if you get caught."

"Don't lie, just don't cooperate. Most people aren't giving names, anyway. If they don't know who you are, they'll just take you to Tonopah and release you. If they do, they'll invent some reason to hold you for good. Now get out of here!"

As the searchlights swept the ridge behind them, they ducked into the indigo dawn.

49

Mercury

One must know the effects of past actions, whence
cometh all sorrow, are inevitable.
One must know . . . that sorrow is a Guru.

—"The Ten Things that
One Must Know" in From
the Precepts of the Gurus
The Wisdom of Buddhism

The sky was even now beginning to glow behind the ridge of hills in the east as Maya and Rio headed across the desert. At first he led them west, as if running from the approaching light. They were moving too fast to talk, stumbling over low cactus in the predawn darkness, tripping on small depressions in the ground. At last Rio turned their course toward the lights of Mercury in the distance. High voltage power lines stretched across their way, and suddenly the spirits were gone. Only the solid, physical reality of ground and plants remained. Maya sighed, half with regret, half with relief, as they passed under the buzzing and humming wires.

The moon had set. Under the power lines, the ground was level and bare of brush and cactus.

"Let's stay on the clear ground," Maya said. "We'll make better time."

"It's the obvious place for jeeps to patrol," Rio objected.

"They're going to find us anyway, as soon as it gets light. We should be as far away from the others as we can."

They ran along the jeep road. Although the path was somewhat smoother, it was still rough enough so that Maya was forced to look down, straining to see obstructions in the dim, light. When she glanced up, Mercury was already closer, a string of brilliant lights that blinded her night vision, forcing her to shield her eyes.

She was tired. She had been running forever through the desert night, with no sleep and her lungs on fire, when they heard, once again, the grinding engine of the jeeps and saw the round lights beaming into the dark.

"Down," Rio whispered. They lay flat against the ground, feeling the light pass over them, hoping the shadows still protected them as the jeep stopped and voices drifted toward them on the wind. Maya stifled another cough.

"Did you check under the power lines?" A man's voice spoke above her.

"Yeah. It's clear. Let's look farther up."

Maya's heart was pounding. We could get arrested now, she thought. We will get arrested soon. Spirits of the night, wherever you've gone, help us.

Their protection held, for the moment. The voices passed them by.

"Let's go," she whispered as the sound of the engine died away. Already the sky was beginning to lighten, and walking was easier. "Let's go and let's not stop now for anything—because in a very short time it'll be too light to hide any longer."

They pushed on, walking fast, almost running again. Suddenly Maya wanted, more than anything, to get to Mercury before the guards picked them up. She would never make it to Ground Zero, but if she could just stand for one moment on Mercury's paved streets, she would have done something for the desert, earned a bargaining chip she could cash in with fate so that Rio stayed free.

She was shaken by a sudden, deep cough. My wake-up call, she thought, my Tibetan bell. Perhaps I'll develop permanent bronchitis as a chronic reminder to stop making every destination a new Kala Pattar to attain. Let Mercury be a town, no more. What matters is only that Rio and I are together in this moment, running in the desert dawn, and he has spoken to me once more.

"You okay?" Rio asked, dropping back. She nodded, and they ran on.

The sky changed from indigo to the barest suggestion of velvet blue, glowing, lightening. They raced against the sunrise.

Time, Maya thought, only a little more time. Twenty minutes. Half an hour. The dawn progressed, inexorable. Now she could no longer see the stars. The sand and rocks and plants began to display hue and color among their silhouetted forms.

Suddenly she heard a voice, and the metallic sound behind her of a radio. "Don't run," Rio cried out, but Maya did anyway, impelled by some primal instinct she couldn't resist. Her heavy boots felt slow and cumbersome, pounding against the desert floor. Suddenly she heard a man's gruff voice behind her.

"Get your hands up, high, where I can see them. Or I'll shoot!"

Maya froze in place. Part of her wanted to laugh hysterically, to tell the guard he was using lines out of a bad movie, but she couldn't speak. Behind her, Rio slowly raised his arms.

"Don't be afraid," he called to her softly. "Just do what they say."

Maya's fear was located somewhere in the vicinity of her throat, a solid lump that hurt when she swallowed. She raised her arms up high.

"Take your pack off, slowly. Keep your hands away from your pockets," the voice said.

"You know, of course, that we're committed to nonviolence," Rio continued speaking in a strong, calm voice. "You don't have to be afraid of us."

"Walk forward slowly," the guard said to Rio. When he and Maya stood together, the guard continued issuing orders. "Lie facedown. Put your hands behind your back. Turn your head to the side."

They lay down, Maya put her face in the embracing, possibly radio-active, dust.

She felt her wrists grabbed from behind and cuffed tightly with plastic bands.

"Get up, now!"

What do I do? she wondered. Is this when we're supposed to noncooperate? What is Rio going to do? With some effort, she raised her head and turned to look at him. The morning light was stronger now; she could see him clearly—unshaven, red eyed, his hair gray with dust, his face creased with lines and streaked with tears and dirt. Even the mountains erode, she thought. Whether you love them or not, whether you abandon them or lie to them or penetrate their secret crevices with the truth, eventually they all wash down to sea. Goddess, I don't want to lose him again.

"What do we do?" she whispered. "Are you going to walk, like they say?"

Rio's mouth stretched into an ironic, vertical grin. "Remember what Tommy said, about how the noble impulse wears off? Well, it just did."

"I said get up!" the guard barked.

Rising from a prone position with her hands cuffed behind her back was difficult, Maya found, sort of like those games in grammar school, three-legged races and such. She made one attempt, lost her balance, and fell. Irritated, the security guard reached down and jerked them to their feet. Now Maya could look around. There were five guards around them, and one was talking into a radio.

"Get their packs," one of the guards ordered another. "Let's walk them out."

Walking with bound hands was also awkward. They made their way across the last few feet of ground to stand in the parking lot on the outskirts of Mercury. Below them lay the main street with its fabled attractions, the coffee shop, the bowling alley.

The sun rose over the foothills, covering the stark, knife-edged ridges with the soft bloom of its golden light, as a young Wackenhut gripped her arm and propelled her toward the back of a closed police van.

She craned her neck to take another long look at Rio, but the guard shoved her roughly forward. Then she was up and into the closed van, Rio following behind her. Metal benches lined each side, and they settled themselves opposite each other, moving awkwardly because of their bound hands.

The door slammed, and they were alone in the dark.

They sat for a long time in silence. He was across from her, but she couldn't really see him, only the outline of his shape in the dim light that filtered through the vents. She could smell sour sweat that could have been his or her own.

"Are you all right?" Rio asked at last. "They didn't hurt you?"

"No, I'm fine. And you?"

"I'm fine, too."

They fell silent again. Maya's wrists hurt where the plastic band cut into them, and her head ached. She had followed him into the underworld, and now she would go quietly mad here, trussed and shackled in the dark, facing his silent rage. Finally he spoke.

"I know that I have to forgive you, if I want to go on living. But it's hard. It's taking me some work."

"I did you a great wrong," Maya admitted. "But I can't give you back those missing years, no matter how bad I feel. So go ahead and hate me. I deserve it."

"I don't hate you. I don't have the right to hate anybody."

"You have the right to be mad and hurt. You have the right to bleed."

His voice dropped so low she had to lean forward to hear him. "But if I'm honest with myself, I have to admit that what hurts the most isn't just that you didn't tell me. It's realizing that your picture of me, all those years, was so different from my fantasy of you."

Maya strained to see through the dark. Her throat hurt, and when she spoke, her voice was husky. "But my picture was about me more than you. If I had written to you, if we had made contact, I wouldn't have had to carry a picture in my head. I would have known who you were."

Rio let out a long breath. "I'm just cutting myself on the broken edges of my own illusions, that's all. How can I blame you for that?"

"What was it you said before, on the rock? I forgive you, you forgive me. Clean slate—new start."

"You were afraid of me, weren't you? On the rock? You were physically afraid of me."

"Only for a minute," Maya admitted.

"That hurts, too."

"It was just something that flashed across your face when you were so angry, that made me think of that night you put your fist through every mirror in our place."

"Well, there you have it. Another great moment in the life of Rio Connolly that's a total blank to me."

Maya slumped back against the wall of the van, but the pressure made her shoulders ache and her wrist joints pulsed against the metal. She leaned forward, but her back felt the strain.

"Try leaning up against the corner," Rio suggested as she squirmed around. "If you brace your shoulders against the two walls, it leaves room for your hands."

"That helps," Maya admitted as she adjusted her position. "How long do you think they'll keep us in here?"

"As long as they want."

"Oh."

"Were you scared?" Rio asked.

"I have to admit that I was. It's been a while since someone's pulled a gun on me."

"Don't be scared. The rough part is over. Now it's just a matter of waiting, to see what they'll do."

"I hate waiting," Maya said. "I'm not good at it."

"I am. I've gotten very good at it. I could be on the Olympic team."

"I guess you've had to learn."

Rio spoke in a low voice, almost dreamy, as if he was talking more to himself than to her. "I know how to do time," he said. "Time is like the gorgon in the old myths. You just can't look at it directly or you turn to stone. But if you look into the mirror of the moment, if you hold that up in front of your face like a shield, you can live through anything."

"Are you scared?" she asked softly. "About what might happen?"

"I don't know." He laughed softly. "You know what's weird? It's how familiar this feels. Comfortable, even, like I've finally landed back where I belong."

"Don't say that."

"But maybe it's true. You know, there's something that happens to people when you're locked up for a long time. You don't have to decide when to wake up or go to sleep or turn off the light, or what to do with your day, or who to call. You don't have to decide anything. The lights go off at a certain time and on at a certain time. Your meals are set down in front of you and there's no choice on the menu. After a while, you get used to it. And that's why, I think, a lot of guys keep coming back in. Because it's familiar. I always swore I wouldn't be like that. But hey, what the hell, I swore a lot of things in my time. I swore I wouldn't be like my father. I believe I even remember swearing I would never leave you.''

"Stop it, Rio. It's going to be okay, it really is.''

"Is it? Or did I turn out to be one of those guys after all, the two-time losers, the ones that make the same mistake over and over again. Isn't that really why we're here, right now?''

"What do you mean?'' Dammit, she wanted to see him, to watch the expression change on his face, to look into his eyes.

"Herb talked me out of doing this action, you know. After I left you on the rock. He was afraid for me. But then he left, and I kept thinking about what you'd said, and I got madder and madder, until I did what I've done a thousand times before. I said, fuck the world—I've just got to do something, anything extreme. And now he's dead, and we're here.''

Maya sighed. "You could look at it that way. Or you could say that you gave Herb the gift of the death he wanted, with someone who truly knew him and cared for him to hold his head and wash his body.''

"Do you really believe that?''

"I do.''

He was quiet for a moment, thinking. "That's worth paying a price for, then.''

"Not the price of your whole life. But I have a feeling we'll slide through.''

"You don't get to bargain, though. Not for something that's really important. You have to be willing to throw it all on the table, offer it all up. I wish I felt as optimistic as you do, but in my experience the universe doesn't make you any deals.''

"There's a power in that,'' Maya admitted. "But it also sounds a bit like your brother's letter—remember? I thought you didn't have to be a hero anymore.''

"Maybe it's a guy thing, like Tommy said. We think we're over it, but we never are.'' She could sense him moving restlessly, shifting position. "I guess all I'm trying to say is that, whatever happens, I'm glad I was there for Herb, at the end.''

"The rest of us didn't know him like you did. We didn't love him. We couldn't have done for him what you did.'' And now I'm doing what women do, Maya thought, buttressing, bolstering, trying to make him feel good. But it's true.

"He was good to me. When I wanted to join Grains, you know, at first they didn't want me. My history scared them. But Herb talked them around. He's an old fighter, you know. Fought against Franco in the Spanish civil war, like your dad. Organized his union. He had a broader perspective on things. I could talk to him in a way I couldn't do with anybody else."

"I wish I'd been able to know him."

Rio let out a long sigh. "God, I miss him already!"

"When he died, I felt the spirits come for him," she said softly, wishing her hands were free to take his hand or pat his shoulder. "He had a good death."

"I felt something, too." He spoke tentatively, as if he were about to venture onto risky ground. "It was like that clean, raw wind on the coast, so strong you can lean against it." Now his voice dropped almost to a whisper. "Remember?"

"I remember. I remember how the light comes down, after a storm, like spotlights poking through the clouds and gleaming on the gray backs of the waves."

"You talk like you write."

"It's an occupational hazard."

"I read your books, you know. But it's better to be with you, to hear you talk even if I can't see you very well."

"Well, maybe the Goddess lost patience with us both and decided that this is the only way we could possibly say certain things to each other. Locked up in the dark, with our hands tied behind our backs so neither one of us can do the other an injury. We've become each other's captive audience."

"Ow! You made me smile, and my lips are chapped."

"I have Chap Stick in my pocket, if I could get to my pocket," Maya said with regret.

"Sometimes these bands are loose enough that you can work them off, if you wriggle your wrists. Mine are too tight."

Maya experimented, but the motion brought sharp pain. "Ouch! No, that hurt. They're too tight."

"I'm sorry."

"It's not your fault."

"Isn't it?"

"No, it isn't," Maya said firmly. "Anyway, we should be proud to be here. In some way that isn't entirely clear to me at the moment, we're stopping them from blowing up the world."

"There is that."

The van was beginning to get warm. Outside, the sun must be fully up. Soon it would be stifling, Maya thought, and I'm wearing my down jacket with no way to get it off or even unzip it.

"So what's she like?" Rio asked suddenly, his voice carefully casual. "My, uh, Johanna's . . . you know, the kid? Do you think she might want to have some contact with me?"

"Definitely. I've got a letter for you in my day pack, and her picture, too." Suddenly a terrible thought struck her. "Oh no!"

"What's wrong?"

"Betty's ashes. They're still in my day pack!"

"In your day pack? You carry them with you wherever you go?" He sounded amused.

"Yes. I carried them all over Nepal—or at least, the Sherpas did. I could never find the right place to leave them. I thought about taking them out of my pack . . . but, I don't know, maybe I had some idea I would leave them in the desert. But that wasn't right." She was too nervous, now, to sit still, but there was no room to pace, no way to be in motion and release her tension. She began to rock back and forth. "What if they search my pack? What if they dump her out, or throw her in the garbage?"

"If they don't actually arrest us, if they just take us to Tonopah and let us go, they probably won't search your pack," he said in a calm voice. "And if they do, you'll just have to tell them the truth. It's so goddamned weird, they might just believe it."

"Thanks! Thanks a whole lot!"

"I'm sorry," he said, but she could hear him trying not to laugh.

"You're not sorry! You're laughing at me!"

"Well, you must admit it's kind of funny."

"Funny! Fuck you, Rio Connolly! After all I've been through— eighteen airplanes in five days and hardly any sleep and then to go traipsing across the desert getting guns pulled on me . . . and then you sit there and laugh!" She was straining against the cuffs but they only cut her wrists more deeply. "You know something, I'm sick of you! I'm sick of thinking about you and worrying about you and feeling guilty about you! I'm sick of your letters and your mistakes and your whole goddamned miserable life!" She threw herself back on the bench, but only slammed her wrists and elbows into the metal wall. A sharp pain raced up her arm, and she began to cry.

After a long while, Rio spoke. "I'm sorry if I hurt your feelings."

Maya sighed. Her head hurt and now she was feeling ashamed of her outburst. "I'm sorry I said what I just did. I didn't mean it."

"You did. That's okay. It's honest. You can always tell the truth to me, Maya. I can take it. How can I blame you for lying to me all those years if I can't take your honesty now?"

Oh, twist the knife, she thought.

"I don't mean to be insensitive about your mother," he went on. "Really, it'll probably be okay."

"That's my line. Only I manage to sound more sure about it. And what if it's not?"

"Don't think about it," Rio said. "When you're in a situation like this, you can't afford to think about what might go wrong. You just drive yourself nuts."

"I can't help it." Suddenly she could feel how little sleep she'd gotten in the last week, how close to the edge she was. She felt light, shaky, as if she might have a breakdown or a breakthrough. "When I think about them, pawing through her bones—it's like the ultimate desecration."

"Maya . . ." Rio began, but she was seized by a spasm of coughing.

"That sounds awful," he said when she was quiet again. "Have you seen a doctor?"

"It's just my personal form of meditation," Maya told him. "And you know what? I'm sick of that, too. I'm sick of the universe trying to teach me spiritual lessons, and sick of trying to accept the perfection of every rotten stupid moment that happens and sick of always trying so damn hard to improve myself! Oh, don't mind me, I'm just tired."

"I've only ever learned one thing that could be called a spiritual lesson," Rio said in a low voice. "I wasn't trying to improve myself at the time. It just came, and saved my life—miserable as it was. I had to relearn it a couple of times—it seems like I have to relearn it just about every day—but each time it comes as a sort of grace."

"What are you saying?"

"You're tired. You're sick—physically, I mean. You're still grieving for your mother. Don't interpret those things as some sort of failure on your part."

Maya desperately wanted to wipe away the tears from her eyes, but she couldn't twist her head far enough to reach them with her shoulder.

"What is it?" Rio asked. "What are you trying to do?"

"Can I wipe my eyes on your shirt?"

"Here," he leaned over and offered her his shoulder.

"And my nose, too?"

"Anything."

Maya wiped and sniffed, and then settled back into her corner. "It's so ironic. I've carried those ashes so long, they're like something I've incorporated into me. I honestly forgot about them. All through Nepal, I kept looking for the right place to leave them, and never found it. I wanted something spectacular for her—I wanted to give her to the Goddess Mother of the Universe herself. And now I've gotten her arrested. Joke on me!" She sniffed again. "It is pretty funny, actually."

"I'm not laughing!" Rio said quickly, but then they both were, laughing and crying at the same time.

"Oh, Goddess, I've gotten poor Betty arrested!" Maya's laugh became a cough. When it subsided, she sighed. "It's a good thing she's dead. She'd never forgive me."

"If we get out of this," Rio promised, "I'll help you scatter her ashes. That is, if you'd like me to."

"I would." Maya wished she could reach out and take his hand.

"And if we don't, if I don't—"

"We aren't going to think about that, remember?" she interrupted him. "It's just a distraction. We were talking, that's what's important."

Rio shifted restlessly. "There's something I want to say, in case I don't get another chance."

"Stop talking like that! It's bad magic."

"It's just this: I'm sorry. I'm sorry how it all came down on you, I'm sorry I didn't love you better. I've been sorry for seventeen years that I had to stop for that drink."

There was a time, Maya realized, when she would have given anything to know she would someday hear him say exactly that. Now she just felt sad.

"It's funny, talking in the dark," Rio said. "Maybe it's better. I've been talking to you inside my mind for so many years. When I do, I can say anything. You always understand. In the dark, I can pretend this whole conversation is a dream I'm having. I'm glad you yelled at me, you know? Now I don't have to worry that I'll blow it, that I'll say something wrong that'll drive you away again."

"I won't go away, Rio," Maya said, knowing as she spoke that she was swearing a pledge. "Whatever you say, whatever happens. We do have a history together. We need each other to sort it out. I won't cut you off again. Nothing you can say will change that."

"Won't it? Well, I guess you already know the worst, anyway."

"What is that? What is the worst, for you?"

"What I said, in the desert, about when the others died. Out of all of it, that's what I feel worst about. Except for losing you. I should have been with them."

"Why weren't you?"

"They threw me out of the Front, about a week before. They said I was drunk, and unreliable. They were right."

"I'm confused," Maya said. "Why did you bomb the Bank of America, if you weren't with the Front?"

"I didn't."

"You didn't?"

"Of course I didn't. If I had, I would have done it right, drunk or not. Nobody would have gotten hurt." There was a note of pride in his voice. She remembered how happy he'd been, building giant letters in People's Park, fixing the toilet, rewiring an old lamp. "I can fix anything," he'd said to her once, but of course there were things that nobody could fix. He went on. "Anyway, I wouldn't have done it. I thought it was a bad target. Too big. Too many factors we couldn't control."

Maya's head buzzed and hummed in the heat as if all her conceptions were swarming and burrowing and trying to find new places to rest.

"Rio, you're telling me you spent fourteen years in prison for something you didn't do?"

"You got it."

"But why did you plead guilty, then?"

Rio sighed patiently. "For the same reason anyone pleads guilty. Because they offered to cut me a deal, and my lawyers didn't think we could win a trial."

"Fourteen years? What kind of a deal was that?"

"I'm out now, aren't I?" he said quietly. "I'm alive, and talking to you. You forget what the political climate was like. They could have ramrodded me right into the gas chamber, if they'd wanted to. And you know, even though there've been times I've been far more sick of my own miserable life than you could possibly be, I still prefer it to the alternative."

"For something you didn't do!"

"It's like I said to Ben, if they want to get you, they will."

There was no bitterness in his voice, she thought. His voice was like the face of the Rinpoche watching his *gompa* burn. "It doesn't really matter if you leave them an opening or not, if you do an action or cower under the bed. They'll goad you or seduce you or, if it comes down to it, get you the means and the material and hold your hand while you light the fuse."

"What are you saying?"

"Remember our old friend T-Bone? He's some high muckity muck in the Justice Department, I hear."

"You mean . . . ?"

"I don't know what I mean." Now, at last, she heard emotion in his tone, anger, yes, and grief. "I know that Daniel didn't like the Bank of America as a target, either, and neither did Edith. I don't believe either one of them set that bomb. I don't believe they deserved to die. But we'll never know what really happened. And maybe we don't need to know. I could sit here and say to you that I'm not a murderer, at least—but maybe in a larger sense I am. I started us off on that path, you know. I pushed us over the edge, from talk to action. I brought T-Bone and Randy into the group."

"I never trusted them."

"I should have listened to you."

Maya's shoulders hurt and her head ached from the steadily increasing heat. Her throat was dry, and the air in the van was sour and hot.

"And now it's possible that old T-Bone is the one who wants to put you away again?"

"Anything is possible. But you can't worry about it, Maya, you really can't. You've just got to go ahead and live your life. Although now that you're here, I can't help feeling that I hope I get to live a little bit more of it outside."

His voice dropped so low, she could hardly hear him. "If they do it to me, if they send me up again, will you write to me this time? Just every once in a while?"

"It'll be my second chance," she said. "My turn to redo something I did wrong before. But it's a second chance I don't want. I pray the Goddess doesn't give it to me. We'll get out of this, I know we will." Still the longer they sat, trussed up in the dark, the harder she found it to believe that they would yet slide through into El Mundo Bueno.

Now the van was really getting warm, and she was starting to sweat. Her skin itched where Claire's sweater clung to her.

"Do you ever really get a chance to redo something you've done wrong, and make it right?" Rio asked.

"Of course you do," Maya assured him. "Sylvia, the woman who trained me to be a Witch, she used to say that the Goddess gives you challenges. And if you don't meet them, she just keeps on giving you the same one over and over again, until you finally succeed. It's sort of the Pagan answer to hell."

"This van is starting to resemble hell. It's heating up. Are you all right?"

"I wish I could unzip my jacket."

"I'll help you." He turned around so that his cuffed hands were toward her, and by kneeling down while she bent over him, he was able to feel for the clasp on her zipper. After several tries, he was able to pull the zipper down. The jacket opened.

"Thank you," Maya said. "That's much better. Can I do the same for you?"

"I unbuttoned mine before they cuffed us," Rio said.

"That's thinking ahead."

"If you wriggle around, you can slide your coat down off your shoulders and just let it hang off your arms, even use it as a pad against the wall."

"That's a lot better," Maya said, taking his advice. "It's amazing how suddenly I feel luxuriously comfortable, just because I'm not as uncomfortable as I was five minutes ago."

"That's the trick," Rio said. "Sometimes you can't do the AA thing of living one day at a time. You have to just take it minute by minute. Maybe nothing really gets much better, but if it gets a little better, that's enough for a moment. That's change." His voice went flat. "Maybe you give up hoping for the big things, but you can hope for a little bit of a breeze or a drink of water. Something small and attainable. Then, when it comes, you can survive inside a great, big despair and hardly even notice it."

"It won't come to that," Maya stated as firmly as if she believed it. "We'll go boating on Stow Lake. We'll wander in the Pyrenees. You know, Daniel said that, years ago, and I didn't even know he was making a literary allusion. I'd never read *Waiting for Godot*."

"I still haven't." Rio laughed.

"If only we had a copy now. It would speak to our condition."

They heard the front door of the van open and slam shut. The engine gunned into life, and the van started off.

"We're moving, at least," Maya said. "That's bound to be an improvement."

"I wouldn't count on it."

"Myself, I've always equated motion with freedom."

The van careered around curves, accelerating and decelerating in a way that threw Maya into the corner and jerked her away. In the heat and the stifling air, she felt queasy.

"Let me sit by you," Rio said. "I'll brace you." He moved over next to her and wedged his feet against the opposite bench. "Is that better?"

"Thanks." His side met hers with an electric shock. She was too conscious of his touch, his sweaty, desert smell.

"How far is it to Tonopah?"

"Three and a half hours."

"That long?" Maya didn't think she could survive that long in the airless, dank cage. She would go mad or pee on the floor, she would throw up all over Rio's shoes. How had he endured fourteen years?

"They won't take us there right away. They're probably just going to bring us back to the holding pen at the main gate."

The van lurched heavily to the right, and she fell against him. I'm going to throw up, she thought. Goddess, that's all we need in here.

"You okay?" he asked, as she righted herself.

"As good as can be expected, given the circumstances."

"Hang in there."

The van swerved and lurched, and they rode in silence. Then Rio spoke abruptly.

"Everybody makes mistakes. I made bad ones, the kind people die from. And maybe I'm not done making them yet. But I didn't die. At a certain point, I figured out that I was just going to have to live with what I'd done and hadn't done, the good and the bad. And overall, I still wanted to live."

Maya allowed herself to lean against him, and spoke gently. "You said you learned a spiritual lesson once. What was it?"

"I don't know if I can define it. I'm not a writer, like you."

"Try. I find myself deeply in need of spiritual comfort, if not motion-sickness pills."

He was silent for a long moment. "I'm not very improvable, for one. I know that about myself. I mean, I have to improve to my utmost just to get to what most people consider their starting point. All I can do, really, is try to be an ally of the rock and the wind and the rain."

"You were that, for Herb."

"Yes," he said after a long moment. "The wind rose. It was right."

"Maybe we're mistaken to always think in terms of bargains and deals and sacrifice," Maya said. "Paying a price for doing what's right—when you think about it, it's sort of a capitalist spiritual metaphor. Maybe we just need to learn to trust that when a choice we make feels right, whatever its risks, then what comes from it is bound to be okay. The means are the ends."

"I'd like to go back, to that rock on the coast, sometime. Do you still go there?" Rio asked.

"We'll go together," Maya said, as an act of magic, sending her will out into the universe. "We'll steal that rowboat, yet."

"Better rent one this time." Rio laughed. "I'll do time for Herb, if I have to, or to stop the nukes, but I ain't doin' time for piracy."

"That's a shame. I always kind of liked you as a pirate."

The van stopped suddenly. The back door was flung open, flooding them with the blinding, desert light.

"Get out!"

Rio stepped out of the van, and Maya stumbled after him, blinking.

"Name?" said a guard with a clipboard.

"Hiroshima," Rio replied. The guard shook his head and waved him on.

"Name?" he said to Maya. "Don't tell me, let me guess."

"Nagasaki," Maya said.

"The Japanese twins."

She blinked again, still getting used to the light. When she turned her head, Rio was gone.

A woman guard marched her across the road to the sound of chanting and applause. The bright light dazzled her eyes, and she stumbled. Fifty feet away, across the cattle guard, a crowd of demonstrators cheered her on. The guard clipped her handcuffs off, and gratefully she pulled loose from the sleeves of her jacket and rubbed her sore wrists.

"Put your hands in front," the guard said, and cuffed her again, but less tightly.

"Where's my pack?" Maya asked anxiously, picking up her jacket with her cuffed hands, savoring her increased freedom of motion. Yes,

Rio was right, if something gets even a little better, it's enough for a moment. Don't think about what might happen further down the line.

The guard pointed to a pile by the side of the road. "You'll get all your belongings in Tonopah. Or if you're booked into jail, you'll get a receipt."

Then she found herself in an asphalt parking lot surrounded by a chain-link fence, locked up with fifty other women.

"Maya!" Alix ran up to her and gave her a handcuffed approximation of a hug. "You got popped! Are you okay?"

Maya nodded. "I'm dying of thirst."

"There's water over there. And a honeyhut, if you need one."

"A what?"

"A Porta Potti."

"Praise the Goddess!"

Alix and Laura drew her away from the guards by the locked gate. "What about the others?" Alix asked.

"Herb had a heart attack," Maya said softly. "He's dead."

"Oh no!"

"I should have been there." Laura began to cry. "I'm a nurse—I could have helped him."

Maya shook her head. "I'm not sure anyone could have helped, even if we had gotten him to a hospital. I think maybe it was the way he wanted to go, you know? Out in the desert, in the middle of an action. And we were all there with him. Rio held his head and bathed his body."

"Oh, I'm glad he was there," Laura said. "He and Herb were so tight."

"But then we had to leave. Ben thought it was too risky for Rio to get arrested with a dead man," Maya said. "Now I have to pee or die."

By the time Maya emerged from the honeyhut, Alix had spotted Rio in the men's pen.

"That looks good," she said. "So far they haven't singled him out."

"What about the others?" Maya asked. "Any sign of them?"

Laura shook her head. "If they got found with Herb's body, I suspect the Wackenhuts would go ahead and book them into the jail in Beatty or Tonopah, not hold them here."

Alix nodded. "That's why Ben would have wanted Rio to get away. Let's hope his luck holds."

Maya took some time to tell them all about Herb's death, and their walk to Mercury. All the while she was anxious. What if I'm wrong about the Goddess, what if she doesn't give us second chances after all?

"Where are the men?" she asked Alix finally. "Can we talk to them?"

"Over there," Alix said. "By that fence." She led Maya to a corner of the pen, where a matching corner of the men's side was separated by a three-foot no-man's-land between chain-link fences topped with barbed wire. She whistled, and when one of the men came over, she sent him to find Rio.

Now that she could see him in full daylight, he looked tired and old and shabby. His face was already turning red in the morning heat. She could see the derelict, the convict. The pirate was not to be found.

I probably don't look so good myself, she reflected. But he was smiling at her as if she were Miss America herself.

"Now I can see you again," he said. "You still look great to me."

"I wish I could say the same for you, but you're starting to look a bit like a boiled lobster. Don't you have a hat?"

"I gave it to Herb. I'll be all right."

"Another interrupted conversation," Maya said. "I never told you about Rachel."

"That's her name?" Rio asked. "Johanna's . . . my . . . the kid?"

"Rachel. Rachel Roberta Weaver. Johanna named her after her grandmother."

"And what's she like?"

A chain-link fence topped with rolls of razor wire separated them, and this wasn't how she'd pictured talking to him. But she was done waiting for perfect moments. Or maybe this moment had a perfection of its own. Maybe the fence had become everything that had ever divided them, a fence of lies and silences, and she had been learning for months how to reach across it, to ally herself with the wind and the rain and the rocks.

"She's a great kid. I'm proud to have helped raise her. Sweet and smart and adventurous and responsible. Really, she's just what my mother and Johanna's mother always wished we'd be. Only now I'm on their side. If she behaved like we did at nineteen, I'd kill her."

"She's nineteen? How the hell did Johanna—did, uh, we get to be old enough to have a kid who's nineteen?"

"In the usual way, I guess. We survived."

"Did you say she's in college?"

"She just started at Harvard this year."

"Maya, are you making that up?"

"No, it's true."

He shook his head. "It just sounds so unlikely. For me, to have a daughter at Harvard. Nobody in my family ever graduated from any sort of college. I was going to be the first."

"Premed."

"She's smart, then?"

"Smarter than you, smarter than me, smarter than Johanna." Maya risked a smile. "She's a good kid. She wants to do public health in the Third World. Like my sister, Debby. You'll like her."

"I'm sure I will." He looked at her, suddenly anxious. "But what will she think about me?"

"She knows about you. She really does want to meet you. Damn— her letter got arrested in my day pack, too!"

"Maya, Maya, Maya," Rio shook his head, "didn't anyone ever tell you not to bring valuables with you when you're going off to get arrested?"

She shrugged apologetically. "I'm the untrained blockader, learning the hard way."

"Well, it's looking good so far," he said. "I don't want to jinx anything, but I'm beginning to think we might really just slide through."

"Hey you, get away from there," one of the guards on her side shouted. "Leave the men alone." The guard started to walk over, and Maya panicked. They would notice Rio, now, they would single him out, they would take him away and it would be all her fault. She moved quickly away from the fence, and Alix and Laura drew her into the center of the crowd of women. The guard strolled back to the gate.

"Are you all right?" Alix saw the tears streaming down Maya's cheeks. "Is he still mad at you?"

Maya sighed. "No, even though he sure has a right to be. I told him something I should have told him long ago. And it hurt. I knew it would."

"Have some water," Laura said, handing her a paper cup she had filled at the large plastic cooler. "Don't get dehydrated."

Maya took the cup with her cuffed hands and drank, somewhat awkwardly. The water tasted of plastic, but she didn't mind.

"It's okay," she said. "We had a good talk, in the van. Nothing like being locked up together in the dark to make you get down to it."

"A truly bonding experience," Alix agreed. "Could be a new mediation technique—what do you think?"

"I think my head hurts."

"Eat chocolate," Laura said. "Just reach your hands into my jacket pocket, and have some M&M's. They'll make everything better."

A large schoolbus pulled up in front of the gate.

"Everybody line up!" the guards shouted. The women waited while the men were herded aboard. Maya could see Rio enter through the door. Then they were directed to follow.

The men had scattered themselves throughout the bus. Maya spied Rio and noted an empty space beside him. She moved toward him, and he gestured at the empty seat with his chin.

In the front of the bus, a radio was playing music that was mostly static. "Cruel and unusual punishment!" one of the protestors behind her yelled. "They're playing Cher!"

"I saved you a place," he said.

She slid into the seat next to him. With a great deal of noise and commotion, the other blockaders were seated and the bus started off.

He turned to her and smiled. "Now that I've kind of gotten over feeling socked in the gut, I'm starting to think maybe you've just given me the biggest gift of my life."

"She is a gift," Maya said. "The storm gave her to all of us, and we all failed her in some ways. In my case, it was a failure of love. Maybe that's the only Pagan sin."

Outside, the desert rolled past, brown and golden under the harsh sunlight. Alix was leading the back of the bus in singing "Ain't Gonna Study War No More," and their voices battled the static on the radio.

"I used you, Rio. I used you as something to define myself against, and so I couldn't see who you were. I'm trying to strip away that part of myself, the part that needs somebody to be down so I can be up, someone to be bad so I can be good. But damn, it goes deep. Layer after layer, like an onion, until you wonder if there really is a core under there."

"There is a core, Maya," Rio said, turning and looking at her, his eyes full of tears. "It's a hell of a thing to have to learn it the way I did. But there is ground, solid ground. Under you, under me."

Where his thigh pressed against hers, a current flowed between them, like the hum of high-voltage power lines.

"Like the bare hills here," she whispered. "Like the contours of the rocks, and the play of colors on the stone, and the raw, cracked dirt. Bare, but not barren. That's how I want to be."

"We can walk on that ground," he said. "Maybe we can even walk away from the past. Not to lose it, but to let it be behind us."

"I asked you what spiritual lesson you learned," she said. "I guess it's only fair I tell you about mine. It's funny how hard it is to put these things in words, even though I do that for a living. But when we were out on the desert, looking for you, something spoke to me, and said, 'Only what is broken endures.' "

He was quiet for a moment, taking it in.

"If that's true, then I should be immortal," he said.

"Maybe you are."

"Maybe we all are. No one gets out of life without a few cracks and fissures, at least. No one gets out alive."

She leaned against him as the bus rounded a long curve, and he allowed her body to fit to his in a way that felt oh so familiar and yet seemed so strange. We aren't even the same bodies we were, she thought. Aren't all our cells replaced every seven years? How long will it be before all of him that was formed in prison is gone?

The radio continued to blare scratchy, inaudible music. Around them the other protestors chanted, joked, and sang. Maya closed her eyes against the glare of the noonday sun.

When she awoke, the bus had stopped, and all the protestors were being herded out the door. She followed, holding out her hands to the guard who clipped her cuffs and set her free.

That's it? she thought with an odd sense of anticlimax. All that waiting, all that processing, all that enforced helplessness, for what? And then, My pack? Where is it?

With a great sense of relief, she spied her day pack in a pile of blockaders' belongings, and grabbed it. The past and the future, she thought. My only true valuables, put at risk on the walk to Mercury. Once again, I hold them in my hands.

Rio and Maya sat on the curb under a shady tree outside the Starlight Casino. The others had gone in to order Cokes and call support and maybe drop a few quarters in the slot machines, in celebration of their release.

Maya reached into her pack, and pulled out Rachel's letter. "Here it is." She handed it to him.

He opened the envelope and drew out the paper. He stared at it for a long moment, holding it closer and then out to arm's length. Finally he handed it back to her.

"This is embarrassing," he said, "but I don't have my reading glasses. And without them, I can't make out her handwriting. Will you read it to me?"

Maya smiled, although partly she wanted to cry. We are mortal after all, the pirates and revolutionaries and the wild creatures pledged to live in the wind, going off in our bifocals to remake the world. Well, why not? She took the letter from him, and read:

Dear—dear I-don't-know-what-to-call-you. Dad? Father? This is so weird. Up until fifteen minutes ago I always thought you were dead, my whole life long. Right now I'm so mad at my mother, and Maya too, I could kill them both for lying to me. And her plane is leaving and I have to write fast so this probably won't make any sense. But in my mind I always called you Dad, when I thought about you. I thought you were in the Land of the Dead and that was sort of comforting. I could talk to you and imagine that you were looking out for me. But now, Dad, now that I know you're alive, and now that you know I exist, I'd like to get to know who you really are. I never believed you were really all that bad. Here's a picture of me. I'll try to

write some more to you, when I can be more coherent. I guess I'll
sign this,

Love,
Rachel

"Read it again," he said when she'd finished, and she did.

"She's calling me Dad," he said. "How strange. I'll have to get used
to it. I never thought I'd be a dad. She sounds nice."

"She's alive and strong and beautiful. With all our failures, that's
still something. And you know what? We can call her on the telephone!
What time is it now in Cambridge? She's probably at class, but later we
can call her. We're free. We can do anything we want."

"Yeah, turn the radio down, turn the lights on and off, unbutton
our own fly—all the things that count."

"We can rent rowboats, and take trips back to the coast," Maya
said. "We'll do it—we'll go back to that rock together, in our reading
glasses and our gray hair. Maybe bring Johanna, and Rachel too. We'll
stand on the peak with our arms out and feel the power of the wind."

"Be careful. I just might take you up on that offer." He reached for
her hand, almost shyly.

"I want you to," she said. "Oh, here's her picture." She took her
hand away from his, to reach again into her pack, brought out the picture, and handed it to him. Then she placed her hand in his again.

Together they looked at the photograph.

Rachel stared out at them, smiling in her high school graduation
picture, bright and new and young. Her features were a map of the place
where continents meet, Europe, Africa, America. Plates grind against
plates, whole ranges of mountains are thrown up and eroded down,
oceans rise and fall, currents change. And her face was what we will walk
toward, Maya thought, the shiny promise of a future that is not yet
broken, and might nevertheless endure.

Wounds did heal, even old wounds, although they might leave
scars and lasting changes. They would make a pilgrimage together, she
and Rio, Johanna and Rachel, back to the rock on the coast, to the valley
where Rachel was conceived. Maya would stand on the rock and scatter
her mother's ashes into the clean wind, the deep water, letting the waves
and currents carry them where they belonged. Waters mingled all over
the earth. Perhaps her father's ashes were already traveling to meet
Betty's. Perhaps they would never meet again. Maybe her mother's bones
would come to rest on the Mediterranean shores of the Holy Land or on a
clear strand beside the Black Sea, or be food for the prey of salmon who
would carry them back upstream. Or maybe, in the long sweeps of time,
they would sink into the seabed and be pressed into rock and uplifted by
the swells of fire below the earth's crust. Maybe Betty would become a

mountain, a whole range, a new Himalaya, Sagarmatha, Chomolungma, herself the Goddess Mother of the Snows. Maybe every mountain, every desert, was once somebody's mother, somebody's bones. And to walk their steep slopes, to trudge across the dry plain to Mercury, was to step upon the shards of body upon body, crying out in their spirit voices, always calling us to awaken to their broken, enduring love.

About the Author

STARHAWK is the bestselling author of *The Spiral Dance, Dreaming the Dark,* and *Truth or Dare.* A feminist and peace activist, she is one of the foremost voices of ecofeminism and travels widely in North America and Europe giving lectures and workshops. She lives in San Francisco, where she works with the Reclaiming collective, which offers classes, workshops, and public rituals in earth-based spirituality.